WHAT IS ALL THIS?

UNCOLLECTED STORIES

STEPHEN DIXON

FANTAGRAPHICS BOOKS

FANTAGRAPHICS BOOKS
7563 Lake City Way NE, Seattle, Washington 98115

Book Design: Jacob Covey
Editor: Gary Groth
Copy Editor: Gavin Lees
Editorial Assistance: Kristy Valenti and Ian Burns
Associate Publisher: Eric Reynolds
Publishers: Gary Groth and Kim Thompson

Distributed in the U.S. by W.W. Norton and Company, Inc. (212-354-5500)
Distributed in Canada by the Canadian Manda Group (1-416-516-0911)
Distributed in the United Kingdom by Turnaround Distribution (108-829-3009)

ISBN: 978-1-60699-350-7
First Fantagraphics printing: August, 2010
Printed in Singapore

To my daughters:

Sophia Dixon

&

Antonia Dixon Frydman

BOOK

1

What Is All This?
BOOK ONE

EVENING.

It's been a long time. I don't know since when. Just a long time. That should be enough to explain it. To say that: a long time. Very long. Since I've been here, I mean. How could I forget? In this room. In this house. On this street. In this city. This state, to be sure. This country, of course. Naturally, this hemisphere. On earth, goes without saying. This solar system, what can I add? This universe, I won't even go into. Wouldn't try. We all go a long way. Very possibly we all go the same way. Maybe we all add up to the same thing. This time: who can say? Nobody, I think. Maybe some people try. Maybe a lot of people try and some succeed. I don't know. But what is it I began to say? That I've never left this room? No, I've gone out. Several too many times. But the number of times isn't important. Let's say I've only been out of this room once. But stayed away for eighty years only to return and never go out again. It would mean I've been out a long time by anybody's standards but only went out once. But that's not what I began to say. It was something about myself in this room. But too late, at least for now. Because my next-door neighbor comes in.

"Howdy do?"

"And how are you?" is what I answer.

"Just fine, and having a pleasant day yourself?"

"Pleasant. Couldn't be better."

"Enjoying the weather and sights?"

"Wouldn't it be crazy if I didn't?"

"Well, please continue to have a pleasant day."

"It isn't difficult to try."

"Then I'll see you then."

"And a goodbye to you," I say.

My neighbor leaves. I try to remember what he said. Nothing much. I look at what he left. Enough for a small meal. It takes little to feed me, and I eat. It tastes all right to bad. But a person has to eat. That's what one of my parents said when he or she spoke to me about needs. That's something I can remember that brings me way back. And a roof over your head. And clothes, if people where you live wear clothes or the climate you finally settle in gets cold.

The landlady comes in. "Hello."

"Good morning," I say.

"But it's evening."

"Then good morning for this morning and good evening for now. For how are you today?"

"Fine, thanks, and you?"

"What's to complain about, because really, what could be wrong?"

"I'm happy to hear that, and have a good rest of day."

"And I'm happy to hear you're happy to hear that, and to you the same, a very nice rest of day."

"Goodbye," she says.

"Goodbye."

She goes. She left something. A blanket for me to wrap around myself and sleep under tonight. It's what I needed most. I had my meal. I've a roof and these clothes. Last night was cold. This morning, this afternoon, now this evening is cold. In my mind there comes a time in these seasons when it doesn't seem it can ever get warm again. Somehow she knew. But of course, for she lives in the same building and so must undergo the same cold. God bless her, I would say. Some people might think I should. Others might say or think I shouldn't. This is a world of many opinions, much diversity and different harmonies and strifes. I could almost say they're what I've come to like most about it, other than for the possibility of the new day.

Someone raps on my window. It's my super who lives on the other side of me. We share the same fire escape. My window is gated and locked. Bundled up like a bear, he signals me to let him in. I wave for him to come around and enter through the front door. He waves no, it's easier getting in through the window now that he's outside. Easier for you, I motion, but for me it'll take four times the effort to open my window than the door. Come on, he motions, you opening up or not? I unlock and open the window gate and window and close and lock them once he's inside.

"Nice to see you again," he says.

"Same here, Mr. Block, and make yourself at home."

"Think by now you ought to be calling me John?"

"John it is then, John."

"Fine, Harold."

"Why'd you come through the window, John?"

"Because you opened and unlocked it and the gate."

"I opened and unlocked them because you waved me to and then continued to wave me to open and unlock them after I motioned you to go around through your apartment to the public hallway and get in my place through the front door there."

"Then because I was out on our fire escape feeding my pigeons and thought it'd be nice visiting you again and, if I did, to get into your place through some other way this time but the front door."

"A good enough reason I suppose."

"Really the only truthful one I have."

"Wasn't it kind of cold out there?"

"Actually, I could probably think up several other truthful reasons, and almost as cold out there as it is inside our rooms."

"One day it might not be this cold," I say.

"Something to look forward to?"

"One day it might even be considerably warm."

"More to look forward to?"

"And hot. Our rooms, out there on the fire escape, the hallways, the whole building, will be hot."

"It's always good speaking to you, Harold. Seems to raise my body temperature by a degree, which these days I don't mind."

"Same here, John. And have a very nice day."

"What's left of it I will."

We shake hands. He leaves through the door. He left a pair of woolen gloves. I put them on. He once said he only had two hands but two pairs of gloves and one day would give or loan me one. He didn't say this time if the gloves were a gift or loan. No note either, which he likes to leave behind. But no matter. They're on my hands. My fingers are already warm. A person couldn't have more thoughtful neighbors.

Someone taps to me on the ceiling below. I get on my knees and yell through the floor to the apartment under mine. "That you tapping, Miss James?"

Three taps have become understood between us to mean yes, and she taps three times.

"Having a good day?"

One tap means maybe or just so-so.

"Not too cold out for you?"

Two taps mean no.

"Are you saying it's cold but not too cold for you?"

Three taps.

"Well, one day it should get warm again, but probably not too soon."

Four taps mean wonderful or great.

"Even hot. Maybe one day even very hot."

Four taps.

"Though let's hope it doesn't get so hot where we'll be as uncomfortable as we are when it's this cold. But that's such a long way off as to almost seem unimaginable."

One tap.

"By the way, I've received a number of very nice things today. A meal from Mr. Day, blanket from the landlady and a pair of warm gloves from John."

Six taps mean an interrogative.

"John...the super...Mr. Block."

Eight taps for good. Then a long silence.

"If you're through now, Miss James, I'll be speaking to you again."

Three taps for yes.

"You're through?"

Two taps.

"What else would you like to say?"

She taps for several minutes straight. Hundreds of taps, maybe thousands. I don't know what she's saying. A so-so here, a great, yes, no and interrogative, but that's all I understand. Then she stops.

"Well, that's something," I say. "Anything else?"

Two taps.

"Then goodnight, Miss James. And stay as well and warm as you can."

She taps "I hope so" and then "Goodnight." I go to bed. I put the blanket over me and tuck it in. I wear the gloves and my clothes. It's cold but not as cold for me as it was. And it could be considered a good day. When it began I had nothing to eat and no prospect of a meal and no blanket or gloves. Probably also been a better day for the rest of them because they gave me these things and for Miss James because she knows it and spoke to me tonight. I turn out the light and wait for what I hope will he beautiful dreams. Really, outside of my friendships and conversations here, dreams are what I live for most.

STORM.

Paul walks to the point. When he was here two winters ago he wrote a story about a writer who came to a similar village to get over a woman in New York City who had stopped seeing him.

In the story and real life she was an actress who was portraying an actress on a daytime television soap opera who was in love with a writer of soap operas who couldn't give up his wife for her.

One night, in the story and real life, she told Paul she couldn't see him anymore as she was in love with—and thinks she'll be marrying—the actor who plays the writer on the show.

In the story and real life he had to sit down for fear of falling down and she said he was beginning to look and sound like one of the more unconvincing morose characters on her soap.

"The writer you're in love with?" he asked and she said "Abe would never act so callow or doleful in real life or on the show." She asked him to leave and he said "Not yet."

"Do I have to call the police?" and he said, "Please, let's go to bed one last time and then I swear I'll go."

Both in real life and the story she said "You've got to be even crazier and wormier than I first thought you were when I met you and then, for some stupid unself-protective reason, changed my mind."

He slapped her face, pushed her into her bedroom and told her to take off her clothes.

In the story he had to pin her arms down and sit on her while he removed her clothes.

In real life he didn't pin her arms down and he thinks she took off her clothes while she sat on the edge of the bed.

In the story and real life she said if he was so intent on physically overpowering her, then she wasn't going to fight back, as she could get hurt even worse that way. "Irreparably, even," she said in real life.

He doesn't remember using that last line in the story; he thinks he felt it would have sounded too banal to be believed. Now he'd use it, and he makes a note in his scratch pad to add that line to the story if the line he might have written in place of it isn't a better one and if this can seamlessly be worked in.

Both in real life and the story she pleaded again for him to leave, and he said he wouldn't. When she cried because she was frightened of the harm he might do her in bed and later, out of self-reproach, when he was through, he broke down, in real life, said he must have been temporarily insane to have threatened her like that, and left.

In the story he held her down, got on top of her and tried making love.

She said something like "As I said before, Perry, you don't have to force me as I'm not about to resist. I don't want to risk rupturing my vaginal walls and maybe as a result restrict my childbearingness and facility for having sex unrestrainedly with other men."

The act was physically painful and difficult for them both.

In real life, a month before that night she said "It's sleeping, Paul; let's wait."

In the story she later said that rape or whatever he wanted to call it, it could have been pleasurable for her if he were the man she was in love with but for her own reasons didn't want to make love with tonight while he most demonstrably did. "But you're not. In every possible way you're unattractive and hateful to me, no more now than before."

He said he could make her attracted to him and she said that was only his insufferable hubris speaking in him again. He said hubris was one of a dozen or more words he'd looked up at least twenty times in the last ten years and would still have to look up again when he got home.

In the story he looked up the word when he got home and gave the definition.

In real life now he doesn't know what the word means and writes it down in his scratch pad and underlines it.

In the story and real life he made an evening call for her from the phone booth on this point a week after the incident in her apartment.

In the story and real life he said something like I'm calling from this point, which is on an icy peninsula a mile out to sea, and where I can hear the sounds of buoys, gulls, bells, waves, fishing boat motors from nearby and far-off, the clinking and pinging of the halyard against the flagpole at the point's tip, and somehow it's the maddest and saddest and happiest and sappiest and sanest phone call I've ever made. For you see I'm both speaking to you while at the same time so totally alone and now being covered like everything else out here including the mouthpiece and coin slots and telephone wires and poles with snow."

In the story she said "I hope you get buried to death and die," and hung up.

In real life she said he sounds awful and there's nothing she can do for him, and hung up.

He phones her and says "Storm, hi. I'm calling you from that peninsula point phone I last phoned you from and which I never would have done if it wasn't around the same time and so soon after seeing some of the same people and the same sea and shore sounds couldn't be heard and the point wasn't as deserted as it was when I phoned you in what a few fall months will be two winters ago."

"If it's snowing," she says, "I hope you freeze your balls off and die, goodbye."

"And if it's raining or let's say the meteors are showering as they are now but weren't then showering? Or the sun's thundering and mountains are lightninging and stars and moon are closing in and the earth's fissuring and oceans are tidalwaving and this village and your city and our country and countries and continents are disappearing worldwide? Day the earth ended—a time-torn title for a short story but a workable theme for one I'd work on if I hadn't used it twice before. Remember the husband and wife archeological team? The last two people on earth who seek shelter in the cave they've been exhuming for years? And just as the cave's crumbling with them in it they discover an intact skull and complete skeleton and enfaced slate and stylus that are probably a million years older than the oldest bones and writing materials ever found of protohuman American, and also the skeleton's digging and cooking utensils that are very much like our own. And what about old Philly Worstwords, who's awakened from a series of dreams of the successive loves of his youth and artistic successes of his middle age, to find his top floor apartment walls collapsing and all the surrounding buildings plummeting? And from that hospital bed in his now towering wall-less single room, observing the dissolution of his neighborhood and then the entire city and countryside beyond. 'Why me?' he kept asking—remember that, Storm? 'Why me, why me, why me?'"

AN
OUTING.

It's raining. The rain stops. The puddles dry up. The night falls. The day comes. It's raining. There's thunder. Lightning can be seen by those who can see or who see it or those who remember it when they saw. Something like that. A master I'm not. I get out of bed. It's time. The rain stops. I suppose the puddles are beginning to dry up.

I wash and shave. I've come a long way. Last night I was asleep. Tonight I'll most likely be asleep. The night after tonight, or tomorrow night as they say, I'll probably be asleep too. And maybe one time during the day of these days I'll be asleep in what's called a nap. But still asleep. A sleep that might last for about an hour. That's about the length of my naps. Though some have been as long as two hours. One nap I had lasted three hours I believe. A long time ago. And one lasted so long that it could no longer be called a nap. But I should get going. I've come so far this time that I feel I want to continue.

I make myself a breakfast of two eggs and toast. I make a pot of coffee and drink two cups of it. I drink a glass of water. I go to the bathroom. What I do there is my business. I dress. I leave the apartment. On the stairway going downstairs I tell myself now's not the time to stop. On the ground floor I repeat to myself now's not the time to stop. In the building's vestibule where the mailboxes are I tell myself I've made it this far this time I might as well try to see it through to the end. On the stoop leading to the sidewalk I say to myself I've made it outside at least but now where will I go? On the sidewalk I'm about to say something else to myself or repeat one of the things I just said to myself when a woman approaches. I raise my hat to her. She smiles. I set the hat back on my head. She passes. I look up. The sun's trying to break through. I look down. Still plenty of puddles on the sidewalk and street. The puddles will dry up faster if the sun does break through. That's elementary, I think. What's also elementary, I think, is that the puddles will increase in size and depth and possibly spill over to form secondary puddles if it soon rains as hard as it did the last two times. What isn't elementary, I think, meaning I'm thinking and have been thinking what is and isn't elementary to me, is to think about the mathematical proportions of sun and rain in relation to puddles, secondary or otherwise, and how much water would be lost in relation to water gained or something like that if it rains again, though if the sun comes out real strong before it rains. Meaning, if the sun comes out real strong, or is really just a sun of normal intensity and warmth for this time in this area, before it rains as hard as it did the last two times or just rains an average rainfall. Oh, better to forget it than try to explain it. I'm not a scientist, mathematician or meteorologist. A weatherman, let's say. To me rain is rain, puddles are puddles, the sun's the sun.

Standing in front of my building I tell myself I can head up or down this street, toward the avenue with buildings and stores on both sides of it or toward the avenue that borders the park. Both avenues are at the end of my sidestreet and have a subway station three blocks south of the corner, though only one has a subway station seven blocks north of the corner, as the station on the park avenue is a terminus. But all that would only be important if I wanted to take a subway, and if I did, if I wanted to go north or south on it, none I want to do.

I walk toward the avenue with buildings on both sides of it rather than the avenue with only luxury apartment houses on one side of it that face the park. The sun's broken through. Most of the clouds have disappeared. I suppose the puddles have begun to dry up. And now it's beginning to rain. A sunshower. I used to love them as a boy. And the rainbow that would come soon after the sunshower. Both of which I still love as a man. But quick. Under cover. Before my only street clothes get soaked.

A woman walks by holding an opened umbrella. I raise my hat. She raises the umbrella. I get under it and hold the umbrella rod right above the handle while she holds the crook. She came from the avenue with stores on it. We walk toward the avenue that borders the park. It's a woman's umbrella, brightly colored and with a thin leather handle and strap, but the canopy isn't wide enough to protect two average-sized adults walking a foot apart from each other, so we move closer till our hips touch. Then our arms holding the umbrella and next our elbows touch. Her hand moves a few inches up the rod, folds over mine and brings both our hands back to the crook. I switch hands on the umbrella so my arm closest to her can go around her waist. She takes her hand off the handle so she can curl that arm around my neck, Now almost the entire one sides of our bodies touch. Even the timing of our strides are changed so when we move our inside legs forward our thighs touch.

We stop. Our cheeks touch. We close our eyes. I don't know if her eyes stay closed but mine do as we kiss. She licks my chin. I suck her lips. She sticks her tongue in my mouth. I press my tongue against hers and then try to reach its roots. We start walking. It's now pouring. The sun's out. Our mouths are still joined but our tongues are back in place. We walk into a lamppost. We laugh and shake our hurt toes. One rung of the canopy's crushed. We've reached the avenue, cross it and enter the park.

She leads me to a spot right behind the park's peripheral stone wall. She takes my hand off her waist and puts it on her breast. My other hand continues to hold the umbrella above our heads. She puts her hands on my back and chest and slides down my body that way without letting go of me till I can no longer reach her breast. Then I can't even reach the top of her head without crouching over her. She's taken her slicker off and is sitting on it on the ground. She pulls up her skirt to her waist, points to herself down there and nods her head. I shake my head. She closes her eyes, opens her mouth wide and keeps it open, puts her arms around my ankles and squeezes them tight. I get down on the coat. It lightnings. It thunders. The rain's coming down harder. I unzip my fly, pull myself out, the way we do it I won't say, though I never stop holding the umbrella over us and not one part of our bodies gets wet.

The rain stops. The sun never left. I hear cars and buses passing and blaring on the other side of the stone wall. Commercial traffic isn't allowed on the park avenue but I hear what sounds like a huge trailer truck. A parks department worker appears on a small hill nearby raking leaves. He sees us and leans with his chin on the tip of his rake handle and whistles. I wave him away. She winks and waves at him to come. He walks down the hill, drops the rake with the teeth part sticking up and unbuckles his belt. I'm through anyway. I get up.

He gets down and takes my place but in a different way. I close the umbrella and make sure I don't step on the rake head as I start out of the park.

There are many more puddles on the streets and sidewalks than before. I'm sure the new process of their beginning to dry up has already begun. I cross the avenue. I feel and hear drops on my hat, which I only now realize I never took off. I look up. It's raining. The sun's gone. I open the umbrella. It starts teeming. I think about the park couple probably getting wet. I run to my building, but the wind or whatever the air pressure against the inside of an open umbrella is called that keeps one from running as well as he'd run if the umbrella were closed, slows down my running to a walk and then a standstill and then begins pulling me back across the avenue as if I were attached to an opened parachute. I close the umbrella. I run to my building and into the vestibule, and after checking the mailbox for mail, run upstairs. I unlock my front door, go inside, lock it, stand the umbrella against a wall and take off all my clothes and hang them up on the clothesline above the bathtub and put my shoes in the tub. I wash, make a lunch of canned soup and two cheese sandwiches, eat them and drink a glass of milk and get into bed. After all the running about and such just before, I'm sure I'll have a good nap. The umbrella. It's probably leaking along the floor and maybe through the floor cracks to the apartment below. I get up. I bring the umbrella to the bathroom, open it and stick it in the tub. I think of taking a hot bath, but there are too many things dripping into or drying off in the tub. I get back in bed. I think of that woman. I'm glad I went out. But I still have her umbrella. Will she be on the street next time I go outside where I can give it back to her? I should have got her name and phone number to return the umbrella, or at least her last name and address so I could send it to her by messenger or mail.

SHOELACES.

Herbert bent down to tie his wife's shoelaces, one hand and knee touching the pavement. A Fifth Avenue bus pulling out of a stop sent exhaust fumes in his direction. He held his breath, finished tying one of the shoes, and looking up saw her large body standing over him like an equestrian statue still draped with its unveiling cloth.

"I'd do it myself if I wasn't so heavy," she said.

"You're not that heavy," he said, and untied and tied the laces of the other shoe just in case.

"But you shouldn't be doing that, Herb. It's not a man's job. I should lose weight; tie my own shoes."

"Don't be silly." That was it. Both shoes tied neatly and tight. Maybe he should have tied double knots so he'd be sure they wouldn't come loose. But then later at home, if she didn't ask him to untie the laces while the shoes were on her feet, she'd make him take out the knots after she'd forced the shoes off her feet, and that always hurt his fingertips. It was a damn nuisance this bending, tying, retying, looking at her ugly scuffed shoes with the stockened big toe sticking out of the opening in front. It was almost the same style his mother and all her illiterate friends wore some fifty years ago. Now maybe if his wife wasn't so heavy and her feet not so swollen most of the time, she'd be able to wear high heels like other women her age and begin to look like somebody. But what wishful thinking that was, and he stood up, spit into his hanky and rubbed it on his dirty hand, then folded it and carefully stuck it back into his coat's breast pocket.

"So many people walk on Sunday it's amazing," she said.

"Not so amazing. We do it."

"But on Sunday? I'm saying, everybody?"

"Sunday's as good as any other day. Less crowded."

"But so many people walking when no stores are open, I can't see."

"So they don't spend money; that's bad?"

"And what do you want them to do, die with every cent?" She looked at her shoes. "You know, I think you tied them too tight."

"Why, it hurts?"

"I wouldn't ask if they didn't, Herb."

"I thought I tied them loose enough. Though you should know what's wrong with them. You're wearing the things."

"I'm not trying to pick an argument. I say they're tight. I mean— I know, especially the right. Now will you please untie them some?"

He was glad he hadn't double-knotted the laces. He started to bend down, his wife now breathing more heavily above him, but quickly straightened up and looked around.

Before, when she had asked him, he also looked, but just quick ones so she wouldn't suspect anything. There were fewer people on the street then and nobody seemed to be looking his way. But now the street was more crowded and people seemed to be looking everywhere. They didn't see anything interesting in front of them, they looked in the store windows. If nothing interesting was in the windows, they looked around the sidewalk. A man tying his wife's shoelaces was interesting, untying them, even more so.

"Maybe I should stand here all day and get my feet swelled till they're limp and blue, is that what you want?"

"No, of course not."

"Then what?"

"Try walking a little more. Maybe they're not that tight."

"Walk and get lame? You'd like that better? You got so much money where you can throw it into some doctor's window?"

"Did I say that?" his voice almost a whisper.

His wife, apparently satisfied with his answer, dropped her scolding finger. A painful expression creased her nose. She looked suspiciously at her shoes and attempted to stand on her left foot. Her fat jiggled and her bosom heaved. She got her foot about three inches off the ground.

"You know, it's really killing me," she said to the back of his head. "You tied them before like a madman."

"What?" He was watching a group of schoolgirls, dressed nicely in sweaters and kneesocks and skirts, jump out of a cab, laugh and fumble over the change they each contributed to the fare, and cross the street. He still heard them laughing, one exceptionally pretty one with her long red hair like silk bouncing, as his wife pointed to her feet.

"I'm saying it hurts, Herb—do you hear?"

He'd stoop down. After all, she was his wife and he knew he had to get it over with eventually, so get it done now and that'd be that. But squatting down, his thighs spread apart, the first thing he did was feel his crotch. His pants were dry. He glanced at them and saw they weren't stained with urine either, which was a good sign. Because lately he'd occasionally let himself go: just short spurts and not from any excitement or anything. It was only that something had gotten wrong inside him like so many other men his age got, and he sometimes couldn't control himself. His wife knew about it, and when she wasn't shouting at him for staining his pants so much, she'd be urging him to see a doctor who takes care of such things. But he'd hold off that visit a week or two longer to see if his trouble would go away by itself. He heard it sometimes did.

A young couple stopped a few feet away to look at the store window behind him. The Tailored Woman was what the store was called, and some very nice clothes and accessories it had also. He looked up at his wife's breasts drooped massively over him. They never looked good when she tried stuffing them into one of her baggy dresses. Maybe in her skimpy nightgowns, when they swung back and forth, unstrapped and partly hidden, maybe then they looked best. But she should only have the figure to go into one of those dresses in the window. And he should only have the money to buy it. A real fortune they must cost. But say he did have the money—what good would it do? A laugh, that was the good it'd do, because she'd never lose an ounce. Money she could but weight never. He looked back at the couple. They were now watching a white sports car zoom downtown. Herb, his legs aching, rose and also watched the car as it screeched to a stop at the corner when the traffic light turned red. With that car the driver could have easily made it through the light, he thought. The car, waiting for the light to turn green, revved its motor and exploded two loud pops through its tailpipes. Then it switched gears, retched, bucked like a horse at the starting gate, and took off down the avenue, turning at 55th Street and disappearing.

"What is it, Herb? You're interested in everything but me today."

"I was looking at that white sports car."

"Car? That was a car? That's a toy car. It couldn't fit three."

"Maybe, but it looked nice and went fast."

"Fast? Marilyn's friend's husband had one, and fast it went into a tree. Lucky he was insured and not hurt."

"For someone who's careless, any car could hit a tree."

"You know him that well to say he's careless? Anyway, can I change back the subject?"

"Huh?"

"The shoes, Herb, the shoes. Because one minute more and I'll be crippled for life."

"Walk over to that water thing there." He pointed to a polished bronze spigot attached to the outside of the store.

"Why?"

"Because you could put you foot up on it, which'd be easier for me."

"You can do it right here. Come on, Herb—for me."

What did she say this morning? "It's a nice day"? "Such a beautiful day"? Some nonsense like that when she said they should take the subway to Columbus Circle, walk along Central Park South on the building side because that's such a refined area, and then go to Rockefeller Plaza where all the pretty flowers are, and from there they'd maybe stop in for coffee and take the bus home. But once on the train she decided to get off at 59th and Fifth instead, and now only two blocks they've walked and already she's asked him twice to do her laces. By 55th Street she'll say she's dead tired, stop, complain, make him bend down and feel if one of her ankles is more swollen than the other, then tell him they should take the Fifth Avenue bus downtown now because her legs hurt real bad and they can just as easily see the store window displays and flowers from the bus. But an idea like hers he never should have listened to in the first place. He should really just hail a cab and ride away without her for once, which would serve her a good lesson. Besides, the Fifth Avenue bus doesn't give free transfers crosstown where they're going like the Lexington Avenue bus does, but try get her to walk the three short blocks to Lexington and she'd holler like he's never heard. So today's the last fall Sunday of the year that'll be beautiful, as she said. But how did she know? The weatherman's her uncle?

"Herb?"

"What?"

"Herb!"

She meant business. He squatted down, for all he had to do was give her one more excuse and she'd jump down his throat even worse. People walk past? What did it matter?

Yell, she could do better than anyone in the world. And the people? Already they started looking like he thought before. But he had no reason to complain. This wasn't his avenue. It was stupid even thinking it was for a second.

He looked around to prove his point. A woman walked by with her very proper-looking blond daughter. Both of them had nice clear rich voices and were smartly dressed, their faces and noses handsome and small—but not in the air like some people. Still, some things he could tell: they didn't want to mingle with you and for your own personal good you shouldn't try to have anything to do with them. Another woman walked towards him, a small dog trailing at the leash she held. Now she he immediately knew he didn't like—a real anti-Semite. He could tell just by her cold sour look like she had a stomachache and then traipsing past him like she owned the street. Because why did she look at him like that? Something she didn't like? His wife? Her beaten-up old shoes? This man on his knee? She didn't like that? Maybe she didn't like anything. Whatever the reason, this street was city property, kept up with taxes paid by all of them, so if she thought she had any more rights on it than they, she was crazy. He, he'd tie, untie, retie, untie and tie again if he liked, and she could go and make faces at them all her life and see how much it bothered him.

He switched his weight to his other foot and began tying the shoelaces just as he'd been taught as a boy to tie them. The black laces wrapped easily around one finger, under the loop, under the loop again, and after pulling tight he had a bow—a good one. But as a boy he was always glad to have people watch him tie, especially when he first learned how and his relatives praised him without his mother's coaxing. But here? Well, for one thing his wife appreciated it, and he guessed that was something. And then it was a good bow as he had said, like one he could hardly make anymore with his rotten fingers, and it was also much neater than when he'd done it as a boy, with the loops of the bow equal on both sides. He undid the laces on the other shoe, even though they seemed loose enough, and retied them also.

"How do they feel?" he said, patting the square fronts of both shoes and looking up.

"Eh?"

"I said how do they feel?"

"Fine."

"Not too tight?"

"No, fine, just fine. Both are perfect, Herb."

FIRED.

"You sonofabitch."

"Just get the fuck out of here."

"You're firing me? Good. Because I can't stand you and this place."

"I'm not firing anyone. You're quitting, and never come back."

"I'll come back for my paycheck."

"Don't bother. It'll be in the mail."

I go downstairs, change into my street clothes, throw my bowtie against the dressing room wall and step on it so the metal clasp breaks, leave the restaurant and head home.

On the next street a man says "Dig it, man, dig it. Right up here, ten bucks, satisfaction guaranteed." He holds out a flyer.

"No thanks."

"Come on, man, dig it, no harm to look. Put it away for later."

I take the flyer and read it as I walk. *$10*, it says. *Girls, muchaches, girls. Complete private sessions.* No extra charges. On it is a photo of a nude woman sitting on a bed. Very young and beautiful, bandanna around her forehead, lots of pubic hair.

I put the flyer into my pocket. I've thought about going to one of these places and felt it would either cost much more than the flyer said or I was afraid of getting a disease or mugged or that the women were being exploited and I wanted no part in that. But now I don't care what happens to me or who's being exploited; I just want to forget the manager and job and looking for another one and have a good time. I only have about fifteen dollars on me, so what can they take? And for a disease I can always get a free clinic shot.

I go back. Man's still handing out flyers, smiles and says to me

"Go dig it, man," and I open the door and walk upstairs. Second-floor door's open and the room I step into is like a small lobby of a cheap hotel.

Woman behind a desk says "Yes?"

"Uh..."

"Want to join the fun? Ten dollars."

I give it to her.

"And eighty cents tax."

"Didn't say anything about tax, not that I won't pay it."

"You mean the handouts downstairs? Look again."

She gives me one. Where it says *taxes included*, it's been crossed out. I don't take out the one in my pocket to see if it's been crossed out too. I give her a dollar and she gives me twenty cents change. "What do I do now?"

"Give your bag to the attendant there and come back."

A man's standing in front of an opened closet. He takes the athletic bag my waiter's uniform and other things are in and puts it on a shelf.

"No tag?"

"Yours is the only bag like that," he says. "It'll be here."

I go back to the desk and say "Now what?"

"You can't do anything without a ticket. Here, give it to your girl." It's like a movie ticket. "Like to sign our guest register first?"

She turns it around and gives me a pen. Register's also like a hotel's. None of the names seem real. *Bob Smith. Jack Brown. Joe. Dick D. Pegleg Pete*. I sign *James George*, which is my real name reversed.

"I'll let you in." She goes through a curtain behind her and opens a door from the inside about ten feet away. I go in. She returns to her desk. Six women sit around a table in the middle of the room. They're pretty and fairly young and either in leotards or brief swimsuits. There are benches against all four walls, and I sit on one. An older man is sitting on a bench across the room. He's wearing a coat on this humid summer day and sunglasses with mirrors for lenses, and seems to be enjoying himself just by looking at the women.

Sit for a while, I tell myself. Don't be in any rush. There's just this guy and you, so you got a complete choice. Listen to how they speak and what they say. Make the right decision from it. Pick the one you think has the best combination of looks and personality and even intelligence and doesn't seem abrasive and will be the most fun. Right after I finish thinking this I choose the youngest-looking woman mostly because she is so young and it seems as if this could almost be her first day here. She's around eighteen or nineteen, less than half my age. She's actually beautiful.

More beautiful than any woman I've ever been with. Perfect features and skin. Long black hair, slim body in black leotards. Long muscular legs, tiny waist and small breasts.

She looks like a dancer. She seems bored and isn't talking with the other women. Radio music's playing and she seems to be listening to it. I go over to her, tap her shoulder.

She looks up. I give her my ticket. She stands, flashes a smile and says "Follow me."

I follow her through the door to the lobby, past the checkroom and desk to a small room off a hallway. She shuts the door. "What do you want, half and half?"

"What's that?"

"You haven't been here before?"

"No."

She seems disappointed and looks around. A bucket of dirty water's on the floor. Looks like someone spit several times in it. She feels the water with her finger. "It's cold. I better get some warmer water to wash you with."

"Don't worry, I'm clean."

"No, I have to. I'll be back. Sit down. Take off your clothes."

She goes. I take off my shirt and hang it on a hook. My pants and shorts on a different hook and then my shoes and socks. I look in the mirror. I flatten my hair back, fold my arms, sit on the bed. The room is mostly this single bed against the wall. No window. Bucket of water and a stool with a folded towel on it. She comes back with a basin of water.

"Got some warmer water for you. And soap. They seem to have none here."

"I don't see any. By the way, you mentioned half and half. What is it?"

"Half blow job, half screw. You want that?"

"Sure. Is there anything else I can get?"

"Nothing I give. Come here." I walk over to her "Hold the pan." I hold the pan. She drops the soap in the water, takes my penis in one hand and starts washing it, "Wait a minute, we got a problem. This thing won't fit in me. I should've asked you to undress before I got the water, but this thing isn't even semi-erect yet." She drops my penis.

"What do I do?"

"Whatever you do, you're not going in me. I'm sorry, but I got some more working to do today and I'm not the biggest girl in the world, know what I mean? You want me to just blow you, that's something different, but not if it's going to take too long."

"I want the other thing too."

"Then pick one of the other girls who looks bigger." She puts the soap on the stool, takes the basin from me and dumps the water into the bucket. She pulls my ticket out from inside her shoe, where I never saw her put it, and gives me it.

"Listen, how can I tell who's bigger than who, because I don't want to run into the same problem?"

"Anyone older than me and with a bigger behind's usually good. Just any of them then, because you see I'm too slight. Use that towel. Sorry. Bye." She leaves with the basin.

I dry myself, get dressed and go back to the lobby. "I still have my ticket," I say to the woman behind the desk, showing it.

"I know. Let me come around." She lets me in. Most of the women look at me when I walk in and then resume talking.

The man with the sunglasses and coat is still there smiling.

There's a new woman, in purple shorts and red T-shirt, but I can only see a little of her face. I change benches so I can get a good look at her. She's cute: small nose, little eyes and pouty lips. She looks at me, smiles nicely, and then looks back at her shoes. Another woman has a gorgeous figure I see when she stands up and looks at me and winks. But her hair's bleached platinum and looks like it'd feel like straw. And she's chewing gum very hard and snapping it, and I don't like hair like that or the sound or smell of chewing gum. Some other time, because of her great body, I might choose her if I ever come back here, which I think I will.

It seems fair, reasonably clean, no hustle, and the women are attractive and mostly young. But now I want someone who seems as if she almost doesn't want to be chosen and who at least has the appearance of being modest, like the one in purple shorts. I go over to her and hold out my ticket.

She looks up. "Oh yeah, I forgot," she says, and laughs. "My mind was lost somewhere." She takes my ticket and says "Over here," and I follow her to a room right off this one. It's three times as large as the first one and has a dresser, chair, sink, window with drapes over it, bathroom mirror screwed to the wall and the same single bed. "Take off your clothes. Water in the sink takes too long to get warm and I want to wash you, so I'll be right back."

"You're not going to believe this…"

"What?"

"Forget it; it's ridiculous."

"No, what? I want to know."

"I'm already very clean."

"Everyone's very clean, honey, but everyone's got to be washed. Only way I know if you are is when I do it myself, okay?"

"Fine."

She leaves. I take off my clothes and sit on the bed. There's stirring behind the wall with the mirror, I stand and look in the mirror and see myself and also some kind of movement behind it. The movement stops but there's still an outline of a head with lots of hair around it, like the woman has. I sit in the chair and cross my legs and keep my eyes on a different wall than the mirror's. I don't want her thinking I'm suspicious in any way she'd think wasn't normal, as I don't want to be asked to leave if that's what they do when they're suspicious of you.

She comes in with a basin of water with a bar of soap in it. "Sorry I took so long. Could you stand so I can get you washed?"

"Want me to hold the pan?"

"Sure, honey, that'll be as good as my resting it on the chair."

I hold the pan and she washes and dries my penis. I put the pan on the chair. She takes off her shoes and shorts and I lie on the bed. "Make some room for me, honey."

"Excuse me." I slide close to the wall. She sits on the edge of the bed.

"What do you want?" she says.

"Is there anything besides half and half?"

"Sure, plenty. Want me to fly you around the world?"

"What's that?"

"I suck you all the way around, ass and cock. You never had it, it's great."

"Do I get to come in you?"

"For ten dollars more. Without coming in me it's only five dollars more."

"What else is there besides that?"

"Sixty-nine. That'll cost you five more. But there you also get to come inside me. If you want to stick it in my ass that's another ten dollars no matter what else we do or where you come in me, because that one takes a little longer and isn't the easiest to do."

"Nah, I don't think so."

"I can give you a quarter fly around the world for five dollars more where you also come in me."

"Thanks, but I think I'd just like half and half."

She takes off her shirt, lies across my chest and holds my penis and stares at it. "What's this?"

"What's what?"

"This stuff leaking out of you. I don't like the looks of it. Sure you don't have something?"

"Positive. It's probably just come."

"I hope so." She wipes the tip with her fingers and puts my penis in her mouth. I play with her nipple. Her eyes are closed while she's doing it. About two minutes later she sits up, wipes her mouth with her wrist, gets on her back and opens her legs. I get on top of her and only go a little ways in.

"Push in all the way, honey. You're not doing us any good hanging outside."

"I thought we'd play with each other a little till we're both ready."

"Why do we got to play? You're ready, I'm ready, come on." I go all the way in, grab her head, shoulders, back of her neck.

"It'd help if you moved a little too," I say.

"I will. I just wanted to make sure you were settled." She moves. I come.

I get out before she gives me any sign I should and roll over on my side.

"That was quick," she says.

"I guess it's been a long time."

"Yeah? If you want, for another five, you can do it again if you think you can be quick."

"I don't know if I can do it that fast again."

"How long you think you need?"

"If I take an eight-minute rest or so and then you play with me a little, maybe a total of fifteen minutes."

"That's too long for another five. For another ten I'll wait the eight minutes with you here before we start again."

"I don't even think I can guarantee anything that fast. I better just forget it."

"Next time don't wait so long to come here, okay? Then you won't have to do it so fast and can get more out of it." She gets off the bed. I do too. Cleans herself with a washrag and sink water and says "Don't you want to wash yourself too?"

"I guess so." I go to the basin and start soaping my penis.

"I'll help." She washes it for me over the basin on the chair, gives me a paper towel to dry it with.

"Thanks."

She puts on her shorts and shoes. I put on my undershorts and pants and sit down and take my socks out of my pants pocket.

"My socks were in my pocket—"

"What, honey?" She was putting her shirt over her head and didn't hear me.

"My socks. I just wanted to explain. They were in my pocket because I already got undressed and dressed here once when another girl right before you—you weren't in the main room at the time—she said I was too big for her when she was washing me."

"Which one was she?"

"Girl in black leotards. Very young."

"Very, very young with her long black hair brushed, straight down in back? Very pretty?"

"Yes."

"I don't know her name. No, you're big all right, though not where you're that unusual. Sure that was her real reason for refusing you?"

"That's what she said."

"She must have never had a baby or be younger than I even thought, though I still don't see why she should be so smug."

"You won't say anything to hurt her job. That she refused someone for what might be a flimsy reason?"

"She's got no worries. Young and pretty like she is, she can turn away twice as many as anyone and still do better than most. Don't feel sorry for her."

I'm all dressed. "By the way, this is for you." There's a sign on the wall that says *Tips aren't obligatory but are welcome*, and I give her three dollars.

"Thank you, that's very nice." She puts it in her purse.

I go to the door. "Well, goodbye."

"Let me leave first, honey." She runs her hands through her hair, opens the door, says goodbye and goes. I wait a few seconds before opening the door and walking through the main room. The older man's there smiling at the women. The woman I was just with isn't around. The young woman in black leotards is sitting and talking with another woman. I smile at her as I pass. She flashes a smile back.

The checkroom man isn't around. I take my bag off the shelf, wave goodbye to the woman behind the desk and start downstairs. A young man's running up the stairs. I go outside.

"Dig it, man, dig it," the man from before says, holding out a flyer.

"You already gave me one. It's in my pocket."

"Way to go, man. Best beauties in the West up there, so use it," and sticks the flyer he was going to give me into another man's hand. I head home.

When I get there I call the manager of the restaurant I worked in and say "If it's all right with you, I'm feeling much better now and just think I got unreasonably hot under the collar before and want to come back tomorrow, all right?"

"Let me think about it. Okay. But no more getting so damn temperamental, or you're through here for good, got that?"

"Right."

"Same time tomorrow then," and he hangs up.

THE
BUSSED.

There were no passengers on the bus when I got on it. "Forty grens," the driver said, an unreasonably high fare for not a very long ride, I thought, and I grudgingly fingered through my pockets and wallet but all I could come up with was a five-tavo bill.

"Can't change it," he said. "And you know the state rules; no free rides unless you're a bona fide disabled veteran or visibly pregnant, so I'm afraid you'll have to get off at the next regular stop."

"Maybe another passenger can change it."

"Who's to guarantee there'll be other passengers?

"Sorry: no money, no ride."

"But I have the money. It's you who haven't the change."

The bus stopped at the corner and the driver pointed past the opened door. "See that bench? It's been systems analyzed to be uniformly comfortable to the average waiting person for a period of up to an hour. Care has gone into the design, development and fabrication of that bench. The next bus is scheduled in thirty-three minutes, which is generosity on the state's part seeing how around this time we don't get but an average of one passenger per tour. And extreme generosity, considering how that one passenger hasn't even the money to pay. The next driver's name is Robinson, by the way, so if you're feeling up to it, give him my regards."

Someone had left the morning newspaper on the bench. "War in Kamansua progresses," I read. "506 hostiles killed, enemy's tally of 51 friendlies dead discounted. President Lax says peace is feasible. Senator Merose calls for investigation of existent sans-culottists in war industry. Senator Servin calls for investigation of unproductive visual and audio agipropaganda. Senator Fleetmore calls for investigation of insane asylums. Says all mental health money should be diverted to war interests. 'Look at us: first in space, first in peace and defense, first in the technological arts, but still with more asylums than any state in the world. I say that if you're not sane to begin with, then no treatment or institution is going to make you sane. I call for a war against the insane,' he said to applauding colleagues. 'Think of the cost, the state danger and disgrace. I say that if one's emotionally ill—a euphemism for what's more validly known as state immediocrities—then that's his problem to deal and live with in another state, because now, as a uni-fied people, in this indeterminable era, with all mankind to consider we cannot afford to...'"

The next bus came an hour later, this one also empty.

I got on, five-tavo bull in my hand and explanation prepared. The driver called out the fare and said Intercom had warned him about me so I needn't bother with useless words. "You've had time to get it changed."

"It's past worktime and nobody's around. What I suggest is you ride me to my stop, and when I get home I'll send Intercom a check for the fare plus whatever expense you think the state might entail in handling it."

"Words, words. Worse, you're making me run behind schedule and upsetting my disposition for future passengers." He drove to the next regular stop. "You're a lucky man to have come even this far. For all I know, it's a subterfuge to con your way home without paying the fare—stop by stop via bus by bus with the excuse of having no change." The door opened, I saw there was no chance in arguing with this guy, and I got off.

All the neighborhood shops were closed. There were no lights on in the windows above the stores. I waited for a hitch, none of the passing cars even slowed down for me, and forty minutes later another empty bus came along. It was the same driver who had refused me a ride nearly two hours ago. "Forty grens, please," he said, giving no sign he recognized me. I began to walk home. The bus remained at the stop, its interior and headlights still on. A man across the street was walking hurriedly, head down as if bucking rain. I ran to him, and seeing me, he ran away. "Stop," I yelled, "I'm no thief. I just want to change a fiver for the bus fare."

He kept running, rolled-up newspaper flying out from under

his arm. It was the afternoon paper. I picked it up and read the headline: "'Victory at last,' President says." "Our state leader is a modern-day messiah," the front page editorial said. And then Senator Fleetmore again—my senator, I only now noticed—thanking the Senate for voting overwhelmingly for his bill barring all future aid and development money for the treatment and cure of the emotionally ill. "Because we all know their only problem is being lazy and unwilling to work and thus survive. Since that is so, I propose incarceration rather than hospitalization. Or, to reduce state costs further, revoke their passports, hand them their extra-state traveling papers, and escort them to the exit gates. I fully expect the House to pass the bill, and the president assures me he'll sign it into law tomorrow evening, as all of us feel the urgency in getting these emotionally ill—a term I use euphemistically, as they're more scientifically known as—"

I walked back to the bus, door opened, and I stepped inside. "Please."

"Forty grens," he said, driving off.

"I beg you to take me to the stop near my home. I'm not well."

"Then you've got to get off. Sick people can be infectious and therefore a living threat to all passengers and personnel."

"But my wife and child have been waiting two hours for me. They usually pick me up at work, but my wife is ill today so I had to return home by bus for the first time. Look, I'll give you the entire five tavos for the ride."

"You trying to make me lose my job, besides getting me thrown in jail? Bribing a public officer, the Book of the State says, is a crime punishable by a minimum of three years imprisonment and the subsequent loss of all statesman rights for not less than ten years after release. I'm sorry, but my duty is to report you."

"I wasn't bribing you. I was giving you the money to hold, with the provision—which I thought you'd understand intuitively— that you send me the change when you're able to, though with all expenses deleted."

"The Book of the State takes very seriously such an offense. It says that the giving of any amount excessive of regular fare to state public officers on state public transportation systems should be constituted a bribe."

I reached for the lever that opened the door, but he swatted my wrist so hard my hand went limp. "Look what you've done," I said, showing him my hand, which was already beginning to swell. "I need that hand for my job."

"You were trying to escape. You're really in for it now, brother, so just sit quietly in the back or you'll be charged with crimes too numerous to memorize. But they're all here," and he pulled a leatherbound Book of the State out of his back pocket—"the rules and punishments and all in simple plain language for nobody to misinterpret."

I sat in back of the bus. We drove for miles and I never saw another car, person or lit store along the road. I saw the first star of the night and made a wish. "Dear God," I said. "Let me be with my family who need me as I need them. I know I'm not considered a religious person anymore, as I guess most people aren't. But I do love my family, offend no one intentionally, speak the truth more than most, and up till now have had relatively little to complain about. Grant me this one wish."

"What are you running on about back there?"

"Quite truthfully, I was wishing."

"The Book of the State," he said, holding the book up, "—the good book expressly prohibits wishing on public systems if it interferes with the driver's capability. My advice is to remain silent or your family will only be a pleasant part of your past."

We approached the corner where I normally would have got off. My wife and child were there, both of them dressed warmly I was glad to see. I'd told Janet not to pick me up at the stop—told her to drink plenty of fluids and I'd see her at home a bit after six. But here she was, puzzled and sad as the bus drove past with me in it. She waved and shook her head to indicate she didn't know what was going on, and I blew her a kiss which met the one she blew me. "I love you," I wrote backwards in my condensation on the window. By the time I put the exclamation point on my already runny message, my wife and child were just dots in my sight.

"Nice looking frau," the driver said. "Some boobs. Things like that really get to me—right here," and he pointed as he laughed. "And some ass. I'm a big ass man and I saw it as we were driving up and she had her back to the bus. You're a lucky brother, all right. What does she call herself?"

I was so distraught I began to cry.

"Can't take a little bugging, eh? Can't take other men even thinking about your wife, that it? Think she can only be yours, legs and neat ass and those beautiful boobs just waiting for you. You're an evil man. Selfish, insecure, dissolute. Good things should be shared, the Book of the State says." He stopped the bus to turn to a page in the book. "Right here it says that, and stop bawling and listen. 'No person has a permanent right to anything. All things are to be shared by the total state. The total state is defined as "everyone within the state who hasn't lost his statesmanship on his own or through his associations."' The Book also says that 'family life, if not in the best interests of the state, can be temporarily disjoined or everlastingly dissolved if...'"

I stared out the window at the earless streets and sidewalks without pedestrians. Where was everyone? Home, enjoying dinner, happily by themselves or with one another.

All I could be secure about was that my family was always safe on these streets. Then I saw another bus behind us, filled with passengers. It pulled up alongside our bus and the two drivers saluted. I tapped on the window at the people getting off the bus, but nobody seemed to hear me. I rapped on the window, banged it with my fists, then put my foot through it and screamed through the hole I made "Please, help me get out. I'm being held prisoner by a maniacal driver. My wife and child are sick and need me at home."

"We're all getting sick," a man said, walking away as he spoke. "The flu and fallout's going to get us all."

Two young men stopped at the broken window. "Nasty mess," one said, and the other laughed at his friend's remark.

"Tell the driver to let me off," I said. "I didn't do anything."

"You make that mess?" the same young man said. "Nasty, nasty," and the other laughed again. "The Book of the State says explicitly," and he removed the book from his pocket, thumbed through the index and then turned to the page he wanted while the laughing man said "That's a very nice copy, George; real nice." "The Book says that the state, and I quote, 'shall not take lightly any indifferent, capricious or premeditated destruction of state property, be it public land, buildings or vehicles.'" And flipping to the index again and then to another section inside the book; "'A vehicle is considered part of the state, and thus public, if it meets any of the following sixteen criteria. One, if the state had acquired the vehicle since the Five-Seventeen Turnover. Two, if the state acquired and then lost the vehicle during the interim of the Preliminary Advance and the initial Letdown. Three, if the state—'"

"I'm being held prisoner for no possible state reason," I yelled.

He turned to the index and then to a page in the book. "'Prisoners, suspect or convicted, who try to cajole or coerce a statesman by looks, words or material enticements, shall have all statesman rights annulled for himself, if not previously done, and his immediate loved ones,'" and the other man kept nodding. "Furthermore, an immediate loved one is defined as...it says here someplace," and he returned to the index.

"You ought to get a book with a good thumb index like mine," the other man said, and he showed him his own book.

The first man found the right page and resumed his reading. "'An immediate loved one is defined as a person who has had a close living association with the offender for two or more months preceding the time of offense, or is a direct genetic offspring of the offender, though not necessarily living with him at the time, or an indirect blood association of the offender, though not necessarily living with him at the time.' Now, an indirect blood association isn't easy to define verbatim or otherwise," and he turned to the index.

I gave them the back of my head and they got the message and walked away. A woman came by. She was young, and by her looks she seemed gentle and understanding. I pleaded with her to speak to the driver to let me off the bus. "I'm innocent," I said. "And I've loved ones who depend on me."

She pulled out her Book, which like the others had the state seal of a blue circle on the cover, and read from a section called Guileful Innocence, quoting authorities I'd never heard of such as Stormberg and Mauser. "Oh, the hell with you," I said, and spit through the hole in the window, and the blob landed on the page she was reading from. She became hysterical, and in seconds had a crowd questioning her. A third bus drove by, stopped, backed up, and parked behind the second bus. Most of the passengers got off, and once they got wind of the story, joined the crowd around the woman. "Look," she said, and showed them the stain my spit had made on the page. The crowd looked angry, even though I swore I was sorry and that I'd only done it to get their attention in some desperate way. "I'm being held for no of tense against the state other than what the driver had either lied or misconstrued as one."

"But no offense, young man," an elderly woman said kindly, "can be worse than the mistreatment of our good book." She read from her copy. "'Crimes considered perfidious in previous eras, such as rape, infanticide, selling or giving of state secrets to state enemies, are still not ranked as base as the purposeful desecration of the Book of the State. Defiling and burning the Book are considered primary crimes. Malicious language about the Book is considered a secondary crime. Permitting the Book to fall into disrepair—a tertiary crime but one not punishable by imprisonment—may be considered a secondary crime if the offender, once admonished, doesn't repair the Book in the time specified or return the Book to the State Book Depository for a new one.' Also: 'Any Book willfully or carelessly allowed to be destroyed, damaged or fallen into a questionable state of disrepair by one's offspring under the age of sixteen—'"

The crowd got angrier as she read and some called for immediate trial and punishment. The driver, to no effect, told the crowd he was a public servant and thus a state officer and had everything under control. He then called Intercom from the bus and asked what he should do, and they said they'd be right out. Someone asked who I was, and my driver took my passport, recited my name and address and said he'd in fact just seen my loved ones a few miles from here at a bus stop. "Then let's get them before they escape," one of the other drivers said, and she and about thirty people got in her bus and started out after my wife and child.

I'd never felt such fear for my family. What did the Book say again about punishing an offender's immediate loved ones—those in close association, the genetic offspring as compared to the adopted children? And was the punishment harsher for the loved ones of a Book of the State desecrator—one who spits on the Book, no less? I'd never read the Book. It had all been such infantile nonsense to me. I'd stuck with the disenfranchised novels and poetry anthologies, books kept in my house illegally and which they'd now find. I had to help my family and didn't see any other way of doing it except by calculated violence, which had to overcome my growing hysteria. I edged myself nearer to the driver, who along with the crowd was waving at and cheering the bus that had pulled away. I found a wrench under his seat, came down on his head with it and, as he was trying to hold onto my legs from the floor, his head gushing blood, I pulled the door lever and shoved him outside, his body knocking over the people trying to get in.

The key was still in the ignition switch. I started the engine, almost had to run over a group of people to get past them, and drove after the other bus. I began gaining on it, this bus pulsing with excited passengers, and through the rearview mirror I saw the other bus behind me, though its headlights gradually getting smaller. I overtook the bus in front, passed the stop my wife and child had been at, and drove to our home. I left the engine running and ran through the house till I found them in the kitchen, both weeping. "Dearests," I said, "get into the bus outside—quick. No time for explanations"—when Janet asked me for one—"just move, move." But she looked even more bewildered, even frightened, and withdrew with Lila behind a chair.

"Goddamnit, do what I say before they get us."

"Who is they?" she said.

"The people: Intercom, psychopaths, latent killers."

"And why should these people be after us?"

"Because we've desecrated the Book of the State—now I said *move*."

"I didn't desecrate anything. And Lila and I can't be responsible for another one of your dangerous acts."

"Because I've desecrated the Book," I said, thinking that even though I still loved her I'd never seen her so stupid, "it means all my immediate loved ones who are either living with me or are my genetic offspring, are almost as responsible as I am."

"Then I'll simply explain that I never loved you and you're not the father of my child. And that I lived with you only because you were emotionally ill and I was paid to be your nurse and cook."

"They're after the emotionally ill also. I read it in the papers before. The president's going to sign the bill into law tomorrow. And one amending provision states that anyone living with the offender for two months or more will also be judged emotionally ill. Now come on, Jan, for your one chance of freedom is with me."

We got on the bus just as the other buses were pulling up, the passengers frustratedly banging their Books on the windows at us—acts of desecration, I thought, tertiary, maybe even secondary crimes that could also penalize their families. I drove on and in a few minutes they were nowhere behind us. Intercom could be close, but I knew these roads well, so I might be able to elude them. Suddenly on the Intercom band a man was speaking to us. "Haven't a single chance, Mr. Piper. Your lines are tagged, Mrs. Piper. Lila, you awake? Seven minutes to capture, friends. Why resist any further? Stop now. Feel relieved. Better an authorized state Intercom officer than a mad state mob. Press button G to confirm message and detail pickup site." I pressed G and roared obscenities till my breath gave out, though no doubt swearing on the state radio was another crime, maybe major.

Then I told Intercom I was shutting them off because their mechanical dictums were distracting my in-flight skills, and smashed in the radio with the wrench and pulled out the wires.

I drove out of the city, through suburbs and then suburbs of suburbs till we entered that part of the state where there was still some untouched land left. I saw a cow and pointed her out to Lila, who squealed with pleasure. Janet apologized to me, rested her head on my thigh and said she was scared but was glad I'd convinced her to come with me. Lila was on my lap, pretending to be the driver, laughing when I told her to pay more attention to the road.

"Where we going?" she said.

"As far to the state border as we can get."

"Drive carefully, darlings," Janet said.

Lila soon fell asleep, her hands still on the wheel. We drove most of the night, over backroads where I hoped Intercom wouldn't be able to tail us in the dark. When the fuel gauge was nearing empty I turned into a dirt road and drove the bus another twenty miles before we were out of gas. I rested Lila on one of the back benches, covered her with my jacket, and in the middle of the bus we settled down ourselves. "Kiss me," Janet said. We were in the mountains, close to the border of the adjoining state. This state also had a Book, though I'd been told by ex-lawyer friends that it had a very progressive policy regarding college-educated immigrants, substituting a few years of unpaid military service as punishment for major crimes committed in another state. In a few hours we'd make the journey by foot. We had to start over someplace, no matter how restrictive it might become there. I kissed Janet. We hugged each other and I told her what my driver had said about her ass and boobs, and she seemed pleased, became giddy and playful.

"Touch my neat ass," she said.

"Don't know if I can. It might be considered an act of desecration. We have to consult the Book of the State first," I found the driver's book, thumbed through the index and located the right passage. "It says here 'All immediate family personal privileges, such as embraces, hand-locking, body-fondling, lip, nose or any sensory coupling such as flesh-conjoining, may be done solely in the privacy of the couple's legally designated residence, or if permitted in writing by the state.' Now, a legally designated residence is defined as—" but her frenzied tongue plugged up my mouth.

GETTING LOST   .

Couple of minutes after she comes home from work she says "If you don't mind, I'd like you to go."

"What?"

"I want you to leave for good."

"It's not that I didn't understand you. Just that you're not kidding, right? And for good?"

"I know it sounds abrupt. But I didn't want to talk about it. I only wanted to say 'please leave' and hoped you would know what I mean and get your things fast and go. That's what I hoped."

"Okay, so I'll leave."

"Good."

"I'm going. Just give me a second to catch my breath,"

"Fine. If you don't mind, I'll wait upstairs."

"No, I don't mind."

"I mean, I just don't want to be around. This is as bad a moment for me as it is for you."

"I know. Or I think I do. Sure it must be. It has to. After all, we've been together a long time. Almost three years."

"That long? I guess so. I'm sorry. Though no hard feelings, all right?"

"Right."

She goes upstairs. I start getting my things together downstairs. I've an apartment in the city but have spent four to five of every seven days here in her house upstate. So I get my things. Books first. Work materials. I put them all in the canvas carryall bag I've lugged from house to apartment to house and back again the past three years.

My favorite coffee mug? Sure, why not? Why leave anything behind? But why not leave most of it? She'd see the mug and know it's mine and my favorite and maybe one day return it with all the other things I'd leave behind and that day we might be able to get something going again. No, don't think like that. It's over, finished, done. Get lost, she essentially said. All right. What I'm doing. Fast as I can and forever. We've tried. We lost. Lot of bull. Then what? What went wrong? Why think about it now? Plenty of time later on. What will happen? I'll pack, upstairs and down, take the bus home with all my junk. If she was nice she'd drive me, as this stuff's going to weigh a ton.

"You couldn't by chance drive me to the city?" I yell upstairs.

"I'd really prefer not to."

"Okay. I understand."

"Thanks. Especially for being so understanding."

She's in her room. Probably lying on the bed. Feeling sad, no doubt. Gets very emotional sometimes. We've had these scenes before. They always worked out, though. I'd pack. Ready to go, I'd say goodbye. We'd be sad. Maybe cry. She'd say "I obviously can't adjust." I'd say "I of course wouldn't expect you to do or give up anything you didn't want to." We'd kiss goodbye. I'd hold her. We'd hold each other. She'd say "Why are we being so silly?" "I don't know," I'd say. "If there's anything really bothering us," she'd say, "why can't we just talk and work it out instead of always taking the worst extreme?" Then we'd make love. Or take a long walk. But be lovey-dovey, though. And later she'd help me unpack and maybe say "How many more times you think we can do this?" But this time it's not going to be like that. I can see. We gave ourselves one last time. And before that, one last time. We really are two different persons as she's said. I'm much more sensitive and creative than her. She's more straightforward and practical than me. Other things. Maybe the way I described us just now isn't true. But I can see why she wouldn't want me around very much. I'm not jolly. I get on people's nerves after a' while. Maybe everybody does. But we don't belong together. Ill-suited, poorly mated, mismatched. I think she's superficial, really. Deep down I want a woman to really give herself to me. Not all the time. But deeply. As I think I did with her. Not all the time. But much more than her. To stick with me. By me. I need that confidence. I said I was sensitive. I'm also insecure. Maybe we all are. And she's not superficial. But I have to know she's there and sexually only for me. But she can't. She likes to see other men.

I get jealous. They like to see her. She says "I can understand your jealousy but it annoys me." So she resents me for annoying her and I resent her for going out with other men. Those two to three nights a week I'm not here. Not for going out with them but sleeping with them. I had to ask. She said "You know I'm unable to lie to anyone, so I have to say I occasionally do." But her not lying isn't altogether the truth. If I didn't resent her sleeping with other men, we could continue as a couple. Those four to five days. But I do resent it. I've tried to sluff it off. Ho-hum. Who cares? What I don't know doesn't hurt me. But it does. It comes out. She's told me to see other women. I can't. "Sleep with them too." But one's enough. She is. I've even asked her to marry me. She really laughed when I asked that. Just a few weeks ago. I admitted it was funny. That I was actually proposing. Saying those words and for the first time too. "This might sound funny, but will you marry me?" I thought marriage was what we both wanted and needed most. Or at least I did. But don't go into it anymore. Just go. Get your things. Leave. Get lost. No goodbye. Take the bus. Go to your apartment. Drink a bottle of wine. Get drunk. Pass out. Do that for two days. Plenty of sleep. Then it'll be over. Simple as that, really. Or I hope so.

I pack all my things downstairs. Only the books I borrowed from her village library are left.

"Could you return my library books here so I won't have to pay a fine?" I yell upstairs.

"Where are they?"

"In the red bookcase, top shelf. About ten of them."

"If they're overdue now, why not run then over yourself?"

I look at the books. "They are overdue. Ah, you're so clever. I'll take them there now."

"You've time to both pack your things upstairs and catch the next bus?"

"It comes at five."

"Okay. Thanks."

Library's just a few doors down the road. Big pillars. Old baby blue colonial courthouse. Sarah the librarian's there. "Returning these," I say. I pay the fine.

"I was going to call you. Two of the books you ordered came."

"Won't be needing them now as I won't be here to return."

"Things not right?"

"Right."

"Too bad. You're our best customer. Hate to lose one of those. County gives us an additional stipend for each hundred books borrowed over what it's set as our regular load. Why not take the books anyway and mail them back in a jiffy bag?"

"They don't treat me like this in the city. I'll miss you and your coffee urn and of course your books." We shake hands. I kiss her cheek.

"Very sweet," she says. "Keep in touch."

I will miss this village. Didn't think it before, but now do. Ribbon mill right on the river. Many of the villagers skating there in winter. Not swimming there in summer yet, but fishing and picnicking and watching the boats and ships. Lovely old houses. Winding bushy roads. Nice fall foliage. The springs here. Big snowfalls. Crazy Mr. McNally, the accepted peeping snoop. Better than the city. City's grimy and stinks and rattles my ears. But can't afford it here on my own. Soes it goes, as Mona and I made up a phrase. Her son. I'll miss him too. Good kid. Likes me. And smart. Together we were like a family. Most times better than most families it seemed to me. She should have thought of that too. Pleasant Street. Three bars and a barber shop and a thrift and a liquor store and Millionaires Mart. Volunteer firemen's parade every July 4th. Village Hall and its slide shows. Even the baying dogs late at night. Raccoons and rabbits and skunks, and a deer once, trying to climb over Mona's garden fence. I'm no longer the confirmed urbanite. Not really knocking the city. Just had enough. But got to get moving to catch the five after five bus.

I go back to her house. Really got all the things from downstairs? Mug? Take it. What else? Fancy supply of marmalades and jams? Take the unopened ones. Paring knife? Cost a lot and the one in my apartment is only good for buttering bread. Antique colander I bought at a lawn sale? Nah, leave them all. Now upstairs.

She's on her bed writing. Looks at me questioningly

"The time?" I say; I show her my watch.

"Good."

"Sure you want me to go?"

"I do. I'm sure."

"What made you finally decide? Because I thought we were all having a good time."

"Reasons, reasons."

"For instance."

"For instance I already told you I don't want to talk about it."

"All I'm asking for is one."

"Just that. That you won't just drop it. Don't persist. One of the reasons is that you persist too much."

"Oh, I see. Nothing I say now will be right. It'll all fall under the category of persistence. Okay. I'm going to get my clothes."

"I'll go downstairs," and she gets off the bed.

"You don't have to."

"I want to. I told you this isn't easy for me either."

"That's right. I remember. Must be tough, my leaving. Oh yes. Very tough, then why the hell did you ask me to leave?"

"Reason two. Cynicism. You can be very cynical. Believe me, it isn't easy to take over long periods of time."

"Better over short periods?"

"Cynicism. Persistence."

"Any other reasons?"

"What do you want? I already gave you two."

"That's it? Just two? There's got to be a third. If not a third, then at least a fourth. Or a sixth. Skip the third, fourth and fifth and just slip me the sixth."

"That too. Reason three, or as you'll have it, six, is your occasional crazy talk. And sometimes it's not so occasional and seems truly crazy."

"Maybe you're only saying it's crazy because you can't understand it. But I don't know any other halfway intelligent adult who wouldn't get it and might even think it slightly funny."

"There's another. Your arrogance. That you think you're so funny and smart when you're not."

"Me smart? Oh no. You're the smart one. Me, I'm dumb. Dumb because I hung around so long. I thought of getting out a few times, but then thought we could work it out. Well, up yours' now. I'm glad we're through."

"Two more. That you lie. That you blow up so easily. And other reasons. Plenty. But especially the one I haven't said yet."

"What? That I get jealous because you see other men?"

"That's another. A very big one. Jealousy, which I can't take. But it's not the one I was going to give."

"Don't let me stop you. What is it?"

"Forget it."

"But I want to know the big reason of them all."

"Reason one. Persistence. Stop it. Leave me alone."

She goes downstairs. I follow her.

"Reason ten or eleven. You hound me. Just what you're doing. Following me, hounding me. Always on my back after I've said get off."

"And one I have against you is repetition. You repeat things too much. You say something and then repeat it till it's dead."

"You don't? You just did. Maybe it's the one thing we have in common." She looks around. "Good. You have all your things packed from downstairs. Now please get your clothes and bathroom things and catch the five o'clock bus."

"Five after five. And reason two for me is your inconsiderateness. For you couldn't have driven me? The last thing I asked from you and you wouldn't? Well, thanks."

"I've an appointment around that time, that's why."

"You could've called to delay it. But that's only part of your inconsiderateness. And maybe you're a liar too. Because before you said it would've been too sad or disturbing for you to be with me during the trip."

"That too."

"Bull."

She leaves the house. I follow her.

"Damn you, will you get your things and leave?"

"Right. One reason in my favor and which should maybe cancel out one of the twelve to fourteen negative ones is that I take orders well. Obedience. Yes, sir. At your command. Goodbye." I salute her, go into the house, pack my things upstairs, stuff what I can't get into the carryall into two shopping bags, and leave. She's nowhere around. I walk up the hill and wait for the bus. It doesn't come. I walk down the hill and knock on her door. She opens it. She's been crying.

"Bus never came."

"Is that true?"

"Swear. Got there before five. Waited for more than a half hour. I didn't want to come back. Honest. You've been crying."

"So?"

"Not about us, of course."

"Don't be reason number whatever it was before."

"I've been crying too. Why are we doing this? Not the crying, but just this."

"I'm not sure. Anyway, what we're doing is right."

"Right. Can I come in and call the bus company to see what's wrong?"

"But be quick."

The bus company man says "Because of road construction the route's been changed from Sunset Drive to River Road on weekdays from seven-thirty to half past six. We posted a notice on the post office and community bulletin boards of all the towns affected."

"You should've posted them at the libraries too, but thanks." To Mona: "I've got to run if I'm to catch the five after six bus."

She sticks out her hand. We shake. "No goodbye kiss?" I say.

"Wouldn't do." She goes upstairs.

"Last chance to keep me?" I yell.

"Bye."

I go to River Road and wait for the bus. It comes I don't wave it down. I go back to Mona's and knock on the door. Her son opens it. "Oh, you got home," I say.

"What are you doing? I thought you were already here."

"Your mother and I had a little spat."

"For good this time?"

"I think so."

"Then what are you doing back with your bags?"

"Burleigh, how can you be so insensitive? You're supposed to feel relatively crumbled that I won't be around anymore."

"I'll miss you, don't worry, but what can I do? I got to go."

He runs past me down the stairs. "Hey, what about a little kiss farewell from you, chump?"

"I don't mean to be mean but I'm in a hurry, Bo." We wave and he goes.

I call into the house "Mona? That changed schedule made me miss the bus again. Can I stay here till the next one comes?"

"No," she yells from her room.

I go upstairs. "Just another twenty minutes or so."

"You didn't miss the bus. You let it go by."

"Okay. I let it go by so I could see you once more."

"Fine. Now that you've seen me, get out."

"Give me a chance to get a good look."

"Don't be stupid again."

"And don't be so insulting," I say.

"You're forcing me to say these things and be this way. I'm getting angry. Frustrated."

"What does that mean?"

"That means don't get me even angrier and more frustrated by acting even more intentionally stupid. That means leave this house. That means start now. That means go. Get lost. What do I have to do, call the police?"

"Last time I thought you were a little sorry I left and glad I honestly missed that bus."

"Last time I might have been but I've thought it over and now I'm not. I don't want you around anymore. Never again. Plain and simple—scram, stupid."

I grab a plant off the washstand and throw it at her.

She ducks and it hits her chin. She screams. Blood comes out. She's on the bed holding her face and screaming. I get down on the floor on my knees and say "I'm sorry, I'm sorry." She pushes me away and runs to the bathroom. I run after her. She has a towel to her face and I say "I should've done that. Got you that towel. I shouldn't have thrown that plant. Tell me what I can do for you."

She goes downstairs with the towel wrapped around her face and goes outside and gets in her car and drives away.

"Where you going?" I yell.

Probably to the hospital. The police she could have called. Or maybe to the police because she thought I'd stop her call. But probably to the hospital our some friend. I got to get out of here. First time I ever hit someone like that as an adult. That finished us, of course. Hitting someone? Worst thing I've done in my life. They hate it. Women do. Especially Mona. Said once when I raised my hand to her "Touch me like that and it'll be the last time I so much as say boo to you. I hate men who knock women around. Hate anyone who abuses with his hands."

"I got excited," I write on the blackboard in the kitchen, "Of course: much worse than that. I'm sorry. I love you both. See ya."

I head down the hill with my bags. No, if's after six-thirty, the bus is back on Sunset Drive. I go up the hill and wait, put on a different shirt and throw the bloody one into the woods. The bus comes. I should have cleaned up her room. Repotted the plant, scrubbed the bathroom sink and floor. I signal the bus and get on it. Andy Maxwell's there.

"How's it going?" he says.

"Don't ask."

"Sit next to me," he says when I sit two rows behind.

"Andy, I'm really feeling lousy right now. Mona and I broke up. Worse. I hit her in the face with a flower pot. She probably went to the hospital for stitches. It's possible I broke her jaw. Not only did I do that to the person I love most, but the police might be after me now for it."

"You never should have got so excited."

"I know. That's what I just wrote her. But what I really can't take now is anything like advice after the fact and so on. Commiseration. I'm miserable. I feel as lost as I ever have in my life. Worse."

He sits next to me.

"Please?"

"Look, whatever you did to Mona, bad as it is, she might have deserved it. She's a bitch. You're much better off split up. You'll feel lousy for a while, but know that she has very few friends here and more than a few who'd like to have thrown a pot at her, though not in her face. She's a complete fake. Thinks she's the hottest goods imaginable and lies blue streaks day and night. She'll do anything to get ahead, and that means buddy screw her best friends and use them as fools. She's also a snob. Loves anybody who's anybody or rich, no matter how rotten that person might be. You did a bad thing in hitting her, granted. But I can well understand how she could push someone to do it. She's just not nice but pretends to be with that big smile and cheerful disposition and charm of hers, and that kind of twofacedness throws people into a rage."

"No, no, she's not like anything you say."

"You don't see it. Or you don't want to admit it.

You're too nice a guy yourself and can't see' anything but good in people and cringe at saying anything bad. I'm not saying these things to make you feel better. I'm also not one to repeat gossip, but only what I see myself firsthand. In time you'll know I'm right."

"I hope not. And I don't want to think about it.

Excuse me but I really want to close my eyes and maybe sleep."

We get to the city. Andy takes one subway and I take another to my apartment. I drink a bottle of wine while I listen to sad music and read the papers. Then I call Mona.

Burleigh answers. "Mom's in bed. She just came back from the hospital and had five stitches put in her chin. Why'd you hit her like that?"

"I feel awful. It was totally my fault. I love your mother, honestly. Please tell her how terrible I feel and that I'll pay all the medical bills and anything else she asks."

"Want me to tell her now?"

"Yes."

He comes back to the phone. "She says to shove it. She told me to say that. And I'll tell you how I feel, Bo. You did the worst thing." He hangs up.

I call Sarah. "Sarah, I hit Mona with a flower pot before. We're really split now, for good. I know I sound a bit drunk, but I wanted to know if you'd go over there now and check in on her. Maybe she needs some help."

"She has Burleigh, doesn't she?"

"Sure. He's home."

"And other friends perhaps, so she doesn't need me. To tell you the truth, Mona and I never got along well. It would have been nice, having a friend living so close, but that's not the way it is. I'm sorry you hit her. That was wrong. But as far as my feeling for her is concerned, she's a mite too pushy and self-centered and a stinker of the lowest degree."

"Really think so?"

"I'm not the only one. Take care."

I call up the Ludwigs, whom I consider our best friends around where Mona lives. Ben says some of the same awful things about her and says his wife Mary feels the same way. "Besides that, she's going to get in a lot worse trouble than a flower pot in her face. She goes out with the wrong kind of guys. One's a pusher. She's brought a couple of them over here between the times you were in the city and when I thought things were dandy between you two. Who knows what she saw in them."

"They were all very good looking," Mary says on the extension. "Nicely built. Big too. She likes men with lots of wild fluffy black hair. I like them also, but not dopes and pigs like these. Like her, they only seemed interested in a good quick time for themselves at the moment and nothing else. Take it from me, Bo, you're much better off without her."

"Am I?"

"We both think you were the best chance she had to improve."

I call up several other people Mona and I know. They all say I should have shown more restraint. Nobody has a nice word for her, though. I begin to feel sorry for her now in a different way. I picture her all alone. Without good friends. Just Burleigh and she. And all these people saying nasty things about her behind her back and even to her face. I see her lying in bed with a bandage on her jaw, planning things, scheming, worried about what the chin scar will do to her beauty, or maybe just sleeping now or in pain. Maybe she did push me too far. Still, I should have held back. Anyway, I don't feel as bad about myself now and that I won't be seeing her anymore. Tomorrow I'll feel better. Days after that, better yet. I'll send her flowers. Make my apologies more intelligible in a letter or two and wish her a long happy life, and then forget her for good. I drink more wine and get sleepy. "Mona," I shout, "I love you, what can I say?" I pass out. All night I seem to dream of her making love with other men and enjoying it. I wake up around three and for hours just lie there with the lights on. "Tough days ahead," I say.

END OF A

FRIEND.

I bump into him. He says "Excuse me."

I say "The same."

He passes. I say "Wait up."

He stops, turns to me. "Yes?"

"You forgot something."

He looks around. "I don't see anything. What?"

"To say excuse me."

"Either you didn't hear me before or you're trying to fool me."

"No other alternative?"

"None I can think of now, but what of it?"

"You're right. You did say excuse me."

"Fine, then. I won't begin to try to understand you." He walks away.

"One more thing."

He doesn't stop. I run after him, tap his shoulder. "Didn't you hear me?"

"Yes, I heard you."

"Good. For a second I was afraid maybe your hearing wasn't okay."

"My hearing, my vision, and I'll tell you, my smelling, are all okay." He starts off again.

I run after him, grab his arm. "Now listen you," he says, pushing my hand away. "I don't quite like this. Not 'quite.' I definitely don't. I don't know you, yet you stop me and immediately try to fool me. Then you talk some gibberish about my hearing to me. Maybe you even intentionally bumped into me. Now it's no doubt something else. Well, I've someplace to be now. Important work. People are depending on my being there. So if you don't mind?"

"But one more thing. Only what I wanted to say to you before I got distracted and asked about your hearing."

"All right. One more thing. What?"

"Your face."

"Yes, my face."

"Yes, that you have a face."

"You're right. How completely absentminded of me. I have a face. Thanks for reminding me. Goodbye."

He starts off. I grab his arm. He swivels around hard this time and says "Stop me once more and I'm going to do something you won't like."

"Why?"

"Because you're provoking me. Detaining me for some ulterior or insidious reason of your own which I think I'm finally on to and am a little fearful of. Now, may I go? Not that I have to ask you. But rather, I am going, and stop me once more and it's the police I talk to next, not you."

"Go on, go on, I'm not stopping you."

"You don't call grabbing my arm a couple of times and saying nonsensical things to stop me, stopping me?"

"To be honest, yes, I'd say I stopped you, but not with nonsensical things."

"Oh? That I have a face?"

"My point wasn't just that you have a face. For we all have faces. All except those poor disfigured people who don't have faces. Not disfigured. People without faces at all, I mean. But that wasn't my point. My point was that you have something on your face."

"My nose."

"Yes, your nose. You see, you knew. I didn't have to tell you after all."

"Don't I know. And excuse me for being so blunt, sir, but you're mad."

"No I'm not. I thought you were more observant than that. Can you take a little more honesty for one day? I'm feeling unusually content with myself talking with you here, not at all mad. That's honesty. That's an honest statement about my life, is what I'm saying, which you might or might not agree."

"I mean in the head, which you knew perfectly well. A screw loose. Daft. Disturbed. Your desperate need for attention perhaps. Your... but I'm not going to analyze you. Excuse me for even having said what

I did, as your mental and emotional states are none of my business. And now I'm going. Stop me again and I will call the police, and after that, who knows? Maybe the courts will decide you belong in an asylum for a while, which I don't think you'd like in the least. Now, have I made my point clear?"

"Good and clear. If that was any indication how you make your points, then you make them very well."

I watch him go. I sit on the curb. I watch the cars and trucks go by. The vehicles. Buses, bicycles, motorcycles, scooters. People go by too. Baby carriages. Not along the street but across it and then on the sidewalk across the street. Lots go by. Dogs with their walkers, dogs without. A battery-powered wheelchair. Two girls on roller skates in the street. Only roller skaters I saw today on the street or off. Day goes by. Night comes and stops. I stay on the curb. I look at the lights of passing planes overhead. I look at the water running along the curb under my legs. A twig floats by. Half a walnut shell empty side up. Piece of paper. I pick it up and read it. It's the label of a pickle jar. Spices, cucumber slices, vinegar, a preservative, and where it's made and by which company and the kind of pickle it is. I drop it into the water and it floats away. Someone must have opened a fire hydrant nearby.

A dog off its leash stops and sniffs the parking meter pole I've been using as a back rest. I shoo it away. It comes back. I say "Scat." It sniffs the pole some more and lifts its leg. I say "Get out of here, beat it, scram," and raise my hand.

"Touch that dog and you're in trouble," a man holding a leash says.

"He your dog?"

"Whether he is or isn't, just say I don't see anyone beating on dogs."

"If he's your dog, tell me, so I can ask you to call him away."

"Why? The pole's public. On a public sidewalk alongside a public street. So that dog has as much right to the pole as you."

"Any sensible person knows people have more rights than dogs. Just the word 'public,' for instance, will tell you that. From publicus, pubes, populus, people, people, not that one should expect anyone else to know that."

"Okay. Maybe some people have more rights than dogs. But for you, I don't think so."

"Whatever you say. But I don't want your dog, if he is your dog— just this dog then—stepping a step nearer to me and lifting his leg again, or I'll summon the police and have it taken away. There's the street for what a dog has to do, not the sidewalk or against a building wall or fire hydrant or parking meter pole, and certainly not against me."

He raises his finger in a curse sign and walks away. The dog follows, does its duty against a parking meter pole a few feet away. Does its other duty on the sidewalk a few feet past that. The man inspects it, hooks the leash on the dog's collar, and they leave. I continue to sit. Those were the only words I said to anyone or were said to me since I saw that other man on the street and tried to speak to him about his face. Then it begins to rain. Someone dressed for the rain and under an umbrella comes over to me and says "Don't you think you should come out of the rain?"

"That your umbrella?"

"Yes."

"Can I get under it?"

"There's only room enough for one. You want an umbrella, buy one. If you haven't the money, work so you can buy one. I don't think that's too unreasonable a solution. But if you want a cold and possibly a fatal case of pneumonia, then you're doing exactly the right thing."

"Thank you for your advice. I think I'll just continue to sit."

"If that's what you really want, I've no complaints."

She goes. I continue to sit in the rain. I begin to catch a cold. Coughs, sneezes, a few feverish chills. The rain turns to sleet and then snow. I continue to sit. I can't see the sky or the buildings across the street because of the snow and now not even the passing vehicles. The rain soaked me, now the snow covers me. I have no coat or hat on and only half a pair of socks, and the water's soaked through the holes in my soles and the protective layers of paper inside my shoes to my feet. Several people stop beside me. They're all dressed for the snow. One of them says "You have to come out of the snow. It's a blizzard. Twenty inches are expected. It's going to last till early tomorrow the weather report says. You'll freeze to death out here."

"You know or have a better place for me to go? I've run out of thinking or looking for them."

"Under an awning. If all the awnings around here are down because the owners are afraid they'll be crushed or blown away, then in a lobby or store. And if not there because they'd rather not have you for whatever their reasons, then in a parked car if you can find one unlocked or in one of those shelters downtown, but someplace warmer and more sheltered than here."

"Thank you very much but I don't think I can do that anymore."

"If you're too sick to, I'm sure we can call some service to help."

"No, I think it's better I just sit."

Someone must have called the police. By this time I'm very sick. The police put a coat on me, carry me to a drugstore and sit me beside a warm radiator till an ambulance comes. I'm driven to a city hospital, wheeled into the emergency section, put on an examining table. The curtains are pulled around me. My clothes are scissored off. The doctor who takes care of me is the same man I spoke to earlier today about something regarding his face. He checks my eyes and ears and after taking my pulse and listening to my chest, says "Personally, I knew you'd come to no good."

I can't speak. I try to, my mouth opens but I'm physically unable to.

"I mean, up to no good," he says. "Not just for everyone else, "but to yourself too. Am I right? Don't bother to answer. You're obviously too weak. But can you take a little honesty now yourself? I'm afraid, my friend, this is the end."

STARTING AGAIN.

"It's so difficult." "What is?" "Just dealing with it." "Dealing with what?" "The rejections day after day, day after day." "Don't send your work out then." "Then they'll just pile up." "Don't do them then." "Then I'll have nothing to do." "Try to do something else then." "I can't. I've been doing this so long." "But if you've had no luck?" "I didn't say I haven't had any luck." "Then little success? Really, what can I say that I haven't already said?" "Nothing, please say nothing. I know you're trying to be helpful but I have to work this out on my own."

I go into the bedroom, shut the door, lie on the bed. She comes in. "I'm sorry," she says, "but I have to work in here." "You can't work in the other room?" "That's where you're working." "I don't think I'll be working there anymore." "What'll you do then?" "I'm not sure. I've just lain down to think about it." "You couldn't lie down on the couch? I'll tell you why I ask you that. You used to work in this room and I used to work in the other. Then you said this room isn't the best room for you to work in and you'd like to work in the other, so I got all my things out of that room, brought them into this room and started to work here. Now you say I should go back into the other room, which means carting all my things back to it, and I now have even more things than when I used to work in that room because I'm much further along in the project I'm working on. But you want me back in the other room not because you want to work in this one but because you want to lie on the bed and think about work. Be honest—is that fair?"

"I don't know if it's fair or not." "Then what I'm asking of you is to think about whether it's fair." "I don't want to spend my time thinking about that. I just want to think about what I might like to do other than the work I've been doing. And I can think better alone, lying on a bed, than alone, lying on a couch." "You're not being fair." "Maybe I'm not, but it is what I want." "What about what I want?" "If I thought about it I'd consider it, but right now I only want to think about what I'm going to work on from now on or at least for the immediate future." "Give yourself a minute or less to think about how my moving into the other room again will affect my work, what I want, and so on, besides how difficult it'll be for me to move all my things back to that room." "I'll help you. I'll even move it all by myself for you." "Okay, I can see there's no arguing with you for now, so let's get it done. But don't ask to move back into that other room once my move is done if you decide, after all your thinking in here, you could do your work much better alone out there." "I doubt I could promise you that." "Excuse me, I'm going for a walk."

She puts on her sweater, takes her keys and goes. I turn over on my stomach and think about what I'm going to do. I could do this, I could do that, work at this, work at that, try this, try that, this, that, this, that. None seem like the right thing to do. None excite me or seem like anything I could or would want to do. This minute I wish I lived alone so I wouldn't have to face her when she gets back. So I wouldn't have to explain anything more to her. So I wouldn't have to help her move into the next room or tell her I changed my mind about wanting her to move there or about not wanting to do what I've been doing the last twenty years. For that's what I decide on now, this second, or just a few seconds ago. Decided it when I was thinking I didn't want to help her move into the next room. Decided to go back to doing what I've been doing the last twenty years. Decided it because none of the other things I thought of doing seemed right for me or excited me and so on, and not doing anything seemed worse than any of those other things I thought of doing and also worse than not doing what I've been doing for twenty years. I fall asleep.

"You haven't moved my things or even started to." For a moment I thought she said that in my dream. But she apparently woke me up by poking me or some other way and said that while I was coming out of sleep. "What did you say?" "You didn't hear me?" "Yes, I heard you, if what I think you said is what you said and not what I thought you said in my dream. You said something about my not having moved your things?" "Yes. Can you tell me why? I've lots of work to do today and I want to start doing it right away." "So do I." "Fine, do your work, but

I can't do mine out there unless all of my work things are out there, and you promised to move them for me, remember?" "I do, sort of, because it was either me alone or both of us, but I've changed my mind. Stay in this room." "What will you do?" "Same as I've always done, and in the old room." "You decided that?" "Yes." "Suppose I said I just now decided I want to move back to the other room?" "Then I'd say that's okay, I'll help you move back there, but not today, or at least not right now, as I want to get back to work right away, and because all my equipment for work is in the other room, I don't have time to move you there now." "Suppose I said I don't care if you want to get right back to work; that I want to move back to the other room right now so I can resume work soon as I can after my things are moved there?" "Then I'd say okay, that's fair. I've put you through a lot. I've asked you to do plenty of things for me and you've never really asked me to do anything like those things for you, so this time I'll put what you have to do over anything I have to." "Suppose I said I don't believe you?" "Try me out." "All right, I'm trying you out. Help me move my things into the other room." "Where should we begin? They're your things, so you know where they should go." "No, I believe you. Or maybe I don't, but I don't want to go into it now because all I want to do is work. I had a terrific idea when I was outside about the work I'm doing and I don't want to lose it." "Good, because I also had a terrific idea when I was thinking just before I fell asleep, and I want to get to it right away." "Then I'll see you." "Want me to close the door?" "Thanks as I don't want to be disturbed by anything. Not your talking to yourself while you work or your equipment going like mad. I've got to have maximum quiet in here to concentrate, or as much quiet as it's possible to get." "I'll have to make some noise out there, you know." "That's all right. What I can't control, I can't control." "Same with me, I suppose."

I kiss her cheek, leave the room and close the door. A few seconds later I hear her working. I sit down at the dining table where my equipment is. I might as well start. I don't have any idea what I'll be working on now, but I should try to start something. I've sat down before with nothing in my head and almost always started something. I can do it again. If I can't do it this time, it doesn't mean I won't be able to do it again. In fact, I just about know for sure I'll be able to do it again, now or sometime soon. If not sometime soon, then sometime in the not too distant future, though it's never taken me that long to start again. So I'm not worried. Start something. Remember that if it doesn't come now, chances are almost nonexistent it won't ever come again.

THE

ARGUMENT .

I enter the room and he leaves. Then he enters the room and I leave. Then I'm about to enter the room as he's about to leave it, neither of us steps aside so the other can pass, and we stop at the door's threshold, facing each other. I say "What do you say to enough of this?"

"Enough of what?"

"This entering and leaving, reentering and releaving. Let's have it out completely or make up without having it out completely, but one way or the other or even some other working-out."

"What other working-out?"

"One not one of the two I just gave you but a new one I haven't yet worked out. I'll just say I'm sorry and you also say you're sorry, and then, all made up, we can both go back to that room or both be outside it, but at least be in the same place together at the same time."

"I don't see any need for making up with you."

"Then you don't see any need for saying you're sorry for what you did or any need for being in the same place at the same time together when we want to be?"

"I didn't say that."

"Do you say it now?"

"Yes on the first, maybe only a maybe on the second. I see no reason for saying I'm sorry for what I did, though I do see the advantage, since we both live here, of thinking we can be in the same room together without getting on each other's nerves. But it was your fault alone, so you're the one who has to apologize, not me."

"I don't see it that way. I say it was as much my fault as yours. And that if we both admit that through a mutual apology, we'll have made up and then we can stay in the same room together."

"I can't admit anything like that because I don't believe it."

"The heck with you then," and I try to get by him.

"Where do you think you're going?" he says.

"Around you, where I was heading to before, so I can get into that room."

"I'd also like to be in that room. So would you please turn around and go into one of the other rooms? Or stay in the hallway here or go outside or do whatever you want to wherever you want to do it? But not in that room till you apologize for starting the argument before, because until then I want to be in that room alone."

"But that's the room I want to be in and the only room I can be in to do the things I want to. It has the books and television set and fireplace, and I want to find a book and read it with a fire going and the television on but the sound turned very low. I don't want to explain why I want the sound turned very low while I read, but I do, it's my privilege why I do, and also my privilege why I don't want to tell you."

"You want to know something?" he says.

"If it's that you're going to accept the mutual apology idea I proposed, I do."

"No. It's that we're about to get into a bad argument again."

"Oh, we're not in one now?" I say. "Now we're still discussing things in a relatively unquarrelsome way. But you want to know why we're about to get into another bad argument? Because you insist doing something you know is impossible for me to allow you to do, which is the main reason we got into the last bad argument that led up to all this. Now please, for both of us, turn around and go into one of the other rooms or outside or anyplace else, but leave me alone in that room."

"Why do you say I'm the one responsible for this argument we're getting into? Because I want to be in a room I pay half the rent on? Because I want to read a book among the many books in that room that are mostly mine? Because I want—"

"Neither of those, nor the third one you were about to give: the television set, which I know you paid for so is all yours. But because you insist on being somewhere that you know will anger another person who also wants to be there. And last time—"

"Don't give me any last times," I say.

"That too. Last time you also refused to listen to my reasons, which was just another reason we had that bad argument. But the last time I was about to tell you of—"

"I said to stop with those last times."

"Right," he says. "Because what you just said is another reason why we had that bad argument the last time, and why we're starting to have one now, which I'm sure you'll say we started equally and I'll say you started alone. Because last time you also told me to shut up about the previous last time and wouldn't let me go on—"

"I don't want you to go on now because—"

"—because you didn't want to hear me explain reasonably and extra rationally, as I'm doing now, that you—"

"I didn't want you to explain, that last time and the time before that, because you—"

"Because I—"

"Shut up," I say.

"Because I was making sense, that's why. I made sense that last time and I'm making sense now. But you can't stand anyone who makes sense when you're feeling really argumentative about something."

"Now I said to shut up. I'm in fact warning you to shut up."

"Don't threaten me. That's what you did the last time, and I won't be threatened, just as I wouldn't the last time."

"Then shut up and stay that way. If you don't, you'll be sorry."

"Sorry about what? That you won't argue rationally? That you won't let me speak what you know is the truth about you? That you won't take responsibility for the bad arguments we have when they're solely caused by you?"

"I'm warning you."

"That I won't bow down to your warnings and feel frightened by your threats and shut up when you tell me to, and all that? I'm to be sorry for any of that? That's ridiculous."

"I warned you," I shout, and I hit him in the face with my fist. He goes down. Last time I only pushed him hard and he fell back but didn't go down. I lean over him. His eyes are closed. I kneel beside him and ask if he's all right. He says no. I say "Nothing on the outside is bleeding." He says "Something in my mouth is, but nothing much." I say "Open your eyes, let me see them." He says "What do you know about eyes when a man's hurt, but I think I'll be okay." I say "I'll get you water." He says "Please do; not too cold." I get him a glass of water. He sips a little, rinses it around in his mouth, spits it back into the glass with some blood. I say "Think you can stand now?" He says "I think so, no thanks to you," and I help him up. When he's on his feet he says "What you just did, hitting me, was unforgivable."

"It was your fault."

"Again, ridiculous."

"I hit you, but you provoked me, so it was as much your fault as mine."

"I didn't provoke anything, and certainly not a fist to my jaw. All I was doing at the time was talking rationally to you."

"But you knew that continuing to talk to me at the time, and probably talking rationally was worse than any other way, would only make me madder. You knew I was already mad. You knew I had a temper. I've exhibited that temper several times, to you and to others, though never so violently. Anyway, let's just say it was a little bit more my fault than yours." He shakes his head and I say "Then forty percent your fault and sixty percent mine, but no more than that."

"A lot more."

"Eighty percent mine then and twenty percent yours. For you have to accept some responsibility for my having hit you."

"None. It was a hundred percent your fault, just like the last time. It's always your fault."

"Not so."

"Always. Always."

"Go to hell."

"You the same."

I grab him by the shirt. He says "Let me go this instant." I let him go, turn around and go into the kitchen and put water on for tea. He goes into the room with the fireplace, television set and books. I go to that room a minute later and when he sees me coming he gets up to leave. I make way for him at the door just as he makes way for me. We pass each other. This time I hear the front door slam, so he must have got his coat and hat and gone outside.

I wait for him for hours. Then I read a book, drink, light a fire, watch television till there are no more programs on, and get in bed and try to fall asleep.

QUESTION.

I'm sitting opposite her. I say "Do you want to?"
    "I don't know."
    "You've time. Waiter?"
    "Yes?" he says.
    "Check, please."
    "Yes, sir."
    "Well, what do you say?" I say to her.
    "I still don't know."
    "You going to make your mind up in the next thirty seconds?"
    "Don't be nasty to me."
    "Waiter?"
    "It's coming right up, sir. I have to write it up first."
    "Forget it for now. Or give it when you feel like it, not to mix you
up. But I'd like another cup of coffee."
    "Another cup?"
    "Another cup. You?" I say to her.
    "I don't know."
    "Have another."
    "I always get a little high and fidgety with two cups."
    "What'll it be," waiter says, "another round for you both?"
    "Two cups, just to play it safe," I say.
Waiter goes. She looks at me.
    "Well?" I say.
    "Well, what?"
    "Well, have you made up your mind?"

"The place is crowded. People are waiting for tables. We shouldn't have ordered more coffee."

"Come on, answer."

"I told you, I don't know. It's not something I can make up about right away—I mean, my mind, your question."

"I knew what you meant."

Waiter brings a coffee pot and pours our coffee.

"Thanks," I say.

"You gave me too much," she says.

"You don't have to drink it all," I say. "I know, but I didn't want to waste it. Coffee beans have become expensive."

"Yeah, but still not as expensive as these restaurants want you to believe. I figured it out once At least not to warrant eighty to ninety cents a cup."

"Would you like your check now?" waiter says to me.

"If you don't have it made out yet, don't worry."

"I have it right here."

"Sure, put it on the table."

He takes it out of his shirt pocket and puts it down.

"Thank you," he says.

"You too. Thanks. Should I pay you or up front?"

"Up front or me."

"Which would you prefer?"

"Long as I'm here, and it doesn't take you too longto check it, you can pay me."

I look it over. "It seems good." I give him a twenty and ten and he goes to the cashier with the money and check. People waiting at the door are looking at us.

"What do you mean you figured it out about the coffee?" she says.

"The coffee wholesalers, they doubled the price of the beans from what it was a year ago, right? You feel the effect of that by the jump in price of coffee at the supermarket, though I don't think any of them raised it by more than fifty percent. But restaurants, because most of them also doubled the price of their coffee—you know, the excuse that the wholesalers did it to them—are now getting four to five times the profit they used to for a single cup."

"But you're not considering their larger overhead in a year and that all kinds of wages and workers' benefits and such are more. Cleaning bills for this napkin, tablecloth, the waiter's jacket, for instance."

"You're right."

"I waitressed for a while, so that's the reason I know."

"I know. I wasn't figuring the rest. Cleaning. Overhead."

"I still don't understand how you got four to five times the profit for a cup of coffee when the coffee growers only doubled the wholesale price of it and the supermarkets only raised it by half. It could be you didn't explain it clearly or it just went past me."

"No, I think it's my fault. Let me try again."

"Here you are, sir," waiter says, "and have a good night."

"You mean 'Here you are, ma'am,'" and I put the tray with the change on it in front of her.

"Oh?" he says. "Well, all right."

"No, I'm only kidding. That was my money. Tonight was my treat, next week's hers. Thanks. You've been very nice, and this is for you."

"Thank you." He puts the tip in his pocket, takes our glasses, the spoon she didn't use and the tray. Our table's clear except for our cups and saucers, pitcher of milk and sugar—pepper and salt dispensers will stay—and my spoon. He knows I drink it with milk. I pour the milk into the cup and stir it. I drink, she sips. She looks at her coffee.

"I wish I had a spoon," she says.

"You drink it black."

"To stir like you. I like to do it."

"Use mine. I'm finished with it."

"You used it."

"Only in my cup. I didn't stick it in my mouth."

"I wouldn't mind if you had. But it has milk on it. I know it's nutty, but I like my coffee absolutely black."

"Lick it off," I say.

"That would look ridiculous."

"Then I will."

"But no milk on it. It has to be licked clean."

I lick it. It still has some milk on it. I lick it all the way in and out of my mouth, and look at it. It's clean. I give it to her and she stirs her coffee with it.

"Well?" I say.

Just looks at her coffee and stirs.

"Come on. Do you? Don't you?"

"That question from before?"

"What *other* questions?"

"You could've asked other questions before."

"I did ask other questions. But I'm asking now about this one, that one, the one."

"I don't know."

"When, then?"

"I don't like to be pushed or rushed."

"I haven't. I've asked you and you said you don't know and you don't know and you don't know. And now we're having another coffee and the customers waiting at the front want our table and the waiter wants us out of here and a question like the one I asked is best answered right here when we're sitting and comfortable rather than when we're on the street and cold."

"Give me a little more time."

"Everything okay?" waiter says.

"Yes, thanks," I say. He goes. Busboy takes my empty cup away.

"If I had had it black like yours he wouldn't have taken my cup."

"That's why I have it black," she says.

"To give yourself more time?"

"I don't know if it's that. More because I like it black."

Busboy passes our table again, comes back and takes my spoon.

"I don't think she's through with the spoon yet," I say.

"Oh, sorry." And to her: "You're not?"

"I don't think so."

He puts the spoon down and goes.

"You could have let him take the spoon," she says. "I'm through with it."

"I don't like them shoving us out of here like that."

"They're busy. It's Saturday night. Dinner hour, the night and time they make about forty percent of their week's tips and the restaurant its earnings and which makes up for all the nights they don't have that many customers. I should be more understanding of them and just drink up and go."

"First tell me yes or no."

"Maybe I should just leave the rest of the coffee and go. I didn't want a full cup anyway."

"Yes or no?"

"And you didn't tip him enough."

"I gave him exactly fifteen percent."

"You didn't. I calculated it. You gave him about thirteen percent."

"You must be figuring thirteen percent of the total bill plus tax. I gave him fifteen percent before tax."

"Oh, maybe you're right."

"Not maybe; I am. And what do I have to do, consult you about everything at a restaurant?"

"Don't get snappy again."

"Why not? You're more worried about the damn waiter, nice as he is, and the restaurant's overhead and cleaning costs, than about me or us."

"Not true, and don't raise your voice to me."

"Ah, forget it," and I get up, get my coat off my chair and say to her "If you're ready, I'll walk you home or wherever you want to go."

"You don't have to walk me anywhere. I'd rather be alone."

"Good, then," and I turn to go, turn to her, "Goodnight," she looks away from me, and I leave.

I go home. Phone's ringing when I get there. "What is it now?" I say.

"What is what?" Murray says.

"I thought it was Vera. How are you?"

"By the tone of your voice, I'm glad I'm not Vera. What're you doing tonight?"

"Nothing."

"Want to see *Challenges*?"

"Sure."

"I thought Saturday night you'd be out, but then thought maybe this Saturday, miracle of miracles, you're not. In front of the Laron at nine?"

"Right."

I hang up. "Right." I grab a plant Vera gave me and yell "Right, yes, sure I want to go to a movie tonight," and throw it against the wall. It breaks, earth and planter parts going several different ways, big stain on the wall, mess on the floor. "Sure I do, goddamn you," and slam my fist through a closet door.

I wash it, iodine and bandage it, dial Murray with my other hand but he doesn't answer. I go to the Laron and see him out front.

"What happened?" he says.

"I called before but you weren't in."

"But what the hell happened? Your hand. It's bleeding through the bandage."

"I suppose you already left. I called to say I couldn't go to the movie after all."

"You shouldn't have come. I would've known something was wrong or you got a better date. But it must have just happened. You get into a fight? Catch it on a knife at home?"

"I just came here to tell you, didn't want to stand you up. I'm not feeling well. I'm going home."

"Okay, I appreciate that. But how bad's the hand? You can't answer a little question?"

I shake my head and start home.

"What's with you? Look, I won't go to the movie. I'll take you to the hospital if you want."

I keep going.

He says "Okay, I'll drop it. Hell with your hand. Forget I asked."

I walk back. "I can't answer because of how I'm feeling, don't you see? I got crazy with myself over Vera and punched it through a door and mashed it, and it was so stupid to do, I'm ashamed."

"That's better. Buzz me if you need me," and he goes into the theater.

I go home. Vera is sitting on my building's stoop.

"There you are," she says. "I was going to wait five more minutes and then send it by mail."

"You mean you finally have an answer for me? Hallelu."

"Answer? To that question in the restaurant? I forgot about that. No. Your set of keys. There was no room to slip them under your door and I didn't want to just leave them there. Here."

She holds my keys out. I take my bandaged hand out of my coat pocket and hold it out to her palm up. She says "What's this, a joke? No, I don't want to know. I know it's bad. I'm sorry if your hand hurts you the way your face now tells me it does, but I've got to be going, goodnight," and sticks the keys into my coat pocket.

"I'll tell you what happened," I say as she crosses the street.

"I told you. Save it for another time."

"I'll still tell you because I believe in answering a question when it's asked."

"Good. You got your big dig in. That should be enough."

"I'll still tell you, and I wasn't trying to get a dig in, because I've nothing to hide from you and I think you'll want to know."

She's across the street, stops, says "All right—I'm listening. What?"

"I'm not shouting it across the street."

WHAT IS ALL THIS? | 81

"You've shouted everything else across, why not this?"

"Come here or I'll go there."

"I'll come. You're hurt. You are hurt? That bandage with blood isn't a fake?"

"The answer is no."

She waits for a car to pass before she crosses the street. "Now, what? If you're not going to act like an ass again with that 'The answer is no.'"

"First, how do you feel about me?"

"About what? Which way? What does that have to do with anything? And when are you talking about?"

"This way. About everything. Your feelings to me. Before and now."

"A week before—we both knew. Now—let's be honest—neither of us does."

"Will you come upstairs with me?"

"Have you been to a doctor or hospital?"

"No."

"Then only to look at your hand and wash and dress it if it needs it."

"I don't feel too well anyway, so that's okay with me."

We go up the stoop and into the vestibule. She gets the keys out of my pocket, unlocks the door, and we start upstairs, she in front.

"What was the question before that you asked me in the restaurant?" she says, without turning around.

"One at the end? You don't know?"

"That's why I asked. I'm curious because of what maybe it all led to."

"I forget also."

"No you didn't."

"No I did. It was an important one for us, though. First the argument and my storming away and eventually smashing my hand through a closet door, which is part of what I was going to tell you I did and why."

"It was much more important to you. But maybe we better forget it because of what it could lead to now. More arguing and bitterness, and that's the last thing I want to get involved in again."

"Now I remember," I say.

"All right. Though I don't believe you. But what is it? Bad hand, sour feelings, potential explosion, but you want to have it out, let's."

"No, I suddenly forget. Tip of the tongue, off it again. Probably because of the damn pain and a headache now. I'll remember it, though."

"Hopefully, when I'm not here, if you did forget."

"Honestly, I did."

We'd reached the fourth-floor landing. She unlocks my door, puts the keys on top of the refrigerator, looks around and says "My God, what a mess you made. What could have got into you?"

"I don't know."

She has me sit on the toilet seat cover, takes my bandage off, says "Look at this; it's awful," washes and dresses my hand, makes me take three aspirins. I say "I still don't feel too well. Could you stay?"

"All right, but on different sides of the bed."

I go to bed and sometime later she joins me. My hand hurts like hell. I can't fall asleep. She says "Your jumping around is keeping me up."

"My hand."

She turns on the light. There's a lot of blood on me and my side of the bed. She says "I better get you to a hospital."

We go to one. They take x-rays and say I broke a couple of fingers and part of the rest of the hand.

After they put in a few stitches and a cast is put on, she says "Whatever it was you asked me in the restaurant that was so important to you then, I would have said yes to if just to avoid all this."

"Who can predict anything?"

"I know. But I only said that about your restaurant question as an expression of how I now feel."

"Anyway, it only proves you never know what can sometimes happen."

"Now I know, and you frighten me and made matters much worse for us, much."

"Don't be."

"I am. You want me to retract it? I can't."

"You'll feel different tomorrow or so."

"No I won't. You scared me silly. Break your hand? Next you're liable to break my fingers and then my face. I feel awful for your hand and your pain and such, but for us you couldn't have made matters worse. I'll get us a cab and see you to your building, but that's all."

"All I ask is that you sleep on it."

"No. It's the wrong time to say this now, but I've definitely made up my mind. No more."

I slam my hand with the cast on it against the hospital wall. She runs away. I'm screaming at her from the floor to never come back, while trying to hold my hand.

OVERTIME.

I do everything he told me to. Then there's nothing more for me to do. I check over what I did and it seems good as I can get it. I wait. I get up, sit down, look at the clock, walk around. Where is he? And she? Where are they? How long do they expect me to sit, stand, look, walk around, wait for them like this with nothing to do? They say they'll be back in an hour, why does it have to be three? If I could go to sleep or take a walk outside and step in for coffee someplace, it wouldn't be so bad. But if one of them caught me sleeping or not here when they got back, it would. They'd think I always slept or went out when they weren't here. Hell, I've waited long enough. I'm taking a walk and will live with the consequences if they find out.

Going down the stairs, I see them coming up. "Where you been?" I say.

"And where you going?" he says.

"I waited so long, I decided to take a walk. Waiting tired me out, and I need some exercise like walking to pep me up."

"Now you don't have to wait any longer, and you'll get plenty of exercise working, so come on back up. We still got lots to do, which you could've started doing before we got back here."

"Like what? I finished what you told me to do and checked it to make sure it was done right. And you didn't leave instructions for anything else to do because you said you'd be back before I was through."

"You could've cleaned up the place."

"Cleaning's not what I was hired for. I left that kind of unskilled work for better pay and more demanding work like what you hired me to do."

"But that's how you could've spent your time. You should've thought of that. Anything can be cleaned. Ten minutes after you clean something it can be cleaned. Soap can even be cleaned. And cleaning or anything like that would've been more productive than getting bored and irritable waiting for us or going out for a walk."

"Maybe for you it would've been more productive, but for me it would've been the opposite. It would've been going backwards from something I worked myself up to be, which might've ended with my being even less productive for you."

"Look, you're wasting our time talking. Let's get to work."

"I'm still so restless from waiting that I've got to take a walk."

"Walking's not what I'm paying you for except when you're doing it for me. You want to keep your job, you come upstairs now and work," and they go upstairs.

I think it over and go upstairs. They've already started working and I join in. Later he tells me what else I should do. Later she does too, tells me, and I do it. At times we're working on the same thing together. Other times we're working on separate things or the same thing out in different parts of the room. Sometimes two of us are working on the same thing and one on another thing. Other times one of us is in the restroom or on the phone or making coffee for us all and two are working on the same thing or separate things in the same or different parts of the room, and so on. Then it's all done. I even worked an hour longer than I'm being paid for and there's more work to come. We put what we worked on into boxes, tape and address the boxes and bring them to the post office and send them off.

"That didn't take too long," he says.

"Long enough," I say.

"About as long as I expected it to," she says.

"But we did it quicker than I thought we would is what I'm saying," he says.

"It might not have been quicker but it would've been sooner if both of you had come back earlier."

"Anyway, we got it done and we'll see you tomorrow," she says.

"About tomorrow," I say to him. "If you're both not there or don't plan to be by the time I get to work, could you leave instructions for me if you're going back now or phone them in early tomorrow so I can get right to work rather than waiting around for you?"

"If we're late," he says, "and I haven't left instructions or phoned them in or she hasn't phoned them in for me, then just clean the floors a little, wash the windows. They're all dirty, the floors especially. Tidy up the place a little is what I'm suggesting, scrub down the restroom and all its parts. If we're really late and neither of us has phoned in your instructions and I don't send them in with somebody else and you've cleaned the entire place where it really shines, give a little paint job to the ceiling and walls. The paint, brushes, turpentine and ladder are in the back closet. One coat. If we're really very late and never got instructions to you and the paint's dried, give it two coats, but no more than two."

"I don't see how I could do more than two coats in one workday. You said turpentine, which means the paint has an oil base. Oil paint takes a long time to dry. I doubt I can even put on a second coat in my scheduled worktime tomorrow if you have me do all those cleaning chores besides."

"So put in a couple hours extra."

"For money?"

"Do it because you like the job. Show me that. And that you want to keep it. Because you complain too much. You ever hear her complain?"

"I've complained," she says. "Plenty of times."

"About me you've complained. That I'm not nice enough to you after work. That I don't take you out enough, show you enough attention and give you enough nice things. About those you complain a lot, but I'm talking about at work."

"About work you're right. I have no complaints. Pay's good and hours aren't too long and work's not too hard."

"So if neither of us is here tomorrow when you get in," he says to me, "and I haven't left or I don't send any instructions to you, clean up the place, scrub everything down, and just don't sweep the floor but mop and wax it. And the windows and every shelf—really get this place into tiptop shape. Two coats of paint. And if you later have nothing better to do but sit around, put a few extra hours in painting the doors and window frames and all the furniture and shelves."

"I'll have to get overtime for that."

"I don't pay overtime."

"Then I can't give you free overtime anymore. I did it today and plenty of other days for months after you promised you wouldn't keep me beyond my normal workday, but no more."

"You only worked nine hours today."

"But I was here for twelve and a half—my half hour for lunch and those three hours waiting around for you."

"You rest at home, you rest here. No big difference, and for all I know the office might be a nicer place to rest than your home, and it'll be even more so after you clean and paint it."

"But it isn't my home. No overtime pay, no more extra hours after my regular workday."

"Then I'll have to let you go," and he asks for my keys to the office, I give them, she waves goodbye and they head toward the park and I go the other way. I turn around when they're a block away and I yell "You bastard!" Neither of them turn around. People walking past look at me and seem to wonder what I'm yelling about and to whom.

"That bastard," I say to people who pass. "That one over there. Well, now he's gone, went into the park. But he is a bastard. A slave driver. Let him get another sucker to work overtime for nothing, but not me."

"These days you're lucky to have a steady job," a woman says. "He fired you?"

"Just now. For what I said. Not giving him hours of free overtime."

"Can you give me his name and phone? I might like to apply for the job now that it's open."

"You wouldn't like it."

"Why? I like steady work and money coming in. Right now I'm jobless and broke. Let me talk to him and decide, unless you're planning on getting your job back."

"Not a chance."

I give her his name and phone number. She says "This is the best hope for a job I've had in weeks. Because if you just lost it, I'll probably be the first one to apply." She goes to a phone booth a few feet away.

"You calling him now? I'm sure he won't be at work till tomorrow."

"What do I have to lose? He's not in, I've lost a quarter. Big deal—I'm not that broke."

"Nobody will be in, so you won't lose your quarter."

"Good, then I'm losing nothing by calling him."

"Time. You'll be losing time."

"What else do I have to lose now?"

"Also your common sense. Because I just said he won't be in, yet you still want to call him. You'd think you'd take my advice because you'd think I'd know. Besides, even if he was in, I don't think he'll hire you. Or maybe he will. Maybe you're just the person he wants, someone who'll knuckle under to everything he tells you to and do any number of free hours' overtime for him."

"If you're saying all this to stop me from applying for the job or just to insult me, it didn't work."

She puts some coins in the telephone and I go home. By next day I've thought about it a lot and call him and keep calling him till I get him at eleven and say "Listen, I lost my head yesterday and I'm sorry. If you give me the job back and if you still want me to, I'll work a couple of hours overtime for nothing today and with no complaints."

"I already hired someone you told about the job. She said she wasn't using you as a reference, though, because you insulted her when she started to call me."

"All I told her was that she wasn't showing good common sense in trying to call you minutes after you fired me, since I knew you wouldn't be back at the office right away and that you were probably gone for the day."

"I did go back a few minutes after I left you. Went to the park but suddenly remembered. I forgot something at the office, and she got me when I was coming in the door. She said you told her you got fired and that she's exactly the opposite of you in that she's willing to work overtime for no pay anytime I want."

"So will I," I say. "And me you won't have to teach how to do the job. Think of all the time you'll be saving—the worker's when he doesn't have to be learning what he already knows; and yours, because you won't have to teach him."

"What time? A few minutes? Half hour at the most? For what's so complicated about the job? I'll miss a lunch, that's all, and what do I do at lunch but sit around and get fat and maybe take a nap."

"You sonofabitch."

"You know, that's the second time you cursed me in less than a day. Yesterday you called me a bastard. I didn't answer or turn around, so I don't know if you knew I heard. I know it wasn't meant for your coworker, as you've no reason for calling her one. How do you expect to be rehired, cursing me like that?"

"You weren't going to rehire me."

"You don't know that for sure, and I won't tell you. I'll make you sweat, except to say I told the woman to call me at noon today to see if I still wanted her to start work tomorrow."

"You're just trying to make me feel as if I really lost something in not working for you. But I'm telling you I didn't, because there are always just as good jobs and better bosses around, and for you to go to hell."

"Three times in less than a day," he says. "I think that's a record for me. Now I'll level with you what was in my mind before you cursed me a second time, and still in my mind but only by a little before you told me to go to hell. I was going to ask you to come back."

"Bull."

"Nothing you say now will make it any worse or better for you. So if you want to stay tuned only to hear what was in my mind before, I'll tell you, which I feel free to do now. I was going to rehire you if you agreed to working overtime for no pay whenever I needed you to, but which I wouldn't be so excessive at, if I have. I thought maybe I'd been unfair to us both in so quickly firing you, since as workers went you were okay, and should I expect anyone better—more reliable or less complaining—in that kind of job for the pay it gets? If you agreed to my terms, then when she called I'd tell her I rehired you but would keep her in mind in case things didn't work out. But when you called shortly before I was going to call you, I thought I'd let you shoot off your mouth and agree to all my terms without my even asking them, which'd make it easier to ask more things out of you in the future. Though I doubt it, because you're so pigheaded, I hope you learned something from this," and he hangs up.

I interview for a number of good jobs after that, but nobody will hire me because of the lousy reference my ex-boss gives me. So I start saying he had something personal against me, which had nothing to do with my job performance or even with reality, but none of the people interviewing me will accept that for not giving them his name and phone number. I finally land a really rotten job that doesn't ask for any references, where I work about ten more hours a week than the last one and for much less money. I also have to put in a lot of free overtime. I never complain about it and I in fact say I'll do it gladly, and after a year there, I get a small raise. It takes another two years before I'm making as much as I was paid by my last boss. But the cost of living's gone way up since then, so in what I can buy with my salary I'm actually earning half what I did at the old job. But like the woman who replaced me there might still say, with so many people being laid off and looking for work for a year or more, I feel lucky to have a job.

CAN'T

WIN.

My agent calls and says "Meet me at the Triad Perry Publishing Company right away." I say "What's up?" and she says "It's very important. Just be there as soon as you can. I'm already on my way," and she hangs up.

I think "Oh God, it can't be anything but good news—the annual Triad Perry three thousand dollar prize and publication of the manuscript in the fall." I leave the apartment, take a cab to the publishing house and walk into the reception room. Quite a few people are sitting on couches and chairs there and a receptionist is behind a desk, a dog sleeping on the floor near her feet. My agent comes out of an office with a man. She says "This is the managing editor, Mr. Whithead," and to him "You tell him, not me." I say "It's bad news, isn't it?" and she says "Depends how you look at it or take it, but I'm afraid it is."

He says "Once more you've been chosen as one of the runners-up in our annual short fiction award," and hands me my manuscript, "If this will be any consolation to you, there were again more than four hundred applicants for the award. So take pride in knowing that for the fourth year in a row you were considered good enough to be one of the five finalists, a remarkable achievement, or at least record, I think."

I shout "Goddamnit," and slam the manuscript on the receptionist's desk and keep slamming it and shouting "Goddamnit, goddamnit. For what the hell stopped you from giving me the prize this year? Because who'd you give it to? And who'd you give it to last year and the years before that? Do you remember? Does anyone here remember? What are some of the names of their books then? Why'd I even have to be dragged down here when you could have used your brains for a change and mailed me the news?" and I throw the manuscript across the room, its pages spilling over most of the people sitting on the couches and chairs. Some of them leap up and snap at the pages before they land on the floor. Others grab the pages off the floor and read them, saying "Hey, this is pretty good....You mean pretty damn awful....It's stupid....Funny.... Makes no sense....What the heck's this passage supposed to mean?...He's got to be kidding himself....No, he should have won....You mean never have entered....Christ, if he had taken first prize and you announced it, your whole company would have been disgraced and laughed out of the publishing business and maybe even financially ruined. Why don't you look at my manuscript for next year's contest if you can't publish it sooner?" and several of them give Whithead their manuscripts.

He piles the manuscripts on the desk and says to me "Listen, don't get so excited. If this will be any consolation to you, and I should have told you this before I broke the other news to you, you did take first prize in the scarf design award this year, which entitles you to a thirty-dollar check and mention in the *Scarf Designers News*." He gives me the check and holds up a six-foot scarf for everyone to see. It's all stripes, but bright stripes of six different colors and with different-colored fringes at the ends of it—not a bad design but not what I had in mind for a first prize today. I take the scarf, stick the check between my teeth and rip it in two and spit the other piece out, and grab a bud vase off the desk and shout "Idiots. This scarf and check aren't what I came down here for either," and throw the vase to the floor. It smashes, pieces going everywhere, one into the dog's rear leg. It yelps, jumps and limps around the room as it cries.

The receptionist runs over to me and says "Before I could have understood your outbursts and rage, but injuring the defenseless dog has gone too far," and she shoves me with both hands and I fall over a chair to the floor. She edges back, shouting "Don't kick me. Don't beat me. Get him away from me." The dog's still limping around the room and crying.

"That'll be about enough of that," Whitbread says to me. And to the others: "What about this dog? Whose is it?"

"Not mine," my agent says, leaving.

"Not mine either," some of the others say.

"Of course," he says. "Not yours, his, hers, the receptionist's, or anyone's. Then what was it doing here in the first place, and what are you going to do about it now?" looking at me.

"Okay," I say. "I'm the one responsible for the broken glass, so I'll look after him, even if he isn't my dog." I put the scarf around my neck, pick up the dog and carry him out of room, take the elevator down and look on the building ten register for a vet. There is none, so I go outside on Fifth Avenue and stop one of the hundreds of people on the sidewalk and ask if she knows where I can find a vet around here.

"For your dog?" and I say "Yes, for this dog, though he isn't mine," and she says "Go east on 53rd, then second building on your left after you pass the pocket park."

The vet's office is on the first floor of a brownstone. I go in, set the dog down and say to the nurse "He has a sliver of glass in his rear right leg. Could you have the doctor remove it? I'm not the owner, but I'll take care of the cost." "That'll be sixty dollars," and I give it, and she says "We're a little crowded in here, so can you wait outside?" I look around and see all the seats are taken by people with pets on their laps and in carriers, and one guy with a parrot on his shoulder, and I go outside.

The nurse opens the front door an hour later and the dog comes out with a bandage around his leg. He seems to be walking all right. "Good, you're much better," I say. I tie the scarf around his collar as a leash, walk him back to the publishing house, take the scarf off and leave him with the receptionist. She doesn't look up, continues typing. The dog falls asleep beside her on the floor.

I go home. My mother and sister are there, and I tell them what happened to me today. The agent's call, the publishing house, my letdown and how mad I got, and the dog and bud vase and consolation prize, and I hold up the scarf.

"That's my scarf," my sister says. "The one I designed and knitted myself. I've been looking all over for it. How come you took credit for it when I should have been the one who entered that contest and won?"

"What're you talking about?" I say. "I never entered this scarf in any contest," but she grabs it from me and calls the publishing house and says "Whithead; give me that chief man Whithead." When he gets on the phone, she says "Look, my brother before is a cheat, an out-and-out lying fraud. He didn't design that first-prize scarf or even knit it. I did, and I'm coming right down there now to get all the publicity I can out of winning that contest and also the thirty-dollar check. Some people might think they can't use the money, but, baby, I sure can."

LONG MADE
SHORT.

Mark phones and says The wind is strong, just right for Rain stops but
The red rose picked by his wife The rose Marlene cut The little girl
comes into the store, At work where I was sorting some I put on my
socks He was walking into the elevator He walked into the elevator
She lifted herself up, came down hard again He pulled, himself out,
got to his feet They both felt good because "Bastard," She started the
car To get started they They started to go downstairs, she holding his
Starling's the hardest part, Mark used to say, lots harder than The
starter gets his gun The gun gets the starter The cheese got the mouse
"Shoot," the starter said. "Shoot the starter," Marcos says. "Marko,
shoot the starting gun already so we can get started," she said. We all
started out together—Marlene, Bea The road started to slope Just
start. Me. Begin. Another way then. Girl phoned Mark's strong but
not so strong where he Mom says Dad whacked his strap Gave her a
note which said "What's Daddy picked up his wife Daddy lifted
Mark's wife above his head Uncle Aunt Bea keeled over, knocking
his The teacher had enough, jumped up from her seat behind the
desk and screamed " The professor stood out in his yellow When I
was a "What the hell," she said, "you think I care? Do it. Go on and
do it." "How can you be so cavalier about it?" he says to her. "Oops,
a cavalier's a man, and a chivalrous one no less, right? But that's okay;
the word here's being used Someone through the window Someone
threw a bottle through his bedroom window, awakening them. Suddenly, glass smashed. Glass smashed, building collapsed. He was
inside it. The building collapsed on the man. Before I knew it, I was
buried in rubble and gasping for air. The building didn't collapse as

they all first thought from the noise, but one wall of it did. A wall of the building collapsed on the girl. A part of the apartment building came off, large enough She's talking to a friend. A young woman's talking to what seems like a friend. A woman's talking to a man at the corner as I'm walking up 113th Street to Broadway, when a At first I thought it was a girl talking Because she was short and slight, I at first thought the person talking to a man at the corner was a A piece from the northwest corner building on a Hundred-thirteenth Street and Broadway "A piece from the corner apartment building," he said, "just when I'm walking up the block, landed on Smashed this young woman's head. He was there when it happened. This is what Listen to this. I'm It happened right in front of him. I'm walking up the steep hill on a Hundred and Thirteenth, about fifteen feet from a couple talking at the corner, when I see this thing in the air coming down so fast that by the time I could get my first word out By the time he can get his first word By the time he yelled his first word of warning By the time I could yell "Watch—," He sees this I see this building piece coming down I see this huge chunk from a building coming down fast, start to yell "Watch out" to a couple on the corner standing under it, when it lands on the woman's head. Blood everywhere, some hitting me and the wall I'm beside. I shout "Oh God no," and sink my fingers into my cheeks and turn around and people are running past me down the hill I just came up and others are hurrying up the hill, no doubt to the woman who was hit, and I say to myself "I must help her, I have to do what I can, I can't just turn my back on her," and I turn around. She's on the ground, blood around her head and running along the sidewalk and a little of it into the street. People are looking at her, some with their hands over their mouths and chests, gestures like that. One man on his knees beside her is looking away with an expression as if he's never seen such a horrible sight. A woman standing near her shouts "She's dead, she's dead, there's no way she can't be dead." There's nothing I can do. And there are enough people here to help her if she can be helped. And I'm feeling dizzy and a little sick and I start down the street to my building on Riverside Drive and then think maybe she isn't dead, maybe that woman was wrong, maybe nobody else will act in a helping way if she is alive, like call 9-1-1 and yell out "Is there a doctor around?," for the avenue's pretty busy, someone could be a doctor or ex-medic along all the passing people, or someone could know of a doctor in one of these buildings here.

Or a nurse. A nurse would know how to stop the bleeding and keep her alive. I run back up the hill, there must be fifty people around her now, and I say "Did someone call 9-1-1 or does anyone know of a doctor near here? We have to get help," and a man says "She doesn't need a doctor. She's as dead, the poor girl, as she'll ever be," and I say "Maybe it only looks like that. We can't be sure, because did anyone check her breathing or pulse?" I'm saying this mostly to the backs of people around her. I can't see even a single part of her, not even the blood anymore, there are so many people in front of me. A woman says "Believe it, she's gone. No one could have survived something that big from so high up. She was dead the second that foot-by-two-foot slab of concrete hit her," and I say "Is that what it was, and so large?" and she points to the top part of the fourteen-or-so-story building and says "Came off there, below the last window on the left; you can see where the piece is missing," and lots of us look and several people move to the street, no doubt to get out of the way in case another piece falls and I say "I can barely see that far, even with my glasses. But please, someone should yell for a doctor and call for an ambulance, if it hasn't been done yet just to be absolutely sure," and a man says "Guy went for a cop; two people, in fact," and I say "A police-man can't help her—oh, screw it," and I push my way through, I'm squeamish and I don't want to but I feel I have to see for sure for that poor girl's sake, and it's an awful sight, couldn't be worse, her eyes are open but the balls can't be seen, part of her head gone, a little of her brains spattered about, it's horrible when something like this happens, nothing like it should, for she was just standing there, talking to a man, if only I had come up the block a few seconds sooner and been looking up and close enough to the building to see the piece falling but not that close to get hit by it, I could have yelled, but in time to warn her, and then maybe she could have jumped away and the piece would have missed her or just hit her leg. Or if I were even closer to the corner, got up the hill even sooner and looked up for some reason and saw the piece breaking off the building, I might have been able to push her and the man she was with out of the way. I cover my eyes with my hands, stay there a few seconds and mutter to myself "Poor girl, poor girl," and then walk out of the crowd. A policeman's walking into it, saying "All right, folks, everybody move; this means everyone." Another policeman comes, an ambulance, police cars and an EMS van. A yellow police strip is set up around the medical team working on her. I cross the street and watch. She's covered completely with a tarp, people near the area are told by the police to keep walking, people who have walked past the area and crossed the street and walk past me talk as if they think she's been murdered or she jumped from the building or had been hit by a car and then moved to the sidewalk. The medical team put her on a litter, take the tarp off and cover her with something much lighter, which almost blows off when they slide her into the ambulance. Ambulance stays double-parked awhile, emergency lights flashing and back door open but nobody in there with her. Man she was talking with, who for about half an hour after stood in the street with this paralyzed face of pain and constantly pulling his shirt collar apart with both hands, is escorted to a taxi by a policeman and helped inside and driven away. Ambulance leaves, police strip is torn down by a policeman and crumpled up and dropped into a street trash can, some policemen and women have a smoke and seem to be laughing and joking about other things and then either walk away or get in their cars and leave, storeowner or employee comes out several times to throw a container of water over the place where the woman had lain, and all this time thoughts come to me about life, death, sorrow, chance, that young woman, my daughters when they'll be her age. I picture them standing under similar buildings on Broadway or even this same building or walking past them. Will I now advise them "If you're walking outside or stop to talk to someone on the street, do it close to the curb"? I think about the woman's parents hearing the news, which they might not have yet. Brothers and sisters if she has, close friends, maybe a boyfriend or even a husband, though she seemed too young to be married. Maybe the man she was talking to was her boyfriend, although he seemed a lot older than she, quick glimpses I got of her before she was struck and little I could make out when she was on the ground, so he was more likely a neighbor or one of her teachers she'd bumped into, since this is a university neighborhood. She was talking excitedly, if I recall right, smiling, animated, big hand gestures, had long hair in a ponytail and seemed to have a good figure, which was what first caught my attention when I saw her from further down the block, then suddenly dead, probably not even for a half-second knew something was wrong, and so on, thoughts like that, all very natural after what I'd experienced. I cross the street and look at the spot where the storeperson threw the water. He didn't seem to like that he was doing it at first, but by the third or fourth time he just poured instead of threw, as if he'd got used to it and wanted to do a good job, or maybe it was because the blood and other things had by now washed into the street. There's still a little blood stain on the sidewalk. A rain or just people stepping on it will get rid of it. I stare at the stain and think I'll picture the woman lying there as I last saw her, but I don't. I think "Does the shape of the stain remind me of anything?" But it's just a blob. I crouch down and touch the sidewalk, I don't know why; maybe I'm just being overdramatic or something, but I move my fingers to the stain and say low as I can "I'm very sorry," then look around to see if anyone's looking at me. Couple of passersby are but with no more than slightly curious faces, as if thinking something like "Why's he tying his shoes in the middle of a busy sidewalk instead of by the building or curb?" I get up Sidewalk was still damp from Smells his fingers and they don't Concrete's still there but One would think the storeowner Or the police; how come they didn't Someone could trip over it, even the smaller pieces, and Tries lifting I try to push the biggest piece Kicks the smaller pieces into the street and then against Asks a passing man I ask another man if he'd help me with Together they "By the way," the man says, "where in hell this big "Up there?" the man says, and he ducks I look up Will more fall Wait a second; how come the police didn't keep the police strip around this part of the sidewalk, in fact block off with police barricades the whole He goes to the curb In fact, why isn't there a policeman here directing all the pedestrians around What is it with this city that Runs to the payphone across Broadway I dial Information, gets the phone number of the precinct for this Tells the woman who answers why he's calling and the location of the "The yellow strip, the plastic yellow strip," I say, "the one that says 'Don't cross' or 'Do not cross' and has the word 'Police' on it" "That is strange," she says; "very unusual, in fact, that none of the—how many officers did you "'Some kind of oversight'?" I Goes into the store, asks for the owner or manager The man says "Oh, I don't think anything else will I stand outside the store warning pedestrians and one couple who stop to talk at the Police car comes and he tells the officers he's the one who called and points up "Mistakes are made," one of Same kind of yellow strip is "I'd also," I say, "because some people who are just talking and not looking could walk right "Don't worry, they're coming," He goes into a liquor I buy a bottle of red wine and a bottle of sake, walk back to the corner entirely cordoned off now

except for "It's far enough away," the officer   Police truck with barricades   He walks down the hill with his   I think of the young woman
and almost feel the impact   Shudders, covers   I go into my building,
take the elevator   He opens the door   My kids run up to me, shouting
"Daddy's home. Daddy's home," pretending it's been a long time, since
I've only been gone   Sets the bag down on the sofa, gets on one knee
and hugs them   His kids kiss   "Why do you look so sad?" my older
"Anything wrong?" his wife says, coming out   "Oh gosh," he says to
her, breaking down, "this poor young...I was going up...she was just
standing...

ASS.

I haven't had any ass in a month. More. Two months, going on three. A long time, and I wanted some. That was all, animal as that must sound. I was tired of doing it to myself. Tired of thinking and dreaming about it, swiveling around to stare after it on the street, reading fiction about it, looking at nude photos in men's magazines, lingerie and swimsuit ads in the Sunday *Times* magazine, going to R-rated movies just to get a glimpse of the pubic area and long looks of bare thighs, breasts and behinds. So I brushed my hair. Shaved. Ten after nine. Little bit late to call but it was worth a shot. And left my apartment.

I made two calls at the corner phone booth. First woman said "Bullshit, man, you only call when you're horny," and hung up. The other call was answered by the babysitter: "Ms. Michaelson is out on a date." I'd check out the bars. Where else could I now hope to find someone to make love with tonight? I looked in the window of the bar nearest my home. It had a tall, beautiful bartender, but all the customers at the bar but two were men like myself: looking for ass; trying to get into bed with the bartender, who, times I was there, I saw was mainly behind the bar to keep their fantasies going about her while selling them twice as many drinks as they'd normally buy. Did any of them eventually end up with her? I doubted it, so to me it was a losing place.

I went into the next bar a block away. It had always been the best place in the neighborhood to meet women. Always crowded, lots of good music playing, and no professional whores. It was much darker now. Just as crowded. Same kind of music it usually played but much louder. All the customers were men, and they were all gay. Several of them gave me friendly looks. I walked right out. "Say, where are you going?—you're cute," one of them said. I looked at the bar's sign and saw the name hadn't changed. There was a notice taped from the inside on several of the bar's small French window panes and one pasted to the lamppost out front:

COME TO THE WEST SIDE'S NEWEST MEAT RACK

Dancing, inexpensive dining
Taped music during the week
Live combo Friday & Saturday nites
Never a cover, minimum, ripoff or
Commercial hustle of any kind at
Our good place
Peace-loving bartenders
Well-meaning bar owners
Sympathetic landlord
We like nice company too
Bring your closest friends

Probably the best bar for me to go to now was one eight blocks from here. I hardly ever went to it because it was so far away. But plenty of single women used to go there, and it was usually crowded at the bar. So if I saw a woman I was attracted to and she seemed unattached, I could go over and stand next to her while ordering a drink or drinking the one I already held. In other words, it wouldn't seem unusual my just standing there before I spoke to her.

So I walked to it. It was a chilly night and I was glad to get inside. The place was crowded. Lots of smoke, chatter, laughing, huge television set on without the sound: basketball, and a new super-stereo jukebox playing a loud rock number almost in beat to the dribbling, passing and dunking of the ball.

I looked around as I unbuttoned my coat. Two middle-aged women sat on the bar stools nearest the door. They looked up, seemed to resent the draft I brought in with me. One flicked cigarette ash to the floor, the other fooled with her false eyelash, and they resumed their conversation. Group of young women at the end of the bar by the dartboard. Two of them playing, other two watching. All four drinking beer from the same pitcher. A pretty woman sitting at the middle of the bar, a man on either side of her leaning on the counter and talking to her at once. Another woman standing not too far from them, looking drunk or stoned. She dropped her cigarette, had a hard time finding it, and when she did, picking it up and then trying to relight it though it was still lit. And several other women, at the bar or seated at the three tables in front, young and not so young, heavy, thin, stacked, flat, pretty, very pretty, short, average and tall, all apparently with men. I went almost to the end of the bar, stepped on a guy's foot along the way, said "Excuse me, I'm sorry," and then "But I said I'm sorry," after he growled.

There was only one bartender, running around like mad and also pouring drinks for the waiters and waitresses for the table customers in the next room. I remember him from the bar that had gone gay. He sort of managed it and never poured a free drink in two years and liked to eighty-six people from that place. One time he told a friend of mine to leave because he thought he was drunk. When Jack refused to go because he said he wasn't drunk, and he wasn't, Gil phoned the police. Two cops came in about five minutes. Their patrol car was double-parked outside with the emergency roof light spinning. Gil didn't have to say a word to them, just pointed at Jack. They went straight to him and said "Okay, wise guy—get." "But I'm not drunk," Jack said. "I'll piss in that ketchup bottle and let you take a urine test of it to prove I'm not drunk. But if I am drunk then I got that way here, so why don't you pull Gil in for selling a drunk beer?" One cop started to unsnap his holster. "I can't believe it," I said. "Come on, Jack." Gil said to me "Good, you're his pal, you go too." I said "Jack, goddamn you, let's go, before you get shot for being a jerk," and pushed him out the door. He never really forgave me for butting in. He said later "I wanted them to take me to lockup and then for Gil and those freeloading cops to pay with their jobs for that bum rap."

"How you doing, Gil?" I said.

"Rick's it, right?"

"Ray."

"Ray. Ray. Right. Nice to see you." He stuck his hand across the bar. He always wore the greatest shirts and belts. My clothes were fairly old and drab and getting threadbare from the wash. We shook hands. "What'll it be?"

"A dark draft."

"All out. Only in bottles."

The bottles of dark were German or Danish and too expensive, and besides, I didn't want to be carrying one around with the stein. I said "Regular draft, then. You got yourself out of Sweeney's, I see."

"Came to where I couldn't make it there, or they couldn't make me," and he laughed. I smiled. So we were old friends. He gave me my beer and I paid and put down a good tip. "Appreciated," and I said "You're welcome." I was going to ask if Sweeney's had new owners—anything to keep the talk going a while longer—but by now he was holding three order slips a waitress had given him and pouring a bar customer white and red wines, and I turned to my left. Those four young women were right by me as I'd planned. The two dart players had each been trying for the last few minutes to end the game with a bull's-eye. One of the two watching the game looked at me and then away. It was a hard look, a quick put-down for faking my way over here and staring directly at her, not at all interested, never could be interested, go away. The others seemed just as hard, though none looked at me. I didn't belong in this place. Didn't belong in any of these bars. It wasn't my clothes that were old, it was me. And my aim was all wrong: to come here just for a beer, okay, and preferably with a friend so I wouldn't have to push myself on someone to talk, but not just to find ass. It had never really worked out for me here or in that bar that was now gay or any of the bars around. In the four years since I'd come back to the city it had never worked out once. Closest I came to meeting a woman in any of these bars was right here about a year ago. I looked at her a long time. She was short, blond, lively, had a nice smile, seemed sexy, homey, thoughtful, uncomplicated, and as if she'd be lots of fun. She was talking to a man and every so often looked at me. Once, she smiled at me and I smiled back. Then she left for the ladies' room and on her way back I touched her arm and said "Excuse me, I know you're with someone, but I'm drawn to you, plain as that, silly and rude as that has to sound." She said "No, I think it's fine. I just met that guy, so I can talk to you, and thought I was the one bugging you before with my occasional stares. You've very wistful eyes, that's why, which you must have been told before and which has to sound sillier or plainer than anything you said to me." Two stools opened up and we sat at the bar. Admitted that these opening conversation lines were the worst. Laughed, talked, bought each other drinks, had hamburgers and fries. Then about six women—women I didn't know she'd come in with—came over and one said "Have to be skedaddling now, Lail." I whispered to her "Stay the night with me—we got something going." She said she knows, and she would, and she told me before she was a singer and accordionist? Well, it's with an all-women hand and singing group in Florida and they had performed in Brooklyn that afternoon and were on their way to Pittsburgh in half an hour to give a concert tomorrow. We exchanged addresses. I kissed her fingers at the door, in jest and for real. We wrote each other and sometimes I called. Each letter and phone call became more affectionate. Then she didn't write back. I wrote again and she didn't answer. I called a few times. The woman who answered always said she'd give Lail my message. Finally I got her on the phone and she said she couldn't come to New York as I'd been asking her to and I shouldn't come to Florida to see her as I then said I wanted to, as there was lately another man in her life and marriage seemed a definite possibility. I said "Hell, I'll marry you," and she said "Sorry, but with this one I know I'm safe."

I said to the woman who gave me the hard look before "Come in here often?"

"What?"

"Do you come to this bar often?"

"What if I do?"

"I don't mean to sound forward."

"Anyway, I don't."

"You don't mean to sound forward?"

"Funny, funny, funny."

"Bull's-eye," one of the players said.

"She got a bull's-eye," I said. "Like to play?"

"No."

"Any of you other ladies care to take me up on my challenge?"

"Got a bad arm," the other woman who'd watched the game said.

"Had enough....Game's too slow," the two players said.

"Might go faster if we teamed up and just one person watched," I said.

"I think we've all had it," the hard one said. "As spectators and playing."

"Terrible drudge, darts," I said.

"Then why'd you want to play?"

"I'm very lousy at this talk."

"What talk?"

"This talk. Bar talk. This bullcrap bar talk. This get-together-and-say-something-to-meet-one-another and introductory-interrogatory male-female what-I'm-not-talking-to-you talk."

"Oh."

"Maybe he shouldn't try it then," one of the others said.

"Shh," the hard one said. They all looked at one another, were holding their laughs in. Screw it: they thought I was foolish or smashed or insane.

"Nothing," I said. "Zero. Zip. Goose eggs. Blah. What am I doing in here? Excuse me."

"You're excused," she said.

They all laughed.

"Oh, you're all so dear," I said.

"You're right; we are, we are."

"I know. It's what I said. You're all very dear. Goodbye."

"Goodbye...Goodbye...Goodbye," her three friends said.

I left. Went home and lay down on my bed with my shoes and clothes on and read, listened to the radio—a talk show, then music—drank, read, drank. I still wanted some ass. I didn't know any women to fool around with except the two I called. Both I hadn't spoken to in months. Where were the other women I once knew? Where were all my men friends? Married. With women. Gone. drunks. Fathers. Abroad. Big successes. A suicide. Turned bisexual. One put away. Another put himself away. Not friends. I didn't know or want to continue to know just about anyone. Ass. That's what I still wanted. There were other bars. Two others around here and both had prostitutes. So I'd pay. A prostitute cost more money than I could afford, but tonight I'd pay. I could get the clap. I didn't care. I cared, but I'd take the chance. I never got it yet. I'd be very careful. The thought of getting it never stopped me before, and I could always get a shot. I put on my coat and left the apartment. "Nah," I said when I reached the street, "I could also get arrested as a john or robbed and mugged."

THE

CHOCOLATE SAMPLER.

"I'm telling you," Mr. Hyman said, "the baby's beautiful. Just beautiful."

"You really like him, Dad?" Sylvia said.

"Like him? My God, what do you think?"

"I mean, he's really funny looking in his way, isn't he?"

"He's wonderful. A grandson like that is just wonderful."

"Who do you think he looks like?"

"Well," he said, glancing coyly at his son-in-law, "and remember, I only saw it from behind the nursery window, he looks like none of you. Tell me, Sylvia, who was the other guy?"

"That's a nice joke to make the day your only child has a baby."

"Don't get touchy. I was only kidding."

"I know. I didn't mean it that way."

"You want my seat, Hank? You must be exhausted."

"I'm fine, Dad, thanks."

"You think they'd give more than one chair in the room," Mr. Hyman said, "even if nobody's in the other bed."

"I'm sure there was another and they took it out for some reason. I'll just lean against this."

"And you, my darling," he said to Sylvia. "You look tired and pale. Place quiet enough to get a nap in?"

"The hospital's great, Dad—really. Good service and everything."

"Food's good?"

"It's better than that. You get choices like I've never seen in a hospital. This afternoon, for instance, they let me have things my doctor ordered me to stay away from during my pregnancy. The aide comes in and says 'Want this?' and I tell her 'Are you for real?' Here—chocolates like this box you brought me? Well, before, never, because of some diabetic thing, but now I can eat them till I get sick. Take one, Dad."

"No, thanks."

"Go on. They're just going to be eaten by the nurses and me if you don't."

"Okay, so you broke my arm."

He picked out a round chocolate with a little loop on top, removed the paper holder and dropped the candy into his mouth, Splitting it in two with his back teeth and drawing out the juices with his tongue, he saw Sylvia and Hank looking at him, so he smiled, chewed more ambitiously than he normally would, and said "It's good. Very good."

"Whitman's makes some of the best chocolates around," she said.

"This I didn't know when I bought it. I just bought, that's all."

"So what time you think you'll be heading back?" Hank said, placing the wrapper Mr. Hyman had put on the side table into the waste basket.

"I just came," he said, laughing. "Let me at least look at my grandson again."

"I didn't mean it that way. I meant—well, you know: tonight. Later. When we go."

"Ohhh—twelve o'clock, maybe. Tomorrow's no work, so it makes no difference when I get back."

"Was it a good trip coming here?"

"It's amazing, Hank. Four hours or a little more than that by bus, and that's it. Red Carpet Service, Trailways calls it, with a real red carpet running down the middle of the aisle. Give you a mealy pillow, a real hostess to assist you, she said. I never knew such a bargain existed till a friend told me last week."

"What'd you eat?" Sylvia said.

"Well, they don't give you a real meal, but for eighty-nine cents more a ticket than regular fare, you can't expect one."

"But what was it you had?"

"A choice of deviled egg or ham sandwich. I had deviled egg plus some orange juice in the beginning and tea later."

"But you never liked deviled egg that I can remember."

"This was pretty good, though, and I was hungry. Look,

I was thinking I should see the baby again before they close the nursery."

"Anything you want, Dad."

"Like to come too, Hank?"

"I saw the kid plenty today. Thanks."

He waved at them as he left the room, went down the corridor and stopped before a window with six babies behind it. Two of the babies were crying, one with a tag above its head labeled: C-25, Riner Baby—Male. He pointed at him and tapped the window and said "Hello. Hello, beautiful one. There, already with a mouth like your little mother, am I right? That's the way she was then, crying, crying. But you'll wake up everyone around you and they won't like you, you know. Shh, shh. Go to sleep like something good. Everybody will love you if you do." He made a few funny faces at his grandson and then waved and smiled at the other crying baby.

"So?" Hank said in the hospital room. "Do you have any idea what I'm supposed to do with him?"

"Something, I guess," Sylvia said.

"What do you mean 'Something, I guess'? Is that supposed to be an answer?"

"Just something, something. Anyway, he'll be gone tonight, so what's the big deal?"

"But it's almost nine now, and I got to walk out of here when they close this place and think of something to do about him."

"Then take him to Lucine and Dave's for dinner."

"You know they invited me and not him. And I've already imposed on them by getting there so late."

"They wouldn't mind that much."

"I'd mind. They didn't know your old man was coming down. No, it wouldn't be right."

"So who knew?" She pointed to her chest. "I knew?"

"Okay, so nobody knew, but must everybody suffer? Why did he even come down so quickly in the first place?"

"Maybe because you sent him a telegram of the birth."

"But I didn't know he'd rush right down. And you told me to telegram him."

"I think he had a right to know—don't you?"

"Of course. I didn't say no."

"So think, then. Think of something."

"I'm thinking," he said. "I'm thinking."

He sat in the chair facing her and put his hand on his forehead.

Sylvia lay on her back, her belly, knees and feet making large bumps in the sheet, her head propped up on two pillows. "Think of anything yet?"

"I'm still thinking." His eyes followed the second hand on his watch.

"Maybe you can get him to go back earlier. Tell him you got something important to do. You know: something involving business and that the dinner you're going to is part of it. He knows business and respects it."

"Oh yeah. Your dad really knows business."

"Just tell him that!"

"I can't think of anything better, so I guess I'll have to." He looked at her. "You know, you really look like you're struggling. You need anything to help?"

When Mr. Hyman returned, his hand on his cheek and his head shaking back and forth and smiling, Hank offered him the chair.

"Don't need it," he said. "After seeing that boy I could stand and dance all night. I'll tell you, he's something. A knockout."

"I'm glad you like him, Dad," Sylvia said.

"Like him? Out of all the kids there, and I studied each of them, he was the nicest looking of all. I don't want to start anything again, but where he got that nose from, I'll never know. A small one like that you don't often get in my family. And when Sylvia married you, Hank, nice a nose as you got, I thought a very small nose your kids will never get. But you got. And two gorgeous blue eyes also."

"The doctor doesn't think they'll stay that way," Sylvia said. "Probably get darker the next few months."

"Maybe it's for the better. Because what would my neighbors think if I brought around a grandson like that with blue eyes and such a small nose. 'So Sylvia married a Gentile?' they'd say."

"Tell them not to worry," Hank said.

"Worries like that I should have all my life. But let me tell you, worries about Sylvia's birth I had plenty. Did I worry." He looked around, tried sitting on the arm of the chair Hank was in, then stood and said "You know, it's really beyond me why they don't have more than one chair in the room."

"Take mine," Hank said, getting up.

"No, sit, sit."

"Then I'll call someone here and get you one."

"Don't bother. A big hospital chair like this one is too heavy for someone to lug in. But tell me. What are you paying for all this, if it's all right to ask?"

"Too much," Hank said. "But thanks to your gift, we'll be able to squeak through just fine."

"I wish I could've given more. Sylvia tells me your folks gave a real nice little something also. That's very kind of them, tell them from me. In fact, when I get back I was thinking I'd phone them and say everything here is just dandy."

"I called and told them," Hank said, "and they'll be here in a couple of days."

"So I'll call them also and tell them. No harm in that. But let me tell you how surprised I was when I got your wire. I nearly fell off the chair I read it—that's the truth. 'A boy,' I said. 'My first grandchild and it's a boy, and weeks early, no less.' Her mother in Boston should only feel as happy as I did. And that little weasel she married also."

"You should have heard her," Hank said, laughing.

"She called before you got here and first thing she says is all this psychological stuff she's always reading about and spouting, and what's good for the newborn infant and so on—things like that."

"I hope you took it all with a grain of salt."

"Mom only meant well," Sylvia said. "The baby was a little premature, so she was naturally worried."

"Of course she meant well," Hank said. "And she's been all right. Helped us out plenty when we needed it, plenty, so I'm not about to gripe. But when she gets into that psychiatric and Freudian and Dr. Spock bushwah, well, let me out—know what I mean, Dad?"

Mr. Hyman nodded, took a candy from the box, peeled off the gold wrapping, and stuck it into his mouth. "It's cream filled. I thought it was a cherry."

"You want one with a cherry?" Sylvia said.

"Sure, if nobody else does. They have them in the box?

Didn't know. Just bought it without asking."

"They do, and a whole set of instructions also. That's why it's called a Whitman's Sampler—so you can sample any of their assortment. Here," and she pointed to the chart on the inside cover of the box. "Chocolate Butter Cream—third square in, second row from the top; that's what you just got." She dug into the box where the chart said Liquid Cherry would be, removed the wrapping and gave the candy to her father. He bit the top half off, held the bottom half, which still had white liquid in it, and said "You know, you're right. It's a cherry. I got it in my mouth right now."

"Told you. You can get whatever you want just by looking at the squares here, and it has an identical layer underneath."

"It's really something," he said. "Anyway, Hank's telegram was a terrific surprise. I thought three weeks from now, a month. I immediately dropped what I was doing, called you—you weren't home, of course, or at work—and took the bus to Washington, though when I got off I realized I didn't even know what hospital Sylvia was in. Hank didn't say so in the telegram—just his congratulations. So I called a couple of hospitals I found in the phonebook and they didn't know, till I asked one operator what's the biggest hospital in Washington, because I remember you once said that's where you'd be. She said 'Washington Hospital Center you must mean,' so I called and they said you were here. You should've told me what hospital, Hank, but doesn't matter. And it's some place, eh? Biggest and nicest for its size I ever saw."

"Dad," Sylvia said. "What are your plans for later tonight?"

"I thought I'd take the proud papa out for dinner before leaving."

"I can't," Hank said. "I already got some place to go to. A sort of dinner-business engagement, you might say. Something I couldn't put off even if Sylvia were having the baby tonight, and I've already delayed it a couple of hours."

"So you go even an hour later. For coffee and cake—around then. Business deals always work out best around that time."

"You got a good point, Dad, but I can't. Let's face it—the kid's here now and I can't afford to pass up any chance for a sure buck."

"So you can't, then."

"But what are you going to do?" Sylvia said. "I don't want you walking around alone and maybe getting mugged. This can be a dangerous city."

"I'll go home by bus like I planned."

"Why not take an earlier one?"

"Because I want to take it at eleven or twelve. I'll have dinner in some nice place near the station and then sleep on the bus. It sort of rolls you, you know?"

"But you won't be getting in till four or five in the morning," she said. "That's why I'm concerned."

"That's not so late for me. Sometimes when I get through clean-ing and setting up at the deli and then having breakfast someplace with the other waiters, I also don't get home till four or five. By the way, you must be tired, sweetheart, so I think we better go before they kick us out." He opened the closet door to get his coat. Sylvia, with one eye on her father, mouthed to Hank that the least he could do was have a celebration drink with him before going to dinner, but Hank pointed to his watch, flapped his hand to tell her to forget the matter, then sliced the hand sideways through the air to say the incident was closed.

When Mr. Hyman had put on his heavy overcoat, he said "You know, I didn't sleep coming here on the bus I was so excited, but going back? Like a log I'll sleep."

"You're lucky," Hank said. "I could never do that."

"It's something you almost got to be born with, I think. He kissed Sylvia's forehead, patted her hand as he told her how happy she had made him today, and said to Hank "I'll go downstairs and wait for you in the coffee shop, okay?"

"I won't have time for a coffee, Dad—I'm sorry. I'm much too late as it is."

"One coffee, what's that? It's the least I can do for you."

"Have a good trip back," Sylvia said. "And remember. Soon as we set things up in the apartment with the baby, we'll have you down for a weekend, all right?"

"And I'll bring him a little something that'll knock your eyes out when I come. Something just beautiful," and he blew a kiss to her and left the room. He walked down the corridor, feeling tired for the first time since he got to Washington, and stopped at the nursery. All the shades were down. Without bending down, he tried looking under the shade of the window his grandson was behind, but couldn't see anything but a small section of the floor. Then he saw a woman's white shoes, another pair of shoes and white stockings, and for a moment the bottom of a white uniform when the first woman came nearer. He tapped the window, thinking maybe they'd raise the shade so he could have a last quick look at his grandson, but neither of them did.

"For a moment there I really thought I was lost," Hank said.

"The least you could've agreed to was a coffee with him," Sylvia said. "After all."

"He's down there now waiting for me, so I still have that problem to contend with."

"But coffee, Hank. Because how long would that take?"

"Too long. You know your old man's not one to let go with just one coffee. But that's still not my reason. If I had the time, I'd do it."

"Oh, well," she said, brightening up. "Tell Lucille all about everything, and that tomorrow's my last full day here and I'll be able to get calls and have as many visitors as I want. Did she say what she's serving tonight?"

"Whatever it is, you can be sure it'll be cold."

"Not Lucille." She took a candy out of the box. "You know," waving it in front of her, "you really get to miss these things when you know you can't have them."

"Candy never made that much difference to me."

"Me, neither. That's what I mean."

He motioned with his head to the other bed, which had a rolled-up mattress on it. "When they going to fill up that thing?"

"Tomorrow, they tell me."

"It's nice here like it is. Like a private room, almost, though without paying for one."

"But there's enough noise on this floor for an entire girls' dorm. I think I'm going to hate it here by tomorrow."

"You'll be home in two days, so don't worry." He leaned over and kissed her lips. When he started to raise his head, her arm, still wrapped around his neck, drew him down again.

"Isn't it wonderful?" she said, peeking his mouth.

"It sure is."

"I mean, the whole thing, Hank. Everything."

"I'm telling you, honey, if you were a man I'd give you a cigar. And the best too—not those cheap things other new fathers give out—because that's how happy I feel. Practically every guy I met got one. Gave out almost a box today."

"Do you like the name Gavin?"

"We picked it out, didn't we? Goes well: Gavin Riner."

"Have you thought more about a middle name?"

"Maybe he shouldn't have one—not every kid does. Maybe we should just give him a middle initial and leave it at that."

"Then everybody would ask what it stood for. No. Besides which, I never heard it done that way."

"I was only kidding, Syl. Just a joke."

"Oh." She smiled. "But think of a few tonight, okay? And I will too."

"Right—and now I think I better go." He reached for his coat in the closet. "Christ, I bet Lucille and Dave will be fuming."

"Not on your life, they won't." When he looked as if he didn't understand her, she pointed to her belly: "The baby, dummy, the baby."

He leaned across the bed while inserting his arms in the coat sleeves and kissed her on the lips with a sticky smack. Then he drum-tapped his fingers along the table till they reached the candy box, and moved his index finger across and down the chart. Finding what he wanted, he pulled out a chocolate and bit into it. She nudged him to show it to her, and he held up the part he hadn't eaten. It was coconut filled.

REINSERTION.

"Dad?" Andy said. "Dad, you asleep?"

His father's eyes opened. He weakly shook his head that he wasn't asleep.

"How do you feel tonight? —Dad, you hear me? I'm asking how you feel."

His father was on his side, cheek pressed against his shiny hands, which were clasped together on the pillow. Three other Parkinson's patients shared the room. The one next to his father was completely bald and bony and looked cadaverous, his mouth hanging wide open and his hands grasping for imaginary hornets and other wasps above his head and on his face and pillow. "Get that one," the man said. "Get that yellow jacket or I can't sleep, I won't." Then he was quiet, his mouth—a hole—still open, eyes shut tight, his teeth in an uncapped paper coffee container on the side table.

"You shouldn't be in this room," Andy said to his father.

His father's frozen stare moved slowly to a glass of flowers on his side table, which the hospital's women volunteer group had brought over during the day with a get-well card.

"They're pretty, aren't they," Andy said.

His father nodded.

"I would've brought some myself, and much bigger ones also. But remember last time when they couldn't find a vase in time and the damn things just died?"

His father tried to smile but gave up and shut his eyes.

"You want to sleep some more? That it? Well, you just sleep, go ahead, and I'll get a chair here and relax a little while you're napping.

I don't mind."

"Every time...every time...every time..."

"Every time what?"

"My mind...my mind...my mind every time...every time..."

"I still don't get it, Pop. You'll have to make more sense."

His father shook his head in disgust.

"Something about how you feel?"

He continued to shake his head.

"Maybe you want the nurse. Do you want the nurse? If you do, just say so and I'll run straight out of here and get her for you."

He shook his head, his expression even more disgusted.

"You don't? Well, then maybe—"

"My mind...my mind...goddamnit, I'm incomprehensible, Andy."

"Don't worry about it. Because look at you, with your sudden rage and articulateness. You're getting better, can't you see? You'll be back to your old grouchy self in no time. And 'incomprehensible'? A word I never heard you use before, except to repeat it mockingly whenever I used it."

"The nurse said..."

"Yes?"

"The nurse said...the nurse said every time my mind... my mind every time..."

"Dad, come on, give it a rest." He took his hand. It was cold, just as before the operation, so what good had it done? The first one turned out to be a failure. And when he and his sister brought him back to be examined the doctors said that, as they had previously warned, it was necessary to reoperate on about ten percent of the cases; drilling deeper and reinserting the tube into the patient's skull and freezing that part of the thalamus they had missed. But they had never mentioned the possibility of reinsertion. All they said was that three to four percent of the patients never fully recover from the operation and another one percent die on the table, almost always because of a previous cardiac condition the desperate patient and family hadn't disclosed. Andy and his sister hadn't wanted him to go through it again, but he insisted. "For what good am I the way I am? A burden, a good-for-nothing burden on everyone if I don't get myself fixed up quick and back to work. And you want to see all my money disappear and then yours too?"

"Dad?" Andy said. "Your hand feels wonderful...it really does."

"Every time...every time..."

"Dad, let me see you give me one of your real good handshakes."

"Someone," the patient in the next bed said, "someone get that yellow jacket...that hornet on the lamp. Now get that one. I said get that one."

"That poor man," Andy said. "Does he bother you much?"

But he was still trying to squeeze Andy's hand.

"Say, now that's what I call a grip. You're getting much stronger. Why, I bet in a few days—"

"In a few days..."

"In a few days you'll be able to pull out teeth just as you used to. I'm not kidding. The surgeon said they got it all this operation. That you're really going to be able to walk by yourself this time."

"This time...this time..."

"Don't repeat everything I say, Dad."

"Every time my mind...my mind...it's my godawful mind, Andy," and he shut his eyes and seemed to be dozing off.

"That's fine, Dad—you sleep. I'll just sit here—till closing, even. I promise."

"Yellow jackets...wasps...hornets," the other patient said. "Huge hornets and flying stinging ants. Iowa's full of them, all trying to keep a working man from his sleep."

He snapped his hands in the air at the insects. Then his feet began tremoring and his legs jerked up and down under the covers and his hands thumped the mattress. "Yellow jackets and hornets and flying stinging ants..."

"Flying stinging ants," Andy's father said, his eyes still closed.

"That's right. Huge stinging ants. Iowa's full of them, the rotten pests. They'll kill you." Then the two men were quiet, their sleeps seemingly untroubled. Andy waited a few minutes, felt his father was really asleep this time, and left the room.

He took the elevator to the cafeteria on the fifth floor, got a cruller and coffee, looked around for a place to sit and saw, seated at the rear of the room, the surgeon who'd operated on his father. He went over to him.

"Excuse me," he said, "but I wonder if I could talk to you for a moment." The young doctor peered up from the coffee he'd been sipping. The nurse beside him whom he'd been talking to, cut his jelly doughnut in half with a fork.

"Pardon me?" the doctor said.

"I'm Herman Waxman's son—Mr. Waxman on the seventh floor?"

"Oh, sure. Nice to meet you. I'll be on that floor in fifteen minutes, so why don't I speak to you then?"

"I might not see you. You fellows seem to come through the floor so rapidly that I've missed you each time. And I work late and can't get here every night."

"Tonight I promise I'll be there at eight sharp. I'll be making my rounds of all the Parkinsonians then, and I'll make a point of looking for you."

"Your coffee's getting cold, Dr. Gershgorn," the nurse said.

"Would you mind very much if I had my coffee with you?" Andy said to him. "I've some important questions to ask about my father's operation."

"Mr. Waxman," the doctor said. "I appreciate and understand your interest and concern and all, but this is my one breaking during an uninterrupted five-hour stretch."

"Just tell me if his operation was a success or not."

"If I can remember correctly, your dad's coming along nicely."

"But his hands are still cold, and almost rigid. And when you saw him in that preoperative exam two weeks ago you said his hands would become warmer and have more movement after the operation. And there seems to be some damage to his speech and mind—even worse than before the first operation."

"I don't recall getting any reports on that. Maybe your dad is still drowsy."

"But it was like that last night. And the nights and days before that, my sister said."

"Well, so soon after an operation—"

"The operation was a week ago, if you'd really like to know."

"Now listen, Mr. Waxman. It's impossible for me to talk accurately about this without his charts and records, so what do you say I see you upstairs?"

"I suppose you're right."

"I'm saying...well, I'm not trying to be evasive or anything, but this is a cafeteria."

"Of course. I'm sorry. My apologies to you both," and still holding his tray, he excused himself and made his way to a table across the room. A woman, whom he'd seen in his father's room but mostly in the visitors' lounge down the corridor, where she was always smoking, got up from another table and sat opposite him.

"You don't mind, do you?" she said. "It's only you're the one person, other than staff, I recognize here, and I hate having coffee alone."

"It's fine; sit." He reached for the sugar dispenser.

"I see you also like your coffee sweet," she said.

"I usually drink it with nothing, but this hospital coffee's such vile stuff that I—"

"That Mr. Waxman—he's your father, isn't he?"

"That's right."

"A sweet old man—just wonderful. Everyone on the floor loves him. He's a lucky man also, having a son who lives close by, coming to see him so much. Don't worry, your lovely sister told me all about you and your important TV news work. It sounds very interesting. And it's nice that he also has a daughter who takes care of him the way she does."

"Sheila's devoted to him. She and Dad have always been close."

"That's wonderful. Now the two boys of my poor husband—you can have as a gift. I'm not even sure they remember he's alive."

"Did your husband go through a similar operation?"

"Similar? The same. There's only one way to cure them so far, and that's the one they both went through. And now reinsertion also, drilling away like they were oilmen digging for riches, instead of well-paid surgeons. But he wanted it. Oh, we couldn't talk him out of it for the world. But it won't do him any good. And for this factory here to go ahead with it and take the last of our savings, was like taking candy from a baby—literally. Have you noticed him grabbing for hornets and such?"

"That's your husband?"

"Myron Dodd, bed number B. He did the same thing after the first operation for a week, and also repeating everything he heard, exactly like your dad does. And last time they also discharged him, saying he was in terrific shape—you should have seen how convinced the doctors were. And in a way he was, walking and speaking fairly well and gaining weight and using his hands as he hadn't done in years. But three weeks after we got him home he collapsed in his chair as he was trying to push a hole through his baked potato, so you can see why I say it'll happen again."

"I'm sure it won't. Just by the statistics they give, the second operation has a much greater chance of success."

"Oh, no. I hate to admit it. What I'm saying is I hate to be the prophet of doom or callous or a person like that, because I know your family is no better off financially or any other way with your problems. But I have a vegetable on my hands for the rest of my life, and so do you. I don't know where we're ever going to get the money."

His father was the only patient awake when they entered the room.

"Andy? That you?"

"He's here, Mr. W.," Mrs. Dodd said, stroking his cheek, "so don't be worrying none. You've a very nice boy here.

And we've just had a pleasant chat and I assured him everything's going to be all right with you. You're a lucky man, Mr. W., a very lucky man." Then she went over to the other patients in the room, made sure they were covered, and sat on her husband's bed.

"Andy—where are you?"

"Right beside you, Dad. Anything wrong?"

"You're here? Good." He moved his hand through the bed rail.

"You want to take my hand?"

He nodded and Andy held his father's hand and kissed his forehead. Then his father said "Lila? Your mother, Lila...I mean..."

"She's home."

"Home?"

"Her home. You've been divorced close to ten years, don't you remember? You live alone with Sheila now."

"And you?"

"You know I live alone too."

"You come and live with us too—understand?"

"You're speaking much better now, Dad."

"Nice girl, nice woman, your mother." The thought seemed to please him. "We never should've split up. It was bad for you kids."

"I don't know. It was good for you two, so I guess good for us."

"No, no. Never should've split up."

"Okay, if you say so. And you really are speaking much better. Keep it up and you'll be out of this place in a week."

"Nice woman, very pretty. Came from a good family, true class. Why isn't she with us, Andy? I mean, I mean, you think after marriage to one woman for twenty years... thirty years..."

"Mom told me she wants to come. I spoke to her yesterday and she was very eager to know everything about you. But coming here means leaving her job early. Also, the long subway ride at night, and this dangerous neighborhood. It's too much for any woman, Dad."

"The daytime. The daytime every time the daytime, Andy."

"Try and go back to sleep, Dad. Just rest."

"But the daytime, Andy. She has a day off Wednesday in the daytime—I know. And Sunday all day."

"You mean you think she ought to come during the day? I'll suggest that to her. She wants to come badly. She told me so just yesterday."

"Today. She'll come today and I'll be better, Andy."

"I'll tell her. She's very concerned about you—as much as Sheila and I are."

"I know. A lovely woman. If we would've stayed together this wouldn't have happened. She knew how to take care of me best. Call her again. Tell her to come. Do me a favor."

"Right after closing tonight I'll call her. I'm sure she'll be here in the next few days."

"Few days?" He looked puzzled. "Few days? Few days?"

"Don't be repeating everything I say. It's not good for you."

"You and Sheila and she come next few days, Andy, and I'll be better."

"I know you'll be better also."

"Also, Andy..."

"Also what, Dad?"

"Also what, Dad?"

"Dad, please. Now I already asked you not to repeat everything I say. Just please."

"Please," he said, shutting his eyes. "Please, Andy... please, just please." Then he seemed to be asleep. Andy, still holding his father's fingers through the bed rail, opened a newspaper in his lap with his free hand. When he raised his wrist to look at his watch, Mrs. Dodd, sitting beside her sleeping husband with her arm around his shoulders, called out from across the beds "We got more than half an hour yet. I checked. I check every five minutes, in fact. It's some ordeal, isn't it?"

ONE   THING.

I said I only have one thing on my mind to tell her. She didn't ask what. Sat there, reading, looking over her shoulder out the window. Then at her hand. Way she was holding it, in what I'd call a relaxed fist, probably her nails. Shut her eyes, seemed to be drifting into thought. Then, when her face tightened, into deep thought. Opened her eyes— popped them open, is more like it, and still without looking at me. She was looking to the side at the coat rack filled and covered with our sweaters, hats, coats and scarves. Seemed about to say something, to me without looking at me or to herself aloud. But she closed her mouth, shook her head, began blinking rapidly as if she had a tic, which she never had before that I was aware of, so I didn't know what to make of it. Blinking stopped, and her irises rose till they were partly hidden by her eyelids. I'd seen her do that before. Put her finger to the inner corner of her right eye as if she was trying to take something out of it. That speck, if that was it, could have been what caused the blinking before, or the blinking might have been her way to get rid of it. Wiped the finger on the back of her other hand. Looked at where she'd wiped. From where I was sitting opposite her—about ten feet away—I couldn't see anything there. Then the book slid off her lap and the bookmark fell out. Could be she forgot she was holding it. Could even be that for the last half minute or so she'd intentionally let it rest on her lap without holding it. Book made a noise when it hit the floor and the sound startled her. Leaned over, picked the book and bookmark up, slipped the bookmark into the book and seemed to look for the page she'd left off at. Seemed to find it, because she held the book in front of her and resumed reading. After that:

little motions of her face, eyes and hands, though none to me. And her foot tapping intermittently, not because of a tic but out of impatience it seemed. All while she was reading or pretending to read, because in more than five minutes—and she was a fast reader—she still hadn't turned the page. I wanted to say "As I was saying before, I only have one thing, or you could even say 'one point' on my mind to tell you," but didn't think she'd respond in any way no matter what I said or how urgently or emphatically I said it. By taking her eyes off the book, for instance. By looking at me. By saying she heard me the first time. By saying something like "I know what you're going to say, knew what you were going to say the first time, didn't think much of it then and don't think much of it now, so don't bother saying it."

She seemed completely removed from me, and not because she was too absorbed in the book to look up or say anything. She knew as well as I that it was a dull and almost unreadable book. Unreadable meaning a chore to read because it was so dully and unimaginatively written and had so little to say. That there was nothing new or intriguing about it. Nothing about it in subject, style, structure or whatever else there is that makes a book interesting and rewarding and grabs your attention from the start and holds it, or the kind of attention she was pretending to give it. When she suddenly looked up. Not at me but at everything else in the room: coat rack, window, wall art we'd collected individually, before we knew each other, and together; her book again, which was back in her lap, or maybe, she was just looking at her lap. Who knows with her, but that's it, I thought, and I stood up and went to the kitchen. Thought I'd make myself coffee or tea. Even a hot chocolate, which I hadn't had in years and didn't even know if we had any hot chocolate mix, or mug of vegetable broth made from a cube. Then got so angry right after I grabbed the kettle to put water in that I slammed it down. At her for ignoring me. For using the book as an excuse not to look at or listen or talk to me. And everything else in the room and on her person like that as a device against me. Ran back to the living room. Didn't actually run but sort of walked quickly, still angry and pumped up to say what I thought of her treatment of me. All the improvisations and stratagems or just tricks, I'll call them. Her nails, which didn't seem in need of any further trimming or cleaning. Coat rack—maybe something to do with it being so filled it might topple over, but it had to be looked at three to four times? And what could be out the window that wasn't there when she looked a minute before?

Same tree with the same bloom. Same back fence in no need of repair. Same redwood picnic table and four plastic chairs. Patch of grass I mowed a few days ago and bushes I recently clipped. Maybe a bird standing on one of those or fluttering in place in the air before flying off. That would be something worth looking at if it was that, for a short time at least. But she still, if just for a few seconds, could have given some sign she was prepared to listen to me. All to most of which I was about to tell her, when she started smiling. Not to me but the book on her lap. Something in it was making her smile, it seemed. Or maybe she was just looking at the book but smiling at what she sensed I was about to say because of the way I'd stormed in here and possibly over that one-thing-on-my-mind I'd never got to say. If it was the book, then something in it that reminded her of something else that was funny. Or a passage or line in the book that was so bad she had to smile. Or she recalled something that made her smile that had nothing to do with the book or me. Or maybe something to do with me but not part of my storming in or that one-thing-on-my-mind-to-say. Something we once did together that was pleasant or funny or both. Something either of us had said to the other or our child had said or done to one of us or both. Or anything. But she'd smiled and was still smiling, so how could I go up to her angrily and berate her about something when she was like that? It'd seem awful or just not the right moment or totally out of sync or whack. Anyway, it'd be a lot more difficult to do than when she wasn't smiling disparagingly or cynically or any other way like that at me. And her smile was real. I know her too long not to know that a smile like that can't be faked. So I turned around, thought of going back to the kitchen to make coffee or one of those other drinks. Thought also of turning back to her and saying there was still one thing on my mind I wanted to tell her, since what was on my mind then and was still on it now had nothing to do with any criticism or dissatisfaction with her. Thought to ask if she had any idea what that one thing on my mind was that I'd wanted to tell her, for I now forget what it specifically was. Thought also of asking what she was still smiling at. But she looked so content smiling that I didn't want to distract her from whatever was causing it. I just wanted to sit down opposite her and look at her face made even lovelier by her smile. And then perhaps, when she was finished smiling, ask if she had any idea what I'd started out to say before about that one thing. It was something concerning the two of us, I remember, and as a result, our child. That's right: that it was silly to continue fighting when we know we always eventually work it out. And work it out to such a degree that we always feel good about each other after, and as a result, our child feels better. So why don't we take a shortcut this time and forget what's eating us about the other and sit together and talk about things the way we do when we're feeling good with each other? She stopped smiling and looked up from her book at me. I smiled, was about to sit in the chair opposite her. She looked down at the book in her lap without smiling. I thought "Give it time," and went into the kitchen to get away from her and not—at least it wasn't in my mind at the moment—for anything to drink.

DAWN.

Lately she's been giving me signs. We were to meet at an art gallery opening and before she got there a woman said of the two paintings I was standing in front of "Look at that. 'January 75. January 75.' How can the painter do even one complicated work like that in a month with so many perfect squiggly lines on top of lines when today's the 23rd and they had to have been here by the 22nd and then before that taken a few days to dry?" I said "I'm not a painter. But you can get that effect by painting one layer of acrylic over a lighter colored layer after the first one's dried, which only takes an hour or two." She said "Acrylic, what's that?" and I told her and she thanked me and walked away and a few minutes later Dawn came. We kissed hello and drank some champagne and talked to a few people she knew and looked at the paintings and got our coats and were about to leave when she said "Let me go to the ladies' room first." While she was gone that woman of before came over and said "Oh, you're leaving? Tell me, what do you do if you're not an artist?" and I said "I write." She said "And I play the piano. What do you write, journalism?" and I said "Fiction." "And I'm a concert pianist. You've been published?" and I said "A couple of books," and she said "Well, good for you. You like Mozart?" "Yes." "Scriabin?" "Sure. Scriabin, Prokofiev, Stravinsky why not?" "You should feel very at home here—this is a Russian gallery. Tell you what. I love to read. So send me your books and in return I'll send you tickets to my next recital." "All right." "Better yet, drop them off at my apartment and we'll have coffee and talk some more and then when I get the tickets I'll send them to you. I live in the Osborne—one block west on 57th here. I'm always practicing between ten and three every day of the week, though I don't mind being interrupted for a short while. My name's Sue Heissmatt—with an e, I and double-s. Yours is what?" "Vic White." "Okay, Vic. I haven't read you but I'm looking forward to it. You have my name and where I live and hours I'm sure to be in, without writing it down?" "It's in my head." "Good. Then hope to see you soon," and we shook hands and she went to the drink table. Dawn returned, and on the street I said "I met a woman there and we got to talking about the paintings we both knew little about and then she started with what we each do. 'Oh, I'm a writer,' and 'I'm a pianist,' and after a minute's total conversation she said why don't I come to her apartment at the Osborne over there one day soon and bring some of my published work along, and in exchange she'll give me tickets to her next recital." "You should do that," and I said "But I'm not interested in her and I don't want to just screw around." "Why not? Every now and then you ought to give things a chance rather than only imagining in your head or on paper how they'll turn out. She might be fun, but do what you want."

A few days later Dawn drove into the city for dinner with me. She yawned at the restaurant a lot and didn't talk much or seem interested in anything I said or our food. And whatever touching was done on or under the table she did reluctantly, it seemed, and as briefly as she could without trying to make me wonder about it or upset me. When we were walking back to her car, she said "If you had a phone I would have called to say I was too tired to come tonight, and I can't stay either. Now I hate even thinking how I'm going to make it home." "I'll drive you," and she said "You don't have to, I'll make it some way." "But if you're so sleepy, what could be better than not driving off the road, and later being carried from car to soft bed? Just let me stop off for my typewriter and writing work," and she said "Really, I appreciate your offer, and any other time you know I'd accept. But I'm going to be extremely busy grading exam papers the next three nights, and I can always get it done much faster when you're not around, all right?" "Of course," and she said "Great, because I'm too bushed to even think about it anymore, and didn't want it turning into another big thing." I said "Another? When was the last other? I'm sorry, excuse me, forget it," and she said "Thanks, lovie." We kissed goodnight and she got into her car. I blew her a kiss and started back to my building, and a few seconds later she passed me without tapping the horn and waving or even looking at me as she usually did.

I called two nights later and said "How you feeling?" and she said "Tired, bored, overworked, hassled, crotchety, queasy and very unrested, but once I get these exams done and grades in, I'll perk up," and I said "I miss sleeping with you, and I'm speaking about just sleeping," and she said "Sleeping alone was never nearly as good as with a warm partner, but waking up alone can usually be." I said "Did I tell you about the ad in *Coda* I answered a couple of months ago?" and she said "What's *Coda*, an international spy trade journal?" "The poet's newsletter that's sent to me every three months or so courtesy of CCLM or CAPS," and she said "I don't have the time to ask what those letters or acronyms stand for, and you're not a poet." "They now let fiction writers in, and I didn't tell you about the ad?" "You might have, and I forgot." "It was for a creative writing position, and I answered it—" and she said "If this is going to be one of your long short stories, I still have hours of work to do." "Five minutes more shouldn't matter that much—consider it your work break." "I took my break five minutes ago." "Okay, I'll be quick. I got an answer back today from the English Department chairperson, a Ms. Liz Silverstone, was how she letterheaded it, and chairperson with a capital C. She said, and I quote, 'While you do not have the MFA we advertised for, still, your list of publications leads us to pursue your application further. I'll add to that: with very strong interest indeed.' That's Ms. Chairperson's adscript in pen, as if the typewritten part wasn't hers." "Hurray, you finally might be paid for your fiction," and I said "Well, I did sell those two books—small press, no advance, and no royalties yet, but they still might come. Anyway, it's only for a year. And I know no long-range plans between us. But if I do get it, and prospects look good, you and Paula might think about coming to live with me there, all living expenses on me." "Where is it?" and I said "Southwest Indiana." "Maybe you better just fly home every now and then," and I said "I of course wouldn't expect you to come. Though you did say you wanted to take a leave from high school for a year to have the time to make a film," and she said "If I make one it'll only be through a Film Institute grant I applied for, which could mean that same time you're in Indiana, I'll be taking courses and shooting and cutting my film in L.A." "You mean you'd go there without me?" and she said "Without Paula too. She'd stay with her father. But listen, yours is the best offer I got all day. Though don't write that woman to say you're no longer interested in the position, just because we wouldn't be tagging along. Get the job first; then decide."

I called at the end of the week and said "I know I'm seeing you tomorrow, but I have to tell someone about the ultimate book rejection I got. It came from a Seattle publisher of up till now only Urgo-Slavonic and Altaic translations but who I'd heard four months ago was looking for an original story collection in English. So I sent off a load then, and today, after a couple of queries from me asking about the status of my collection, I got a jiffy bag with half my stories missing and my novella just sort of tossed in there and paginated like so: 5, 14, 78, 24, 2, though six of its pages also missing and the ones that were there either mangled, minced or decapitated. Thinking this peculiar, though also relieved they didn't accept my work but having anxieties they may have kept the rest to publish as a chapbook, I searched for a note and found at the bottom of the bag not only a standard rejection slip with, you know, 'Thank you for the opportunity to read this,' but also burnt matches, cigarette butts, wilted lettuce leaves and pieces of a Vienna roll." "Maybe they were trying to tell you that you send too much of your work at one time," and I said "But they did everything but vomit into the bag before stapling it up." "Then I don't know. But maybe they were also saying 'We're a small house new in this particular line. So next time give us a while longer to consider your manuscript without besieging us with queries a month after it's arrived.'"

I took a bus up to see her the next day. We went to dinner at some friends of mine she'd never met and when we were driving back I said "So what do you think of them?"

"They certainly are a couple, with that always working things out to perfection and complete integration and staying two feet away from each other so they don't step on the other's toes. It all reminds me too much of my own marriage and which I never want to go through again." Later, when she was undressing in her bedroom, she said "I feel uncomfortable now because I don't feel anything like having sex tonight, and with all your hints hidden in suggestions before, I think it might tick you off." I said "No, it's fine. We'll just go to bed. Or I'll read downstairs and for now just you go to bed." "My uncomfortableness comes only because the last time you got angry when I didn't feel like making love," and I said "That last time was after a couple of weeks when I was sort of expecting it or wanting it very much but didn't think, or only thought of myself, and reverted again to being the same old schmuck." We went to bed, read awhile and shut the lights. She started crying about fifteen minutes later. I was holding her from behind, thought she was already asleep. I asked what was wrong. She said "I'm feeling a bit skittish, hopeless, edgy, skew jawed, doldrums. Maybe it's my mother, or my period about to pop. But she was so strange on the phone today that it scared me, and I'm also beginning to dread more and more facing a hundred-thirty kids every school day." "This will seem hackneyed," I said, "but I promise you'll feel better after a good night's sleep. If you want I'll massage your neck and back till you feel more relaxed." "No, thanks." "Come on, I'll do it just the way you like. Turn over." "I'm too sleepy, so don't waste it. And I'll be okay. You're a love. What's the time? But why should I care? Tomorrow's Sunday."

Next morning she went to the bathroom, shut the door, came back with her hair brushed, face scrubbed, got back into bed, chin up close to nine, smiled, teeth had been cleaned too, sucked my thumbs, twiddled my nipples till they got hard, moved in her front, positioned me. later we took a long walk and talked and laughed a lot and, preparing and eating lunch, had fun impersonating various musical instruments in solos and duets to Paula's frenzied conductor's hands. All right. Now we're tight. Nothing seemed wrong. In and out, that's how we sometimes go. Does she notice how Paula adores me? Does it make a difference that I feel like Paula's father too? What do her friends say? Do they like me? Does she notice when I anonymously clean her toilet bowls and sweep all her rooms? "Make you tea?" I said "No, thank you. I mean, you bet. For you often bemoan I never need or take anything from you but some of your better spontaneous lines, but from now on I'm going to say yes, yes'm, yes." "Good," and later: "Let's visit the Whipples without calling them," and I said "You two go; I'd just like to read." "Reading, reading. It won't be as much fun if you don't come along, and remember what you resolved?" We drove across Tappan Zee Bridge and she said "Look!" "What?" "Balloon moon over Tarrytown and it's not even dark yet," and I said "Okay, but never surprise me like that while I'm driving." We burst in on the Whipples and their two kids and four hounds, who never stopped licking and sniffing us, and I said "Someone, throw them a couple ducks, will ya?" We all went to their Pizza and Brew. Rip Whipple winking back and forth at me and the miniskirted legs of our waitress, and I said "Uh-huh," but thought "Who cares? I got Dawn," and held her around the waist while we ate. Driving home, I got lost, just as I got lost driving out there. Paula said "Darn, he got us lost again, Mom," and Dawn said "Vic's a good loser, you have to admit that. And now we can see what these Scarsdale dudes and dudettes do in their rooms late at night besides watch their tubes." When we got home Paula went right to her room to make pompoms for her class, and Dawn said to me "I have to be up early tomorrow. Deep dreams," and kissed me and went upstairs. The phone rang. I was reading downstairs and started for the kitchen, but Paula ran to Dawn's study upstairs and said "Mom, it's a man who said in a kind of deep rough voice 'Dawn Bodein in?' but refused to give his name. Dawn got out of bed. I moved to the bottom of the stairs to listen. It was Peter, though she didn't say his name, but it had to be him because he'd been calling once a month for months, and last month I answered the phone and he said in a kind of deep rough voice "Hi, Dawn Bodein in?" and I said "Who is it?" and he said "Just tell her a friend," and I said "Well, I hate to tell you, but she left for Toulouse for two years," and he said "Could you let me speak to Dawn, please?" and I said "Dawn Please or Dawn Bodein? We're rather unique in having two Dawns here," and he said "Either, and I don't mean Dawn Either," and

I yelled "Dawn—Friend's on the phone," and she got on and I left the kitchen, and later she said "What did you say to Peter? He thought you were insane." "Who's Peter?" I asked, and she said "Just what you described him: a friend." She was speaking on the phone in a normal tone and with the door open, so she probably didn't think I'd be listening downstairs. It also had to be Peter because one of the first things she said was "But it isn't for Friday—sure you can make it?" and laughed, and I'd seen Peter's name on her wall calendar every three weeks for several months under Friday. Also, because she said "Works out perfectly. Sunday I'd have to be in Brooklyn Heights anyway to fetch Paula at her cousin's where her father's dropping her off," and I knew Peter lived in Brooklyn because of a number of things I'd picked up: a letter envelope from a Brooklyn Peter, and so forth. I went away from the stairs while she was still on the phone. I didn't like hearing her joking and teasing and laughing with a guy I knew she was sleeping with. At a restaurant dinner in my neighborhood a few weeks ago she said, after we'd talked about lovers and serious relationships we'd had before we met each other, "I think it's only fair to tell you something, even if you won't like it. I guess I'm having what one could call a relationship with another man. But it's really nothing much and isn't going to go anywhere, and is the only one I've had since I've known you."

I said, mainly because saying what I really felt—that I hated she was screwing someone else, even if only once every three week could damage our own fragile relationship even further and where she'd probably drive home after dinner rather than spending the night with me, "It's not important. You see who you want and I'll do the same. And also, when we want, we'll see each other, like tonight, but slow, we have to go slow as you've said," and she said "Boy, is that a relief that we can both finally say that." So I went back to the rocking chair in her living room. Drank another glass of wine while I read. Then Dawn got back in bed—her bed squeaks—and I turned down the heat and shut the lights downstairs and opened the front door and said "Here, Snuggy Snuggy; here, Snuggy Snuggy," and got the cat back in the house and locked up and went upstairs. Dawn was reading in bed. "I thought I wanted to sleep, but got the urge to read. Let me read you a poem by Anne Sexton. It's about a witch." I listened to it lying on my back in bed while she was sitting up, I kissed her waist while she rubbed my hair and read, and then her navel and legs and then her vagina, and she said "No, I can't do it while I'm reading a poem. I mean, you can't do it. I mean, I just can't read a poem while you're doing that." "So stop reading," and she said "But I want to read, and if you want me to do it silently, I will. She committed suicide, did you know?" and I said yes and she finished reading the poem. "What do you think of it?" and I said "I liked it," and she started reading another about snow. I rested my head on her chest and hand on her thigh, and listened. While she read she took my hand off her thigh and pressed two of my fingers into her clitoris and read a few more lines while she continued to press my fingers down and rub them around. She said "She's too much. I can hardly ever get through more than two of hers at a time," and dropped the magazine to the floor and kissed me. Later, she said "How come we never encourage each other verbally when we make love? People have told me it really gets them off." "I prefer being quiet except for the normal sounds." Later, she said "That was great. I don't know why I felt so much like it tonight, but I obviously did," and I said "Me the same on both," but thought "You felt like it because Peter probably oozed on about it over the phone and how you both hadn't done it together for more than two months. So you thought of him and your upcoming weekend, and maybe he's very good in bed, and also of me, no doubt, and it was enough to get you hot, dear Dawn, eh not? and also the poems." "Goodnight," I said. "Goodnight, love," she said. She cuddled up to me. We went to sleep.

Next morning, her alarm clock rang. It was still dark out. She had to get up for school and Paula to wash her hair before going to school. I did my morning exercises in the bedroom and went downstairs and sat at the table with my coffee while they finished their pancakes and juice and milk. Dawn wiggled her fingers at me to get my attention, and said "I'm going to the city Tuesday night for my dance class. I'll drive you back, okay?" and I said "Sure." "Also, I've been thinking we need a little vacation from each other," and I raised my eyebrows, and she said "I'm saying that I'd like it if we didn't see each other this weekend—that's all right, isn't it?" "What's the real reason?" and she said "I already told you the real reason." Paula got up, and Dawn said "If you're through, bring in your dishes, please?" Paula went into the kitchen with her dishes and started washing them, and I said "What I mean is what's behind the face of what you said?" "Face? What face? I don't understand, I just want to do some things by myself this weekend, okay?" "By yourself? Does that mean alone or without me?" and she said "Whatever I want to do—what's so wrong with that?" "You've a date—for all I know, you've two—so why didn't you just say it and that you've probably had your share of me for the time being, and what's troubling you is that I haven't had my share yet of you." "I don't know about you, but I can't go through these things so early," and I said "I'm sorry, but I can't help it. That's how I immediately felt. Maybe it's your fault for bringing this on too suddenly for me." I went into the living room with my coffee and sat in the rocking chair. The cat jumped onto my lap and stayed there. Dawn came in and got down on her knees beside me and stroked the cat and rested her arm on my legs and said "I shouldn't have said anything before I left. That's what you used to do before I'd leave for school when you had something I didn't want to hear or wasn't ready or sufficiently awake for just then, and it would mess up my whole day." "Forget it, it's all right," and she said "Though it does make me a little fearful for us again, but no big deal." I said "No, it's had its effect," and a couple of tears were coming out and she saw them and I thought "Goddamn fucking tears," and got rid of them. "Oh crap," she said, "I should have just stuck to ending it between us when I got back from Turkey," and I said "What a thing to say. Turkey was a summer and a half ago." "But I'm no good at periodically readjusting the relationship with the same man." "Look, I'll never be able to work here today. If you don't mind I'm going to start the vacation a day earlier and take the express bus in." I set the cat on the floor and went into the dining room to put my typewriter, which was on the table, back in its case. She came into the room and said "Maybe vacation was the wrong word to use. I meant by it that we could both use a short break from each other—for a couple of weeks or so." Paula yelled goodbye from the kitchen. We yelled goodbye, and she left through the back door, probably because she didn't want to pass us to get to the front. "I've got to go too," Dawn said. "I don't like leaving it like this, but I for homeroom." She put on her coat and got her briefcase and books, I got my typewriter and canvas totebag, and we left the house and walked up the hill behind it to where her car was. She said "Listen, either be here or you're not here, but that's okay, right?" and I said "Right, and have a good week." "Okay. You too. A great creative one," and kissed me and got in her car and started it up and smiled and waved at me. She was trying to placate me with that smile and wave and those last remarks because she knew I was feeling hurt as I'd been again and again the past two years when she decided to "break us up for two weeks, a month, her vacations, her separations, no doubt her other men besides Peter, her other times with other people, when she was feeling claustrophobic with me, as she'd said, and maybe when she gets too close to a man she always has to draw back, as she'd said, and so on. But I don't want to go into it again. Then why am I going into it again? But anyway, anyway, she was there on the flat part of the little hill, warming up the car not fifteen feet away from me, and when she drove off she probably thought "Who the hell needs the aggravation? I should be asking myself. Let him get used to me and my ways and what I can and can't do now, or let him go screw himself. No, that's too hard. Just let him go and maybe for good." And I was standing there a few feet away from where I said goodbye to her, thinking "God, I love her so much I don't know why I hate her." I don't know what I'm saying. I know it's going to be a lousy day. I should take the bus. I must take the bus. Just get the hell down there and take the bus already, stupid, and I start down to the stop.

THE

WILD

BIRD

RESERVE.

We're walking through the park when we hear a groan from behind the bushes.

"What was that?" Jane says.

"Sounded like it was from in there."

"I know, but who is it?"

"Want me to take a look?"

"No. Let's keep walking. I'm afraid."

"Why? It could be a harmless drunk or sober man having a heart attack. You push on a ways and I'll check it out."

"I said don't. It's no joke. We shouldn't have come this way. The path's too narrow. The bushes and boulders are too big."

"We're in the heart of the wild bird reserve, that's why the denseness. Part of the eastern flyway in fall and spring."

"Then let's fly away." Our boy in the stroller throws his bottle to the ground. "Don't, Jim. Stop throwing things." She gives the bottle back to him. "I think he's made." She leans over his back and sniffs. "He's made. Please?"

"I'm still concerned about that groan."

"What for? Nobody in his right mind should've been in there."

"But say we read tomorrow it was someone who got killed. Worse than the heart attack. Someone who bled to death because nobody came in time. We could read that."

"We won't."

"We could."

"I'm going and so are you. Now let's go." She pushes the stroller. Jim throws his bottle out. She picks it up and offers him it.

"I wouldn't give it back."

She drops it into the stroller bag. Jim tries sliding out of the stroller frontways.

"You'll break your feet, Jim," she says. "Now in. I said in."

"We'll move quicker if I carry him. Because it's going to start pouring again."

"It wasn't a good idea cutting through the park."

"Too late. And there's better tree shelter along the way."

"Maybe that's what that groaning man was trying to do—save time. I hate this city."

"One incident. That's all it ever takes you."

"You're right. I like this city. But I hate people getting beaten up on and robbed and raped."

It starts to rain. "Want to keep going or duck under this tree?"

"What do you think?"

"I don't know. You're in a rush to get out, aren't you?"

"It's tough knowing what to do. Get drenched and give Jim a worse cold. Or stand under here and risk getting hit by lightning or mugged."

"Let's ask Jim then. Jim? Should we stay or go?"

"Shou," Jim says. "Ba-ba, ba-ba."

"He wants his bottle," she says.

"No chance."

"Did he at least make up our minds about staying or going?"

"Would you stay here for a second while I go back?"

"Me? Here? Without you? You'll loan me a gun? And put him down till we decide."

"I like holding him."

"If we suddenly have to run you'll be too tired from holding him by then."

"But say we do read or see on the TV tomorrow—"

"Oh, sure. Drop by drop. His last words to the police were 'I heard a couple and their son Jim pass by. They debated helping me. She convinced him not to. He convinced her he was crazy enough to. Jim wanted to crawl back and throw his bottle at the mugger. The one thing they agreed on was they were tired of picking up his bottle.'"

"Ba-ba, ba-ba, ba-ba."

"Okay, let's go," I say.

"Now? When it's a waterfall?"

"Then we'll stay here."

"You didn't get the word from Jim yet."

"Okay, Jim? You don't want to go under a waterfall and get a worse cold or even worse."

"Ba-ba, ba-ba."

"He's really hot for his bottle. Maybe if we had some milk in it."

"Don't start," she says. "He drank it all. What we should have in it is water from one of the fountains we passed, but they all had to be torn loose from the ground. This city."

"There she goes again, folks."

"Well, this city, this city. Where I can't even get water for my son because of the creeps who like kicking fountains down?"

"Whenever we can't get water for him he's your son."

"Our son. But those creeps. I think it's stopped."

I stick my hand out. "Still coming down pretty hard."

"I like it under here. I can say that. Like our own arbor. Or whatever it's called. A private retreat in the storm."

I put my arm around her shoulder and hold Jim up to us tight. "If that—"

"You're getting his neck wet from my hair."

"If that man was mugged, I hope he was at least also under a shelter."

"Oh, thanks. But if he was, then I'd wonder what he was doing there. Looking to meet men, probably."

"Or he loves nature and wanted to step further into it. A bird watcher, maybe. Someone might have jumped him from behind just to get his binoculars."

"Why from behind? Those guys will attack you right from up front."

"You're so sure his attacker was a man?"

"I don't even think anyone was attacked. But it's not something a woman would do."

"They would. They have. Girls too, in groups and gangs. Certainly some of the girls I've taught. And starting at age eleven and twelve."

"Something would have to be wrong with them then."

"Ba-ba, ba-ba."

"You think ba-ba means something other than bottle?" I say. "Like weh with him means wet and tub water and puddles and numbers one and two and maybe also rain."

"Weh, weh, weh."

"I at least got his mind off the ba-ba."

"I'm going. I don't care if it's buckets. Now put him down."

I put him in the stroller and push it downhill. "Weh, weh, weh," Jim says. We reach the park drive and I pull under the eaves of the Swedish Cottage.

"We're soaked through as it is," she says, "so don't stop now."

"Still afraid? We're away from it, and maybe we can call the police from here."

"Sure. See anybody inside? Nothing but the puppets. Hello, puppets. Which'd almost be nice for Jim to look at some other day. But you weren't afraid? That groan before was one spooky scene."

"I wasn't for me, though I was a little for you two."

"That's why I want us to get on."

"But we're safe now. And Jim shouldn't get any wetter. Stay here. Dry him off. The towel in the bag's still dry, and I'll be right back."

"Why? Let the police go snooping around. There's an emergency box over there. Not around—to your left. On the traffic light pole. Call them and you'll have done more than most anyone would."

The box is in the rain. Its cover is hanging off. Above it, the glass police sign two lightbulbs were once in has been smashed out. "I don't think it's working," I yell.

"Try it."

I pick up the receiver. "Officer Tanner," a voice says.

"I'm speaking from near the Swedish Cottage. I want to report that I heard about ten minutes ago what seemed like a male groan in the general vicinity of the bird refuge woods up from Eagle Hill."

"A groan? Wasn't a tree swaying? Did you look?"

"I tried to. My wife got scared. We've our kid with us."

"No personal threats against you, though? Or a description of anyone you saw there?"

"No. Only it did seem very ominous to us."

"All right. I'll have a car make a check."

"I didn't give you the exact location of the spot."

"You said the Cottage callbox. If there's anything wrong around there, we'll find it."

"But up the hill from it, up the hill. Hello?" No answer.

I run back to the cottage. "No?" she says. "Well, if they won't do anything, it must be nothing."

"But at least if I go and find nothing, I'll know there was nothing."

"It could also mean the man with the groan is dying behind a bush you didn't look behind. And suppose in your great search the mugger tries to get at Jim and I here?"

"You're by the road. There are cars."

"Where? You see one?"

"They'll be by. And right up the road's the path to the park exit and buildings and lots of traffic."

"Then walk me there."

"It's pouring."

"I don't care. He's already soaked. He's probably got pneumonia, so what do you want for him next—to get cut up and thrown into the underpass? And me too. I've got pneumonia too. We all do. Now walk me out. Oh, I'm going."

I grab her arm. "Use your sense."

"And you stop the crap. I'm going home. You go where you want. Call me if you're killed."

"Okay. But hustle, though." She goes. "And put the towel around his head." I run up the hill to where I heard the groan. But Jane and Jim. I run back down and catch up with them as they're leaving the park. "You all right?"

"Can I even talk? I'll choke on a mouthful of rain. Find anything?"

"Only got halfway. Then I thought someone might pop out at you." We cross the street. "You can make it home now?"

"I can, but I'd like help."

"I'll get you a cab."

"If you're lucky. They're all filled."

"Then hurry home. But I only came back to check on you."

"Please don't go back. If anyone's been mugged, he's crawled away by now or been found, I'll start a fire. I'll put on hot soup and make us toddies. I have to get Jim changed and fed and down for a nap. You can start the fire. But help me, Sol."

"Get under." We get under the canopy of a building facing the park. "Sir," I say to the doorman, "could you loan me your umbrella so they can get home? We're on this sidestreet two blocks down, and I'll bring it right back."

"I need it to get my own people to the street," he says.

"I'll give you a dollar to loan it."

"That has nothing to do with it. Even if in two minutes I can make that much in tips with it."

"Then I'll give you two dollars."

"Weh, weh, weh."

"Listen, if I had another umbrella..."

"Frank," a woman coming out of the building says. "A cab?"

He opens the umbrella and goes into the street and blows his whistle.

"If a second cab comes along can you hail it for us?" I say.

"If another of my tenants doesn't want it."

"Please, Sol. Let's just run home."

"She's a little frightened," I say to the woman. "We were in the park and thought we heard someone being mugged."

"That's nothing unusual," the woman says.

"At least we're safe here. From the rain and muggers."

"You'd be surprised. Only last week my purse was snatched on these steps. Fortunately, I don't carry anything but duplicate cards anymore and a ten-dollar bill if they demand money. But right here. I yelled for Frank. But he was working the elevator because our regular man was in the men's room."

"One of those coincidences."

"That my purse was snatched and not some other tenant's?"

"That the elevator man was away and Frank wasn't here to protect you."

"My next-door neighbor, Mrs. Reeves, was threatened with a broken bottle right in front of Frank's eyes."

"No," Jane says.

"She says no. A few months ago. He was on duty then. But this young girl slipped around him while he was tying his shoelaces and threatened her in the lobby."

"A young girl?"

"No more than twelve, Mrs. Reeves said."

"Twelve is the age I told her it can start," I say.

"Twelve? Dr. Melnick—the professional office off the lobby? Three boys of about ten or so rang his bell and walked in and terrorized everyone in the waiting room and the doctor himself. They got in through the service entrance when no one was looking and snuck upstairs. Ten-year-olds. Kids."

"Ten sounds pretty young for it," I say. "They were probably older."

"Nobody bothered to ask them for their birth certificates. But the doctor's an obstetrician, and he said one of them could even have been eight."

"Not eight," Jane says.

"Got your cab, Mrs. Fain," Frank yells from the street. "Son of a B," when it's grabbed by someone else.

"You're not fast enough," she says. "But that was Dr. Melnick. They took a satchel of drugs, which turned out to be emetics. Much as I pity and think I understand the poor thieves, I hope they swallowed them all. And of course everyone's money and wallets when they announced they had guns. Even a little girl's purse with only buttons inside. And then raced past the doorman. But those are the youngest I know."

"I thought around eleven would be the youngest," I say.

"And remember, this is only in one building. And we usually have a doorman on duty. And the elevator man, porters, the super, the handyman—all kinds."

"We only have two locks and a front door into the brownstone almost anyone can get in," Jane says.

"That's all? But there's my cab. Nice talking." She gets under Frank's umbrella and he takes her to the cab.

"It's let up a little," I say. "Want to make a run for it?" I fold up the stroller, lift Jim, hold the stroller in my other hand, and we run home.

"It's terrible," Jane says, putting dry clothes on Jim. "But now that I'm here I can't get that groan in the park out of my mind."

"Well, stop about it. Because you were the one—"

"I know. And I know I stopped you from looking into it. I only hope that if a man really did groan, he's safe in his home now and all right."

I get her umbrella and put on my raincoat. "Don't forget the water's on."

"Where are you going?"

"Ba-ba, da, ow?"

"You won't forget the water? I don't want it boiling over with the gas still on."

"The window's open. You going to the park?"

"For a quick look. I'll be very careful. I'll take a hammer with me."

"Fine. Show it to the mugger and he'll be sure to use his own hammer or rock on you. That happens. Weapons are supposed to touch off corresponding weapons. That's why the London bobbies—don't go."

Coat buttoned to the top. Galoshes, rainhat. "Have a hot toddy waiting for me."

"You stupido."

"This may be the last time you'll see me."

"What's that supposed to mean?"

"It means do you want those last words of yours to be your last to me?"

"Now you're really talking stupid."

"Right. Bye, sweethearts." I kiss her cheek and feel Jim's forehead. "His cough's worse but his nose is dry now." She carries him into the kitchen. "Goodbye." She doesn't answer. I leave the apartment and walk to the park. I close the umbrella when I get to the park entrance, as it's keeping me from walking fast. But why walk fast and lose my breath, if there is someone to run from? I open the umbrella.

I reach the part of the path where I heard the groan. Nobody's around. It's still pouring. "Hey, anybody in there who needs help? We were by here before and heard some noises. Hello?"

I close the umbrella and hold it by the spike. But if I have to swing it, it'll probably open and throw me around, and it hasn't the weight to come down hard. I leave it by the path and pick up a stick. It's so rotted that half of it stays on the ground. A rock, then. But if I throw it I'll miss, and carrying it I'm more likely to get a stick over my own head before I get close enough. I need something to knock something out of someone's hand. If he's got a gun, forget it. I'll just drop what I have and run. A stick, a stick, but would I use it if forced? I'd have to, even if my built-in drawback is I'm not a natural attacker and never whacked any adult's head with even an open hand. I find one. Two inches across. I break it with my foot to about three feet long, peel off the twigs and swing it around. Good size, right weight. I walk through the bushes. No one. I'll check behind the bigger bushes and rocks. Only then I'll be satisfied.

A man. Face down on the ground and hat flattened over his head. Pants pockets hanging out. Shoe off and sock rolled down that foot. I touch him, listen to his back. No sound or response. I don't want to turn him over and possibly see his face smashed, body or face knifed. But how else will I know if he's alive? And if he is? First yell for the police or help, and if nobody, then over-the-shoulder fireman's carry, best way I know how. I shake his foot. "Hey, you, can you hear? I'm here to help." I take his hat off. Left side's okay. Eye is closed and lips are warm, but I can't feel or hear his breath. "Listen. We'll both take it slow. But I want you to know I'm not the person who did this to you, if that's what's keeping you so quiet."

I'm trying to turn him over when I hear a noise behind me. It's a man, leaning against a rock, opening an umbrella, foot on my stick. "You do that?"

"Him? I heard his groan before and came back. That's my umbrella. What do you want?"

"Why do you say what do I want?"

"Because you're just standing there. And this man could be dead. So if you're fixed on robbing me as you might have done him, fine. I'd give what I have except I left my wallet home."

"I didn't rob him. Never saw him before. For all you know, he could be the one who did the man you heard groan."

"Then where's the man who groaned?"

"Maybe in the lake. You look all over? The big tree over there? But enough. Give it here."

"What?"

"'What? What?' Yours and the man's wallet. Quick."

"I told you."

He flips the umbrella behind and from somewhere produces a knife. "That's great. For something I don't have?"

"Quit stalling."

He's waving at me to give. I'll jump backwards and run. I jump backwards and trip. He moves for me. I throw a rock at him and miss. Stupid thing to do.

A boulder's behind my back. He lunges at me as I stand up. I feint right and he slits my coat and I think nicks my arm. I grab the hand holding the knife and wrestle with it. We kick, claw, knee, elbow and hook a foot around each other's leg and fall over the man, who says "Huh?" On the ground I bite the guy's ear but don't want to bite through it as I should, when the lobe pops and he's screaming and the knife drops. I'm spitting out his blood when I kick the knife away and go for the stick. He goes for the knife. I say "Don't move." "Eat it," he says, and moves and sees my stick coming down and swats at it, and the stick breaks his wrist, or something breaks. He howls but still reaches for the knife. I swing at his head, but at the last instant, his shoulder or neck. He falls on his back and is moaning. I pick up the knife, try closing it, but there must be some trick to it, and I throw it into the woods. "Move once more and I'll break your head in."

He's biting his lips and trying to keep his eyes on me while feeling around his wrist. I think I also broke his shoulder or some part of his neck. That top left side of him seems misshapen when before it didn't. And he's bleeding a little from it and from the lobe very badly. My own blood's coming out from under my coat sleeve, but not much and mostly mixed with rain.

I turn over the older man. He's been knifed in the stomach and chest, judging by the holes there and the blood on his clothes. "Sir?" He's breathing and seems to be looking without seeing. I say to the other man "Stay where you are till we're out of here, and then you better get out fast because I'm calling the cops." He's squeezing his eyes tight but nods. I fit the stick in my belt, put the older man's hat in my pocket, sit him up, stick gets in the way so I toss it over the boulder, lift him over my shoulder and grab his legs in front and go through the bushes and start down the hill.

I set him against the cottage door and put his hat on his head. My own hat's been lost somewhere and the top three buttons of my coat's been ripped off. He's a little guy, with his pants and hat way too big for him and his jacket sleeves coming down over his hands. Maybe I've been carrying him wrong and making him bleed more and damaging his insides worse with his belly and chest banging against my back as we walked. "Listen, don't move. I'm calling the police from the phone here and will be right back."

I run to the call box and pick up the receiver. No officer answers, so I say "Hello, is there a policeman there?" I do this several times, then say "Hey, where the hell are you? This is an emergency. Oh, damn," and slam the receiver down. I run back, pick the man up and hold him in my arms and carry him toward the park entrance that way, stopping every hundred feet or so to sit on a bench with him in my lap. I look for a police car when I reach the street. A regular car stops and the driver says "Anything wrong?"

"He got knifed in the park. We better take him straight to a hospital."

"Who knifed him?"

"Not me. Some man, I think. And if it was him—look, will you open your back door?"

"Not in my car. I'm sorry. It's not the stains. I no longer trust anyone in this city."

"Then you shouldn't have stopped."

"I thought it was something else. A man carrying his son." He drives off. I rest on the curb with the man in my lap.

"You both going to get wet that way," a truckman yells, driving past and blowing his air horn.

I carry the man to the apartment building a block away.

"What are you bringing me?" Frank says.

"That Dr. Melnick." I go into the lobby and reach under the man's knees and ring the bell and try to walk in as the sign says, but the door's locked.

"Since he had the robbery," Frank says.

The peephole opens. "Yes?" a woman says. "This man's been knifed," I say, raising him in my arms a little so she can see his face. "In the park. He needs help fast."

"Call Roosevelt Emergency and say you want an ambulance immediately."

"I thought the doctor could help till they come."

"The doctor doesn't handle emergencies except for his own patients. Excuse me." The peephole closes.

"Could you call Emergency for me? He's been knifed in a few places and it's been a long time."

The peephole opens. "If I do, they'll ask me to identify myself and think the man's one of the doctor's patients, and he'd be responsible. It's best you call. Excuse me." The peephole closes.

"I'll call," Frank says. "Stay here, sit on the bench, even, but just see no delivery men or strange types sneak by. They're all to go through the delivery entrance around the side." He goes through another door in the lobby.

I lie the man down on the bench. "Just take it easy," I say. "We've an ambulance coming."

The elevator door opens. "What's this?" the elevator man says.

"Frank went to call for an ambulance. This guy's been knifed."

"I better get a mop." The elevator rings. He gets in and takes it up.

A delivery boy chains his bike to the canopy pole and comes in with a box of groceries.

"All deliveries are supposed to be made through the side entrance," I say.

"You work here?"

"The doorman Frank told me to tell you."

"Then mind your own business. It's raining outside, can't you see? What he do, pass out?"

The elevator door opens and two women walk out.

"Will you go around the service entrance with that?" the elevator man says. "You've been told before. I've told you myself."

"The service door's locked."

"Bull, it is. Around. Around."

The boy puts the box into the bike basket, covers it, unlocks the bike and rides off.

"Is he a tenant?" the older woman says.

"Person from outside who had an accident," the elevator man says. "Frank's phoning for an ambulance."

"If he was hit by a car, you could have broken his bones even more by carrying him in here."

"I didn't. He and Frank must have."

"He was robbed and knifed in the park," I say.

"That's terrible. And he's bleeding. But Frank's taking care of it?"

"Yes, ma'am," the elevator man says.

"Then could you see about my car? It's a long gray one and should be around now."

He goes under the canopy and says "It's pulling up, Mrs. Phelps."

"I hope he recovers," she says to me. She opens her umbrella, the other woman gets under it with her, and they go to her car.

"They're on the way," Frank says, coming into the lobby. "The police, too, when I said it was a knifing."

"Is your phone a pay one?" I say.

"Go through there and ring the elevator bell. Say you want to use the house phone and I've given you permission to."

I ring for the service elevator. It comes, the delivery boy and another elevator man inside. I go to the basement with them and dial my home.

"Where've you been?" Jane says. "I think Jim's really got pneumonia. His temperature's not too high, but he's coughing much harder and having trouble breathing. The reception said Dr. Blum will call back in a few minutes and might come over. You shouldn't have gone."

"It's just a bad cold or virus. They'll give him something in the office, and by tomorrow it'll be over like the last times. Be more independent, will you? And listen. I found that man. He'd been knifed and is in real bad shape. The guy who did it, or another one, got me in the arm too."

"Oh, my God. Bad?"

"I haven't had time to look. Can't be much if the bleeding's stopped. An ambulance and police are coming. We're in the lobby of the same apartment building you and I were in before."

"Then the doorman's there. You've helped enough. You belong here with the baby, and if Dr. Blum comes he can look at your arm."

"My arm's nothing. And there's that doctor on the same floor here if I need one, remember? Also the ambulance doctor. If they want me to go to the hospital with the man, I'll call you from there. If not, I'll run home. Keep Jim warm. Put the vaporizer on if you have to. I've got to go now, Jane."

"It's always everybody over us."

"Not true."

The ambulance people and police are in the lobby. A policewoman asks me several questions. The man's wrapped in a blanket and wheeled outside.

"Can I go with him?" I ask her.

"What for—he your friend?"

"No, I told you. Just that I've been with him so long I want to see how he turns out."

"You come with us and we'll write up a detailed report with the detective, and then you can go anywhere you like."

She drives me to the police station. I tell a detective the park story and give a description of the guy who attacked me.

"He sounds like everyone else," he says. "Why didn't you call the park precinct when you first heard the man groaning?"

"I did. The officer said he'd send someone."

"Maybe he did—I don't see anything on it yet—and they didn't find anything or went to the wrong spot. Those bushes can be thick."

I call Jane. She doesn't answer. I call Dr. Blum's office and a nurse there says the doctor told Jane to take Jim to Emergency at Roosevelt.

I cab to Roosevelt. Jane's in the waiting room. "They're working on him now. He's going to be all right, but they asked me to get out because I was so distraught I was upsetting him. Croup. Your son has croup. They say I'm lucky I brought him in when I did. His larynx.

If it wasn't for your floundering back and forth about the man we would've been home long before and gotten Jim out of his wet clothes and spared him all this."

"He had a cough when we started out today. It could have been the early stages of croup and we didn't realize it."

"You wouldn't believe it, Sol. He was like strangling on his own breath. He suddenly had so much trouble breathing that I thought he'd die. I started giving him mouth to mouth, when Blum called and right away he said croup and rush him here. I got Helen to drive us. Good thing I know someone on the block with a car. You probably would've taken him out in the rain looking for a cab."

I ask about Jim at the admitting desk. The woman says "That your wife? She's very worried, but everything's going to be fine. We've a great staff here, especially for emergencies."

"Would you also know about a man brought in more than an hour ago with serious wounds in his stomach and chest?"

"Two in the last two hours with knife wounds and another who was fed glass."

"The two with knife wounds."

"One died, one didn't."

"Mine was Caucasian and kind of elderly and very short."

"He died. You knew him? We'd like getting in touch with his family."

"I only found him in the park. I should have got him here sooner."

"In the park. That's what the police account said. It's always such a job getting these men located if they don't have identification on them. After a while they just get shifted to a medical school."

"The nurse said we can see Jim now," Jane says.

We go to the treatment room, Jim's about to be moved to the children's wing upstairs.

"We've got his breathing controlled and his temperature's already down," the nurse says. "What is he, asthmatic?"

"We were told it was croup," I say. "Seemed like an asthma attack. You ought to check with his pediatrician or a doctor upstairs. Okay," she says to Jim, "here we go through the big building. Ready for a long ride?"

"Ha-dah, beh," Jim says.

"Look at him. Knows what a ride means. Cute kid. Where's he get his orange hair?"

They put him on a gurney. "Hold my hand now," the nurse says. Jane takes his other hand. The hospital aide tells me to walk in front of the gurney in case there's lots of traffic in the halls. I walk in front and push open the doors as we leave Emergency.

"You'll be just fine, Jim," Jane says.

"Oh, yes," the nurse says.

"If your father wasn't so concerned about the whole world, you needn't have been brought in here at all."

"Oh, yes? What he do?"

I turn around. "Watch it," the aide says. "I don't want to ram in to you."

I step to the side. "Incidentally," I say to the nurse, "would you know of a man treated in the last hour or so with a broken wrist or arm and broken shoulder or some part of his neck that he could have gotten from a heavy stick?"

"Not that I know of, and I've been here all day."

"Who's that?" Jane says.

"The guy in the park who knifed me."

"Did you get that treated yet?"

"It's okay. A detective sprayed methiolate on it and bandaged it up."

"You should get a tetanus shot," the nurse says.

"They told me."

"I don't want to say I saw it coming," Jane says, "but it wouldn't have happened if you'd stayed home with us like I said."

"Ba-ba, ba-ba."

"Is he asking for his bottle?" the nurse says. "They almost all say it that way."

"You'd really be much more help to your son by continuing to run interference," the aide says. "We've had some bad accidents here when two gurneys coming from different directions collided."

"He's been hurt," the nurse says.

"I didn't know that."

"Don't worry, I'll do it," I say.

"Better I do it if your arm's really that bad," Jane says.

"Hot soup," the aide says as we approach a crowded cross corridor. "One baby Jimbo coming your way."

THE

BABY.

"You wanted it as much as I did," she says.

I say "I did want it, that's true, or thought I did. But now I don't, and I don't know what to do about it because it seems too late to get rid of it."

"Rid of it, you say? Rid of it? Rid of what? And why 'it'? Why not 'him' or 'her'? It's more than an it. He is more, she's more. No, you wanted a him and I wanted a her and now we have him or her whether you or I like it or not, and I'm going through with it. You don't want to, you can leave. I'll take care of him and her on my own. Or the baby. What have I been talking about? That's what it is— just a baby. But to you, just a goddamn pain in the ass."

"It's because it's changing our lives so. The baby is. And will change it even more when it comes, and for years. It was nice, right—nice and uncomplicated without it—so why do we want to screw things up now with it? Excuse me—with the baby. It's got months to be born yet, but it's a baby. Okay. But I won't get as much of my work done as I want with the baby around. You'll be up all night, and I'll be up because you will, and because fathers just are today with newborns—the father I'd be, anyway—and that'll be the pattern of our lives. Being up, feeding and cleaning him, the kid getting sick, and schools, clothes, all those forced nights at home when I want us to be out, determining our vacations and trips by him, boxing in our lives in every kind of way. I didn't think of all this when I first consented to having it, or her, or him."

"You should've. But as I said—oh, I said all I had to about your leaving or staying, though naturally I want you to stay. But if you're asking me to choose you over the baby—there is no choice. The baby's been in me too long and I can't give it up now. So make up your mind and then do whatever," and she goes into the bedroom and slams the door.

I stay there and in a few seconds I hear her crying. I say "Beth, Beth—ah, the hell with it," and go into the kitchen and get a bottle out and pour a couple of inches into a glass, throw some ice in, swirl it around with my finger, and drink. I drink it all down in a minute and then go back to the bedroom door. It's quiet. I knock. She says "What?" and I say "Is it all right if I come in so we can talk?" "What about?" she says. "What do you think what about? Look-it, maybe there's a way we can work this out. Mind if I open the door so we can discuss it?" "Go ahead."

She's lying on the bed, her stomach sticking up. It's her stomach that first made me think if we weren't doing the wrong thing by having the baby. I liked her stomach before she got pregnant and even better when she was two months pregnant. She was always a bit too thin for me, and also, though I had no real complaints about this, too small-breasted, and the pregnancy the first two months expanded her both ways a little. But by the fourth month, though I liked it, and still do, her breasts getting even larger, her stomach really started to get big. Although it was almost cute, her stomach then—plump but hard; it wasn't a big dumpy stomach. Now she has a big dumpy stomach and has had it for a month, though it's still pretty hard and I know it isn't fat. She's in her sixth month and I almost can't stand to look at it, though the odd thing is that from behind she looks almost the way she always did. Still, I can take the stomach, since it'll only be that way another three months and for a short time after. What I don't think I can take is the sudden irreversible big change in my life once she has the baby.

"This is what I've been thinking," I say.

"Yes, what?"

"Give me a chance to say it. It isn't so easy. This is what I've been thinking. Though most people might say six months is too late in the pregnancy to abort or induce a—to get rid of the fetus; why beautify the words?—maybe there's a doctor who thinks otherwise and we should try to get him. Then—" she puts her hands over her ears "—listen to me. Then, in two to three years, let's say—when I'm feeling more up to making the big plunge and also sharing you with someone else, is what I mostly mean—we can try again, this time for real."

"You finished?"

"Yes."

She takes her hands off her ears. "Please get out of this room," she says very calmly. "In fact, do it immediately or I'll scream so loud that the neighbors will be banging on the walls and calling the police. I mean it—now!"

I don't know if she means it, but I do it. I shut the door. I hear her crying behind it. But really crying. Those are loud sobs, the kind I've maybe only heard three times from her and make me want to run in and throw my arms around her and say "I'm sorry, I'm sorry, I'll never say anything like that again." But I go into the kitchen and pour myself another couple of inches and drop in some cubes and start drinking it before it's even cold. I drink it down in less than a minute. I'm starting to feel a buzz. Tears come. Alcohol tears; I recognize them. They come when they wouldn't have without the drinking. I feel awful about what I've done. I want to apologize but know if I try to go in now she'll tell me to stay out, no matter what nice words I use. She's that hurt and mad. She'll say she doesn't want to look at me again or be married to me anymore, and I wouldn't blame her for saying anything like that. I really did want to have a child. I was happy when she first told me she was pregnant. I excitedly told everyone that we were going to have a baby. I loved her body when it first changed. Not just the bigger breasts and stomach, but also her nipples when they popped out a little and the circles around them changed. I loved our lovemaking when she was two and three months pregnant—the freedom of it. And later, after the third month, that she most of the times had to be on top since, when I was her belly hurt when I pressed into her. I loved accompanying her when she bought maternity clothes and things for the baby. Loved being on the subway or bus with her when she was visibly pregnant and asking some young kid if he'd mind giving her his seat. Loved that her appetite grew to almost as large as mine. Loved that at times she looked like a fertility goddess. Loved being extra solicitous to her and how appreciative she was. Loved thinking up names for the kid with her and talking about how we'd raise the child. How different we'd be than our folks were with us. All that—loved it, loved it—so why the change? Why not tell her once and for all that I want to go through with it and I won't change my mind again? It'll be nice having a child, I can say—nice, and fun. I'll see so many new things about life, or at least remember lots of the old ones. I'll have so many new things to talk about with her. Holding a child will be fun and nice. Playing with it—even feeding it—even cleaning it, though not fun, could be nice. Why shouldn't it, once I get used to it, since it'll bring such relief to the kid? So what if it'll cost more than we can probably afford now to have a child and bring it up? So I won't get all the work done that I want to because of the child. There'll be all those other things and more to make up for it. And it's wrong to back out now. So go in there and tell her just how wrong you know you've been. Tell her. Go on—go in.

I knock on the bedroom door. She doesn't answer.

"Beth, please, it's me, can I come in?" Doesn't answer.

"Beth, you asleep? Listen, I've been thinking about the way I acted before and I've finally begun to understand some things about it and I want to talk about it with you." No answer. "I'm going to open the door, then, and come in, okay? I won't if you don't want me to, but really have a good reason for it, because that's how much I want to talk about it with you. Beth?" Nothing. "Okay, then I'm going to come in. After all, something could be wrong that you're not answering, so I'm also coming in for that: to see that you're all right." No answer. "Okay, I'm coming in."

I try the door. It's locked. "Beth, you can't lock the door on me." No answer. "All right, I'll give you time to think about what you're doing, but think about this too. I'm very, very sorry. Put even another very on that. Sorry for making you cry and disappointing you in all sorts of ways. But most of all sorry for telling you I didn't want the baby and wanted to quote unquote get rid of it. I want the baby now. I know how unfair I've been. It was unbelievably wrong of me, unbelievably, to first get excited over having it and then not wanting it for my own selfish reasons, which were stupid reasons too. I want it very much now and want us to be a wonderful family. You don't have to answer any of that right away. I'm going to the kitchen, to make myself a little drink, so take your time in thinking about what I said."

I go into the kitchen. I'm really feeling a buzz now. I should eat something or soon I'll be spinning. I get cheese out of the refrigerator, also ice for my glass. I put some cheese on a piece of bread and eat it while I pour myself a couple more inches. I sip it, finish the cheese and bread, then drain the glass. I pour another. It's stupid to drink like this. When I do, I just get sentimental. I'll get so sentimental that I'll tell her I want even more kids than one. Two more, even; three, tops.

So what? Important thing now isn't how much I believe what I say but to make her happy. To undo what I did. She won't throw me out. She'll accept my apology even if it's a bit flawed. She almost has to. It's to her advantage. She'll be mad at me for days. Maybe one day. She's good in that way. Then she'll begin believing what I say, and that crisis in my life will be over. I know I'll get to like having a kid. It's natural, this worry over it. It could even end up with my loving it more than anything I've ever loved in my life. That's what I should maybe tell her: "I know I'll end up loving the kid more than anything in my life, or as much as I love you, but in a different way, of course." That's what she'll like hearing. I even believe it, or at least feel I could. But I should tell her that before the booze makes me forget it. Through the door if I have to and extra loud to make sure she hears.

I finish the drink and am really feeling a buzz. I also feel sexy. I'd love for her to get on her knees so I can do it to her that way. That way, of all ways, seems to be the easiest for her, and it's certainly a good way for me. I want to first hold her face to face. To tell her my thoughts about love and the baby and her and then I want to kiss her and have sex with her the way I want to.

I go back to the bedroom door. "Beth?" No answer. I knock. "Oh, just come in," she says. "Door's unlocked."

"Beth, honey," I say, opening the door. She's sitting at the desk with a sheet of paper in front of her and pen in her hand, "I have something I think very important to tell you."

"First I want to read you the poem I just wrote about us, you mind?"

"Sure, please do. Okay if I lie on the bed while you read?"

"Do what you want." She holds the sheet of paper and reads. "'Night is a misfortune sometimes, day is a lifesaver sometimes, night he comes and lies, day he goes away, night is what I have to sleep next to him, day I can rest alone with the child, night is when he talks about death, day is when I sense my baby's breath, night is gruesome, day is toothsome—' What does toothsome mean? I wrote it down because it sounded right and sort of rhymed. I can always change it later."

"I think it means 'pleasing.'"

"Then I was right. 'Night is toothsome—' I mean 'day is toothsome,'" looking back at the paper, 'night is when I feel bloated because of the presence of him, day when I feel so light, airy and thin, day because he's away, night because we fight, day because I fly, night because I cry, day and night, night and day and night, but I will have my baby despite him, I will love it every night, every day, come what may as the poets say, so good day, night; good morning, noon and night, day.' You have the picture?"

"It's a good poem. For a first draft, which it'd have to be, one of your best and maybe could even get published."

"Don't try to flatter me. The picture. You have it?"

"I do. But don't say good night to me till after we make love."

"That's both dumb, callous and horrible."

"I said it wrong. What I was doing was taking off from your poem with that day and night business. And I wasn't kidding and flattering you when I said it was a good poem. I meant it sincerely. I loved it. It expressed so much. It had feeling in it. Feeling which I haven't been able to express in anything I've done or think or feel or whatever in weeks...in months. It had feeling, anyway. And that's good."

"What did you want to say?"

"Can we talk like a married couple who possibly still feel something for each other or at least where each is willing to listen to the other for a minute? Because I want to tell you something that's even more than very important."

"What?"

"Could you come over here and sit with me?"

"No, talk from there. What is it?"

"I want to have the baby. I was confused about it before. I thought it would complicate my life and ours together I didn't know how much. It took some getting used to. Now I'm used to it. Please forgive me. I want us to be a great big beautiful family, okay?"

She's been looking down, now she looks up at me. "Took a bit of drinking for you to say and feel all that."

"Yes it did. Couple of inches."

"Probably more than a couple. Probably a quarter of a bottle."

"No, not that much, but I'm not drunk. I'm buzzing but not drunk. The feeling's real, though. Will you please believe me?"

"Is it all right if I take a day or so to even start believing you?"

"Take all you want. Just don't turn me out."

"You'd have to leave on your own—I wouldn't force you. I kind of need you to help me the next two and a half months, because things aren't going to get any easier for me. And to help me out after, naturally."

"Count on me. I'll take care of you more than you can deal with. Now please come here?"

"You come over here. I'm the one who's pregnant. And I want you to read my poem inside your head. Do that and then we might go to bed. Bed and head. I like that, don't you? But I won't put it into my poem. My poem's done. I won't change a word of it. I'll even keep 'toothsome' in, even if it doesn't mean pleasing."

"It does though. I'm almost positive about that."

"Fine. What a natural instinct I have for words. I'm being facetious, of course. I stink as a poet."

"No, you don't. You don't do it enough, that's all. But when you do, they mostly work. That one was a gem."

"Now you're being sweet. Look at you-you're acting like a sweetheart. I'm almost beginning to believe what you say about the baby. I'm almost tempted to go over to you in bed without you first coming here, but I won't till you read my poem in my head. Not memorize it. Just read it once quietly to yourself. Come over."

I get up and go to her. She holds out the sheet of paper. I take it and look at it. It's blank. I turn it over. Other side's blank too.

"Can you remember it?" I say. Because if you can or any part of it, you ought to quickly write it down."

"I only want to be close to you now, is that enough?"

I put the paper on the desk, take her hands and stand her up. We hug.

"Oh, you big stiff, now it's all right with you, huh?" and I nod that yes right now it is with me.

ENDS

.

Started. I'm going. Really moving. No stopping me now. Look at me fly. Fly is to run. Faster than the sound of speed. Speedier than the fast of sound. Sounder than the speed of fast. I don't know. I don't care. Makes no dif what holds up. Just to be on my way. Just to stay on my way. Right to the very end. The top. I'm there. Stop. The end.

I've reached the end. Very nice here. It is. It isn't. Plenty to do here. Nothing much. Nowhere to go but down. No fun. No sights. I sit. I stand. What to do? Let me see. I sit and stand and rest and sleep and stand and nap and eat and sit and stand and think what to do. What to do? I don't like it much at this end. I'll go back to where I began at the other end. Somewhere back there where I can do some other things and maybe go another way. But not just to stay right here. I go.

I'm heading back. Still in a rush. Places I've seen. Things I've done. All much the same. But all much different. Not bad going back. Seeing the same things from another way is what I meant. A long tunnel down, like. A long passageway down, like. Those are about the same. That's all right. Everything's all right. And maybe things have changed at the other end since I was last there.

I'm here. Back. At the other end. Hurray. Where I first began. It's changed somewhat. Or I've changed somewhat. Or I've or it's or both have changed a lot to somewhat. Could be. Don't know for sure. But it has changed. Or I have. Don't know for sure. Said that. Say something new. I can say I like it better here than at the other end. I can't say I like it better here than at the other end. They're both pretty much the same. So many things beginning to seem the same. Both places no place to go but the other way. Up or down. Back or back. Depending which end I'm at. I go.

Toward the other end. Places seen, things done. No longer the novelty of seeing it again coming from the other way. And still no better point to it all, it seems, than to reach the other end. I stand still. Maybe that's the point. To see the same thing till it means something to me. But standing still I find is seeing the same thing till I get tired of it. And going slower than before is seeing the same thing only more of it. And going faster than before is passing the same thing only less of it. I'm bad at definitions. But haven't time to clear them up. In a rush not so much to get to that other place but to pass through here.

I'm there. At the other end again. Seems the same. I'll stay to see if it stays the same or if I'll see things I've never seen before or in a way I've never seen. I stay. I sit. I stand. Still too much the same. It's almost exactly the same. Maybe even more than almost exactly the same. It is the same. Other than for my staying longer than my last time here. I can go back. I can stay at any of the places in between ends. I can stay here. I choose none. But that's choosing one. And I want to move. I choose movement, not a place. I jump up and down in place. That's moving without moving. That's being in the same place but not being in it. That's seeing at different levels. It means a lot of things but ultimately nothing. I choose going back. I don't choose, I just go back. Maybe there'll be some place to pass through in between ends this time. You never know. I go.

On my way back. Still no place to pass through in between ends. Maybe that point's past the last place where I can see it hasn't changed. I pass that place and that, and that place hasn't changed. Nothing's changed. Maybe none of what's to come has changed. Maybe only places I've just passed but can't see from here have changed. I turn around.

I start to the top end from the middle. The place I called the top end that first time I reached it only because I started out that first time from what I thought was the bottom. But it wasn't. And the top's not the top. And the top's not the bottom and the bottom's not the top. The middle's the middle, though, or as close to it as far as I can tell. And all the places I couldn't see from that so-called middle point I just left haven't changed too. And going a ways farther, all's the same too. Maybe things will start changing or have been changed by the time I get a quarter way from the top end. I reach that three-quarters' point, or as close to it as I can tell, and still nothing's changed. Maybe some of what's ahead will change or has been changed when I get halfway into the top quarter or a quarter way into the top eighth. But nothing's changed. Neither the halves of thirty-seconds or sixteenths of sixty-fourths. That's the same and that's the same too and that and this and everything I pass. They're all the same. I reach the top. It's the same too. What to do?

I'll stay here for the rest of my life. To go back would be foolish. Maybe things take more time to be changed than I thought, so why not this place over any other? But I find after a long time that if I only have a day left in my life I won't be able to stay here for the rest of my life. That foolishness is easier to live with than boredom. So I start back. It's all the same, of course. No new breakthroughs in between. I dig. I claw. I tap for hollow spots. No new breakthroughs in between. It's the same. But I mind less now. I begin to like that I come to expect. No, that's not so. I just accept. I reach that so-called middle point. I could turn around now and head back. I could go back and forth between middle point and top end or between any two points including the two ends, but what would be the point of all that? I haven't been for the longest time to what I first called the bottom, so I continue to that end. Things might have changed. Or better: For the longest time I haven't been to the bottom of all the places I've been to, so there's probably a better point for going there than anyplace else.

I reach the bottom end. I decide to stay where I first began. I stay. I want to go. I try jumping in place so as not to go. I try walking inches away and coming back. I try walking in circles, crawling in figure eights. I try jumping in circles, crawling backward in figure eighty-eights. I try everything I know and can do. All the numbers. All the positions. All the movements and combinations of numbers, positions and movements. I say stick it out as long as you can. I say why stick it out as long as you can? I try, though. I stick it out. I can't stick it out any longer. I go. I stay. I return. I rest. I reach. I stay. I stick. I go. I jump. I walk. I rest. I try. I crawl. I reach. I stay, go, return, walk, run, reach, rest, combine, stay, jump, crawl, try, rest, reach, stay, stick, go, combine, return. I try the thirty-seconds. The sixty-fourths. The one hundred twenty-eighths. The two hundred fifty-somethings. The five hundred something-somethings. It's the same. No change. It was never so good as it was when I first was at those two ends and for that entire first run. It was next never so good as it was when I first returned to that bottom end and during the second run. It was after those never so good as it was when I first returned to that top end and during that third run. I think about all those for a change. I think about it all till I've thought about it all, and that too becomes unchanged.

WHAT IS

ALL THIS

?

Dirk drove to Helen's house to pick up their son. It was his weekend with Roy—once every other, which he and Helen, without lawyer advice or court decree, had congenially agreed to a year ago, when they separated and she filed for divorce—but she had different plans for today.

"Donald invited us to the city for the weekend. Roy can't wait, as Donald's been telling him what great wooden planes they'll make and how much fun Roy'll have sleeping in the balcony-bedroom setup Donald's built in his studio. But what happened to your phone? I called before, around the time I figured I wasn't going to hear from you. Called collect, but the operator, checking with her records office, because at first I refused to believe what she said, told me that as of yesterday, your phone's been removed. Why? What puzzles me most is that you paid good money having a phone installed, and one week after it's in and when you really could've used it, you have it removed. Weird. I've definitely made up my mind, Dirk: Sometimes you're absolutely weird. Were all sorts of incoming wrong numbers getting you down, as they did in L.A. last year? Maybe I'm being unfair, but you at least had that phone for two months, which suggests you're getting better, which means progressively worse. My point is that Roy could've reached you if you had a phone, and now he has to wait for you to call. Next time, I suppose you'll have your phone taken out the day after it's installed. And the time after that, if any phone company is insane enough to let you have a phone, you'll ask the telephone serviceman to remove the phone right after he's packed up his installation tools to go. But, admittedly, all that's your business now," and she yelled down the hall "Roy? Is your knapsack packed? And your daddy's here."

Roy came out of his room, his unhitched overloaded knapsack hanging from a shoulder by one strap. He rushed up to Dirk, kissed him, said "You coming to San Francisco with Mommy and me?"

Helen said no, "Your father has once more made the mistake of driving down without first calling."

Roy talked excitedly about his trip, how sleeping in a bedroll at Donald's was going to be like camping out in the woods. "And he says I can look out the windows there and see mountains and ocean and even look through a telescope to the stars. Do you want to sleep with me?"

"Dirk has his own flat in San Francisco, which you can probably stay at next weekend, if he doesn't mind." She looked at Dirk for confirmation as she sipped from her mug. "Want some tea? You've that old desiring expression again. I didn't make enough for two, but if you think you need it for the drive up I'll put more water on." She went to the kitchen—Roy to his room to find his cowboy boots—and returned with two smoking mugs of tea. His was very sweet, just as she liked it, with two to three tablespoonfuls of honey in it, the liquid well stirred. "Is something wrong with the tea?" she said. She sipped her own tea as a test, seemed about to spit it back, swallowed, said it was too tart, too lemony, "Uch, it's just awful," and they exchanged mugs.

"You like it tart, I like it sweet—our respective predilections, if you like; natures, so to speak. You like the shade, New York snow, barely endurable Eastern winters, depressing poetry, music and films, and decomposing flowers to paint. While I like the sun, warmth, California spring, summer and everything happy and silly that goes with it, including getting a tan. You always put down that silliness in me. No, not always. We got married and everything was nice for a couple of days and then you suddenly became stern and critical, you very definitely changed then—and started doing your unlevelheaded best to kill off my own silliness. What do you say about all that now? Donald's very much like me, in a way: Opposites now detract. Sometimes he's terribly silly, does cart wheels in the street; more than that: just dumb, foolish, indescribable things—he gets along with just about everyone. He's able to cut off his equally serious work almost immediately and simply have a gassy time. And so far, he and Roy get along great. He's teaching him about camping and carpentry and all kinds of ocean-creature things and even how to write out their names on your old electric typewriter. All three of their names apiece, including the Mister and Master—Roy wouldn't settle for less. Roy," she yelled, "will you move it along? It's past noon."

Roy hobbled into the room in one boot, said he was still looking for the other.

"You don't wear cowboy boots on Saturdays. Just Tuesdays and Fridays—you know that. "

"There it is," Roy said, and he crawled under the couch, came out with the boot and sat on the floor to put it on.

"I said you don't wear those boots on Saturdays. Find your moccasins, jack boots, even your mukluks, but I want no more diddling around."

"Please?" Roy said, and he stood up, walked a few steps and fell over; the boots were on the wrong feet. Most of his clothes, books, toys, tools and crayons fell out of the knapsack and Roy screamed "Damn it." He threw the knapsack at his dog, who had just come into the room, and was snapping his crayons in two when Helen picked him up by his ankles and began tapping his head on the rug.

"Idiot," she said.

"I give up," he said.

"Idiot, idiot, idiot."

"Mom, I said I give up, so let me down."

She stood him up on his feet. They looked crossly at each other, Roy serious, Helen mocking, then started laughing, and hugged. The dog, Sabine, got between their legs. "Ummm," Helen said, still hugging Roy with her eyes closed, "just ummm."

They all left the house. Dirk got on one knee to pick weeds out of the gravel driveway as Helen, Roy and Sabine got into her car. "Call next time," she said. "And if you're going to Ken's thing Sunday night, maybe Don and I will see you there," and she started the car, he stepped aside, and they drove away.

He weeded the driveway clean, got in his car and was in the freeway's speed lane doing 75, miles from their house, when he saw them in the rearview mirror, Roy and

Sabine standing on the back seat, looking out the rear window, Helen wanting to pass. He flicked on the directional signal and switched lanes. Helen flashed a begrudging thanks as she drove alongside him. Roy spotted him and beamed and waved. Dirk waved back. Roy now waved with both hands and shook Sabine's paw at him and nudged Helen's shoulder to point out Dirk driving behind them in the adjoining lane. Dirk floored the gas pedal, but her more powerful Saab was still increasing its speed and distance over him. Roy displayed his tool kit, took a hammer out of it and made hammering motions in the air. Dirk smiled, nodded. Soon there were several cars separating hers from his laboring Volks, and Roy blew him a kiss.

Dirk turned on the portable radio strapped to the front passenger seat by the seat belt. The *Warsaw Concerto* by Richard Addinsell, the announcer said, and the name of the orchestra, conductor, pianist, record label and the LP number and time of day. Dirk hadn't heard the piece for years. When he was thirteen or fourteen, it had been his favorite music—this same pianist on both sides of a 12-inch breakable record that, at fifteen, he jokingly broke over his brother's head. He tuned the radio in, listened to the loud dramatic opening, switched to AM and the telephone voice of a woman who said "Certainly, Dr. King's death is sad, as every assassination and sudden making of a widow and four fatherless children is sad. But who's to say he wasn't asking for it a little, you know what I mean?" and the broadcaster's enraged denouncement of her bigotry and proclamation of her stupidity and the loud click of his hanging up, and Dirk turned the radio off. A car honked behind him. He was straddling the broken white line between the two left lanes, and while he edged into the slow lane, an elderly woman cut into the speed lane, narrowly missing his rear fender. From across the middle lane, they looked at each other. She frowned, glared. Dirk let his tongue hang out and crossed his eyes, as if he were being strangled. She accelerated her huge Mercedes to 80, 90; in seconds, he was left far behind. He took the San Mateo exit to the restaurant he liked best in the Bay area, at the outskirts of town.

They'd had their wedding reception there, unusual Japanese and Okinawan dishes made special for the feast in the tatami room upstairs. Lots of the guests got drunk on shochu and high-grade sake illegally flown in that week from Tokyo through the owner's secret contacts at JAL; most of the other guests got stoned on Israeli hashish smoked in the spray-deodorized johns. Irises, cherry blossoms, rose incense, paper slippers, friends' children sitting on the foot-high tables and guzzling from sake carafes filled with soda, handfuls of cold cooked rice thrown at the couple as they left. Later, he picked rice out of her hair; together, they painted "peace" in fluorescent acrylics on their bedroom window overlooking the beach at Santa Cruz; in bed, she said how life was best when she had the sun, health, loving man and a backward and upside-down view of "peace" from a comfy new mattress all at the same time; but where, she wanted to know, will they go from here?

A card, hooked over his front doorknob, read that he hadn't been home to receive a telegram; and penciled on the other side was the deliverer's personal message: "The gram's been slipped under your door."

"If you have no objections," Chrisie wired from San Luis Obispo, "I'll be driving up for weekend with two girls."

Chrisie's younger daughter, Sophie, was genetically his. He'd met Chrisie at a New York party three summers ago, he in the city to be with his dying sister and grieving folks, she on a week's vacation from the man who was still her adoring hot-tempered husband; and minutes after their orgasm, when he was squirming out from under her to breathe, she said she was convinced she conceived. "Preposterous, granted, but I felt it, just as I felt it with Caroline three years ago, their infinitesimal gametic coupling before, as explosive as our own."

He rolled up the canvas he'd been painting on the floor, put away his income-tax statements and forms—Federal, state, New York City, six jobs in one year and once three part-time jobs a day, and he was going to be penalized for filing late—shampooed his rug with laundry detergent, washed down the baseboards with diluted ammonia, dusted every object in the place a two- and five-year-old could touch or climb up on a chair and reach; on his knees, scoured the bathroom tub and tiles and soaped the linoleum floors with the now ammonia-maimed sponge.

He left the door unlocked and hauled two bags of linens and clothes to the laundromat down the hill. A girl was in front, her smock cut from the same inexpensive

Indian bedspread he used to cover the mattress on his floor. "Spare change?" she said. He never gave, but today handed her a quarter. "Thanks loads," and "Spare change?" to a man approaching the laundromat with a box filled with laundry, detergent, starch and magazines. He said "I work for my money." She said "I work for it too, by asking for spare change." He said "Dumb begging kid," and she said "Dear beautiful man." And he: "You ought to be thrown into Santa Rita with the rest of your crazy friends," and she: "And you ought to drop some acid." He: "And you ought to poison yourself also."

She: "I wasn't referring to poison." "Well, I was." "Spare change? Spare a dime, a nickel, a penny, a smile?" "Out of my way, pig," and he shoved her aside with the box and went into the laundromat.

Dirk read while his laundry was being washed. His were the most colorful clothes in the machines. A few minutes before the cycles finished, he got up to stick a dime in the one free drier, but a woman beat him to it by a couple of seconds. "You got to be fast, not slow," she said, and stuck three dimes into the coin slot.

"Spare change?" the girl said outside.

A man set down four shopping bags of laundry and opened his change purse. "Oh, no," and he snapped the purse shut, "I forgot. I'll need all the change for the machines. The coin changers have been vandalized so often this month the owner's had to seal them up, and now she's got to take them out, as they're still being forced open. People are violent and nuts."

One of the driers stopped. A woman sitting under a hair drier and another unwrapping a candy bar signaled with their hands and eyes and candy bar that the machine wasn't theirs. Dirk touched the arm of a man on a bench with a hat over his face, who was the only other person in the room the drier might belong to, but the man still slept. Dirk removed the warm clothes from the drier, folded them neatly and stacked them in a basket cart. He was throwing his wet clothes into the drier when the man who'd been sleeping before squeezed Dirk's wrist and said "Don't any of you people have the decency to wait?"

The telegram read: "The girls and I won't arrive till tomorrow. Husband, parents, complications, love." Dirk drank a few vodka and tonics and fell asleep, awoke in the dark with the radio on and went outside. He had a Moroccan tea at a Haight Street coffeehouse, where many young people were drawing, writing, playing checkers and chess, talking about police harassment, pot planting, Hippie Hill freedom, the Bach cantata being played, democracy now but total revolution, if that's what it's going to have to come to, tonight's rock concerts at the Fillmore, Avalon, Winterland, Straight. A man sat beside him, pulled on the long hairs of his unbrushed beard and braided matted hair and said "Hey there, joint's getting real artsy. Very beautiful old North Beach days. Culture with a *Das Kapital* K. Loonies just doing their dovey ding, am I tight?" Dirk shrugged, the man laughed and patted Dirk's shoulder consolingly. A girl at the next table shrugged and the man said "Yeah, North Beach *si* and now the Haight. You're all gonna burn out famous," he announced to the house. "Like Ginsberg, Kerouac, Ferlinghetti, me boys, me best, me fine old friendlies who bade it ballsy and big. So try and refudiate me in five years, fiends, that all of you who pluck to it haven't made buns of bread," and he finished his coffee, chugalugged down all the milk in the table's cream pitcher and left.

Dirk was on his way home when a girl stopped him on the street and said "Can I crash your pad? I'm alone, in real trouble, it's just me and I won't be any bother,

I swear. The pad I was supposed to flop at won't let me in. These four guys I was living with there all of a sudden split for Los Angeles—ran off with my records and clothes while I was sitting it out in jail. Look at this. The creepy keeper gave it to me this morning as a sort of graduation diploma and safe-conduct visa out of Nevada." She showed him a paper that said she'd been arrested and released after five days for vagrancy, loitering, wayward minor, accessory to crime, resisting arrest. "Resisting arrest, bullshit. They just clamped on the cuffs, felt my tits and dumped me in a smelly van. We were selling speed, made our contact, two cats and myself in Carson City—America's worst dump. Ever been there? Don't ever go. The creepy keeper said 'Now I'm warning you, sis, don't be turning back.' And when we left the diner with our contact, twenty Feds jumped out of the shadows with guns cocked like puny movie gangsters and threw us against our truck, arrested us all."

While they walked to his place, she told him she thought she was pregnant again. "I had a kid in Hartford last year, gave it away. My rich German-Jewish father told me the baby was very ugly after he told me how much he was forking over for my bills. Best of hospital service, never had it so good. And he was kind of sweet too, like an overconcerned expectant father expecting his first child, and then, with my society-minded momma, had me committed. But the state released me after four months, though my folks wanted me in for at least a year but were too cheap to pay for a private crazyhouse, when they found I was still getting pills and grass and was caught balling one of Connecticut's prize mental deficients behind a bandstand during a Saturday-afternoon dance. Ever been to Hartford?

Don't ever go there, either. That's what they told me in Carson City. Said 'Don't come back for six months minimum,' and I said 'Six months my ass, I'm never coming back, none of my friends will ever come back, you lost a good tourist trade with us when you locked me

172 | STEPHEN DIXON

up, and this giant Swedish matron, she was very congenial when she wasn't forcing my box open every ten minutes to see if I was stashing anything inside, she just laughed, laughed and laughed."

Dirk gave her one of the two tuna fish salad sandwiches he made. She said "It looks so pretty and sweet, lettuce flouncing out of it like a dress, and sourdough's my favorite of all nonmacrobiotic breads, but no, thanks. With the last kid I gained 46 pounds, I'm ten pounds overweight as it is, so I'm only going to start eating again when and if I find I'm not pregnant. Look at that view. Golden Gate from your own place. Do you ever really look outside—I mean, really? Too much. You ought to raise your mattress to window height, make it with a groovy chick while you're both stoned on hash and eye-popping the moon. You do all these paintings? Do them on pills? Well, don't ever get on them, don't even hold them, they're worse than anything besides junkie's junk, which can actually be a good trip the first time but the shits when you have to start paying forty bells a high. You're a real housekeeper. Just look how clean this place is. You ought to wear an apron—a clean flowery one. I'll make you one, if you get me some thread things and paint and an old clean sheet. Floor recently mopped, books in place, bed made, not even a curly body hair on the rug, and pardon me for all my luggage"—she lifted her average-sized pocketbook with her pinkie and reset it on the floor—"but I feel utterly helpless if I have to travel light."

They drank tea, she showered and said she was sorry, but she had soaked his bathroom floor and then drenched a few towels in trying to wipe it up. "When I was living in Hartford, I wasn't such a slob. In fact, I was a real housekeeper then, also: cooked, cleaned, deveined the shrimp and cracked the crabs, just obsessed with ridding my place of flecks and specks, as my mother is and you must be. But now I haven't made a bed in eight months, no, nine, except for the five days in Caron City's most depressing jail. You have kids? You look like you have a half dozen. That you and your boy in the sailboat? Is your wife as blonde as he? I never want kids, never want to get hitched. Marriage is for con men who give charm for money and that Mongoloid I balled who'll always need lots of help and love. For everyone else, it's me me me me. My childhood was the worst. My mother's a hysterical bitch and shrew. My dad's got a gripe against because he always wanted to screw me and now because he bought me a thousand dollars' worth of clothes to keep me in Hartford just two days before I split for the

Coast. Two cats came by the place I was staying at and said 'Let's take you away from all this,' meaning my apron and housekeeping chores, and I said sure, anything; there wasn't anything happening in Hartford since I gave that ugly baby away. So I packed those clothes in two valises I stole from the college boys I was living with—they did much worse to me in the past, so don't even begin to twinge and twist—and we made it across country without a bit of flak, never for a moment being anything but high. I've now been in every state but Alaska and Hawaii—Carson City, Nevada, my forty-eighth. And I have no clothes, maybe two dimes in my wallet, my father would just piss if he knew and my mother's aching to put me away for life. And most everyone who knows me says I'm wasting my time. That I've more than a one-forty I.Q. and ought to use that natural intelligence in writing about all I've seen and done, but with a humorous aspect to it, as there's far too much sad seriousness in literature and the world as it is. And one day I will. Just as soon as I land a pad of my own."

He offered her a sleeping bag on the floor and she said that was exactly what she needed for her rotten back. They went to bed. "Hey, look," she screamed, "I can see the moon. It's getting a little past the half stage. My God, it's being eclipsed by the earth—our earth. What do astrologers say about eclipses of the moon? Are they special nights, do any of the signs undergo any change? I bet you're a Gemini. Geminis are the worst. Yes, I'm sure you're a Gemini. Well, I'm a Taurus, we'd never get along, and my name's Cynthia Devine."

The room was very dark when he awoke a few hours later to Cynthia talking about her magnificent view of the totally eclipsed moon. He put her hand on her knee and she felt his chest. "You have a very interesting heartbeat. I've never slept with a man with such a rapping heart." Her hand moved down his body and she said "Ooooh, now I know why it's rapping so fast. But stop, will you, because then I can say tomorrow that it was a lot better sleeping here than in jail. There I got a crummy mattress on a wooden plank with no privacy. I wasn't even allowed to see daylight till they traipsed me across the yard for a health exam. The doctor gave me these pretty blue antibiotic pills and blood-red capsules for what he said was my venereal disease. I told him 'Vaginal infection, Doc, not V.D. A vaginal infection I've had for a month,' and which I still have now, till he finally apologized. Prison doctors are always trying to stick you with the worst. But he was fairly nice, all told. And Sheila, the matron, wasn't half bad, either, when she wasn't trying to get into my pants."

Someone knocked on the door. "You get your share of telegrams," the deliverer said. "When this one came this morning, I was sure it was my fault because you didn't get the two I slipped under the door and this one was trying to find out what was wrong."

"I started out this evening," Chrisie wired from San Luis Obispo, "and then returned home. Let me know if you think I should really come. Call. Love." And her phone number.

He walked Cynthia down the hill, to show her where the public phone booth was and to cash a check at the drugstore for himself. "Goodbye," she said, shaking his hand. "I think we—no, I'm glad we didn't—oh, maybe it would've been fun if we had, as it's always a crazy farce with somebody new, though it's also nice sleeping peacefully, for a change, without someone's hands tearing into me. I've got to call some guys I know. They were staying at a flat around here before I got busted, and if they've already split, then I'm truly screwed. Maybe I could phone my dad for cash. I can get him at business now, just after he's returned from a three-martini lunch. He's really quite beautiful when he's smashed, and thanks."

The druggist smiled. "You made the year 1968 on your check instead of 1969."

His 85-year-old landlord was pulling out weeds from around one of the fifty or so signs he'd painted and then erected in the front yard. The sign read: Stop Being An Accessory To The Crime Of Fratricide—Don't You Know All Wars Are Silly? "I've just come from distributing my peace pamphlets downtown," Mamblin said, "and you wouldn't believe the wonderful reception I received from so many of our courageous lads. 'Peace first,' I told them—'love, learn and grow. Jewish and Christian wars must end,' I said—'gardens, not battlefields. A mental revolution, not a physical one.' One young man from Santa Monica, of all places, said that after listening to me, he would think about resisting the draft. He said I was a man of God, which I disproved scientifically—a walking institution to peace, he tried to make me, which was nearer the truth. But I've unfortunate news for you also, Dirk. Mrs. Diboneck dropped by much too early this morning and complained that you've been coming in at all hours of the day— playing the radio too loud, waking her. Having wild parties, orgies, she said, and that you're also running a hippie haven in your apartment downstairs. She's old, a good woman, knew my wife, been here close to twenty years. And you know I had trouble with the tenant before you, he being a bit queer with men in a sexual manner and shooting out all my lovely leaded-glass windows and causing a mild heart attack for Mrs. D. But what do you think of my latest sign?" He pointed past a couple dozen older ones to a new one with gold-painted lettered bordered by red; I Have Arisen From The Dead. "Did it yesterday, after a long stimulating conversation with a young Welsh lady who happened by while I was weeding. It has no Christian significance, of course, other than its possible mockery of mythological Christian belief—but the symbolism's what I like. I have arisen from ignorance, mediocrity, mindlessness, myths, lies, half-truths, superstitions—I have arisen from the deaf, dumb, blind and spiritually dead. And being you're one of the truly good people in this city and a disciple of mine, I think— I don't precisely know what to make of you yet, though you're being carefully studied, Dirk, phrenologically and every other way, so be on your guard—why don't you work matters out with Mrs. D. yourself? I only don't want her waking me up again before nine."

Mrs. Diboneck's typewritten note in his mailbox read: "I would appreciate if you would not slam the door so vigorous. It shakes everything and scares me to death.

I accomodated your wish last week ago by using my T.V. and Radio allmost never. So be a Gentleman and hang on to the doors!! Thank You."

Using Magic Markers, he made a quick small drawing of the view from his room. Red towers of Golden Gate Bridge, gold spires of St. Ignatius Church, green park, blue bay, yellow ocean, purple sky, brown, black, orange and pink hills and mountains of Marin County, and rolled it up and was about to stick it into Mrs. Diboneck's mailbox when he saw her watching him through one of her lower door panes. She stepped onto the sidewalk, clutching her house dress together at the chest. "I'm sorry I complained to Mr. Mamblin before, Mr.— but what is your name? But the noise, dear Lord, one would think a children school down there directly below with what I hear and you make. Why, why? I ask myself an old woman without any answers, and the radio, so loud I can't hear myself phone talking when it isn't waking me out of sleeps and naps I need and all such things, or is it your TV you own? But is it not possible, may I ask, that people live in this building, too? I don't want to speak about it more than now and never again to Mr. Mamblin if I must, so be reasonable, please, a nice young man and your blond boy so sweet, and we will remain kind friends. Otherwise, I must one day call the police if Mr. Mamblin does not, which to me even with my illness seems cruel but no matter can I help taking this being forced by you," and she dropped a small bag of trash into the garbage can standing between then and returned to her apartment. He put the drawing into his billfold and went to the post office.

"Five cents a card is still quite the bargain," the clerk said, "what with all the other postal rates raised and the cards staying the same. A two-dollar bill? Where you been hiding it? And a John Kennedy for your change." He made a drawing on one of the cards of a laughing man running through a forest followed by a galloping sixtailed five-horned four-eared three-tongued two-nosed one-eyed horselike creature called The Multimal and addressed it to his son in San Jose. Beneath the address he wrote "Attention: Love to you and Mommy,"

"I arrived at the exact instant this thing was being delivered," Chrisie said, holding out a telegram, as she and her girls cautiously walked down the long steep rickety flight of outside wooden stairs.

"Decided not to come after all," Chrisie had wired from San Luis Obispo this morning. "Why not drive down here instead, Love," her address and the number of the main connecting highway, 101.

"Remember Dirk, Caroline?" Chrisie said to her older daughter, and Caroline said "No, when are we going home?" "Remember Dirk, Sophie?" and Sophie, two in a month, said "Dow? Dow?" and painted her hand with his purple marker. "Remember Chrysalis, Dirk?" Chrisie said, and he hugged her, made bacon and eggs for the girls on his two hot plates, gave them juice in clean paint glasses, set up Sophie's portable crib, unrolled a sleeping bag for Caroline, later placed a triptych screen between the section of the room the girls were asleep in and his mattress on the floor.

He and Chrisie had tuna fish salad sandwiches, wine, carrots, cookies, grass, got under the covers, turned down the electric blanket, tuned in a Vivaldi piccolo concerto, watched the lights of a low-flying plane pass his window and cross the full moon. A dog from the house below his began to bay.

"Harrp Easter," Chrisie said when he awoke, handed him a wicker egg basket filled with candy eggs, jelly beans, chocolate bunny and new electric razor. Caroline said "Merry Easter, Dirk," and showed him a similar basket with a baby rabbit inside sniffing the green-paper grass. Sophie was standing in her crib, nibbling a blue candy egg.

Two conductors wouldn't let them on their cable cars because of Caroline's rabbit. The conductor of the third car patted the rabbit's head and asked if he could feed it part of his apple. The car rattled along Lombard street, was very crowded. A woman said to Dirk she would have thought twice about getting on a cable car if she had known a rodent was aboard. A man hurrying to catch up with his wife, who had suddenly jumped off the car to take movies of what her guidebook said was "the world's crookedest street," nearly knocked Caroline off the rear platform. The rabbit got out of a basket, as Chrisie was picking up Caroline, and disappeared into a storm drain. They got off the car, and Chrisie and Dirk made a show of looking for the rabbit. Dirk blew the highest note of his harmonica at the man, who snarled back "Hippies," and resumed his smile and pose for his wife's camera. Caroline stopped crying after Chrisie told her the rabbit had joined its Northern California family underground and Dirk gave her his Kennedy half dollar and harmonica.

They took the next car, Dirk holding Sophie as it headed down to the Wharf. She was met, smelled, her mouth bubbled, he kissed her sticky fingers, felt her firm back, rubbery legs, grazed his face across her thread-thin hair, which was getting blonder than Chrisie's lemon-colored hair. They got off at the turntable, Chrisie said how touristy the whole area was, got on the same car for the return trip up the hill, went to Golden Gate Park, where a radical New Left political party was sponsoring a be-in, and got up to leave an hour later. The sound equipment was bad, not enough music was being played, Chrisie was getting paranoid at the number of people openly turning on around then, and the field was too crowded and the girls could wander off and there were too many political speeches being made and most were too virulent. "The black man," the black woman candidate for the state's 18th assembly district said, "and the white man had all better start working together fast to end the repulsive criminal police power in this fascist town, or else the whole Bay Area's going to go up in flames, a lot of noninnocent people going to get accidentally wiped out, the entire state and country might even get cooked, and I ain't just bull-jiving, brothers and sisters."

"We simply don't work together, fit together, do anything well except sex together," Chrisie said in his apartment, "and even that we can't be too certain about, Dirk. I liked you better when I first met you—even liked you better during that last disastrous weekend in L.A. I like you better in your letters, prose paintings, painted postcards and grunts and silences for phone conversations. I think you only see me because of Sophie. You're so compulsively solitary, while at the same time, so hungry for companionship and maybe, maybe even love. Most people we both know agree to my theory about you, or have even volunteered a similar one of their own, that there are really three of you—and, we can say this unhypocritically while realizing you probably represent, in an exaggerated form, the condition of us all. The pleasant helpful exterior, the bored angry man inside, who keeps distorting the fake amiable face, and the third you, who's inside the second you and who deeply wants a close enduring relationship with someone but can't find his way out. I've thought about it a lot, Dirk, so maybe you can think about it a little after I'm gone. Blaise didn't know I was driving up. Nobody knew except my father, who called as I was leaving the second-to-last time and asked why I couldn't spend Easter Sunday with them. I told him because I was celebrating it with a friend, and he said which friend, as he thinks he knows all my friends, and I said *a* friend, and he said male or female friend, and I said male, of course, though we're strictly platonic, but only because he's a brilliant young scientist fag. I finally had to divulge your name, John Addington Symonds—I love playing literary jokes on my dad, if only to let the snob know how really uninformed he is—and gave a bogus address, which they're likely driving to right now. This place is like a monk's room other than for the paintings. Though David Lieberman became a monk and he still paints. I think Blaise is going to cut up your painting when he discovers where I've gone. I'd hate for him to do that. You painted it for me without my asking you to, and it's going to be worth a lot of money one day. Everyone who's seen it concurs with me on that except my father, who says it's too psychedelic and you ought to try another art form. That one looks like a sexed-up vagina close up. And that one there has always been my favorite—an immense forget-me-not, which was my pet flower as a girl. But *suicide*—no, it makes me anxious, tense. You should have sold it when that very suicidal man wanted to buy it from you, just to get it out of the house. Show me all the new ones, Dirk. I like that one; that one's fantastic; that one's another great pulsing vagina; I don't like that one—another *suicide*. This one should be reproduced in an alternative newspaper's centerfold; this one hung on a busy street corner; this one hung above the bed of a couple who want to but can't conceive; this one given to Blaise to cut up. Can I make you a liverwurst and cheddar on rye? Are we getting along better than we did last night? Do you have any more Miracle Whip for the girls' tuna fish salad?"

The telegram to Chrisie from her husband read: "Don't bother returning less you bring back two fresh loaves Larraburu extra-sour sourdough white."

They drove to the party where Helen, Donald and Roy might be. Sophie in his arms, Caroline behind them, blowing into the harmonica, they climbed the steep flight of stairs, were greeted at the top by the host, who was the twin brother of the man who'd invited Dirk. He shook their hands, seemed disappointed. "Cute kids," he said, "the little one a girl? Coats over there, head's through there, drinks in there, nice to see you—Dick, is it? Julie? I never remember names and especially not children's, and he greeted the childless bottle-bringing couple behind them with a long noisy hug. "Wendy, Harris, glad you could come, glad you could come."

Ken, the host's twin, said he was happy to see them, lifted Caroline and swung her, kissed Sophie's head, Dick's cheek, Chrisie's lips, said "Soft, soft, like morning mush. Bar's over there, head's back there, I guess you know where you put your outer dugs and I'm the bartender, so vodka and tonic for everyone except the teeny kids. Orange pop on the rocks do you, Caroline, my dear?" and he put her into a soda carton and carried her to the bar.

Helen was in the living room, dressed and groomed meticulously in a floor-length harem suit, different from Chrisie, who in less than two minutes had washed her face and brushed her hair and ran a wet washrag over her armpits, and thrown a wrinkled paisley smock over her body, with nothing on underneath but sheer panties she could hide in her fist. "So this is Sophie," Helen said, and took her from his arms and kissed her nose. "She's a darling, a dream child," and held her high. "She should be on television, promoting very pure white soap. She looks nothing like you, Dirk, except for her thin hair." Chrisie's uneasy smile failed; she looked weakly defensive, sullen, said nothing; they were all handed drinks by Ken.

"Special," he said. "Drink this and two more magically appear in its place."

"Why'd you come, Dirk?" He had gone to the bedroom to get their coats. The party was dull and the children's presence was annoying the host and guests. "Why'd you come, or does it matter? You knew this'd be an adult party. If you came with Chrisie alone, I'd say fine, big deal, you're fully out of my life now and I think it'd be wonderful for you if you ended up marrying her and possibly even hilarious. She seems nice, quiet, down to earth, attractive, and good to the girls, though expressionless. She has no expression. I could never understand that in a woman. Ken says she looks like a wasted hippie. Surely, you didn't think Roy would be here. Because if you did, and he was, what kind of message would you be trying to send him? Oh, well." She put the headset back on to listen to the music being piped in from the living room stereo. "Unbelievable. The Chamber Brothers doing *Time Has Come Today*. Like having the speakers built into your brains—four big beautiful spades coming on like Gang Busters in your skull. Want to hear?" She gave him the headset, he sat beside her on the bed. She got up, shut the door, got back on the bed and stretched out on her stomach. He felt her thigh, she laughed and turned over and stroked his neck. She said "Roy's being baby-sat at Donald's by this wild old Russian countess, if you're interested." She said "Donald's in this super cutting room downtown, editing his totally insane flick, if you're interested." Drank from her drink, his drink. Said his tasted better, sweeter, would he mind if they exchanged or just shared? Touched his waist, said she thinks he's lost weight. "It looks good; you've been getting much too heavy. You look best when you're slim," Signaled she'd like the headset back. When he put up his hand for her to wait awhile more, she said she thinks the host has another set. She left the room, returned with the second set, plugged it into the jack, lay beside him, both on their backs, listening to *Time*, which must run for around twenty minutes. She asked if he could do it quickly; she could. Donald's way above par, and all that, but he'll be editing film all night and she wants to fuck, does he? "And then, you're still my quasi-legal husband till June and such, but no rationales or threats, can you do it quickly? I can." He helped her kick off her panties, she helped him unbuckle his belt. He got on top of her and both moved to the group's howls and the beat of "time ... time ... time ..." Their headsets got in the way when they kissed. He tried throwing off his set and got one earphone off and was prying out the other phone cord still wedged behind his ear, when the doorknob turned, the door was being pushed, Helen's wrist was pressed to his mouth and her teeth clenched tightly when Caroline yelled "Dirk," as they came together, "I'm tired, Dirk, and Mommy wants for us to go home."

"We don't often accompany each other that high and far," Helen said, as she took off her headset. "Did they make your ears hot too?" She kissed his forehead, slipped into the Toon's bathroom. He unlocked the door, gave Caroline her coat, helped Chrisie on with her sweater, took a sleeping Sophie in his arms, shook Ken's hand and waved to the host, who seemed delighted they were going, said from across the room "Nice to meet you, Dick; nice to meet you, Chris; come back again real soon."

"Did you two make love?" Chrisie said during the drive home. "I thought that's what you were doing and didn't want to bother you in the room. It was Caroline who insisted we go. And when Helen opened the door and came over to the bar asking for a second set of earphones, I had some crazy idea you were going to do it with those things on. What was it like? You smell like a marriage bed now. I wish we could do it with sound ourselves."

In the apartment, the children asleep, he and Chrisie began to make love, stopped, she said it was usually better when he was hard, she'd understand if he couldn't or didn't want to right now but she felt it was something more. "Feel like it Dirk, that's an order, or almost an order. No, no order at all; it was nothing, maybe a confession, forget I said anything. But even if talking about the act usually kills it, I still feel I've got to do it at least once before I leave. My femininity's at stake, my whole well-being's in peril, the children's futures are in jeopardy; besides, we haven't done it in half a year and you were usually so good at it before; do you mind? Strange how things change."

Chrisie and the girls were in the car, Dirk on the sidewalk. "Will you be coming to Obispo?" she said. "Though I suppose I should continue coming here, what with Blaise and a rabidly uptight father and a mother who's always spying by for butter and mommy-sissy chats and demanding to know who painted those erotic watercolors. No, I'll come here, or maybe we should just start living together. Blaise would love that. He honestly would. He wants to be alone also, so you two could sort of switch. And you cook better than him. I like to cook also, but you cook so well I'd let you run the kitchen. And your sandwiches. I think I'll fly up and get us all killed next time, just for your sandwiches. You ought to open a sandwich shop. Just make sandwiches any old way you like and I'll be your only waitress. We could retire in ten years and live for as long as we liked on the Costa del Sol or any one of those other Costas or Sols. But you do make delectable sandwiches, Dirk, and thank you for buying me two front tires. I didn't know the old ones were bald. I didn't know that people got blowouts from bald tires. I thought that even new tires could get blowouts. Goodbye, Dirk." He stuck his head inside the car window and they kissed. "Goodbye, Dirk," Caroline said. He opened the rear door and kissed her. "Goodbye, Dirk," Chrisie said. He extended his head over the front seat and they hugged, cried, kissed. "Goodbye, Dirk," Caroline said, and he laughed, kissed her cheek again, closed the door, keeping his thumb pressed to the handle button, to make sure the door stayed locked,. "Goodbye, Dirk," Chrisie said, and he stuck his head through the window and they kissed. Caroline was still flapping her toy bunny at him as their car entered the freeway on ramp. During all these words, embraces and gestures of departure, Sophie had remained asleep in her child's car chair hooked over the back seat. What, he thought. What, he wanted to say, what is all this?

PRODUCE.

Suddenly, one of the front windows broke and a fire started at number-three cash register and I knew right away what had happened. Someone had thrown a Molotov cocktail through the window. Because just before the smell of fire and smoke had covered over every single smell in the store, there was this smell of kerosene that had flashed in and out of my nose.

"Hey, I'm burning, I'm burning up," Nelson Forman said, first very surprised to see his clothes on fire, then running from his post at number three with flames coming out of his back.

"Get a blanket," a woman customer said. And when I yelled "Where in hell am I going to get a blanket in a supermarket?," she said "Get a coat, then, something to wrap around him, at least."

But this was a hot, sticky August day and not a person in the store had even a jacket on, not even the register clerks, though it was compulsory for them. Nelson ran up aisle A, flames still coming out of his back. Everyone, including a dozen or so customers and the delivery boys and all the clerics, except the two who were using the store's only working fire extinguisher to put out the small blaze at number three, just sort of looked dumbfounded and helpless at Nelson running up and around and down the aisles, wailing his head off, till I tackled him from in front, a perfect tackle right below the knees, so his whole body would buckle and fall backward and lose an extra yard and maybe even loosen the ball from his hands, and rolled him on the floor on his back till most of the fire was out. Then I flipped open five quart bottles of cranberry juice, the nearest liquid I could reach, and poured them over him till the fire was doused, and rested from the ordeal, with my breath coming on hard, while all three delivery boys uncapped quart and half-quart bottles of tomato and pineapple and apricot-orange juice and spilled the contents over Nelson, even after his clothes had stopped smoking.

"Anyone call the police for an ambulance?" I said to the manager, and he repeated the question to the customers and staff surrounding Nelson and me, and they just looked at one another, some shaking their heads.

One man, speaking for his wife and him, said "We didn't; nobody said to."

"Well, someone call the police for an ambulance," the manager said.

"Want me to do it, boss?" Richard, a food bagger, said,

"Dial 9-1-1, Richie."

"Nine-eleven, right, that new police emergency number, right away. Which phone should I use—the one in the office or the pay one in back?"

"The office, and quick, now, Nelson's hurt."

"What I do, what I do for this?" Nelson said, his eyelids and nostrils fluttering, and just my trying to blow away the ashes on his chest that were the remains of his short-sleeved white shirt caused him great pain. He seemed to be going crazy and his hair smelled singed like burned chicken feathers and we were both getting more soaked by the second from being in this large puddle of juice. Nobody seemed to want to get near us or even get their shoes wet.

"How do I keep him from going into shock?" I asked the manager.

"Put his legs up on that olive-oil can there and keep his head straight down."

"No," a woman said, "you put his head up on something soft and his legs down."

"Which do I do?" I asked the manager.

"Let's keep him flat, then. The police will be here in a sec."

A combination of different sirens was heard in a few minutes and then police came and firemen with picks and fire extinguishers and what looked like gas masks and then ambulance people from the local city hospital. Nelson was given oxygen and put on an IV and treated briefly for his burns and was being wheeled out of the market on a gurney when he threw off his oxygen cup and yelled "Boom, damn bomb went boom. And I saw the man who threw it, saw the bum who went boom."

"Hold him there for a moment," a police officer said to the bearers, but the doctor said he'd have to insist that Nelson not be detained.

"Just one quick question, please." And to Nelson: "Who'd you see throw the bomb, son? I'm saying," when Nelson looked at him blankly, "the person who threw it, I mean. You know him? Could you give me a description of him?

"The person was a man," Nelson said. "Threw it right through it, right at me, right through the window at the Heinz beans I was ringing up. Went boom. That man went boom. And the boom went off like a bomb and burned my back, the bum, my back."

"Is that what happened. Don't worry, you'll be fine and dandy in a few days, son, and take care."

"Good luck to you, Nelly," one of the register clerks yelled out. "Safe recovery."

"Now, what happened?" the police officer said to me.

"And please say it nice and straight and slow. Shorthand's not my profession."

My wife asked if anything had happened at work that day, as she asked almost every night when I first got home and immediately went to the bathroom to wash my face and hands and sometimes take a shower, and I said "No, nothing much."

She said "Oh. It's because this time you look more tired than usual, so I thought something might be wrong. Like a beer?"

"Yeah, a beer—no, an ale. I'm dying for one ice-cold."

"You bring home any from work?"

"No, I didn't even bring home a beer. I didn't even bring any groceries. There was a fire at work, that's why."

"A fire? So, now what are we going to do for supper?"

I was counting on a chicken from you, Kev. Why didn't you stop at another market? Or, better yet, phoned me so I could shop somewhere near here. I would've, even though we don't get the discount like at your C & L."

"Someone threw a Molotov cocktail through the store window and Nelson Forman nearly got burned to death." She asked who Nelson was and when I told her, she said "Was he seriously hurt?"

"I said he was nearly burned to death. That means nearly being burned to death. The hospital I called said he has second- and third-degree burns on about fifty percent of his body and that he's still critical and probably lucky to be alive."

"Which is worse, second or third?"

"I don't know. I don't even know if first is worse or better than second. All I know is that fifty percent body burns is very bad, very critical."

"You should've phoned me, Kev. You phoned the hospital; I admit that's more important, but you should've also phoned me. Now we have nothing for supper but eggs, unless you want to go and walk the ten stupid blocks to the market."

"Is that the closest?"

"And the only one. It's almost seven and that's it in about a square mile around here that stays open. I think they're worried about robberies and such. An enterprising chain should open a store nearer the project, stick an armed guard in it and stay open till nine or ten at night and make a fortune. You ought to suggest it to C & L."

The phone rang just around the time we normally sit down to eat. "Who is it?" I said, angry, as if everyone in this time zone should know that most families have supper at this hour, and a man said "Wimer, Kevin Wimer, you're in charge of the C & L produce section at Bainbridge, correct?"

"Sort of assistant in charge. Finerman's head."

"Finerman, that's right. There was a fire in your store today, caused by a particular labor-trouble reason I'll disclose this very minute, if you're not in a rush. There's a movement going on for better wages and working conditions by the ras-, black- and loganberry pickers of this country. And your food chain has continued to sell these products, even though we've expressly requested it to boycott all the big growers of them till they've fallen in line with the few smaller growers who've raised pickers' wages to the national minimum and improved the pickers' living and working conditions while they're on the job. Were you aware your store was firebombed today?"

"Sure. One of the clerks got fifty percent of his body burned, both second and third degree."

"I heard. And it's terrible. But if it's only five percent second and forty-five percent third, it wouldn't be that bad, am I right?"

"You are if second is worse than third, but it could be fatal the other way around."

"I'm very sorry for this clerk. But if I related to you some of the living and working conditions these pickers have to endure, you'd see they're almost better off dead than alive."

"The pickers can always get other jobs, can't they? I mean, there's no Government law saying they can't."

"Are you a union man, Mr. Wimer—I mean a good one? Then you, of course, know you can't be fired from your present position without an exceptionally good cause, correct? And if you've any complaints that can't be settled by you directly with management, then the union settles them for you, correct? The pickers formed a union, but the major growers won't recognize it, so no complaints are settled in any way except the way the growers want, and that's always to the extreme disadvantage of the pickers. These pickers are relatively uneducated but very honest people, usually from a foreign-speaking minority, good family men, they know how to pick fruit, like the outdoors and accept gladly their means of livelihood. And now all they want is for their legitimately formed union to be recognized and honored by the growers, so the union can bargain directly and fairly for better wages, decent wages, the most minimum of national-minimum-wage-act wages, and for the most commonly accepted working and living conditions, which means a portable privy near their work area and dormitories that weren't built ages ago for pigs. Now, is that asking for too much?"

"No."

"Then support us by joining the boycott movement against the illegal growers. We're asking you—and, incidentally, this is in full accordance and sympathy from your own union organizer, Mr. Felk, at Local 79—to refuse to sell ras-, black- and loganberries in your store. And, in fact, tomorrow, in the street outside your supermarket, to publicly dump and destroy the berries you already have while TV news cameras of two local stations here take pictures of you doing it, all of which we'll be instrumental in setting up."

I made a few whews and good Gods into the phone and asked the man to repeat what he'd just asked me to do, which he was doing when Jennie walked over with a blackboard that listed the ingredients that were going into her "New Superspecial Famous Northern California Egg Dish tonight, which includes sweet cream, Swiss and parmesan cheese, scallions, peppers, pimientos and fresh chopped oregano and parsley," and said "Who's on the phone?"

I said "Union business." And to the man: "What's your name, if I might ask?"

"I'll give my organizing name, which is Backspot, Now, what do you say?"

I said why not ask the head of produce, and he said Finerman was too old, besides being in complete agreement with the berry growers and management against the pickers. "Do what I ask, Kevin, and it might be the spark to make our Eastern boycott successful. We don't want any more firebombing. Innocent people get hurt and it looks bad for us, besides. Just dump the berries at ten a.m. tomorrow, which the stations say is the latest they can cover the story, because of previous camera commitments. We swear we'll use every pressure we have to keep you on at the store, if they decide to fire you, and if that's impossible, then your union has promised to place you at even a higher wage at a pro-picker store. You'll also be stamping your own special mark for the same things your union fought for and won only twenty years ago. Now, what do you say?"

I said I'll think it over, but he said I had no time. I said why didn't he get a produce head of one of the giant, more influential markets to do it and he said because my store was in the news now and to gain back respect for the movement, that firebombing had to be whitewashed from the public's mind. "What you'd do would mean that even though one of your favorite colleagues was severely burned, his fellow employees still thought so much of the movement that they forgave the firebombing and were, in fact, placing direct blame on the market owners for selling those berries."

I said oh, what the hell, I'd do it, and he said I'd see him in front of the store at ten, then. "You'll recognize me as an ordinary pedestrian with the most unordinary happy grin an ordinary pedestrian ever had. Pickers around the nation will never forget you for this. You're a credit to your profession and local."

I didn't care about being a credit to my profession. I never had any illusions my job was difficult, or needed many physical or mental skills, though I did have to use some better judgment and really strain a muscle or two when I worked for a small market five years ago and had to get up before the pigeons do to select and buy the store's produce line right off the trucks. Now I open crates that are delivered twice a week to the market, make sure the fruits and vegetables look appetizing and salable to the customers, which mostly means using the right fluorescent lights and straightening out the food and spraying it every other hour to give it that just-picked or rained-on look and odor, put up the price signs that management directs us to from its offices in another city and occasionally use my own mind by writing and installing cute and clever sayings on the more perishable items, such as "Act like this fruit is your mother-in-law: Please do not squeeze." But I agreed with just about everything Blackspot said about improving the lot of the pickers, was bored with C & L after three years and didn't mind losing my job, with two weeks' severance pay, if I could get another one. And it'd be a kick seeing myself on television, having my wife, friends and relatives all seeing me, which'd be the most exciting thing to happen to me since my plane came back with me and my National Guard unit in it from an overseas emergency Middle East crisis several years ago and my crying wife and family nearly suffocated me at the airport gate.

"How'd you like to see me on television tomorrow night?" I said to Jennie when she set that superspecial northern-California egg dish in front of me, and she said "And how'd you like to see me in a brand-new Valentine gown?"

"But I'm serious." And she said "And so am I. Wouldn't I look spectacular? Now, eat up." And to that five-monthold thing in her belly: "You, too, mister, and don't be letting me know if you think the dish is too hot."

The eggs weren't very good, too bland, which not even salt would improve, which surprised me, with all the different herbs, spices and ingredients she put in it. When she asked how it was, I said "Great, fine, though still not as good as one of your plain cheese omelets or fried egg marinara, so maybe this should be the last time we have it, okay?"

"I like it. The sautéed pepper I could do without, but I like it." She ate all her eggs and, without asking me or anything, spooned half of my eggs onto her plate, while I just sat there, thinking about how I was going to get the berries to the street tomorrow before the manager or Finerman got wind of what I was doing.

I got to work a little earlier than usual and cleaned up the produce section a half hour before the store was to open at nine. The window from the bombing the day before still had wooden planks and tape over it and the store still smelled some from the fire, even though we had used several cans of bathroom spray. One of the girl food clerks said that just before she left work last night, the manager told her the company wasn't going to replace the window till the weekend, just to show the agitators that we didn't think a broken window was going to lose us much business and to also show the neighborhood how difficult it was providing them with the wide selection of food products we thought they wanted. I told her I thought a broken window was sure to lose us trade, not only because it looked bad but also because it reminded customers that more agitation might come if the dispute wasn't settled and, worse than that, of Nelson's near death.

"How is he, you know?" she said, and I said I'd been thinking of calling the hospital; in fact, would do it right now, since I had a few minutes before the store opened, and went to the office.

"Good morning, Kevin," the manager said. "Everything straightened out up front?" He said this almost every time I saw him and he meant was the floor swept in my section and was I getting the more perishable items that wouldn't last the week right up on top for everyone to see or at least working with Finerman ordering replacement produce, since the company prohibited markdowns on its fruits and vegetables. This was really his office, he made us very aware of that; made us feel uncomfortable whenever we had to use just one of the three desks in it. And he red-circled the check-in numbers of our timecards if we clocked in three minutes late more than once a week or two minutes late more than twice a week and even complained to our department superiors if he thought we were spending too much time in the washroom, which happened to be within seeing distance of his desk overlooking the store, as I guess everything else was, except the stockroom in back, where the staff took their breaks. That was why I was a little jittery and maybe too hesitant when I asked if he'd mind my using the phone to call about Nelson. He said I needn't bother, he had called himself last night and the hospital said Nelson's doing satisfactorily and it wouldn't know of any improvement in his condition for two days. "He has those kinds of burns."

"I'd still like to call, if you don't mind, and find out if he just might have improved overnight."

"I never knew you and Nelson were that close."

"We weren't, exactly. I mean, Nelson liked me and me, him and we had lots of respect for each other, as we were both on the company softball team that made the league playoffs two years ago, Nelly at short and me at second."

"It's also that the company's been complaining to me recently about the excess calls from this phone, and on both exchanges. That they're completely out of proportion to the excess calls of their other stores. They even sent me a notice to post on the bulletin board, which I haven't done, because I thought a brief mention of it at our next staff meeting might serve as well."

"I'm sure they could make an exception with this one."

"I'm sure they could, too, if this were the only exception. But I can't be explaining to them why each excess call of my employees—or at least the calls I find out about, because I'm not always in this office—is an exception. I'd be explaining to them all week, if that were the case."

So he wasn't going to let me use the phone. He didn't care about Nelson, except that he had to be replaced by a less efficient man at the register and that might lower the day's profits a fraction of a percentage point and—good God!—how was he ever going to explain that to the company. He didn't care about the pickers or even his own employees. And if it had been me burned and Nelson who wanted to call the hospital, it would have been the same excuse: excess calls. I said "Thank you," I don't know for what, and called the hospital from the pay phone in back. Nelson was doing satisfactorily, a woman there said, though chances of his complete recovery wouldn't be known for at least another day.

"You see the TV cameras?" Mary Sarah, another food clerk, said when I got back to my section. "They're setting up outside—two of them from different stations. What're you think they're for?"

"Probably to film the scene of yesterday's bombing."

"And the paper today? There was a picture of our market, real as life except for the boards, and another of Nelson, all bandaged up, waving from his hospital bed, although he looked so grim and weak, it seemed maybe strings were making his fingers move. My hubby, Mike, and I talked about it and couldn't decide what all that degree business meant. Though because third sounds so much the worse over second, we almost agreed it wasn't, because that would have been too obvious, so we wouldn't have even considered the question in the first place. Do you have a clue?"

The store bell rang, everyone got to his post, the doors opened and the usual early-morning surge of customers, eager to get what they believed were daily-delivered fresh produce, bought grapefruits, oranges, peaches and tomatoes and raspberries that had been in the boxes and bins out here, or in the refrigerated cases in back, for a few days.

"It's getting so exciting outside," Mary Sarah said, coming by after the early rush had ended and squeezing and thumping a melon to see if it was ripe enough for dinner tonight. "Could you put this away for me?" she said, which I did. "And the newspaper article said it was all because of those things—those berries there," and she pointed, to the four crates of different kinds of berries that in a half hour I was going to dump into the street and destroy. I'd already figured out how I was going to do it. I'd wait till Finerman went in back for his every-half-hour-on-the-half-hour smoke, and then I'd stack the crates on one another and carry them outside.

"Morning, Kevin." It was Mrs. Blau, another morning regular. For six months in the cold season, she bought nothing but anise, artichokes and apples; and during the warmer months, it was plums, peaches and carrots with their tops. "You shouldn't be selling those things," she said, meaning the berries.

"I know that, Mrs. Blau."

"I should be boycotting your store for selling them, because by having them, you only encourage people to buy. Haven't you seen the television reports?" I told her I hadn't and she said the educational network last week devoted an entire hour to the plight of the berrypickers and the cynicism and greediness of the growers. "The pickers are the most underprivileged and underpaid workers we have. Because of that, they're forced to live in hovels and have too many children, thereby causing even more future problems for them and the world. I shouldn't even be in this store, do you realize that? And maybe I won't," and she handed me the plums, peaches and carrots I'd weighed for her and tagged, clipped and marked, said "I'm sorry for putting you through so much unnecessary work, Kevin," and left the store.

It was nearly ten. The cameras were set up and a couple of policemen were keeping pedestrians away from the equipment and newsman, whom I recognized from a local evening news show as one of the most well-known television reporters on the city scene. People were trying to get his autograph while he held a sheet of paper up in front of him and was practicing his report to an unmanned camera. Suddenly, Mary Sarah was right on top of me, excited and out of breath and saying "You know what Paul Dougherty of WYBT just said outside about you, Kev?" And Larry, the youngest food clerk, said "What, Mary, what?"

"He said that you, Kevin Wilmer, have just smashed all the grower-grown berries that hadn't been picked by union-member pickers, as an act of protest against the growers and as a form of allegiance or something to the boycott movement, though I don't know if he was talking about you or the pickers, now, Kev."

"What's all that about?" Finerman said, his cigarette pack and matches already out of his pocket and in his hands, as he was on his way to the stockroom for a smoke.

"What's all what about?" I said, stacking a crate of raspberries on a blackberry crate.

"What Mary Sarah said."

"Paul Dougherty said you dumped and smashed berries outside," she said. "But you didn't do that, did you Kev? I would have seen it from number six, or at least heard about it."

"That's true, you would've." I had three crates stacked now, lifted them up, told Larry to put the fourth and last crate on top of the three I held, and started for the door.

"Where you going with those?" Finerman said. "Now, put them down and explain to me, Kev."

I would have, the situation was getting too unsettling and scary for me now, but everything had been arranged, which I had agreed to, and I'd feel even worse and more stupid having had all those television men come out here and set up their equipment for nothing. "I've got to put these berries away, under manager's orders," I said.

"Then you're going the wrong way, if that is what you're doing," Finerman said. "Storeroom's in back. Kevin?

Now, you come back here this instant, Kevin."

I was walking through the door. Finerman, as I'd thought, didn't try to stop me physically, though by now he must have known what was happening. Larry, Mary Sarah and all the delivery boys followed me outside, mumbling to one another that something fantastic was about to happen.

"Okay, fellas," Paul Dougherty said, and the cameras began shooting film of me. Paul Dougherty was reporting off camera that I was leaving the market to demonstrate my solidarity with the pickers' movement for higher wages and better living and working conditions. Behind me, Mary Sarah said "Now I get it; now I understand," and

Larry said "Oh, Jesus, and I was the one who put the last crate in his hands. You think I'll be fired?"

I looked around for Blackspot, but there was a whole slew of ordinary-looking pedestrians grinning and smiling as I almost never saw them do on the street. I walked to the curb, set down the crates, lifted the top crate and was about to turn it over into the street, when one of the three boys standing beside me and hamming it up for the cameras said "As long as you're going to throw those away, can we have some?" I said no, though I honestly didn't know what to say. I hadn't planned for anyone to bring up what I could see was a perfectly legitimate request, and when he said "They're just going to go to waste, anyhow," I told him "All right, but only one basket apiece, understand?"

They took a basket each from one of the crates on the sidewalk and then it seemed that everyone in the crowd other than my coworkers and the television people and one unhappy, ungrinning, very ordinary-looking man except for a purple birthmark the size of a glass coaster in the middle of his forehead began grabbing baskets of berries out of the crates and carefully sticking them into their shopping bags or just eating handfuls of berries right on the street, as the three boys were doing. The crowd emptied the three crates in less than a minute and were grasping for the berries in the crate I was holding away from their reach, when I threw that crate to the ground and quickly stepped on and smashed the berries rolling every which way and then almost everyone in the crowd joined in stepping on the berries with me.

"We're pressing wine," someone said. "Down with the illegal growers," Blackspot shouted at the cameras.

"Up with the C & L fruit men," a woman said, and that was the cheer the crowd liked best. "Up with the C & L fruit men," people shouted. "They give away free berries for nothing."

The cameras picked up on all this. Paul Dougherty was reporting the story as if a last-ditch game-winning touchdown had just been scored. It was almost a surprise to me not to be hoisted to someone's shoulders and paraded around and hip-hip-hoorayed to.

Later, Jennie and I sat down for the evening news.

I'd told her something special was going to be on that we should watch, as I hadn't mentioned what had happened at work today. She said she better see how the chicken was doing in the oven, but I said "Sit tight, just for a second."

There were a lot of reports about Vietnam and Africa and the UN and our country's gold crisis and the city's impending school crisis and then the store I was in. "Oh, gosh, I can't believe it; you were right," Jennie said. I told her to can it, I couldn't hear. Off-camera, Paul Dougherty, while the screen showed me leaving the store, was telling a different story from the one he'd begun to recite when the incident actually took place. Now he said that what had started out to be one individual's protest against the major city supermarkets' nonadherence to the ras-, black- and loganberry boycott turned into a major neighborhood fun-in. "Kevin Wimer was the principal figure in the demonstration. But the neighborhood, a polyglot of race, creed and culture, wouldn't let Mr. Wimer have his protest without them eating it, too." The television showed the loud frantic activity of people stealing the baskets and popping berries into their mouths for the benefit of the cameras, and Paul Dougherty said it was like a "modern-dress Cecil B. De Mille-presents scene of Bacchanalian Rome." The last shot showed me walking back to the market with the empty crates and Paul Dougherty, in the foreground, and for the first time on camera, saying "So what began as a plucky individual's protest against a segment of the giant corporate structure ended up as the best gesture of neighborhood goodwill and all the free publicity that accompanies it that a supermarket chain could hope to get. I guess you can say 'Berry sweet is revenge.'"

"What'd he mean with that last remark?" Jennie said.

"I don't know; too highbrow for me. Maybe that my stunt backfired."

"Did they can you?"

"The manager said he'd speak to upper management about it. Meanwhile, because they're short of help in the produce section, I should stay on. But there are always other jobs."

"We got bills, you know, a baby coming on, and chicken costs money, especially if you don't get it at twenty-percent off." She went to the kitchen, yelled out "You're a fool and a showoff, Kevin Wimer," and, a little later, that dinner would be ready in five minutes.

Blackspot called. "You weren't at first forceful enough with those three kids, but thanks, anyway. Nobody won or lost, but it at least drew some much-needed nonviolent attention to the movement. I was wondering if you'd join our picket line tomorrow against a pro-grower Food-O-Rama on a Hundred and Sixty-eighth. We need marchers badly."

"I'm still working," I said. "But because of my general all-around foul-up today and sympathy for the movement, I'd like to give a few dollars to the pickers. Where do I send it to?"

"We're having a full-page ad in all the city's newspapers on Sunday. It'll mention just that matter and also the address of national headquarters where the donations should go."

The phone rang a minute later. "Let it ring," Jennie said. "Even pull out the jack, since there'll be no end to those calls," but I left the table and answered it. It was Nelson's wife, Rita. She said she hadn't seen the story on television herself, but a couple of her friends called to tell her that one of Nelson's coworkers had come on television to say that not only did Nelson deserve to get burned but the whole city should be torched if the mayor and city council and all the supermarkets and their customers don't support the berry boycott. I told her that wasn't true about one of Nelson's coworkers and wondered what news program her friends could have been watching. "It certainly wasn't the one my wife and I saw, and the other station covering it filmed the same scene." Then I asked how Nelson was and she said "Oh, fine, absolutely fine. How else would he be with half his body charred to shreds and all the pain that goes with it, which no amount of drugs seems to help."

"But is he improving any? I mean, Nelson and I were friends at work, so I'm interested. Everybody at the market's concerned, customers too."

"Oh, yeah," she said, "a lot you all care."

"We do, a lot, me, especially. That television report your friends gave was totally false."

"Well, the doctors say he'll live, thank God, though with so much of his body burned, they say he'll have to get skin grafts on the parts burned most," and it occurred to me that she if anybody would know the answer as to which of the two degrees was worse. I first said "Listen, and I swear to this, I'd be glad to give some of my skin to Nelson, if the doctors think the color is right and all, as I've big thighs and an even bigger behind and I know that's where they take the donor's skin from." Then I told her about the question that had been bothering me for two days now and which was worse, if she didn't mind my asking, second- or third-degree burns?

"Well, the main difference, Nelson's main doctor told me—" but then she broke down. I felt very bad for her and said "Now, come on, don't cry, Rita. It'll be all right; everything'll work out okay," but she said "I can't talk anymore; I've been like this since the firebombing. Oh, what's wrong with this world, anyway?" and hung up.

I stood there a few seconds with that sobbing plea of hers still in my head, then went to the dictionary in the living room while Jennie was calling me back to the table in the kitchen, but all it had in it were the words "second" and "third" and "first" and "burn" and "-s" for the plural, but no word "degree" after them, neither with hyphens, separated nor anything. I decided I'd never get to know the answer to this question. That none of my friends knew and nobody at work knew and that maybe the only person who could tell me would be one of those great skin-doctor specialists like the one working on Nelson, who wouldn't give me the time of day on the phone if I called him, he'd be so busy. Then I remembered my promise to Rita and I said out loud "Good God, what the hell you get yourself into this time?" and I all of a sudden felt stomach-sick and woozy, because just the thought of being operated on for skin for Nelson's grafting scared me to no end now. I hoped Rita would forget my suggestion, or maybe in her condition she hadn't even heard me make it, but I had promised her and I knew I'd have to go along with it if I was asked.

THE YOUNG MAN

WHO

READ BRILLIANT BOOKS.

At the state unemployment office this morning, David met a woman in line who told him, after giving him the once-over and then deploring the long wait and interminable California rain, that she had five beautiful daughters at home from whom he could just about take his pick if he liked. "You seem that good-natured and sensitive to me," she said, "and just look at the way you read those brilliant books. And then, strange as this sounds, sonny," and she looked around the room suspiciously and then stretched on her toes to speak into his ear, "I think it's high time they began seeing men who aren't always so stupid and wild."

David thought the woman was a little eccentric, so he politely told her he wasn't interested. "What I'm saying is that, enticing as your offer sounds, I'm really much too busy with my studies to go out with some women I don't even know."

"*Girls*," she said, "not women. Young gorgeous, unattached girls, the homeliest of which looks like nothing short of a glamorous movie starlet. And who said anything about going out with all five of them? *One*, just one, we're not perverts, you know. And my daughters are smart and obedient enough to realize that what I say is usually the right thing for them, so you can be sure you'll have your choice, like I say."

"Thanks again," he said, as he was trying to finish the last few pages of the paperback he was reading and then get to the one sticking out of his jacket pocket, "but I'm afraid I'll still have to say no."

"Why no? Listen some more before you shut me off. One's even a blonde, though with fantastic dark black eyes. You ever go out with a blonde with fantastic dark black eyes? Ever even seen one, no less? Take it from me, they're the most magnificent female creatures on God's earth, bar none. Writers write endless sonnets about them, swoon at their feet. One handsome young biochemist actually wanted to commit suicide over my Sylvia, but I told him he was crazy and he'd be better off discovering new cures for cancer, instead. And listen: Each of them has a beautiful body. You interested, perhaps, in beautiful bodies?"

"Of course I am," and he closed the book on his finger. "I mean"— he tried to harden his face from showing his sudden interest—"well, every man is."

"Like Venus and Aphrodite they have beautiful bodies," she said dreamily. "And cook? Everything I know in the kitchen and my *cordon bleu* mother before me knew, I've taught to my daughters. Now, what do you say?"

She was next in line now and the clerk behind the window asked her to step forward. "Listen to that jerk," she whispered to David. "Someone like that I wouldn't let one foot into my house. Wouldn't even let him say hello on the phone to my daughters, even if he was pulling in five hundred a week from his job. But *you*?"

"Madam," the clerk said irritably, "if you don't mind?"

"*You*," she continued with her back to the clerk, "sandals, long hair, mustache, face blemishes and all, I'd make an elaborate dinner for and introduce to my girls one by one. Then I'd give you a real Cuban cigar and Napoleon brandy and show you into our library till you made up your mind as to which of my beauties you want to take for a drive. And you want to know why? I like brains."

"It's nice of you to say that," David said. "Because nowadays—"

"Brains have always been taught to me by my father as the most important and cherishable part a man can bring to a woman. Clerks like that dullard don't have brains, just fat behinds with sores on them through their whole lives. But you I can tell. Not only because of your intelligent frown and casual way you speak but also how you concentrate on your brilliant English novel here," and she slapped the book he held. "So, come on, sonny, because what do you really have to lose?"

"Okay," he said, smiling for the first time since he met her, "you broke my arm. But just for dinner, if that's all right. And only to meet your lovely family and have a good home-cooked meal for a change, with some stimulating conversation."

"Now you're being smart." She wrote her name and address on the inside cover of his book, told him to beat her home around six and went up to the clerk's window to sign the form for her unemployment check.

"You act like you don't even need the money," the clerk said, shoving the form in front of her.

"This paltry sum?" she said for everybody to hear. "*Peanuts*. But I and my employer put good money into your insurance plan, so why shouldn't I make a claim for it if I'm looking for work?"

"Next," he said over her shoulder, and David walked up, said good morning extra courteously, as he didn't want to give this man even the slightest excuse for becoming unfriendly and ultimately overinquisitive about him, and answered the same two questions he'd been asked since he started getting the checks.

"Did you work any days last week or receive a salary or payment of any kind for any type of labor?"

"No, sir."

"Did you make an effort the last week to look for work in your field?"

"Yes, sir."

"See you tonight, then," the woman said from the side, twiddling her fingers goodbye as David signed the form. "And don't worry about any fancy dressing for our cozy dinner. We're informal people—very informal, though we're not exactly beggars, by any means."

That evening, David shaved himself twice with his electric razor, as the rotary blades were in serious need of a sharpening, and trimmed his full mustache so that none of the hairs hung over the upper lip. Then he dressed in his only suit and tie, brushed down his curly hair with hair oil till his skull was flat and shiny, and patted after-shave lotion on his face and neck and then at the underarms of his jacket, which needed a dry-cleaning.

But then, he thought, it wasn't every day of the week a lonely, sort of homely-looking guy like himself was invited to sit down at an elegant table with five beautiful young sisters.

The house he drove up to turned out to be in the seediest part of town. It was small and boxlike, sticking out of a garden of tall weeds like an ancient, run-down mausoleum. He rang the bell, much less hopeful of any grand time tonight, but, surprisingly, the girl who opened the door was as beautiful as her mother had said. She was about twenty, black-eyed and as well built as the famous Venus statue in Paris, whom she also resembled above the neck a great deal, he now noticed, except for the long blonde hair. "Come right in," she said in a sweet voice, and David, feeling his neck knot up with excitement, managed to squeak out that he was the man his mother had met this morning and invited to dinner.

"You're Sylvia," he said. "I'd know you anywhere by your mother's glowing description." He stuck out his hand, but instead of having his fingers squeezed seductively as he had imagined, he was jerked past the door and thrown halfway across the room. When he got up a few seconds later, a bit dizzy and his pants ripped at the knee and all set to ask what kind of silly practical joke she was playing on him, he saw her locking the front door with a key, which she promptly dropped down her bra.

"Now, how's that for a quick-change routine?" Sylvia said with a voice much tougher and throatier now, though that smile of unwavering sweetness remained. "Years back, I was in show business, so I know what's what with costumes and makeup and things."

David tried to stay composed by examining the rip in his pants. "It's a damn good thing this is my oldest suit," he said, and looked up to see what reaction his remark had made and saw her peeling off her face skin from the forehead down and then her gorgeous blonde hair.

"A voluptuous goddess of love I can only pretend to be for minutes," the woman he'd met at the unemployment office said, "but a svelte water nymph I could play for you for hours. Not much padding then to bother my tush and ribs and hamper my walk, you know what I mean?" She placed the wig and Venus mask in a hatbox—neatly, as if she were preserving them to wear again—and unzipped her dress, removed the socks from her bra and bandages wrapped around her buttocks and, from her waist, a tight black-satin cummerbund. When she finished rezippering and hitching, and patting her gray hair back into place, she said "Well, now, Davy boy, what do you say we get down to business."

"Why you big fraud," he said. "I mean...why you big incredible fraud."

"Sure, I'm a fraud. What then? You saying you would've come all the way out here just to see an old bag like me? But look who's talking about frauds. We're on to you, you know, the way you take unemployment-insurance money from our Government under somebody else's name and Social Security number—a good pal of yours in Paris who you send a hundred bucks to every other week. We checked, so don't think you've been invited here just for your good looks, you weasel. At least I worked for my unemployment money—twenty miserable weeks I worked, which isn't one day over the minimum and which I don't ever expect to do again. But sit down." She motioned him to a chair. "A sense of decency I at least still got for your likes. You want a drink? Some good gin? Oh, stop shaking your head like a clod. You're not getting out of here till we've had our say, so you might as well sit back comfortably with a drink."

"About that unemployment insurance," David said uneasily. "Well, that's my business—my worry. And if you've brought me here to extort hush money out of me, forget it. I'm broke, flat, *rien*—*comprenez-vous français*? So I'll be leaving," and he stood up and confidently stuck out his hand for the key. She laughed and slapped at his fingers and yelled in the direction of the stairs "Georgie? Little Davy's here and he's getting impatient. You want to come down?"

From upstairs, a man answered in a soft, lilting voice: "I'll be down in a sec, sweet."

"You'll be down in a sec, nothing. Get your skinny ass here this instant."

A thin, sickly-looking man in his fifties came hurrying downstairs. He was panting, still full of sleep, a few days past his last shave and scratching his undershirt nervously when he gave David a limp, wet hand to shake.

"Pleased to meet you, son. Sylvia's told me some very encouraging things about you. Very."

"You see," Sylvia said, edging David back into a couch beside Georgie, "my husband and I have decided you're just the man we need for our work."

"That's right," Georgie said. "We need a smart boy with brains."

"What Mr. Peartree means is that simply the idea of you carrying through your plans to finagle the Government is a good sign to us. Besides which, of course, we can always use it against you if you don't go along with what we ask."

"Sylvia told me all about it," Georgie said. "Amazing. Just terrific. No, really, pal, because not many guys can get away with conning the Federal Government anymore."

David said "Not that I'm committing myself to anything, but I still don't know what you have in mind or even what the wages are for your mysterious work."

"Twenty dollars a day," she said, as if it were two hundred, "and judging from what we have on you, consider it philanthropy."

"You're getting a bargain," Georgie said. "Take it quick before she lowers the offer."

"Offer for what, goddamnit?" David said, and Sylvia, telling him to control himself for a minute, went into a long detailed account of what they had in mind. She and Georgie were basically uneducated people, she said, and as he could see by just looking around their home, these weren't the best of times for them, either. So what they needed now was an educated person to write bright convincing letters to all sorts of big American companies, complaining about the products some woman they'd made up had bought and how much trouble and even serious harm these defective goods had caused this woman and her family.

"We give you the names of the products," she went on, "and what you do, and which we know you're capable of because of your strong English-literature background, is think up something wrong with these goods, type up a nice neat letter telling about it and then sign our Mrs. O'Connell's name and our address. From these letters we expect all kinds of small and semi-large cash settlements, and if not that, then tremendous supplies of these same products Mrs. O'Connell's complaining about, which should keep us in most of our home goodies for a solid year."

"A friend of mine," Georgie said, "once wrote a letter to a cigarette company, telling the truth about how the cig paper had pinholes in it, which made the things unsmokable. In a week he got back a hand-signed letter from the sales manager himself, saying how sorry they were and he should know how untypical his experience was and for his trouble they were sending along two cartons of the same brand he made a stink about. Two cartons—can you imagine? Just think if he was a brainy guy like yourself and wrote an intelligent letter telling how he found some chemically tested rat hairs in his smokes."

"Letters like that," Sylvia said, "which shouldn't take you more than two days. Then you get your forty dollars and our sincerest promises that we won't leak a word to the Government about your little insurance embezzlement. Is it a deal?"

David had nineteen more weeks to go on his friend's unemployment insurance, which came to—after he'd subtracted the biweekly hundred dollars he sent to Paris—around two thousand dollars, tax free and clear. He really had no choice but to go along with them, so he said he agreed, though reluctantly, he wanted them to understand, and promised he'd be at their house for work bright and early the next day.

"Listen," Sylvia said sharply as she unlocked the door, "bright and early it better be. Or around nine a.m. tomorrow, the U.S. Government gets an anonymous tip concerning one David O. Knopps, you know what I mean?"

David returned to their home the next morning and got right down to writing the letters. The Peartrees already had a long list of the names and addresses of the companies he was to write to, so what he had to do was think up something wrong with the company's product, begin the letter with a brief, courteous description of what the difficulty was, mention that she (Mrs. O'Connell) had never written a letter like this before, make no monetary demands or threats about possible law suits but just say that she wanted to "bring this oversight to the attention of your organization, as I'm quite sure you'd want me to do." Then he was to sign her best wishes and name, and in a postscript, assure the company that "although my five daughters and I are slightly less confident of your product these days, we bear no grudges against you, realize that big institutions as well as small individuals can make mistakes, and that we've no plans to stop using your product in the future."

Working an eight-to-five shift, it took David three days to complete these letters, all typed on personally engraved stationery, with Mrs. O'Connell's name and the Peartrees' address, that Greorgie had a printer friend run off. The first letter, to a big soap company in Chicago, took him more than two hours to compose and type. The letter suggested that one of its employees—"perhaps an anarchist or somebody, though with jobs being as hard to get now as they are, I'm hardly the one to place a person's work in jeopardy—had substituted sand for soap powder in your jumbo-size box of Flashy which, if you must know, ruined my almost-new washing machine and an estimated value of $296 worth of clothes."

After the first few letters, he became more adept at grinding out these lies and was able to knock off a new one every fifteen minutes.

One went to the president of the country's largest canned-soup company: "Unbelievable as this may sound, sir—and because of its importance, I'm directing this letter to you—the bottom half of a white mouse was found in a can of your cream-of-chicken soup, which, when dumped into the pot, gave my aging mother such a fright that she's been under heavy sedation ever since." Another letter went to a chocolate company in Georgia that, in its magazine ads, prided, itself on its cleanliness: "You can imagine our shock, gentlemen, when we discovered, after removing the wrapper of our family's favorite candy for more than thirty years, that your milk-chocolate bar had teeth marks in it and a tiny end square bitten off." And about a hundred other letters, all quite civil and somewhat squeamish, all initially self-critical for even thinking of writing this giant reputable company in the first place, all very crafty and subtle, David thought, in getting his main message across: that in one ugly or harmful way or another, the product had caused considerable psychic or physical damage and Mrs. O'Connell wanted some kind of indemnification.

When the letters had been read, edited and approved by the Peartrees, and a number of them retyped by David, they thanked him for a job well done, gave him his wages and a ten dollar bonus for the quick efficient way he had handled his chores and, like his closest uncle and aunt always did, waved goodbye to him from their front steps as his car pulled away. He drove home, merrily humming a peppy tune along with the car radio and convinced that he'd done the only right thing for himself in going along with their scheme. Now, with a clear mind and sixty extra dollars, he could resume collecting his friend's unemployment checks without fear of being caught, with that money complete his master's thesis on Henry James, whose work he disliked but at least understood, and begin applying to English departments of the better universities for a teaching assistantship as he went on for his Ph.D. He had a good life ahead of him—the academic life, which was the only one he could contend with and still be financially secure.

A month later, Sylvia called, asking in the most gentle of motherly voices if he'd care to drop by one afternoon that week for homemade peanut-butter cookies and tea. When he refused, saying how much he appreciated the offer but was too tied down in completing his thesis to even go out for the more essential groceries, she said "Lookit, you jerk. You drag that fat butt of yours right over here, or my next call's going to be to the state unemployment commissioner himself."

"Call him," David said. "And the head of the F.B.I., while you're at it. But remember; Whatever you have on me goes double for you and Georgie-boy with your mail scheme."

"What mail scheme? That was *your* scheme, Davy, if you don't know it by now. We got two God-fearing respectable witnesses, me and Mr. Peartree, who'll swear under oath that you threatened us with force to use our home to accept your goodies from all those companies and then to even buy them from you, which is why they're in our house. Those were your signatures, your words that went into those letters, because we sure don't have the brains and education for that kind of prose. You couldn't pin a thing on us without going to prison for twenty years yourself, which doesn't even account for how much time you'd get for your unemployment insurance theft. So, how about it? You going to take down our new address and zip the hell out here, or do I make my next call to that state commissioner, police or F.B.I.?"

The Peartrees lived in a much better neighborhood now, David observed as he drove along their street. And entering their home, Sylvia bowing him in with a wily grin as if she never had any doubts about him rushing over, he was surprised by the number of boxes and cartons in the living room of so many of the products he'd written about in his letters for them. Flour, sugar, fruit juice, canned soup, cellophane tape that wouldn't stick, alkalizers that wouldn't fizz, ballpoint pens that leaked onto eighty-dollar blouses with the first stroke, linens that tore apart in the first wash—enough food staples and home supplies to keep them going for a good year, as Sylvia had said.

"But no money to speak of, those misers," she said after conducting a tour of the four other rooms, each of them almost furnitureless but with enough boxes and cartons of linens and food and cleaning products to make them look like the storage room of a small neighborhood grocery store.

"Though what we got we owe all to you," Georgie said. "Some smart boy you are, Davy, And my Sylvia's some great judge of people, in choosing you."

David told them to stop buttering him up with such ridiculous bull jive and level with him straight off why they summoned him here.

"So, feeling a bit ballsier than before, eh?" Sylvia said. "Okay. We've another deal you might be interested in." When he flapped his hands at her to forget it, she said "Only one more; we're not gluttons. Now take a load off your feet and let me speak." While Georgie prepared him a Scotch sour, Sylvia explained that with all this food around, they still hadn't a good stove to cook it on or even a decent bed to put their new linens on, so all they were asking of him was to steal the day's receipts of a movie theater they had in mind, which would be enough money to buy the big-ticket items they need and keep them going for a while.

"Oh, just a small theater," she quickly said when he jumped up from the couch and headed for the door. "And not the box office itself, which would be too risky. All you do is approach this little squirt of a manager from behind, ask him into an alley, take his money satchel, which he's on his way to night-deposit, and bring it here. The way we planned it, he'll never even see your face; and then you get a hundred for your labor and we say our final goodbyes."

"It'd be impossible," he said. "I'd be petrified, too scared out of my wits to say a word," and he turned away from them and, unable to control himself any longer, started to cry into his sleeve. But they saw right through his ruse, he thought, glancing up, even though he was weeping real tears. When he was finished, had wiped his eyes, having made sure to irritate them, and after Sylvia had restated what they had on him, he said he might go through with it if they didn't insist he use a gun. "I'd rather go to prison than terrify some innocent guy with a weapon. I'm sorry, but that's how I am."

Around one that evening, Georgie drove him to a bar in a nearby suburban town, bought a couple of beers and, from the bar window, pointed across the street to a very short fat man leaving a darkened movie theater. The man was holding a black bag, which Georgie said contained about six thousand in ones, fives, tens and twenties—"None of it traceable. And no heavy change, either, which he leaves in the theater. We also understand this idiot refuses to call the local police station for an escort, since he doesn't like shelling out the customary twenty bucks tip they expect for the four-block ride. Now watch him, Davy. At the end of the street, he went left, though if he wasn't in such a hurry, he'd continue along the better-lit avenues to reach the bank. Halfway up that shortcut is an alley, which we'll want you to suddenly pop out of, say a few standard, words about his money or his life, take the bag, order him to lie on his belly and then impress upon him to stay put and silent for five minutes maximum or by the time he gets home he'll have found that an accomplice of yours had done some terrible things to his family. It's all very simple. And once you get back with the bag and we see you haven't opened it—we have ways— we promise, and you have my solemn oath for both Syl and myself, to leave you in peace for the rest of your life."

David told him that if he was able to draw up the necessary courage to carry out such an act, he'd do it tomorrow. He knew the Peatrees were sure he'd go through with it. And in a month—if all went well, and the theft seemed simple and quick enough if everything was like they said—his thesis would be done, he already had offers from two good Eastern schools for assistantships while he earned his doctorate, and again that idyllic image of his future appeared; David as teaching assistant for three years, then instructor, assistant professor and ultimately as a full professor pulling down a nice sum at a job at which he only had to put in about twelve hours a week, besides all the long vacations and breaks and paid sabbaticals and research and travel grants. Considering all this, he didn't feel one night's scary episode was too great a sacrifice to make to help him realize these goals. And he was twenty-five, too advanced an age to have to start at a new profession from the beginning.

The next night, David, sweating profusely and shivering, could barely stand straight by the time the manager, holding the black bag and with a sunny after-work smile, came waddling up the sidestreet. When he was adjacent to the alley, David stepped out behind him and said—louder than he'd planned, though no one else was on the street—"All right, fella, if you're wise you'll hand over that...I mean... what I'm saying, fella, is...just give me that damn bag already, you big fool—you know what the hell I mean. Keep your eyes shut and in front and your face on the ground."

The manager swiveled around, just when Sylvia's Venus mask slipped below David's chin, and called him a disgrace to everything good in life and then tugged at the bag David was trying to wrestle out of his hands. David, not knowing what else to do but realizing that, small and slight as he was, he was still a half foot taller and much stronger than the man, slammed him in the mouth, which sent him sprawling. The manager threw the bag at him, curled himself up and said "I want to die, I want to die this very instant," and began sobbing. David patted his head. "Look, I'm sorry, but this money's not even for me. I had to do it. They're after me. My whole life depends on it. I've kids and everything else to take care of. Just keep quiet and stay here a few minutes and don't say you saw my face, and I swear everything will be okay," and he ran out of the alley, got into his car at the end of the street, and drove to the Peartrees'.

The total take of the robbery came to a little more than two thousand. Georgie said "I told Sylvia to tell you we should wait till Wednesday, when the show changes and every lonely dud in the area goes to the movies. But no. She's always got to have her way."

"Maybe the manager's been cheating on the owners," Sylvia said. "You also get his wallet, Davy?"

David was still shaking from the robbery, and flashlike images of that tiny man curled up on the ground and bawling made him so depressed that he had to stretch out on the couch, "What you say— wallet? Never a wallet. Wasn't asked and wouldn't do. Would've been too much like a real crime."

She stuck a hundred dollar bill in his shirt pocket and told him to forget it. "It's over, done with. Your first is always your worst. Fortunately, this one's your last. Now, drink up this nice brandy Alexander Georgie made for you, and let's call it a night."

Before leaving, David asked them to promise they'd never contact him again. "If you do, I'm calling the cops myself. I don't care anymore. Prison would be infinitely preferable to going through another night like this. That poor man, lying there like that."

"That fat disgusting thief," Sylvia said. "I'm sure a few hundred dollars of the receipts are in his wallet right now. Anyway, we earned enough, so you'll never hear from us again. And to prove how sincere we are, I'll get the Bible for Georgie and I to swear on," but he told her not to bother.

David changed his residence that week. Without telling the land-lady where he was going, he rented a one-room cabin on someone's dilapidated ranch in the hills overlooking the campus. Working without letup, he finished his thesis in a few weeks and so now stayed in the area only till the English Department gave the work its approval. His friend had returned from Paris much earlier than expected and resumed collecting his own unemployment insurance. For money, David now worked as a bartender in one of the beer joints that serviced the college community. Two months after he'd last seen the Peartrees, they turned up at the Oasis, took two counter seats and asked David, whom they greeted as if he were just another well-thought-of bartender, for a large pitcher of beer and two cheeseburgers, medium rare.

"Go somewhere else," David whispered. "This place is hot."

"And maybe you could rustle us up a side order of French fries," Georgie said. "Crisp. Make sure to tell the cook we like them crisp."

"Please. Things are finally going well for me. I've a girlfriend. We're going to get married. She's going to have a baby—my first child—*mine*, you hear? In six months, I'm going to be both father and husband, so leave me alone."

They listened patiently. Then Georgie said "You ain't got no girl. We know all about you. Where you live with the cows and what poor decent people your folks are in Idaho and what a fine university you settled on near Boston, and even that your buddy Harold's back and you haven't been able to cheat the government anymore."

"You look terrible," Sylvia said, shaking her head. "An apron on a man is such an unmasculine-looking thing. What're you making here—three-fifty an hour plus tips?"

"That's right," David said, "and it's more than sufficient."

"What about your expenses East? Motels, gas, food, car upkeep and just living there before your college money comes in. Throw that apron away and come home with us.

Next job we got for you we pay seven hundred—just think of it. That's probably three weeks' earnings here for just one day's work, and we don't take off for taxes and Social Security."

"Definitely no," and with a hand he tried his best to make tremble, he served them tea with lemon and a stale doughnut each. "I'm sick. My mind: it forgets. Even this job's too much. Got into a car accident last week. Because of my dizzy spells since, my doctor thinks I've a concussion or worse. I'm going crazy, is the truth, and a crazy man can shoot off his mouth without knowing it and ruin all your good plans."

"Then you're better off not working here," Sylvia said. "And don't worry about your mind. For this job we need muscle, not brains, and looking and acting like a lunatic will even be an asset. You see, we've gone into the loan business with most of the theater money you got for us, and our very best customer won't pay up."

"And this guy's about the same height as the last one," Georgie said, "but much older—more than seventy—besides being an out-and-out coward. He's a horseplayer, a real loser, and all you've got to do is talk tough, flash him your cold sparkling teeth and maybe give him a slight rabbit punch below the ears to show we haven't just hired a blowhard for the job. That should be all we need to get back our money with interest, and then we leave the loan business and move upstate to invest in and help run my brother's dairy."

"As you can see, David," Sylvia said, "we want to get out of the rackets as much as you. We're getting on in years and just want to lead a simple country life again and not always be rattled by thoughts of policemen at our door. But we can't go unless Abe Goff pays us back what he owes. So come on: Do we have to be spiteful and tell your boss you spit in our teas and later tip off the police about your last theft? You know, that movie-house manager said in the papers he'd recognize your face even in his afterlife."

David knew damn well what the manager had told the papers. At least ten times he'd read the article about the night the man got held up, had the movie receipts stolen and his wallet, ring, five-hundred dollar watch and three-hundred dollar cufflinks taken from him after he'd been beaten unconscious. He wasn't sure how eager the manager would be to recognize him, since he must have collected a bundle of money from his insurance company for his own personal loss, but David still couldn't take the chance. He wasn't, though, about to give in to the Peartrees so easily as he felt he had always done, so he begged them in a sickly voice: "Listen. You've got to find another patsy. I'm hopeless. As I said: in the worst physical and mental shape of my life."

"College life has ruined you," Sylvia said. "Made you soft, parasitic, vulnerable and a little stupid, which for us is a perfect setup. Besides, you're obliged to us up to your neck. So now, do I start by phoning your boss," whose home phone number she waved in front of him, "or do you leave this place for good tonight and do what we say?"

The following night, David went into Abe Goff's cleaning store, shortly before closing time. Abe, another little guy, had photographs of victorious racehorses and mud-caked grinning jockeys hanging around the room, and on top of the cash register a shiny bronze of Man o' War. He seemed annoyed that a customer had come so late, but quickly gave David his most accommodating professional smile and said "So, what can I do for you, young man? Suit, coat, shirts, two pairs of pants with the cuffs removed? Let me guess. Old Abe's the best guesser you ever seen. Your girlfriend's yellow mohair G-string that she had French-cleaned? You come for that? Well, no tickly, no stringy, friend, so let's have it," and he stuck out his hand for David's cleaning ticket.

David didn't say anything more than he'd been instructed to. "This is from the Altruistic Loan Company," he said, with a face—without any effort at all—empty of emotion and hard. Then he grabbed Abe by the neck with one hand, punched him twice in his surprised but still accommodating face with the other hand and, when Abe was on the floor, moaning, coughing, pointing feebly to what he muttered was a bum ticker, kicked him in the chin and heard a bone crack, though he'd aimed for his shoulder. Then he fled to the street, past a screaming woman carrying clothes to be cleaned, and around the corner to where his car was parked. His instructions were to drive to his cabin and wait there till they contacted him. But he drove to their home and continued to bang on the door till Sylvia let him in with a remark that alluded to his unique idiocy. He brushed past her and searched through a few cabinets till he came up with an unopened bottle of Scotch. He had downed three quick drinks from the bottle by the time Georgie, in his pajamas and yawning, dragged himself downstairs.

"We've created a Frankenstein," Sylvia said, pointing at David, who was now filling up a tumbler of Scotch.

"I nearly killed a man tonight," David said, drinking up. I've had it with you both, which is what I came here to tell you."

"So who's asking you for more favors?" Sylvia said. "Go home, sleep it off. Even take that cheap bottle of Scotch, if you want."

"I can't go home. They'll find me. I've been recognized, I've got to stay here—just until you get your money from Goff and I my money from you—and then I'll be heading East and out of your way for good."

"You're heading nowhere but home, and you're never going East. You're into us plenty. Even Abe the cleaner will testify on our behalf. He knows the rules of this game, which is just another thing you're too damn smart to be aware of. Now, enough. Your college security is gone, so realize that. It was an illusion, anyway, for you haven't the heart and mind for the good academic life, as you do for our kind of work. Be satisfied you've the makings of a fairly competent criminal with a financially secure future, and you'll feel much better with your lot," and she headed upstairs. "Lock up after you get him to leave, Georgie, love."

Georgie didn't like the prospect of that. Stepping back and smiling amiably, he said "Come on, son, go home peaceably. We don't aim for no rough stuff."

"Why not?" David said, stumbling forward drunkenly. "Get rough. Throw me out, you skinny wreck. I'm as crafty as the two of you now and surely as mean." He slapped him—not a hard slap, as he felt a little sorry for the sickly guy—but Georgie's reaction to it was as if he'd received a powerful blow to the face. "See what you created?" David said. "A monster of Frankenstein's, rather than the doctor himself." He slapped him again, this time so hard that Georgie fell back for real and nearly toppled over. "See what you made me do, Georgie boy? I was just a mild-mannered relatively honest thief when you first met me—but small-time, barely out of my diapers. Now I'm some tough goon full of rage and violence, perhaps even a possible killer." It was obvious Georgie sensed something bad was coming. He stepped back but was too slow and David's foot caught him in the groin. He fell to the floor, clutching himself, and David pounced on him, howling like a wild man and tearing at Georgie's thin hair. Then he turned him over on his back and began slapping his face with both hands so fast that they became one whirring motion in the air.

Sylvia, running and screaming hysterically all the way from her bedroom upstairs, leaped on David's back and tried to pry him off Georgie. "Let go of him, you big boob. Let go or you'll kill him," and she scratched and punched David from behind till he rolled over in a semifaint and lay face up on the floor, peering at their crystal chandelier, when she slammed a heavy ashtray on his head.

He remained on the floor, pretending to be unconscious. Through a slight parting of his eyelids, he saw Georgie sit up and take a Scotch on rocks from her as he whispered if she was going to call the police as she had said.

"Not the police, but the unemployment office you can bet on it. You want him to get away with what he did to us?"

Georgie shook his head and drank.

"And if he is so dumb as to blab on us," she said, wiping his face with a towel and running her hand through his hair, "we'll say 'Sure, we know that horrible young man. Met him at the state office building myself and tried to mend his ways and lead him back to the Lord's path. Then we saw the Devil was hopelessly inside him, laughing at us, besides Mr. Knopps' being one incorrigible pathological liar himself.'"

"But who we going to have work for us?" Georgie said.

"Even if Abe coughs up, we won't have enough money for long, and I'm in no condition now to find a job."

"A woman. Women are more dependable and gullible, carry out orders better and take more guff. And there's a lot less chance they're potential maniacs and killers, as so many of these overpressured students seem to be."

"Make her a blonde," Georgie said. "They're always prettier and get away with more, and they're weaker in spirit, I read someplace."

"And this one I'll find at the city art museum. We want a cultured one. I'll put on my old lady's costume, Grandma Moses mask and go up to some starry-eyed single girl and make small talk about beautiful paintings and such. Then I'll bring up somehow all the antique jewelry I have, that being the rage among girl intellectuals and artistes these days, and say how I don't need it, my being old and not so attractive anymore, and it would be a sin to sell it, since it was actually given to me and I don't like profiting from anything I got for free. And once she comes to the house, I'll give her the jewelry, you'll take a nice photo of us, just to prove she was here, and then I'll contact her and say that unless she does us a small favor, I'm calling the police to report she stole the jewelry from me. I'm sure a beautiful young woman will be able to do a job for us that five Davids couldn't carry out."

"Ten Davids," Georgie said. "Twenty Davids, even. Now you're using your brains, sweet. Now we're really going to hustle us a pile of cash." He told her to pour herself a Scotch and then raised his glass for a toast. "To beautiful young women," he said.

"To beautiful young women," she answered, "and no more brilliant young men," and they clinked glasses, gulped down their drinks and, laughing and giggling excitedly, poured themselves another.

David stood up, feeling the bump on his head, where she'd hit him with the ashtray, and with his handkerchief, wiped the back of his neck, which she'd opened up with her two-inch fingernails. The Peartrees kept on drinking and laughing, giving no indication they knew he was still in the room. He grabbed the bottle of Scotch away from Sylvia, guzzled straight from it, and yelled "Bastards, hypocrites, swindlers, animals. You'll never get away with your new scheme—not in a dozen years," but Sylvia only cupped her free hand to her ear, asked Georgie if he recognized the kind of bird that was cooing from the tree outside the loggia window, and pulled out an unopened bottle from the case of Scotch underneath the couch and poured them each another.

David left the house with the Scotch under his arm and drove away. He didn't know where he was going, except to first pick up some documents and papers and a few books and clothes at home. He was free of them, though—that he could tell and that was the important thing. The loss of his job and their seven hundred dollars, his possible imprisonment and dreamlike academic future, didn't mean much to him anymore. His security was an illusion as Sylvia had said. Though maybe some university in Paris or London would take him in with a criminal record or even if he was still wanted by the police in his own country. They do weird things in Europe, like give their top literary prizes to known murderers and bank robbers, so he didn't know. So, good, that was where he was going, if he could somehow find the means to get there and stay alive till he does.

NIGHT.

Night. Blooming night. Bleeding night. Here it is. On him again. Dusk to dark. He has to do something quick. Pulls down the shades. Even with his lights. In his room. In every room and every place in his rooms. Under the covers. Inside the closed closets. Behind his book. Can't escape it. It's still out there. Where? Turn around. Who? He. What? Night. Don't you see? Everywhere night. Damn you, night. Another damn night. Dark. Stars. Moon. Moons. Galaxy and clouds. Meteorites. All that. Can't stand that. Enough.

He goes upstairs. Climbs flight after flight. First he left his apartment. He reaches the roof. Door locked. Damn door to the roof locked. Padlocked. Hates that kind of lock. That lock's not legal by city law. Read that some place. Could turn this walkup into a firetrap. Landlord, you've done something illegal. Lots. But this? Why this lock at this time and place? He walks down flight after flight of stairs.

He goes outside. First he passed his apartment. It's a city street. So a city block. Row of attached brownstones on both sides of the block. Avenue up the block and avenue down. He's lived on this sidestreet for years. A typical city sidestreet. Typical for this city, he means. Twenty-five to thirty five-story buildings to a side. A ten- to twenty-story apartment house at all four ends. Parked cars. No parking spaces. Manholes and streetlamps. One to two people walking on the sidewalk on each side. He goes into the next building's vestibule. Door to the building's interior is locked. He rings all the tenants' bells on the mailbox. One person says "Ruth?"

"Yes," he says.

"That's not Ruth. Go away."

Click. She's gone.

Another answers back on the intercom "Who's there?"

"Delivery."

"Delivery, hell. I'm not expecting anything."

"I mean special delivery. Mail."

"My eye. I'm calling the police."

"Do."

"I will." Click.

He goes into the next building's vestibule. That door to the interior's also locked. He rings several tenants' bells. One person ticks back without asking who's there.

He walks up flight after flight of stairs. Five to be exact. Five's a lot. He reaches the roof. No padlock. Good landlord. Just a hook. He unhooks. Landlord who obeys city laws. He bets the tenants here even get hot water and heat on wintry days. And a fuse box that can be found and windows that don't fall out as one of his did this year. For three days he waited for the windowman to come. The landlord said he'd called for one. When the windowman didn't come, he put in the window himself. Windy three days. Learned something though. How to put in a window. He asked the hardware store man how. The man didn't know but gave him the phone number of a windowman. The windowman said measure your window frame, get glass cut quarter-inch shorter than what you measured on all four sides, get glazier points and a cold or brick chisel, and you got it made. A paint scraper will do to push in the points, the windowman said. The windowman was right. It worked. A window. That didn't rattle or fall out. But now he's on the roof. Night. No stars or moon. City. Lights of this city. Other apartments, People cleaning, cooking, talking, watching television, playing, making love. Night not so dark because of the city. But what did he come up here for? Answer that. Who? He. Had a purpose. What? To destroy night. To forget night. No. He doesn't know. Yes he does. He came up. Why? To look at night. No. Came up. He came up. To what? To somehow efface night. Erase night. Which? Both. But how? He had a theory. Not a theory. A solution. He had something. Now nothing. Night again. That's it. He had a theory of a solution he would try out up here tonight.

He'd yell. That's what he was going to do. Yell. Just yell. Yell away night. So he yells.

"Night. Damn stinking night. Smelly night. Here again, night. For what? That's what I'm asking. Why? Why you damn night? Damn starless night. Damn darkness. Damn whatever you are and look like. For what? I'm asking. Me. My name. My history. My present. Everything. Why? Why night? Why day? No. Just night. Day I can take. But night. Why do you come and always come and never stop coming and stay for as long as you stay? Answer me that. I want an answer. Why do you come and come and so often? Every day around here, which is often. Too often. Damn often. Night. Damn you, night. I detest you, night. Can't stand you, night. You depress me. I'm depressed by you. Night's depressing. You are. I get. And sick by you. Your darkness, Your length and stars and starlessness. Your moons and no moons and meteorites. This nothing to do almost but but sleep and read at night. Night. Why night? I used to love you so, night. If not love than tolerate you, night. But now? Not now, night. You miserable night. Why these miserable nights? Why this night? These nights. Nights. Night? Damn you, do something, night. I can't stand another night of you always being around me, night. Of your always sure to be there night after night. Of another sultry night. Any kind of night. So do something, go somewhere, I'm ordering you to, night, night, night."

But no use. It's still there. Moon even comes up. He goes downstairs. First he puts the door hook back in its eye. Then he goes downstairs. Flight after flight.

BOOK

2

What Is All This?
BOOK TWO

NOTHING

NEW

.

Now is the time for all good men to Now is the time for all good men
One day she decided she had She'd had enough of the desert and
him and packed to leave. Suddenly, a man jumped out of a fifth floor
window I was walking under. His folks came to dinner. I was rowing
by myself across the ocean when I saw He called his brother. "Jim,"
he said, "there's something very important I have to tell you." She
took her dog out for a walk and saw the same man she'd seen the last
few times walking his dog. A boy was standing on a balcony waving
down at me when the balustrade broke. I was holding my father's hand
through the raised bed rail when he made that noise in his chest and
seemed to expire. They were getting bored with each other. They both
knew that. We both agreed we were getting bored with each other. We
spoke about it. Talked. One day. Yesterday. We talked yesterday about
how we were getting bored with each other. We were sitting in the
kitchen drinking coffee. It was morning. Soon after we woke up. This
morning, they'd got out of bed and washed up and dressed and he
made the bed and tidied up the room while she made them breakfast,
and now they were sitting at the kitchen table drinking coffee when
they both agreed they were getting bored with each other. All right,
enough of getting into it. Now let me get on with it.

"The truth now, Lou, and only the truth, so help you God," I said,
"what do you think of our living arrangement so far?"

"I was wondering when you'd speak," she said. "Not specifically
about that. But it's been at least five minutes since we said a word to
each other."

"You haven't said anything in that time yourself."

"That's what I said. *We*. But I'm usually the one to start the conversation. If it wasn't for me we'd almost never speak."

"Anyway, you're exaggerating. It can't be five minutes since we last spoke."

"We haven't said a word since I poured our coffee, right?"

"I guess so," I said.

"And your coffee was nearly boiling hot when I poured it, right?"

"Not 'nearly boiling hot.' The water boiled and you poured it into the pot and after it dripped through you poured the coffee into our mugs. That would hardly make the coffee nearly boiling hot. I'd say it was quite hot. Barely sipping hot. But surely not nearly boiling hot."

"All right, it was barely sipping hot. Both of us sipped it with difficulty right after I poured it into our mugs, or you did; I just watched you and saw by your expression it was too hot. But since that time you told me the coffee was too hot to drink, we didn't say a word till we were able to drink it normally, and both our coffees are black."

"True. So what's your point?" I said.

"I can't believe you don't know it by now."

"That it would have had to take at least five minutes for our coffee to get from the barely sipping to easily drinking state?"

"I'm no heat or time scientist, but from my experience with coffee I'm sure it takes at least that long to get to that drinkable temperature it reached when we started talking again."

"I agree."

"So what I'm saying, of course, is that for five minutes we didn't say a word. And we sat next to each other all that time, not eating or reading but just glancing at each other or around the room and occasionally barely sipping the coffee."

"You'll probably next say it's because we're bored with each other. Have nothing or very little to say to each other. But it could also be because the coffee's much better than usual today, not that it isn't very good every time you make it."

"Don't try and get off the subject with flattery. Especially about my no-better-than-average coffee."

"It's always better than average. And I'm saying what I feel. Your coffee today was damn good. I don't know if it was a new blend or different grind or what previously untried thing you did with it. I know it wasn't a new pot. So maybe we were just using those silent five minutes thinking about this great coffee."

"Were you?" she said.

"A little. For about fifteen seconds. But we might've been musing about other things. Our different work. Your daughter. What we dreamed last night. And we didn't get much sleep and we're both usually pretty listless the first half hour after waking up, so we probably didn't have the energy to speak."

"We've always spoken—I'm saying, 'just about always'—more than we do now in the morning no matter how tired we've been. Tomorrow we might even speak less than we did today. There'll be six-minute silences soon, then seven, no matter what the coffee's like in temperature and quality or how long we've been up or slept."

"If the coffee's really bad tomorrow, I might have something to say about it."

"You don't like my coffee," she said, "you make it."

"That's not what I meant."

"Anyway, after you've said whatever it is about the coffee tomorrow morning, you, and probably me too, won't have much more to say to the other. In other words, each day we've that much less to say, it seems, so why do we bother staying together when we're obviously bored with each other?"

"You're bored with me?"

"Please, you're not bored with me?"

"Answer me first. I asked it first."

"That doesn't necessarily mean I have to answer you first."

"Just answer it first, then."

"Only if you then answer me back honestly,'"

"I promise," I said.

"Yes, I'm bored with you. Now, are you bored with me?"

"Yes, I'm bored with you, or with myself..."

"No hedging. Be honest. You promised. You're bored silly with me, period."

"No, I'm bored with myself, comma, and because I am, I'm also bored with everything and everyone else. This is someone else's philosophical statement or Indian- or Chinese-religious belief, which I always felt was much too simplistic for me before, but feel it applies to me now."

"No matter whose statement it is or what land it comes from, we're bored with each other and have to separate."

"I felt you were getting to that."

"If you did, then you should have said so or asked me to confirm it, so we could have avoided all this getting-around business to what we finally got to now."

"If I had, then we really wouldn't have said much to each other. For it wouldn't have seemed right for us, after living this long together, to just wake up, wash up and so on and sit down for breakfast and over coffee say right off that we're bored silly with each other and must separate."

"Whether it does or doesn't, we are and so know now what we have to do."

"We've been bored with each other before."

"Never like this," she said. "Admit it. We've absolutely nothing to say to each other anymore."

"This conversation hasn't been that boring."

"That's because all we've left to talk about is our boredom, and we can't talk about that subject for very long without it becoming boring and then very boring and then the most boring subject of all. If we don't resolve the problem now, then all we'll have to talk about the next time we speak at length, for I'm disregarding the 'Answer the door, please, Louise' and 'Don't forget to get a package of cream cheese,' is how boring we are to each other. And since we already spoke about it before, that conversation will have to be less interesting than it is now. And the third time we speak about it will be even less interesting than the previous time, and so on, until we won't be able to speak about it, it'll be so boring, and then we *will* have nothing to say to each other but 'Answer the door, please, and don't forget the cream cheese, Louise.' It'll just be silence between us. Eight minutes. Ten. Broken, perhaps, only by directions, orders and simple requests. Maybe we won't even be able to say these because our boredom and presence together is disturbing us so. Half hour to an hour of just no conversation at all while we're having coffee together at this table. Could you stand that? I couldn't."

"I'd rather wait till it happens before saying how much I couldn't stand it. I might like it for a while, for all I know."

"What about what's already happened? The five minutes of no talk. You liked that?"

"It wasn't bad. I stood it. I thought about things other than us. Something in my childhood, for instance."

"I'm not interested," she said.

"It's similar to now. When I was five or six. I can't know how old I was. Seven, even, or nine, though I doubt I could've been older than that. Sitting at the kitchen table with a glass of milk and my mother saying, while sipping a cup of coffee... I know coffee was part of it, as steam was coming out of her cup, and she never drank anything else hot like that, not even cocoa or tea, that I couldn't leave the table or say another word, just as she wasn't going to say another word to me, till I finished my milk."

"I'll ask. Did you?"

"She eventually gave up, let me leave without finishing it. It must have become too boring for her, once she drank her coffee, sitting there without either of us saying a word."

"Well, I won't, and I am not your mother."

"I know. You're my girlfriend, or sweetie, or once was."

"Which could be another thing, Herb."

"That can come back. But before it does, I feel the conversation should come back. And with this conversation, our conversation is coming back."

"I already told you. This conversation is self-destructive in that it destroys itself by our having it. And now that we've had it—and I have had it, Herb, I have—this conversation is destroyed. Make it easy for us both. Agree to separate, which means, since I live here with my things and child and you only with your things, to leave the apartment agreeably. Find someone or somewhere to live with or at, or do what you want once you leave here, like travel, but don't try to have anything more to do with me once you leave, as I won't with you."

"I could and would if only I didn't enjoy these little conversations, which only you of the two of us think are finished and from this point on or thereabouts can only get more boring and self-destructive. But let me think about it. My first inclination is to say you're probably right."

"Maybe what I say now will help you make the decision. If you don't leave, I will. It'll be more difficult for me, just as it'll be difficult to stay without your share of the rent. But what will be more difficult than either of those is staying here if you plan to stay, even if you pay all the rent."

"I think I plan to stay with you and pay all the rent, and not because I want to be difficult."

"Then Rae Ann and I will have to leave."

"Then wherever you go I'll try to go too and pay all the rent, even though I know for a while I'll be making myself difficult."

"But why submit yourself to what you have to admit, this sophistic argument aside, will be almost total and then total boredom between us?"

"Because I still feel, no matter how boring you say our conversations will get, that if we continue to stay together our conversations will become interesting and soon we'll have a close relationship again."

"It'll become horrible. You'll make me mad. I'll yell at and curse you. I'll plead with you to stop bothering me. I'll say it's bad for me, you and my child. I'll call you a child. I'll call you worse. I'll have you locked up if you persist. People will call you asinine and mean, childish and insane. Particularly, your family. They and your friends will say you're thoroughly wasting your time in trying to live with me. Face it, Herb, we were once close but now aren't. There's nothing left between us. Or only the least thing left, which is like a residue of what once was. Or more like a residual, which like insecticide residuals are more effective against insects than sprays are. This analogy might not be exact from A to Z, but you'll get what I mean, and of course I'm not saying you're an insect. But once the residual is applied, it stays around. Sprays go away and are really only effective when sprayed on the insects directly. But, if you're an insect, just try to casually walk over the residual or even leap over it in the kitchen. It gets on your feet—I'm assuming the insect's not wearing shoes—because it's been applied in too wide a space for just about any insect to stride over or leap across. And after it licks some of the poisonous residual off, it dies. So you can't avoid it. And you more than anyone I know like to go into the kitchen, at least thirty times a day. The residual covers every entrance to the kitchen, surrounds every opening and hole. Because the insect, in its own way, knows after a while it can't go into the kitchen without dying, it must separate from that room. Separate from me, Herb. I am that kitchen. Find another kitchen to get food from. Agree to leaving alone or staying here alone or whatever you want to do so long as it doesn't include being with me, because obviously the kitchen can't separate from the rest of the apartment to get rid of the insects. No matter what, I'm not saying another word to you till you agree to one of those types of separation I mentioned."

"I think I can agree to one of them. Let me think about it."

I thought about it. Briefly. About other things. Mostly. We continued to sit at the table. She reheated what coffee was left in the pot and poured us each a half mugful. Then I thought about something my sister and I used to do as kids. If we both happened to say the same word or words at the same time, we'd immediately hook our right pinky fingers together and one of us would say "What comes out of an old lady's pocketbook?" and the other would say "Money." And the first would say "What color is it?" and the other would say "Green." And the first would say "What comes out of a chimney?" and the other would say "Smoke." "What color is it?" "Gray." Then the first would say "Make a wish and do not speak till someone speaks to you." And we'd each make a wish and neither of us would speak till someone spoke to one of us. Then the one spoken to would ask the other one something so that one would be free to speak. I said to Louise "I was just thinking of something Caroline and I used to do as kids."

She didn't say anything.

"It relates to what you said just before, just as what you said related to what my mother said when she told me she wouldn't speak to me again at the table, nor would I be allowed to say anything or leave the table, till I finished my milk. You did get the idea about not speaking to me from that, didn't you?"

Drank her coffee.

"The coffee's not as good reheated as when served fresh."

Didn't speak.

"Of course, that goes without saying, doesn't it?"

Put down her cup.

"Anyone who drinks coffee knows it's better when just made than when just reheated, or really when reheated anytime after it's been made."

Silence. Looked away from me.

"That is, when they're both served at a reasonable temperature. When they're both served very hot or, for me, iced—not that I'd then see the reason for reheating it first—they're both undrinkable, right?"

Looked at me. No expression.

"All of this said, of course, after I already said that it goes without saying that reheated coffee isn't as good as fresh."

Stood up.

"I was also thinking before about the first time we met. Do you remember where and when that was?"

Got a valise out of the coat closet and went into our bedroom. I followed her.

"Forget the when, then; just where?"

Began packing.

"It was in a movie house. The Embassy. Before the picture began, I sat down next to you, about halfway up the middle aisle, three or four seats in. About ten minutes into the movie, I had to go to the men's room. I asked if you could save my seat for me, and do you remember what you said?"

Silence. More clothes. Went into the bathroom and came back with some of her toiletry to put in the valise.

"You said nothing, Louise. You put your finger over your lips, just as my sister and I used to do right after we'd said the same word or words at the exact same time, and went shhh to me. Do you remember that? Do you remember what I said to you after you did that?"

Closed the valise but couldn't snap it shut. Opened it, pushed the obstructing sweater sleeve further in, and snapped it shut.

"I said 'How can I ask you to save my seat without asking you to save my seat?' Do you remember what your response was?"

Went into Rae Ann's room. I followed her.

"Face a bit strained with anger, you went shhh to me again, which I've already said isn't saying anything—it's just making a sound. To save my seat, though I didn't think this would work—it was really a last resort—I put my book on it, and when I got back I was relieved to see no one had taken my place. Do you remember when you first said any of what I'd consider real words to me?"

Got a knapsack out of the closet and started packing some of Rae Anne's things.

"Outside the theater. It was a pleasant summer night, do you remember? July 6th, a Tuesday, to be exact. After the movie, I'd got out of our row first, intentionally hung back for a few seconds and then followed you up the aisle. Admiring you, I admit. You probably didn't know I was right behind you. Did you?"

Put her hand on her hip and looked straight at me.

"I stopped you in the lobby, not outside the theater, and said 'Excuse me. I didn't mean to be annoying before, as I think you thought I was. But every seat seemed to be taken and I had to go to the men's room and didn't know how to ask you to save my seat without actually asking you, which I know I've already told you inside the theater, other than for the men's room part and that I thought every seat was taken.' Do you remember that?"

Resumed packing.

"Then do you remember what you said right after I told you that?"

Went into the bathroom and got Rae Ann's toothbrush and hairbrush and a few hair ties and threw these into the knapsack.

"Then did you know my sole reason for stopping you in the lobby was to start some kind of conversation because I was attracted to you?"

Raised her eyebrows as if she'd forgotten something. Shook her head. Tied up the knapsack, put it over her shoulder, went to our bedroom, picked up her valise, snapped her fingers, dropped the valise, got some personal papers out of the top drawer of the dresser and put them into a knapsack pocket, picked up the valise and went to the front door. I followed her.

"All right. You give up. Or maybe you didn't forget. Did you? Do you know what I'm still referring to? You said, after I stopped and spoke to you in the lobby, that you had been too engrossed in the movie to be bothered a single second by me in the theater or to try and save my seat. I said I was sorry. You accepted my apology. We continued to talk in the lobby. Then we went to a cafe nearby for coffee. I was the one who suggested it. Over coffee, I asked you out for dinner the next night. I don't think you wanted to. It wasn't because you had to be with Rae Ann. She was with her father for the summer. I in fact think I even had to work very hard to convince you to come to dinner. But the next night, when I was walking you to your building, we made a date for that Saturday. And then, for the rest of the summer, we saw each other almost every day. And after that summer, we saw each other several times a week, sometimes going on-weekend vacations together, a couple of times with Rae Ann. And the next summer, a month-long camping trip in Canada with that very knapsack. Then we rented this apartment together, and of course, except when either of us had to be out of the city, we saw each other every day. By the way, do you remember what kind of movie it was?"

Pointed to herself.

"Right. That kind. Silent. You can say it. I won't bite you if you do. A revival of the best of the silent films, the movie theater billed the series as. We saw several others in the next month. But that day—that first time we met—no piano accompaniment, as there was supposed to be. Do you remember why?"

Opened the door.

"'The pianist,' the theater manager told the audience before the movie began—"

Left. I got my keys, locked the door and went downstairs. She was sitting on the building's stoop.

"'The pianist,' the theater manager said, 'broke his hand the previous day and they couldn't find a replacement in time and, unfortunately,' he said, 'there are no silent movie piano pieces for solo right hand.' Then he said 'That wasn't nice to say, for the pianist is still in great pain.' Now is that a coincidence? The pianist's hands were silent. The silent movie. The theater was silent during the movie except for sporadic coughs and cracking of candy wrappers and things, and of course me. That you originally said shush to me. That you now say we've nothing left to say to each other. That you refuse to say anything to me now. The coincidence factor ends, though, because the traffic is certainly noisy, as is the garbage-receiving contraption at the back of that sanitation truck, and noises from other places. That window being replaced. The plane, now, overhead. Even this mosquito near my ear and now yours," and I swung at it and missed. "But the other coincidences are something to speak about, aren't they?"

A car with Rae Ann and her father pulled up. I looked at my watch. Right on time: nine, when he brought her back every Monday morning after having her for the weekend. Rae Ann kissed him goodbye and got out of the car with her overnight bag. He waved to Louise, she smiled and waved back, and he drove off. Louise grabbed Rae Ann's hand and they walked down the block, knapsack over her shoulder and valise in her other hand.

I walked after them. "Louise, I was lying before when I said I was thinking about how we first met. I didn't think about it. I was only trying to use that as a guise. I thought that by mentioning it, you'd think wistfully about that night and even get a kick out of it, and agree to staying in the apartment with me."

Hailed a cab and they got in.

I ran up to their cab window and said "Say something, Louise. Then say goodbye to me, Rae Ann."

Louise put her hand over Rae Ann's mouth. Rae Ann was looking at me at that moment but I didn't know if she was going to say anything to me. The cab pulled away. I went back to the apartment, and in the kitchen I ate till I was stuffed. Then I sat in front of Louise's electric typewriter and turned it on. The quick brown fox jumps over the lazy   The quick brown fox jumps over the   The quick brown fox jumps

INTEREST.

They're not interested in me anymore. They say they are. They say it to my face and over the phone. They say "We're still interested in you." They're not. I know.

How do I know? I know by the way they say it. When they say "We're still interested in you," they don't say it enthusiastically. They say it without enthusiasm. That's one way how I can tell.

Another way is that they don't look straight at me when they say they're still interested in me. They look away. Or half at me, half away. That's another way how I can tell.

How do I know these are signs they're not interested in me anymore? Have I asked them directly? I have. I've said "You look half at me, half away from me when you say you're still interested in me." I've said "You don't say you're still interested in me with much enthusiasm. You say it unenthusiastically, is what I mean." They said I was wrong. "Dead wrong," they said. But I still know they're not interested in me anymore.

How do I still know, or rather, why? Because, although they've said over and over again they're still interested in me, they do nothing for me. Have they once in the last few months sent my projects to people who might be able to accept them or do something with then? They haven't. I can say that knowledgeably. Have they once in the last few months spoken about me enthusiastically to people who might be able to accept my projects or do something with them? They haven't. That I can't say knowledgeably, because when I asked them if they'd spoken about my projects to other people who might be able to accept them or do something with them, they said they had. I asked "Who?"

and they said that was a secret. I asked why was it a secret, and they said if they told me why it would no longer be a secret. I said "That's an answer for a child," and they said it was the only answer they were going to give. I said "Why?" and they said "Let's not go any further into it. Let's just not."

So how do I know they haven't sent my projects around to these other people in the last few months? Because I've asked these other people if they'd received any of my projects in the last few months, and they all said no. I then asked if anyone who's supposedly interested in my projects has spoken enthusiastically to them about me in the last few months, and they said they'd rather not say. Then has anyone, I said, spoken to them in any way about me or my projects in the last few months, and they said, again, they'd rather not say. They said that was their business, not mine. Meaning, I should stay out of their business or what they think isn't mine. I knew what they meant. They didn't have to spell it out for me, and I didn't ask them to. Maybe I should have, but I didn't. I didn't because I didn't think it would get me any place with them. I also felt it might make matters worse for me with the people who are supposedly still interested in me, and with the people they speak to. I also felt lucky to have even gotten to speak to these other people—the people in the right places, I'll call them, who might be able to do something with my projects. The truth is, I didn't speak to them. I spoke to the people who say they're still interested in me, but only wrote to the people in the right places, and they were kind enough to write back and answer me several times over a period of a few weeks.

Where does that leave me? I know that the people who profess to be still interested in me, are not. They're definitely not. Maybe not "definitely," but I can say I'm almost positive they're not.

Why am I almost positive they're not still interested in me. Because of the reasons I've already given here. Anyway, nothing has come of their professed interest in me for months. In fact, nothing has ever come from their interest in me or anyone else's interest in me and my projects, except for my being initially encouraged by their saying they were interested, which made me produce even more projects for them to send around.

So what am I going to do? I'm about to give up on them. I'll probably make that decision tonight: whether to give up or stick with them. If I stick with them, I'll probably have to accept their lies that they're still interested in me and are sending my projects to people in the right places, or at least speaking enthusiastically, or even just speaking about me to these people, when I'm almost positive they're not. After all, I've tried everyone else who can send my projects to these people, and I've also tried sending my projects to them myself. I couldn't do anything for myself. The people in the right places I sent my projects to said I should get someone to send the projects in for me, that they don't look at them when they come from the producer of the project himself. And all those people who sent my projects to these people tried hard in the beginning, but their interest soon waned. Now that, I also know to be a fact. Because in the beginning they all sent me proof they had sent my projects around to the right places, and then these proofs stopped coming to me. And each time, after I'd stopped getting these proofs for months, I also asked if they were still interested in me and were still sending my projects around, and they all said they were. But this is the first time I also asked these people in the right places if they'd received any of my projects the last few months, and the answer to that I already gave.

What now then? Maybe I should ask the people who say they're still interested in me why they haven't sent me any proof the last few months that my projects are still being sent around. I could do that. I've asked them just about everything else, and it is a question I don't see how they could get out of answering. Because what could they say? If they say "Yes, we have proof we're still sending your projects around, but forgot to send them to you," I could say "So send them to me now." If they then say they don't have them anymore, I could say "Why not? What happened to them?" If they then say they lost them or they were accidentally destroyed, I could say "Tell me another, because that excuse is the oldest in the books. Besides," I could say, "I spoke to all the people you supposedly sent my projects to, and they all said they haven't seen any of my projects in months." If they say "That's not true, or you misinterpreted what they told you," I could say "There are two ways for you to prove it's not true or I misinterpreted what they told me, and either will do. One, by having these people tell me by phone or letter that they got my projects, or, two, for you to come up with those written proofs and send them to me."

Asking them that question about the proofs is another decision I should make tonight. I don't know if I will. What I mean is, I don't know if I can make the decision by tonight, or even make the other decision about whether to give up or stick with the people who say they're still interested in me. Because that second decision really depends on the answer to my question about the proofs in the first decision, and there still might be something about this situation that I haven't as yet figured out.

BIFF.

This weekend.
What?
I said let's get away this weekend.
What?
I said we'll go away this weekend. For a trip. Just to be away.
What?
You telling me you still can't hear?
Is that what you were saying all the time before?
No. I was saying we should get away this weekend. Someplace.
What?
I said—can you hear me now?
Are you still there, Biff?
I'm sure you can hear me.
I can now, almost, but not before.
You mean, everything I said before?
I don't quite hear you.
I said, all the time before, you couldn't hear what I said?
Is that what you said the last time you said something?
Yes.
Though not all the times before that?
The times before that you have to know I said something about our getting away this weekend.
What?
I'll call you back.
What?

I said I'll call back. This connection's ridiculous. Something's at least ridiculous. And we're sounding ridiculous.

What?

He hangs up, calls back.

Hello?

It's Biff. Can you hear me?

Hello? Is that you, Biff?

Yes.

Biff? Hello? I still can't hear anything. Anyone there?

He hangs up, calls back.

Hello?

It's me again, Jane.

Hello? Who is it? Shout if you have to, but I want to know who's there.

IT'S BIFF.

Hello? I give up. I hope it's not someone staying silent just to upset me. But if it is someone I know and want to speak to—

It's Biff, Biff.

—then call back, okay? Anyway, I'm hanging up.

Good idea.

Biff?

You can hear me?

Suddenly I can.

You're not playing a joke on me?

Why would I do that?

You might not have liked what I was saying. That you and I should go away this weekend.

What?

Oh, come on.

This time I was kidding. But where would we like to go?

Say, a cottage on the ocean.

Why the ocean?

Then a cabin in the woods.

No, I mean it's that I could never see the ocean in the summer.

Bad eyes?

Bad joke. I don't like sitting around getting sunburned. I think it's so unromantic, getting unhealthy. Burnt skin, healing creams. White marks where the bathing suit straps were, bed soaked with sweat from your shiverings.

Then we'll rent a dark dank cave with a single warm bed. Would that satisfy you more?

I hope it's not just a bed you think makes for romance. Anyway, I can't go.

Why not? Before, you sounded as if you could.

Before, I was curious what travel suggestions you'd make. I'm curious about a lot of things with someone I only recently met. Especially that he asks me away for a weekend in a single bed. But as I said, I can't.

The single bed was a joke. But why?

Personal reasons.

Too personal to tell me?

You, yes.

Thank you.

Another thing I'm finding out about you is your infantile sensitivity.

You'd be the first woman to think or say that.

That can't be true.

It isn't. Several have.

Another about you is that you're a bit of a liar, or fibber, but can't keep to your fibs when it might benefit you or please another.

Is that an honest, dishonest or tomato aspect?

Tomato aspect? Tomato aspect. Good God. Another unpleasant aspect of yours is your numerous unfunny jokes.

And one of yours I'm pretty well fed up with is your criticisms of me. And fed up with your tomato aspect as well.

I'm sorry. And I think I better go.

My infantile sensitivity again?

Partly.

You prefer your infantile sensitivity in men to be more adult, right?

I prefer none at all.

An insensitive man, then?

No, I don't. I'm getting mixed up. You're making me mixed up. I really have to go.

This conversation's gotten us nowhere. It's in fact set us back a ways. Because I originally called with a nice attitude to ask if you wanted to go away this weekend.

You did. That's true. And I don't. That's true too. Or rather, I can't.

I already told you why without being explicit. For now that should be enough.

Listen. I'll see you.

Fine, if that's the way you feel.

It seems the way you feel.

You know how I feel? How nice. Maybe this conversation hasn't been a waste of time after all. But call again if you like.

You mean that?

I said it, so I meant it.

I'll see you then, Jane.

Have a good weekend.

You too.

He calls back.

Hello?

You said call back, so I did.

I'm wondering if I meant right away.

Then you didn't mean it—see?

Let's say I did mean it. What's new?

Well, now that you ask, I was thinking if you'd like to spend part of the weekend with me in the city.

Actually, I was planning on going to the beach to develop a slight case of sun poisoning. But now that you asked.

You serious?

No. I really am tied up this weekend, Biff. Honestly ...Biff. What a strange name. That your real one?

Biff Junior's my real name.

Is Biff Senior still with us, I hope?

And Biff Senior the first. You see, I'm the third. But my dad didn't like to be called Junior, so he eliminated his. But when they had me, he liked the name so much that they named me Biff, also. Not Biff Also. Biff Junior.

It would seem if he was so devoted to individuality, he would have wanted you named Biff Also. Or Also Biff. Or Biff Biff. That would be the best one, I think.

I don't. And I don't like talking about my name.

You don't? I forgot who first brought it up. Must have been me. Well, I'm sorry if it was.

Yes. So, anyway, you're busy this weekend.

Tied up in knots, I'm afraid.

I'll come and rescue you.

Touché, but no thanks.

Not to stay; just to cut the ropes.

Touché encore, mon Biff, but I'm sorry. I definitely can't see you this weekend.

Not so much where we have to go out or anything. We could meet for coffee somewhere.

Sorry. I'll explain some other time, but right now I can't.

Someone there with you?

It's not that. Or it might be. Whatever it is, I'm not saying. It's none of your business, that's why.

I think it is.

Think what the heck you want, but I'm not going to ask why, because it isn't and you know it.

I thought you were interested in me, that's why I said it.

I thought I was also, to a certain extent, but when you come on like this?

Like what?

Let's see, where were we? Look, I have visions these conversations are only going to get worse for us. So sometimes it's best to let them drop, wait a week or so, and then call back. Or I'll call back. But right now, whatever there was forming between us, is being grounded.

Are you saying, with me?

You really didn't think I meant you and I?

Yes, I have to admit that.

Then either the connection was bad again or you're just plain stupid. See you, honey.

He hangs up, opens a beer, takes two swigs. calls back. The receiver's picked up but nobody answers.

I don't know who should be sorry, me for hanging up like that or you for calling me stupid.

What I said was that either the connection was bad again or else you're stupid. I didn't call you stupid outright.

To me it still sounds as if you did.

Then the connection was bad again just now or you truly are stupid.

He hangs up, finishes the beer, calls back.

I'm being silly now, maybe even stupid, calling like this. But it must mean something.

Maybe that you like making an ass of yourself on the phone and I either like helping or hearing you make one of yourself. Or maybe you're itching to know something more about me that you didn't and you're finding out because I'm doing nothing to hold it back. Or else you're working for the Secret Service and you're keeping me busy with your calls till they pound my door down and arrest me for something. Or maybe it means I've run out of reasons to explain all your calls and I really don't want to talk to you anymore today, or I don't know what. Why?

Why, what?

You continue to call me. Because you know I won't call you?

It could be I like speaking to you.

You call this speaking to me? You enjoy this? That's so silly. You're silly.

I'm going to hang up on you if you say anything more derogatory than that.

Hang up, then.

Just don't say anything more derogatory than silly. You may call me stupid, ignorant, foolish, dumb ox, hateful, aggravating, insufferable, all the others, but not, and I repeat, not silly or very silly. I don't want to be called silly or very silly.

What would happen if I did? You'd hang up?

I promise.

Then you are very silly.

No, I don't promise, because I feel you're about to call me very silly.

Now that's the first clever thing you said since your first call today.

Then I must sound very stupid to you at times.

Oh, very. At other times, extremely. And a couple of other times, profusely. But sometimes, no. You have said clever and even witty things before, but not since that first call.

Dark dank cave with only a warm bed in it, after you said you didn't like sunlight—that wasn't anything but stupid to you, right?

Wasn't that in the first call? And I didn't say I disliked sunlight. And the remark wasn't clever, no.

Bad eyes?

Bad eyes? Oh, yes. Old, old joke. What about your having a minor physical ailment in your insides to get out of going into the army—no guts.

That's very funny.

Of course it isn't. The reason I said it was to explain when I first heard it. Years ago. When I was a freshman or sophomore in college and the older boys were still fairly successful in being rejected by the army—

Deferred from.

Deferred from for physical reasons they made up or exaggerated. Let's see—another one.

All right. So my bad-eyes joke wasn't funny.

No no, wait a minute. There's one more the boys used to tell. That's right. I've stomach trouble.

You've stomach trouble. I see.

No, you don't see. You're not supposed to say anything, in fact, except maybe an oh-yes, but certainly not an I-see. That could lead to your bad-eyes joke again. But after you do say something to my stomach-trouble line, I say yes, I get sick every time I think of myself in the army.

Not bad.

It's said differently, I didn't tell it right. I never could.

None of us can.

No, some can. But there's one more and then I'll stop.

Please, no more. I don't think I could take it. I've stomach trouble also. I get sick every time someone tells me a bad old joke.

Okay, bit of a joke theft, but you're getting there.

Few years with you and I'll be a real comedian.

It would also probably save you a few thousand dollars in phone bills, but don't let me give you any ideas.

Oh, I couldn't see us communicating any other way but by phone, even if we lived together a couple of years.

Lived together? Say, really now, just put that notion out of your head.

No, listen. The idea is for us to live together for two years but to only communicate by phone. In other words, being the phone addict you obviously think I am, if you wanted me to go out for groceries, let's say, you'd pick up the phone, even if we were only ten feet from each other and this was a one-room apartment we shared, and dial the other phone in the place, and I'd pick it up and you'd tell me what you want at the store, and we'd talk like that. What do you think?

I wouldn't see any reason for it.

Now you're the one with no sense of humor.

I think a sense of humor has to have some sense. In this one, it's just projecting your fantasies a bit, wouldn't you say? Besides trying to intrigue me.

That's legitimate.

Right now, it isn't. Look, to be honest with you there is someone else. I don't want to go into it, but someone, and whatever he thinks of me, someone.

He craps on you, right?

I'm not going to answer that.

Why not? If he doesn't, say so.

I give up. Goodbye.

Don't go.

He calls right back.

Jane?

Right after this call, I'm phoning the phone company to take out my phone.

I don't like being hung up on.

Then don't call me.

Even though I've hung up on you, I think it's an exceedingly wrong thing to do. You could be nice.

The nicest thing I could do for you is convince you never to call again.

I wouldn't have. And this will be my last call. Only you sounded— something in your voice and what you said—a little sad, so I called back.

What bull. And I'm not sad. I can handle my own affairs quite well.

But he does crap on you, right?

Give up, my friend.

Biff. And give up I will. I told you, my last call. But he does, and that's always the case. With me, I mean. Whenever I'm interested in a woman, she's not. She's interested in someone who isn't interested in her, and he probably with someone else who's not interested in him, and the same with someone to her, and so on and so forth and ad infinitum, absurdum, exhaustum and dum de dum.

The dum de dum I like best. But that isn't always the case and not necessarily the case with me now.

Not necessarily but not absolutely not.

Not absolutely not, then. Or not the case absolutely in perpetuity for all time then, not. It just isn't so. And it's still not your business.

I don't believe you, but maybe that's my problem. What I wanted to add though is that it's also reversed for me too. When a woman likes me, I'm usually not interested. Not because she's interested in me, but that the ones who get interested in me I'm not interested in to begin with.

Never?

Almost. With you it's the other way around.

I never said I wasn't interested in you, Biff. Just not right now.

Why not? Let's forget all the others. We'll just go away, or stay here, but develop something, become friends. Talk and have fun and anything you want to do anyplace you want to do it at.

That's very generous of you, but again, I can't right now.

Then when? Because we could just go, that's what I'm saying. I could pick you up in half an hour.

Impossible.

Then an hour.

Impossible till one day I tell you it's not. When, who knows? Most likely never. If you can't accept that, stop calling.

Will you call me if I don't you?

For the time being, no. Things have to be settled first.

Like that guy who craps on you? You like being crapped on?

I don't like the word, expression, meaning or even the implication or symbolism or anything else about it in any tense or form. Don't mention it again, please.

That this fellow craps on you?

Biff?

I'm sorry. That was a mistake. I felt like saying something mean.

You feel like that a lot. That's why you shouldn't bother with me. It can't be healthy for you. And if you like me like you say, then don't bother with me. Find someone else.

There isn't anyone else.

First you have to find her.

I'd love to. You think I like making a fool of myself on the phone? I only do it because I think you're worth it to go through all this crap with you and letting you see what's really inside me.

That's a line.

You joking?

A trick, an act, a masculine stunt. A universal ploy, then, used by men and women alike, said for your own gain. Me, me, me. It never ends. I can't even say goodbye.

He calls back.

Call me once more and I'll pull out my phone. I mean it. Leave me alone.

He calls back.

I thought you were going to pull out your phone.

And you with your last call ten calls ago, what about that? Anyway, I thought it would cost too much having my phone repaired. And what excuse could I give the phone company—some maniac wouldn't stop calling me?

You could have said my calls were obscene.

I could have, but now I don't feel like pulling it out. No strength. Anyway, I could just leave it off the hook. Besides, I'm going out. Bye, Biff.

Will you call me sometime if this thing with this fellow is ever through?

I don't think so. Goodbye.

If you say you'll call sometime if this thing you have is ever over, then I won't call again.

Call all you want. What I've decided on now is a new number. Unlisted. I want to be away from all callers. You, everyone.

Even him?

Even him. Even you. Even who? You're such a cluck. Did I ever say there was anyone else? Even if I did, I didn't reveal much because I said it was too personal. So why do you persist?

I persist–

Oh, you persist because that's the way you are. Because you got it sealed in your head you're interested in me and that we could be great together. Oh, yeah. Because you like my face. My neck's so nice. My eyes so blue. Sky blue blue. My lips are so symmetrical and full, you never met anyone with such lips. So soft, not chapped. How sweet. My sweet tweet lips. Or you like my perfume, though I don't wear perfume or cologne. You adore my legs. Long strong thin legs. Tiny feet. Legs like an athlete, dancer or gymnast. Did I like sports when I was a girl? You're amazed by my waist. What size belt could I possibly wear? Why do I ask? Because I once knew a woman who had a very small waist, but yours seems even smaller than hers. Or you like my hair. You always had a thing for long straight black hair. The way it shines. It can also look blue. Pitch black or rich blue in the night light. And so fine. How many times must you take a shampoo a week? How did it ever get so long? Don't the ends break off at that length? Or you like the way I stand, walk and run. An athlete again. My voice. The way I talk and move. Especially the way I move. And most especially my mind. If there was nothing else about me, you'd be attracted to my mind.

You do have a good mind.

Of course I've a good mind. That's what I'm saying. That you say it. That you want to be with me for all these things. My unpolished fingernails. Because I eat health foods and don't wear lipstick and no makeup and I'm slim and my clothes and I can make jokes and talk lively and I seem sympathetic and no guises and am friendly and everyone seems to like me, and I can't stand it. I can't stand it. Your comments. Now don't call. Do not call. Don't—you hear me?—call. You do I'm gonna get my big brudder to come over your house and knock your block off, ya unnerstand? Now goodbye.

Wait.

He calls right back.

Your dialing finger must be exhausted.

I have a push-button phone.

You would.

You don't approve?

Who am I to disapprove? And for someone who makes as many calls as you, it obviously serves a purpose.

I don't like to dial. And never liked the sound of the rotary part going backwards after my finger went around. I also don't like waiting, even for a half second, for the rotary part to rest after each digit's been dialed before I can dial again, or the frustration, after so much dialing, if the line's busy. Now it's so easy. Just push push seven times for the city or ten for long distance, and I'm there or I'm not.

You've sold me, despite the additional expense.

It's not much more. About as much per month as having an extension.

You have one of those too?

Three.

Three? How big's your apartment?

Two rooms, and kitchen and bath, all of which have a phone.

Why a phone in the bathroom? No particular sexual or scatological hangup, I hope.

The bathroom's separated from the rest of my place by a long hallway, so I have one there in case I get or want to make a call.

Wall or standup?

Both. It can be attached to a wall hook or set down on a flat surface. Again, push push, peep peep, and my phone call's made.

Those do seem like the appropriate sounds for a bathroom. How does the one in the kitchen go, chop chop, squirt squirt?

Push push, peep peep. They're all the same.

Are all the colors the same?

You're not really interested.

But I am. Who wouldn't be? A man who has four phones in one apartment?

But all the same number.

I know. Three extensions and the original. Are you more attached to the original phone than the others because it was your first?

I got them all at once. I had four in my last apartment also. I always felt I needed them. I don't like running from one room to the other and have the caller wait for me for five or six rings.

But it's natural to wait for someone to answer.

With me, people calling avoid that wait.

What they don't avoid is your calling.

You've avoided calling.

I said your calling. But it's getting late.

You've some place to go?

Yes, and I have to get dressed. Look. Now that we're speaking so congenially, would it be too much to ask you to understand that I'm short of time and you're tying up the line and that I'm expecting a call?

From that man?

The one who occasionally craps on me, yes, him. You must feel content now.

I was wondering why you didn't leave your phone off the hook before. Most of the times I called, you probably thought was him.

Right. All the time, right. In everything you say, right. Seriously, though, we've had our nice little chats. Now free me for the time being?

You're free forever.

Thank you. I hope you mean it too.

What can I say to convince you?

Not what you say but what you do. Don't call back?

Got ya.

Okay. You said it. Now remember. Bye.

He calls back.

I forgot to say goodbye.

Goodbye, Biff.

Goodbye.

He calls back.

You disappoint me, Biff. I thought you were being serious.

I'm never serious. I should have warned you. And I've just pulled a great grand joke on you that maybe backfired a little. Because if you believed what I said about anything before... My getting upset. My acting silly and sullen or weird and especially that I was serious in this sequence of calls, then you don't know me at all. You've been taken in, though I miscalculated how deeply you'd believe it. And now I want you to have a wonderful weekend with whomever you want to be with, and that's all.

Thanks. You too.

Me too, what?

A good weekend. Be happy and well. Long life and... goodbye.

Goodbye.

He calls back. The line's busy.

He has another beer and then calls back... The line's busy.

He calls three hours later. The line's busy. He calls an hour after that.

Yes?

It's Biff, Jane.

He calls back.

Now listen, you big dope. Will you stop annoying Jane?

Who is this?

Whoever I am, I'm not a big dope. Leave her alone or I'm putting the cops on you.

Not yourself?

Stop being a schmuck. Can I level with you? You're tormenting the hell out of her. Who could stand someone phoning every minute. And look at the time. It's past two. Grow up. You're interested, she's not, then don't bother. Simple as that. I know what you're feeling. Who hasn't been through it, but that's the way it goes.

Isn't that true? Whenever you really care for a woman, she doesn't for you.

Not always. This time it didn't work out for you. So forget it.

Do you care for her?

I care, I care.

You don't crap on her?

He says do I crap on you? —What man doesn't crap on a woman and she on him in return or before the fact? What's important is if in general the relationship works. That.

Does it with you and Jane?

What's it to you? We get along. We like each other. So now leave her alone. Be a good guy.

I love her.

You hardly know her.

She told you that?

I know. Accept that I know. And if she wanted to see you, she would. She's an exceptionally honest, straightforward person. If you love her as you say, that's good, but it should also mean you wouldn't want to hurt her as you're doing. It isn't nice. Be nice. Maybe this sounds overrighteous. And giving advice isn't my line. But on something like this, you've got to take it like it comes.

What is your line, crapping on girls?

Oh, brother. Your wasting everyone's time. Hers, yours, and what's maybe not as important, mine.

Sure, sure.

Okay. I don't know why I said that. Maybe thinking humility would get you to stop. Worst of all, you're wasting my time. I'm sleepy, I worked hard today, and I don't want to hear this damn phone ringing all night.

Ah, the truth comes out.

Truth, yes, shallowness, no. What can I possibly say to convince you? Jane must have said it all. She'd nodding her head. She's making like she's cutting her throat. Maybe my throat. Oh, the phone's. She wants me to hang up. Who could blame her. And as entranced as I am with our talk here, what do you say we call it quits for the night? It's very late.

You're starting to sound like Jane now.

So, Jane and I are pretty close. But it does seem dumb to let everyone on the phone know you're a misfit. Even dangerous. People get put away for less. But I don't think you actually are. You're just very distressed over being rejected.

Deferred.

Not deferred; rejected. She doesn't want you no way. You've struck out. Zero. What more can she say—get lost?

Let her say it.

Listen: get lost. Take a walk. Scram. Vamoose. But leave her alone. For your own sake, you have to.

Take care of your own problems.

I said leave her alone, you dumb creep, is that clear? Now I tried to be nice before, but if I have to break your dumb neck to get you to stop, I will. I mean that.

You convinced me.

And I'm not saying this for selfish reasons. You've got to have some consideration for others and yourself too.

No, you're right.

Peace, then, brother.

Peace.

He calls back.

Do you mind, brother? We're screwing.

He calls back. The line's busy. The line's busy ten minutes later. He goes to bed, calls her.

No one can be as crazy as you.

Wait, Jane. I'm sleepy myself. Drunk, besides. No, that was said for affect. What I meant—

Go to sleep, Biff.

What I mean is now that I know you're in no way interested—

I can't pretend. I can't say yes, you're right. Everything would sound too absurd to say. I can't even hang up on you again. That would also seem absurd. You have to just hang up on yourself and fall asleep and never call again, because there's nothing else I can say or do for you.

Jane? Jane? You still there? Don't answer, then, but you're still there, somewhere by the phone. Well, I love you, Jane. Beery and sleepy as I am, I hope you know that. I never told you that on or off the phone. I did your friend. I know it's a little late to tell. Late o'clock and late for us and so on. But now you know. I'm also sorry for all my disturbances today, and to you too whatever that fellow's name is. The man you're with or I hope were. And whatever he said to me about me was right. And he didn't seem to be crapping on you, as much as

I know you don't like the word. He seemed all right. He implied I should act more like a grown man, and of course he's right. He told me I was tormenting you. I wish he wasn't right on that, but how could I believe he's wrong. I'm sorry, Jane. You listening? Well, listen, then— I'm very sorry. This whole day's been awful. It started off horrible with something I didn't even tell you. And then those calls. How do I ever get out of them or forget all this? I've never done anything like it. They just built up. If you had said yes for the weekend, they wouldn't have happened. I would have come over, tonight, or last night, because it's now morning, with the car. Driven us to where we would have gone. Who knows if from there we might not have gone on for years or for life, even, and I never would have done anything remotely like those calls. But it snowballed, as they say. Snowballs in summer. It can happen anywhere, anytime. Jane? Is the receiver on your bed? Are you on your bed? Alone, or both of you? Are both of you listening to me now? Well, I love you, Jane, I do. And you, whatever your name is, I don't love you, but if you're there—well, you were very kind. He was, Jane. Smart. Thoughtful. He blew up at me because I was asking for it. I'm sorry. I hope you're both happy and well, if both of you are there. And have fun together, if he's still there. Though I wish I was in your place. His place with you, Jane, if he's there or not. But that's all right. I mean that. Jane? I can't talk like this. It sounds crazy, talking to myself. It does. But I have to say something. You knew I wouldn't like it. You're a real shrewdy. And I know this is my last call to you. Even if you hung up or said call me again, it would be my last call. Listen to me, Jane. I've only a few more things to say and then I'll be gone. You probably thought there's nothing left for me to say, but you'd be wrong if you thought that. There is. You see, I felt forced into making those calls. Maybe some spirit got hold of me inside, but it wasn't really me. That's nonsense, of course, spirits. I mean...please say you're there and listening, Jane. Then just say you're there or listening. I've never in my life talked to myself like this. It's a new feeling and I don't like it. New for me. I mean new in that I've never in my life called anyone so many times in a row. I think I already said that tonight, or something like it, but it's true. And surely it wasn't important what I had to say. Everything. We both know that. Nothing was. But I felt compelled. That's it. That's what I meant by my being forced to make these calls. Compelled, now and all the other times with you, but less so now. And I know it wasn't in any way a joke. I realize it was the worst thing I could do to you. And it won't ever happen again. I'm saying I'll never be like this again, Jane. I can't. I learned. I promise. It was so totally uncharacteristic of me. I mean it. Totally. Jane? You there? Well, speak.

LEAVES.

I'm sorry but I'm not going to leave. Even if you slipped another message under my door and this one begging me to go, I won't leave. You could send a half-dozen messages if you want, two dozen if you like, and all typed on the finest stationery or written in the most elegant hand, but I still won't leave. You could have anyone or any number of people you know or I'm supposed to know slip under my door any number of messages that you or they as a group dictated and someone else wrote, but these aren't going to get me to leave. You or anyone else could phone me a hundred times in succession and all night long and all day tomorrow and the day and week and even the next week and month after that if you think it'll do any good, but it won't get me to leave. You could send a satchelful of telegrams of any kind including ship to shore and anniversary and get-well singing grams, but I still won't leave. I'm telling you, I will not leave. I won't even stick my head or foot past the door to give the impression I'm about to leave. I won't even make a single move to open the door, even so much as to get closer than I already am to the door, for as I said before, why should I give you even the slightest hope I'm leaving or even thinking of leaving, as there isn't anything I can see that'll change my mind to get me to leave.

Of course you could try coaxing me to leave by pleading through the door. You could say "Would you do me this very one favor and leave?" Or "Would you please, without any more fuss, get your things together and leave?" Or "Listen, I've been reasonable and fair up till now, haven't I, so what do you say you leave?" Or "Haven't we had enough of this trying to wheedle and coddle you, so will you please just leave? Then will you just plain leave? Then will you just leave then, spelled l-e-a-v-e, and please?"

But no matter how emotional and assertive you get through the door, I'm not going to leave. Even if you said in a much angrier voice "All right, that's more than enough now, are you going to leave?" I wouldn't leave. Or "Okay, do you hear what I say?—I want you to leave." Or "Fun's fun, but I've taken all I'm going to take from you, so leave. Now I'm more than asking you to leave. I'm more than even telling you to leave. I'm saying you have to leave. Once and for all now—you've got to leave. Now I don't want to say this again—leave. This is the last time I'm telling you—leave. Did you hear me, I'm ordering you to leave. I said, I order you to leave. Now I want you to get out of there or I'll really do something more than just order you to leave. Now get yourself straight the hell out of there, as you're forcing me beyond the little self-control I've left to do something more than just order you to leave."

But nothing you say or how or where you say it will force me to leave. Even if you screamed those threats from the street up to my window, I wouldn't leave. I wouldn't leave even if you got several people to yell from the street and outside my door that the only right thing for me to do is leave. That I'm spiting nobody but myself if I don't leave. That I'm not doing it by the book or following any of the traditional or unspoken rules. That whatever little game I'm playing is up. That I should know by now that no place is anybody's for keeps. That when you have to leave you have to leave and that's all there is to it. But no matter how many of you yell from the street or through my door that I'm driving the lot of you beyond whatever self-control you have left to do something more than just order me to leave, I still won't leave.

So go on and give the most rational arguments and doomful warnings imaginable, but you have to know by now they won't make me leave. I've yakked about it through the door to you, yowled so loudly the whole block must have heard, sent my own telegrams and other dispatches and made calls why it's impossible for me to leave. But you never seem to understand why I can't leave. Or if you do understand, then you still can't, or refuse to believe if you can, that nothing you or anyone else can say or do will ever get me to leave.

Of course you could do more than just yell from the street and behind my door that I'm forcing you to do something more than just order me to leave. You could tap on my door and ask to be let in so you can try and reason with me why it's in my own interest to leave. Or even rap on my door and demand I let you in so you can reason and then insist, or just insist without giving any reasons, that I leave. Or you could bang on my door with another person, both of you asking and then demanding, or just demanding I leave. Or bang on the door while trying to force it open, so you could get in even if I tell you I don't want you in, or barge in without first asking if I'll let you in, and then demand I leave. Or bang on the door while someone else is kicking the door and two other persons are trying to pick the lock or force the door open and several other people are shouting behind the door and from the street and the roofs and windows of the buildings across the street that I leave. But the door's quite strong and secure with several bolts, latches and locks, so no amount of picking, kicking and shoving's going to force it open.

You could, of course, then pound on the walls of the two adjoining vacant apartments, while other people are banging and kicking my door and trying to force it open and shouting from all the other places I mentioned and throwing pebbles and bags of garbage at my window to get me to leave. Or you could climb up or down the building's fire escape and yell from the landing outside my window that I leave. Or throw a rock through the window and shout through the broken pane while other people are shouting from the street and roofs and other windows and fire escapes and kicking and pounding on the adjoining walls and my ceiling and floor from the vacant apartments right above and below mine that I get straight the hell out of here. But listen to me. Even if you get all those people to do all that or they do it voluntarily and you also stick your hands past the broken panes and rattle the locked window gate while screaming bloody murder at me, I'm still not going to leave.

Of course your eviction methods might get more vicious and tactical than that. You might try driving me out with smoke- or stink-bombs or even some kind of narcotizing or tear gas. But I'm still quite the limber fellow, I want you to know, and prepared myself with a thick pair of fireplace gloves, so anything you toss in goes right back out the window at you. Or you might be able to bust open the door by snapping the latches and locks with a crowbar and then push aside my dresser and upturned bed and storm in. Or maybe you'll just saunter in after you push everything aside and say "Picnic's over, my friend, so do you leave peacefully or do we have to come up with some other way?" And once you again see your sweet talk doesn't work: "We've had it up to here with you, do you understand? Now get your ass out of here this second or I'll pull you out with my bare hands. Or knock you down and tie you up and, with a little help, carry you to the street. Or just drag you out by your hair, not caring a damn for the lumps you'll take from the bumps along the way and down the stairs."

But you're not about to drag me anywhere while I'm chained to the radiator, and none of your bullying's going to get me to say where I stashed the key. What you'll then most likely do is try to rip the chain apart from the radiator. But this chain's the strongest made these days, and try boffing me stiff so you can cut it with a hacksaw, and I'll wrap it around your ankles and tug on it till you give up and wobble out on your knees. This is a small room, big enough for maybe two or three people and the radiator, toilet, dresser and my massive bed, and I've been here so long I know all the ins and outs of the place better than anyone, so don't think you're going to strong-arm me to leave.

You could then think the time was right for sound reason to work, and say "Why don't you use your common sense already? With all the damage we've done to your window, door and walls, your room's not worth living in anymore." And when I remain silent: "What I'll have to do, if you don't unchain yourself or give me the key, is clean out your kitchenette, including the removal of your little fridge, sink and hot plate, and then stop all food deliveries from coming in and maybe even get your water and plumbing turned off."

But what will you do when you find out I'm staying here no matter how poor and unsanitary the conditions are and that I prefer starving to death than leaving? Only thing I can see you doing after that is unbolting the radiator through the ceiling of the apartment below mine and dragging the radiator out with me still chained to it and swatting away at you from the other end.

Once you drag me out of the room, you and a few of your workmen could pick me up still chained and carry the radiator and me downstairs. Or if that's too hard, lift the radiator over the windowsill, past the crowbarred window gate onto the fire escape and from there into a crane shovel, and with me, still attached, forced to follow, lower the radiator and me to the street.

You'll have to do one of those things to get me out of here while I'm still chained to the radiator. And if you do drag or carry the radiator and me downstairs or manage to lift us over the windowsill into a crane shovel, you have to know by now that nothing's going to stop me from coming back. Even if I'm still chained to the radiator because you couldn't find the key, or I've lost the key and, as punishment or just to keep me from returning here, you've left the radiator chained to me, I'll find some way to drag myself along with the radiator step by step up the stairs. If I can't drag myself and the radiator, then I'll find some tool or rock to file or chip away at the chain or radiator till I'm either free of the chain or have detached it from the radiator, and then only chained to the chain I'll drag myself upstairs.

I suppose the only way you could then stop me from getting back here is to erect a wall around the building and cement up my window and door and maybe remove the fire escape and stairs. But in time I'd find some way to reach the building and get to my floor and through the cemented-up window or door, so the only way you can really ever stop me from coming back would be to remove the building.

Only then would I be able to say to myself that not only were you able to force me to leave but also from getting back to my apartment. I don't see how there can be another way for you to stop me from returning, so you might as well raze the building now. And as long as you're going to have no choice but to demolish the building, suppose I unlock the door myself, leave the room and go downstairs to the street.

THE FORMER WORLD'S GREATEST RAW GREEN PEA EATER.

He hadn't spoken to her in ten years when he decided to call.

"Hello?"

"Miriam?"

"Yes, this is Miriam Cabell; who is it?"

"Miriam Cabell, now—I didn't know. Whatever happened to Miriam Livin?"

"If you don't mind, who is this, please?"

"And Miriam Berman?"

"I asked who this is. Now for the last time—"

"Arnie."

"Who?"

"Arnie...well, guess."

"I'm in no mood for games, really. And if it's just some crank—my husband handles all those calls."

"Then Arnie Spear—satisfied, Mrs. Cabell?"

"Wait a minute. Not Arnie X.Y.Z. Spear."

"The very same, madame."

"Arnie Spear the famous sonnet writer and lover of tin lizzies and hopeless causes and the world's greatest raw green pea eater?"

"Well, I don't want to brag, but—"

"Oh God, Arnie, how in the world did you get my number?"

"I'm fine, thank you...have a little pain in my ego, perhaps, but how are you?"

"No, I'm serious—how'd you get it?"

"I bumped into Gladys Pempkin coming out of a movie the other night. She told me."

"How is Gladys?"

"Fine, I guess. Haven't you seen her recently?"

"I've been running around so much these days, I hardly see anyone anymore. In fact, the last time with Gladys must've been a good year ago."

"Your name," he said, "—Cabell. That's your new husband, isn't it?"

"Fairly new. We've been married two years—or close to two. I wonder if you knew him."

"Don't think so. You happy, Miriam?"

"Happy? Why, was I ever really unhappy? But maybe I should toss the same ticklish nonsense back to you. How about it?"

"I'm happy. Very happy, I suppose. Really doing pretty well these days."

"I'm glad."

"Whatever happened to Livin—your last?"

"That bastard? Listen, I made a pact with myself never to mention his name or even think of him, so help me out, will you?"

"What happens if you break the pact?"

"What do you mean?"

"I mean if let's say we suddenly begin talking about him. Do you declare war on yourself and sort of battle it out till one or the other side of you has won?"

"That was a figure of speech I made. And why would you want to talk of Livin when you never knew him? Anyway, tell me how Gladys looks. Last time I saw her it seemed she was hitting the bottle pretty heavily or at least on pills."

"She seemed fine. A little tired, perhaps, but not much different than the last time I saw her—which was with you, remember?"

"No, when was that?"

"I don't know. About ten years ago or so."

"I can only remember old events if I'm able to place in my mind where I was at the time. Where was I?"

"In this coffee shop on Madison and 58th. The Powder Puff I think it was called."

"No, I don't recall any such place."

"It folded about four years ago. I know because for a few months I had a magazine editing job in the area and used to walk by the shop daily. And then one day it was suddenly empty of everything but a couple of sawhorses and there was a For Rent sign up. Now it's a beauty shop."

"Wait a minute. Not some incredibly garish beauty shop? With lots of pink and blue wigs on these wooden heads in the window and with a refreshment counter in front serving tea and cookies?"

"I think that's the one."

"Do you know, I once went there to have my hair done—isn't that strange? It's not a very good place, which is why I only went once. They dry all your roots out."

"Well, that's where we last saw each other. The place has always been particularly meaningful to me—almost as a starting point in a new phase of my life. Because if it wasn't for what you told me in there that morning, I doubt whether I would've become so conscious of my hang-ups then to leave the city, as I did, and get this great job out of town."

"Excuse me, Arnie. You're still on that beauty shop?"

"Don't you remember? We met there for coffee—when it was still a coffee shop. It was a very intense scene for me—holding your hand, and both of us unbelievably serious and me trying to work up enough courage to propose to you. Well, you mercifully cut me off before I was able to make a total ass of myself and told me, and quite perceptively, I thought, what a shell of an existence I was living and how, instead of trying to write fiction about a world I knew little of, I should get a job and move out of my parents' place and see what things were really like. I was so despondent after that—"

"Yes. Now I remember."

"Remember how torn up I was? I was a kid, then, granted, or just awfully immature, but it was very bad, extremely crushing."

"Yes. I hated that last scene."

"So, right after that, I quit school and got a cub reporter slot on the Dallas paper my brother was working for then—more copyboy than cub reporter, really—just so I could be away from you and the city and all. And later, well, I did become a reporter and moved up fast and then went to Washington to cover local news stories for several Texas papers. And then the correspondent jobs overseas seemed to pour in, none of which I could have taken if I were married at the time or seriously attached."

"Then things have worked out in their own way, right?"

"I suppose you can say so."

"And you've also seen a lot of the world, am I right? I mean, Europe and such?"

"Europe, Central America, Rio and Havana, and once even a year's stint in Saigon as a stringer for a consortium of TV stations. I've had a good tine."

"I'm glad."

"I've been very fortunate for a guy who never had a thought of going into news—very."

"I'm not someone who reads or watches the news, so I never had the chance to see you. But it really sounds like you've done well. And there can't be many things more exciting than traveling. Besides the fact of also getting paid for it."

"Even then, it's not as if I've had everything I exactly wanted—like the wife and kids I always spoke about."

"That's right. You used to speak about that a lot."

"It was way too early to, but I did. Or the home. The relatively permanent home with some grounds I could putter around on my days off, for basically I'm a family and fireplace man and I'd be a self-deluding idiot to deny it. But I've been quite lucky all in all."

"I'd say so. In ten years? You've done a lot."

"Yeah. Well, then last night, when we were in the lobby waiting for the movie to break—"

"You were with someone?"

"A friend—a woman I see, although nothing serious. So, I spotted Gladys, and I don't know, I just ran over to her and for some reason threw my arms around her—something I never would've done ten years ago, as I had never cared for her much. But things change. I was actually exhilarated at seeing her. And we naturally got around to talking about you."

"What did she have to say about me?"

"Nothing much."

"I ask that because she's always had a savage mouth. Always spreading lies about people—me particularly, though I was one of only a few people to even take a half interest in her. She's another one I made a pact with myself never to speak of or think about. She's said some filthy malevolent things about me—to mutual friends, no less—which, in another age, we'd be cut off the line if I repeated them."

"For me, she's always had a special ironic place in my memory. Because if you remember, when we finally emerged from that coffee shop ten years ago, Gladys was walking past—the last person we wanted to see at the time, we agreed when we saw her."

"Now I remember. That bitch was always turning up when you least wanted her."

"She saw us and smiled and began waving an arm laden with clanky chains as if this was just the most beautiful day in the most beautiful of worlds for everyone in it. I remember her vividly."

"You always had an excellent memory. I suppose that's important in your field."

"That among other things. But that incident comes back amazingly clear. Even the kind of day it was, with the ground freshly covered with the light snow flurry we had watched from the coffee shop."

"That part," she said, "I'm afraid I don't remember."

"Everyone has a few scenes in his life that stick out prominently. And not just extraordinary or life-changing events—that's not what I'm driving at so much. For instance, I can remember supposedly insignificant and meaningless incidents that occurred twenty to twenty-five years ago, and also what kind of day it was then and how everyone looked and even what they were wearing down to the pattern of their dresses and ties."

"What was I wearing that day?"

"That day? —Oh...that green suit you had. And a trench coat. The tightly belted coat I especially remember, even that the top button was off and you said that right after you leave me you were going to head straight to a notions shop to replace the button."

"That trench coat. I got it at the British-American House and did it ever cost a fortune, though I at least got a few years out of it. But the green suit?"

"A green tweed, salt and pepper style. It was a very fashionable suit at the time—the one you most preferred wearing to your auditions."

"Nowadays, I just go in slacks."

"You usually wore it with a white blouse and the amber bead necklace I gave you, and so I always felt somewhat responsible for the parts you got."

"I forgot about that necklace. You know, I still have it."

"You're kidding."

"I wasn't about to throw it away. It's a nice necklace."

"How does your husband react to your sporting these priceless gems from other men?"

"Jack? He doesn't think a thing about my clothes—not like you used to do. But he's very kind and sweet. A very peaceful man who knows where he is more than most anyone, and extremely generous and perceptive in other ways. He's a dentist."

"Just about my favorite professional group—even if they hurt."

"But he's not your everyday dentist. He specializes in capping teeth for actors. In the last fifteen years, I'd say most big New York stage and television actors who've had their teeth capped, had it done by him. That's how we met."

"You had your teeth capped?"

"Just four of them. The upper front."

"But you always had such beautiful teeth."

"Well, a number of people who know about things like this thought my teeth should be capped, if I wanted to do soaps and TV commercials, and I agreed. They were a little pointy—the incisors, especially—like fangs. They look much better for it—honestly."

"What could a job like that run someone?"

"Couple of thousand, but that's with two cleanings and x-rays and everything. And you have to consider the labor and time involved. I was in that chair for months."

"Did Dr. Cabell make you pay up before he married you?"

"Oh, we got married long after that. You see, about six months after I paid up completely, he phoned me out of the blue and mentioned something about my having missed one of my monthly payments. I said 'Can't be, Dr. Cabell, there must be some mistake,' and he said he'd look in to it further. He called back the next day and said I was right—I was paid up in full. That's when he asked me out to lunch—to make up for his misunderstanding, he said—and the next year we were married."

"It sounds as if he was initially feeding you a line."

"Why do you say that?"

"Why, because, and I say this quite harmlessly, it has all the earmarks of a line. Which is all right if it works, I suppose, which it obviously did."

"But you're wrong. He, in fact, told me in that second call that I might think his bill call was only an excuse to contact me, but that it wasn't. He really did think I wasn't paid up."

"Then why didn't he have someone in his office call you about the so-called overdue payment? He has a big practice, I assume, so can't be doing all the billing and appointments and such by himself, and it'd seem a lot more professional doing it that way."

"Jack feels that something like that—when he has the time, and he tries to make time for it—ought to be handled by him alone. He's a very informal man, Arnie, despite his imposing office and successful practice, and he's told me several times that there's already too much impersonality in the city between patient and dentist. Also, he likes to chat."

"You're no doubt right. It's absurd of me to even have brought up such a petty issue. But I suppose I've been hauling around this vision of you of being a person too clever to fall for that kind of palaver, we'll call it."

"Fall? What are you talking about? I married the man. Even if he was giving me a line with that call—which he wasn't—what's the difference now? It's all water under the cesspool or something when you married the person, isn't it?"

"Naturally."

"Oh sure, you really sound convinced."

"Well, despite what I said before about how it's okay and such if it works, I'm against lies and deceptions of any sort, what can I tell you? I don't like hypocrisy. I've seen too much of it in my work and I simply don't like it."

"That's right—I forget. You're the big world traveler and interpreter of newsy events."

"All right, I happen to be a journalist—a newsman, if you like. And I write and report on things that turn my stomach every day. In politics, diplomacy, business—"

"You were also always a big one for the soapbox, if I remember. Even in college; always the big speech."

"No, you're not catching my point, Miriam."

"Oh, I catch on. I haven't been asleep these past ten years. But one would think that during this time you might have changed. But you still have to beat the old drum."

"I'm not beating an old drum. I was simply saying—"

"And that you might have learned some tact. Because to call up an old friend and insult her husband as if he were a first-class hypocrite and schemer, well, uh-uh, I'm sorry, that's not showing much tact. That's not using much brains, either, if I can say so without you jumping down my throat."

"I'm not jumping down anyone's throat—especially not yours. I happen to like your throat, just as I liked your teeth. Truth is, I once even loved your throat. I'd never try to hurt you—and I didn't intend to insult your husband. I'm not even sure I did, but let's drop it."

"Why don't we."

There was a long silence before he said "Miriam, Miriam, you still there?"

"Yes. And I have to go now, Arnie. The baby—"

"You have a baby. When I spoke to Gladys—"

"It's not mine; it's the child of a friend in the building. I'll have one, though. We're working on it."

"I'm sure you will. And then it's been good speaking to you, Miriam."

"A little rough at times, but I'm glad we can still say it was nice after all."

"Don't be silly. And also— Well, it might sound asinine to suggest we meet for lunch one time this week, but I will be around for that long. And it's what I originally called for."

"It's probably not a good idea right now, so maybe another time."

"A quick coffee then. Just for a half hour or so, and if not at a shop then perhaps I can even come up to your place. It'd be interesting seeing you again, and then these scenes of ancient college boyfriends popping up after so many years have almost become proverbial in books and movies by now. You know, where the husband just stands aside while these two sort of conspire in their talk about those dreamy goofy college days. And then the husband having a fat laugh about it with his wife when the silly old beau goes."

"Not a good idea, really. I've never been much for conspiracies. Call up again when I'm less hassled by work and getting a new apartment furnished, and I'm sure we can spend some time together. I love talking over old times with good friends."

"So do I."

He said goodbye, but she didn't hear him; her receiver had already been recradled. He bought a newspaper and walked the twenty blocks to Penn Station, since he had more than an hour to kill. About fifteen minutes before the train was scheduled to leave for Trenton and his sister and two nieces waiting on the platform for him, all eager to see him after his two years away and planning a family party tonight to celebrate his return before he went abroad again, he rushed out of the club car and called Miriam.

"Hello? Hello? Hello?" she said, and after her fifth hello, hung up.

He called back a minute later and the woman who answered said in a stiff Operator's voice that the telephone he dialed was no longer a working number. The next time he called it was a thick rolling Bavarian voice that answered, saying "Isolde's Fine German Pasty Shop, dis is Isolde speaking, vould you like to place an order to go to hell?" He said "No, thanks, I guess not," and hung up.

JACKIE.

"The badly decomposed body of an unidentified man was found floating in Billowy Bay off Motorboro Airport at 4:15 p.m., Tuesday, by a Port Authority police officer."

So?

Know who it is?

How could I?

Jackie.

Jackie. Jackie Schmidt.

I see. Jackie Schmidt. Floating in Billowy Bay. What's that, a little article?

Under "Area News."

And you can tell who it is just by reading this little thing in the paper?

I'd known he was thrown in there. First shot, then thrown.

Does it say anything about the guy being shot?

Doesn't have to. I know.

But if he was shot, wouldn't they also say it?

They haven't found out where yet, but they will. And there can't be another unidentified man thrown in the same day? Of course not.

It doesn't have to be the same day. It takes time to get decomposed. In fact, it couldn't've been the same day.

How long you think it takes?

Days. Maybe two weeks. Badly decomposed, three. That's when they threw Jackie in. Shot, took his clothes off, boom, in the water. Today's Wednesday? Then three weeks today. It's him.

So what are we going to do about it?

Nothing. It's done. Jackie's dead. I knew about it. Now I read about it, I was only telling you, thinking maybe you knew, and if you did, then who from? And if you didn't, that you'd probably be interested to hear.

You mind my making an anonymous call to this paper so his wife could know?

Jackie not coming home for three weeks, she knows. So will everyone in time.

How? He's unidentified and decomposed. And no clothes you say? Nothing at all?

Stripped clean. Wristwatch. Socks. Even his gold star.

I don't know why they didn't say "naked" or "nude" in the newspaper, but all right. Did he also have no fingerprints on when you people threw him in?

I didn't throw anybody in. Neither do I know who did. I just know some people who know who did and why and how. Gambling debts. But in bad, and loans. Worse. Taking on more big debts with another group and not paying off the first one a dime before he went in deeper, and then telling both groups to go eat it. Now if he'd just been in deep with the first group and told them to eat it, they would've only broken his arm. But taking on two big debts way over his head and telling them both to eat it and then going to another city to take on a third, well, that got to be too much. The first two met, and with the third's approval, elected to dump him. As for his fingerprints, I guess not. Why bother, for they'd also have to kick out all his teeth and fill in his chin cleft and scars. Besides, they didn't want to make it impossible to identify him.

Then you'll have to explain to me, because I'm still fairly new at this. Why only take off his clothes and go part way with the unidentification, when they know Jackie has a record and will eventually be indentified? Time to give them a cover or get the people who did it away?

No. They thought it'd be a good lesson to whoever might think he can beat out on two big debts to two vaguely related groups and to tell them both to eat it besides.

But how are these people who are supposed to get the lesson supposed to find out it's a lesson and also one meant for them? By reading of an unidentified decomposed man found floating in the bay who could've got there through a long sleepwalk? How did the groups even know it was going to make the paper, nothing as that article was? And if it did, that it'd even be read?

Whisper and word started getting around a month ago. "Jackie's betting heavy. Jackie's welshing. Jackie's in very steep. Jackie won't cough up a note for them and told them both to eat it raw. Jackie could get a jaw broken, talking and acting that way. If anyone's a pal of Jackie's, give him the word? Jackie's missing. Hey, anybody seen Jackie or heard from him the last few days?" Then, body found. "Hmm, bay you say? Isn't that where they usually drop guys that welsh big-time?" Tomorrow or the next day we'll read he'd been shot with a small caliber bullet so close and clean that it almost got lost behind the back hairs of his head. Everybody will know by now who it is and what for. As for the newspaper—if it hadn't gotten in, somebody would've informed them. What's really important, though, is that the people this lesson's directed to get to know it slowly till it sinks in.

These groups never seemed that clever to me to plan it so smooth.

Listen, we're not psychologists and know beans about the subject, but in what these groups do and their customers, they are. They haven't studied it but just know.

So I forget my call and even thinking about it?

You'll see for yourself. Jackie's wife will claim the body in a few days and there'll be a funeral and we'll attend.

We were his such good friends and nobody will mind we're there?

No one. Neither his wife, who'll be compensated for the lesson. And the people who did him in will even expect it of us, and some of them will be there too. They play it decent, very orderly and good manners, something Jackie didn't do or have. That was his problem. Not much brains too. Hand in hand with his gambling, that can kill you. Being a smartass besides, you're dead.

I'll remember that.

It can save your life.

Look, a life worth saving might as well be my own. You know, I don't think I like this business anymore. Money's good and not too many hours and so far steady, but too much excitement for me and you never know who to trust. Your friend's your friend one day, and next day you're fingered by him on maybe even a lie, and there you go with his thumb pressed into your throat goodbye.

There's a lot depending on it for everyone, that's why. You just got to do what's expected of you till one day you get the right to give orders. That takes time and you got to want it but not ask for it. No matter what, it's true you should never think you're absolutely safe. Like with any job, any business. Draw your own parallels.

But even when you're right up there, company president and the rest of it, you can be giving all the orders and still get it in the head.

Not if you do nothing wrong. Everything's protected. Or let's say, all your moves are almost already made. Sure, accidents happen, flukes out of nowhere. New people move in, alliances fall apart and develop, but then you got to know who to be for. All in all, though, you got to stay in line.

But what you're saying makes it seem even more impossible. This one, that one, time comes along, how do I know I won't be dumb enough to pick the wrong one? You saw with that phone call. Suppose I'd made it and some power person found out and thought it a very bad move. And for all I know it could've been my third to fourth very bad move in a short time and they might decide that's the max so now I also definitely belong away. You could've told them of all the moves I made that I didn't know were so bad, and this last one, coming from someone else, could've been the clincher.

Me? Your best friend? Tell on you?

They can give you reasons. I've heard that it can happen. You know it yourself. No, I really want out, but total.

Too early. You got too much put in—and they with you the same—for you to go so immediately. You have to step back very slowly till everything you do's being done by someone else or among a crew and you're so unnoticed, you're out. Something like that. But takes time. Anything else is suspicious.

Then I'm leaving the area.

Forget it. They see a small hole, means someone's missing. You're not around, means it's you. They find you, you'll have to explain. Most times, to be extra protective of themselves, they won't believe you whatever way you say it. You should've thought of all this before you came in.

How could I have known?

Come on. You heard of it, read about it, grown up with it, seen it in the movies and still do. Well, it's not so far from all those combined where you should've known what it was like beforehand.

Poor Jackie.

Stupid Jackie, you mean.

Poor. Because he's dead. Little I knew, I liked him. Oh, let's shut the light.

I want to read some more.

The newspaper ink will make your fingers dirty.

I can live with it.

You feeling like a little physical activity before I turn over?

Not tonight, love, not tonight.

The article about Jackie?

It's not that.

Then good reading.

And you, sweet dreams.

THE

CLEANUP

MAN.

"That's it, I quit, I can't stand it anymore," and I put the broom into the closet and go downstairs to the locker room. The boss comes. "What's this? What happened? If it's Pete again, I'll sack him."

"No, it's not Pete, though he gives me a hard time all right. But it's not him. I'm tired of this job. I've been at it too long. Tired of all this kind of work. I get no satisfaction from it and I don't think I ever did, not just here but in every place. I don't know, but I've got to get out of it for good."

"What satisfaction you want? You sweep the floor, you clean the dishes and occasionally bus some tables. What possible satisfaction can you get in that, except in doing a good job? And you do a good job with your sweeping and cleaning and when I ask you to bus, not to say the way you take care of the windows. Those windows shine. And when they shine, people see them and know it's a clean place I got and they come in and sit down and want to be served and eat and drink and spend money. Customers compliment me on those windows. So I compliment you and on everything you do besides. So why do you want to quit? Satisfaction, that satisfaction that artists and scientists and great teachers get from their work, will never come to me or you. But just small satisfaction, like those people complimenting me on my windows and food, and a compliment or two from me to you and just in your own self about the good job you do, that you'll get. And that you deserve, so stay. I'll raise your salary if you want—ten cents an hour starting when you came in today."

"It's not the money," I say.

"Don't be a fool. It is so the money, or has to be in some big way. Because what else you live on: the garbage you wipe off the plates or sweep up in the corners of the dining room? Maybe you do find something every now and then on the floor you don't tell me about, like a diamond earring or dollar bill or a customer's bracelet. That you deserve too if the person who loses the earring or bracelet doesn't come in to say she lost it, though whatever loose money you find is yours no matter who comes in to claim. But money you earn is what you live on. And ten cents more an hour, though not a lot to most people, to you comes up to almost five dollars a week, which you can certainly use. So ten cents an hour raise you'll get, and starting first of this week, not today."

"It's not the money. I don't want a raise. I wouldn't say no to it if I stayed here, but I wouldn't stay here for a dollar more an hour. Like I said, I'm tired of the job and it's probably tired of me, whatever that means."

"Fifteen cents an hour then, but that's my limit. At four-eighty an hour with the new raise, you'll be making more than just about any restaurant cleanup man in the city."

"No, please, I told you—"

"Okay, you got it. Twenty cents an hour raise, but only because you're so damn dependable, though don't try to hold me up for more. That's almost nine dollars more a week you'll be getting, plus I won't even tell you how much it costs me in those two big meals a day you eat. Of course, you'll have to work a little extra harder for it. I don't give raises away like that just any day of the week."

"Really, I'm through with this line of work. I have to try and do something else, but I don't know what."

"Then why leave? Leave, and I can't say you did anything but quit. And if you quit, the state won't give you unemployment insurance."

"I don't want any."

"If you could get it, you'd take it—don't tell me. It's probably what you're planning to do anyway."

"No, I wouldn't. Jesus, over three years I've been here, and you don't know me at all. You see, I've cleaned up for you and all those other restaurants for twenty-some years because I never tried to do anything else. But I want to be... Well, I want to do... Ah, the hell with it. Sorry. And I've got to go."

I put my apron on the bench, change into my street clothes, wipe the kitchen crap off my shoes with a paper napkin, and say "So, I'll be seeing you, and I hope no hard feelings," and start upstairs.

"Go, then," he says, following me. "But you made a fool of me by not taking my pay raise, which I'll never forget. Use my name as a work reference to someplace not even close to what you had here, and you'll see what you'll get. I'll go out of my way, even, to make sure you don't get hired. And if I hear you're working in some joint, I'll call the manager there and tell him what I think of you. I won't say you stole. That, you never did, which is another reason I prized you. But there are other things I can say that will sound almost as bad, especially that you left me stranded today with five hours to go on your shift. That's almost as bad as stealing, as far as we're concerned. And if I can't get someone in for you in two hours, just as bad and maybe worse."

I buy a newspaper outside, go home and search the want ads for possible jobs. Computer programmer, machine operator, bank teller, and so on—nothing I could do, and they all say no on-the-job training. Pile clerk and messenger I could probably be hired as, but they seem no better and interesting as jobs than what I've been doing.

Next morning I get into my best clothes—my dress clothes, which aren't much, but something—and go to a dozen or more employment agencies. The interviewers all tell me my experience and education qualify me for nothing much better than what I've been doing: cleanup man, dishwasher, busboy. I want to do something more challenging and personally rewarding, I tell them, and I'm too old to be a busboy.

"Busboys come in all ages," the last interviewer says. "A man can retire at sixty-five as a busboy and get a reasonably good pension if he belongs to a good union. I'd suggest you find work in an expensive restaurant as one. If you work fulltime as a busboy and your waiters are fair with sharing part of their tips with you, your earnings should add up to more than you'd make as a cleanup man in even the best-paying restaurant. If you're interested, I have a new listing here for one."

"I'm too old to be called a busboy is I guess what I'm saying. I also feel I'm still young and healthy enough to hold down a better kind of job, and also, for a change, one cleaner. Maybe I should go back to school for something."

"By your looks, you're in your forties. You want my opinion? You're also too old to return to school to study for a new profession. For an education, maybe—just to get one is what I mean. But that's what you want? Go ahead—everyone can profit from more learning at any age. But I don't expect you have much in savings? And just going to school without working at the same time, unless you want it to take you a few years, is one luxury I don't think you can afford."

I buy the evening newspaper, go home and read the want ads. Records assistant, operation analyst, registered nurse, data processor (manual)—half of them I don't even know what they mean. There is an opening for someone to clean offices but that would be more of what I was doing and the ad says I'd need a car. It gets depressing, reading these ads, and I drink more than I usually do and soon I'm feeling drowsy. Well, maybe a good night's sleep is what I need, and tomorrow I can start out fresh in looking for a job.

My ex-boss calls just as I'm getting into bed. "So," he says, "find anything yet? Bank president? Water engineer? What?"

"I'm still looking. What do you want?"

"You sound different—your speech slurry. What is it? You became a drunk already in one day since you quit on me? Because you never drank at work that I know, or much ever."

"All right, I'll be truthful with you, for what do I got to lose? I had more to drink tonight than I'm used to. It's depressing looking for work when you know there's nothing much for you but the same lousy thing. And one full day of it and I think I got the picture what's out there, not that it's going to stop me from keep looking."

"You know, you really got me mad yesterday," he says.

"Oh, yeah? Well, if I made things tough for you, I'm sorry."

"Shh—listen to me. And mad not just for that raise business and that I had to wash dishes for three hours myself. But as I said, good cleanup men are a rarity in this city, and great ones like you are a find I'd never let any other restaurant owner or manager know of. Start drinking on me, though, and I wouldn't let you work another minute in my place."

"Who says I want to work for you. I, in fact, don't."

"Wait'll I finish, first. I think so highly of you that if you do come back as my cleanup man, I'll also start training you under the cook. 'Sous chef'—do you like the title? Because for an hour a day, we'll say—or let's just call it 'sous chef apprentice'—that's what you'll be. Cooks are good-paying jobs and can also be very creative ones—not in my place so much but in others. And when you've learned enough, which, granted, takes time and the cook wants to go on his break, you can fill in for him instead of me or the salad man, and get plenty of practical experience. Then—though who knows when?—you really proved you can handle it, I might even put you in for him on his day off, though you'd have to work an extra day a week to do that, and with your regular wages. That might take a year. It might take two. And I'm only training you that one hour a day as I said. Though train as many hours as you want on your own time, if the cook doesn't think you're getting in the way, but only after the eight you work for the restaurant, which includes the one I'll pay you for to be trained. So what do you say? It's a big step up and can lead to who knows what. In two or so years you could be filling in for the cook on his summer vacation, and for real second-cook wages. It'll mean I'll have to get a cleanup man to replace you, like one of those bums, who'd make anyone look good, on your day off. It's even, when you think of it, being extremely generous on my part, after the treatment you gave me. But I felt the offer worth it if I get a verbal guarantee of your cleanup work for me for two to three more years. And starting at the last salary I offered you, with regular increases, of course, which was what?—four fifty-five an hour?"

"It was up to four-eighty before you raised it another five cents."

"Hey, mister, you drive a hard bargain and got too good a memory, but okay: consider yourself the winner. Now, as for your current drinking problem, we'll call it an off night, right? Because I still appreciate you, and even if nobody else in the restaurant says to your face they do, I know they all think you're a big plus for the place running so smooth."

He says he'll see me the regular time tomorrow, and hangs up. I slam down the receiver. I kick the chair and throw the ashtray against the wall. I slam my fist into the lampshade, and the lamp goes flying over the couch and the bulb in it explodes when the lamp hits the floor. The room's dark, and that was my only lamp and bulb. I turn on the ceiling light switch, but that bulb went out a couple of years ago. I finger around for the ashtray pieces on the floor, and after nicking myself, give up. Now I know what was wrong with me all these years. I never once lost control.

CHINA.

Every morning at eight the guards march us into a room for TV interviews and three hours later march us back to our cells. And every noon the guards march us across the prison yard to another building for radio and newspaper interviews and three hours later again order us into double formation and march us back to our cells. And every afternoon at five and in the evening at nine they march us into the communal lounging room to read political pamphlets and listen to lectures and recorded ancient Chinese music and then march us into the communal TV room to watch televised interviews of us done a day or two or even a week or month before—we're never quite sure since we're always clean-shaven and well-groomed and dressed in the same blue uniforms for these interviews and answer the same questions with the same answers to the same interviewer. After two hours of this they march us back to our cells and I usually fall quickly asleep: tired from all the marching, bored to fatigue with the prison routine, a little sick from the unpalatable food we get or else kept awake with hunger pains because I refused to eat this food, another day done—I'm always thankful for that. Because during the seven hours allotted us for sleep our releases might have been arranged and morning could mean our start out of here—though I often wake up tired, probably because in my dreams I usually march too. Tonight I marched across Chinese and European but mostly American landscape, flanked by the nine air force men who are prisoners with me, though accompanied by what seemed like the entire military service including the commander in chief, all of us singing a marching song I don't ever remember hearing and keeping in step, as we don't do here, to cadenced numbers as we paraded past flag-waving crowds. "Hup, two, three, four; ein, zwei, drei, vier; uno, duo, trio, fouro..."

But this morning my cell door's open. Now that door's never open except for the few seconds it takes the guard to march me in or out of the cell and when my food's brought and he directs me to stand at the farthest point from the door with my nose and knees touching the wall. And no breakfast has come, no guard to tell me what kind of American pig I am today or why my breakfast hasn't come or even why my cell door's open. I stare suspiciously at the door. Then, with my back to the remote control camera that focuses on my cell all day, I relax on the floor mattress, happy with this one break in prison monotony since we were all brought here seven months ago from a prison that didn't have radio and television studios.

I dream some more about marching. This time it's across the George Washington Bridge to New York, though I've never been on that bridge or even to New York or New Jersey. I march up to the automatic tollbooth, toss a pocketful of change, keys and tissues into the toll basket, and when the sign flashes "Okay, Yankee trash, march ahead," I march toward the graceful hills of hometown San Francisco turning pink and yellow pastel in the twilight and suddenly becoming the gray and black glass slabs of neighboring Oakland.

I wake around noon, my cell door's still open. My lunch hasn't come and I'm hungry, as I shoved aside last night's meal. And there are no sounds from the cell corridor, no voices or car and truck noises I sometimes hear past the three inchwide slits in my outside wall, a foot above my highest jumping reach. How odd, I think, since every day but today I've been awakened by the guard who calls me pig in several Chinese languages, and a few minutes later he'd place my breakfast on my cell floor—plain white rice and hot black tea, the best meal of the day. Later I'd join my fellow prisoners in the corridor and we'd march down many halls and through many electronically controlled doors till we got to a compound the size of a national soldiers cemetery, which we marched across to the TV studio for another round of interviews on our spy flight over China's territorial air space, something we've done every day except Chinese patriotic holidays for half a year. In the studio we'd take our regular places on a double row of benches and then, one by one, would sit in the only chair in the room other than the interviewer's and be interviewed.

At first we refused to be interviewed, feeling it would embarrass our country and families, look disastrously bad on our service records and, once we were released, land us a stiff term in an American stockade. But Chinese officials showed us American newspapers and videotapes of U.S. news programs that quoted high American officials about how we hadn't been on an electronic and photographic intelligence gathering operation as the Chinese had charged, but had been forced down by an air-to-air missile over open seas during a routine meteorological run and that America had done everything possible to get us released and now China had to make the next move. For three years Chinese officials told us China could never make that move unless we or a high American official admitted to the spying mission. Since we already saw two American presidents say on TV that America could never admit to a covert flight it didn't make, we thought that instead of marching our lives away in a foreign prison, we'd encourage China's next move by telling the truth without revealing any pertinent information about the flight. We felt that once China got all the propaganda value out our confession as it could, it'd release us to our military, whom we'd take our chances with by pleading emotional and physical breakdown during our capture. That was six months ago, and up until yesterday we were still being interviewed and the questions were always the same.

"Were you flying over Chinese soil?" the interviewer asked each of us, and each of us said "Yes, sir, I was." "Are you repentant you were on a spying mission over China?" "Yes, sir, I am." "Why do you want your country to disclose the truth about your spying mission?" "I love America and want it to be a truthful country so it can have the respect of the world. And also a personal reason, sir. I want to return to my loved ones in the States"—though on that last score I always said "Because I'm tired and bored with this place and the food's inedible and I know I'll never get used to sleeping on an inch-thick mattress on a hard cold floor and also because I want to finally find a loved one." I have no loved ones or family, except for an aunt who's been in an asylum since she was twelve and, for all I know, might be dead by now, God be with you, Aunt Rose, crazy since birth I was countless times told. I was sure the Chinese accepted my one digression from the prescribed dialogue because it gave a touch of realness to the interviews. Anyway, they never objected and my line always got a loud laugh and whistles from my buddies, even after they heard it a hundred times.

I go to sleep and dream of marching again, this time across the Pacific. I pass an island, and a beautiful Polynesian woman in a grass skirt and no top waves to me from a cliff and says "Aloha, Jamie, welcome to paradise now and give all those pretty boys a kiss from me." Those boys turn out to be my fellow prisoners again, all of us marching single file. "Ahoy there," a captain on an old whaler says, "where you off to, mates?" "China," we say in unison, and he says "China? Why that's unoccupied alien soil—a country we don't even have relations with." "China, nevertheless," we say. "We know of a good Cantonese restaurant in Shanghai and a bar in Canton where you can either get shanghaied or buy for a week or weekend a real live China doll to have relations with."

The door's still open. It's dinner time and no dinner's come. I wish for the nightly rattle on my door of the dinner guard's truncheon and the only joke he, or for that matter, any other guard ever made to me in English: "Arise, hair horse man, purloin meat and soiled potatoes." I'd knock a message out to the next cell, but we're not allowed to. "Do not communicate clandestinely," the prison commandant told us the day we got here, "or you will lose many privileges." "What privileges, sir?" Captain House, our commanding officer, said. "Food, sleeping and washing privileges." "That is expressly prohibited by the Kobenhavn Code regarding military prisoners, which states that basic human needs may be suspended during certain urgencies only to the extent that they are similarly suspended for the prisoners' keepers." Commandant Ep said China respects that code as much as America respects China's borders. But since I apparently have no food and washing privileges to lose today and have slept all I need to for the next day, I knock on the wall to the adjoining cell.

Knock knock, I knock, but Junior Walker doesn't answer.

Knock knock knock. Knock knock knock knock, one or two knocks every so often louder or more rapid than the last, along with an occasional SOS, but I get no response. A word from the guards that I've lost all my privileges for the next day would be a welcome response, but no guard comes. Maybe I should stick my head out the cell door and see if a guard's around. "Any prisoner so much as sticking a single finger joint through the cell-door window when opened," Commandant Ep said that first day, "will be afforded the most serious punishments for this act." "Please specify what punishments," Captain House said, "so my men can know what to expect, which is clearly stated in article six of the internationally recognized Sashburton-Tang declaration." "Let your men expect the most serious punishments that life can assuredly ill afford." "Thank you, sir." And to us: "You heard the commandant, men. No sticking not even a single joint through the door window unless you want to be afforded the most serious of punishments that life can definitely not afford, agreed?" "Agreed," we all said, slaves to living, our voices one. "Thank you, Captain House. Thank you, Commandant Ep."

I fall asleep and dream of marching again, though now I'm the officer in charge of a company of hotdogs, sizzling steaks, baked potatoes, bottles of French Bordeaux and chilled American Chablis, fresh-cooked deveined shrimps with a cocktail sauce on top and lemon wedges on the side, all-marching five abreast till I command the food to halt and one by one to march up my body and into my mouth. The marchers become disorganized and retreat once they reach my waist and disperse when they land back on the ground. I begin eating my fingernails and then my fingers, but my hunger's still not sated. I bellow "Deveined shrimp, bottles of white and red, franks, steaks, spuds, re-form into single lines and march into my mouth, hup, two, twice, no; mut, rut, vier, hup."

I hup myself out of sleep. It's morning. Door's still open. I pound on the cell wall and yell "This is Jamie Namurti, goddamn you, and someone answer me right now." I scream that I'm starving, "dying of thirst besides," and for the benefit of the remote control camera I grab my belly and drop to the floor in pain, but no doctor with food or guards with warnings about penalties incurred by prisoners for cutting up in their cells come bustling down the corridor to me. I stand up, raise my middle finger to the camera, and stick my head a few inches past the door.

Nobody's in the corridor, the cell block seems deserted. I shout at the camera the only Chinese words I can think of: "Mao Tse-Tung, Chiang Kai-chek, Tao teh-king, Li Po, I Ching, dim sums"—those meat- and fish-filled delicacies I used to get in San Francisco tea parlors between classes at the Art Institute—"Kiangsi stew, mushi pork with three extra pancakes, sweet and sour bass with steamed bows and all the cold rice beer I can drink," but nobody comes to order me to quiet down.

"Abe, Pule, Rick, Dom, Junior, Milkmore, Eunstman, Coneymile, Captain House," but none of my fellow prisoners answer. "Commandant Ep," I shout. "Soldier Hsi"—the guard who likes to call me pig. "Han, Tz'u, Shih"—the three guards who bring my food. "Chin, Chan, Tun, Yin, Shan, Shu, Wong, Wang, Wing, Went, Wu"—names I yell because they sound Chinese. Then I say to the camera "I'm sorry, but my hunger and thirst have totally overwhelmed my self-protective instincts and common sense. At the count of three I'm going to have to leave this cell to find the kitchen, though all you have to do is say 'Don't come out,' and I won't. So please don't squeeze any triggers.

Do not use guns under any circumstances. So I'm stepping outside my cell now—one, two, three," and I throw my only bar of soap out the door, but no one shoots at it. The soap bounces a few times before breaking apart like a soda cracker. "Next, I'm coming out—the real Jamie; no inorganic impersonation. Presenting—your attention, please—the one and only in the gorgeous living flesh," and I step gingerly into the corridor, look around, do a brief frenetic Navaho dance of peace I learned from my father, end it with a leap in the air and my heels clicking just before I hit the ground. Nothing. And all the cell doors are open I see, as I slide down the corridor's linoleum floor. And no grimacing guards in the glassed-in monitor room at the end of the corridor, though all the monitors are on, showing, among other things, our ten empty cells. Maybe my fellow prisoners were shot, but why would the Chinese shoot them and leave me? Or taken out for questioning and I was left behind by mistake, my cell door—last one at the other end of the corridor—left open by mistake; by mistake, the corridor door left open also and the monitor room left empty. But I'll never know unless I try to find out.

The kitchen's on the same floor as the cell block and seems to have been deserted in a hurry: food still in stove pots and tea in cups. I drink lots of water and eat about a quart of cold rice. Then I go downstairs, announcing along the way that an unarmed peace-loving American prisoner by the name of Jamie Namurti is heading this way, admittedly unauthorized to be out of his cell but please don't shoot, as he's an intensely harmless chap who only wants to know why no one's around and why his food wasn't brought to his cell and why his cell door and the cell block door and, it seems, all the doors in this prison were left open.

Nobody's in the building, so I walk across the compound to the radio studio and then the television one, but they're like the rest of this ghost prison. In the television studio, I sit at my regular place on the bench to think what I should do next, rise as if ordered to by Guard Tu and sit in the interviewee's chair, face the lifeless camera and make the kind of confession I always wanted to.

"No, you goddamn ninnies, for the three hundredth time I was not on a spy flight for America and, in fact, am not in the American Air Force or even an American. I'm the legitimate handpicked rightful revolutionary heir of the great Mao—rather than the bureaucratic New Class fakes now in control—so you're all under arrest. Actually,

I'm the great-grandson of the illustrious Sun Yat-sen by a previously unknown pre-teen marriage arranged by my great-great-grandparents, so now you're all most certainly under arrest. All kidding aside, me and my fellow flyboys here, well, we were over China not to spy on her but to seek asylum in her, when one of our country's most effective anti-asylum missiles caught us in our contrails, knocking us for a few unaeronautical loops though not hitting our plane in time to stop us from landing it on your munificent soil. The truth is, and I see no reason to lie or joke around about it anymore, we were on a spying mission for China against American fleet forces in the Pacific when Vietnamese naval batteries, thinking we were scouting for an expeditionary brigade of Japanese to reestablish military imperialism in Asia by Asians, gunned us down. Okay: our sole reasons for transgressing your territory was to end the border dispute between Indonesia and Malaysia, return Sabah to the Philippines, Thailand and Cambodia to the Khmer, reunite the Koreas under the Silla kingdom, Japan under the Yamoto priest-chiefs, Burma under the Toungoo dynasty and China under the Kalmucks, and really get things moving again in Asia, really get the job done. The absolute truth now? I want to go home. I miss my mad Aunt Rose, I adore my loony Uncle Sam, I'm even a little crazy about you, China, wherever you are, whatever you might be."

I stay in prison for three more days, sitting in Ep's elegant office chair and giving the most extravagant orders imaginable to a thousand functionaries, sleeping in his bed with a photograph of his beautiful wife, smoking all his Cuban cigars and drinking his plum brandy, cooking up wild tasty dishes in the officers' kitchen and working myself back to pre-prison shape in their pool and gym. But I'm very lonely and also curious to know what's going on outside, so I fill a knapsack with food, canteens of water and a blanket and go through the main gate and head south, thinking that with a lot of luck and muscle I might reach Kowloon, walk across the bridge to Hong Kong, and sneak onto a ship leaving for some country like Japan or Australia.

I'm on the road for a day before I see another person. The man's walking toward me, but seems too frail and old to get any intelligible information from, so I salute him and walk past, but he yells "You there, Yankee fan, you part of occupation forces blitzing south instead of west as I past heard?" I run back and hug him and say how happy I am to speak to someone in English again, "though I haven't a clue as to what you're saying to me."

"Suspect it's my English then, which I haven't spoken since one New Zealand missionary lady learned it to me in Nan-ch'ang some thirty years ago. Name of Dot Gentle, a Mrs.—you know her, familiar with her good looks and name?" I tell him I'm not and ask why the road's so empty. He says he's surprised I haven't heard about China's newest and perhaps greatest disaster. It seems that American bioresearchers were testing a new nerve agent in a Taiwan proving ground when, because of an unforecasted storm, several chemical gas clouds blew across the China Sea. Once the gas reached China it was discovered it had no effect on the nervous systems of Chinese inhabitants but worked with unintended superlative results as a herbicide, for in a week this agent acting as a multiplying virus spread so fast that most of the arable land in the Fukien and Kwantung provinces were made infertile and the crops were destroyed. By the time American bioagricultural scientists could come up with a counterreactant to the herbicide, a civil war had started between the more reactionary political faction, which insisted China declare war on America for its chemical invasion, and the group in power, which said that war with America would be national suicide for China and so it was the reactionary faction that had to be crushed. Diplomatic relations between China and America were once more restored, arms and food were sent in from the States, and the two countries were now fighting side by side against the rebels. A new era in international peace and cooperation will begin once the war ends, world experts have said, though by the time it comes most of China's cities and farmlands and maybe a quarter of its people might be destroyed. Right now twenty million homeless Chinese are plodding this way from the ravaged South, eating everything in their path like twenty billion locusts.

I give the man half my provisions and head back to the prison. With its solid walls and vast food reserves, it'll be the safest place to stay till the Americans come; and where I know I won't starve.

It takes me a day to get back, but the prison's locked. I ring, and a caged window in one of the gate doors opens and the eyes of Commandant Ep appear.

"You leave something behind?" he says, and I tell him I want to get back in, since I heard that living's going to become extremely hazardous outside.

"Can't do. Orders from loyalist command state that I and my soldiers return from the front, where we had previously been ordered to go to fight, to occupy the prison against all possible enemies of China and also against the expected onslaught of the landless millions migrating north. This prison will soon be of indispensable use to China and even more so when the war ends, and the government doesn't want it recklessly torn down. Besides, you've no right requesting entrance here, as officially you're no longer a prisoner. I, myself, once ordered to do so by loyalist command because of American material help and armed intervention on our side, pushed the button that released the doors of the ten American cells. Why you didn't leave with your colleagues, or more like it, why they left you behind, is something I didn't understand. Fleeing as I did to fight the rebels, I never had time to find out, but it was probably because of your disagreeable pushy nature, which even now you do openly employ. What you and your colleagues did with this new freedom was of no concern to me, till I learned several days ago that you're all, by far, not thought of as free men in your own country. On the contrary, very important American leaders have recently denounced you for lying, for the purpose of making prison life here easier for yourselves, about being on a spy plane over China. For this crime you'll each, when caught, receive a reported prison term in America for many years."

"We told the truth about that flight. Each of us, in fact, was given a few hundred dollars extra a month because of the risks of that flight and many others, and you know that as well as anyone."

"Let me be frank with you, Soldier Namurti, although later at your trial say I told you this and I'll deny it with a rage. One of America's quick bargain-table conditions for its material help and entry into our civil war was that loyalist China retract all of its espionage charges against America, as America didn't want to ally itself with a country that on record still considered it a liar. Naturally, the charges were withdrawn—I understand that the rebels, once the war had begun, would have agreed to the same conditions for similar American assistance—and now your country accuses you of giving aid and comfort to what at the time was its enemy."

I walk away while Ep is deciding out loud whether reimprisoning me for the oncoming Americans is worth having to feed me during these food-shortage times, and head north. South is where the famine and refugees are. And from the east, the old man told me, American forces are moving west to join with the loyalists to smash the rebels for good, and I don't want to be captured by them, flown home for a treason trial and maybe put away for life or possibly even executed.

I walk for days till I come to hills that seem to have plenty of woods for protection, and climb the hill that had the best view of the valley. Two Chinese are living at the top—a girl of about seventeen and a boy who's around five. They're frightened when they see me and hide behind a clumsily built lean-to for two days. I make no attempt to befriend them, though do make a point of exhibiting my dried fish and seaweed and bag of rice. When they come out and walk hesitantly toward me, she says "Lin," and touches her chest, and I touch my chest and say "Jamie." We shake hands, the boy hugs my waist, and I give her the rice to cook, since what I forgot to pack is a cooking utensil. She later accepts my offer to rebuild their lean-to, and the day after I give them my blanket for the cold nights, she asks me to sleep inside.

A few days later we see an army of refugees on the road that takes a week to pass. In a month, the American troops pass, and the month after that another American army comes from the east. The war must be over, because the second army brings materials and equipment instead of weapons. From our hill cover we watch the Americans repair the road, the Chinese refugees in the backs of trucks return to the south, and then the Americans widen and repave the roads into highways and level the trees and huts and farms along the highway and replace them with American-style ranch houses and then suburban track developments along with shopping centers and malls, trailer courts, industrial parks, a sports complex and an oil refinery, and farther off we see a six-lane freeway approaching. The smaller hills around us are cut down to bumps, and more developments rise on them and also on the planed-down steps of the larger hills.

One day two non-Chinese climb up our hill with surveying equipment. Lin, her brother Chu, and our baby Sun Goddess and I hide behind a clump of trees and watch the men eat lunch, take lots of land measurements and then discover our two-bedroom cottage and garden and chicken coop. When they start walking in our direction I throw a rock at them and shout "Don't come any closer or I'll drop a few grenades on your heads." One of them says "Hey, you're American. Well, nice surprise, brother, and welcome; we're Americans too. The war's been over for three years, haven't you heard? Nothing to be worried about anymore—this country's been pacified. The whole of freaking Asia's been pacified. China and Stateside are the greatest of buddies now. And any man who can build that shack with just the material he found lying around and who knows with what tools, should have no trouble tying in with the big boom going on here. So come on out, fella, we're your best friends." I yell that I'll give them to ten to get off my property or I'll start zeroing in on them, and they leave.

They return the next day with about a dozen American and Chinese soldiers and three other Americans. The three new civilians present themselves as diplomats with the embassy in Beijing and ask me to come out peacefully as I've no reason to be afraid. Everything's okay in China again, they say, but this hill has to be surveyed for a road and housing development that are going to be built on it with American help, and I'll be amply compensated for my house and land which are directly in the builders' way.

We've been so happy and healthy up here, and now I don't even know why we brought another child into this world. But I have to act quickly before they come into the woods and corner us and break up my family and send me back to the States to stand trial, and Lin, Chu and Sun Goddess to live without me in that ugly emptiness out there for the rest of their lives. I give the signal and we start to run, Sun Goddess light and laughing in my arm and Lin and Chu right behind me, running fast as we can. We dart around the soldiers, who don't seem able to make more than lazy attempts at trying to block us, and after a long sprint we stop to catch our breaths, and hear the diplomats shouting down to us. "You're making a grave mistake, buddy—you've no idea what you're doing. If it's a psychiatrist you think you need, well, hey, we have all that free for you now also—free for everyone in this country, including the Chinese. Come on back, pal, as there's just no reason to run." But we're already a third of the way down the hill, safe and free from them for the moment, and they're not going to get their hands on us without one good hell of a chase.

SHE.

She called and said "Can I stop by?"
"Sure, what's up, how are you?"
"I'll tell you when I get there, all right?"
"Of course, see ya, goodbye,"
and two hours later she rang from downstairs
and I buzzed her up,
my room cleaned, floor washed down but not ammoniated,
as I didn't want to give the scent I was doing
it for her.
New sheets—fresh, I mean, and bed, which is also
my couch, remade twice till it was right,
most of my books out of sight or in place in my
one bookcase,
books on my table and desk turned cover-side down
so I wouldn't seem pedantic,
everything on my desk stacked and aligned,
my new eyeglasses opened on top of my typewriter.
If she asks "Those yours?," I'll say "Yes, for reading,
and only nineteen ninety-five at Cohen's, Delancy and
Orchard, and that includes the eye examination,
bathroom and kitchenette cleaned too and everything
put away.
Two croissants bought in a run so I'd have time
to do all that cleaning and tidying up,
old clothes thrown into the closet,
but what should I wear?

I had that thought: Which turtleneck jersey, blue,
green or black? They're all clean,
and which pants of the five pairs I found in a pile
on a garbage can on the street the other day
and washed in the Laundromat down the block,
even the gray wide-wale corduroys that said
Dry Clean Only,
all of them my length and waist and no Cuffs,
the way I like mine.
Shoes and sneakers and flipflops paired and lined
up at the end of the short hallway by the door,
bedspread flattened out again in my only room.
"Your tomb," she'd said a number of times,
but not for a while.
Then my face shaved, hair brushed back,
anus, genitals and underarms cleaned with a wet
washrag, the washrag then folded neatly over
the bathroom towel rack.
She might comment approvingly of my new headhair
curls which have formed in the two weeks since I
last saw her, painting on the wall also picked up
on the street since then: large studio oil of chair
turned upsidedown on a studio cloth with many folds,
draped sidetable with teapot, several birthday
candles in their holders and can of Ajax on top,
and she might say "Where'd you get that
—off the street like most of your furniture?"
and I'd say "Yes, a studio portrait, appropriate
for my studio apartment, and the chair sort of
symbolizing my life right now,
and also the way I acquired it:
that somebody would just toss it out."
"You writers," she might say, or something like,
if the conversation came to that.
So she came—knocked on my door and never mentioned
the painting or my hair—and tells me what I knew
she would and had prepared myself for,
and I told her why I hadn't called her the
last two weeks and that I'd been thinking the

same thing: "We just don't click together anymore
after almost three years. And it's not that I
don't love you, but—
Actually, I do love you, but like a croissant and
some tea? The croissant's fresh."
"I'd love to but I haven't time and am meter-parked.
I'm glad you're taking it this way and not getting
angry as I thought, and was a little anxious,
you might. But you know, I've always said,
from the first time we met, that I needed a complete
year of freedom, for I went from my first husband,
and that was for ten years, right to you,
and because I was so young, he was the first
man I knew. Let's face it: I just haven't done
what I've wanted with my life—you have to understand,"
and I said "I do."
"So that's it. Nothing more needs to be said,
I think. And you never know what the future
will bring. Gigi"—a good friend of hers—"broke
up with her boyfriend once—severed their relationship
irrevocably, as she put it—and two years later
they resumed, though a few months after that she
broke it up for good, but anyway, we'll see,"
one arm in her coat sleeve—"Why'd I even take
this off? The boiling heat in this apartment"
—other arm trying to shove past the lining of
the other sleeve.
"By the way," she said, "the camera I left here.
Can I have it back?" and I said "Bottom drawer
on the right, under the T-shirts, to perhaps forestall
it being burglarized."
"You New Yorkers. I'm so glad I don't live here."
She stood the whole time, even when she laced her
shoes right after she came in.
She found the camera, briefly looked at her face
in the small Mexican mirror above the night table
—something I'd also found on the street—checked
her permed curls—"I wish mine were natural like yours,"
she once said—flicked the front ones with a finger

and said "Don't get up. I'll see you," and blew me
a kiss and left.
I was still on the bed, and after she left, I said
"Okay, I won't get up if you insist."
We'd pecked lips when she first came in.
She didn't try to dodge me or anything like that,
so I thought it was a good sign. When I'd pressed
down harder on her lips, she pulled back and said
"No, that's enough. Things are different now."
Shortly before she left I asked if she'd read anything
interesting lately, and she said "The selected letters
of Joyce—it recently came out and was reviewed,"
and I said "Oh? Me too. The one with lots of heretofore
unpublished erotic if not masturbatory letters between
Nora and Joyce when they were still fairly young,
right around your age. What a coincidence."
"Not much of one. You got me started with him
—I'd always resisted, thought he'd be too difficult
—and now my passion for his life and work is
out of control."
"I get blamed for everything. . .something my father
used to say about himself," and reached across the
bed to the night table and turned over the book.
"The letters, see? Just so you wouldn't think I
was lying to accrue some advantage with you.
Hardbound or paper?" and she said "Same as yours
—what do you think? I only have so much money,
so even six dollars was a sacrifice, but I had to
have it."
Her last words before she told me not to get up,
she'll see me, and blew a kiss and left.
"Sorry it didn't work out," I'd wanted to say, and
what would she have answered? Probably just a shrug.
I'd also given her a book due at her library in a
few days and which I'd checked out and was going
to mail back. She said she'd read a few pages of
one on artistic creativity I'd left behind and was
a couple of weeks due, and found it very dull.
"What do I owe you for the late fee?" and she said

"Grace"—the librarian of her town's small library
—"said you have your own card, something I didn't
know—I'd always thought you were checking them out
on mine—and that she'd collect from you next time
you're there. I didn't say anything."
Made coffee, read today's Times in bed while I sipped
from the mug, tried to stay calm but couldn't.
Stripped down to my boxer shorts and exercised—
pushups, situps, swinging from the chin bar between
the bathroom's door frame, running in place.
Drank several glasses of water.
Ate carrots, celery, raw cauliflower florets, peanut
butter on crackers and thin slices of Swiss cheese.
Squeezed the croissants in their bag into the
refrigerator's tiny freezer. Never cared for them,
or haven't since I lived in Paris and had one with
jam and café au lait almost every morning in the
back of a café while I read the Herald Tribune.
Walked across Central Park. Bought her daughter
a beaded necklace for Christmas from a jewelry crafts
stand in front of the Met on Fifth.
Walked downtown in the park thinking "I don't feel
too bad. A little better than I thought I would,
in fact. So she's gone; so what? I'll see. Could
lead to something good. New woman I might even be
more taken with, and she with me and with greater
constancy. Someone who lives in the city—maybe even
on the West Side, so I won't have to go so far to
see her—and who's marriageable but never married,
or if once married, no kid, much as I adored hers."
Wished we'd had the baby she aborted without my wanting
her to. "Are you kidding?" when I said a year ago
"Let's get married and keep the kid." Oh, if only
she'd wanted it too, but the hell with it. "Do you
hear?" I said in my head. "The bloody hell."
Saw places in the park we'd walked past, commented
about, rested at. Zoo Cafeteria we'd sat outside in
the cold, pretending it was a ski lodge, though I,
unlike her, had never skied, and had hot chocolate

and shared a warmed-up roll.
Tonight I won't feel so good. But with a little
vodka and a lot of wine, I'll be much better tomorrow.
And day after that, not great but just fine, and
every day after that, always better.
I exited the park at Central Park West and 72nd,
headed to a liquor store near Broadway for a bottle
of wine. When goddamn, on Columbus near the corner,
she was unlocking the driver's door of her VW bug.
I ran up to her while she was putting a shopping
bag on the front seat, and said "Do I know you?"
and tried to kiss her.
"No way," she said, swiveling out of my grip.
"I know you too and have read your stories. You
and your surrogates never stop with a civilized kiss.
By the way, I never asked—how's your mother?"
"The same, the same, but do you mind if we don't
start that how's-so-and-so talk today, okay?
I'm sort of fed up with it."
"I thought you wouldn't get angry," she said.
"Who the hell's angry? I'm not. Say, how about
a coffee for old friends' sake?" and she said
"Got to go. Only came down to quickly see you
and do some Christmas shopping. Now I have to get
back to correct papers and prepare next week's classes."
She got in her car, door was still open, and I said
"Boy, you're sure not going to suffer."
"What about you? You've said yourself you only
give your suffering over somebody three days.
Then they're out of your mind, which I find healthy."
"That was two months after I first met you and we
split. Not three years, and half of it living together.
Screw it," and I waved with my back turned to her,
and instead of going to the liquor store, I headed
for home.
Few seconds later, I heard footsteps running up
behind me. I turned, but it wasn't her. Some young
father pretending to run away from his young son.

BURGLARS.

Something's wrong. I unlocked the door to my mother's apartment as I do every night to check up on her and take her garbage out, and a breeze blew past me into the public hall. It's winter and very cold out and during this time of year she always keeps her windows closed.

I go in and see from the foyer, papers floating to the kitchen floor. I run to the kitchen. Her pocketbook's on the floor, has been turned inside out and its personal papers and coins are scattered about.

I yell "You sonofabitch, I'll kill you," and open a kitchen drawer for a knife, but right away know I'll never use it on anyone. But I can hit a head with a hard object if I have to, so I grab a candlestick out of a cabinet and bang the base against the counter and yell "You better get out the way you got in here or just peacefully identify yourself to me and leave through the front door, or I'm going to beat your thieving head in," and go into the breakfast room.

A window to the backyard is open and two of its bars have been pried apart. The backyard door is locked and I open it and go outside, and nobody's there. I check the downstairs bathroom. The light's on, there's a cigarette in the toilet bowl and a faint odor of cigarette smoke. I flush the toilet, then think I shouldn't have—police might have wanted to examine the cigarette—and go upstairs.

The ceiling light in the girls' room is on and all the dresser drawers have been pulled out, nothing inside them but clothes of my five brothers and sisters from ten to twenty years ago. I look under the bed, inside the closet, throw open the door of the bathroom right outside the bedroom and shove the shower curtain aside.

My mother and I run to the front of the apartment, turning on the lights as I go and glancing around, and listen at her door. I hear breathing, she seems to be sleeping. I turn on the night light in her room. She dozed off in her house dress, closed book on her chest, afghan she'd knitted, covering her. I make the same quick search: closet, bathroom, under the bed, candlestick ready to come down on the burglar's head, though I'm almost sure he escaped through the breakfast room window and over a backyard fence right after he heard me open the front door.

I put the book on her night table and turn off the light. I search the baby's room next to my mother's, the linen closet, living room, boys' room, which is now unused like the baby's and girls' rooms and where I slept with my older brothers in bunk beds for about fifteen years.

I phone the police from the kitchen, then yell from the backyard "Attention, neighbors who have backyards on these streets. A burglar, about ten minutes ago, broke into my mother's apartment here and climbed over one of the connecting fences to get away, so turn on your yard lights and all your rear room lights and make sure your rear doors and windows are locked tight."

I repeat the message and then return to my mother's room and shake her shoulder. "Mom, it's me, don't worry," and I tell her what happened. She puts on a robe, is very shaky and I have to hold her arm when she walks downstairs. I make us both a drink. We sit in the breakfast room while we wait for the police. It's now her sitting room of sorts, where she embroiders and reads and watches TV. There used to be a table and eight chairs in here when the family had breakfast together every Sunday and dinner together almost every night.

She says "This never used to happen on the block when you kids were growing up."

"I know, I know."

"We used to keep the front door unlocked during the day because of all you kids running in and out, and nobody but someone we welcomed or invited ever came in."

"You started locking the front door about twenty years ago, when all of us were grown up or could be trusted with keys, but I get your point."

"But double bars I didn't have on these windows till three years ago, and only because a couple of neighbors got burglarized from the backyard, but the thieves still break in."

"I'll get more bars put on. Stronger ones. Maybe even gates, if you can overcome your aesthetic distaste for them, but you'll be safe."

"It's not my safety I'm worried about. At my age, though I don't want them here, they can come and go, so long as they don't do it while I'm asleep. It's just that

I hate to see these things deteriorate the way they have, for everybody's sake."

"Your safety is important. You're just talking like that because you're flustered and upset. You're healthy and can live lots of years yet, so we're going to make it extra safe for you here. Unless you want to give up the place and come live with Marion and me."

"Never. I like my privacy even more than you do. And we'd end up barely tolerating each other after a few months, and I'd probably sour your marriage a little besides. You will sleep over tonight, though, won't you?"

"Sure. In the boys' room. Marion would want me to. Then early tomorrow I'll call the locksmith."

The police come, write up a report and give us a prediction and statistic: we'll never again see what was stolen and this was only one of an average of ten burglaries a day in this precinct.

One of the policemen picks up the silver candlestick and says "This what you made your noise with to chase the kid away?" They already determined it was a strong man with a crowbar who pried the bars apart and a small wiry kid who slipped in. "Think you would have used it on him like you did on the countertop?"

"I don't know, now that you say it was a kid."

"Even if it was a kid, you think he came empty-handed and wouldn't have used his weapon on you, and believe me, he had one."

"Then I suppose I would have had to protect myself with this stick, though I wouldn't have liked myself later on for doing it."

"No," my mother says, "I wouldn't want you hitting any child, even if it meant he took everything from me."

"Even if it meant he'd bash in your son's brains protecting you?" the policeman says.

"There are ways. There have to be. Talk, for instance. He was a junior high school teacher, so he knows how to talk to boys and girls."

"*Talk.* That's years ago. When I was a boy, and I've got at least ten years on your son. Anyway, you'll have to take it to a silversmith to get the dent out, if you can find one these days. Looks like an antique."

"It is," I say. "A wedding gift to my folks from my mother's parents more than fifty years ago."

"You want the truth after all this time?" my mother says. "I only told your dad that's where they came from. It's fifty years old, all right, but I bought the pair of them in a department store for myself so he'd think my parents were even more generous than they were."

"He never knew?"

"Why would I have told him? It was only a harmless fib. Now it comes out because of this robbery and I don't want to tell real lies for the policeman's report. Otherwise, I would have kept it to myself for life."

THE   .

LEADER

Hitler was coming to town and he wanted one of us girls. Young, he liked them young. "How young?" I asked the prostitute who told me this.

"Young like you," she said. "That's what I heard from a friend of mine who's still a prostitute in Berlin. She was in a house that Hitler went to—oh, that was a long time ago. Now he doesn't go to houses. We just go to him and he or one of his aides selects. Anyway, he specified young—at least twenty years younger than him. That was ten years ago when he was first becoming our leader. Now it's maybe thirty years younger than him—who knows? So you got a good chance to be the winner, sweetheart."

"Did your friend say what he's really like in person? Because I don't think I could take doing it with such an incredibly powerful and famous man."

"He's all right."

"She say that?"

"She didn't say much. Just that she didn't get him. She was already too old. And that he took the youngest girl in the house, who also happened to be the prettiest and best built, so nobody was sure if he picked her only for her being young or pretty or her build or what. She had big boobs, that's what my friend said. Big and high and a tiny waist and hips that were in proportion to her breasts and long legs. And she was blond."

"He prefers them blond too?"

"It's difficult to say what he prefers. Remember, this is all second-hand. I don't know what other houses he's been to or if he's changed his taste much in women since then, but he's seen plenty of women, I understand. That's what a general friend told me. Not a friend— a client, a one-shot deal. He came in here a couple of years ago for a supposed quickie and said before we did anything 'You know what?' I said 'No, what?' He said 'Did you know I'm on Hitler's personal general staff?' I said 'No kidding, that's great.' What else was I to say? He said 'Wouldn't you like to know what Hitler's really like?' I said 'Yeah, yeah, tell me,' because I could see he was aching to say it. I didn't actually care then or now, but you do?"

"Well, yes, in a way. After all, he is Hitler. The leader of the entire continent. Maybe one of the greatest men ever."

"The hell with Hitler, and you know it. And the hell with all the continents he conquers—though don't breathe a word to anyone I said any of this. Oh, go ahead. Tell the world—what do I care? I'll say I never said it. No, that never works anymore. But I couldn't give a toot what Hitler's really like. Just give me my money, get your cookies, and go—next customer, please, know what I mean? But he was a general and, if he was telling the truth, on Hitler's staff. And he had plenty of money to throw around also, so I said 'Of course, I've always been eager to know. But he's very nice, though, am I right? Sort of like a god.' I said that to make sure he knew whose side I was on. He said 'He's a god like you say, but a real god.' I could see he was having second thoughts, as if I might be an informer or so patriotic that I'd run out and blab if he said the least thing critical of Hitler. 'You would like him,' he said. 'He goes for girls like you and makes them excited with his godlike qualities, and I'm not just talking about the spiritual and moral, you understand?' 'Not exactly,' I said. 'Because maybe I shouldn't be telling you this, General, but I heard from a prostitute friend who's now dead that he likes girls much younger than me—half his age, preferably–and with big parts in all the important places, no disrespect meant, is that true?' He said 'The cut of the female figure doesn't matter to him so long as it's perfect for him.' Now that can almost mean nothing or two things, which can also be nothing if you can't or don't want to figure it out, so I dropped the subject. After, which is way after, for that was a weary old general who I think fought his greatest and maybe last battle on me and in the end won at an enormous sacrifice to himself, he said 'Want to know what Hitler's really like?' I said 'Didn't you ask me that before?' 'Did I?' he said, and I quickly said 'No, it must have been someone else,' for he seemed angry. He said 'Who? You know people who are talking disparagingly about our great leader?' 'No, just some harmless lieutenant in the tank corps I saw a year ago.' 'You go to bed with lieutenants?' he said. 'No, I only overheard him downstairs when I was wandering through the main room looking for a lost brooch. Me, I save myself only for colonels and higher.' Anyway, Hitler's coming to town to check the military base, I suppose, and his first stop after he detrains is the Forest Hotel. We're all to be in a room there when he or his aide comes in to make the choice. And no men for any of us till after the selection, as he wants the one who's picked to be, at least for the time being, pure."

Two hours later the madam, Mrs. Dorfer, came into our room and said "Knock knock, darlings. Get your finest finery and most daring undies on, as we're going to Hitler's hotel."

We all get into a couple of officers' cars Hitler sent over. Seven of us girls packed in to each one, which was almost the entire house. Lotte and Ilse were left behind. They were obviously too old—girls Mrs. Dorter saved for soldiers and townsmen who had drunk or gambled too much and were down to their last marks. During the ride I asked the girl next to me "Excited?"

"For what? None of us has more than an eight percent chance of getting him. This was also supposed to be my day off, and besides that I'm coming down with the sniffles, so with my luck it'll probably be me."

"But Hitler. Just that you might see him up close."

"Yes, Hitler. Maybe you've a point. Truth is, till now I didn't even think there was a real Hitler. He's so easy to impersonate and look like, and that voice—even my brother fooled me with it once on the phone. I thought there might be four to five men dressed like him making speeches and shaking their fists all over Europe—something thought up by some military and industrial geniuses to get our economy rolling again, and knowing the national mentality, what better way? But real or not, I was never one of his bigger fans. He comes in like hailstones and thunder, and thinks we're going to take over the whole western world? You ever read world history? I did—before, when I was becoming a teacher, plus all the best literature there is. In the end, we got to lose. You can only stick it out so far and for so long before choppo, you get your head and hands cut off and, if you're not looking, your behind too. So big deal, I quietly say in my own way—Hitler as a client. No, I thought it over. Years from now if I'm alive and I tell people that, they'll say 'That miscreant and baboon? He brought the great German nation to its lowest ebb yet. You had the devil himself in you.' But believe me, if I wind up with Hitler I don't move any more for him than I would for any other man, unless he puts a cocked gun to my head. And with his responsibilities and heavy worries and past decisions, you think he's going to do any amazing tricks in bed? That's for the newsreels. Like all deep thinkers I've had, it'll take everything he has for him to get started and then stay with it, so I suppose I will have to move a little more for him than with others, just to get the job over with."

"Well, I'm excited at the prospect," the girl on my other side said. "It's like a fantasy come true. When I was a young girl—I am not old—I fell in love with him right after they jailed him for that putsch. His face—so sensitive and brooding, yet sweet. And his presence, defiance and physique. That was then. Maybe now his body's a little changed. But I wrote him a letter, even. When he got out of prison he wrote me one back. He said 'Your faith in my cause inspired me and inspires me still. We will win.' That was very nice. I kept the letter, knowing it would be valuable one day, but my ancestral home was bombed early in the war and everything went up in it—I won't even specify what people were inside. But from that prison sentence till now I have adored him. If I was chosen over all you girls it would be like for some other women making love with the world's most famous movie star who they've been writing about in their diaries for years. And he's still very handsome and gallant like one, wouldn't you say?"

"Very," I said. "Do you know anything about what kind of girl he prefers? I heard he likes them extremely young."

"I don't know, though I'm sorry to hear what you said. Perhaps if he'd succeeded with that putsch and we were in the same situation now, only ten years earlier, my chances would be better. But I wasn't a prostitute then, so I guess I lose out no matter what."

"I've a good idea what he likes," a girl on one of the jumpseats. "Helga, the cleaning lady in our house, told me he only likes girls with big derrieres. She said years ago she was a girl in the most elegant house in Hamburg, and Hitler, who'd just become chancellor then, came in with Goebbels or Göring—though I know those two don't look alike, I always get their names mixed up because of the G and O. They were some pair, she said, Hitler and the other one. Joking, playing the piano, throwing money in the air. You should speak to her. She has funny stories to tell about them just from their one trip. But Hitler took the girl with the biggest buttocks. She was also very young, chunky, and kind of happy-go-lucky, and had short black hair."

"Someone else thought he liked tall blondes with tiny waists," I said.

"I'd heard that too. So I asked Helga again, but she said Hitler definitely picked the stubby black-haired and Göring or Goebbels chose a tall blond. But you got a nice derriere—not fat, but just big and broad enough to qualify. Mine? Too small and firm, I think—coconuts, which lots of men prefer. If Helga's right then I guess I should count myself out too. Though I'd love to be the one selected. Not just for the money involved but because it'll be one hell of a story to tell for the rest of my life."

"Did Helga say what kind of man Hitler was like?"

"Only the girl he was with saw him. But she did say something quite strange happened soon after Hitler left. The girl fainted dead away in the room she'd used. They thought she was overcome with being with the new dynamic chancellor, and maybe he also had something unique going in a physical and amorous way to have had such an effect on a young pro. They revived her with salts, but she said she couldn't speak about what happened, nor could she work anymore that night. For two days after, all she could speak was gibberish—his stress, his anxieties, how it isn't easy guiding an entire nation and maybe becoming the future number one leader of the world. They got her a doctor, but the third day after she saw Hitler and without allowing herself another man, she really cracked and had to be taken away."

"She must have been very immature," I said. "I know I wouldn't let myself go like that if he picked me tonight."

"You never know. Have you ever had a truly great man?"

"You mean a powerful figure—world famous, like a great artist whose name everybody knows? Once; Johann the tightrope walker."

"You had him? Out of the air I'd think he'd be ungainly and tense."

"Sort of. But he's called the best ropewalker in Germany and so maybe the rest of the world, we can say, can we not?"

"We might."

"Even still, he fell. Two weeks ago—I read it in the paper. Broke both legs and his spine entertaining our troops. He was the most famous man I ever had, and just average in bed. Wanted things done, wouldn't do much, peter out, come back, give him a few wiggles from below and you're done with him. Nothing out of the ordinary. Normal."

"Maybe that was a bad day for him, or a very good one. Maybe all aerialists and the like only think they have to come to us, but don't do well because they get most of their fulfillment on the ropes and bars. And like our leader, just think of all the tensions they come to you with. Everybody watching them, one false move and so forth, some people even hoping they'll fall because that could be more exciting than just his high-wire walk. But Hitler's problems are much different than any other man's, so I don't want to prejudge him too hard. Though I do think he'll be an experience to make love with just because he is who he is and all those pressures he has to release."

The cars stopped. "Everyone into the hotel," an officer said. "Leave your pocketbooks and accessories in the cars." Soldiers all around— naturally, security was tight. So many flags above the entrance, and the lobby never seemed so clean and bright.

We were led into the dining room. Only now, nobody was there except maybe fifty soldiers on guard. The middle of the room had been cleared except for fourteen chairs in a row for us girls. We were told to sit. A few minutes passed. Then the commanding officer said "Everyone rise." The soldiers stood at attention, and all the girls rose. The door from the kitchen opened, and out first in front of a group of officers was Hitler, who walked quickly and was in full uniform and knotted tie and holstered pistol and with his hat and swagger stick under one arm, but instead of those riding boots I'd always seen him in photos and newsreels, he wore highly polished black shoes. He walked past us with the commanding officer, as if we were this officer's troops he was inspecting. He was taller than I thought he'd be, and he didn't look well: pale and fleshy in the face and with big bags under his eyes. His hair style and mustache were the same as always, and his paunch and the way his body drooped were no different than most men his age. He also looked a little annoyed, as if with just one glance he knew that none of us were what he'd had in mind and that he was wasting his time here. Then he smiled.

"That one," he said, pointing the stick at Vera, the girl who'd been wanting him since the Putsch. "No good. Sorry, my dear," he said, sort of bowing, and the officer snapped his fingers and a soldier escorted her out of the room. Vera, who threw her hands to her mouth and screamed in delight when she'd thought she'd been picked, left sobbing. Hitler walked past us all again and kept shaking his head.

"Stand straight and tall, girls," the officer said.

"No, that's all right," Hitler said. "They're standing fine. That one," and he pointed the stick at Gretchen, who had the biggest buttocks and maybe the best shape of any of us. "She's quite charming looking, but her age is against her. Please," he said to the officer. "To save them this embarrassment, you should have left behind the types I asked you to. Excuse me," he said to Gretchen, and the officer snapped his fingers and she was escorted out.

Of the twelve girls left, maybe only Reni had a behind that came close to being as big as mine but still compact, if that was what Hitler liked most in a woman. She also had a bigger bosom and tinier waist and was blond and almost as young as me, so I thought he'd pick her. Then, maybe Hetta next, who was the real beauty of the bunch though perhaps too tall and slim for him and like me a brunette, with maybe long-legged Frieda and me coming in third.

"You," he said, pointing to me. So I was out too. "I would like her. She has a bit more sparkle in the face than the others and a seemingly cheerier disposition, though you are all so nice for taking the time to come here today and Colonel Beineman will see that you are adequately recompensed. Thank you," and he saluted us with the stick and left.

The rest of the girls crowded around me. "Oh, Gerta, you are so lucky," they said. "You clever girl. I bet you winked at him and showed him a peek of what you had, isn't that so?"

"The winner and new champion, perhaps," Clothilda said, raising my hand above my head. "You will be fantastic. He will adore you and be fantastic. Play your cards right, my darling, and you can take that other whore's place and give orders in all his castles and feed his huge dogs."

"Just be careful and return to us safe and sound," Mrs. Dorter said.

"The rest of you please return to the cars you arrived in," the commanding officer said. "Mrs. Dorter, see Colonel Beineman, and you, please," he said to me, "come with me?"

I got into the hotel elevator with him and two guards. "You have nothing that can be construed as weapons," he said. "Barrettes, nail-files, clippers—mind if I search?"

"And if I did?"

"I'd have the matron do it. I don't take liberties with women, madame."

"Search me."

He searched me during the elevator ride. "You're clean. Now be good to the leader, you hear? He doesn't need to be counseled or consoled, just relaxed. Say only pleasant and reassuring things to him. Beautiful day today—words to that effect. He won't find them rude or dumb and he will understand your unease. And don't be aggressive or suggest anything unless he asks you to. He likes politeness and warmth. In other words, do what he says to do, and you will be amply rewarded, and if he comes this way again soon, you'll be his choice for a second time."

"How long do you think it will be?"

"This is between you and him. And I forgot: be responsive too. Whatever he does, say you like."

"Though I know he's not like anybody else, I do that with all my clients unless they're suffocating me with their weight or trying to murder me. Any other advice?"

"None I can think of. After it's over, he'll tell you so by leaving through the door to the adjoining room, and probably without saying another word. Then you get washed and dressed and see me outside your door."

We walked down a hotel corridor where a lot of soldiers were. "Can I ask you one more thing? Why do you think he picked me?"

"He already said. He liked you. Your disposition and sparkle and such."

"Some of the girls said they heard he only likes us young and with big buttocks and larger breasts than mine and maybe blond and a very narrow waist, which mine—though flat—is not. Any of that true?"

"He likes all kinds. Young, maybe, but most men do. But you with your brown hair and others with red or black or even dyed to those. But no more of this. Here is his room. Just go inside and undress and get in bed under the top sheet. He'll be in soon."

I went inside and undressed and got in bed. There was an uncorked bottle of Moselle in an ice bucket by the bed. I'd like a drink but didn't know if I should take one. I'd wait. There was fruit too. And tiny cheese and wurst sandwiches on a silver tray. Truth was, I was getting nervous and would like something to eat and drink to calm my nerves. For what would I say to him? How was I to act? He'd see through any pose I put on. *La guerre* goes well, *mon general, n'est pas*? No, that wouldn't do. Whatever I'd say: no jokes. And suppose he didn't like me nude? My simple little appendectomy scar might put him off. Then he'd say so and I'd leave if he wanted me to, easy as that. I don't think he'd get angry. And he had so much power. That was what frightened me. I must be on my guard what I do and say. People who it seemed hadn't done or said anything had disappeared. Not anyone I knew, but friends of friends. All for a good cause, I'm sure, but some say no. But who was to say what was the good cause? A man with so much power could establish his own good cause. That was true. Just keep the words functional and complimentary and wait for the signals from him, that was the best way.

The door to the next room opened and he came out. He didn't say anything, just looked at the ceiling, blinking his eyes as if the light there was too bright for him, then looked at me. He was in slippers and a bathrobe. Very nice one too. Velvet. Red, with black piping and a thick braided rope. Stern, though, and it didn't seem a smile would ever come.

"Hello," I said.

"Hello. You're a very attractive young lady—you know that, don't you?"

"I've been told."

"Hasn't gone to your head yet, has it?"

"The Moselle?"

"The Moselle? Oh, the Moselle. No, not that. You want some? Maybe you've had some."

"I haven't. I thought I'd wait."

"You should have felt free and helped yourself. I wouldn't have minded." He was still standing by the door he'd come through, bathrobe still tied. "Did you think I would have got upset if you'd taken a glassful?"

"I thought it would be politer and more respectful of me to wait till you got here. It's your wine. I'm your guest and these are your rooms. I would wait till you offered it, that's what I felt."

"It's the hotel's wine. They gave it to me. The best Moselle, they said. Let me see." He came over and read the bottle's label. "Good, but not the best. So now it's our Moselle and I will only drink a glass if you'll have one too. No, that's not so. But drink a glass or two. Don't wait for me."

"Do you want some? I'll pour it for you."

"Yes, pour it. Why not? And I'll offer you sandwiches. That way, we can be polite to each other and give each other different things."

"Thank you." I poured the wine into two glasses, held his glass out for him. We clicked glasses. He first, then I clicked his. I drank all my wine. He only sipped from his.

"You drank so fast," he said.

"Because I'm a little nervous. Uh-oh, maybe I shouldn't have said that."

"Nervous of me? Don't be. And say anything. I am in here like all other men. And you are young. And have nice breasts. I like them."

"Thank you."

"I won't tell you why. That might embarrass you. You'll have to guess. All women's breasts are nice, but yours especially so. But I still won't say why."

"I'll think about why you think they're nice later on."

"Do. It's good to have something to think about later on."

"You mean after you leave?"

"No, always. Always to have something to think about but not always to think about it. Activity. Physical and of the mind. Both you can't do very well together at the same time, now can you?"

"I don't think so."

"Don't say so or agree with me unless you believe it."

"I won't."

"Then what do you really think about it?"

"About what?"

"That physical and mental activity can't go hand in hand together very well. And then, not too much of only one without the other coming soon after it, and on and on and on and interchanging themselves like that till you sleep. Thrust yourself into experience and then reflect on the meaning of it. But all reflection and no experience makes us mad. The opposite, and we are nothing but brutes. Now who previously said that?"

"I've no idea."

"Guess."

"Goethe?"

"Very good. You're educated. Or look straight at me and tell me you didn't read my mind."

"I didn't."

"Something happened. Or perhaps it is that you're just plain smart."

"I went through your schools. And almost became a nurse."

"You should have. And I'm excited by you, you know? Educated, or a mind reader. Both would do." He sat on the bed. "Oh, I completely forgot." He offered me the plate of sandwiches. "Eat, go on. You're young, maybe still growing. And you'll grow bigger, stronger, and wiser and maybe even telepathic if you take the headcheese."

I took the headcheese sandwich, though I never liked it because it's gelatinous and all those foot and mouth parts.

"Don't take it just because I suggested you to. What's your favorite tea sandwich here?"

"Headcheese."

"Truth now."

"Actually, I prefer an unadorned cream cheese, but they don't have any here."

"What they didn't supply for us here is not what I asked you." He seemed miffed.

"I'm sorry, you're right. I was being selfish. Out of all these, the hard cheese on the black bread there. I like that best of all."

"Then put down the headcheese."

"Headcheese is nice too."

"No, put it down. Eat what you like. You don't get that many opportunities for that now, am I right? Food is generally scarce. Not for me—I won't lie to you. But I'm sure it is for you. So here you have a choice. More than a choice—you can have all these sandwiches when you leave. Tell the commanding office that I said so."

"He'll believe me?"

"It's what I usually do. He knows. You only don't get them if you don't tell him."

"I'll tell him. Thank you. All the other girls would probably like some too, so we'll divide them up."

"Do that. Very generous." Then silence. He sipped his wine, was looking away from me. I didn't think I should say "Don't you want to remove your robe?" as I would have with any other customer by now. No: wait for the signals. He was paying more, for one thing. And he was who he was and would do it at his own time. And I'd made too many mistakes already. Though who could say—maybe he wanted me to take the lead. Maybe he was shy and unassertive in bed...but someone would have said, or maybe they hadn't heard.

And maybe the commanding officer also didn't know and was only guessing at the right approach when he said don't be suggestive or aggressive.

"Would you like to come under the covers with me?" I said.

"In time."

"Of course. In time. I'm sorry. I knew you knew better what to do. I think I said it out of force of habit. That's the truth now, even if my saying that about habit and all it alludes to might also be the wrong thing to say. But I'm getting in deeper and deeper, but I also have to admit I'm feeling more than a little nervous in your presence and I don't know what to do about it."

"Calm yourself. As I said, I'm not unlike any other man in many respects. Act natural. I want that. Not fright or anxietude. I chose you because you seemed the one young woman downstairs who'd be least afraid of me and so would do what I want her to."

"I'm not too different. A few of the other girls would have been like that too."

"Yes, but I chose you."

"Thank you."

"Come all the way out of the sheets this time and I'll sit on the bed more."

We did.

"Very nice breasts. Strong body. You are very nice. And you will be very nice to me too, all right?"

"Of course."

"Lovely hair. Kiss me." I kissed him. A little kiss. "Soft lips. Lovely lips." He stood up and untied his bathrobe. He still had all his clothes on underneath except his jacket and belt with revolver. He got undressed, touching my thighs and forehead every now and then. Nude, he looked his fifty or so years in physique. He sat back on the bed. "I'm tired, though not much."

"I've time. Really. And energy—all you wish."

"Touch me. Hard if you like. Don't worry. Everyone can take a little hurt."

"Down there?"

He nodded. I held and rubbed him.

"Now I'm going to lie on my stomach and I want you to do something."

"I think I know what it is," I said.

"No, you don't. Not even with your educated guess. I want you to urinate on me."

"I couldn't."

"Yes, you can. It's easy. And you must have done it to others. And everyone can urinate a little at most times. So do it."

"Where?"

"Waist up, but principally on the top of my head. Now, please."

I stood over him. "It's not as easy for us to direct it," I said. I urinated on his shoulders first and then made it up to the top of his head.

"That's good. Thank you, Now defecate on me."

"I could never do that. And I never have."

"It's harder, but try."

"No."

"You don't want to?"

"It's not that I don't want to. I'll do all the other things you want."

"You can sleep with twenty men in succession in one evening—that's true—that's maybe an exaggeration—so you can't do this for me once?" He was getting angry again. "Please, dear—what's your name?"

"Gerta."

"Please, Gerta, be nice. You said you'd be very nice, And you had the face of a nice girl, which is also why I chose you. So you do it once in your life. What's that?

Once, and it's done. What is it even having it done to you once? And after, you can run to the bathroom without making an excuse. I don't ask for this all the time, I swear. Now, I'm ready."

He put his head face down into the pillow. I got over him again. "It might take time," I said.

"All the time you need." His head was now right below my behind. A funny thought I had was that I suddenly felt like one of his bombers circling over an enemy town. His head was the town center—the primary target, where the enemy's command post and warworks were, and maybe I sprayed it and a little of the town's outskirts before with my urine like bullets. If I told him this now, would he laugh? No—no jokes. Serious business with him, bombing, and I better get serious too. But a town eager to get bombed—pleading for it, in fact? Enough. Must concentrate. I tried. Nothing. His head turned a little to the side and one of his eyes was now visible and looking up.

"How are you doing?" he said.

"Soon."

"Good. If you need another glass of wine, take one. Take two."

"I think I'll be all right without it."

"Better to take it, and fruit."

I drank standing up on the bed with him still flat below me. Poured myself another glass and drank that one down too. I reached over for a pear, bit into it and threw it back into the bowl, but I missed and it fell to the floor. He didn't stir. I got over him again.

"I think you should be ready," he said.

"I just about am." It came. First direct hit on the town center, and he moved his face back into the pillow. He made noises like a man making noises during the sex act rather than at the end. Then it was over. The enemy town was totally destroyed. Mission accomplished and with a first strike also, or whatever the expressions are that air force people use. "Excuse me," I said.

"I understand."

He was still on his stomach with his face in the pillow, though you'd think he'd want to get out fast too. I got off the bed and went to the bathroom and cleaned myself. I looked in the mirror. Hitler, I thought. Nobody would believe it. Or rather: for my own sake, nobody was ever going to have a chance to believe it. He didn't have to tell me that. The woman he lives with: she does it to him too? Has he always done it this way and only with young women? She isn't that young. Nice figure, though: I don't know about her behind. But he said no—"I swear," he said, "not all the time." But that girl who cracked up after being with him. Having someone like him plead for you to do such a thing must have been too much for her to bear. Suppose she once worshipped him. She might have been to rallies or at least seen newsreels of rallies with him speaking to half a million cheering people. If only she could have been like me. I'm not tough but I've been around long enough to take the healthy way; in many respects he's inferior, a crazy pathetic pervert, simple as that.

I left the bathroom. He was gone. And the soiled linen was gone and a perfume had refreshened the room. I dressed and left. The commanding officer was waiting outside the door.

"So everything went well?" he said.

"I think he was satisfied. He didn't complain. I treated him as nice as I could, just as you said."

"If the report back from him is a good one, then I hope we'll see you again." He snapped his fingers. The same two guards came over. "Drive her home in an officer's car or to wherever she wants to go."

"Home," I said. "And thank you." We shook hands. The guards and I walked to the elevators. "Wait," I said, "there's something else. Hitler said I could have all the sandwiches in the room."

"Forget the sandwiches," one of the guards said.

"But he said I should ask your officer for them."

He ran back and knocked on a door. The officer came out. "She says he told her she could have all the sandwiches in his room."

"Then get them for her."

"You must come with me, sir. I'm not allowed in unless with you."

They went into the room I was in with Hitler before. The guard came out carrying the tray of sandwiches and gave me it. The officer went back to his room.

"But it's silver and belongs to the hotel," I said. "Hitler only said the sandwiches, nothing about the tray."

"If my officer says it's what I should give you, nobody will mind."

I held the tray, offered each of them a sandwich as we rode down in the elevator. They each took one. I thought maybe one of them would ask me what Hitler was like in the room. As a test of my silence, perhaps. Or maybe because of his curiosity on the subject concerning such a man, he might lose his head for a moment and ask. If one of them did, I'd say "I'm sorry, it's something you know I can't talk about, and if you insist, I'll have to report you to your officer." That would be the right answer. I also thought that maybe one of them, if he didn't know what Hitler was like in the bedroom, would want to pay to be the first one to make love to me after Hitler. But, that too, neither of them asked.

THE GOOD FELLOW.

"Help."

Lenny said it to himself, though for a moment he wanted to say it out loud.

"Help," he said softly. He looked around the Student Union cafeteria. Thank God nobody had heard him. His voice was normally deep and resonant and carried much farther than he liked.

A novel was opened in front of him on the yellow table. Underneath it was a cup turned upside down, as a prop. He was getting a headache. He was astigmatic and had broken his glasses a month ago, but hadn't replaced them because Student Medical Service didn't cover eyeglasses and a new pair would set him back thirty dollars. He gently massaged his eyes through the lids.

He'd been on the same sentence for the last five minutes. For sure, he didn't want to read. He looked through the all-glass wall to the outside: there were no windows in this ultramodern room, which was about the size and as brightly lit as a big city's airline terminal. The moon was nearly full tonight, and low, so low it seemed caught in the eucalyptuses in the distance like a helium balloon. If he were with someone now, he'd ask why.

"Question," he'd say. "Why is the moon so frigging low tonight?"

This person could tell him it had to do with the time of year or the vernal equinox or something. But a simple answer, which he should have known and this person might have picked up in a high school or college general science course. People remembered so many more things than he. He wasn't a well-informed person in anything but literature, and even that, mainly twentieth century fiction.

"Question," he'd say to this person beside him or even a group seated around the table. "What do you say we go to the Dunes for a burger and beer?" The Dunes was the most popular off-campus hangout. There you could get dark or regular beer in huge pitchers and a real California hamburger, which was grilled and came on a warm sesame roll with tomato slices, onion slices, shredded lettuce, relish, mayonnaise, mustard, ketchup, spices and a bag of tortilla chips or garlic-flavored potato chips on the side. Lenny was from New York and was used to having his hamburger broiled and stuck on a cold bun with only a single pickle round on top.

"Question," he'd say. "What the hell am I doing back in college after graduating six years ago. Forget it; I know." He was here on a much-coveted creative writing fellowship for a year that carried with it a three thousand dollar stipend and a chance to meet book and magazine editors from the East, scouting for new writers. He'd also come to meet female students, all tanned and blond and built for the beach. But he hadn't had much opportunity to meet them. The English Department parties he'd heard fantastic stories about before he got here, were almost nonexistent, and the one he went to—the first one he futilely drove around looking for in the hills above campus for an hour—was boring and stuffy and he felt totally out of place. And because he wasn't going for a master's like the nonfellowship students in the graduate writing program, he only had one three-hour class a week. Each of these workshops the past two quarters was composed of intense-looking and opinionated students and some professors' wives. The exception, this past quarter, was Miss Prettyface Louise, a senior—she was allowed into the class because her fiction and criticism was on a level with the graduate students, the teacher said—who sat with her thighs locked and breasts high and eyes demurely down. He could go for her and would call her now if she wasn't betrothed.

"Question," he said to himself. "Why'd he drive to campus just to sit in this cafeteria for two hours? You really want to know? I haven't met any women at the Dunes—they all seem to come in with guys or in groups of women that want to be left alone—and I thought this place would be a good one to, since I'd also been told writing fellows were considered choice company and prize catch by a lot of the unattached literary-minded women on campus. If I met one, or really anybody here to talk to, and I could convince this person to come with me, then to the Dunes for burgers and beers. For you see, I'd become almost a nightly regular there and want to show the bartenders and barflies that I don't always have to come in alone."

Maybe he should call the other writing fellow and invite himself over. B.J. Aimlace was married and quite sympathetic to Lenny's loneliness out here and often said he had a standing invitation to visit them anytime he liked. They lived more than an hour's drive over the mountains, in a rented house facing the beach with an ancient redwood growing out of the living room roof. Lenny had been there once, during the first quarter. B.J.'s wife, who after dinner shared a hashpipe with her husband, which she said always made her feel more congenial if not beatific, suddenly swung around to Lenny and said "I loathe you." Just like that. "I truly loathe you, Lenny Polk. You're so infuriatingly straight." Mercedes was English, and her long articulated drawl on the word "loathe" made her opinion of him seem that much more virulent. B.J. lit up some more hash, shrugged when Lenny again declined to take a toke—he'd told them he was frankly afraid of drugs like these and could never see himself driving home along winding roads turned on—and passed the pipe to Mercedes. Lenny didn't say anything to her about her remark; he only smiled helplessly at both of them as if there were no excuse for his loathsomeness and lack of courage. Then he whispered to B.J. if she'd been serious. "She's more likely just after your ass," B.J. said. "I am not," she said. "That's a big fat lie." "Believe me, if she truly loathed you she would have fled to the bedroom and singly sulked." Little later, Lenny said he was getting tired, thanked them for a delicious dinner and great time, and sat embarrassed while they stood waving goodbye to him from their porch for the ten minutes it took to start up the car.

He stared at his book for a few minutes. Then he turned the page, though he hadn't finished it yet, just in case anyone was watching him. At the next table, which was a flaming red, a very attractive girl sat down with a mug of tea. A heavy girl with bad skin sat across from her, biting the top off of a tall chocolate freeze.

"So what did you think of him?" the attractive one said.

"Who?"

"You know—him, the lead, the one with the brows."

"Oh. I thought he was cute."

"You mean great."

"Yes, great. That's the word I was looking for. I also liked the way he moved."

He wondered what movie actor they were talking about. Or maybe it was someone in the university's graduate theater program. If it was a movie actor—brows? Doesn't immediately register—then he'd probably seen the picture. There were four theaters in town and he went to just about every movie they played. Movies were an effective way to horn into people's conversations, mentioning from the next table he'd over-heard them and apologizing for what could be considered eavesdrop-ping, but he'd seen that movie and enjoyed or had some problems with it too. He also always tried to toss in something clever and perceptive so these people would have more of a reason than similar moviegoing to ask him to join their discussion and perhaps later their fun. He'd done it successfully last spring in a Paris bar favored by Americans. A Smith stu-dent who'd just sat through two straight showings of *Dr. Strangelove* in French and was dying for someone to clear up a lot of what she obviously missed in the film. She thought his comments elucidating and brilliant, especially when he explained the more hidden scatological meanings of some of the characters' names. Later that night they made love in his cramped hotel room, which he'd been living in for several months while he tried to find a job and learn French, and the following morning she left with her college chorus for a concert in St. Paul's in London. If she'd given him her correct American address and last name he would prob-ably go home now and write her a long funny letter or lonely poem.

The heavy girl finished her freeze, snapped the plastic spoon in two, and stood up. The other girl stood up too, glanced past Lenny as if searching for someone in particular, and they walked away. She hadn't touched her tea.

He'd call Louise. Her dorm was nearby and they'd already met for coffee three times in the evening, though never for more than twenty minutes. He was at the stage where he thought he might take her hand and hold it. Through one ridiculously juvenile pretext or another—"There's something there that needs to be brushed off"—he'd touched her wrist and once even her cheek and kept his hand there a few seconds, and so far she hadn't objected.

A girl answered the phone.

"Is Louise Robbins in, please?" he said.

"Nope. This is her roommate Penny."

"Louise?" It suddenly sounded like her. "Is that you?"

"Daddy? Uncle Rootie? Father Travers? Who is this? Penny Wolfgang, speaking."

"It's me, Louise, Lenny Polk. What gives?"

"Oh, hi, Lenny. That routine was for someone else. How are things?"

"Just fine. I was around campus and thought you might like a quick coffee at the Union."

She laughed.

"You see, I was first going to see a film at University Aud," he said. "Part of that Ukrainian film festival they've got going every Thursday night. And then I got caught up in a book, and thought—" but she was still laughing. "What's so funny?"

"Nothing, why?"

"You were laughing. Listen, Louise, if you can't meet now, would it be too past your curfew to meet me in the next couple of hours?"

"I can stay out till two if I really have to."

"I thought eleven was the latest."

"No, two. If I really have to, I can sign out for three and have a friend sign me in by morning. As it is, you caught me in bed." She giggled, as if she'd said something naughty. "What I mean is, I'm in my jimmies and about to sleep into bed. I mean, sled into sleep. I mean—I'm high."

"High?"

"Hi, Daddy. Hi, Uncle Rootie. Father Travers? Grandpa Wolfgang? What I meant was that I'm high on life, Grandpa. Life's what intoxicates me. Solely, life's what makes me high."

"You don't think you can have coffee, then."

"Not tonight, Leonard. Thanks."

"How about us driving to San Gregorio Beach sometime this weekend. I hear it's rough and rustic and gorgeous."

"I'm going to my future in-laws this weekend, though I don't know which day."

"Then the day you're not going."

"I better keep both open."

"They keep a close tab on you, no?"

"I suppose, because Hank's in New Zealand, they think they have to."

She laughed. He also laughed and figured it was for the same thing. It amused him when she spoke about her fiancé being in New Zealand. He'd gone there half a year ago to get his PhD in abnormal psychology. She was to follow him out after she graduated, four months from now. Lenny suspected she was a virgin. She'd spoken about "perhaps a certain sexual inexperience for a California girl my age" when they talked, over coffee, about a Henry Miller novel he'd read as a college freshman in the smuggled-in version from France and she was reading for an American literature course. And she'd written explicitly about the inhibitions and frustrations of a virgin heroine who resembled her in looks and read that story in class, but refused to answer—and the writer-professor who ran the program said she was "within every realm of her rights not to"—when one of the male grad students pumped her on whether the protagonist was herself. Lenny had never made love to a virgin. He didn't think he'd ever even had a chance to the past ten years, not that he'd know what to do, though he was eager to test his delicacy in such an event. He felt that with Louise, whom he felt tender to, it would be extraordinary, though maybe not for her.

"Well, I guess that's it then," he said. "See you Monday."

"No class Monday, didn't you know? It's Washington's Birthday—or Lincoln's. I forget which."

"Ronald Reagan's. To celebrate the good governor's fortieth year in show business. But one or the other's all right with me. So long as it means a day off from class and I can get in another afternoon to write."

"Oh, I don't feel that way yet. I guess I haven't been writing that long, but I love our seminars and everybody in it. But I'll be signing off now, Len. Little Louise Robbins, now flying away."

He went back to the cafeteria table and finished reading two full pages, but they were mostly dialog. Nathaniel Vest was one heck of a writer, he thought, and I'm probably one of his few readers to take an entire week to complete half of *Miss Lonelyhearts*. He looked at the moon again. It was still pretty low, though seemed to have risen a bit. Or maybe he was just sitting lower in his chair than before, so the moon was actually higher than he thought. Today is Thursday, and there won't be another class till a week from Monday. At least in class he talked and joked and could look at Louise and got into an occasional literary argument. And after the seminar he always had a coffee and pastry here with B.J. and sometimes Louise would come along with a few of the tuition-paying grad students, who read very well though wrote rather poorly and usually criticized his stories he read in class more severely than he felt they even overexaggeratedly deserved. "Hang Washington," he said. There were classes on Lincoln's birthday this year so why not Washington's? Another thing he didn't know the answer to.

He stuck a napkin between the pages and closed the book. He got up for another coffee, stretched and yawned and looked around. It was getting late; not many people here, and he didn't recognize anyone. If he did, he was sure he'd ratchet up the guts enough to walk over to that person's table and ask if he might join it, even to someone he'd only met briefly or to a girl he'd never met but was sure she was in some way connected to the creative writing program. But he didn't recognize a soul.

THE TALK SHOW.

Enraged, the writer walks off the stage and out of the television studio.

"Where'd he go?" the host says. "Hey, Mal, where you going? God, that guy walks fast. Come on back, will ya, and let's be friends. Then let's have a walking race. Okay, we'll just stare at each other while the announcer reads sonnets. And you didn't sing that old Irish ballad you promised us. Sure, you can go. Made a mint with his last two novels—not that I'm knocking it, you understand. It's the international way, *comprendo? Nicht so?* Bet you didn't know I spoke Chinese. But me? Walk off once like he did, and that, my friends, would be show business, as they say—forever. And bestsellers I don't write. Some people will even say I can't write, and there won't be many who'll take issue with them. Because anybody here read my last book? Come on, don't be ashamed. Stand up if your belt and garters are on tight. Say, let's not all rise at once. Anybody even remember the title? What was that? Be brave and shout it out. No, it wasn't *Gone with the Wind*; but thanks, Mom. Huh? No, not *Madame Bovary*, either—but Flaubert, right? And you people thought I never went to college. *Crime and Punishment*? That's what the readers thought I inflicted on them. *War and Peace*? A good description of what went on between the editors and me. It was...*Madame Bovary Returns*, the hopeful horticulturist in the front row says. We're all quipsters here. No, I said horticulturist. That's a hearts and flowers man with brains. *Swann's* what? Never heard of it. *Oedipus Sex*? Never saw it. *Be a Wolf*? Who even wrote it? And is that a nice thing to advise a married man? *Dead Souls*?—you said it, brother, not me—is what I think I have in devoted readers here.

The Trial? What this guessing game's getting to become. But *Wild Walter's World.* There it is. My autobiog. Born with a silver spoon and golden locks in my mouth, which is why I talk this way. My mom never took them out because she thought they might improve my face. Someone once suggested it be retitled to *Crazy Publisher's Catastrophe*, because you know what that book sold? How many fingers you got on your hand? Not you. Our orchestra leader just held up six fingers on his right hand and seven on his left—but the fiddler next to you. The one who got his hand caught in a giant metronome the other day and had to have a few fingers removed. Well, his hand—the one that was operated on. Count how many fingers he's got left. Subtract two. That's how many copies my book sold. I still got it home. Under a broken kitchen chair leg. In the same brown paper bag they sold it to me in. My wife didn't want it on the bookshelf because we already had a book there. And our youngest daughter refused to sit on it to reach the dinner table and our mutt still thinks it's the oddest-looking fire hydrant around. Truthfully, it sold pretty well and in more languages than I knew existed. And starting this month, any one of you out there and in this audience can be one of its two million paperback owners. *Wild Walter's World.* I said the title too low? That was *Wild Walter's World,* folks. Not *Wild Walter's World Folks,* but just *Wild Walter's World.* Okay. Now, did our guest really leave? He's not back there smoking a cigarette somewhere? Daphne, you checked? Nobody? Dashed out of the studio with our library prop and ordered his chauffeur to drive him home? Well, this is a very intellectual show tonight. And before introducing our next eminent author—and it beats me how we're going to carry out our literary discussion format if it's now just going to be me and him here. Or 'I.' All these brilliant writers around the joint are making me unsure with the language. Maybe we could bring up some members of the audience to join in the discussion. They'd like that, right? Yeahhh. Anyway, before we do that, time for plugs. Have you always had a deep-seated yearning to write great novels and story articles and lead the happy enriching life of a successful author, but everyone said you had to have a household name, like Ivory Soap, or your work would never sell? Well, the Westport Famous Writers Correspondence School—I'm joshing. But this all but indescribable product I have here and which is really something to write home about, folks, as it can literally do the magical polishing work of a thousand and one genies..."

DREAM.

Paul tries to remember the dream he just had. In it he was sitting at his New York desk in the home he and his ex-girlfriend Tilly rented for three years in California, writing the story he's currently writing about another woman who recently broke up with him. His brother John entered the room. John's been turning up regularly in Paul's dreams and began doing so about five years after the small plane he was in disappeared over a jungle and was never found. Paul asked him if he'd done any writing since he was away. John said "Quite a lot, but I haven't let anyone see it and for the time being I won't be sending it around." Paul didn't tell him about the feelings he was suddenly having that John's writing would turn out to be much better than his own. He did say "One language can never seem to support two brothers close in age as serious writers, and maybe that holds for the world as well. And when it becomes known you're alive, I'm sure book and magazine editors will be pounding on your door to get you published, while with me, after so many years of a thousand submissions and few acceptances and no notoriety or catchy news story about a derring-do life, it'll continue to be just the opposite. I also think how silly the stories I've written about the impact on a young man whose idolized writer, doctor, composer, explorer brother was lost on a freighter, blimp, space module, single-prop plane over a desert, rain forest, mountain range will seem to readers now that you've reappeared and your writing, once you let it get published, becomes known. Where have you been the last eight years?" John said "How are Sis and the folks?," shook Tilly's hand and patted her son Ezra's head as he left the room. During the entire dream, Ezra stayed beside Paul, his cheek pressed against Paul's thigh while his arms were wrapped around his leg, even when Paul was bent over the desk correcting his story or striding across the room to greet John. Ezra looked the same as when Paul last saw him two years ago. Tilly looked about ten years older than she is, wearied, scrawny, captious, mordant, lined, riled, severe. She was with her new boyfriend, who was squat, hirsute, jumpsuit, shaggily bearded and nattily haggard, and he seemed dismissive of Paul and every so often said "Bah" or "Ah" to him and busily scribbled in a notebook a story he was writing. Ezra never loosened his hold on Paul's leg, his sad silent face gaping forlornly into space. Tilly's parting words to Paul were "So nice to see you again, and wait till you read the breakup story I've written and is being published about us."

"Send it to me when you get the galleys," he said, and went back to his correcting, thinking why should he finish this story when no doubt Tilly's and her boyfriend's stories will also prove to be much better than his own? Without taking his eyes or pen off the page, he placed his hand on Ezra's head. "My boy..."

P.

Now, he would like to, in this day and age, right here, on this very spot, today, not tomorrow, this time at present, from these moments right now till he says stop, oh don't be ridiculous, come off it, who would have thought it?, let the gentleman speak, I'm truly amazed, he's saying he'd like to, what are you talking about?, where do you get that stuff?, will wonders never cease?, I declare, does he ever, I'm truly amazed, poppycock, baloney, you slay me, horse manure, beans, where does it all come from?, be with a woman like the woman in the story he wrote who was, act your age, grow up, don't make me laugh, how you do come on, big joke, stop kidding yourself, breaks me up, laugh a minute, or as he thought the young woman he saw on the street every working weekday morning was, oh yeah, go on, pull my other sleeve, no thank you, oh you kid, that's what you say, maybe I'm wrong, in a pig's eye, bless my heart, it's got bells on it, what a crack, a crock, soft, warm, loving, sweet, sensible, strong and kind, come come, now I'll tell one, like fun, well I'm a monkey's uncle, do you feature that, better you than me baby, tell it to the Marines, it beats the Dutch, funny as a rubber crutch, get off my foot, ouch you're killing me, as I live and breathe, I'm truly amazed, pshaw, sheet, shucks, I'm from Missouri, you don't say?, it's true, says you, I'll be jiggered, what a nerve, shut my mouth, clap my trap, shiver my timbers, blow me down, strike me dead, for crying out loud, what now?, dog my cats, tickle my willies, goodness, gracious, my stars, heaven and earth, dear me, for Pete's sake, what do you know, twaddle, indeed, zounds, fiddledeedee, gadzooks, gad so, good lack, the devil you say, t'ain't so McGee, pile it on, blimey, bushwah, hogwash, hooey, hoopdedoodle, nibbledenoodle, my word, bilge, bosh, bah, balderdash, pishpash, pashpish, what piss, rubbish, raspberries, horsefeathers, hominy grits, sticks in your throat, in your hat, don't give me that, bullcrap, far be it from me, I see, oh brother, let's hear another, hind, wind, string, tweet, tensible, hoving, soft, sift, saft, shift, insensible, reprehensible, findensunable, ope sopperer, mope slopperer, nope whopperer, op cropperer, plop, flop, clop clop, now now, there there, warm warm, simmer simmer, down down, cool off, go slow, steady as she blows, easy there mate, calm yourself, come to your senses, smarten up, get hep, be wise, mind out, relax, take a seat, load off your feet, watch your step, look sharp, here comes cookie, you'll be okay, thataway, I believe you, sure we do, what rot, enough of that.

Not someone like the woman in the story with that Italian or was he an Englishman? Certainly someone like the woman in the story who nursed him and then bussed them through barriers from one to another enslaved land. Not someone like the woman aloft on the trapeze who licked his lips, eyelid and forehead as she let his wrists go. Maybe someone like the woman who stayed imperturbably beside him in their apartment building the revolutionaries or reactionaries were about to blow up. Nor someone like the woman he and their son stalked to make sure the jazz musicians she favored didn't beat on her face. In the story Terry said "Do you mind if I go, Po?" and all he had to do was say no and she wouldn't as she wanted to stay while he preferred her away and didn't care where or with whom as long as she averted getting hurt and returned before he left for work so he said "If that's what you want, have fun, one on me, whatever that might be, double entente, trouper disentendering," nigh about the turn in their tie when he was proroguing his own going owing to Oz. He should call Oz now to explain some things. "Oz, it's Dad, I've got to squeak past for x-reasons I plant cain." Better a letter dispatched to friend Helen Elmen's house with a note attached saying "Pleez geev this to Ozie as a surpreez." Oz wants a sprise. Set a purise for I's, Pi? Lap, sid to read, Up, God be raised. Arms, snoogle and cud. Now Oz's turn to read. Words downslide up. I know what that picture means. High, farrer than the sky. Down, em tie or uv gah to may. Wraah, doe wanna go to beg. Swish off de lie, turn on dee on. I doe wan de be in de dar alo, so key bo begroo door oen. I luf you. Police, whir all my haar. Hey you, Poor, you're so bear en me t'me. Dearest Osbert, I still think of you as one of the wisest, slyest, hippest, flippest, slickest, wickedest, stingiest— Dear Oz, I feel you're now old enough to understand that the reason I left so suddenly two years ago wasn't as a result of anything you or your mommy did but— Back, give me piggypack. Glass, let's click-click. Wipe, my milk slight spilled lips. Run, I'm won. I'm faster. Going to be strongaller. Dear Sir, prior to our phone conversation on or before the evening of September 4th, I spoke with your mother, Mrs. Wong, who during the same call, but in advance of our own dialog, broached what I think is a particularly important subject re our mutual concerns and one which I believe should be more thoroughly developed in our future written conversation. Most Reverend Master, may I humbly beseech your indulgence for the callous indifference and ofttimes deplorable inattention I've displayed in relation to— Your Grace, Reader of Ghosts, Liver of Kings, Nero's Pleasure Peeper, Detector of Gearls, what explanation could I afford to put forth, without the most diligent distortion of truth and ensuant likeliness of a good garroting, that could enucleate any further what you have undoubtedly discerned through my absence and all but silence. Buddy, Chum, Crony, Confidant, Partner, Best Friend, Bosom Pal, greetings, salutations, hail, hey, hi, hiya, ullo, halloo, hoo-hoo, hist, pist, yo-ho, oh-le-ee-oh-lei-ee-yoo, howdy do, how de do, how d'ya do, are you? I'm fine, long time no see, miss ya, kiss ya, love ya, wanna be with ya, what can I say? maybe one fine day, try to understand, so hard to explain, though know full well, realize straight out, be aware of to the very end, that O, ah me, woe betide, poor dear, alas, lackadaisy, have mercy, what a-pity, so sorry, but do me a favor, just one thing I ask, bear in mind that, regardless of whatever else happens, despite anything anyone might tell you, needless to say, remember too, take care. Godspeed, look after yourself, best of health, peace be with you, don't want to hear any bad reports, be good, keep in touch, stiff upper lip, compliments to your mom, kind remembrances home, fond memories from afar, with all due respects, excuse the liberty, in deference to, best wishes, most affectionately, I remain, friendly yours, may God bless you, through thick and thin, through years on end, till hell freezes over, sincerely, always and forever and a week of Sundays and month after month and year in year out, yours truly till the cows come home again for a dog's age faithfully, Paul, P, Pi, Po, Pum.

STORIES.

This afternoon—

Yes, what this afternoon? What?

Just a second. This afternoon I, uh—let me see; it started like this.

Like what?

Let me think. That's right. I was out walking and—

So what happened when you were out walking?

Give me a chance. I'm telling it. You keep butting in.

Butting in how?

Like that? Like saying "Butting in how?" Like saying "Like what?" Like saying "Yes, uh, what this afternoon? Um, well, tell me, come on, what happened, don't hold it in, what, what, what?"

I don't remember saying the last of those things. The "Like what?" and maybe some of what went before it, I admit to saying, but not that "Um, uh, well, what, what" stuff.

I was exaggerating. For effect. To show how much you butt in. But you don't expect me to remember everything you said all those times you butted in.

No, I don't. That's true. But go on. Where were you? Something about the other day—

This afternoon. Right. Doing your three-mile daily run.

Walking. I said I was out walking. And I don't run that far anymore. Six miles a week total. Mile a day. Sunday I take off.

How come? You used to do three to six miles a day without taking a single day off.

I'm getting up there in years, man, what do you think?

That shouldn't stop you. Look at those guys who are fifty-five, sixty-five, even seventy-five. The women too. Let's not forget the ladies. One's around eighty. I see her lots of times when I'm in the park. Running. Well: walking-running. Maybe not even that. Maybe only walking fast, if that. But going. Arms pumping. And not walking a little faster than normal just to look at the birdies and trees. She's out there for good healthy exercise, and has the exercise suit to go with it: light blue with a white stripe down the jacket arms and trouser legs, and a sweatband around her forehead. Eighty, if a day.

You want me to go on or not?

About what you were saying before? Sure, why not?

Because suddenly you're telling a story about a running-walking woman in a blue and white exercise suit. Really, who cares?

And who cares about your story, if you want to know?

You did, it seemed. I came home, you said "What'd you do today?" and I started to tell you, and probably would have been finished by now if I didn't have this slight speech problem which—

And what's that, by the way?

My speech problem which enables you to butt in.

I meant, what exactly is this speech problem you say you have?

You're saying you don't know by now?

Would I have asked if I did?

Yes, you would have. To distract me. To butt in again. Because you know what speech problem I have. My problem with speech. I go "Uh, um, what, oh, this afternoon I was, well, uh, walking"—like that.

You're not doing it now. I mean, you were in imitation of yourself, and before that in your exaggeration of me. But just now you spoke clearly, precisely, uninterrupted—by me or yourself—and articulately. Definitely articulately. For example, the way you said "Yes, you would. To distract me. To butt in again. You know what speech problem I have. My problem with speech." I think those were your words, minus or plus one or two. And amazing how I remembered them, no?

They sound like the words I used. And you're right: I did speak clearly then. But that's my point. Which is—

What?

Will you let me finish without any more "Whats"?

Okay, what? I'm sorry—I mean, what? Damn, I can't help myself. I'll be quiet. I will. So, speak. Go on. Oh, God. I'm really impossible.

You're intentional, not impossible. You were having fun on me, intentionally, or making a joke of me. But something. What were you doing, and why? Don't answer that. Two questions? I'll be here all night. Let me just finish my story. Then, if you wish, we can talk about other things.

Is that what you really want?

Yes.

Then go ahead. Your story. I'll just listen. But let me find a good place to sit first. I don't think I can stand another second. I know I can't. It's been, well—if I say it's been some day, and emphasize the some, you'll know what I mean. That's the kind of day it's been.

I see.

An incredible day. Unbelievable. First I get lip from the chief exec; then, from the one right under him. Then another exec comes in, not as big as the first two, and gives me lip, and all for different things. Three lips in a row and the day isn't even an hour old. That's a record for me. For all I know, maybe a record for all working mankind for the first hour of a working day. Then I get a phone call. Who do you think?

Let me guess.

Ross. Ross wants this, Ross wants that. Ross says I didn't do it right yesterday and to do it right today. Ross lets me have it. Ross, if you want my opinion, is a louse.

If you say so.

I'm definitely saying so and have said it, and not just today have I said it, because not just today has he been a louse. He's almost always a louse. Or close to being almost always a louse as any person could be. Ross, in other words, is an A-1 louse. Then I get another call.

Don't tell me who from.

You're right the first time. Benjamin. Benjamin also with the barbs and complaints. Not as much of a louse as Ross, but he's closing in. In a year or so he'll be solid competition against Ross for louse-of-the-year award. In ten years, the way he's going, and the way I know Ross will stay or even get worse, they'll be the sole competitors for louse-of-the-century award, or at least the decade. Yes, the decade. Louse of the decade. So far, Ross had that prize wrapped up, but Benjamin could give him a run for it. An A-2 louse, Benjamin is, know what I mean?

One and two. Ross is one, Benjamin is two.

Right. A-2 louse. He said to me "Remember last week?" I said "Last week?" He said "Yeah, you know, don't kid me: last week. I wish I could forget last week also," he said, "forever, because you really cost us, kid, you really did. Don't do it again, damnit—don't," and he hung up. I'm in big trouble with the company; big, big trouble.

Sounds like it.

Three of the top hotshots and two of their underlings, all down my bed? But that's not even half of it. Or it is half, but there's plenty more. I go out for lunch today and who do you think I see?

Um—

You got it. The one and only. And oh, still so goddamn beautiful. I died when I saw her—a hundred times. She walked right past me. Didn't say hi—not a peep. Didn't say zero or even look at me—nothing.

She must have it in for you.

She hates my guts. It's been how long now?—and it's interesting when you think how different our feelings are for each other. Love and hate. Love and hate. If a cup of hot coffee had been near her, she would have dumped it on me and then hit me over the head with the cup. A mug? Even better, because it would have been heavier. Good thing I was standing by the entrance when she passed, away from any food. Know why she feels this way about me?

No, why?

Because— Haven't I told you before?

Come to think of it—

Because of everything, that's why. Everything I did and she didn't and the other way around. Everything I said and she didn't and the other way around. That last week we had. That last month and maybe that entire last year too. I thought she'd get over it. Well, it's obvious she didn't. What could be more obvious, am I right?

From everything you've said—

So that's lunch. But it's not over. I haven't even sat down yet. We're still waiting for a table, Hesh and I. Then it's our turn, the woman who seats the customers says. Maitre d'? Nah, place isn't fancy enough for that. Hostess or host. She points to our table. We start for it when a waiter comes tearing down the aisle shouting "Hot soup, hot soup." I don't know about you, but to me that had always meant "I got food of any sort on my tray or in my hands and I'm in a rush because I've too many tables to serve or this one customer's been kvetching like mad that my service is too slow, so let me by fast," or something like that. Not necessarily hot soup, is what I mean, right? A warning for people to get out of the way. A blinking red light for them to stand back if they're going to cross his path. A verbal word to the wise to "Watch out, I'm barreling through and nothing's going to stop me, so if you get hit it's your own damn fault." So we step aside. The expression's always meant the same to you, hasn't it?

Sure, I suppose so, though I don't know. Yes.

Of course, yes. Hot soup. What else could it mean? So we've stepped aside, but no, this guy actually has hot soup on his tray, two big bowls of it, not cups, and he trips over his own feet or something, and it goes all over me. Hot soup. Not a drop on Hesh. Just me.

That's terrible.

Scalded—my wrist, my neck, the creep. They had to take me to the hospital.

No.

No, they didn't. Just wanted to see if you were listening. You were, though I did get a little burn on my hand and greasy noodles and crap on my jacket and shirt. I'm suing the joint. Captain Brey's might have the best lunch in town for the money and a reputation as long as—well, as long as anything; one of the best. But to me, from now on it's just a joint I'm going to sue, and you watch me, buddy, I'm going to win.

Where will you eat lunch now? You go there almost every day.

What does it matter where? Their waiters should be more careful. But that's not all.

There's more.

Would I say "But that's not all" if there wasn't more?

That's what I meant.

Don't tell me.

It's true. You said "But that's not all," and though I said "There's more," I said it uninterrogatively because I knew there was more. It's just an expression I use. Doesn't mean anything more than that.

Well, there was more. Plenty more. I left that joint with the stained jacket and shirt and also a stained silk tie. I forgot to mention that. My tie was destroyed. I went straight to Tabor's—without having lunch, you understand—and bought a new jacket and shirt and tie and brought the other jacket and shirt—

The dirty jacket and shirt.

The stained, ruined, probably forever-useless jacket and shirt to the cleaner's to see if they could be salvaged. The tie I kept in a bag for future proof against Captain Brey's. Wait till the judge sees that tie when I pull it out of the bag. The stained jacket and shirt I'll have photos of. Someone at Tabor's—the stockboy. It's his hobby, photography—always carries his camera with him—and he took them for a small fee. Buying the jacket, shirt and tie went smoothly enough. Chose the clothes, gave my charge card–easy. I'm wearing them now—what do you think?

Oh, nice, nice.

Cost me a pretty penny, but I'll get it back. But the cleaner's. To make a long story short—to abbreviate it, in other words, because I realize I've been running at the mouth too long, and you're getting to look uncomfortable standing there. Why don't you take a seat?

I like standing.

Someone standing while I'm sitting and talking always gives me the feeling that person's about to run away. Come on, sit down.

No, really, what happened? I'm not tired and I won't run away.

Then your day couldn't have been too rough.

Actually, that's what I was about to tell you when—

Before you go into your story, let me finish mine–especially at the most harrowing part. I was robbed. It's the truth. At the cleaner's. Cleaned out at the cleaner's. Taken to it. You know the expression.

Yes.

Well, I was, and so was the cleaner—Mr. Samet—and so was his tailor, Archie, and his presser, Nat, and his seamstress, or whatever she does with her sewing machine in back. What's her name again?

The woman, around fiftyish, with blond hair?

Redhead. What blond do you think works there?

So I'm a little colorblind. I thought she was a blond.

That's not being colorblind; you can't see. Her red hair is a light red, yes—almost orange—but several shades away from being blond. Anyway, we were all robbed. Hesh, the lucky stiff, walked me part of the way there and then ducked into a luncheonette to eat. Two hoods came into the shop with guns out and emptied the cash register and took everything we had. Wallets, pocketbook, watches, rings, change—even my new fountain pen. The one Lillian gave me.

The one for your birthday?

That one. A hundred dollars it cost her, she said.

She told you the price?

I asked her. When she gave it. I wanted to know how valuable it was, just so I'd take better care of it.

A lot of money for a pen.

Did you ever see the way it wrote? And it never leaked. I wanted to have that pen for life. I'm so mad.

I can see why. It's been quite a day.

But I'm not even finished with it. See what I mean about it being unbelievable? I went back to work penniless, though they did leave me my keys. I thought of calling you to come over to bring me money to get home, but one of the women at work loaned me a twenty. But the cabby couldn't break it—wouldn't, is more like it—nor would he let me out of the cab in front here till someone walked by who'd be able to break it. I didn't want to fool with him. He was insane. Wouldn't listen to reason. Ranted, raged—I thought he was going to kill me. Tell me, how does a man like that get a hack license?

I suppose the Taxi Commission doesn't give them the tests they used to years back—police checks, things like that. I hope you got his number.

I got it, all right, but think I'm going to use it? He said he had a club and I wasn't to leave the cab till someone—but I told you that. I even told him, keep the twenty, but he wouldn't hear of it—said that would be as if he'd robbed me. No, I don't want him coming around and clubbing my head if I pressed charges against him. He was an A-1 psychopath. All I eventually told him was "Anything you say, sir, anything."

Good thinking, and just the right tone.

You bet. And someone did come by who could break the twenty. I gave the cabby the fare and a big tip, so he wouldn't go crazy if he thought I didn't give him enough, and left the cab, came into the building and took the elevator up. It worked fine, for once—no bumping and then stopping between floors. Put the key in the door lock. It slid right in—sometimes it doesn't and gets stuck. And everything seems fine here. I see Angela did a good job cleaning up.

We pay her enough.

Do we ever. So?

Yes?

So, what about you?

Your day finished?

If you mean was that everything—no, I didn't tell you all. Something very strange did happen at work when I got back after being robbed. And there was also something one of the policemen at the cleaner's said when I told him "You mean you're not going to finger-print the glass counter both robbers put their hands on?"

What did he say?

No, I've talked enough. You. What happened today?

Really, when I think of it, nothing.

Come on, tell me. I think I've a few minutes before I have to start getting ready to go out. Lillian's picking me up here. What time is it?

Five after six.

Five after? Oh God, she's supposed to be here at six.

Your watch accurate?

I set it this morning off of the radio clock.

There you go, then. Sorry. I have to shower and shave.

It's all right. Your stories are always much better than mine anyway, and you tell then much better too.

Do I? I wouldn't say that. And you'll keep her company if I'm not out in time, okay?

NEXT TO NOTHING.

Once more. I want to try it once more. I don't want to be told I can't.
I don't want to be held back in any way. Verbally, physically, whatever,
no. I want to try it again and will try it again and I'm trying it again
right now and I don't know just yet whether it works.

It doesn't. I can see that. I don't know why I tried. I tried because
there was nothing else to do but try. I don't know how true that is, but
I was in my house. There was nothing to do. I'd read the papers and
finished a book, I cleaned up the house and did my exercises for today
and for tomorrow too. I ate for two days too. I tried to sleep and dream
but I couldn't. I was, in a word, restless. In two words, very restless.
I walked around outside and in and told myself I was doing nothing.
Then said aloud: You are doing nothing. And I was, though I was really
doing something. I was saying out loud you are doing nothing. But that
was almost doing next to nothing. I wanted to do something more than
that. I wanted to do something. I wasn't. All I was doing was saying I
was doing nothing. All right. So I sat down, which still wasn't doing
anything much more than nothing, and thought about what else I could
do, which was doing something a little more than doing nothing or next
to nothing. But how long can I think that before it too becomes doing
something that's just about nothing? So I got up and walked around
thinking about doing something more than just next to nothing, but
I'd covered that thinking when I was sitting. So I went into my study,
sat at the typewriter and began typing this. It is something just a little
more than doing next to nothing, but if I continue doing it, though I
don't know what I'll continue doing if I do, it'll be something that's just
about next to nothing. To avoid doing that, I'll try something else.

I write—of course *I* write—and of course I write, though maybe not of course for both, because someone else could be writing this, or I could be dictating it, even if I say I'm not. But I am writing and not dictating this, I swear, though I also swear I'm a good liar, but I'm writing this and what I write, which would be the start of the first paragraph I write if I deleted, as I think I should, everything that precedes is:, is: Up you go, there you are, now you help me, and I stick my arm up, she leans over and grabs my wrist and helps me up. I get on top of the wall where she is, say Ready? and she nods, and we both jump down to the other side.

So what do you think (I say)?

That we go right back over (she says). I don't like it.

You don't like what?

It here. This place.

What about this place, or why?

We don't belong here. We've heard terrible things about it. We might be trespassing; it could be dangerous. I don't know, but let's go back.

We've come to explore, that's why we're here. We've seen the wall countless times from the other side, said several times we wanted to see what's on the other side. Now we're on the other side for the first time and we see what's on the other side, which looks almost like the side we came from. Let's go further in to see what's further in.

(To me that's almost writing nothing at all, or worse than nothing, though writing next to nothing could be worse than nothing if I keep it. Maybe I should chuck it all from the start. Or go back over the wall when she first asked us to and continue from there. Or climb over the wall for the first time with or without her but try to forget I've been over this wall before. Instead I'll just go a little farther in from where we are now over that wall and see what I find. For sometimes things just happen, like a wild dog might appear and try to bite off my leg. What I mean is how will I know what I can or can't find if I don't look for it and give myself the time? Of course by continuing from here I'll be stopping myself from finding what I might just find if I started from a place farther back or completely over again, so what it boils down to is my wanting to go on because I normally wouldn't and because I am here and don't expect to be here again, even if I realize this can be worse than doing nothing at all. I should delete this entire paragraph, or at least cut or correct certain parts, like the "of course" that starts the previous sentence and "so what it boils down to" and such. But because that's also what I've always done—cutting, correcting, retyping, making better, maybe making worse—when all I want to do is go further in and see what happens and explore, this time I won't.)

A dog appears out of the woods. Look, a dog (she says). Here, doggy, doggy, here. It seems like a nice trained dog.

I don't think it is (I say).

The dog growls, barks, Lucinda jumps. (I am not Lucinda. My name's Hank, in real life and in this what I write. I also see I didn't have to say who Lucinda wasn't, because this being a first-person piece, Lucinda—at least in this country—obviously can't be me. But I now see why I felt I had to say something about who Lucinda wasn't: Lucinda could have been the dog. But I've never seen that dog before or known its name. Instead of saying I wasn't Lucinda, I should have said the dog wasn't, since I didn't want to give the impression it was the dog who jumped. I know there's some flawed logic in there or whatever it's called if flawed logic isn't it, but I'm not going to go over it and delete or correct it or any of the other flawed logic and possible grammatical mistakes that precede and might follow this paragraph, since all I want to do is go further on and not get sidetracked so much.)

Go home (I say). I think Lucinda thinks I said it to her, because she runs to the wall.

Help me over (she says).

I didn't mean you when I said go home (I say). But I'll skip sticking the "I say" and "she says" in parentheses, I don't know why I started it; I've never done it before. I'm sure I did it for pedantic literary reasons: that it might come out meaning something more than if I wrote it in a more normal way. I'm frequently trying for something new and most of the times it doesn't work. But I'll keep the parenthesized "I say" and "she says" I have in so far, even if I know they didn't work. But where was I?

I didn't mean you, I say, but the dog.

I'm going home even if you didn't mean me, as I don't want to deal with dogs or anything else here. I've seen what's on this side, or seen enough, and now I want to get back over to the other side, not so much to go home, although I just might. Now help me over.

Wait; let's go further in.

Help me over, I said.

And I said just a little further in.

Dog barks and snarls and then rushes at me, and I don't move. I read to do that some place, or rather, I once read to do that and not show any fear. So I stand still and say to the dog without what I think is a sign of fear in my appearance and voice: GO HOME! Or rather: GO HOME, the exclamation point being redundant and unnecessary, I think, just as I think the word redundant or unnecessary is redundant or unnecessary if I use one or the other. And I put the command in caps because I of course yelled it, which is why the exclamation point was redundant or unnecessary: for how loud can I seem to yell on a page without my having to say I yelled very loud or I yelled so loud I must have been heard a city block away? In other words, for I didn't explain that well, I don't think an exclamation point adds anything to the capital letters when I'm yelling. And why the "of course" from above, since if it was of course, why say it was? There's probably a good reason, or just a reason, forget the good, the reason being idiomatical, I think. Anyway, the dog snarls again and snaps at my pointing finger—I'm pointing at it but not too close to its open mouth, and that arm of the pointing finger is the only part of my body that moved—and turns and goes. Dog does: disappears into the woods.

Come on, Lucinda says. I also don't see why I don't use quotation marks for dialogue. I don't usually like it when others leave them out. You have—I do—the writer does—more flexibility with quotation marks. For instance, if I write a line like: —Come on, Lucinda says (or: Come on, Lucinda says), but with a period after says rather than a comma, it could seem as if I want a character to say aloud "Come on, Lucinda says," rather than just "Come on," which is what I intended up there. I think I've almost made a case against quotation marks with my example, so let me give a clearer one. I've time? Because I usually like a tight piece, and these explanations and examples are dragging this one out. But last one and then I'll try to go straight through.

If I write, and I'll put the example on its own line to make it even clearer:

—Come on, Lucinda says, giving him his hand, how do we know I'm not having a character say "Come on, Lucinda says, giving him his hand"? It's possible, and so is her giving him his hand. His hand might have been torn off by the dog and she picked it up and gave it to him to take to the hospital, while she fought off or distracted the dog so he could escape, to get it sewed back on right away. Or else she might have found his hand somewhere, or the dog dug it up and brought it over to her—an artificial hand, perhaps—and given it to him because she knew it was his. Or she might have taken his left hand, we'll say, and put it in his right hand when he still had both hands attached to his body, artificial or not, or because he had no control of his left hand because it had been permanently maimed during a war. Or the control he didn't have might have been when he touched her when he knew she didn't want to be touched, and to show she didn't want to be touched, she put his touching hand into his other hand, whether the touching hand or the one she put the real hand in was artificial or not. Or both his hands could have been artificial, and she didn't want to be touched not because they were artificial but because she simply didn't want to be touched by him, or at least not on the place he touched her.

It's obvious I still can't explain this properly now, or correctly, not properly, or clearly, which is just another example, or two of them, that I can't explain this clearly now. Nor do I want to go back to try to correct or delete all or part of what I've written since Lucinda said "Come on." As I said, and if I didn't, I'm saying it now: I just want to push on.

Lucinda says (but in the new way) "Come on." I say "No, you come with me." She says "Please, help me over the wall. I have to get away from here. It's too spooky, dangerous. Foreboding—that's the word. There are signs all around that say do not enter. (Or Do Not Enter.) We've heard awful things about this place. There's a couple supposed to live near here who eat any children who wander over the wall—exaggerated, perhaps, but just that people say something as horrible as that must mean something about what kind of people the couple are. So, help me."

No, I say.

Now that's the example I should have used before. Not that "Come on, Lucinda says" or "Come on, Lucinda says, giving him his hand." And I didn't intentionally leave out the quotation marks around "No" just to make a better example, but now that I did, I think it is. Because by saying "No, I say," which that *No, I say* above could have meant, it could have meant I was saying both "No" and "I say"—the "I say" to emphasize how much I was saying "No."

That explained it only a little better than my previous examples explained what they were supposed to be explaining, and I said I wouldn't get sidetracked again from whatever my intention was in doing this piece, which after getting sidetracked so much, I forget. What was it? To let something go? "Going to let my mind go," I think I said, whatever that means. What does it, if that was it, the intention, for if it was, exact or otherwise, that "Going to let my mind go," I now don't know. I read back but can't find it. I know it's there, but I read back too quickly, maybe because I just want to push on, not back, which also might have been my intention, or the only one. Sounds familiar. Was it? My intention, sole or one of? I ask Lucinda if she remembers if I mentioned what my intention was in starting out to get here, other than just to climb over the wall and be here, and she says "What?" "Nothing about my wanting to just push on or letting my mind go, or something else?" and she says "Not to me you didn't." "Didn't mention it, you mean?" and she says "Far as I can remember, yes."

Hell with it and the woods. I'm not going to push on if I don't know why I'm pushing on, though I don't see why I can't if I don't, but hell with it as I said. I realize all that could be an alibi of sorts. How so? That I just don't want to go through these woods yet, out of tiredness, disinterest, lack of courage, etcetera—normal reasons, in other words, so there it stands. What does? The issue, the issue.

"Let's go over," I say, and she says "Where?" and I say "The wall, of course," and she says finally, because I thought you still might have meant the woods." I say

"To go over to the woods? What the hell would that mean if I'd said it?" and she says "Don't get testy again. I thought you might have meant it as another word for through them," and I say "Why? Have you ever heard me use the word 'over' that way before?" and she says "You never made up words that I know of, or used words in any way other than what they were meant for and people could easily understand, but I thought this time might have been the exception. It's obvious I shouldn't have thought that." "You shouldn't have," and she says "All right, so I shouldn't have and won't anymore, if it's going to irritate you so much, but let's go over in the way you said." We go to the wall. I give her a boost. She makes it to the top, gets on her knees and stretches down and gives me her hand and I clasp it and she says "Ready?" and I nod, and she pulls me to the top.

We jump to the other side. She takes a deep breath and says "Don't you like it better over here?" and I say "No, I don't think so." "Then go back over, but without my help this time," and I say "You know that anytime I want to, I could, because I don't need your help." She says "Catch me," and runs toward home, and I chase her and she lets me catch her and we roll on the grass and laugh and kiss and make love and then go home. At night, I come back and stare at the wall.

THE
PHONE.

"Answer it, Warren," she yelled through the partly opened bathroom door. "Warren, you there? Answer the phone and tell whoever it is I'm busy and I'll call back."

Warren was in his bedroom down the hall. He ran to his parents' room, picked up the receiver and said hello.

"Hey, there, fella, how are you?"

"Daddy, that you?"

"That's me, sure, who else?"

"Where are you?"

"In a hotel. Away. How's everything home? Your mother?"

"Fine. Today we went to the park and I fell off the swings, I didn't get hurt, but Mommy said she won't let me go on them anymore."

"She's probably right. You're getting too big and fat for those things. If the clothes don't fit—I mean the shoes, don't buy them, which I suppose can be applied to you and your swings in some far-off way. Say, Warren, you want to get your mother on the phone for me?"

"She's in the bathroom and says whoever it is she'll call back."

"Tell her if she calls back it'll cost her two dollars station to station. Tell her that now."

Warren dropped the receiver on the bed, ran across the room, stood , pressed up against the full-length bathroom door mirror and breathed heavily on it, leaving several moist clouds on the glass. He knocked on the door, yelled through the opened part of it when he got no response, his voice high above the shower splashing, "*Mom*. Dad's on the phone and says to hurry or it'll cost you dollars to call him back."

He fingered a wavy streak through the runny mirror blotches. "Mom? I said Dad's on the phone and he wants for you to hurry."

She turned the shower off. "Tell him I'll be there in a minute. I have to dry myself."

He took two large hops and made a bellywhop on the bed. The receiver jumped up when he landed and fell to the floor. He walked two fingers across and down the bedspread to grab it, while his father was saying "Hey? What in God's name is going on there?"

"I dropped the phone. I'm sorry."

"Where's your mother?"

"Getting dried. Where you calling from, Dad?"

"San Francisco."

"Where's that?"

"Where's San Francisco? What do they teach you in school? In California. In America."

"How far's California?"

"A long way—too far to walk. About three thousand miles from you, but you'll learn all about that when you get up to geography."

"I'm in geography."

"Then maybe you haven't come to it yet or you learned it and forgot. What's holding up your mother?"

"She said a minute. When you coming home? Mommy said she didn't know."

"Soon, probably—depends on a lot of things. Look, do me a favor and ask your mother to really hustle."

"I think she's coming." He ran to the bathroom door, listened, ran back. "Yeah, I can hear her putting on something. How come you didn't day goodbye when you left? I didn't see you."

"No time. You know me when I have to make one of my flights. Rush-rush. Besides, what are you talking about?—you were sleeping. You've been good, though—not giving your mother any backtalk?"

"No."

"Good." Silence. Warren wanted to end it in some way, to speak of something interesting that had happened to him the last few days, but he couldn't think of anything that his father wouldn't get angry at or think too dumb to even be worth talking about. He heard him light a cigarette–that snap-snap-snap of his old silver army regiment lighter he'd said was almost no use to him for all the trouble it gave but which he'd never give up because of the great memories it brought back. Warren felt rescued when his mother came out of the bathroom. She was in a bathrobe and had a towel around her head.

"He's three thousand miles away," he said, handing her the receiver. "In San Francisco."

"Ken?" she said.

"I'm fine and dandy, thanks, and you?"

"Oh, just wonderful. Never better. Where are you?"

"San Francisco. Didn't Warren just tell you?"

"That where you headed the morning you snuck out, or did you make a stop in Vegas first?"

"Who snuck out where? And why would I go to Vegas? I put some duds in my bag and sort of stole out of the room so you wouldn't wake up. Considerate, in my abstract silent way, you can say."

"Listen, did you call to be the funnyman or tell me your travel plans, or what?"

"I called—and notice how serious my voice is now—to find out how you are, and of course Warren too. And then, when I get the true picture of our latest falling-out, and also the business side of my trip out of the way, I thought I could better make up my mind about the whole thing."

"What do you mean *true picture*?" She looked at Warren, who was sprawled on the bed, listening to her part of the conversation and whatever he could pick up from his dad's.

"Excuse me, Ken. Warren, could you leave the room?"

"What for?"

"Don't give me the 'what for'. Just do as I say."

He shrugged, as if her last words had sounded more reasonable, and shut the door behind him.

"Warren was listening," she said. "It isn't good for him—learning all about our difficulties this way."

"Don't worry so much about him. He's capable of accepting these things much better than you think."

"That still doesn't make it right. Jesus, he's only eight."

"Then maybe it's inevitable that he knows. And maybe, also, if you'd listen a little more closely like him—"

"All right, what is it you really called to say?"

"Part, I told you. Also, that I probably wouldn't've rushed out like that or even be here, for that matter—because the business could've waited—if it wasn't for you. You know, in the things you do that burn me up so much and what you say and all."

"Come off it."

"There you go again—you see? I knew this call wouldn't be worth a plug nickel for all I'd get out of it."

"Because you're not making sense, that's why. If you used your brains first before you said something, you'd get somewhere."

"And somewhere I haven't got by using my brains?"

"I'm talking about the phone."

"That nice apartment and car and all your clothes and your fur piece and my job and your forty to fifty pairs of slacks and everything else I got just by sitting around on my ass?"

"You know I wasn't referring to your work...or that you're not a good provider. You are. That's not what I meant."

"It's pretty clear what you meant. But look, I called up with a nice gesture—to make things right. But if you have other ideas... I'm saying, if you don't want things right again, or you don't think things can ever work out between us again after that last fight, then fine. That's just fine. That's really fine and dandy with me."

"Oh, stop with all this defensive nonsense why you called. I'll tell you once and for all why you called and save you the trouble. First of all—"

"Now cut it right there, Bobbie, I'm warning you."

"You're warning me what? Reason number one is you want me to apologize for our last battle as I've always done in the past, right?"

"Wrong. I called because—"

"Reason two is—"

"Will you give me a chance to speak?"

"—after I get you off the hook by saying it was my fault and I want you to come home, you'll want me to phone your mother—just so the dear woman should worry none, know what I mean?—and tell her everything's hunky-dory between us again, as I finally realized, sweet sensible repentant Barbara finally realized she was in the wrong. Number three-"

"Enough with your stupid numbers. Are you going to listen to reason or not?"

"Whose? Yours? That's not reason. I don't know what it is. It's doubletalk. Because I'm sick and tired of kowtowing to you every time you're in the wrong and refuse to admit it or you're feeling sorry for yourself because you're in the wrong and refuse to admit it. This row you'll have to smooth over by yourself—and that's with both your mother and me—because I've taken all I can from you."

"Who the hell's asking you to call my mother? Why are you blowing this thing so out of proportion for?"

"Because I can see it. Your standing there acting like you always do—like a spoiled pouting child waiting for an apology."

"When, always? Name one time before."

"August 2nd, 1969, at eight-fifteen in the afternoon. How the hell do I know, but there were plenty. My point is you never admit when you're wrong, and I do."

"Now that's a lot of crap if I ever heard any."

"Now that's a lot of crap if I ever heard any," then thinking how ridiculous it was mimicking him and how silly she must have sounded. She set the receiver down and ran her hands up and down her face.

"What'd you say, goddamnit?" his voice muffled in the bedspread. "Bobbie?"

"Excuse me a minute. Ken, I have to go to the bathroom."

"Can't it wait?" but she placed the receiver on the bed and went into the bathroom. She splashed water on her face, stepped on the scale, stepped off it and threw her robe and the head towel over the sink, and stepped on the scale again. She stared down and waited for the arrow to stop jiggling. Oh, give it up, she thought, her weight still fluctuating between 105 and 110. She put on the robe and went to the phone.

"Sorry, it was urgent," she said.

"Urgent? You could've had two drinks at the 21 and gone to the John there for what your little urgency just cost me."

"That's right, you're calling from San Francisco, aren't you."

"Yes. And it's not eight at night here and special low-evening long distance rates, either."

"That's right. I believe there's a three-hour difference in our time zones, which means you still probably have light. What can you see from your window?"

"Other windows."

"No great big beautiful bay and mountains and ocean and ships going to Tokyo and Bangkok and places?"

"Windows. Actually, a curtain. I drew the curtain because of all those other windows. Come on, Bobbie, what do you say we cut out all this sarcasm and biting remarks for a while, okay? Let's just say we're both in the wrong as we were for our last squabble, and begin something from there."

"So now we're both in the wrong. My, we are making progress. I'm sorry, Ken, but I'm not accepting any compromises."

"Okay, so I admit I was compromising—but only to get you off the hook this time."

"Just try unhooking yourself for a change, all right?"

"Do me a favor? Forget I called?"

"Whatever you say," and she hung up. She went into the bathroom to dry her hair.

The phone rang. Warren, reading a comicbook on his bed, waited for it to ring five times before he ran to her bedroom to answer it.

"Hello?"

"Hello, sweetheart, how come you didn't answer sooner?"

"Hi, Granny. Mom's in the bathroom with that hair dryer going on. I'll get her. Ma?" he shouted. "Grandma Ruth's on the phone."

"How is everything at home?"

"Fine. Dad called. He's in San Francisco. Ma?" he said, interrupting her next question, "Grandma Ruth wants to speak to you."

"I said, Warren, your father called? How long ago?"

"I'm not sure; not long. Ma?"

"Did he mention anything about when he's coming home—or your mother? Warren, are you listening to me?"

Just then his mother pushed open the bathroom door and took the receiver out of his hand.

"Hello, Ruth, what can I do for you?"

"My God, Barbara, right away I can hear how angry you are."

"It might sound like that, but I'm not. How are you?"

"But I can hear."

"All right, you can hear, you can hear, but how are things with you?"

"Wonderful, thanks, but I'd like to know what's this I hear about Kenneth and you. I haven't the exact story, of course, but whatever it is, it can't be more than a little fuss."

"It's much more." She waved Warren out of the room. He gestured he'd sit on the bed and wouldn't speak or listen to anything said on the phone, but she continued to shake her head for him to leave, and he stamped out.

"Why is it more than that?" Ruth went on. "A spat, like everyone has spats, and then it's over. Be smart—make up. I know something about how a wife should act. She thinks she's in the right—and even if she is, she should forget it or maybe just believe she's right but not say so. For if it makes them happy and builds up their ego, why shouldn't you give in sometimes, am I right?"

"No."

"Don't be a little girl, Barbara, angry for nothing, holding malice till it hurts. Do what I say and everything will work out fine."

"You honestly believe that?"

"Answer it yourself, dear: what else could happen?"

"Well, there's always what I think of myself after that lie—there's always that. And then tell me one thing that's gotten better between us after I've given in to him because you said I should, my own folks said I should, just about everyone I know said it."

"If everyone's said it, then it must be the right thing to do."

"Oh, artfully answered, Ruth, but I can't believe you believe that deep down. Haven't you been reading the papers? We're wearing our own fashions, breaking down all the discriminatory practices. Women shouldn't sell out to men anymore."

"Please, you can't change him. That's how he is, was, and will always be, so accept it."

"Then it's never going to be good again between Ken and me till he does change—and you can tell him that when he phones you."

"He said he was going to phone me?"

"Also tell him not to constantly kick me in the face as to what the call's costing him when I'm trying to talk over some very important personal things."

"He said that? That's not like him."

"That's just like him. Your son's the big sport when he wants to make an impression. Just come over here and I'll show you all the nice things he's told everyone we know he's bought me."

"I can't come over today, but thank you."

"I was only kidding—never mind. You'll probably be speaking to him soon—I mean, grant to me that I know by now how he operates—so tell him where I stand, all right? Also tell him—let's see; what should you say? That this time it's different. That I often think it's not worth the trouble being married to him anymore. And for sure he can't come back to the apartment till he takes responsibility for these fights and separations and that he's going to do something to prevent them in the future."

"So he's responsible, so you're responsible—what makes the difference in the end? After all, you're husband and wife, married almost ten years and with a lovely home and a son to consider, so you'd think one of you would be big enough to accept the blame and then forget it. Because listen, Barbara—"

"Ruth—please? No more," and she said goodbye and hung up. She figured Ken would call within the hour. He'd walked out on her three times the past two years, after calling her the worst names possible, and always Ruth later called her begging for a "beneficial to both" reconciliation brought about by Barbara's willingness to accept the blame. And always she said she couldn't but would ultimately, just to end the matter and for the sake of their son, say something like "Okay, maybe it's a little bit more my fault than yours; so it's over; come home."

She had a good idea what would happen next. He'd call his mother, who'd tell him only a little of what Barbara had said and certainly none of the tough talk and give him advice how to handle this tricky situation. Then, nervously picturing the call he still had to make, he'd light a cigarette and smoke it down slowly. Finally—feeling emboldened by the cigarette and the shots of scotch from the bottle he always carried in his suitcase—he'd tell the hotel operator he wanted to place another call to New York. His approach would be like the ones he used in the past. He'd say he knew he wasn't totally innocent for this most recent rupture, but could she tell him with a straight face that her hot temper and insults and inflexibility weren't mostly to blame? It was always so easy for him, she had always made it so easy for him, that she could just puke when she thought of all she'd given up in herself since she married him. She lay on the bed, thought of taking the phone off the hook so she could avoid the inevitable ugly scene, decided against it, as he was going to call sooner or later so be done with the damn thing no matter how bad it might turn out, and tried dozing off for a few minutes and only reopened her eyes when Warren tiptoed into the room.

"You sleeping?"

She shook her head.

"What are you doing lying down then?"

"Resting, can't you see?"

"I'm sorry."

"No—I'm sorry. I'm actually just lying down here waiting for your father's call."

"He say he'll call again?"

"No. But I have an intuition about such things—a feeling."

"What things?"

"Things like that. About what people will do who are very close to me like your father and you. That he'll call."

"How long you think he will?"

"I can't predict it with any great exactness, not being the expert in these feelings that some people claim to be, but I'd say soon."

"Will you let me speak to him?"

"You know it." She inspected her nails. Most were jagged, uneven, the nails on the right hand bitten down so far the last few days and the cuticles looking such a mess, that she had to turn the hand over. She got out her manicure set from the night table.

"Why'd you send me out when Granny called? She say I did something she didn't like last time she took care of me?"

"Why, did you?"

"What did *she* say?"

"Now you're doing a bit of conniving like your father sometimes does, you know? Even at your age, which I'm not sure is so cute. I had personal things to discuss with her—nothing about you."

"What personal things?"

The phone rang. Warren lunged for the receiver, said "Daddy, that you?"

"Yeah, how'd you know?"

"He says, how'd I know?"

"Tell him I had an intuition," she said.

"A what again?"

"Here, give me it. Ken?"

"What's going on there?"

"I was only telling Warren to tell you I was feeling slightly intuitive tonight."

"About what?"

"Ask your son."

Warren stuck out his hand for the receiver.

"What in the world's that supposed to mean?" Ken said.

"The phone, Mom, the phone."

She mussed up his hair—he grabbed the receiver while she still held it to her ear—and said "Wait till I'm finished and I'll call you to it," and pointed to the door. He shook his head, slapped his hands against his sides when she continued to point and smile, and slammed the door behind him.

"Now you made me get him mad," she said.

"Get who mad—Warren? What the hell were you you doing there, talking riddles? "

"All I said before is that you should ask your son because he knows. In fact, he knows too much already for an eight-year-old."

"You know, I don't want to appear dense—it's a very unattractive pose for a man my age—but you're really making a lot of sense to me, you really are."

"What I'm saying is that if you don't want Warren to know too much about our difficulties, well, then I don't have the solution. Maybe we should get a housekeeper or maid—somebody, at least, who will occupy him during his more restless moments and occasionally answer the phone. It's just every time I'm left alone with him or the phone rings when I'm in the shower, let's say, he uses answering it as a pretext for barging into our room and asking me a lot of embarrassing questions."

"So slap him down then, that's all."

"Brilliant. No, I think the nanny idea is the best one."

"What nanny idea? You might not believe this—you probably never thought you had such a schnook for a husband—but I think I lost a little of what you're saying."

"It's all quite simple. What I want is for us to have someone look after Warren weekday afternoons and to answer the phone when I can't, or maybe the alternative is to get a phone extension in the kitchen."

"Why an extension?"

"So Warren can answer it there and then tell me I'm wanted on the phone, without him having to come into the room to answer it. We can call it Warren's personal phone—something he'll like."

"His personal phone—right, I see."

"But it's important, Ken."

"I know it's important, but enough's enough, agreed?"

"But it sounds as if you don't think it's important. You're not worried about the extra charges for the extension, are you?"

"Now don't start up on me again, Bobbie, and I'm not kidding anymore. And let's stop all this silly jibberish, as I'm just not up to it now."

"Then I don't know, Ken. If we're ever going to get any privacy around here with that boy... I mean, the only way I can see his personal questions and overcuriosity letting up on us is if we—"

"Okay. For the seventeenth time—I heard, I agree. You say you want a nanny for the kid, fine, you'll get one. We'll bring her all the way from Ireland if we can't find a good one here, and not steerage, but good accommodations on a plane or ship. And what else was that—an extension? You want a phone extension? Fine again, great, even two or three or as many as you think we need, and all push-button Princesses if you like, and any color you want, even pink. But now, you going to listen a moment as to why I called?"

"I'm listening, dear, I'm listening."

MR.   GREENE.

It was a beautiful day, clear and dry, the orchards soaked by the early-morning downpour and smelling of fallen fruit and fresh buds. Life fantastic, I thought, when something hard was shoved into my back and a voice said don't turn around.

"Don't turn what?" I said, turning around and seeing a man holding a handgun.

"Didn't I say not to?" and he split my head open with the gun butt, and while I lay on the ground howling for help but not sure if my words were coming out, and trying to divert the stream of blood running into my nose and mouth, he shot me twice in the stomach and once in the head.

I woke up. Usually when I have dreams like this I'm somehow able to startle myself out of sleep before the bullets come, though not before I'm clubbed. But this morning I was awakened by the sounds of a sanitation truck being fed garbage. My wife stirred on her side of the bed and asked what time it was, though she knew as well as I that the city Sanitation truck made a punctual seven o'clock visit to our apartment building every weekday.

"Seven," I said, and she said "Oh," and shut her eyes for another ten minutes. Then we got up, washed and dressed and started preparing breakfast.

"I had an incredibly creepy dream this morning," I said at the table as she set before me my Wednesday breakfast of poached eggs on buttered toast and half a tomato. "A man hit me so hard that it feels as if my head still aches."

"Sounds like the dream you had two nights ago, or was it three?"

"Three. But this time I was shot. Twice in the stomach and once in the head."

"Ug," she said, "I'm glad I sleep peacefully," and wrapped my lunch sandwich in aluminum foil and stuck it in a paper bag with an apple and lots of vegetables. "You'll be late."

I kissed her on the lips goodbye. "Be careful," she said. "And please don't run for the local again. I don't want you getting another heart seizure, as this place gets very lonely without you."

I was sort of hustling like a marathon walker to the subway entrance when a man said "Like to win a free ticket abroad just by answering a few questions, sir?" I stopped and this well-dressed young man approached me carrying a briefcase. "I'm with the Transiberian Travel Service," he said, "and we're conducting a very essential poll." I told him I was in a hurry to get to work, but remembering my wife's advice on the subject and curious about the free trip abroad, I told him I could spare only a minute. "Wonderful," he said, and reached into his briefcase for what he said was his short question and answer sheet concerning potential intercontinental travelers and transoceanic flights and pulled out a very rusty Luger.

"In broad daylight?" I said, and he said nobody was around but if someone did come by before I stopped stalling and handed over my wallet, he'd be forced to shoot me. "You can't do that; this is supposed to be a civilized society. Hasn't there been enough violence in the world already?" Just then a woman turned the corner and headed our way. I quickly reached for my billfold to give the man, but he said "Too late." He pulled the trigger; the bullet grazed my arm. I begged him not to shoot again, but a bullet tore through my throat. The man ran off. I was on the ground, dying, no doubt. A few people kneeled and stood above me, first asking me and then one another what they could do to help. Then two hands stroked my head and the voice belonging to them said that someone had gone to call for an ambulance. "Don't worry," she said, "you'll come out of this alive. I've witnessed three street shootings this year and the victim has always lived," and I passed out.

The radio alarm buzzed. It was 7:50—fifteen minutes later than I usually got up. "Jan," I said, "it's 7:50. You set the alarm for too late again. Get up; I've barely a half hour to get out of the house."

"I think you were the one who said it," she said, turning over and shutting her eyes.

I touched her back; she felt so soft and warm. I snuggled into her from behind and fondled her backside.

"You feel so soft and warm," I said.

"Can I sleep another five minutes?"

"You can if you let me lie close to you like this. In fact, sleep for another hour. I'll make sure Frilly's all right and get out of the house by myself."

"You're a love," she said, and made a kissing sound. I lay close to her for a few minutes. Then I got up, checked our baby and saw she was safe and asleep, made two poached eggs on buttered toast, a dish Jan always complained was too much trouble making for breakfast—and after sticking a container of yogurt and dietetic cookies into my attaché case for lunch and again peeking into the baby's room to see that she was all right, I left the house.

I started down our quiet suburban street to Charlie Ravage's house at the corner, as this was his day to drive us to town. "Say, Mr. Greene," a man said, signaling me from the passenger seat of an expensive new car, "do you remember me? I used to be your next-door neighbor in Lumpertville—old fat man Sachs." I walked to his car and told him his name was as unfamiliar as his face, but maybe he'd gotten a little thinner since the time I was supposed to have known him.

"I've actually gained twenty pounds." He opened the door and pointed at me what looked like a sawed-off shotgun and invited me to step inside the car for a business conference, "No fuss," he said, "and you'll be able to leave with your good health intact."

"How'd you know my name and where I used to live?" I said, sitting beside him when he moved over.

"Oh, Mr. Greene, I've watched you numerous times coming out of your garish pink house, all fresh with your darling wife's adoring smells still on you and with your low-caloric breakfast in your gut. I know all your history and comfortable habits, especially the precise time you leave for work every day. Eight-fifteen, am I right?" and I nodded and asked what he had in mind doing with me. "You're the vice-president of the town's most prominent bank, aren't you?" and then described the relatively simple bankrobbing plan he'd devised. He would drive me to town, I'd get the bank guard to open the front door, he'd follow me in, disarm the guard, I'd open the bank's safe and in a matter of minutes and before the bank officially opened, he'd be gone with about fifty thousand dollars in untraceable cash. "Not bad for a half morning's work, wouldn't you say?"

We drove to town. I was let in the bank, George the guard was disarmed, bound and gagged. I opened the safe, the man took all the paper cash in it and then bound and gagged me. I could have set off one of the many hidden alarms before I was tied up, but the chance of saving the bank thousands of insured dollars and getting a bonus if not a promotion wasn't worth the risk of being shot. Just as the thief was about to leave through the only side door, George freed himself and ducked behind the tellers' counter. The alarm went off; the entire bank lit up, and customers waiting outside for the bank to open began banging on the windows and door. The man tried the side door, but because of the alarm all the exits were automatically locked from the outside. He shot out a window and was about to leap through the opening when a police car pulled up in front. He reloaded the gun, said "This is what you get for hiring loyal but dumb bank guards," and while I pleaded for him not to shoot by shaking my head from side to side, he pulled the trigger and in an instant it seemed I'd lost my chest. Someone ungagged and untied me, through darkening eyes I watched the man gassed out of the president's office and taken away; then I was lifted onto a gurney and slid into an ambulance. I was given blood, and just before an oxygen mask was put over my face I asked the doctor if she thought I would live.

"No question about it," she said, but by the tone of her voice and the look of the attendant next to her, I knew I'd never reach the hospital alive.

"Dad," someone said—my son or daughter. "Dad, get up." It was Ford, my six-year-old son, who since his mother died four months ago when some madman seated behind her in a movie theater shot her, woke me up every morning. "It's past eight. Dad, and you're going to miss your first class."

"Eight? Why didn't you wake me sooner?"

"My alarm didn't go off. You set it wrong again last night. But Frilly's already making your breakfast."

Frilly, my ten-year-old daughter and a lookalike for her beautiful mom, kissed me when I came into the kitchen. My regular workday breakfast was on the table. Two five-minute eggs, just as I liked them, not boiled for five minutes but spooned into the saucepan and covered after the gas under the boiling water had been turned off, and corn muffins that Frilly had made the previous night. "Get your math home-work done?" I said, and she said "Math's a snap. I can whip through it in the short ride to school."

The school bus honked twice, and the kids kissed me goodbye, I walked them to the bus, told them I hoped they'd have a gloriously happy day at school and that tonight we were going to dine out fancy for a change and later catch the concert at Civic Aud.

"Morning, Mr. Greene," the driver said, and I said "Morning, Will; great day out," and waved at my children waving at me till the bus was out of sight. I got my briefcase, which Frilly had laid out for me with my lecture notes and a bag lunch inside, and rode to campus on my bike. The air was chillier than I was dressed for and I was sorry I hadn't taken a sweater, which I usually throw over my shoulders and tie the sleeves at my chest.

"Cooler today," Sam Rainbow said, cycling past me from the opposite direction and wearing a sheepherder's coat.

"Hiya, Professor Greene," one of my former grad students said, a pretty, intelligent young woman in a short skirt and high boots. She had such gorgeous legs. I stopped, said "How are you, Roz? Magnificent morning, isn't it? Listen, if you're not in a hurry, how about a quick coffee with me in the campus lounge?" and she'd just said she'd love to when I heard a barrage of gunshots and she flopped to the ground.

"Oh, no," I said, "not again," as people were dropping all around me, some hit by bullets, others dodging behind bushes, cars and trees. Roz had been shot in the head, part of her brains on my sleeve. There was nothing I could do for her, and I was still out in the open. I ran for a car parked about thirty feet away, but the sniper in one of the top floor windows of the Arts and Sciences building cut me down with a bullet in the foot, and while I was crawling the last few feet to the car, another bullet in my back. I regained consciousness after the shooting had ended. "We got him," a man told me. "Some overpressured poly sci student who went nuts. Don't know how many got hit, but that dead bastard sure'll serve a good lesson for anyone else thinking of using a repeater against innocent people like that. And don't fret about yourself, Professor. Doctors here say you'll be up and walking again in a matter of weeks," which, when I began heaving blood and feeling as sick as I ever felt in my life, I knew was a lie. "Have somebody pick my kids up at school," I said, and he said "Sure, sir, anything you wish."

"Happy birthday to you, happy birthday to you, happy birthday, dear Daddy, happy birthday to you."

That was what I woke up to this morning after all those disturbing dreams. My wife and two kids singing the happy birthday ditty on my fortieth. "Thank you," I said. "Thank you one and all for reminding me what I most didn't want to be reminded of. And now, if you can bear with more of my impoliteness, I have to hurry and get dressed."

I took off my pajamas and grabbed my underpants. "Aren't you going to shower first?" Ford said, and I said "Why? Do I smell so bad that you don't think I can wait till I get home tonight?"

"It's not that. We're all meeting you at your studio later where Grandpa's coming to treat us to dinner and a show."

"Has that been agreed to by your mother?"

Jan said "On your birthday, Saul, you know your father always takes charge."

"Agreed, then," and I got in the shower. My family undressed and got in with me, and though it was crowded and we each did our share of horsing around under the spray, we did manage to get our bodies soaped, and Frilly even got in a shampoo.

We sat at the kitchen table for breakfast. Frilly lit candles, and when I said "At breakfast?" she said "It's a special occasion, did you forget?" and handed me a box wrapped with the front page of today's newspaper and decorated with quartermoons and tentacled suns and stars. Inside were two nylon brushes, a number 14 and 17, which I needed badly. I hadn't sold a painting in months and I was again starting to put the touch on my closest friends. Ford gave me a pound tube of Mars black and Jan presented me with twenty-five yards of the best unprimed duck canvas. "You're all saints," I said, "and I worship you as others might worship the great god Moolah, but now I gotta get going and live up to your faith in me."

They walked me outside. I unchained my motor scooter from the building's fence, hugged my family and headed for my studio, which was in a municipal-run building of artists' lofts in the poorest section of town.

Once there, I promptly began the completion of a huge painting I was calling "The Birth of the Earth," and was working feverishly, laying on heavy long strokes of the Mars black with my new 17 brush, when one of the other artists in the building knocked on my door and said I was wanted on the pay phone downstairs.

It was Jan, saying don't worry, everything will be all right, I should prepare myself for some pretty rough though not totally catastrophic news—while I was practically screaming for her to come out with it already—but a boy had entered my father's junior high school classroom without a late pass and when my father told him to go to the guidance office to get one, the boy shot him in the hip. "But Dad's okay," she said. "He's going to live; be thankful for that," but my knees wobbled and I fell back against the wall and slid down to the floor. She said, when I told her where I was sitting, to stop acting like a wimp and meet her at the hospital right away.

I went outside and signaled for a cab. One stopped, and I ran to it, but a man beat me to the door. I told him that not only had I hailed the cab first but that it was possibly a dying father I was going to see, and he took out a handgun from a concealed shoulder holster. I feinted left, sprinted right, but the man shot me in the leg and, after I bounced off a car fender to the street, he stared straight down at my face and cursed me before putting a bullet into my head.

"Saul, Saul, what are you still lying there for? You have to get up," my wife said, leaning over me and looking distressed. Had I really survived? I thought. Was I in a hospital or still on the street? "And what about Dad?" I said.

"What about him? Because if you aren't out of bed and dressed in half an hour, we'll miss the 11:15 to Morganburg Lake, and the next train doesn't leave till three."

I got up, began dressing, told Jan about these scary repetitive dreams I had overnight, and she said the rich food she made for dinner last night must have affected me. "My stomach didn't feel too good either when I woke up." I asked if the kids were all right and she said "Sure, why shouldn't they be?" I didn't want to alarm her with the very real fear the dreams had left in me, so I said "Because of the food. How are they feeling?"

"Those two? They've stomachs like a shark's. That's because theirs haven't been tampered with years of cocktails and cognacs."

We all sat down for breakfast. Frilly already had her swimsuit on under her sundress, and Ford, while eating, was stuffing his schoolbag with books, sports equipment, and little action figures. Then we cabbed to the station and boarded the train.

I was looking out the train window at the fields and farms we passed and feeling a lot more peaceful than I had this morning, when a woman shrieked at the front of the car. Another woman screamed, a man yelled "Turn the damn thing up," a radio was made louder and a newscaster, trying to hold back his sobs, said "There's no uncertainty about it now: Senator Booker Maulson, without question the nation's leading spokesman for the underprivileged and poor and its most ardent activist for world peace, was shot in the back of the head while making an Independence Day speech to a picnicking crowd of thousands."

"God help us," Jan said, and started crying. Frilly broke down also, and Ford pulled my arm and asked why everyone was so excited.

I went to the front of the car where most of the passengers had gathered around the radio. The newscaster said Maulson was killed instantly and his murderer beaten to death before police could pry him away from the outraged mob. Many of the people in the car were now weeping uncontrollably. The woman beside me said she was sure Maulson's murder was part of a worldwide conspiracy: "People just don't want peace, that's all." Two men who seemed to be traveling together told her Maulson had got what he'd been asking for, with all his peace marches and speeches against big business and the military and war. The man holding the radio said these men were talking cruelly and stupidly, and out of respect for Senator Maulson, his grieving family and the millions of people around the world who will mourn his death, they should shut their mouths. The men said they didn't have to, this was still a democratic country where freedom of speech was accepted as nearly a sacrament, and this man was an ignorant liberal patsy who maybe ought to be shot in the head himself. The man handed the radio to his son and jumped at the two men. He knocked one of them to the floor and kicked him in the face and was beating up the other one with his fists when the man on the floor shot him in the back.

I pulled the emergency cord. The train stopped and I led my family to the rear of the car, where I forced open the door and we jumped out. We'd follow the tracks to the last station we passed, about six miles away, and from there take a train back to the city. Then, Jan and I would decide on doing one or two things: buying a used car and finding a quiet, remote part of the country to live and work in, or using all our savings to fly across the ocean and settle in a much safer and saner land.

We'd walked a few miles when Jan said we should stop: she and the kids were exhausted. We rested on a shady hill near the tracks.

I felt tired and tried to fight off sleep because of the dreams I might have, but I soon dozed off. Someone was shooting BB holes through the windows of our new house. "Come on out or we're going to come in and drag you out," a boy yelled through a bullhorn.

The telephone rang. The woman who answered my hello said "They've just killed your son at school, and because he's the son of yours, we're all glad."

Our neighbor, Mrs. Fleishman, yelled from her window across the narrow airshaft. "Two army men smashed down our door and shot Mr. Fleishman and then threw him down the stairwell. Help me, call the police."

I called the police. The officer said Mr. Fleishman deserved to be killed and so did I. "Without doubt, Mr. Greene, your family's next. None of you people can think you're safe anymore," and when I asked for his badge number, he said "Shove It Up, Nine One One."

Mrs. Fleishman screamed for me again from her window. "They're coming to get me now, Mr. Greene. Hurry, call the police."

My wife came into the bedroom. "Three state troopers are at the door. Should I let them in?"

"Of course, let them in. What did we do that we have to be afraid of?" Right after she left the room, I shouted "No, no, Jan, I was wrong."

Frilly was being dragged out of the apartment when I ran into the living room. I started after her down the stairs, heard a gun discharge, and covered my eyes. Jan demanded I go to the window to see what had happened. Frilly had been shot by a firing squad as she stood against our building's courtyard wall.

"Six soldiers and Marines are at the door," Jan said. "They say if I don't let them in they'll shoot the doorknob off."

"Where's my gun," I said, "where's that damn gun?" Jan said I didn't have a gun. "You've always been firmly against even holding a gun. You don't even know how to load or shoot a gun," and I said "I've got one, all right," and searched frantically through our dresser and pulled out Ford's cap pistol and aimed it at the front door and pressed the trigger, and real bullets came out, I had firing power in my hand, I kept shooting at the men Jan had said were behind the door and yelling "You're all dead, you bastards; I'm getting back at every last one of you; you're all getting exactly what you deserve," and the door crashed to the floor, the men fell in after it, about ten of them and half of them dressed like soldiers and state troopers and police, and all dead, I had killed them all.

"They're dragging Frilly away again," Jan said.

"Ford, where's Ford?"

"They're dragging Ford away also. Stop them, Saul. Do something before I go crazy right here."

"They're killing my dog," Mrs. Fleishman screamed. "Help me, Mr. Greene. They're murdering my dear Dovetail with bullets."

"Dad," Frilly said, "you're sweating something awful. Mom's awake and says we should get a move on."

Police cars and ambulances with their sirens going were speeding on the country road paralleling the tracks, no doubt heading to the train we'd been on. I asked Jan how she was and she said "Still sad and frightened but not so tired anymore. I slept also and also had bad dreams."

I told her I'd carry her to the station on my shoulders if she wasn't so tall and big-boned, and she laughed, said she could make it on her own, that maybe we should have stayed to help that poor wounded man and his son, that she supposed we shouldn't feel too guilty, as there must be several other people on the train, including a doctor and nurse or two, who could do a much better job than us. Then the four of us resumed our walk to the station, calmer now, on probably the worst day of our lives.

PIERS

.

He dials the California number Chloe sent him last week when she
wrote that she and Lucia had finally found an interim home. She
also said they'd be driving east for a vacation in a few weeks and was
Pennsylvania before or after New York? He hasn't seen them in three
years. He wrote about that last afternoon with them in a story that
opens with Chloe saying she's pregnant by him, though she was living
with her husband at the time, and closes around two years later with
Chloe and Lucia driving onto the San Francisco freeway on their way
back to L.A., though in real life the cities were reversed, as he wanted
the story to end with the letter A because it began with the woman's
name Zee. Nobody noticed the alphabetic artifice or the twenty-four
others he planted in the story, as they haven't in the story where all
the men have names that could be women's, like Robin and Dale.
Or in another where all the city names start off with Saint, San or
Santa and the women are named after ores, alloys, metals, gems and
semiprecious stones.

"Chloe's on the property but a half mile through the woods from
here," a man says. "This long distance? Give me your number and we'll
have her call you back on our magic free telephone."

Last commune she lived in was vegetarian, Chloe wrote, and so
authoritarian that when they found her and five-year-old Lucia sharing
a beef jerky, they forced Chloe to eat six bowls of cold porridge made
from organically grown hand-ground oats, and Lucia three. Lucia
became so hysterical after the third bowl that she had to be injected
with a tranquilizer, and they were evicted the next day. Always mistakes, she wrote in another letter, all but the last he's included in an

epistolary story composed solely of edited versions of the letters she's written him the past few years, with all the people's names switched around and the same dates and locations other than for the exact building, RTD and box numbers reproduced.

This year she fell in love with a junkie, she said in the letter and story, and the year before that with an alcoholic, and she hoped both would say "Ah, at last a woman who turns me on, someone to communicate with, to *be* with; now I can throw away my junk, my gin, my jive, forget my literary critiques and satirical cartoons and great American hovels and go off with her and start a farm and finally do something worthwhile." One man she recently met at a psychodrama, the incident he closed the story with. "Everyone was putting him down. So I said to him 'What you want and need most is to mount a woman and really jam it all the way in there, am I right?' Everyone hooted at me to sit down, but the man said 'Lady, you just knocked the nail on the nose. But no chick will let me do it because they think I'm too horny or homely or both.' 'Well, let's first end this pressing need you have, and after that we can get down to the weightier issue of why you think you're homely or have to be horny, but not in front of these unfeeling creeps.' The rest of the psychodrama participants began beating up on me when I refused to be mounted in front of them, and when the man tried tearing them off me, they broke a few of his teeth. They only let us go after they'd ripped, bit, scratched and clawed most of our clothes off and some of our hair and skin, and later in my place we went to bed.

He turned out to be leery, weirdy, a bad lover, a born loser, I think syphilitic and infanticidal, maybe even sapropelic and homosexual, certainly sadistic, sodomitic, satanic, septic, scabietic, scrofulous, carious, dystonic, dyspeptic, dysuric, the worst. Mistakes. Always mistakes."

She calls an hour later. "Piers?"

"Hey, Chloe, how are you?"

"Fine, thanks, how are you?"

"And Lucia?"

"Fine? Family's doing fine? You know I'm untalkative on the phone."

"Um, glum...to hear you say you're untalkative on the phone?"

"Very untalkative on the phone."

"Lots of untalkatives on the phone."

"Can't we stop with the untalkatives on the phone?"

"To find out if you're still writing your journals?"

"Daily. I was in fact logging today's account when they said you wanted me to call back, which I also wrote down. And now, as I'm talking to you, I'm trying with my other hand to transcribe everything you said before, as this is an unusual event. So far I've the journal question, your untalkatives on the phone, 'Um, bum,' and 'And Lucia?' and 'Hey, Chloe, how are you?' Verbal equivocals and punning abound in your talk, Piers. Despite everything I've done and might do in my life, do you think I'll post-Chloe be known wholly as Lucia's madonna and your occasional chronicler and letter recipient and one-time mistress as Kafka's Milena now is? But we're starving and haven't any food and neither does the main house, so we have to drive down the maountain to the supermarket. Lucia wants to speak to you too."

"I don't think I'm prepared."

"You need a script? It's all right—she doesn't know who you are. And unlike me, she likes to speak to anyone who calls. Here."

"But I've never really spoken to her before. Help me out if it gets rough. And don't forget to come back. Chloe? Chloe?"

"Could you repeat that for my journal jottings starting from to her before?"

"Hello," a girl says.

"You speak," he says.

"I speak. Lucia speaks."

"You wouldn't remember me, Lucia. I'm Piers. Did you, about a month ago, get a postcard from a person named Piers?"

"Postcard?"

"Do you know what a postcard is?"

"He says postcard," she says away from the phone.

"Tell him they're neither made from recycled paper nor nourishing."

"Lucia," he says, "did you ever get a postcard over the phone?"

"I know a postcard."

"Good. Because, you see, I'm a long ways away. So far away from you that if you got on a plane to fly to the city I'm in, it would have to be in the air for many hours to get here. And a regular postcard takes days and days to get to you, so to speed things up I'm going to send you one over the phone instead. Do you understand?"

"Yes."

"Fine, then; here goes. A postcard for Lucia over the phone. 'Dear Lucia.' That's your name, right?"

"Dear Lucia Maria Dorn."

"Good. 'Dear Lucia Maria Dorn. I'm sending you a postcard from a place far away that takes hours to fly in the air to and I hope you like getting my card very much. Love, your friend, Piers.'"

"What?"

"I just sent you a postcard over the phone. There's not much room to write on a postcard, so I had to keep it short."

"He's sending a postcard on the phone."

"Lucia, how old are you?"

"Five."

"Five. I see. Do you like to go swimming?"

"What?"

"Swimming. Do you like to run through the forests with the animals?"

"Are no animals here. No pets allowed."

"No wild weather-wise animals like woody woodchucks in the woods?"

"No."

"Skunks, chipmunks?"

"No."

"No raccoons, baboons?"

"No."

"Goose, moose? Grouse, mouse? Cockatoos, kangaroos? Chickadees, wallabies?"

"No, no, no, no."

"Well, then, do you like to fly in the sky with the magpie and other birds?"

"Are no birds here."

"Do you like to swim in the ocean with the fish?"

"No fish."

"Sure, there are fish."

"He says there are fish here."

"In the ocean, I said. I didn't mean in fishtanks. And you're near the ocean. I know where La Honda is. I used to live around there. And you and your mom and I once built a whopping bonfire on a beach nearby that burned through the night, but that was too far back for you to remember."

"I remember."

"You remember the potatoes we roasted? The wieners as big as big bed pillows we toasted?"

"We have to go for food now."

"She's right, Piers. We gotta go."

"She speaks; does she read?"

"Only the words 'flash' and 'cards' on the giant flash cards I hold up. 'Giant' she only knows by my accompanying drawing of one, and 'I' she thinks is a bed on its headboard, and the flash card set doesn't have a card for 'hold up.'"

"I also wanted to know when you're driving east."

"To...know...when...I'm...driving...east. Got you. To that I say 'I don't know if I am.'"

"You can stay with me. There's enough room."

"In the unlikelihood that I even start out from here and then get past my friends in Pennsylvania, I'll stay with you if I don't get stuck in New Jersey, yes."

"And if I flew out tomorrow on a twenty-seven-day excursion flight, would I be able to stay with you?"

"My camper's too small for us all."

"No double sleeping bags or available space in the main house?"

"If he...means...he and I...then I...tell...him—"

"Stop that."

"I'm with someone else."

"No one else. You and I. Someone else you can always be with. You and me. Woman and man. Man on woman, woman on man. Side by side, grunt to grunt, stomach to stem, my woman, my man."

"To fall in love?"

"We'll see. But just to be with me."

"For two weeks?"

"Three weeks. Past the excursion flight mini-maximum into the unknown beyond. I don't know. That's the unknown. I don't know if that's the unknown. What do I know? What I knew? What I know now? That's it, no. Even what I knew as the well-known turns out to be unknown again and again. What I know is that I can't say I don't know anything, as that's not implicit in my saying I don't. Nah, maybe not even that. But you're with someone else. A man?"

"He is. I am. Quote he is, I am, unquote. I'm sorry. It's exhausting enough chattering this stuff over the phone. And my despicable compulsion to write everything down simply because I began doing it when I was six. For you, I'll tear up this journal page. Book 85, page one twenty-two, lines nine through eighteen. I tore it up. Eliot's piaculative and I'm not sure about Pound's, but now mine. Did you hear the tear? There's a lit fireplace a hand's toss away from here and the expiatory ultimate would be for me to throw in my hands. The penultimate would be this entire journal's death fire. Naturally, not my other eighty-two books, as throwing them in has no estimable sacrificial grading and is less likely to occur than self-immolation, and I'd also sear my arms pulling them out as Nora did with *Stephen's Arsonist*, and then I couldn't drive. And Lucia can't both reach the floor clutch and steer. And we've really got to go. I hate belaboring the point, but the all-night supermarkets in the valley don't stay open all night. There was a suit to that effect and the county ruled that 'all-night' means only till midnight. The stores could stay open past then if they liked, but they couldn't put 'all-morning' on their signs unless they meant to stay open till at least noon from twelve-o-one on. 'Bye."

"Don't go."

He turns on the TV. The movie is about a young writer who trains to New York from Texas with a huge novel and falls in love with a rich woman twice his age. His editor is secretly in love with him and warns him about the older woman and her circle of culture hounds. "They have a single gift and unsparing craving of preying on talented writers and transforming them into puny hacks in half the time it takes me to edit their hulking novels. Leastwise with me the author has every right to reject my deletions and corrections, which if stubbornly done to excess could mean the manuscript's rejection no matter how fat the advance. While none of her young men have had the grit to resist being regaled and eventually devoured for new meat by the insatiable Hazel Brawn and her highborn ravenous friends."

"Since I've the lifelong incurable disease of *cacoethes scribendi*," the writer says, "they'll either find me stuck in their throats or be suffering from my cramps and blocks, but massively incapacitating."

"I still think you'll be what they eat."

One of the commercials ends with Anne Hathaway saying to Shakespeare, who's slavering over the cardigan sweater she bought him after he fretted about being chilled at his desk and unable to finish *Richard III*, "As someone once said, Bill, 'All's wool that wraps Will.'

Or was it 'Ill's Will no longer with his garret chill'? No, I think it was 'All's better in belles lettres with a swell Metre sweater.'"

"You mean," Shakespeare says, "'All's ill that rends Will's.'"

"Aye," Anne says.

"'Neigh,' I should have the beleaguered Richard say." While watching the movie, Piers writes Lucia a letter. He folds the writing paper into quarters and with magic markers draws a picture in each square. The top right one's a self-portrait, the caption beneath reading "Hello, Lucia, I'm Piers, the man you telephone-talked to the other night, remember? I decided to send you this letter instead of a post-card—think back. As you can tell from that <u>think back</u>. I don't like repeating words like <u>remember</u> in so short a space made even shorter by the little space I have to write, and I'm sorry not only for this long sentence, which could have been broken up with a period in place of a comma twenty or so words and a contraction ago, but also for using plurisyllabic words like <u>repeating</u>, <u>remember</u>, <u>shorter</u>, <u>little</u>, <u>sentence</u>, <u>contraction</u> and maybe even <u>sorry</u>, <u>broken</u>, <u>period</u>, <u>comma</u>, <u>using</u> and maybe even <u>maybe</u> and even <u>even</u> and surely <u>surely</u> and <u>plurisyllabic</u>. I'm sure I left out one or two but not <u>one</u> and <u>two</u>, as they're not pluri-syllabic words. Though if I hadn't used all those underlined words in that sentence before the last (please turn over and continue reading in box 1), the sentence would have read 'As you can tell from that I don't like words like in so short a space made by the space I have to write, and I'm not for this long, which could have been up with a in place of a or so words and a, but for words like and and and and and.' Not that I couldn't find any meaning in that quoted sentence no matter how unwittingly it was written, but I would have used an *an* instead of <u>a</u> in front of <u>in place of</u>. Anyway, I promise not to write any more big words like <u>anyway</u> and <u>promise</u>. But since I don't know if you can read these big words I promised not to write, I'll just write them without assuming you can't read them or that they can't be easily taught to you. By the way, I don't have yellow hair but felt I should use that color in my self-portrait, since I already drew my face red and neck blue.

"The above drawing in square B is my dictionary. I don't think you'll be interested in seeing it, but a book is an easy thing to draw.

"Above is my typewriter. I write stories and letters on it. This letter to you, though, I'm writing by hand. I could write it by foot, but I have slippers on. The man in the first joke tells bad squares. Turn that sentence around a bit and you'll see what I mean when I say 'Maybe that's what makes his red so face.' Turn <u>red</u> <u>so</u> <u>face</u> around and you won't have a proteron hysteron. Keep turning and you'll get dizzy. (From now on TPO means <u>turn page over</u>, so TPO to box 2.) Getting back to the more rollicky topic of sad jokes and bad oxymora, I guess in my second letter my face will have to be purple, which might be your primary art lesson, though I won't tell you what I heard or said to make my face that way.

"This is my room with me lying on the floor in front of a television set. The figure on the screen's left is a woman. The one on the right a man. Now the man's on the right and she's on the left. Now they're falling together onto the bed. Now a blanket's on top of them. Now a cat jumps on the blanket and snuggles in between them. Now the light fades till the screen's dark. (TPO to box 5.) I can't draw all these movements and different shades of light in the little space I have for the TV screen in my drawing, so I'll leave the figures the way I drew them: two vertical sticks, the ganglier one standing for the man, the small tire surrounding them being my TV set, which is on loan from my parents so I could see the presidential debates tonight: I don't own: do you? One day I hope to see you where you live or where I love, which as I told you on the phone is many hours away from you in New York by plane. That's bad English (please continue on page 2), but the only language I know well enough to illiterately know. The man in squares A and D on page 1 makes veriberi bad jokes, or tries to joke, as he just tried to, and unfailingly fails, as he just succeeded in unfailingly failing again, and again. What is the color of dumbness, which is the color I'd draw the man's face in those two pictures if I hadn't already drawn them read I mean red. That's even worser English, and what I just wrote then the worsest, and there can't be any worse English more than that, except maybe that, if I hadn't capitalized the <u>E</u> in <u>anguish</u> and made it <u>i</u>. By the way, what I seem to be poking with a big stick in my self-portrait on page 1 is this letter I'm writing to you.

"P.S. The movie I'm watching ends with this rich lady getting sick from a strange disease known as kakemonomania scribbledibblebe, and the fiction writer in the film, ten years younger than I and much better-looking and whose name I think is Dom, saying, as she lies asleep in her hospital suite, 'I've had enough of you and your lowdown friends for a lifetime, Mrs. Brawn, and I just wish I had the guts to say it to your face,' which he actually is doing, since he's standing over her and she's lying on her back. The young woman editor, which to make a long story short is a worker who makes short sentences and large spaces out of toiled-over compressed passages and long paragraphs, loves Dom or Rom or some hom-nom like Strom or Pom but only one of thorn, comes to the hospital room, and she and the writer kiss and hug. The unedited editor says 'You were truly in love with her, weren't you, and there's nothing in life worth living for more than that, in spite of it often ending in agony, fiasco and utter distress,' and he nods yes-s-s. 'Will you two idiots get the H out of here,' the older woman says. 'I'm exhausted with you both and want to get some shuteye before I die,' and they smile at her, she at them, they leave the room and race downstairs and through the lobby.

She whistles for a cab and they run to it hand in hand, while the doorman yells after them 'That sure must've been a quick recovery,' for you see, Lucia (as the closing credits and cooing music come on and the cab pulls away with the couple visible through the rear window kissing to beat the band), when the two of them came to the hospital separately a few minutes ago (TPO), the doorman saw they were very sad.

"No, no, all wrong. Say, who do I think I'm writing this letter to anyway? I'm about as adept at sending off epistles to bissles as I am missles. I mean missives to missies as I am apostles. But there again: too much effort. Too many wisecracks, lies, cricks, tricks, and gimcracks. There again. Never ends. In edition t' ill wit y'll git whit I premised mit (pleez T to new P last time)," and he draws a fullscale facsimile of the message-address side of a picture postcard, writes her name and address underneath a canceled stamp of a straddle-backed Don Quixote attacking a tilted windmill, and on the left side of the meticulously printed "Made in Spain (reproduction prohibida)" he writes: "Dear Lucia: Here's the picture postcard I said I'd send. Having fun. Hope you are too. Wish you were here. Wish I were two. That heroic grave structure on the card's front is not the posh posada my apartment's in but this country's largest bibliocrypt photographed right after the heaviest snowfall in a hundred years. Warmest regards to your mom. Love Piers."

He goes out and mails the letter and calls Chloe an hour later.

"Hi, is it too late? Lucia and I had such an enjoyable talk before that I thought we could do it some more."

"She's in the camper, not feeling well. I shouldn't have even taken her to the store with me."

"That was sudden. What's it, something serious?"

"Hey. It's presumptuous getting anxious over the phone when you can't in any way help. It's an earache, which she woke up with today. Painful, yes, but she'll be out extroverting tomorrow morning after tonight's antibiotic kicks in, so don't be unnerving me with your concern, okay?"

"Suspension points."

"You must have a fat roll to make all these calls."

"Last term's teacher savings—want some?"

"No," she says. "I've always felt that once a person's given material things, he resents the receiver and feels cleared of any emotional responsibilities he might have had. And I never felt you were obligated to give and don't want you to feel you are."

"I'd like to. I promise to remain emotionally sniggled and spiked. And you can't be doing too well."

"We're always short. Now we're on Welfare, but it provides. There is one think it won't take care of and which I'd really like to do. Primal therapy. If I'm accepted, they can't take me for a year, and then I'd have to have the two thousand to pay for it, money before words. If you care to contribute when the time comes, I'd be very grateful."

"What is it?"

"What two of the Beatles went through."

"Next will you be jetting to the Maharascal's Indian ashcan for a real treat?"

"They did that before Primal—all four. But don't be superficial. Till now you've suppressed it and we could talk."

"My transmisanthropicization tonight."

"I don't know what you mean. And if you've that much money to throw around, apply for Primal."

"Have I never given you my views on psychotherapy for creative writers? It mars their handwriting and reduces their typing speed."

"This has to be what happens when someone talks to you twice in one night. And you say you want to fly out and nestle with us a spell?"

"*Mit* out *mein* hurts."

"And if Lucia wasn't here?"

"Why shouldn't she be? Just the holy family we of us, campering in your damp hamper or in a fleecy sleepy caul in the copse. What do you say?"

"Same. A man who left me a year ago, and last month wanted me desperately back. Or my back desperately. Either way, I was alone, so why not? It'll probably end with my heart efflorescing and then picked, plucked at and scrunched underfoot, 'Keep Off The Grass' and 'This Vegetation To Be Regarded Not Discarded' signs not worth standing. Another heavy relationship fraught with ambiguity and me once more forsworn against men per se and fi-dy till the sun god hisself sweeps me off his feet, seats me on his stick and streaks me to his utility closet. Not now. He's here. In this very room searing marshmallows while his ears roar. You know I can't leave a man but the reverse. Man a leave can't I know? What I'm waiting for is one who will swear his everlasting love and positive intentions to me. Would you ever do that?"

"I could."

"You might, as a device, in again, out again, win again, but I doubt I could really count on you. But if you do come out here, we'll drive down to see you. Lucia and I. In short, I'd like us to at most remain friends."

"No," but she's hung up.

KNOCK

KNOCK.

He knocked, I went to the door. Or she knocked, I went to the door. First I said "Did someone knock?" Then I listened as I stood in front of my chair to see if anyone behind the door was going to say something after I said "Did someone knock?" But first I listened as I sat in the chair to see if anyone was going to say something after he or she knocked. No one did. Then I said "Is anyone there?" No one answered. Then I got up.

I was sitting in the chair I'm sitting in now, wearing the clothes I have on now, my right leg crossed over the left as it is now, a book in my lap as the same book's in my lap now, reading, which I'm doing now. I was in the middle of a sentence when he knocked. Or she knocked. For it could have been one or the other who knocked, or even both. First he could have knocked, then she could have knocked. Or the other way around: first she, then he, but each knocking once and her knock coming right after his or his right after hers, for there were two quick knocks in succession; knock knock, like that. Or both could have knocked at the same time, each holding back the force of his knocks to about half a normal knock to make it sound like one person knocking twice.

Or it could have been two men or two women who knocked, instead of one and one. And he or he or she or she could have knocked, once, and right after that the other person could have knocked once. Or both of either couple could have knocked, twice at the same time, though each holding back the force of his knocks to about half a normal knock to make it sound like one person knocking twice. Or both of them could have knocked a half knock the first time, then one of them could have knocked a full knock right after that. Or the other way around: first one of them with a full knock, then two of them with a half knock, but in either case the sound made would be that of one person knocking twice.

Or it could have been any one of a number of other possibilities of two knocks made in quick succession on my door. Such as three or four people knocking twice at the same time, but each person holding back the force of his knock to about a third of a normal knock if it was three people knocking at once, or about a fourth if it was four, though in the end sounding like one person knocking twice on my door.

Or three to four or more people knocking once, with each person holding back the force of his knock to the fraction of the total number of people knocking. And then one person knocking a normal knock right after that, making it sound in the end like one person knocking twice: knock knock, like that. Or the other way around and all the numerical possibilities of three or four or more people knocking twice on my door. Such as two of them knocking once at the same time, each holding back the force, of his knock to about half a normal knock And then three to four or more people knocking right after that at the same time, each holding back the force of his knock to a third or fourth or fifth or whatever fraction of the total number of people knocking at the same time. Though in the end this double knock sounding like one person knocking twice on my door.

Or it could have been a half to a full dozen people who knocked on my door and all the numerical possibilities of their knocking and whichever way around. But each person, if let's say all twelve knocked at the same time for the first knock, holding back the force of his knock to a twelfth of a normal knock or as close as a person could get to that. And then each person who participated in the second knock, if let's say the door this time was knocked on by nine of these twelve people at once, holding back the force of his knock to a ninth of a normal knock or thereabouts, with perhaps from one to eight of these nine people making up in the force of his knock for what the eight to one of these people lacked, in force, though in the right proportions to everyone who knocked at the same time so it wouldn't come out sounding in the end like anything more than the second half of a person's normal double knock.

More than a dozen people I don't think could have fit around my door to knock on it, unless a dozen or so people had stood by the door and another dozen or so had sat, crouched and lain on the hallway floor within reach of the door. Then the dozen or so standing people could have knocked all at once for the first knock, each holding back the force of his knock to about a twelfth of a normal knock or as close to that as possible. And right after that the dozen or so sitting, crouching and lying people could have knocked at the same time for the second knock, each holding back the force of his knock to a twelfth or thereabouts. And again, if it was necessary, with from one to eleven of these dozen or so people making up in the force of his knock for what the eleven to one of them might have lacked, though in the approximate right proportion to everyone who knocked at the same time so that this double knock by about two dozen people would come out sounding in the end like one person knocking twice: knock knock, no more than that.

I don't think more than two dozen or so people could have stood, sat, crouched and lain around my door and still have been able to reach it to knock. Though about three dozen people could have lain on their stomachs on top of one another in five or six even piles facing the door and knocked that way in whatever combinations they'd decided on beforehand and in all the right proportions to one another so it wouldn't come out sounding like anything more than one person's double knock.

And I suppose some four dozen or so people could have fit around my door to knock on it if about three dozen of them had lain in those five or six piles and the fourth dozen of them had suspended themselves from the ceiling around the door and had themselves fastened to the walls on the sides and above the door and to the ceiling upside down above the door. But all of these people facing the door or at least within a knock's reach of the door. And every workable numerical possibility of these four dozen or so people knocking on my door, and whichever proportion of knocking they chose, or perhaps someone standing behind the piles but not in reach of the door, chose for them. Though in the end their knocks on my door, directed or not directed in any way by someone else, sounding like two normal knocks in quick succession by one person: knock knock, not much more than that.

For instance, the double knock I heard could have been done by two of those four dozen or so people making the first knock, each holding back the force of his knock to about a twenty-fourth of a normal knock, which could be possible, or something close to it, if well worked out beforehand. Followed right away by each of the second two dozen or so people knocking his one twenty-fourth of a knock. With perhaps both these knocks having to be made up in force by one to a few knockers for what some to many of the knockers lacked. Or even reduced in force by some to many or almost all the knockers if one to a few of the other knockers couldn't learn to hold the force of their knock to even a half. But in the end the sound coming from these five to six piles and the dozen or so people hanging from the ceiling and fastened to the ceiling and walls would be that of one person's normal double knock on my door.

Or all five or six piles around the door could have knocked the first knock, each person in each pile holding back the force of his knock to the fraction of the fifth or sixth of the total single knock allowed each pile if they want to make it sound like the first half of one person's normal double knock. And then two persons from the same or different piles could have knocked on the door at the same time for the second knock, each holding back the force of his knock to about half a normal knock.

Or the double knock I heard could have been done by one person suspended above the door while the forty-seven or so other people looked on. Or even while all forty-seven or so slept, or half of them slept and a quarter of them looked on and the fourth quarter of them had their hands raised in knocking position in front of the door but didn't knock.

Or one person fastened to the wall above the door could have knocked once, followed by a person at the bottom or top or squeezed somewhere inside one of the piles knocking the second knock with one or both hands, and if the latter, holding back the force of each hand's knock to about half. Or out of the four dozen or so people it could have been ten who knocked at the same time for the first knock. Five of them from one to five piles knocking with both hands and four of them hanging from the ceiling knocking with one hand and another person fastened to the wall knocking with one hand or even a foot. Though each person holding back the force of each hand's knock or that knock from a foot to about a fifteenth of a normal knock, or as near as possible to that. And for the second knock, a dozen or so people from any of the positions around the door could have knocked with both hands, or if they were fastened to the wall or hanging from the ceiling, with both feet or even a foot and hand. But each person holding back the force of each hand's knock or knocks from his feet or knock from his foot to make the sound of about a twenty-fourth of a hand's normal knock, which even with a lot of practice would only be barely possible. Or at least holding back the total force of both knocking hands or feet or hand and foot to make the sound of about a twelfth of a hand's normal knock, with perhaps one hand or foot making up or holding back a little to a lot for what the other hand or foot of the same body lacked in force or gave too hard.

Or the double knock I heard could have been made by three hanging and fastened people while the forty-five or so other people looked on or slept or spoke with their hands or silently with their lips or had their hands or feet in position to knock. But each of these three people knocking two hands and a foot against the door or two feet and a hand against the door, and all knocking at once and each of them holding back the force of his knock from his hands and foot or feet and hand to about a ninth of the sound of a hand's normal knock. Or at least holding back the total force of each of his triple knocks to about a third of the sound of a hand's normal knock.

It's also possible that someone, hanging freely by the chest in a sling or fastened to the wall at the waist with his limbs free, could have knocked that double knock, or the first or second part of it, with both hands and feet at the same time. Or even with his hands and a foot and head or feet and a hand and head, though holding back the force of each of whatever four of these five body parts he's using to make the sound of about a quarter of a hand's normal knock. Or at least controlling the total force of the knock from four of these five body parts, to make the sound of a hand's normal knock.

I don't think it's possible that anyone could have been that coordinated to knock four of these five body parts on my door at the same time and still have been able to not only hold back the force of each of these four parts or control the total force of their combined knock, but to also make up or reduce in force for what a few to the rest of the people knocking might have lacked or given too hard in their share of the knock.

The knocking of more than any four body parts from the same person at the same time I don't think anyone could have done and still have been able to control even the total force of the knock from these five body parts.

More than four dozen or so people I don't think could have fit around my door to knock on it. Unless an additional two dozen or so people had stood on ladders and chairs behind the people lying in piles and used long sticks which, when struck against the door, made the sound of a hand knocking. But these two dozen or so people would probably have only been able to reach the door with their sticks if the people hanging from the ceiling in front of the door had raised themselves to make room for the sticks. But not raised themselves that high where they now couldn't reach the door with any of their body parts including the elbow, buttock, shoulder or knee, or where they also interfered in the knocking movements of the people fastened to the wall. Though some of these hanging people could still have been able to knock on the door, even if they had raised their bodies out of reach of it, if they had used long sticks. And those fastened people now blocked from the door by the hanging people, who had raised themselves in front of them to make room for the sticks of the people on ladders and chairs, could still have knocked on the door if they had used curved sticks.

So it's possible that the first part of the double knock I heard could have been made by all two dozen or so people on ladders and chairs each holding back the force of his stick to make the sound of, about a twenty-fourth of a hand's normal knock, or as close as possible to that. Followed right after by a few people on ladders and chairs knocking one or two sticks apiece on the door, along with several hanging and fastened people and some from the piles knocking from one to three of their body parts on the door. But each person in this second knock holding back the force of whatever body part and stick or other thing he might be using to the closest possible fraction of the total number of body parts and things being knocked on the door at the same time to make the sound of a single hand knock. Or at least holding back the total force of the number of things he's using to make the sound of about an eighth or twelfth of a normal knock, if let's say he's knocking two or three things on the door at once and the total number of things being knocked on the door at the same time is twenty-four. And with some to many of the knockers making up or reducing in force for what from many to one of the other knockers might lack or give too hard. But no more than twenty-four body parts and things being used at the same time for that first or second knock, as I don't think anyone, if he's only knocking with one body part or thing, can control the force of his knock to make the sound of more than around a twenty-fourth of a hand's normal knock. And no more than three things being used by a person for either knock, as I don't think anyone can control the sound of the knocking of more than three things at once if more than one person is knocking at the same time. And whichever way around each of these six dozen or so people wanted to knock on my door. Or someone in or out of the hallway wanted them to knock on my door. Or which the majority or even the entire six dozen or so people had chosen by voice vote or ballot before they came into the hallway, or by some kind of silent signal once they got into the hallway. Or their previously selected representatives had chosen for them by voice vote or ballot outside the hallway, or by signaling or ballot inside the hallway once these six dozen or so people were set up in their positions around my door. Or some person or couple or group had told them outside the hallway some way, or told them inside the hallway in some silent way, not only how to knock, and how many times to knock, and the reason or reasons why they should knock, but even the reason or reasons why they had to practice and where they had to practice to knock. But in the end, the sound from all the body parts and things being used by all the people who knocked on my door would be that of two knocks in quick succession by the hand of one person: knock knock, like that.

I open my book. I begin reading from the beginning of the sentence I was in the middle of before when I first heard that double knock. I finish the sentence and am reading the next sentence when someone, male or female, or maybe two males or two females or one and one, or even a trained dog or either a male or female and a trained dog, or either one male or female and two trained dogs, or up to around six dozen or so people and trained dogs of the same sex or evenly or unevenly mixed, knocks two knocks in quick succession on my door.

I put the book down. First I put a bookmark on the page I was reading and shut the book. But first I uncrossed my legs and continued to hold the book open and listened for any sound or voice or bark or sniff behind the door or human or animal scratching or more knocks on my door. Then I shut the book and said "Yes?" No one answered. Then I stood up and put the book on the chair and listened. No sound. Now I go to the door and say "Who's there?"

THE
NEIGHBORS.

Someone rang his bell several times, then said "Mr. Samuels—you in? It's only me, so open up."

Bert closed his book, leaned forward in his chair to listen.

"Mr. Samuels, I'm telling you, it's not the city or real estate people; it's Anna Kornman."

He walked quietly to the door and put his ear against it. He of course knew who it was, her ugly singsong voice as recognizable as any he'd ever known. It's just he thought she might be with those people she mentioned.

"What do you want?" he said. "And who is it I hear out there with you?"

"Hear? What do you hear? There's nobody with me. And I got some real important news to tell you."

"So tell."

"Not from behind the door I won't. What do you take me for?"

"Sure the police aren't waiting with you to grab me?"

"Grab you? This is America, isn't it, and you've done nothing wrong that I know."

"Okay." He opened the door, looked both ways in the hallway as Anna came in, then slammed it shut and locked it. Some plaster above the door fell and splattered when it hit the floor.

"Excuse me," he said, looking at the crumbling plaster and peeling paint hanging from the ceiling.

"Excuse you I should say. You think I was the Gestapo or something the way you act."

"Just being cautious."

"Yeah, but to snoop around and slam the door like that I never saw."

"I know what I'm doing. As for the cheap paint job, that's just another thing you got to expect from piker landlords."

He bent down, wriggled his shoulders till he heard the bones crack, and shoveled the plaster pieces into his palm and dumped them into an empty ashtray on an end table. "So out with it," he said, brushing his hands. "What's this urgent thing you got to tell me, because I'm very busy."

"You sit around here doing nothing all day and you call that busy? Remember, I made this trip for your benefit."

"I'm sorry," he said. "Now what is it?"

"Nothing that important, seeing your attitude."

"If it was nothing, you wouldn't've come. I know you, Anna."

"I could've come just to talk to someone, and given that 'important' business just to get in here. It gets lonely, only you and me in this empty old building."

"Anytime you want to move, just say the word. The new owners will gladly hand you a relocation fee of a couple of thousand easy and cart you out like you was a princess."

"All I said was this place still unnerves me some—especially the painted X's on all the windows of the tenants who left. A shiver, a real shiver I get when I see them." She clenched her teeth and wrapped her arms around her chest, as if she were standing ankle-deep in snow. She sat, banged a cigarette pack against the arm of the couch, and pulled out the cigarette that popped up and put it between her lips. She fingered through her pockets, came up empty-handed, and looked at Bert searchingly.

"Excuse me?" he said.

She pointed to the end of her cigarette and mumbled something through it.

"I don't smoke, but thank you."

She took the cigarette from her mouth. "My God, you think living in the same building with you thirty years I know you don't smoke? But matches you got for your stove, right?"

He handed her the box of matches he kept in the side pocket of the coat he had on. Then he looked away, not wanting to catch another glimpse of her cynical, grinning face.

"So you don't smoke, eh? Well, it's nice you at least got ashtrays."

She struck a match against the flint on the box. With one eye closed and the other squinting down her nose at the flame she held to the cigarette, she drew in a satisfying first drag. Three puffs quickly followed, leaving her surrounded by smoke.

He waved his hand before him, though he stood about ten feet from the nearest arm of the smoke. "Now what is it you came to say?"

"Give up you don't," she said, laughing large holes through the smoke in front of her.

He just stared at her.

"First of all, those real estate people were here to see me yesterday,"

"I know that."

"So, to come I didn't have to at all, I see."

"Did I say I knew exactly why they came?"

"Yeah, but everything I say you seem to know beforehand. Who knows; maybe it's not that important to tell anyway," and went to the window.

What she probably means is she had nothing new to tell him, he thought. Because for one thing, she knows he misses nothing going on in the building. Especially now, with everything being so quiet—even the radiators stopped knocking two weeks ago when the landlords were allowed to turn the heat off to freeze them out—the slightest noise outside moves him to the window. Few days back it was a bunch of cats fighting. Later that day, drunks arguing over a bottle of booze as they sat on the entrance steps. Two mornings ago it was a policeman, bundled up in earmuffs and a nicely tailored blue coat, running his nightstick against the courtyard's brick wall and looking for vagrants who might have moved into the unoccupied apartments for the night. And yesterday, the three men she referred to, representatives of some big outfit that had bought the building from Mr. Shine and wanted Anna and himself, now the only holdouts, to leave so they could raze the building and put up a seventeen-story luxury apartment house in its place. It was curious why they also hadn't come to see him as they'd been doing regularly the past few months. Probably they gave up with his shrewd bulldog-like stand and were now preparing their final, higher offer. He smiled, just at the possibility, but hoped they'd hurry up with it before he came down with pneumonia and was taken away in an ambulance and forced to give up the apartment because of his absence.

Anna was standing with her back to him by the window, blowing smoke rings against the pane. Just look at her, he thought. Looking like the same skinny wreck she was thirty years ago, even though she's wearing several sweaters and God knows what else under her housecoat. What does she think she's staring at anyway? Maybe a few months ago—when they first started to hold out—there were still a few old people sunning themselves in their beach chairs along the courtyard walls, but now?—nothing. It was so like them to take the first offer and run out of here, when if they'd listened to him they could have, all sticking together, milked the landlord for way more. Already, just Anna and him, he's worked the real estate men up to two thousand, and before he's through he figures they should get four thousand each, plus the maybe five hundred extra for moving costs. After all, their reasons for staying are as valid as the company's for tearing the place down, for the building's still in good condition and was getting decent rents. And then, what are they planning to put up anyway?—for he's seen the architect's drawing of the apartment house nailed to the empty brownstone next to his. A nice drawing they'll be putting up, with plenty of trees and pretty shrubbery around it, but an apartment house it isn't. Someone's got to be blind not to see that this cheap white-tiled tombstone will be completely run-down and a hazard to its tenants in five years, but just let him try and argue this point, let him try and tell the city what he knows and has seen in other similar new buildings, and they'll call him a crank and a crackpot like they do to all the poor people his age and maybe find some way of stopping his Social Security checks and locking him up for good. So he keeps quiet on this, and that he's holding out for all he can squeeze out of them. Instead, he argues he's grown very attached to the apartment—why not, after more than half a lifetime here?—and he could never get another like it in the city for the same rent, and there's also his civic rights, so no amount of money or pressure will ever force him to leave.

Anna was back on the couch. Down to her last drag, she blew the smoke through her nostrils and snuffed out the cigarette in a tea-stained saucer she'd been using as an ashtray.

"Excuse me," he said, "but you couldn't have used the ashtray? I eat off that plate."

"It has that paint and plaster in it and I thought it'd burn up."

Oh God, he thought, how this skinny, frightened-looking woman has stayed in the building and resisted the real estate people so long remains a mystery to him. She's obviously cleverer and stronger than she makes herself out to be, and is probably out to profit from her stay as much as he is, but he still has to hand it to her for sticking with it—though for the life of him he'll never tell it to her face.

"You're so quiet," Anna said. "Anything wrong?"

"No."

"You think they'll come back today? They're getting pretty persistent."

"Depends what you told them yesterday."

"You ask like I caved-in to them."

"Just curious, that's all."

"Well, for one thing, I told them nothing. They just talked, and I'll tell you something: they were very gracious, very gracious indeed. Hats off on their laps and everything—you should've seen them."

"Nice clothes I know they got."

"Dandies like that in my living room, I ask you. Even being so polite to ask me if I'd mind them smoking."

"So what happened after?"

"'*Mind?*' I told them. 'I should mind? Smoke all you like,' I said. 'Me, I also smoke.'"

"I meant, what they say about getting you out?"

"You know: the same old story. If I leave they'll give me bonuses to knock my eyes out."

"What are they giving now?" he said.

"I didn't ask. But they mentioned fifteen hundred, maybe sixteen. They weren't too definite."

"Four thousand they'll give at least—but what's the difference? To me it wouldn't matter what they offered."

"Same thing I told them. I like the Upper East Side, I said, and a place like this I couldn't get nowhere else, so horses it'll take to move me to Brooklyn."

"What they say to that?"

"First, that I'm your stooge—and which I'll tell you I didn't like hearing such a lie. And two, that if they wanted, they could have the city down our necks before we know it—and with no promises they'll then give us what they originally offered. They said the city's very sympathetic to them, with half their planned apartment house already half-rented out."

"This I can believe," he said. "All the city wants is property taxes—

that's all; no concern for the little man—and bigger and more classy the building, more the tax."

She nodded, got another cigarette and tamped it on her thigh. Bert stood up after she lit it, and walked to the window. He hated the stench of tobacco, especially cigarettes. She waved a cloud of smoke away from her, and said "Truthfully, Mr. Samuels, how long you think we can hold out like this?"

"I don't know. Indefinitely, maybe."

"I don't think I can do it that long. It's almost December now, and soon it'll be much too cold with no radiators going, five sweaters and heaters or not."

"So give up then—go!"

"No need to get so excited."

"But it's obvious you're caving-in to them. So just do it and be done with it I say."

"Be done with what? Please, be reasonable."

"So don't then," his voice toning down.

"I'm not. For look, some rights I got also, no? Throw me out into the street, who do they think they are? Build for us cheap you think they could do instead."

Rights my eye, he said to himself. But ask her to give the real reason she's holding out, and she'll say with this big innocent look "Me? I should do that?" If she'd only admit the truth once, he'd probably tell her why he's staying too. It'd be good getting it off his chest to someone, and then united in purpose like that they might be able to drive the relocation fee up to five thousand.

"Did they say anything more about me?" he said.

"Some. They said 'You know him well?' and I said 'Well? For thirty years I know him, and very well. A nice man, quiet and friendly'— that's what I told them."

"Thanks."

"It's the truth. Then they went on about how you're all the trouble. That they think you're crazy and for my own safety I shouldn't be in the same building alone with you, and how they can't even speak to you anymore, since the last time when you threw them out. Crazy, I said, you're not. And for you to throw them out I couldn't understand."

"They accused me of holding out only for the money, which you can understand made me upset."

"That they told me also. Something like you'll get no more than you deserve and what's the going rate. What did they offer you if I can ask?"

"Doesn't matter."

"How much, though?"

"Same two thousand they offered two weeks ago."

"You've been offered two thousand? Then I'm going to get two thousand. Moving costs excluded?"

"Maximum of three hundred," he said, "but if it costs less I can't keep the balance."

"Keep? Just watch me try to move for three hundred with all my furniture. 'Brooklyn,' I'll tell the mover, and he'll laugh in my face."

"They say anything else about me?"

"That was it. It was sort of like you wasn't living here in a way."

"Not living here? Oh, I'm living here, and they know it full well. Excuse me a second."

He strutted into the kitchen, put water in the kettle, and set it on the stove. Gas and electricity and water they still had, thank God, he thought, but only because he was smart enough to contact, after the city didn't get back to him, a tenants' protective organization, saying how he thought his unhumanlike landlords were about to shut everything off.

"You know what especially made me uneasy," she said when he got back, "was the way they blamed me for pushing back the demolition date. I mean me, I should do that?"

"Doesn't bother me none." He put his cup of tea on a side table and sat down.

"Yeah, but yak-yak-yak they went on about the extra workers' costs and that from their own pockets it's coming."

"Don't believe a word they say."

"So from whose pockets does it come from—yours? Mine? I don't like it."

"Forget it. Just tell yourself you're right."

"I tell, I tell, but what good's it do if my heart still goes out to them some? I know deep down they're wrong, but like my late husband I always believed business is business, you know? And here they already paid for the property—two brownstones and this building, no less—which must've cost them plenty the way this neighborhood's changing."

"Quadruple they'll get back, those cutthroats."

"Maybe. But in a way they've acted all right with us and been fair to the other tenants here. I mean, give in a little, Mr. Samuels."

"Give in, you ask me?" his voice rising.

"I didn't mean it that way."

"You have the nerve to ask me to give in?"

"I told you that's not what I meant."

"Listen, I know exactly what you meant. So if you're going to be talking like that, better you do it somewhere else."

"And somewhere else I will." She stood up, smashed her lit cigarette into the saucer and started for the door.

"You should get your head examined if you think I'll stay in this room another minute with you."

"Now what I say?" he said, thinking maybe he was too rough with her this time. He reached for her arm, but she pulled away and grabbed the doorknob.

"Don't give me that nicey-nice what'd-I-do? business again—please. For plenty I've taken from you—everything from watching you not offer me tea to your hurling insults."

"So I got a little temperamental. So everyone does once in a while."

"Crazy's more like it. And when you act like this, I don't know what else you might try, like those men said." He stared at her a few seconds and began laughing.

"Look, you got your hand on the doorknob, so use it. Then take all you can steal from the landlords and get the hell out of here."

She muttered something under her breath and tried opening the door. As he continued to laugh at her, she kicked the bottom of the door, unlocked it, and charged out.

She did just what he expected her to: slammed her front door shut a good five minutes after she'd slammed his, walked noisily through, the hallway and down the stairs. He went to his bedroom window, waiting for her to storm out of the lobby, through the courtyard, and across the street, heading, he was sure, to the drugstore phonebooth a block away. He raised two Venetian blind slats and peered through them just as she came out of the lobby and glanced up at his living room window. She was carrying her mesh shopping bag, a bag of garbage and a bundle of old newspapers—but she wasn't fooling anyone. First thing she'll do when she's away from the building is get rid of all that bogus junk and hustle to the phone to haggle with one of the realty people. Later, when they can't agree to what she'll call her final offer—cunningly made much higher than what she expects to get—she'll tell them to come to her home, where they'll settle, her knowing all the time the advantage of bargaining in the very apartment they so desperately want.

He stood at the window till she returned, a celery stalk and packaged bread sticking out of the mesh bag filled with groceries. A costly trick to fool him, he thought, and look how it worked. He waited behind his door, listening till she was upstairs and in her apartment, and then went back to the window. He stayed there for more than two hours—even moved a chair to it so he could sit on it—and was surprised, by the time his dinner hour rolled around, that the realty people hadn't shown up.

Four days later Bert saw the three men enter the building, and then heard them climb the cracked green linoleum steps leading to the third floor. He stood by the door as they walked down the hallway, one of them, apparently wearing metal plates on the heels of his shoes, clicking along like a tap dancer. They stopped at Anna's door and rang the bell. She let them in, and in an hour showed them out. "Thank you very much, and good day, gentlemen," she said, and one of the men: "And thank you for tea, Mrs. Kornman." Bert expected the men to ring his bell next, since after disposing of her they'd naturally think he could be had for the same price that very afternoon, but they went down the stairs.

He rushed to the window and opened it a little, hoping to catch something in their expressions and movements and what they were saying that'd give him an idea of how they accepted her last offer, which would help him decide what his should be before they ultimately forced him to leave. All he saw were their secret, lineless faces—no smiles or looks of disappointment—and the creased tops of two of the men's hats, and the third man's black slicked-down skull, since this fellow was holding his fedora and combing the hair above his ears. All three talked softly, moved swiftly, and carried briefcases under their arms. Then the hatless man stopped as the other two walked on, slid the comb into his coat's breast pocket, carefully placed the hat on his head, and grabbed the briefcase by its collapsible handle, letting it dangle at his side. He ran to catch up with the others, who were waiting at the curb, and all three walked silently side by side, crossed the street, and headed downtown.

Bert waited for Anna to knock on his door—certain she was the type who'd want to boast to him about how much she'd shrewdly extorted from the company. She never came, so three hours later, after he tramped up the second flight of stairs with the evening newspaper, thinking she'd hear him and throw open her door, he rang her bell.

"Yes? Who is it?" after he rang a fourth time.

"Bert," he said, thinking, Who else could it be, you liar.

"Who, please?"

"Bert Samuels, from the third floor. Remember me?"

"Just a moment."

"Just a moment?" he said under his breath. Why, she should be hung upside down by her toes, the ugly witch, he thought, picturing her waiting behind the door, smoking a cigarette or filing her nails.

She opened the door, seeming to withdraw her halting smile just as soon as she gave it. "Would you like to come in? Though why I should be so polite to you after your treatment of me the other day, I don't know."

"I'm fine here, thanks."

"Have it your own way." She flipped an unlit cigarette out of her hand, almost like a magician pulling something from his sleeve, stuck it between her lips, and tried to light it with a silver table lighter. "Needs fuel." She put the lighter and cigarette on a little table by the door and searched her housecoat for matches.

Bert forced a smile. "Say, I saw those fellows leave before and wanted to know if they had anything new to say about me."

"You? Nothing much. Why should they?"

"Oh, stop it. They must've said something."

"Only about me. They offered—you know: like they always offer."

"So come on; what happened?"

"What happened, what?"

"The money, the money! How much you finally take to leave?"

"You think I took? Is that what you're driving at all this time?"

"Look, I'm nobody's fool. All along I knew you were holding out and using me just to get more cash from them."

"What, are you altogether insane?"

"Goddamnit, I saw you myself running to the drugstore to phone them. Thursday—right? Yeah, Thursday late."

"To dump garbage and for my groceries I went for Thursday. Always Thursday the groceries. Friday's too crowded, and Saturday's my holy day. I eat and throw my trash out, you know, no matter how some people live."

"Anna, I know what you did, so why bother arguing? I didn't come here for that."

"Then what is it you came for? The first day since last week I speak to them is today—*today*; but did I expect them? I didn't. They drop in from nowhere, no letter, just unannounced, and now I think I'm glad they did."

"Glady for the money you mean."

"Money? What's money to me? Enough I got without theirs. To you, maybe—to a stingy hoarding old man like yourself it's the world—but to me? Pride's more important. It's living here, you, always insulting me like I'm an animal, that'll make up my mind fast. So I'll tell you, Mr. Samuels, before I only got excited and threatened to go, but now, don't tempt me into really going."

"So you're leaving this week then, right?"

"I wasn't leaving no time till you helped me decide this very moment. Now I'm going to call them tomorrow morning and say that anything they want to give me is good enough just as long as they take me away from this madhouse."

He didn't believe a word she said. All he wanted was for her to admit she sold out—just that simple satisfaction—and also to know what amount she sold out for, since besides using the figure for his own bargaining purposes it'll give him an opportunity to tell her what a monkey they made out of her. But she'd turned around, ignoring him and appearing to be deep in thought, and then said "You'll have to excuse me, but I got a lot of packing to do and might as well start it now, so if that's all you got to say, goodbye."

"There are some other things I'd like to speak over with you before you go, would you mind?"

"I don't know what other things, but if you do come in, please leave the front door open." She motioned him inside, and after flitting around the apartment a few minutes, opening closets and drawers and pushing a couple of empty boxes to the middle of the floor, she started refolding the sweaters that had been neatly crammed inside the television console cabinet.

"Go right ahead," he said. "Just don't even think I'm here. Mind if I sit?" She nodded, and he sat down and watched her build a pile of sweaters two feet high. She went into the bedroom, came out in a dress a minute later with the three sweaters she'd had on underneath her housecoat, and added these to the pile.

"When they were here they said I could have a one-bedroom in Queens, not Brooklyn," she said, "—a building they got a big interest in and which they said is newer and in better condition than this one, though not so near a market. I think I'll take it anyway—temporarily. I mean with my legs acting up again it'd be a nuisance looking for a Manhattan place just now."

"Sure, sure."

"You still don't believe me? Mrs. Scarlisi—you remember, nobody I was friendly with, but from apartment 45? She's there, and they told me she likes the neighborhood very much except for that market problem. So she takes the bus when she doesn't want to walk, and though they don't come regularly like our buses, they're regular enough. I think I'll call her later."

"Just stop with the talk and tell me how much you got, all right?"

"Got I didn't get. All they said was it'd be a tidy sum if I decided to leave."

"How much a tidy sum?"

"Five hundred for the moving costs, and I can keep the balance what I don't pay the movers, fair?"

"Sounds fair. But for the last holdouts they got good reasons for being big sports."

"Didn't I tell you last week they were fair people?" She went into the bedroom and returned with a suitcase and some dresses. She started folding the dresses and putting them in the suitcase.

"When did they say they'd be back to see me?"

"Like I said before, they really didn't mention you."

"Not even if I was also ready to move or not?"

"Not even if you was still living here." She clasped the suitcase shut.

"Yeah, I'll bet. Anyway," just as she was about to protest, "what'd you finally get for signing away your rights to this apartment?"

"For the last time: I signed nothing; they only offered."

"All right, all right, but try telling me they gave you more than two thousand."

"They offered a lot more."

"Twenty-five hundred?"

"A little less."

"A little less? You took *less*?"

"Less they said they'll offer than twenty-five hundred, but it's still more than I ever thought they'd offer, so for me it's plenty."

"Because you don't know better, that's why. And then taking so little you ruined my chances of getting much more. For what you get: twenty-two hundred? Maybe twenty-three? Why, four thousand clear before the five hundred moving costs you should've got, or a stupid fool like yourself I've never seen before. Goddamn you," he yelled, "you screwed up everything, and he kicked a hole in one of the empty boxes and kept kicked the box till it was across the room. He walked in circles around the room, slapping his forehead and wringing his hands and saying "What could've possessed me? Why'd I ever trust her? What am I to do now? All this time here for practically peanuts, peanuts," and flopped down in the easy chair and pounded the chair arms with his fists and shouted toward the ceiling "Moron, absolute moron, I'd like to tear off her rotten hide," and shook his head back and forth several times and then leaned forward with his hands in his hair and shut his eyes.

When he'd simmered down a couple of minutes later, she was no longer in the room, her suitcase was gone, and the bedroom door was closed. She has to be in there, he thought, because if she went past him out the apartment he thinks he would have heard her. He sat up and calmly waited for her to come out. If it takes till tomorrow, he'll wait, he thought, though before that he'll shut the front door. He's going to apologize, say something about being unable to explain exactly what took hold of him just now, but he's definitely sorry, as sorry as a man could be. After rewinning her confidence, or a good part of it, he'll very politely ask her to hold out against the landlords with him for just two weeks more. She didn't sign anything, he'll say, so in that regard they're in luck. After two weeks, they'll each be a cinch to get four thousand clear and the five hundred moving costs they promised her, plus a freshly painted three-room West Side apartment, a new demand he just came up with—so the hell with the long bus rides in Queens; there'll be good markets and services right up her block. After all, he'll point out, doesn't she owe him at least this extra stay in the building, for in a way it's actually she who made him so upset before when she misled him into believing she signed the relocation agreement. And then who knows: the realty people might get so panicky after two weeks that the two of them could even pull in more than four thousand—maybe even five thousand, five and a half.

The last figures will knock her right off her feet, he thought, and be what he needs to have her go in with him.

The bedroom door shot open, just as he was going over the pitch he'd give her. Anna, lugging the suitcase and dressed in a moth-eaten Persian lamb coat with this veiled black hat pushed down on her forehead and hiding most of her face, hurried by him before he could say anything but "Wait." She went out the front door, down the hall, and hobbled down the stairs. He ran to his living room window, raised the blinds all the way and saw her trudging lopsidedly through the courtyard. This time she didn't look up at his window, though he had opened it so he could stick his head out and was prepared to smile and wave and even plead with her.

BOOK

3

WHAT IS ALL TH

What Is All This?
BOOK THREE

CONTAC.

He was in the local Fairway, buying groceries for dinner tonight. A few hours ago he and his wife and her son returned from Lake Tahoe a day sooner than they'd planned. It has become too expensive for them and Ginny had caught a bad cold there. Just before he left the house he asked what she'd like for dinner tonight and she said "Something soft and simple; I also have cramps. You decide, Rod— you know food better," so he decided the softest and simplest meal they could afford was meatloaf and yams. He'd make them after giving Jess hot cereal and toast and while Ginny continued to sweat out her cold in bed.

He got two medium-sized onions out of a bin. They were going for four pounds for twenty-nine cents—a good buy; they wouldn't come to more than five or six cents. The mushrooms he usually chopped up and put in the loaf he'd skip tonight. Even though they were on sale, sixty-nine a pound was still too high, considering how much money he had on him.

He counted what was in his wallet and pants pocket: three dollars and seventy-five cents. He could make a good meatloaf with that, buy a few essential breakfast goodies and still have a little money left over. They'd gone with friends to Tahoe, shared a cabin near the ski lift area for five dollars a day per couple. He'd taken forty dollars with him, but with gas, two quarts of oil for their old car, rented tire chains, rent, $1.25 mittens for Jess, dollar woolen cap for his own frozen ears, cigarettes for Ginny, grocery costs split among the three couples, a few dollars tossed away on the slots and electronic blackjack machines at the casinos, he didn't have enough money for both Ginny and him to ski. They drove to Heavenly Valley the morning after they arrived, and while he looked after Jess, Ginny, who was much more of a skier than he and had brought her own skis, went up on the slopes and had a good time, he was glad about that. He wanted to get up there also, but it was only after the first day, when he learned what the equipment rentals and ski lifts costs and that his almost equally strapped friends couldn't loan him a tenner, that he knew he wouldn't. "I'll take care of Jess tomorrow," Ginny had said. "All day, so you can have some fun," but how could you have fun there without money?

Driving back home from Tahoe he told Ginny they'd have all the money they need if they moved to New York. He'd come to California single, a grad student in English at Stanford, but by the time the two-year fellowship ended he was married to a woman with a small house, three-year-old son and broken-down car, all from her previous marriage, and a hundred-ten a month in child support. Since then he'd given up pursuing his doctorate, as the English department didn't think he had the makings of a scholar and wouldn't renew his stipend—his main reason for going to grad school–and tried getting a reporting job for the local newspapers and editing journals and books for the university press and teaching language arts in a junior high school. But he didn't have sufficient journalism experience for the newspapers and couldn't pass the tough three-hour editing test for the press and didn't have the education courses needed for a teaching license and was told he'd have to go back to college to get them. He was broke. He'd been broke, on and off, for six months. He mowed lawns, clipped hedges, parked cars, tended bar at the faculty club, modeled for art classes with only a strap on—his eyes cast down when unsuspecting acquaintances showed up to paint or draw and saw him posing. Christmas season he got his first fulltime job since he left school: temporary salesman in the men's sportswear section of a Palo Alto department store, where he taught himself how to steal.

His wage was $1.89 an hour. He felt he deserved more for all the work he did and that he needed at least three dollars an hour to live on, so he stole the balance from the store. He'd make out a change requisition slip for twenty dollars, take thirty from the cash register he shared with other salespeople, go to the gift-wrapping counter, which also made change for them, hand the girl the twenty and requisition slip, and while she was checking off different change rolls, he'd take

out his handkerchief, sniff into it and stuff if back in his pocket with
the ten dollar bill.

He did this once every workday for the last five of the six weeks he
had the job, but all the money he'd earned and stolen was gone now—
mostly for overdue house and medical payments and upkeep of the
car. So he told Ginny he wanted them to go to New York. That while
looking for editing and writing jobs, which would be easier to get
there, he'd work as a per diem sub in junior high schools, something
he'd done before. In New York he was certified. He was a second-step
sub, which last paid twenty-nine dollars a day. At the store he used to
work three more hours a day than he put in at subbing, and even with
the ten dollars he stole daily, which he didn't tell her about, he still
didn't make as much. But this was her home, Ginny said. She and her
ex-husband had moved here from Michigan two years ago and, like
so many new residents, she wouldn't dream of living any other place.
"I got a home, so why should I rent a dingy, cramped apartment? And
there are great schools in this district. Jesse won't have to get molested
or run over every other time he goes out as he would in New York. Nor
will I have to fuss with his snowsuit, like I did in Lansing, whenever I
just want a quart of milk at the store."

He was in luck. Ground chuck was going for fifty-nine cents a
pound, twenty cents less than usual, but all the packages of it weighed
at least a few ounces over a pound. He figured this was a standard
tactic of the supermarkets: give the customer a break on the price but
recover some of that loss by prepackaging the minimum amounts in
much larger portions.

"Can I only have a pound of chuck, please?" he asked the butcher,
who was weighing and labeling sausages before sending them through
the noisy wrapping machine.

"We don't have any there?" she said.

"None I can find. It's for a small meatloaf, so anything more than
a pound will only go to waste at our house.

She seemed annoyed she had to interrupt her sausage work. She
turned over several packages of ground chuck so she could see their
weights, selected one, unwrapped and weighed it, picked off a little
meat, reweighed and priced it, put the meat in a new plastic tray,
slapped the label to the bottom of it, placed it on the conveyor belt
to the automatic packaging machine, where the meat was flattened
and wrapped.

"It's a special this week," she said. "You're getting a terrific buy."

"It's good chuck—I know. We use it often."

Walking away, he thought Why'd she have to act like that? She didn't give him that hard a time, but she should realize, without thinking twice about it, that some people didn't have much money—that was an established fact. She probably got a dozen requests like his a day, and most for the same reason, he bet: every penny counts.

He got a can of tomato juice, three yams, a carrot, two small potatoes, which he'd grate into the meatloaf and was cheaper to use than bread crumbs, and a canister of salt—they were even out of that. Then he saw the Contac. "5 Days & Nights' Continuous Relief for $1.49," it said on the package. "Approximately a penny an hour," it continued underneath, but $1.49 was still too much for him, so he'd have to steal it. Ginny had a bad head cold, and he had to be out early tomorrow morning looking for work, so couldn't afford staying up half the night with her suffering. And Contac, maybe the best of all cold medicines, was also the easiest to steal, its package compact and slim enough to slip into the side pocket of his jacket.

He took the Contac off the shelf, put it in the jump seat of the shopping cart, pushed the cart to the first aisle he found empty, looked both ways, and slipped the package into his pocket. He got a quart of milk and stick of butter and was now ready to leave. He had all the ingredients he needed, for a meatloaf—eggs! but he was sure they had some at home—and medicine for Ginny. In his mind he saw the tiny little time pills working as they did in the TV ads—drop by drop releasing the medication into the animated bloodstream and giving almost instant relief.

There were eight checkout stands, all ringing up sales like mad, with about four baggers hopping from stand to stand and cheerily bagging the goods. He chose the stand that was third to being furthest away from the office. Someone, maybe the manager, was behind the large picture window, looking out, then at his desk to some paperwork or something, no doubt an old pro at sensing and spotting shoplifters, so Rod had to be careful. Third from the end, far enough away from the office but not that far where he might draw suspicion.

The checkout girl had waited on him a few times. She was slender and smallwaisted in her neatly pressed uniform and had a bright open face like his wife's and was a far cry from the female clerks in New York City supermarkets. Here, most of them looked as if they'd gone from some mild success as high school cheerleaders to working fulltime as checkout clerks, a decent enough job, he supposed, till you went to college or professional school or got married and started having babies. In New York, the clerks wore street clothes and were generally older, tougher and had a better sense of humor than these girls, but didn't much act like they respected or trusted their customers.

"And how are you this evening?" she said, her foot on the switch that brought the merchandise tread nearer to her.

"Fine, thanks." The man behind the window seemed to be writing, then raised his head with his eyes closed, as if trying to remember something. "We've just come back from skiing."

"That sounds like fun." She smiled and put the onions on the scale.

Five cents, she rang up, just as he'd figured. Then fifty-eight cents for the chuck and fourteen cents for the yams and eight cents for the potatoes and three cents for the carrot, which he'd also grate into the meatloaf as his mother did, for added body, she said, or was it flavor? Salt, butter, tomato sauce, and two packaged pecan pinwheels for thirty cents, which he got off a rack by the cash register. That would be dessert for Ginny and Jess. He should have picked up a Boston lettuce for a simple salad. He calculated he had enough money for one, and any other time he'd go back for it, but didn't want to risk going through checkout again.

"Dollar ninety-seven," she said. He gave her two singles; she handed him three cents and some Blue Chip stamps. "Was it snowing?" she said, bagging his groceries; all the baggers seemed tied up at other stands.

"Excuse me?"

"You know: in the place where you went skiing. Was it snowing there?"

"Fortunately, only a little," and he knew she didn't suspect a thing. "We didn't even have to use the snow chains we rented—that's how nice the weather was, although there was more than enough snow on the ground to snow on."

"I like to ski, my boyfriend and I, but just the costs of the ski lift and equipment is enough to keep us from going, Oh well, we'll get there yet." She gave him the bag and said "Have a good night."

"Hey, you too," he said, touching his pocket to make sure the Contac was still hidden by the flap, and left the store and headed for his car in the parking lot.

"If you don't mind?" a man said behind him.

It was useless to run. And he couldn't quickly come up with a reasonable excuse why he stole the Contac. He even became sloppy. "My kids," he said to the man he'd seen behind the office window and who had the words "Buzz Walker, Store Manager" embroidered on his work jacket. "I can't afford these expensive drugs," he went on as the man held out his hand for what his eyes said was in the right side pocket of Rod's jacket, "and my littlest one is very sick with a head cold."

"I'm sorry about that. But you know we can't be letting people steal what they want because they got financial problems. As it is, if your kid's real young, these capsules are no good for anybody under twelve."

"Is that so? I didn't know that."

"Says right here on the directions." He pointed to the package Rod had given him. "What are you trying to do, kill your kid?"

"I still can't read it. It's too dark out here, and my eyes," squinting as if he had serious trouble with them. The manager looked at him skeptically and then told him to forget it.

"But for both our sakes, shop somewhere else from now on, I got too much work as it is without these dumb hassles," and he went back to the store, scratching the back of his neck with the Contac.

Considering the situation, Rod thought, the manager had been all right: fair, not self-righteous; not coming on strong with a speech about possible police trouble for Rod and making him grovel before he let him go. The manager knew how tough it was for some guys to pay the bills and keep a family going out here. But more important was that he had his own job to protect, his own family to support, so the organization that was paying him had to come before any individual feelings, especially when it concerned someone he didn't know. If Rod had this guy's job and was pulling in around two hundred a week and no doubt getting a discount on the food, he'd have acted the same way, though he wouldn't have been so careless as to wait till the shoplifter made it to the lot with his theft. You can't take him there. Too many legal loopholes. The shoplifter could put up a stink as to what was public or private property that could bring the entire company to court and maybe cost the manager his job. Rod would have stopped him after he'd paid for his groceries and was about to leave, or better yet, so as not to make a commotion, cornered him in some quiet spot in the store. Like the manager, he would have been fair and sympathetic though

WHAT IS ALL THIS? | 425

also resolute in not condoning the theft. And after he'd let the thief go, though also telling him never to come back, he'd write a report to the chain's headquarters in Oakland, recounting, very subtly and self-effacingly, the terrific job he and his staff were doing in keeping down shoplifting, giving this one as an example, but saying he confronted the guy in the store. A promotion, bigger-than-usual Christmas bonus—who knew what could follow a number of such reports, most of them false or exasperated. But if he worked for a company that was paying him a good wage, he'd work his butt off for it, put in as much overtime as they wanted him to, and always push himself for advancement and never steal.

He picked up a Boston lettuce at the supermarket in the next shopping center, pocketed a package of Contac and brought the lettuce to the checkout stand farthest from the balcony office overlooking the front part of the store.

"Hi, how are you?" the girl said, smiling at him as if he were a familiar customer, though he'd only been here once. "Only one item? You could've gone to the express register," and he said "This one was moving fast, and only the lettuce because I forgot to get it before." She rang up the lettuce gave him his change, "Have a nice night," and he said "Thanks. You too."

He knew he wouldn't be caught this time. He hadn't looked uncomfortable, which he was sure he did the last time, or dallied to decide which checkout stand to use or tapped the jacket pocket at the stand or felt the flap on the way out. It had taken one casual look around in the drug aisle and a cough that doubled him over as he slipped the Contac into his pocket, and now he was in his car and driving out of the lot, and he wanted to howl and cheer but tempered his appearance to that of a tired worker who'd never sully his family's reputation or jeopardize his future for such a petty theft.

Home, Ginny yelled from the bedroom "Rod? I'll be up and fix us dinner in a moment."

He told her to stay in bed: that he was more than happy to make supper for the three of them. He put together a meatloaf and put it and the yams into the oven.

Jesse came into the kitchen. "Make me cereal. Make Jess cereal, Rod."

He kissed him on top of his head, lifted him into the highchair and in a few minutes had two slices of cinnamon toast and a bowl of instant oatmeal in front of him, with milk, butter, wheat germ and sugar on it. "For you, Jesse old king."

"It's hot," Jesse said, waving his favorite spoon in the air. "Cereal too hot for Jess, right?"

"I'll taste it," he did, and said "It's okay; it won't burn you."

He held the package of Contac behind his back and went into the bedroom. Ginny was in bed. "Guess," he said, and when she said "Hmm, let's see," and then gave him that artfully dumb expression of hers of being completely taken in by his surprise, he produced the Contac.

"You're a mindreader," she said, pushing the covers aside to sit up and take the package. "I need them so badly, and you knew, Teeny, you knew." She tore out one of the capsules and held it between two fingertips. "Do you think they work as well as those silly ads say? I got one heck of a cold on that trip."

"They better work at the price."

She looked at the price on the package and whistled. "Dollar forty-nine? For ten pills? That's crazy. You're really extravagant, really too good to me," and she swallowed the capsule without water. About thirty seconds later she said "You're not going to believe this but I'm already feeling much better. I bet it makes me sleep better too. And listen," and she breathed in and out extra loudly, "I think it's already unclogging my nose."

MEET
THE
NATIVES.

Henry Sampson was awakened from a deep sleep by children yelling at the top of their lungs. He edged his body across the bed, picked at his Baby Ben. Eight-forty, he saw, squinting at the clock. Goddamn, he thought, it's not even nine, and Sunday, no less, so why can't the school lock its gates and help a man get some sleep? He shut his eyes and hugged the pillow to his ears, but still heard the kids in the schoolyard that faced his windows, now choosing up sides for Capture the Flag.

"Timmy you're with me. Laura, get over there. Larry, Mary, Walt with me. Sylvia, Carole and Junior with Louie. That okay with you, Louie—five against five?"

"Fine with me."

Henry moved the pillow from his face. The sides were unfair the way he looked at it—one team having two more girls than the other—and he was surprised Louie hadn't put up a squawk. And really, this should be the healthy unperturbed attitude he should always take to their games—even squeezing a bit of it into the What the Native Children Do section of the Washington guidebook he was writing—if these kids weren't the reason for most of his present troubles. He had come here, after having saved enough money as a waiter in New York, two months ago—in April, when the weather was still cool and dry, the windows of his cheap second-story apartment barely open and the neighborhood quiet. His goal was to write his fourth guidebook— a glib, witty first-person up-to-date account of the city's high spots, night life, places to see, tour, eat at, drive by, and plainly avoid. In the first six weeks he completed most of his research, browsed through all the public buildings, monuments, memorials, museums and parks worth noting, and part of the day, when it was still quiet outside and the temperature comfortable, written what he considered to be the most exciting imaginative prose of any of his books.

Then the weather changed, the days and nights becoming hotter and stickier than he'd ever experienced. This was a valuable piece of information left out of most of the Washington books, and he already included it in the What to Wear section at the opening of the book. (DC's weather is ideal for the gracious Southern clothing store owner. Here there are truly four distinct seasons—the fall and early spring being as delightful and pleasingly capricious as any city in the U.S. But the heat spells of late spring and summer? Let me inform you, dear travelers. It would be as insufferably stifling as the muggiest of Middle Eastern and Asian cities I've lived in if not for the ubiquitous air-conditioning.) And with the late May heat came jarring street noises, loud arguments and TV sounds from surrounding apartments, and the disturbances in the schoolyard of St. James: from the 8:25 morning lineup to the P.T. classes and after-school games of the neighborhood, kids. A week ago he decided that only at night and on Sundays would he ever find the peace to get work done at home. So during the day he now got up when the first few kids came into the yard, downed a quick breakfast and spent most of the time walking around the city, reading and napping in Rock Creek Park, editing copy there that he'd written the previous night when he'd drunk—too much—and going to another tedious double feature in an air-conditioned theater.

All of a sudden it was silent outside. Maybe the kids had been kicked out of the yard or went to play somewhere else. He relaxed in bed, felt himself getting sleepy, for a while imagined himself playing Capture the Flag, freeing all the prisoners. Henry the Kid beating the other team home with the flag and being congratulated as he scored the winning point.

But a boy shook him out of his thoughts: "By the count of ten you pimps better be over that line or you lose the flag. One, two, three, four, five, six..."

Henry wanted to yell for the boy to get the hell away from his window.

"Capture the flag. Free him, free him," a boy and girl screamed as Henry got out of bed. "I got the punk," another boy shouted as Henry turned the shower on in the bathroom and put his head under it.

When that didn't cool him off and calm his nerves, he got in the tub and let the cold water rise around him.

He ducked his head into the water and thought God, if this isn't nice, so nice, so perfect, so goddamn completely perfect, and came up for air, held his nose and dropped underwater again. It was so peaceful and comfortable in the tub that he pictured himself working here. He'd seen it done in a movie once—Spencer Tracy or Clark Gable sitting in a half-filled tub, typewriter and writing paper on a wood plank set up in front of him like a bed table, a cigarette stuck confidently to his bottom lip as he knocked off the last few lines of a prize-winning news article or novel. Confident and cheerful now himself, he scrubbed his face and hair with a washrag and through a soap bubble forming on his lips began to sing "Oh Suzanna."

"Oh Suzanna, oh don't you cry for me. For I come from Alabama with a banjo on my knee."

It was all he know of the song and he repeated those lines twice more and was giving out with what was possibly his highest range since his college chorus days, when a group of intentionally clashing voices outside joined in with him. He got up and slammed down the window. He still heard them mimicking him, so he threw on his ter-rycloth robe, drying himself with it as he went into the kitchen, and yelled from the partially opened curtains "Will you kids please stop!"

They continued to sing—the entire song.

"Didn't you hear? Now you had your little joke, so can it."

He couldn't see them. They were behind a row of bushes inside the yard's mesh fence, about fifteen feet from his building. The only other time he shouted at them was last week. They were fighting among themselves, whistling, screeching, cursing, and rattling the fence when one boy climbed it, then throwing, pebbles at the boy when he was perched on top. "Stop that; you're going to kill him," Henry yelled, and the kids scattered and the boy climbed down on Henry's side and ran away. Now he felt he was their target, and a regular sitting duck also. Having finished the "Oh Suzanna" song, they now baited him with the first stanza of "Lulu had a baby, she named him Sunny Jim." By the time Lulu got excited and grabbed Jim by his cocktail, ginger ale, five cents a glass, Henry was in the bedroom, angrily zippering up his Bermuda shorts and prepared to show his face at the window for the first time to them and demand they stop bugging him.

They'd ended the song when he reached the living room, and didn't follow it with anything. Relieved, he flopped into the easy chair with a book. It was one of the forty-odd history and guidebooks about Washington he'd borrowed from several public libraries—the main purpose being to condense what this writer and others had said into tiny sections of his own book. The trifle of his book, as his unpublished books on Philadelphia, New Orleans and San Francisco has been similarly titled, was: *Henry Sampson's Modern Guidebook to Washington, DC*. Below that would be the subtitle: "Your most perfect little companion to all places for all people. Meet the natives and their environment and be as comfortable and knowledgeable as you would in your own hometown."

He never got to know these other cities that well, having only enough time and money to stay in Philadelphia for a long weekend and never having the bus fare to get to New Orleans. And he'd only spent a few hours in San Francisco—where he first came up with the idea for a series of guidebooks—before shipping out on a World War II troopship to Australia. The Washington book would be different. Not only was he getting a true feeling of the city but the writing was more informal, something his other books, which now seemed like staid travelogue scripts, entirely lacked. These would be the keys to getting it published. And publication would create such a demand for his previous books, once he changed them to first person and did a bit more personal research and lightened up on the language, that he didn't think it'd be more than a few years before he'd be known as one of the most readable authorities on American travel. He was musing about all this—the money, notoriety, delicious free meals and luxurious hotel accommodations that would accompany his success—when he heard the children shouting outside again.

"Louie, you're the stupidest ass I ever seen,"

"You are, you mother."

"My mother, what?"

"Just your mother, you mother."

Henry tried to ignore their argument. He sat at his work table, typed "–37–" on the upper lefthand corner of the page, and continued typing and erasing for two minutes and six satisfying lines. "One especially intriguing area often missed by most tourists is DC's own Chinatown, which is only a stone's throw from the Capitol Building. It's made up of an assortment of exotic shops run by native Chinese, some of the wares, a reliable source informed me, reputed to be smuggled straight from Red China, and under the very noses of your congressmen, no less! One particularly hospitable Mandarin restaurant I had several outstanding dinners at is the..." He was looking through his dining-out notebook, which didn't list the restaurant he'd eaten in but only the more expensive places he'd jotted down many of the dishes and prices from the menus posted out front, when he heard another shouting match in the schoolyard.

"I said get your freaking hands off me, Ronnie," a girl said.

"What're you, crazy?" the boy said. "I wouldn't touch you with a cruddy pole."

"Yeah, I bet," she said; "On your mother's life," he answered, and so it went, till Henry ripped the page out of the type-writer and bunched it up and flung it to the floor. "That's it," he said, and he rushed out of the apartment and down the service stairs to the rear entrance. He calmed his rage once he got outside, moved closer to the schoolyard till he stood under the plaque above the door in the fence—a mutilated crucified Christ dangling over the school's name and motto, both written in Latin.

"Pighead Sylvia's got a hole in her sock," a boy was singing to "Glory, Glory, Halleluiah," but stopped when Henry entered the yard.

"No need to stop," he said. "You have a pretty good voice, in fact, although the words are a bit nasty. Anyway, I only came down from that building there to ask if you kids could tone it down some."

They all stepped back a few feet. He smiled and tried to think of something to say that would make them trust him. His eyes settled on tough-looking girl with messy hair and holes in her socks. Has to be Sylvia, he thought, laughing to himself. And the short kid there is probably Junior. He was trying to determine which ones were Ronnie and Louie when a boy came forward and said "Yeah, and who chose you to tell us what to do—God?"

Which intolerable bastard is he? Henry thought, but said "And who might you be, my good friend?"

"I might be Ronnie Peterson, that's who, and I'm not your good friend." He turned around to the others and squeezed his nose, and they all laughed uneasily.

Of course. The more the boy talked and swaggered, he knew it could only be Ronnie; the one who yelled the loudest, complained the longest, had the foulest mouth, constantly tried to feel up Sylvia and was always bullying someone. How many times had he heard his ugly shrill mouth, pictured these pugnacious mannerisms. Ten pages. Ten pages at least he could be advanced in his book if it wasn't for this one kid alone.

"Look, Ronnie...that's your name, right? What are you—ten, eleven, twelve? So you're old enough to understand what I mean. Because every day I'm awakened by your loud games—"

"I'm not here any morning but Saturday and Sunday, so don't be blaming me for those other days."

"Who's blaming anyone? I'm just saying I've got a very important government night job, and sleeping Sunday morning means a lot to me."

"Well, I don't know, mister, because Sundays this yard's a public playground for everybody, and today's Sunday."

"The yard's also part of a religious school, and because today's Sunday you should treat it with particular respect."

"It isn't my school."

"It's others', though—Catholic people. And it means a kind of holiness to them that took almost two thousand years to create."

"Well, school's closed today, so it isn't nothing."

"That's right," a boy said, getting next to Ronnie.

Henry tried to put the voice and face of this boy together.

Then it clicked and he blurted out "Timmy Santangelo," he located a word that had been on the tip of his tongue; "Timmy Santangelo."

"How'd you know?" the boy said, then glanced at Ronnie. Ronnie returned his dumbfounded look.

"Don't be surprised," Henry said. "I've been hearing you kids so long, I'm bound to know your names. Let's see now," and he ran his finger across his bottom lip as he observed a tall thin girl. "You're Mary," he said, and she nodded. "Mary...? Mary...?"

"Mitchell," she said, covering her face with her hands and giggling. "Mary Elizabeth Mitchell." Some of the other kids inched up as if they wanted to be identified too.

Henry pointed at one of the boys, closed his eyes and thought Who the hell could this one be? Louie? Maybe Walt, or Larry, even. He knew it'd floor them all if he could say the boy's name when he opened his eyes.

"That's Junior, mister," Ronnie said. "And the little shrimp next to him is Walt. And after Walt is Louie and Carole. But what do you want to know for—you a cop?"

"Far from it," he said, wishing Ronnie had given him a few more seconds. "And also, I think I deserve something like a little more respect from you. After all," and he stepped closer to Ronnie, who suddenly looked frightened and yelled "Run, you dumb pimps, run," and all of them except Ronnie and Timmy took off and stopped about twenty feet away.

"Why'd you tell them to run?" Henry said. "I'm not after any of you."

"Just take a walk, mister."

"That goes double for me," Timmy said, catching his thumbnail under his top front teeth and snapping it at Henry.

Jesus, he thought, he's seen cocky kids before, but these two take the limit. So what does he do now? If he turns around, they'll jeer him till he reaches his building, and then let him have it under his window for a while, embarrassing him in front of his neighbors and of course prevent him from getting any kind of work done. All he can do is stand firm where he is and let them know he means no harm, though this time directing his entreaties to the other kids.

"Listen, boys and girls," he yelled at them. "The reason I came down here—"

"Yeah, for what?" Ronnie said.

"Was I talking to you? —The reason I came down here," he shouted over Ronnie's head, "was because—"

"Ah, you already said that, so stop it."

He lunged forward, just to grab Ronnie's arm and maybe cover his mouth till he finished what he'd started to say, but Ronnie dodged out of his reach and Henry tripped and fell. Lying on the ground, he heard the slapping of the boys' sneakers against the asphalt as they ran to their friends. When he looked up, all of them were laughing and pointing at him. He thought he must really look a sight. What with his knees scraped and arms dirty and blood trickling out of his stinging right hand, which had broken his fall. Really looking like the prize patsy of all time. He wiped his hand with a handkerchief, dabbed the knee cuts and tied the red-blotted rag around one of them. He stood up, laughing along with the kids.

"I feel like a real kid again, with my knees scraped and all," he said to Ronnie and Timmy, who had moved to within ten feet of him.

"Well, you don't look like one."

"He looks like a donkey," Timmy said, and repeated it to the others. One of them hee-hawed back.

"Hey," Henry said. "When I was your age we also used to give the older guys the business. But when we went too far with it we also knew they had a perfect right to pin back our ears. So how about us calling a truce now and you kids running up to Columbia Road and having a soda each on me—okay?"

The two kids smiled, "Sure, mister, anything you say," Ronnie said, and held out his hand.

Henry reached into his pants pocket for his money clip, and when he couldn't find it, searched through his other pockets for a spare dollar and change.

"So?" Ronnie said.

"I left my money and keys home. Usually, I never leave without them. Wait here and I'll throw a couple of bucks down from my window."

"Quit stalling. What you're going to do is throw down burning hot water on us, you mean." He waved over the others, and once together, they all laughed about something and ran to the other end of the yard.

He watched them awhile, thinking he'd give his eye teeth to know what they were saying about him. He looked at his slippers—another thing that must have seemed funny to them—tried to think of the least humiliating way of leaving the yard, and finally, with a helpless shrug of his shoulders, started for his building.

It was quiet when he got to the apartment. He cleaned his cuts, sat at his worktable and thought he'd once been very much like Ronnie and Timmy. You put up a valiant resistance—you're the leaders, so it was expected of you in front of your friends—but once the old grouch left, it wasn't fun to rib him anymore. So you walked away, even felt petered out by the excitement, and you forgot whatever you were arguing about with the guy.

When some kids in the yard—he didn't bother to look outside or try to place their voices—started up again a half hour later, he decided to call it a day. He changed into slacks, put in an attaché case a box of fig newtons, cold bottle of No-Cal root beer, two books and the first thirty pages of his manuscript, and left the apartment.

He spent the next few hours in Rock Creek Park and felt unusually good there. He couldn't quite explain why but it could have been the glowing sun, his dream-filled sleep on the cool grass, the pleasure in watching people—kids playing quietly, babies and their adoring mothers and elderly couples picnicking in the shade, and especially this beautiful girl in shorts teaching her Great Dane to hurdle benches. She was alone, lived on his street three blocks away, so if it wasn't for the possible misunderstanding of her giant dog, he might have approached her. Later, while walking back from downtown where he went to the National Gallery and took in another double feature and had dinner at Scoll's Southern-style cafeteria, his original intention just to delay his return home, he felt that today had been his best day so far in Washington. (Life in the nation's capital around early dusk has all the tranquil flavor and drowsy lush charm of the Old South. So prepare to rest your tired feet along the Potomac, weary wanderers, and some places dip your toes in it, or take a leisurely stroll along the old C&O Canal, hearty visitors, and enjoy the most soul-stirring balminess of any city in the U.S.) And in a way this was true. He'd never liked living alone, although he understood the present necessity of it to write his books, but if there was one American city where a single man could enjoy himself—free museums, plenty of safe clean parks, ratio of single women to men around five to one, price of alcoholic beverages much cheaper than in most cities because of no state taxes—it was Washington. So really nothing should bother him again when there was so much to see and work to get done—especially not the minor annoyances of those kids outside. In the morning he'd buy a huge fan at Goodwill, close the rest of the windows and write six hours every day no matter what, have the book finished in a month and rewritten and sent off to the publisher a few weeks after that, which should be just around the time his money was running out. Then when the book was at the printers— a New York editor of a fairly large house had expressed interest in it and in fact was the one to suggest the first-person approach—he'd be off celebrating somewhere, with not a care in the world except for the forthcoming reviews and the size of his royalties, which he had a strong feeling wouldn't be anything but very good.

He opened the door to his apartment and heard the screams of children, but thought Hell, it's getting late, so it won't last too long. In the bedroom where the screaming seemed even louder, he calmly took off his shoes and socks and stepped into his zoris. When he was in the kitchen getting a beer, he only found it amusing when a girl yelled hoarsely to her mother that she didn't want to go home.

"Crybaby Sylvia's a nincompoop," a boy shouted. She yelled back "You stupid garbage bag" and other things before she was dragged off screaming by her mother.

Poor Sylvia, Henry thought, laughing out loud. Poor, poor Sylvia, He drank down the beer and a shot of bourbon, berating himself for not taking this super-cool attitude to their disturbances from the start. He got up for another drink.

He was sitting in the easy chair by the window, drinking his fifth beer and bourbon and staring at the gray silhouette of the school against the starlit sky, when he heard two of the remaining children telling Mary she was it.

"No I'm not," she said. "It's dark and I have to get home."

"Come on," a boy said—which one, he once knew, but now couldn't tell. "You can stay a little longer."

"Can't," and she was gone.

Henry swung at a pesky fly, felt relaxingly high from all the alcohol. He heard a bell chime somewhere the quarter hour of eight or nine, then Timmy saying "See ya tomorrow," and the rattling of a stick against the steel wire fence as he left the yard. Now it's quiet, Henry thought. At last—the sole advantage of living in the rear of a building and not facing the street. He slumped back, his shirt soaked through from the drinks and heat, and was dozing off when he heard a loud thumping in the schoolyard followed by a much softer slap. The thumping sounded like something being slammed against something else—a fist against one of those big bags boxers practice on, even, but couldn't be that—but the slapping sound?, when the noise stopped.

About ten minutes later, while he was trying to balance the empty beer cans on his chest like a pyramid—three, two and now the sixth on top—the same noises started up again. He put his nose against the window screen, couldn't see anything, and yelled "Hey, what the hell's going on down there?"

The sounds continued, thump-slap, thump-slap, while he tried to figure out what they could be. Ball against a wall, of course. Has to be.

"Hey, is someone throwing a Spaldeen against a wall or something?" The thumping continued. "For crying out loud, don't you kids ever stop playing? Enough, already. Beat it! Take off! Let some people around here get some peace and quiet for a change," hoping a neighbor or two would join him in scolding the kid. He decided nothing would stop the racket short of a trip downstairs himself. He yelled through the window "I'm coming down," grabbed his keys and money clip off the dresser, hurried through the building and into the backyard, stumbling over a bush in the dark. He got up—same god-damn hand from before, he thought—and walked through the school gate and saw Ronnie Peterson, only dimly visibly from the moon and the lights in the apartment buildings, casually tossing a basketball against a handball wall.

"What're you doing with that freaking basketball?" he said, rubbing his bad hand against his pants and going over to him.

"Throwing it." He didn't move a step.

"But why the hell now—when it's so dark?"

"You don't have to curse, you know."

"Okay, then just why now?"

"Because my punchball I couldn't see."

"But do you have to play in the same spot all day?"

"I didn't. We all went home for lunch and came back only after dinner."

"Look, I don't mean to seem unreasonable, kid, but isn't it a trifle late for you and your ball to be out?"

"I got permission. Tomorrow's no school. And listen, mister, you're as drunk as can be. I can even smell it from here, so why should I listen to you?"

"Don't get fresh with me, Ronnie. Take some advice and don't act so tough when your friends aren't around to back you up."

"I don't need them. You don't scare me. And don't be coming nearer or I'll get my dad to break your nose in."

"Say, I'd like that. Go on, call him—well, go ahead," not sure if he was up to facing the boy's old man if he did take his bluff. "Because I'd really like to speak to Mr. Peterson about his dear considerate son."

"Maybe later. Stick around. He'll be here soon to get me." He poised the ball over his head, threw it against the wall, and retrieved it effortlessly when it bounced back to his chest.

"Now didn't I ask you nicely just before? I mean, don't you think you're just banging the ball out of spite."

"Shove off, mister," a slight quiver in his voice.

"Well, what, then? I mean, what do you want from me—my blood?"

"*Meada du sombrero*, mister—you know what that means in Spanish?" Henry shook his head, and Ronnie said "'Go shit in your hat.'"

He swirled around and threw the basketball against the wall, didn't see Henry's fist coming down on his face. The blow caught him square in the cheek and sent him sprawling. The ball rebounded past them, banged against the fence with a ping and rolled jerkily a few more feet before stopping. Henry charged over to him, and was pulling at Ronnie's shirt and hair when a woman screamed behind him. He jumped up, looked around as if others were watching him, looked at Ronnie, whose eyes were closed and he wasn't moving, and ran to his building.

Someone pounded on his door half an hour later. "Mr. Sampson? It's the police. I want you to open the door."

"Be there in a jiffy." He was sitting in the easy chair, downing his last beer. The pounding became more insistent. Henry yelled out "I have to put on some clothes before opening up, you know."

"Just open it now."

He unlocked the door. Two policemen were in the hallway, and behind them two men in baseball uniforms held up a woman by her underarms. She was sobbing and sweating and saying in a Southern drawl "That's him, that's him. That's the filthy crazy bastard I saw nearly kill my boy." The ballplayers just stared at their spikes, as if they'd been tapped at random by the cops to hold this woman and didn't want to get any more involved than that.

Henry was so sickened by her wet pulpy face that he had to turn away. He also didn't like her pointing at him as if he were a common ignorant dipso like herself who'd just committed an unprovoked brutal act. Because there were things to explain. Plenty of things— all proving how justified his attack on her son had been and why it could be labeled a clear case of self-defense.

She pulled away from the men and tried to punch Henry. A policeman grabbed her wrists and tried calming her down. He said "Yes, ma'am...All right, ma'am...Now everything's going to work out just dandy, ma'am, so you take it easy, you hear?" The other policeman took down Henry's name and address and began asking a lot of questions Henry found to be embarrassing. Yes, he was not a permanent resident. No, he could not say he had any present visible means of support other than for a little savings. Yes, it's possible he struck the face of a boy known as Ronald Gregory Peterson. Yes, he had a pretty good idea why he did it. No, he'd never been in trouble in Washington before. Yes, he might have had some difficulties with law enforcement agents in other cities.

And then other questions, some even more disturbing, Henry feeling too dizzy and confused to answer them and really only thinking of a paragraph he wrote last week for the Tips the Natives Know section about the ruthless almost Gestapo-like tactics of a lot of the police here and which he'd have to revise. Because he had to maintain more than a semblance of truth and fairness in his books if they were to be worthy of publication and sell. And these two here—the first policemen he'd spoken to in this city—showed courtesy and considerable understanding and tact, far unlike that fat slobbering Texas cop who arrested him on a street a year ago, when all Henry had wanted from several prostitutes and strippers were statistics and humorous anecdotes for the Strictly Male section of his uncompleted Houston-Galveston book. (Tourists concerned with the current widely discussed issue of law and order in our nation's major cities will be pleased to learn that the 30 police—and this opinion is not only mine but that of many very discerning and influential Capitol Hill friends—is probably the most honest, intelligent and well-mannered municipal protective force in America. Besides being unusually effective in keeping the city's crime rate down beyond a reasonable low, considering the poverty that exists in some outlying areas here, the police are also helpful and friendly to residents and tourists alike in dealing with matters of a noncriminal nature. In a way, they remind me of those handsome white-uniformed Carabinieri in Naples and Rome. For whenever I approached one for street directions or really any topical or historical information, he would first salute me, smile, even bow a little, and then very graciously and patiently offer his help.)

WHO
HE?

Always home for dinner on time, shirt smelling of work: sweat, from all the teeth he pulled out, and the chemicals he used there for plates and fillings.

Scrubbed his hands with a nail brush before sitting at the table—"My fingers have been in all sorts of mouths, so need two to three washes"—my mother at one end, he at the other, various numbers of kids on either side.

"Eat all your plate," he'd say to me. "When I was your age we felt lucky to get one square a day."

Not "What happened at school today?" but the job I had after.

"Everything still good there? Getting to work on time and not giving them any trouble? You never want to lose or quit a job before you have another one. How much you making now? They don't hint you're due for a raise soon? If you do have a few extra bucks a week hanging around in your pocket, you don't think it's time you started contributing to the house? I did at ten and never stopped. It costs us a small fortune to bring up seven kids."

When they didn't want us to know what they were saying at the table, they spoke Yiddish. He'd taught it to her so she could speak to his mother. His father, a weaver and darner, had spoken a broken English, but only Yiddish at home.

"Go lie on your stomach in a bathtub," was one of the curses he translated for us. Others: "May his head get so small to fit through the eye of a needle. May the rest of his life be like a hand caught in a jackal's jaw. May he have no sons to say kaddish for him, and if his wife does give him one, then a son who turns into a goy." I didn't understand why he found them so funny.

"Monkey Jew bastard" was the worst thing he could call a person. "Not at the table, Labe—please," my mother would say.

"Who he?" he often said when we were speaking about someone he didn't know. "Who is he?" I once said, and he said "You too? God, won't any of my kids ever know when I'm poking?"

Home with newspapers he found on subway seats and in public trash cans, yellow with piss a couple of times and once with spit on it, but he said "So what's the big deal? You just tear that part of the paper off and read the rest. And look what I've saved over the years by not buying the afternoon dailies: several trees."

When one of us said "Why do you have to be so cheap?," he raised his hand and said "Shut your trap, you nobody," but never once hit any of us except a few times with a newspaper.

He gave my mother spending money every Friday at the dinner table. He'd come home, scrub his hands, sit down, take out his wallet and say "Here, for the week." Sometimes she'd say she didn't know how she could keep the house running on so little, and he'd say something like "What, what I gave isn't enough? Okay, then—take everything I got," and throw some more bills across the table at her or slap the money down in front of him and tell one of the kids "Pass it to your mother."

In a good mood, he'd take a wad of bills out of his pants pocket, unwrap the rubber band around it and say "they aren't all ones either. Who's gonna count what I took in just for today?" When one of my brothers or sisters would give the figure, he'd say to us "See why I want all my sons to be dentists?"

They argued at least twice a week at the dinner table. When it got really bad I'd get up and start to bring my dishes into the kitchen, and he'd say "Where you going? You didn't excuse yourself." I'd say "May I please be excused?" and he'd say "Get the hell out of here if you can't take it."

He'd eat the half a grapefruit right down to the white rind, then hold it up, squeeze it in half and drink the juice left in it straight into his mouth.

Got arrested for steering, for a cut of the fee, his patients or women they knew to doctor friends for illegal abortions. He spent two years in prison, lost his dental license and had to give up his practice, and went broke paying for his lawyers.

"Did it standing on one foot," he liked to say about his prison term, but that was all he spoke about it except that he met lots of very respectable and educated people there—"Judges, important business-men and politicians"—many of whom will be future patients of his, he said, once he gets back his license.

"If I had a nickel I'd build a fence around it," he said whenever we asked him for one, and then he usually gave.

Insisted we kiss him till his dying day, he used to say, "just as I did with my father."

"Pick me a winner," he'd say when I put my finger in my nose. "Get me a green one this time," he also used to say, if he didn't say the "pick me a winner" line.

I was ashamed of his frayed pants cuffs and shirt collars, stained ties and pants, broken shoelaces and other men's shoes he wore. Dead men's shoes, given to him by their widows, of several sizes from a too tight to a floppy 11.

"He's a diamond in the rough," his best friend told my mother before they got married, "who'll continue to adore his mother much more than he ever will you."

He said he was happiest when he was at his office, seeing a stream of cronies there, and working on people's teeth, especially extracting a deep-rooted tooth out of a big man's jaw. "If I can pull it out with no Novocain, even better, I've been blessed with two strong quick wrists to do it, if the guy sits tight, with little bleeding or pain and no swelling after."

Pulled one of my mother's molars out two nights before their wedding. "In her parents' kitchen," he said, "and without anesthetic. She was an ideal patient; not a tear or peep."

He supposedly had a woman or two on the side now and then, my mother said, but she never believed it: "He was too stingy to."

To keep what little hair was left on top of his head, she massaged his scalp several nights a week for years.

"I'll admit," she said, "your father and I never had a problem in bed, except when he'd been terrible to me that day. But he always said 'Let's work things out before we go to sleep so we can have nice dreams and wake up okay,' and for the most part we did."

Rare times we saw him loaded, and it always seemed to be after they came home from the annual Grand Street Boys gala, he'd throw all his change on the kitchen floor for us to pick up and keep. Then my mother would usually say "That proves your father's had too much to drink. Always when there's an open bar. One of you want to help me get him into bed?"

I can't remember him ever holding my hand when I was young, teaching me a sport, helping me with my homework, seeing one of my teachers, taking me to a ballgame or park, stopping to talk to me on the street, going anywhere alone with me but once a year to buy me clothes wholesale at a patient's factory downtown. He did used to take a couple of us to Broadway shows once or twice a year because the theater manager, for free dental work, would give us seats that hadn't been sold. We'd show up in the lobby about twenty minutes before the play began, the manager would be called out, he'd say "Let's see if anything's available," and we'd wait while he checked. There were always seats for us, though we'd have to be split up, my brother or sister and I in the balcony, my father in the orchestra.

"It's not what you know but who you know"—quote he used most. Or "Remember this: it'll help you out in life. It's not what you know but who."

"I failed with my sons when none of mwent into dentistry," he used to say. "Artists you had to be. Writers, reporters, part of the intellectual elite. You'll all learn soon enough that you went wrong, but by then you'll be stuck for the rest of your lives at what you're doing."

He'd stand me up on the kitchen counter in front of his friends and say "Sing 'God Bless America' for us." His friends would applaud when I was done and give me a nickel or dime each. One man gave me a new dollar bill once. My father took it from me and said "Better I keep it for you for the time being. Otherwise, you'll lose it." When I asked him for it a while later, he said "What dollar you talking about? I've given you way more in change over the last few weeks. All you kids ever ask me for is money."

He used the word "schwartzer," and I said "You shouldn't say that word." He said "What're telling me, that I'm prejudiced, against them? I'm not. They're in fact great patients, paying up much faster than the Hebes and never once bouncing a check."

Three of his five siblings died of diphtheria and influenza when they were very young. His surviving brother looked like a wolf and was a bookie most of his life and died of a blood clot in his brain when he walked into a streetlight pole. His sister came to the apartment one Sunday a month with a jar of glutinous soup she made and greasy cookies and onion rolls she baked that were still warm. They always spent at least an hour alone together, talking very low so no one would hear them. After she left, my mother said things like "I wonder how much cash she got out of your dad this time after one of her sob stories. He's a sucker for everything she says, just as he was for his mother." Or "I can imagine the loathsome things she said about me and which your dad, of course, let her get away with. I never liked his family. Only his father. A sweeter, sadder shlep never lived."

He liked to call me "junior boy" because I was small for my age and the fourth and last son. At first I liked it—he said it affectionately and sometimes rubbed my hair. But when I got into my midteens I asked him to stop calling me it—it made me seem too boyish. He said "I can't; it's gotten into my blood." "Junior boy, junior boy," he'd say mockingly when I was in my twenties and angry for one reason or another or indignant over something, usually politics or the state of culture.

"You can fall in love with a rich girl as well as a poor one," he said, "so why not one with money? But never bring home a girl of whatever financial means who's not Jewish."

"I get along with everybody," he said, "which is why I've done well as a dentist, and when I lost my license, selling textiles. Be like me, smart and not a wiseguy, and you'll get somewhere. Go on like you're doing—a cynical sour-puss—and you'll end up a flop no matter what field you go in."

"The whole world's trying to steal from you—remember that," he said. "But what most of them don't have is our *Yiddische kop*, so take advantage of what God and we gave you. You don't, that just shows what a schmo and easy mark you are."

Some nights after dinner he'd say "Get me one of my cigars out of the humidor." He'd give me the cigar band, sometimes slip it on my finger, and a matchbook for me to light the cigar. Then he'd sit back in his easy chair, content in smoke. "Boy, does that feel good after a long day. And better when you have such a terrific kid lighting it. Thanks."

"Where'll all your writing get you?" he'd say. "To the nearest soup kitchen if you're lucky. Give it up before you really start suffering because of all the disappointments you're bound to face."

"You drink too much and you got a filthy mouth," he'd tell me when I was in my twenties. "You'll just make enemies and never get a good-looking levelheaded wife. She'll think: 'That's gonna be the father of my children when there are so many more refined sober guys out there who have a steady income? Not on your life.'"

Most of my teeth he worked on he ruined for me. He didn't take x-rays when I had a cavity, saying he didn't need to: when he was drilling he could see with his own eyes where the decay ended, which meant that a year or so later the tooth usually started aching again. He did give me Novocain, but the minimal amount, so it always hurt when he used the drill on me. When I was sixteen I paid for two root canals with another dentist with money I was making as a delivery boy after school and Saturdays. My father never asked me about my teeth after that and I never told him about the other dentist, but he knew. Otherwise he would have said, as he used to, "You haven't had a checkup in a while. Let's set up a time next week." Before he got his license back he worked on our teeth and several of his old patients' in a friend's office, always at night after the other dentist had left.

Walked out on some of his dinner checks, half to save money and half as a game. "I love putting something innocent over on people," he said. "What about the waiter or waitress?" I said, and he said "Oh, don't worry your head; I always leave a tip."

When I got in front of the TV set, he'd say "What's your father, a glazier? Get out of the way."

His family was very poor and he worked every day after school and all day Sunday starting when he was eight. "Saturdays, because we were Orthodox, I rested like the rest of the neighborhood, though if my folks had let me I would've worked that day too after attending *shul*.

"Went straight from high school to dental school—that's the way it was then; it wasn't that I was especially good in the sciences. But I applied myself, burned those candles—and lots of those nights they were candles, which were cheaper than gas, or electricity, when our building finally got it. If I could do it, you can too, if you changed your major again and went back to being pre-dental. Of course, I could've spent four years in college and then gone to dental school, but who had that kind of time to waste? I wanted to start making some real money and move my folks to a better apartment and buy my mother a fur stole, and things like that."

Had the largest dental practice and the first purple opentop car on the Lower Eastside. "I saw that car as an advertisement for my practice," he said. "All the girls were after your father," my mother said.

"Not only did he have a good income but he also had hair then, so was quite the catch."

Also said about his time in prison "I did it dancing, something I always felt good about, that I didn't whine or act like a fruitcake while I was there."

My younger sister and I were told he was a major in the army dental corps in San Diego—my mother even got out the atlas to show us where San Diego was—taking care of the teeth of soldiers who were about to be shipped across the Pacific to fight the Japanese.

"After his release," my mother said, "with his license taken away and all our savings gone and the war still on, so no opportunity for him to make a pile of money—that time was the hardest for your father, I think worse than being in prison. It was also the bitterest period of our marriage, and we've had some beauties."

Worked in a war factory in Brooklyn when he got out. After the war, he sold shoes and then paints and then textiles and quickly did so well at it that in a few years we were able to keep a maid.

Forced to give up dentistry for good because of his worsening Parkinson's disease and diabetes. For a couple of years he was falling down on subway platforms and streets after work, and strangers had to help him home. "Thank you," I'd say at our front door or in the building's vestibule when I'd see them through the peephole, "I'll take him from here."

The last few years of his life I'd shave him and clean his dentures and give him his shots and exercise him and clean him up after he went to the toilet and come in every night around twelve—I'd rented an apartment on their block to help out my mother with him—to give hid his pills and turn him over so he wouldn't get bedsores and to make him comfortable for the rest of the night. Sometimes I got mad at him while he was lying in bed—that he'd just pissed or shit right after I'd changed his diapers—and would turn him over too hard or curse him under my breath or curse my own fate out loud that I had to be coming here every night to take care of him. "You want to do the right thing," he said a few of those times, "but it's just not in you, so you shouldn't even try. Don't help me from now on. I'll live longer without it. Anything's better than you acting like an animal to me."

When my parents were first introduced, he was a handsome dentist with a thriving practice and she worked as a receptionist in a doctor's office during the day and at night and Saturday matinees danced in a

West 42nd Street musical review. He used to meet her at the stage door two to three nights a week and give her flowers and boxes of candy. "You laugh," he said to me, "because you can't see anyone your age doing that today. But then, if you wanted to win a beautiful girl nine years younger than yourself, that's what you were expected to do."

"I couldn't get her to bed so I had to marry her," he said. "But I already knew that bad girls you sleep with and nice ones you marry. Look at your mother. It's obvious she doesn't like me talking about it, but I think it's an important lesson all my sons have to learn."

"Hook up with a *shiksa*," he used to say, "and she'll wake you up in the middle of one night and start shouting into your ear how much she hates Jews. It's bound to happen eventually, so stick with Jewish girls. Much less confusion with your kids later on, and they're prettier than *shiksas* and make the best wives."

"When we were kids we went barefoot in the summer to save on the shoe leather," he'd say.

"We had so many relatives and *landsleit* living with us in our small apartment on Ludlow Street that we had to sleep in shifts, sometimes two to three to a single bed."

"It was two for five to go to the movies then—two people for five cents. So I'd stand out front of a movie theater and say 'I got two, who's got three?' and always got someone to go in with."

"No matter what a cop or teacher smacks you for, you deserve it. Always respect authority."

"This is my youngest boy," he said to a couple of his cronies in his waiting room. "Maybe not the sharpest of the bunch, but so far the hardest worker and the one most interested in making money, so the son I have the highest hopes of following me into dentistry. If he doesn't become one, like the other three, I'll really consider my life a flop."

"Dad emotionally cool?" my mother said. "It's just a front. He doesn't like showing his deeper emotions around you kids. Afraid it'll give you the wrong way to act and later make you vulnerable to people who take advantage of sensitive men. So he wants to always look chipper and strong, even tough, able to endure and stand up to anything. But weeks after your brother died he was still crying to himself to sleep every night. With his mother, he was even more inconsolable. At least with your brother he let me hold him in my arms sometimes, though don't let on to him that I told you."

"Why would you want to move out when you've got free room and board here?" he said to me when I started looking for an apartment after I graduated college. "Stay with us till you have a pile of dough in the bank and can afford a long layoff from work. The food's good, bed's comfortable, you have your own room now, so if you want to be left alone to type your head off in it, the room's quiet enough with the door shut where nobody's going to complain."

"Don't be a dope," he said when I told him I'd stopped signing up for my weekly unemployment insurance check because I was no longer looking for work. "You and your last employer put good money into that plan, so take it while you can. If you were doing something really illegal, that'd make it a different matter. But you want to write and just live off your savings, do it when the government checks run out."

"I don't care what you say," he said, "that girl's ugly as sin and dull as dishwater and is making a fool of you if you think she's good-looking and has a nice personality."

Went through the apartment a few times a night turning off all the lights in rooms nobody was in. "You people," he'd say, "must think I've got stock in Con Edison."

"Get off the phone," he'd say on the extension when I was trying to rake a date with a girl or talking to a friend. "I've only been on two minutes," I'd say, which was usually how long it was before he picked up the extension, and he'd say "It's been ten minutes, don't tell me. The phone company charges by the minute, you know, and not a single flat fee for the call. Besides, I'm expecting some very important calls from my patients, so say goodbye."

"Close the icebox door," he'd say when he saw me looking inside the refrigerator for something to eat, "or get what you want fast. You're spoiling all the food."

"You already eat like three Greeks," he'd say sometimes when I'd open the refrigerator or breadbox shortly after dinner, "you want to make it four?" "I'm a growing boy," I said once, "you've said so yourself," and he said "Yeah, don't I know, but give it a little rest, will ya? You're eating us out of house and home."

"That woman's got a beak and bad breath on her that's driving away fine prospects," yet he made a match for her as he did for lots of his patients. "I hate to see two people lonely," he said, "so when they sit in my chair and tell me they're looking for somebody, I almost immediately know which of my other patients is the right one."

If the couple got married—several couples did—he hinted to them that he expected as a thank-you for bringing them together a new suit from Harry Rothman's or four custom-made shirts from the Custom Shirt Shop.

"When I was a boy I walked to work even on the worst days to save on trolley fare. Thunderstorms I'd go through—blizzards like we don't get anymore—and I never got even a cold or where the weather stopped me from a single day's work."

I kissed his lips on his hospital deathbed, something I'd never done with him—it had always been the cheek—and didn't want to do it then but for some reason thought I should. I was alone in the room with him when he died.

I knew he was dead; everything about his body said so and I'd heard a death rattle and put my ear over his mouth and heart. I didn't check his pulse because I was never good at finding it on anyone but myself. I wanted to kiss him with nobody around before I summoned the hospital staff and they examined him and declared him dead and shooed me out of the room so they could clean up him and his bed. From a pay phone down the hall I called my mother to say Dad had died peacefully and then my brothers and sisters. I had lots of change on me because he'd come into the hospital in a coma and we didn't think his room needed a phone. Kissing him was something I think he never would have done with me if I were the one who died, and why should he? He had more sense than me in many ways—he never did anything unless he was sure he wanted to—and no fake sentimentality. I'd come every day to the hospital—it was an easy cross-town bus ride from my apartment—and stayed the last two nights there sleeping on a couch in the visitor's lounge and every hour or so looking in on him and sitting by his bed and dabbing his forehead and cheeks with a towel if they were wet and swabbing his lips with glycerin swabs if they were dry. He probably would have done what he did with my youngest sister, who died in the same hospital of cancer when she was twenty-three, though like him the cause of death was listed as pneumonia: visited me after work the first two days, stayed half an hour and then gone home to have dinner. And after those two visits—maybe even after the first—said to my mother "I can't go anymore"—this is what she told me at the time—"It's too tough to. I can't take seeing one of my kids in this condition." So he wouldn't have seen me alive after the first or second visit and would have left it to my mother to tell him how I was doing, I'm almost sure of it. With my brother he never had to go through any of that because Gene drowned and was never found.

"Kiss me, I'm your father, and I don't deserve it after the nickel I just gave."

"Listen to me, I'm your father, and you know anyone else better to advise you with your welfare in mind? I've been around; I know the ropes. Believe me, I won't steer you wrong."

"Leave the house for good, why don't you," he said a couple of times. "All I ever wanted was for my kids to be civil to me and for there to be a bit of peace in my life. But I can't have any of it when you're always kvetching and squabbling with me and making speeches and getting angry at every third thing in the world."

I think what hurt him most, other than the deaths of my sister and brother and of course his mother, and more my brother than my sister since she'd been sick since she was five, he said, "and we never thought she'd live as long as she did," was that while he was in prison my mother got him to go along with a name change for all the kids. "She forced it on me. Shoved the cowers of attorney at me and said 'Sign them or I won't be there when you're released.' I should've told her to stow it, but for the sake of keeping the family together, I didn't. She was ashamed of my last name because I was all over the newspapers in this big graft scandal and was doing time and she said all your lives would be ruined by having my last name. That people remember, but she knew damn well they forget or don't care. As for me, I never regretted going through any of it except for losing my dental license all those years. So I had to find another profession when I got out, and it worked. I was a terrific salesman; made a bundle and would've stuck with it but I loved dentistry more. But I'll never forgive her. She did the worst possible thing she could do to me, and all out of spite. That's why I get so mad at the dinner table sometimes. I see you kids and I think of it, and it makes my blood boil."

"Change your last name back to mine," he said a few days after my eighteenth birthday. "You're of legal age now where you don't need both parents' consent," and I said "I can't." "Why not? Come on, please, change your name back and I'll give you anything you want within reason." I said "I wish I could, just because I know how happy it'd make you, but with the other kids keeping the name we have now, it wouldn't be a good idea. I want to have the same last name as them, and they all want to keep the name they've had for almost fifteen years." He said "Look, what am I asking for? Just for one of my sons to carry my name—the two older girls will marry and get new ones— and I'd pay for all the legal costs involved," and I said "Honestly, it's just been too long." "Ah," he said, "you were always such a weak jerk. Get out of my sight."

FOR A QUIET
ENGLISH SUNDAY.

"You know, it sort of looks like spit in a way."

"My God," she said, "what does?"

"Nothing," he said. "I was just thinking out loud."

"No, really, what? I wasn't being cynical. I'm interested."

"The rain driveling off the arch there. Also the way it snacks against the sidewalk."

She looked at both places. The rain didn't look like spit or anything close to it. But if he insisted . . .

"You're right. It does resemble it."

"Resemble what?"

"Oh, come off it, Peter—like what you said. Like spit, then, I suppose."

"You couldn't quite get the word out for a moment, could you." He laughed in that ridiculing way he knew she disliked, half to himself and half aloud. But she wouldn't let it upset her, since that was what he wanted. Then he'd have excuses.

"Well," she said, "it's never been one of my pet words. But I will go along with your description."

He turned away and looked at the doorway's granite arch, which had been shielding them from the rain the last five minutes.

Then, without meeting her eyes, he shifted his blank stare past her to a row of Georgian townhouses across the street, the slicing rain looking more now like snow or sleet than anything else. She wondered what he was thinking.

"What are you thinking, dear?" she said.

"Nothing much."

"I hope you're not angry with my remarks before, I was only trying to be accommodating."

"And my most profound humble thanks to you m'lady," and he swept his arm in front of him and bowed low to her in mock gallantry. Straightening up, he said "Now what do you say we drop the subject and walk?"

"It's still raining."

"Just a ways—I promise. Then we'll duck in someplace for coffee."

"Now that's the most intelligent idea you've had since you suggested lunch."

He walked out from under the arch, and she followed him. The rain had let up a bit and the cloche hat she'd bought yesterday was all the protection she needed. But he was walking much too fast again—acting like a disgruntled schoolboy and not making any secret of wanting to lose her, though she wouldn't let on she knew. She'd play his little games, have coffee and tolerate his moody silence and get him back to the hotel for a nap and later some cocktails.

"I certainly appreciate you're harping on that again."

"But you would rather be alone—I mean: right?"

"If that's what you want me to say, okay."

"You'd rather be with that woman friend you met on your last buying trip—isn't that true too?"

"Again, if that's what you want me to say, okay."

"Stop mimicking yourself. You sound simpleminded."

"Then stop being a pain in the ass. Stop bugging me."

"All I want is for you to say if you want to be alone. An honest yes or no. I'll find something to do without you."

"You really expect an answer to that? Because all your suspicions and assertions have been groundless since you first started up about this fictional beauty."

"Sure they have. But ever since we landed in Ireland you've been beating the drums to get to London like some breathless Romeo."

"Oh yeah, I can really see myself doing that."

"Who is she, Peter?"

He stuck his palm out and squinted at the sky. "It's stopped raining."

"Thank you for the weather report, but all right, when did you first meet her?"

"Who?"

"Just tell me. I'm no kid anymore. And I'd never ask if I felt I couldn't accept the answer. I've been half expecting it for a couple of years."

"Make sense: expecting what?"

"Hey. Why don't we just separate for the afternoon right here? You could then do whatever you want without me and I could finish my shopping."

"Knock it off, Cyn, I'm tired of it."

"It's for your benefit I'm making the suggestion."

"And again, I appreciate it to no end. Your considerateness is an absolute wonder to me."

"Yes," she said, eyeing his composure and not as sure now. "Let's see then." She placed her hand on her chin. "You know, I really don't know how many hours I should give you—for the truth now: how long does a man need to make love to a woman he hasn't seen in four months."

"Four months."

"With me you hardly take four minutes these days."

"I do my best."

"Your best—but never mind. Tell me, did you drag us around this wet neighborhood because she happens to live here? I'm not complaining about the choice, mind you, because it's a lovely part. London can be so pretty, and so clean."

He looked away from her to a few cars passing.

"Well, then is her apartment done up Modern? Neo-Victorian? Old Depression? No furniture at all? Poor dear, and quite an inconvenience for the two of you, but maybe you can fix that. All right, if the topic fails to interest you, then just tell me what color hair she has. Women are curious about such things. It's probably a well-brushed mousy brown, although you've always preferred real blond—long and artsy-like and casually billowing over the shoulders like those California college girls you said you used to flip over so much and who never gave you a tumble."

He continued to look at the street, then at his shoes, then at her new suede walking shoes, the soles caked with mud because the storm had opened up on them while they sat reading in a little park nearby.

"Don't stand there gaping like an idiot at nothing—pretending she doesn't exist. I saw her envelopes in your pockets—even in your billfold once. She writes you at the office, right? About once a week from what I can make out. For a moment she thought she had him:

his bottom lip dropped and his face froze. She was excited at the prospect of his spilling the whole story of the woman and thus clearing up the fuzziness of it in her own mind, because just by his silence and cunning avoidance of the issue she was starting to feel like a fool. But now he returned to his old maneuvers, gazing out at the street, at nothing at first, then at a passing bus, trying to give the impression he wasn't concerned with anything she said.

"That last one got you, didn't it? Well, you needn't have looked so worried. I didn't pry inside the envelopes. That's not saying I wouldn't have, but I just never had the chance."

"Those letters you refer to—that is, if they're the same ones I'm thinking of, were business correspondence from a silver company in England."

"London, England?"

"The main office is in London, yes. But the factory's in Edinburgh."

"And this company always makes it a practice of writing you on salmon-colored stationery and with pale-blue feminine script?"

"Knock the ways of British business if you want, but it's what helped send us over here on the cuff."

"And doesn't that make me delirious. But the owner, or salesperson, couldn't by any chance have the first name of Margaret?"

"If you mean Miss Pierce—she's their corresponding secretary. She must be a damn efficient woman from what I can make out, though I've never met her. Both times I was in the office, she wasn't there."

"It's a lovely name, Margaret—as if it fits for this quiet English Sunday. Seems any woman who'd have it would be the type to light your fires, eagerly mix you drinks and such, and later make perfect shy love."

"This one's probably a pursy seventy and maybe an Anglican deacon on the side."

"If I ever wanted to be named anything, it was Margaret. I think I would have been much different for it."

"I kind of always preferred the name Morris for you myself."

"Would you like my being called Margaret? If you did, I might even change it for you."

"If you feel that name would suit you better, fine. Now let's get a move on then, sweetheart, though to where, I don't know."

She sailed. "Just lead the way, my dear." She looped her arm through his and they began to walk at an even pace. After a minute, he broke away from her and walked ahead. She kept abreast of him for a while. Then he walked faster, his arms and fists pumping back and forth like those people in sweatsuits she's seen on the park side of Central Park West from her apartment window, looking as if they were in a speed-walking race.

"I can't keep up with you," she said.

"You have your thirty-dollar walking shoes on—so walk."

She stopped, wheezing from nearly running a block alongside him, and said "I was right before. You do want to hurry off somewhere without me. Every action of yours says so."

He stopped and trotted back. "When are you going to give up on that worn-out crap?"

"When you start telling the truth."

"I can't insist what I say is the truth. And there are people around. This is getting embarrassing. You'll just have to start believing what I say, that's all."

"But you do want to walk much faster. At least admit that."

"Yes, I want to walk faster. It felt good, but not for the reason you have. I just feel like moving today—almost like running like a kid."

"So why don't you then?"

"Yeah, I can really see myself doing that too."

"I'm serious—run. Don't let me hold you back."

"If you don't shut up, I will."

"But that's what I'm saying—run. I'm being honest with you, and you're a dope not to take me up on it. Say your goodbyes and run the hell away from here, back to the hotel for your things and then back to this neighborhood or some other, or wherever, but run, goddamnit—just go."

"Oh, screw it then," but he stared at her a few seconds as if waiting for her to change her instruction, and then began walking in the direction they'd been heading, quickening his steps when he was a few feet away from her and then starting to run. People on the street turned to look at him as he ran past. At first all she could think was how silly he looked from behind, his jacket waving and his buttocks jiggling and his legs cockeyed and flailing as if this were the first time he'd tried running, although he more likely forgot how to run as he used to or was running that way because he'd been out of shape so long. By now he was more than a block away, surprising her with his wind and at a distance much farther than she expected him to get in such a short time.

SEX.

I think life is worth living just for the sex in it.

Say that again?

Life. Life can be worth living just for sex.

I see.

I believe that.

And I see. But what happens when you get old and there's no sex. You commit suicide?

Old people do it. Once a year and hurray, today's the day, and maybe every sixth federal holiday.

They can do it almost as much as us. Though it takes longer and the men have less juice to squish out and the women are a little drier down there. So I'd use a lubricant, that's all.

Oh, wiggle me one of your drier-down-heres—I love that.

It's true. In the *Times*. There was a study. A report of one. If you'd read, you'd know.

I still don't think so. The heart, the sudden palpitations—who'd have the guts to? You go slower, side by side. There are ways. Whatever, will you try to hustle it *up* a little?

And don't give me that. about my reading. It doesn't have to be newspapers.

Just be quiet and move, twitch, do something because you're becoming a dead weight on me again,

You're also supposed to move.

Let's just keep a lid on it till we're through.

Right. You about through now too?

I was through two minutes ago.

You never said anything.

Said? What the hell you think my screams were about?

Those were screams? I thought that was you complaining I was too heavy.

Those were sexual moans. I hit the top, I yell like everybody else, except maybe you.

I yell; I scream.

You titter. You go meow like a pussycat—and then fall off and doze or pretend to because you think it's cute. You're a boy getting his first screw. You're hopeless.

Thanks. I'm still not done yet, so thanks. My uncle, my whole family, say thanks.

Don't blame me.

No, I'll blame my uncle, my whole family—thanks.

You had your chance. When I'm up there that long I'd think you'd get there too.

Well, I wasn't.

You had time.

What's time got to do with it? I was enjoying the nuances, the textures, each little speciality of the act. Gradually building to the peak of all time, or one of them. Then you came in with your sex-is-life line. Life is worth living, etcetera. Anyway, will you get off me?

Maybe I can still work it out.

Work it out on some other girl, not me.

Give me a minute more.

Minute more on someone else, now off.

Hold it. I'm there. Just give it another shake or two. Oh, that's it, that's it.

Oh, that's it, what? I'm not doing anything. God, you're a load.

There.

Bull.

No, there, I did it.

You did what? You did nothing.

Feel it down there yourself.

Whatever stuff might be there is from me, not you. Wow, what a zero I have in you.

Zero; that's a hole. That's you.

Then I got a one, but a limp one. You're the worst.

That doesn't help, by the way if you want there to be a next time.

The mind remembers—the subconscious—even if I don't.

Next time? I really look forward to that.

You never know. It just comes.

I come; you don't.

Oh? Next time I'll get in the same place from the other side when we're all turned around and going cookies, and send you to heaven, baby, send you to heaven.

Send me into a state of frustration and depression, maybe.

I might as well be doing it to myself.

It's never the same.

There are ways. Chopped liver, somehow. There are also other men.

And other women.

That's what I'm telling you to do. But not with me again. How could I?

When you get the itch, you just lie on your back, or I get on my back with my itch, and—

No, sir. Don't even think the possibility exists.

Sobeit, my love.

Good. Now how about getting off, up, dressed, out and far from here.

Right. Up, out, off, dressed, out, up, away and far from here—got it. But in that order, or should I start from the last first or first laugh?

How did I meet you?

Excuse me?

How did I ever meet you, and why? What did I see in you and how? What was it that brought us to this? What in God's name kept me going with you? I'm asking myself. What the hell was I thinking?

What are you talking about?

Why you? There must have been a dozen other guys in the bar, so how come you?

You were attracted to me at the time. Now you're not.

I wasn't attracted. It was because of where I happened to sit at the bar—next to you.

Maybe you sat next to me intentionally.

I sat there because it was the only stool left at the bar. Maybe the person before me was a woman who you also bored to death, but she was smarter than me and left.

The person before you was a man.

Maybe you bugged him to death and he left. But that still doesn't explain it. And don't give me that you remember who sat there before me. It was too long ago.

Two months to the nose, almost, and I do. It was a man. He had blond hair, and probably still does. And was around my age, build, height, handsize, and he said he was a film editor or something. He talked a lot about film, carried film books. Several on top of the bar getting wet.

I should have met him. He should have held out and bugged you out of the bar. Then your stool would have been the only one available and I would have taken it and talked to him and maybe liked him and given him my phone number, and two months later I'd be here with him, instead of you.

He was gay.

The truth now.

He wasn't. Or didn't seem so, at least. In fact, he said "No chicks here, for my money," and left. That's what he said.

You remember that too? I don't believe it.

I'm telling you. I came in, sat, drank. He was already there and didn't seem too interesting. He mostly spoke to the soldier en the other side of him who was getting worried this man's books were getting wet.

The soldier sounds nice. How come I don't remember him? You'd think I'd remember someone in uniform. Because he also left before you got there and was replaced by another man. A drunk, though nicely dressed, who was in his own world singing songs to himself out loud. Said he could be a singer again, was at one time.

Oh, yeah. Funny guy, in a raincoat, but a fool. Right. And after ten minutes of this fool singing and right in this man's ear most of the time, he got up—the editor did—and said to me "No chicks here, for my money," and left. Then you came in.

I wish I hadn't.

No matter what you wish, face the music—you came in and sat down.

Who was sitting on the other side of you—just in case I had gotten your seat?

Skip, the ex-actor, who's an unbelievable eighty-two. Sitting there when I came in and when we left.

I like Skip.

Maybe you should have tried something with him.

Don't be obnoxious.

I'm not. I like Skip too.

Not that he's unattractive. I mean, don't be obnoxious about him. He's beautiful—a beautiful man—and gentle and witty and filled with wonderful interesting stories about his travels and professional life. And he's had his heartaches, too. Losing his wife early. Throat cancer that forced him off that soap and practically killed his acting career. A son who couldn't care less that he's alive, and grandchildren he's never seen. He's told me. He's told you. Don't dash his memories.

Who's dashing?

Spoil them. Crap on them. Don't insult the old guy. He's great. I love him.

Getting pretty hot there between you two.

God, you're stupid.

Don't call me stupid.

Dumb, then. Because why do you say such stupid things?

Sometimes... forget it.

No, what? I'm sorry.

Sometimes I have to. Sometimes we all, for whatever our reasons, say dumb stupid things.

That could be true. I thought you were going to say something more insightful than that, but okay. Anyway, you now want to get your clothes on?

You see—I did come. Look. There. It isn't piss.

Maybe it's your juices finally coming out now from way back in your body. Once those little guys get swimming I don't see them going back down your tubes to your testes and that other place they're made in, just because you only got them halfway up.

I'll get another batch all the way up now if you let me.

If there was ever non-love talk between two people, this is it. Are you a necrophiliac?

No.

A lover of dead bodies?

I know what it is.

Because if there was ever a dead body to make love to, mine's it. Though don't try.

I've ways to get you going.

No way friend—none. This body is closed, a mausoleum. Door locked, key lost, at least for you. Nothing. For you, nothing ever again.

I know—I'd even bet—I could get you interested.

No. Because I won't let you. That pencil looks better than you. Just get it out of your head. All your schemes. The BS about bets.

Why won't you give me a tiny chance to try?

Because I don't want to. Simple and plain. I don't like it with you. With anybody like you. I also hate this talk—hate you for talking it. It's dead-body talk. Antisex. Necrospeech.

Gets me going. Look, take a peek. You can say you're not attracted to that?

Jesus, what do I have here? Go. Really, your clothes on, the door way behind you. Something. But beat it.

That gets you going? I'll do it. Yes ma'am, just watch me fly.

Don't. Please, don't be sick.

I was only joking. I'm not sick. That's what happens when I'm frustrated. But more so that I can't get what I truly want to say to you across. The nice things. Though I once did it like that with a woman. The one I lived with. It was fun. It might seen crazy now, but she wanted me to, would ask.

I don't want to hear about it.

"Squirt like a fountain," she used to say. Something like that. She was from the West Coast. That was the term they used there, she said—Oregon. "Shoot," I think it was, instead of "squirt." Or "make." That's it. "Make like a fountain," she used to say.

She must have been as sick as you.

Why? She wasn't. I loved her, she me. We were together for three years. She had a son, was once married, and for those three years I was his surrogate dad. But after being with someone that long you often try out experiments or throw a few comes away. That night we did it that way. Big deal—no harm. She'd done it like that with her husband. I think we also later made it the more normal way together, so I got in two instead of one, besides all that fun.

I never did it that way except when that was all I was doing with boys.

Make believe I'm a boy.

Uh-uh. From now on you better get used to doing it to yourself and in your own apartment till you hook up with someone else.

It's not the way I'd prefer it now, either.

Fine. But I'm serious. You and I—we're no more.

Okay, you said it.

Then you understand?

Right.

Good. I'm getting dressed. Please do too.

Come on, what am I asking for? Then I go, and for good, as you said.

Enough.

Honestly. A quick one. Then I never call or come back.

I said no. I don't want it or feel like it.

Then I'm going to have to take it.

Try, and I'll kick your nuts in.

Go on. I'd like that.

You really are crazy, you know? Just take off.

I want it, though.

You want to prove something's more like it. Well, not with me. No time. And don't get crazier or you'll have more than trouble from me. The police—I promise you.

What will you say? I've been banging you every other day for two months. You'll say you suddenly don't want to?

Don't start with me.

Let me just touch it.

Hands off. Not even a look.

Once, and more than a touch, and I swear I'll be fast, and then I'm gone.

Get away.

Please?

Get the hell off of me.

Just a little fun-making.

Stop. You're hurting me. I'm not ready.

Get ready!

I can't. It doesn't work like that. And you're already in deep trouble.

Get ready, because I'm coming in.

You craphead.

Oh, I love that.

You mother, you bitch, you whore. Get off. You're heavy as shit. I don't want to. Not now.

Now.

You're hurting.

Now. Oh good; that's so good.

Shut your mouth.

You want me to keep it shut?

Shut your mouth. Let me out. Get out of here. Off me. Please.

I'll shut up if you want. I'll be quiet.

Be quiet.

You won't complain.

I'll complain. I don't want to do this.

Complain, then. That's actually not so bad. Complain all you like.

I won't complain.

No, complain.

I won't say anything.

Then, good. Neither will I. Let's just enjoy it.

I can't.

Try.

All right.

You won't blame me?

Yes. No.

Say you won't blame me.

I won't blame you.

And you don't.

I don't.

And that you like it this way a lot.

I don't.

Neither do I—not a lot.

Please be quiet.

It's not a bad way, though, is it?

Quiet.

I will. But what I'd like to know is why we have to do it this way so often.

This position?

No, just doing it.

Not often.

A lot of the time, then.

Not even that.

Then once ever week or so... you got to admit that.

Shush.

THE

KILLER

Falling feet first in the air I get the feeling if I wanted to save myself I could simply flap my arms and fly back to the bridge. Fly in loops and all kinds of stunts under and around the bridge, in fact. In fact, if I could fly like that I don't think I'd want to die so fast. I'd first fly to wherever in whatever way I wanted to and then die by flying someplace I could only die by flying to, like straight into a building or mountainside. I flap my arms. I start to fly. I fall into the river. But I'm not dead yet. I'm zipping further down in the water like a heavy spear but more like a sleek fish. I don't mind drowning but I don't think I'd want to drown that fast if I could swim for a while like a fish. I'd swim to the ocean's floor and see its strangest sea creatures and rock formations and flora, and then when I'd seen enough I'd kill myself some way like swimming deep when I knew I didn't have the breath to get back to the top in time. Or else off a huge waterfall to jagged rocks below, or I don't know but somehow like a fish when I no longer wanted to swim but just wanted to die.

I try to swim and start but stop because I can't, and give myself up to drowning, but pop out of the water like a stick and onto my back. Somehow I made it to the top, but I didn't want to. I didn't even want to reach the water alive. I wanted to die in flight as I thought people did when they jumped from so high a height, and I was sure if the free fall didn't kill me the impact of my body against water would. Maybe the way I fell stopped me from being suffocated in the jump, and the way I landed—there was barely a splash—stopped me from being smashed. But I survived and I'm now unable to sink. This river is near the ocean and the ocean might be depositing a lot of its salt in this part of the river, and that salt bed, if it's called that, might be keeping me afloat. But I could be wrong, as I know as much about oceanography, if that is the science that deals with ocean salt accumulating in the river's delta or basin or whatever the right word is for the river area the ocean flows into making it even saltier than the ocean, as I do about aerophysics, if that is the science that deals with the speed of sixteen feet per second—or is it thirty-two?—that an object falls at once it reaches its maximum speed if there are no obstacles in its way.

I let myself go all over as I do when I want to completely relax myself, but I still can't sink. It would be nice, though not as nice as swimming like a fish or flying with my arms as wings, to float around like this for as long as I want, though only if I were able to navigate myself and go at a faster speed. But I am able to float, as I wasn't able to swim or fly, so maybe I should float out to the ocean and somehow across it and then after a long journey down all those foreign coastlines, but more realistically just down our domestic ones, to find a way to kill myself by floating, such as going up a river where the ocean's salt line ends and making sure I'm in the middle of this very wide river when I start sinking so there'd be no chance the current could carry me alive to land.

I try to float faster by kicking my feet. But I can't get up sufficient speed to make floating interesting enough to want to stay alive for the time being, so I turn over on my stomach with my head in the water to drown. But by some natural means or I don't know what, I'm flipped over on my back. I turn over and try to swim, thinking maybe the force of my strokes and kicks will keep me on my belly long enough to swallow enough water to drown, but I'm flipped right over and floating on my back. Now what animal or insect do I remind myself of and in what environment does this animal or insect's automatic flipping-over movement take place? The closest one I can think of it a dead fish in stagnant water being prodded onto its stomach by a stick, and once the stick's taken away, flip back over to one of its sides. And what science would deal with the phenomenon of my being flipped over when I try hard as I can not to? Probably a couple of them, including oceanography.

I turn over on my stomach and while I'm being flipped back I gulp a mouthful of water, thinking if I do this repeatedly I'll swallow enough water to drown. But the moment I'm on my back again I cough up the water. I try it again and again, but my body won't allow even a small portion of water to stay past my throat.

It seems I'll never get to do what I want in this water and I'll have to float like this till one of the river's boats picks me up or I'm washed to shore. Either way, I'll be pampered with warm drinks and blankets and eventually they'll find out what I was doing in the water and word will get back to some newsroom and I'll be made into this dumb folk hero whom nature kept alive despite his most earnest efforts to take his life, which will make it even tougher for me in the future to find a solitary way to die. What I should do is backstroke to a remote shore before daybreak, get back to the bridge and my car, and find a way to kill myself where there'd be no chance I'd survive.

But which way is shore? It's either east or west, if I'm still in the river, or north if the current's carried me to the ocean If I'm in the ocean and swim to shore as if I'm in the river, I'll be on my back all night without reaching land, always parallel to shore though perhaps progressively further away from it if the tide pulls me that way, and so tired by daybreak that I won't have the strength to backstroke to shore once I sight it or out of range of a would-be rescue boat. And if I'm still in the river and backstroke to shore as if I'm in the ocean, I'll be swimming all night up the river, also too tired to backstroke to shore once I see it or away from a passing boat. The best thing is just to float till daybreak comes, conserving my energy for when I'm able to see where I am in the water.

I close my eyes. Sleep would strengthen me further and even seems possible. But if I'm now in the ocean I might float too far out to swim back to land. I'll wind up floating along till a boat discovers me or I starve to death. Starving to death seems the better of those two, but how can I be sure I won't be rescued hours before I'm about to die? Then I'll be rushed to shore and hospitalized till I recover and hounded by reporters and the police who'll want to know what I was doing in the ocean and how come my car was left on the bridge and several types of scientists who'll want to know all the scientific reasons why I was able to survive my jump and stay so long afloat, making it even less likely I'll find, for the time being, the necessary privacy to end my life.

I decide to backstroke to shore as if I'm now in the ocean. That way, if I'm actually in the river and found there before I reach shore, I'll probably be looked at as just a routine near-drowning rather than the person of note I could easily be turned into if I were found floating and dying way out in the ocean. And if I'm in the ocean, then by back-stroking to shore I'll either reach shore or by daybreak be closer to shore than if I didn't swim to it, or be somewhere in the river between its two shores if I now, by some luck, happen to be in the ocean at the river's mouth.

To find land, which is north of the ocean, I have to find the North Star. And to find that star I'll have to first find the Big Dipper, as one of the few things I know about astronomy is that the top star of the ladle of the Big Dipper points to the bright North Star. But to find the Big Dipper I'll have to find both Dippers to see which is the larger of the two, because for all I know the Little Dipper might also have a bright star off the top of its ladle.

I float several complete circles, but all I can come up with is one Dipper. It isn't a very large Dipper either, as I remember the Big Dipper getting in the summer or winter. If it's in the summer that the Big Dipper gets much larger, then the Dipper I'm looking at, and which does have a fairly bright star off its top ladle star, would be the Little Dipper, which I remember gets proportionately larger the same season the Big Dipper does. So if that medium-sized Dipper up there is the Little Dipper in its larger summer size, then the fairly bright star off its top ladle star isn't the North Star.

Instead of swimming on my back to this bright star, and I figure it's a fifty-fifty chance it's the North Star, I take what I consider a sixty-forty chance to reach land and that's to conserve my energy till morning by floating to wherever the currents take me. By not swimming I realize I might be reducing my chances of drowning, since if I backstroke all night I might get so tired that the automatic reflex or survival instinct or whatever it is physiological that's probably respon-sible for my flipping over and also preventing me from swallowing any sea water, might stop functioning. But I float, all the time trying to compensate for the decrease in my drowning chances by keeping a sharp eye on the sky for that second Dipper. If I find it I'll be able to positively identify the North Star, follow it to land, if I'm in the ocean, or up the river and then to land, if I'm now in the river or that part of the ocean the river flows into, and get to my car, if it hasn't been towed because of my illegal parking by the bridge, and drive it off a cliff somewhere or, better yet, into my air-tight garage where I'd keep the motor running and asphyxiate myself, something I would have done instead of jumping if I hadn't concluded beforehand that the surest way of successfully killing myself was to jump from the middle of the south side of that particular bridge.

I float all night without locating the second Dipper. The sun rises and I don't see land. But now knowing where west is, I backstroke till I'm exhausted in the direction of what, because of the moving sun, is growing to be less of a chance of being north or south.

I see a boat and swim toward it, thinking if I get on it I'll pretend to my rescuers that I fell off my own small boat, ask them to let me rest in a private room, as I'm feeling ill and very tired, and in that room find a means to kill myself—a knife, scissors, piece of glass which, if it isn't broken I'll break soundlessly, a sheet to hang myself from a pipe or a sturdy hook overhead if there's one.

I get within a few yards of the boat and yell for help. A man sees me and runs to the front of the boat. The boat slows down, turns around, a rope is thrown to me and I climb onto the deck. They men who help me up speak a language I've never heard. They crowd around me and. pat my back, rub my hair and kiss my cheeks. A man who wears what looks like a captain's hat runs to me from the front of the boat and throws his arms around me, lifts me up and grunts and grins at having rescued me. I thank them in English, but nobody seems to understand me. I shake the captain's hand and place my hands under my chin in a way which in my country means I'm sleepy. He nods and speaks to one of the crew. The young man goes below deck and returns with a tray full of food. "No, no," I say. I yawn and close my eyes dreamily pretend to snore, which have to be sounds and signs understood in every country. The captain says "Ah-oh," and sends the young man below deck again. The man returns with bottles of whiskey and glasses for us all. The captain raises his glass to me and says something and they all slug down their drinks. He puts his hand over my lips to stop me from drinking to the first toast, but the second, fourth and sixth toasts I'm allowed to drink to. Then he escorts me to the pilothouse, points to his wallet and gestures he'd like to see mine. He takes out my driver's license and speaks into a radio set, the only words I understand being my three names roundly mispronounced.

I yawn and stretch my arms and mime a man lying down and plumping a pillow and sticking it under his head and pulling a blanket up to his shoulder and falling asleep, and after I'm finished the captain says "Ah-oh," and sends the young man out of the room. The man returns with dry clothes and sandals. I put them on and sit in a chair and feign dozing off, hoping they'll be as nice as they've been and carry me to an empty room so I can continue my sleep in quiet. I hear shushing sounds from the men. A blanket is tucked around me. After about a half hour I stand and beat my chest to show I'm fully awake and inhale deeply as if I'd like some fresh air and open the door so I can perhaps find a way to kill myself outside the pilothouse. The captain shakes his head and finger as if he understands what I want and I'm going about getting it the wrong way. He opens the door of a water closet, waits outside it till I'm done there, walks me to a sink and makes motions of a man washing his face and hands, and after I've done that, he leads me to the eating area next to the galley and sits me down at a table and orders a man to bring me breakfast.

After breakfast the captain takes me to his cabin. He points proudly to several framed photos on a wall. One is of him and a woman in a wedding dress arm in arm. Another of four beaming children sitting on the grass, with the captain and woman hugging each other behind them. Another inside a frame bordered with black ribbon is of the captain and woman and four children, all much older now, standing behind an elderly seated couple, who are kissing each other's hands.

The captain offers me the top bunk, a brandy, pulls curtains over the portholes, puts on pajamas and gets into the bottom bunk. In the dark he says something in his language, which I suppose means sleep well or pleasant dreams. I say "Goodnight or good morning," and the room is silent. Only the boat's engine can be heard. For now I'll just think and sleep. Later in the day I'll try to find a way to end my life. A sharp fishing knife, since this seems to be a fishing boat, to slash my wrists and bleed to death in an out-of-the-way section of the boat. If there is no such section, I'll jump into the ocean, which I assume we're in, when none of the crew is watching, and preferably in the night. Maybe this part of the ocean doesn't have the salt accumulation the other part had, if that was the reason I couldn't sink. Or else maybe the reflex action or survival instinct or whatever it was that kept me flipping over on my back and stopped me from swallowing the salt water, won't work so well this time or at all.

But suppose one of the crew finds me after I've just slashed my wrists or sees me in the water and jumps in and saves me? Then they'll know I was in the water to commit suicide the first time they found me and they'll lock me in an empty room or brig with my arms bound behind me and take me to wherever the boat's going or to my country, but certainly hand me over to the authorities who deal with people who try to kill themselves. I'll be locked up in jail or a mental institution till the authorities are sure I won't try to kill myself again. That might be for weeks, maybe even years, because who knows what standards are used for releasing potential suicides in the captain's country or even in my own. If these standards are now fair and progressive, how do I know they won't be reversed during the years of my confinement, meaning, for example, that would release me today if let's say I was confined for the same reasons five years ago, might in the future, because of the new harsher standards, get me ten years, fifteen, maybe life.

Or suppose I manage to escape in the water without anyone seeing me and another boat comes along and rescues me no matter how hard I try to avoid it? Or else I get so cold in the water or frightened of being attacked by sharks I see or irrationally fearful of sharks I imagine I see because of the hallucinations that come to someone freezing to death, that I signal that boat and it rescues me and the new captain learns I jumped off another boat and probably a bridge and I'm locked up and later turned over to the authorities. Or else this new captain might not learn of my previous attempts and I again try to commit suicide by slicing my wrists or jumping overboard and I'm discovered with my wrists bleeding, or saved a third time from the water, or else they don't see me in the water but for the same reasons of freezing or sharks real or imagined or something else I'm rescued and locked in a brig till I'm turned over to the authorities who deal with people who try to kill themselves again and again. No matter how progressive the standards are in whatever country I'm taken to, I still won't be released because of my three to four consecutive suicide attempts till the authorities are absolutely sure I won't try to kill myself again. That might mean, in my extreme case, the surgical removal of some part of my brain to prevent me from killing myself. Which would mean living a total hell for the rest of my life without any chance to kill myself though perhaps with occasional dim ideas I should. Or maybe the surgery doesn't work, as my jumping and drowning attempts didn't, and I'll try in some way to kill myself again and this time fail because of my own panic or weakened condition brought about by the surgery. Or else the authorities might detect through some special tests that I'm going to try to commit suicide again, and they'll order the doctors to cut deeper, pump me up with chemicals or alter my genetic code, leaving me as much dead as alive, more dead than alive, but for the rest of my life not alive enough to try to kill myself.

I never should have jumped. I should have worked out my suicide better. I certainly won't try to kill myself on this boat and possible bungle the act, maybe even injuring myself while doing it to the point where even if no one finds out about the attempt I'll end up physically incapable of making another suicide try. What I have to do now is contrive a foolproof excuse as to what I was doing in the water. Another as to why my car was left by the bridge. Others to cover the possibility of my being seen on the bridge or falling into the river. And once the press, public and authorities and scientists are done with me after I get to land, I must resign myself to living a quiet, modest though noticeably content existence till the next time I try to take my life.

A HOME
AWAY FROM
HOME.

Downstairs, his father was watching TV. Ray was in his old room upstairs trying to keep his eyes open and his mind from drifting, as there were still lots of things to take care of before he flew back to California.

His father had to be put in a nursing home, that was the main thing. He was ailing, incontinent, periodically incoherent, in constant need of attention and his condition was only getting worse. It'd be ridiculous taking him to San Diego with him, as Ray's house was too small and he knew they'd be at each other's throats the day they got there.

Ray had looked after him a month now, after a neighbor had phoned and said his father was too feeble to stay by himself anymore. He was tired of changing his father's bed every day, doing all that laundry, emptying and scouring his urinals and setting them strategically around the house, tucking him into bed so he wouldn't fall out, turning him over twice a night and waking, showering, drying and dressing him and for breakfast sticking two eggs in boiling water for three minutes when every day his father demanded they be scrambled in chicken fat or at least fried sunnyside up.

He'd only put off placing him in a home earlier because the old guy had begged, pleaded, "I'd get down on my knees if I could to stop you," blubbered real tears as he said "Just another week. Ray. Wait till the Sunday after next, please." Always the stall. And last night he said "I'll die in a week's time if I'm put in a home. I know it, sure as I'm sitting here watching TV."

Ray went downstairs. "Pop? I'd like to speak to you."

"Speak to me later. Ted Soloman's got a good show on tonight."

"This is more important than Soloman. I've got to be getting back to California."

"When?" He pressed the TV remote in his lap, and the sound went off. "You going back tomorrow? Good. Tonight? Even better. Not that I won't miss you. But it'll be nice having the house to myself again," and he turned the TV sound back on. A comedian was still talking about his freeloading brother-in-law.

"Now this mooch," the comedian said, and his father laughed, "is such a sponge on me that just yesterday..."

"I'm not going back tonight. Things have to be settled first. Number one, we've got to discuss that nursing home."

"What nursing home?" The comedian became a raving mute again, right on a major punch line. "You going to work in one in California?"

"You're going to a home—now, you know that. It just depends when. You've got to realize I teach in San Diego, and by staying here with you I'm losing all my paid sick days for ten years."

"You sick? Take some of my medicine then. Got more than I can use in two lifetimes, those thieving doctors."

"I spoke to the nursing home administrator today. He says they've a waiting list a mile long—that's how well respected and popular this home is."

"Popular because it's cheap."

"It's not cheap. I'll be paying more for you there than I would at Grossinger's Hotel."

"Then send me to Grossinger's. There I'd at least get to meet interesting people and eat good, filling food. And what a choice. You ever see the menu they got up there?"

"The food's supposed to be excellent at this home also. And this Mr. Kramer, the administrator, told me—"

"Better food than at the Concord, Grossinger's has. That's a fact. Been to both resorts, and Grossinger's is without doubt the best. I only wish you were in the resort business."

"So do I. It'd be a nice healthy life."

"Healthy life, my eye. Money. You'd make money. Piles of it, though you'd probably have your first stroke by the time you're forty. And with three college degrees, those guests would give you twice the respect you get from your junior high school delinquents."

"Junior college, and they're good kids."

"Whatever they are, but you won't listen to me. You never have. So what do you say you let me watch some entertainment for a change," and he switched on the TV.

"This Mr. Kramer," Ray said over the ad, "he says he's held your place as long as he can. That if you don't take it in two days, we'll have to give it up. That I'll have to forfeit my thousand dollar deposit besides, and he doesn't see the prospect of another vacancy for three months."

"Somebody'll die before then. Old people always do, especially in nursing homes."

"Listen, it took me a month—will you shut that thing off!" The television went dead. "A month of constant badgering to finally get you this bed, and I don't want to give it up. I promised Mom I'd see you were well taken care of, if anything happened to you, and this is the best way I know how."

His father looked sad, then indignant. "What're you always going on about your poor mom for? Is it you want me to think about death?" Ray shook his head. "Well, you're successful at it, even if before it never enters my mind, close as some people might say I am to it. All I know is that death's my world's worst enemy—but you? It's always on your mind, day and night."

"I didn't know I was upsetting you so much."

"Worse than that, you're a depressing joke. Okay, we both loved her. But she's dead and buried now and we're left here alive with each other, so let her rest in peace."

"Fine. Now let's get back to what we were talking about. The only solution left is for you to try the home for a month. If you don't like it, I'll find you a place more comfortable."

"You're a liar. For you saying you'd fly East just to make me more comfortable? Once I'm in that home, you'll forget me for good, just as you forgot to invite me to California."

"If you mean for a visit, I was always too busy with work. But if you mean the homes there, you wouldn't like them. Who would you know there but me? And you'd leave in a week, it gets so hot."

"You don't want me out there because you don't want me around, period. That's okay. You're no bargain yourself. But I'm willing to admit how bad off my health is, so if that Hudson River home you got lined up for me is so important to you, have them hold my place for two more weeks. If it's not too difficult to understand, I just want a last two weeks alone by myself here and then I'll go."

"Impossible."

"Why? Just leave, that's all. Get Mrs. Longo down the street to look in on me twice a day, and I'll be okay. So I mess up the house a little—big deal. Then, in two weeks, I'll go to the home, but in my own way. No help. Nothing. Just me in a cab with nobody around to make a fuss over me. Then the realty people can sell the house, the junk people can have the furniture, and with the money you get from them you can help pay the nursing home. My own Social Security and the little savings I got should take care of the rest."

"You serious?"

"Serious as anything. Move my bed near the john and I'll be all right. When I want groceries or something, I'll phone and they'll deliver. Is it a deal? Because believe me, it's the only one I'll make."

Next day, Ray called Mr. Kramer and asked if he'd hold his father's place two more weeks.

"Can't," Kramer said. "Those beds are too scarce as it is. And I'm not getting a dime from yours, and I've maybe ten families hounding me to put their fathers here for the rest of their lives. What better offer could you give me than that?"

"My father will also be there for the rest of his life. And he's a very amiable man who won't give your staff the slightest trouble."

"All my patients are amiable, Mr. Barrett, I've no complaints: they're all dolls. I'm sorry, but you have to have that bed occupied by tomorrow, or it's off my reserve list, and also gone is your deposit."

Ray arranged for Mrs. Longo to look in on his father for the next two weeks. That afternoon, after seeing that the refrigerator was full and a bed was set up near the downstairs john, he kissed his father goodbye and trained to the New York town overlooking the Hudson where the nursing home was. He greeted Kramer in his office, said how glad he was to meet him after speaking with him on the phone these last weeks, and asked to see his father's room.

"You want to inspect it before he comes, that it? Right this way, then. It's really heartening to see such a devoted son," and he led Ray to the second floor.

"There it is," Kramer said. "Even from the corridor you can see how much cheerful sun it gets."

Ray walked into the room, said hello to the three patients there, and sat on the one empty bed. He kicked off his shoes, stretched out on the bed, and told Kramer that for the next two weeks he was going to be staying here. "I made a deal. And if you'll hold on for a minute and not get so hysterical, I'm sure I can make you understand."

"So how are things looking to you today?"

Ray opened his eyes. It was Mrs. Beets, an 82-year-old resident from the next room, nudging his shoulder.

"Fine, thanks, and you?"

"Terrible. My palsy's never hurt me worse. You want to see how bad my hand shakes?"

"I was sort of taking a nap, thanks."

"Naps you can always take, but my hand here's shaking more than even yesterday. I think it ought to be photographed for posterity by a TV news show, just so young people can see how fast a human hand can shake."

"Leave him alone, Beetie." It was Mr. Spevack from the next bed. He was 78 and on his back all day, as he'd recently had one of his legs removed because of some rare bone disease.

"I was only showing him my hand."

"Show it to the Marines." After she left, saying she had a painting class to attend anyway, Spevack raised himself a few inches and said "Never saw such a bad palsy case in my six years here. But tell her that once and she'll never leave us alone. Sleep well?"

"So-so."

"Sleep, go on, don't let me bother you. Man's best healer, sleep." And after Ray felt himself dozing off again: "What about your stomach? Acting up again?"

"It was never acting up, Mr. Spevack."

"And the sugar in your blood. Very important, you know."

"It's perfect. On my honor."

"How can you be sure? Check. You always got to check. You take a urine sample this morning?"

"As I told you when I got here, I'm only holding this bed for my father."

"Why doesn't he come visit you, your old man? Shame on him. Son in a dreary place like this and his dad doesn't visit? It's not right. Now, if you were my son…"

"If he was your son," Mr. Jacobs, another patient in the room, said, "you wouldn't have to come visit him. He'd always be in the bed beside you, talking and dreaming of his pretty ladies."

"That'd be nice," Spevack said. "My family always around."

"What you say?" Jacobs said. "Can't understand you. Put your teeth back in your mouth."

"I said it'd be nice having my whole family around. Just like the ancient Chinese."

"What? You reminiscing again? Wake me up when you're through, as I've heard it all." He shut his eyes, and between snores said for them to wake him when the dinner cart rolled down the hall. "I'm starving, though who can sat the garbage they give us here,"

"I like the garbage," Spevack said to Ray. "Doesn't give me heartburn, which Mr. Jacobs should appreciate the value of. He's had four major strokes and is working on number five, because you see the way he sneaks the salt shaker from under his pillow and sprinkles it on his food like it was air?"

"So I push off tonight or a week from now," Jacobs said. "Isn't anyone outside who'd care except maybe the social worker chap who checks up on me here, and him you can have on a silver platter. That's why I sleep so much. When the end comes, let it happen during a beautiful dream."

"He's got nobody," Spevack whispered. "You at least got a father and a good future in San Francisco., right?"

"San Diego."

"Mr. Zysman knows all about California also. Didn't you once live near San Diego, Mr. Zysman?"

"You joshing me?" Zysman said from under the sheet, as he never showed his face. "I was in L.A.—literally nearer the North Pole." He was the youngest official patient in the room—68, and up until a few months ago, if Ray could believe everything he said from under the covers, he'd been a man about town—"A gadabout with two young cuties pinned to my arms, dinner every night at Sardi's or the 21, and still a big-time operator and heavy backer of movies and shows." But his Fifth Avenue apartment caught fire with him in it, most of his body had been burned, and he'd sworn never to let anyone see his body and face except professional people—"Doctors and maybe a few of the prettier nurses, but that's where I draw the line."

"Come on, Zysman," Jacobs said. "Throw off the wrapper and tell us about those gorgeous young ladies in Hollywood."

"I can't. You want to see a body of just scar tissue? And I used to be such a handsome rake. With a full head of hair and a big chest and powerful ticker and still able to get it up when I wanted to with the most exquisite and demanding showgirls. Now look at me."

"I'm looking," Jacobs said, "but all I see is a big lump under the sheet. Come on, show us that thing you used to dazzle your show-girls with."

"Never." He burrowed deeper under the sheets. "Not today, tomorrow, or in a million years."

"We should all live so long," and Jacobs went back to sleep.

"They should get Mr. Zysman a private room or curtains he can pull from under his sheet," Spevack said. "But every time he asks, they say they will, and then you never hear of it again. You should've gotten into one of those nicer homes I hear about in California, Ray. There they treat you like a golden-ager should."

"Food, everybody." It was Mrs. Slomski, one of the nurses' aides. She wasn't the most pleasant woman and seemed to drink on the job, but most of the men liked having her around. She was occasionally exuberant, told raunchy jokes and, for a few extra bucks, snuck in food for them they weren't supposed to have.

"So how are you today, people?" she said.

"Sleeping soundly," Jacobs said.

"And I'm not quite ready to sit up," Zysman said, "so could you please slip my tray through the hole I made in the covers?"

"No chance. Today, good friend, you're seeing the light."

"Lay off the guy," Spevack said. "It's his business if he doesn't want to come out."

"But God's own handiwork is our there for the viewing," she said, pointing to the treeless parking lot and the home's other wing. "Not only that, the doctor ordered it."

"What doctor? Name me names."

"Doctor Gerontology, that's who. He said: 'Mrs. Slomski, I think it'd be beneficial today to have people see Mr. Zysman, and Mr. Zysman to face up to people seeing him,' though naturally I can't tell you the doctor's real name. Professional courtesy and all that." She placed a tray of food in front of Spevack and then tapped Zysman through the sheets. "You coming out, sweetie?"

"If you insist on seeing me," Zysman said, "put a screen around the bed."

"Enough dillydallying, Mr. Zysman. First of all, all the screens are in the new wing. Secondly, I raised six kids and saw to my own dear parents till they were in their nineties, so it's not as if I don't know how to handle people."

"I said to lay off the guy," Spevack said. "He's got a bum heart and everything that goes with it. You continue and I'll report your drinking habits to Kramer's office. You're probably tanked up even now."

"You think they don't know? They encourage it, in fact. Drinking and drug-taking are the two professional hazards that all nursing homes accept from their personnel, because how else could we bear looking at so many crotchety old men? Two."

"Have some pity, Mrs. Slomski," Ray said. "If Mr. Zysman doesn't want to come out, respect that wish."

"You, Mr. Barrett, should think to mind your own business. Talking about disgraces, you're the worst. Occupying a bed that rightfully belongs to a senescent is one of the most despicable crimes against hunan nature a person could do. To me, you don't even exist."

"I'll be occupying it for one more week. Then my father gets it."

"Listen to that lie. You're running away from the world, that's what you're doing. Or maybe writing an exposé for a scandal magazine. We're wise to you—the whole staff. We all think you're a misfit," and she swiveled around to Zysman, said "Three," and flung the sheets off him. When they first saw his scarred body—his gloved hands covering his eyes and a scream so tight in his throat no sound came out—everyone but Mrs. Slomski had to turn away.

"Get a doctor," Jacobs said, "My heart. My heart can't take such a sight."

Mrs. Slomski daintily put the sheets back over Zysman. "Now that wasn't so terrible," she said. "The truth is, you don't look half so bad as you think. It's all in your head. Because nobody here hardly winced except for Mr. Jacobs, and you know what an old fuddy-duddy he is, besides being a great one for a practical joke. Take it from me: what I did was therapy. And now that everyone's seen you, how about coming out on your own accord and eating these nice goodies?"

Zysman didn't move. After about a minute Mrs. Slomski said how her curiosity just seemed to get the better of her at times and lifted the sheets off him though held them up in front of her so nobody else could see him. She let the sheets fall back on him and said "Know what? I think the poor man's dropped dead on us."

Ray phoned his father a week later and said the two weeks were up.

"Yeah? So what do you want me to do?"

"Have Mrs. Longo pack your bags and drive you here so you can take over the bed."

"Look, I don't know if I'm ready to go there yet. Why don't you fly back to California and let me work things out on my own."

"If I leave now, I not only lose the deposit, which is a lot of money to me, but they'll take the bed away from us also, and then where will we be? No place. It'll take a month or two to find you another home or another place in that one. Believe me, if I had the strength, I'd come and get you and, if need be, carry you here myself."

"You feeling sick?" his father said.

"Why do you say that?"

"Your voice. It's weak. And this business about your strength."

"That was just a figure of speech. All I have is a little cold."

"Give me another week. The extra time will do your cold good, and then I'll be there to take over your bed."

Ray didn't tell him about Zysman and that he felt his death had in some way started the decline of his own health. He'd never seen a dead man before, not even in the army. He lost ten pounds in a week and, for unknown reasons to the staff and himself, wasn't able to hold down any solids. And Mr. Lehman, the patient who now had Zysman's bed, was screaming again, something he did half of every day and night, till Ray told himself he'd had it here for good. He threw off his covers, said "Let my dad find his own home if he wants, but I'm getting out," and jumped off the bed, but crumpled to the floor. Nothing was going to stop him from leaving, though, and he stood up but his legs collapsed again, Spevack rang for an aide, who put Ray back to bed. At first Ray thought it was the flu. There was a bug going around the home, though he'd never heard of a flu that made his hands tremor and his up-till-then 20/20 vision so bad that he had to be fitted for thick corrective lenses. When the doctor made his rounds the next day, Ray asked if anything more serious than the flu could be making him feel so sick and weak.

"If you were forty years older," the doctor said, "I'd tell you your illness was simply another common geriatric problem that someone your advanced age had to accept. But you're 33, if your chart is correct. So all I can say is that your condition is caused by some minor, though unique fluke in your metabolism, and that it won't be long before you're feeling as healthy and vigorous as a man your age should."

Few days later, the barber came around for the patients' monthly haircuts. As he snipped Ray's hair, he asked if he wanted any of the gray touched up.

"What gray hair? I've got as many as you've got fingers. Just finish the trim."

"You patients here," the barber said. "You're all as vain as the high school Casanovas I cut," and he held a mirror up to Ray's hair. Not only was it partially gray on the sides and top, but it was thinning in spots and there were lines on his face that a fifty-year-old man didn't have and his neck was beginning to sag. What the hell's going on? he thought. Just a couple of months ago he was so youthful-looking that other teachers on the campus often mistook him for one of their students.

Every day after that, he studied the increasing changes in his face, hair and neck. And every day he phoned his father, who was less inclined than ever to go to the home.

"I've been getting these disappointing reports on you," his father said, his voice more resonant than Ray had heard it in years. "From your Mr. Kramer, who says you're an unruly patient and giving everyone there a hard time. That isn't like you. Place getting you down?"

"I'll say it is. Believe me, I'd be on the next plane to San Diego if it wasn't for this damn flu."

"Flu? Before it was just a cold. You got to take better care of yourself."

"Flu, eye trouble, maybe the early signs of ulcers and a urological disorder—I'm not kidding you, Pop. But once I'm better, I'm getting the hell out of here, with or without my deposit, and then you'll have to find your own nursing home."

"Fine with me, because I'm feeling so good I think I might not need a home after all. Fact is, I'm feeling as good as I ever have in my life. Would you like me to visit you?"

"How? If you use up all your strength getting here, then make sure it's when you're coming to stay."

His father came the next morning, looking better than Ray had seen him in ten years. He'd lost weight, his face was rugged and tan, he had an energetic gait, even his spirits seemed up, and with him was a very pretty young woman in her late twenties or so, whom he introduced to Ray as Ms. Amby Wonder."

"Amby, meet Raymond."

"How do you do?" she said, extending her hand. "Any friend of Barry's is a friend of mine."

"Friend? This is my son. Raymond Barrett—don't you recall my saying?"

"Oh, yeah. Barry did mention you. So, pleased to meet you too, Raymond."

"Who's Barry?"

"Why, your Daddy, most certain. Barry for Barrett. Isn't that what everyone calls him?"

"Who is this woman, Pop—your nurse?"

"You won't believe this, Ray," and he moved closer to the bed so Amby wouldn't hear, "but she's my girl."

"You mean your daughter? Someone not from Momma?"

"Girl like in woman. You don't understand?"

"I'll tell you what I don't understand? I'm looking at you and I almost don't recognize you. You seem several inches taller than when I used to walk you to bed and tuck you in. You got a glow on your face you never had. And your clothes—right out of a stylish men's shop. What've you been doing, taking rejuvenative pills?"

"Sure, why not? Great stuff, those—you want my doc to prescribe you some? Take two after rising and four before bedtime, and whoopee!" and he twirled around twice and squeezed Amby into his body.

"Pop, you're embarrassing me," Ray said, glancing at his roommates.

"That's one of your problems: too self-conscious. But listen, it's not just the pills. It's my new disposition. Mrs. Longo suggested I see a psychiatrist. I said 'What, me, a shrink?—never.' But she harped on it and to get her off my back I went, and in just five sessions he got me, straightened out fine. He said 'Throw away your sadness and walker and get yourself a piece of ass,' and that's what I did. But you?"

"What about me?"

"Your scalp, for one thing." He ran his hand through Ray's hair. "Even I got more than you."

"It's from the flu. But it'll all grow back."

"And that nice red color your hair used to have? That'll grow back too?"

"I've been worrying a lot lately, and a little gray won't kill me."

"I still don't like it. Ailments, balding, your face kind of sickly-looking. I think you should be in a real hospital. Want me to admit you into one?"

"I'll be okay, I said. In a few days I'll be up and out, and then it's goodbye to New York forever."

"I'm glad, because you can really use that warm California sun. As for Amby and me, we'll be getting some sun also. In Antigua. If you're really not feeling that sick, then we'll be flying there tomorrow."

"You crazy? Pills, psychiatrists or whatever therapies you're on— they can't keep you going forever. You're committing suicide. You should take it easy—rest, like me."

"Let him go to Antigua if he wants," Amby said. "His doctors say he's as healthy as a horse, and you should be happy to see him having fun."

"Don't give me that claptrap, young lady," Ray said. "I don't know how much dough you think he has and how much of it you're planning to finagle out of him, but I think you should know first that he has a very serious heart condition."

"Heart condition?" and she laughed.

"And diabetes, liver trouble, glaucoma, plus a half dozen other equally enfeebling afflictions. He's an old man, if you must know the truth," and Amby kept on laughing, his father coining in with her. "His doctors said long ago that a person in his condition can barely stand the strain of walking, less any great globe-trotting with an adventurous young woman—a tramp."

"Now hold off, Ray. Amby's a fine young lady."

"She's an insidious conniving tramp who's going to ruin your life. So get her out of here—I don't want to look at her anymore."

His father took Ray's hand and shooed Amby out of the room. "Calm yourself, Ray. You're upset and tired, besides not feeling too well. We're only going for a week. When we get back, we'll come see you again, okay?"

"You won't find me here."

"Then in San Diego we'll come visit—but just take care."

"Don't bother visiting with her. I won't have you both out there, and not because I don't have room."

"Anything you say. But relax, son." He put his fingers on Ray's temples, as he used to do when Ray was a boy and had a headache, and rubbed them so gently that Ray soon felt himself falling asleep. His father whispered goodbye to the other patients and left the room.

"Dad?" Ray said a minute later, jolted out of sleep by a pain in his side. He dragged himself out of bed to the window, and opened it. "Dad?" he shouted to his father hustling through the parking lot with Amby. "You're being used, fleeced, swindled by a pro. You've got to get out of her scheme fast before she takes you for every dime you have. Now you're coming to San Diego with me when I'm feeling better, you hear? We'll take long ocean walks, sit out in the sun, talk over good times, go out for nourishing dinners, and see all the better TV shows together. We'll take good care of each other is what I'm saying, and I'm going to have to insist on your coming, you hear? I said, do you hear? Goddamnit, Dad, you get so headstrong where you can't even listen to me anymore?"

PALE CHEEKS

OF A

BUTCHER'S BOY.

Max Silverman figured he had about the softest job in the Bronx: assistant manager of a large five-and-dime on Jerome Avenue, under the El tracks. Most of the administrative duties were handled by Mr. Winston, the manager for fifteen years, so all Max had to do was roam the aisles to prevent kids from pocketing merchandise, relay Mr. Winston's orders to other workers and fill in for him when he wasn't there, and do a little bookkeeping and stock-control work at his mostly empty desk in his windowless office in the back of the store.

Then another recession came, this one, as the newspapers put it, the worst economic downturn since the end of the Korean War. In a month, four salesgirls were fired on the spot. A few days later, after the President had said on TV that all reports of a serious recession were grossly exaggerated, Mr. Winston gave Max a check for his salary and three weeks' severance pay, told him how much the company appreciated his efforts to raise the store's sales volume during this unfortunate reversal, and regretfully said goodbye.

The two times Max had been laid off in the past, he blamed it on the ineptitude of government and the greediness of big business moguls and stockbrokers and the like, whom he pictured smoking fat cigars and playing cards beside the pool at some swanky West Indian hotel, while he and other victims of their bungling, and schemes were being tossed into the streets. But this time he didn't feel so had. The way he looked at it, he hadn't been fired as a common laborer, which is all he was in the past, but that part of management which had to be sacrificed for the economy to survive. And then his mother, who was planning an early semi-retirement for his butcher-father on

Max's future earnings, took it lightly—even lifted his spirits a bit by saying she'd heard he had an A-1 reputation as assistant manager and would be sure to get a similar position sooner than he thought. But after a month of job-hunting and Wednesday morning visits to the State Unemployment Office, where the lines each week seemed to get longer with men much better dressed and groomed than he and who looked much shrewder and so were more likely to find work, he became depressed, lost what confidence he had, and once more was blaming his being unemployed on the President, Congress, the New York Stock Exchange and top executives of huge corporations and businesses.

A week later, after having no luck at three employment agencies before it was even ten o'clock, he became so disgusted with everything that he decided to call it a day. He took the subway back to Burnside Avenue, waved to his mother as he hurried through the apartment, and shut his bedroom door behind him. Putting on his pajamas and yelling to her that nothing was wrong, when she asked through the door, he got into bed and soon fell asleep, a cigarette, which he'd taken only a few drags from, still lit in the ashtray on his night table.

That afternoon, his mother braved a look into his room. Seeing him sleeping soundly, she pushed his door till it banged against the wall. Max rustled around, opened one eye and peered at his mother, who was mumbling to herself and fidgeting with a dish towel.

"Max?" she said, bending over him.

"What?" he said drowsily.

"Max!"

"What, for Christ's sake?"

"You sick or something, lying there? Before, you said you wasn't, but your cheeks have lost all their rosiness."

"I'm fine, Ma, thanks."

"If you're fine, why you lying in bed like you're sick?"

"I don't know. I'm tired. And frustration, not finding work. I thought maybe my luck will change with a good night's sleep."

"Night? Three in the afternoon is night?"

"What's it, three?" he said, shutting his eyes and trying to doze off.

"What then, midnight?" She pulled a wristwatch out of her housecoat pocket and dandled it above his eyes. "You see what time it is?" nudging him till he opened his eyes and looked at the watch.

"Yeah, three."

"Three it is. That's my point. So what are you doing still lying in bed?"

"Don't worry about it, please," he said, getting up. "It's just a day's rest. Now if you don't mind?" He grabbed her elbow and escorted her out of the room.

"You'll end up a no-good loafer if you make sleeping in the day a habit," she said from behind the door. "Get a job, why don't you. Only then can you sleep; then you'll have the right to. Max? You taking in what I'm saying?"

That evening Mr. Silverman was unmoved by his wife's story of their son's behavior. "Things are tough all over," he said, opening a beer. "A lot of good intelligent workers are unemployed now—good young butchers in the market, even—so don't be concerned if he's discouraged for a day or so. It's only natural."

"But why should he get discouraged? I mean, five or six jobs he could've got today if he looked hard enough. But no, he's in his room all day doing what? Sleeping off all his chances, that's what."

He lifted, his shoulders and murmured that he supposed she was right. "Your worrying, though's, not going to hold up dinner, I hope. At the table we'll have a little talk with him."

She summoned Max to dinner a half hour later, but he said through the door he was too tired. She immediately got worried, because for Max to miss or pass up one of her Thursday meatloaf dinners meant he was either working late or drastically ill. She went into his room, turned on the ceiling light, and felt his head.

"Ma, I told you already, I'm just sleepy."

"Sleepy? You got how many hours sleep today and you're still sleepy? No, something's wrong with you; I know."

He moved his head away from her hand and shut his eyes.

"Please, Max, I got meatloaf on the table, so come eat it while it's hot."

"I'll eat it cold tomorrow. I always liked it better in a sandwich with ketchup on it."

"You'll eat nothing cold tomorrow. I'll throw it out the window before I give it to you that way. Now I'm not kidding, Max. Supper's ready and you're holding up your father."

He propped himself up on his elbows and stared at her. She'd seen this pose of his before and nervously grabbed his flannel pants off the chair and tried ironing the cuffs between her thumb and forefinger.

"Here," she said, holding out his pants.

"Here, nothing," and he slapped at the swaying pants in front of him. "I'm warning you, Ma. If you don't leave the room I'm going to a hotel for the night and tomorrow find my own apartment.

She left the room, saying, as she closed the door, that she'd make two meatloaf sandwiches for him tomorrow when he looked for a job—just as you like then, with lettuce and ketchup and a little sprinkle of salt."

Next morning Mr. Silverman tiptoed into Max's room, his old underpants hanging loosely at the crotch. He carried the first section of the *Times*, which he'd just finished reading during his usual half-hour stint on the john. He said "Jesus, how do you stand it; it's so cold in here," and shut The window. He shook Max's shoulder, and when he heard his awakening grunts, asked if he wanted to ride downtown in the subway with him.

"No thanks, Pop," Max said, his voice muffled in the pillow.

"You still feeling sick?"

"I was never sick."

"Then maybe you should get up. It's quarter of eight."

"Quarter to eight?"

"Sure, quarter of eight. Be smart and get to the agencies first. That's what I used to do when I looked for work."

"Friday's the worst day for looking...you know that. Besides, it'd be silly going downtown now when I got an interview in Brooklyn at noon."

"In Brooklyn?" his father said, chattering from the cold. "You'd travel all the way out there for a job?"

"At this stage of the game I'd take one in Newark. You should get dressed. You're freezing your ears off."

"But in Brooklyn it'll mean a good hour and a half ride from here. That's before seven you'll be getting up if the job starts at nine."

"So I'll get my own apartment there—I don't know. I'll tell you about it later tonight."

"But why should you pay rent when you got your own room and plenty of food here? Look, don't get desperate, all right? A good job you'll get Monday, so just sleep your worries away today."

When he returned to his room, his wife asked if Max was getting up.

"He still looks a little sick," he said. "Why don't we let him sleep?"

She jumped out of bed and went to Max's room.

"Max!" she said, throwing open the door.

"Yeah, Ma?" he said, his head under the covers.

"I'm not fooling around now. Max. Get up this instant. You got to get a job."

"Like I told Dad, Ma, I'll go later—in an hour or so."

"You'll go now!"

"I said later. Now, please?"

She threw the covers off him. He was curled up on the far side of the bed, one hand under his head.

"Max, you was never a loafer. I'm surprised, really surprised," and stormed out of the room, leaving the door wide open. He got up, shut the door, opened the window a few inches, picked the covers off the floor and went back to bed.

The only movement he made from his room that day, besides going to the john a few times, was a quick trip to the kitchen for a few slices of seeded rye and a knife and an unopened Velveeta cheese, and another trip into the living room two hours later for a book of *Reader's Digest* novel condensations, which he'd purchased for ten cents and a coupon through the mail. His mother, who always cleaned the apartment thoroughly on Mondays and gave it a good going-over on Wednesdays and Saturdays, twice opened his door by bumping it with her vacuum cleaner as she turned the doorknob. Both times, after saying "Excuse me, that was an accident," and peeping into his dark cigarette-smelling room, she slammed the door shut and continued vacuuming the hall outside his room another ten minutes.

Max admitted to himself he was never that reflective a person, but began thinking a lot as to why he refused to leave his room other than for the toilet and snacks. First, thinking about the psych course he took in his second and last year at college, he blamed it on his mother's strong pushy nature and his father being kind of meek and browbeaten and such. But that was a lot of nonsense, he thought, No matter what he felt about them, he still couldn't tic staying in bed to all that Freudian crap he'd read in his textbook and heard long discussions of in the City College cafeteria. So next was that he did it because he did it and that was that. He liked this one better because it fitted his concept or image or something about himself in the way he made decisions; quickly and forcefully, without time-wasting thought or going back on it. Anyway, that was good enough for now, and he opened the *Readers Digest* book, lit a cigarette, and knocked off a condensation of Uris's *Exodus*.

That evening his Uncle Barney, the sage and Ann Landers of the family, and knocked on Max's door. He walked in when he didn't get a response, and sat on the bed.

"Is it all right if we talk nicely—with the light, too?" Barney said; turning on the night table light and squeezing Max's foot through the covers.

"The folks call you in?"

"Stopped by on my own. Just wanted to see how my favorite nephew's doing."

"What time is it?"

"Time for supper, kid, so what do you say? Though we were only dropping by, your Aunt Dee and me are thinking of gracing this happy household by eating over tonight."

Max turned to the wall-side of the bed. "See you at the table then, okay?"

"Come on, kid, what's happened to you? You used to be such a go-getter—a real driver for the almighty buck. Believe me, I know what I mean when I say if you don't get up now you'll be chained to this bed like an addict."

"I can't right now, Uncle Barney—just try and understand."

"What do you mean 'can't'?"

"Just that something around me—a voice, even—is telling me to stay here another night. Then when I leave, the whole world will open up for me. Not exactly that, but something like it."

"Huh? What's with this voice stuff? Listen, the only things you'll get staying here so long are bed sores and a free ticket to the loonybin. I've always done right by you in the past, haven't I? So I'm telling you now, kid: get up."

Max rolled over to face him and said "Will you just get out of here already and let me sleep? And shut the light before you go, because you turned it on when I didn't ask you to."

"Okay, okay, you're going off your rocker and I won't waste my breath on you anymore; okay," and he shut off the light, left the room and shut the door. Max then heard from the hallway his mother carrying on the way she did over the newly dead: "Oh my God; what am I going to do? Oh my God."

He wasn't bothered much after that. Twice his father tried to make contact through the door, with a couple of taps and then some mumbling about Max's health and appetite and did he need anything?

Max answered the first time with a grunt that he was doing fine, don't worry. But the second time, feeling sorry for his father, he said that he'd see him the next morning when they'd go to the Bronx Botanical Gardens, something Max had been promising to do with him the past ten years. The Gardens were only a twenty-minute ride across the Bronx, but neither of them had ever been there.

Saturday morning his parents closed their eyes or turned away each time Max went to the bathroom or sneaked into the kitchen for a snack or cup of coffee. On Sunday Max dry-shaved himself in bed, leaving the start of his first mustache. Later that day, while lying in bed, cigarette smoke rising from the ashtray balanced on his chest, he concluded that he was no longer staying in bed for any just-plain-old-Max reasons, as he'd believed, but as a one-man protest against the lousy economic conditions in this country. He saw himself staying here for weeks—a sort of fast-unto-death that Gandhi threatened the British with in India—the word getting out to neighbors and friends and through them to the newspapers, who'd write him up as someone protesting against heavy unemployment and the so-called reputable captains of industry who caused it. In time, others would join his protest—thousand upon thousands of blue- and white-collar workers staying in bed, eventually causing many big businesses and corporations and factories to close down. Supermarkets, department stores, movie theaters would suffer. *Time* and *Newsweek* would devote cover stories to the news; TV would run half-hour documentaries on it. It would an end up with a meeting of the frightened big guns of the financial and industrial world, who'd end the recession and after that work together with the federal and state governments to building a new and sounder economy. Sometime after, before the eyes and ears of the nation, they'd credit him with having alerted them to how serious the situation was and for having driven some sense into their heads. Because of the notoriety he'd get, he'd soon have a top executive job, with a huge private office and plenty of pretty secretaries within reach, and become a known force in the business world. All these things were up for grabs for guys like himself: "The Takeover Generation" that *Look* devoted an entire issue to; the young entrepreneurs who were on the way up by the use of their wits and initiative and because of their courageous, dynamic actions.

He awoke an hour later. At his feet were the *Times* and *Tribune* with the Help-Wanted sections on top, which his mother must have put there during his last nap. He kicked them to the floor. "Who needs you?" he said, and shut his eyes and tried to get back to sleep.

Monday, Mr. Silverman left for work, calling Max, through his bedroom door, a hopeless mental case and wishing on him a Multitude of the worst Yiddish curses. Mrs. Silverman, too distraught to say anything, went about her morning household chores. But around noon, with all the rooms dusted, carpets swept, scrubbed and mopped with pine disinfectant, she could no longer restrain herself. She barged into his room with a shriek, waking him.

"Get up, you bum, before I call the police."

He pulled the covers over his head. His mouth felt parched and sour. He'd brush his teeth soon as she gave up and left the room.

"I said to get up, you dirty loafer, or I swear I'll throw you out of the house myself. Don't think I can't, because I can. Max, do you hear me? Get up this instant."

He turned over on his back, sneezed, said "Excuse me," and reached to the night table for a cigarette and matchbook. He lit up, shut his eyes, and exhaled.

"All right," she said, dusting the top of his dresser with her hand, "you're not going to listen to ne, so I'll try this. How long you going to make us suffer this way?"

"Until the recession ends."

"What do you mean 'the recession ends'? Talk sense."

"Okay; I just don't know."

"You just don't know what? I'm listening. I'm your mother and it's natural I'm interested in what you have to say."

"I'm telling you, I don't know. But something wonderful will come from all this, something that'll benefit all of us. You might not realize it yet, but you've got a great social reformer on your hands."

"Does that mean you're not leaving today?"

"I don't think so."

"Tomorrow?"

"Like I say: I'm not quite sure."

"You mean never, then, don't you?"

"I don't know; it's difficult to judge."

"Well, just tell me so I'll know better than to have my friends and family come over and see our disgrace. Next week? A month? A year? Just so I know, Max."

"Maybe."

"Maybe what? Listen, you're thirty, so act like thirty. For fifteen years you felt like working. I did too before I had you, and your father for his whole life. So why all of a sudden you feel you can't get up and get work? Believe me, if that's what you really think, then all I can say is you're a freeloader and a bum."

"I'm sorry, honestly I am." He took another drag and stared at the ceiling fixture.

"That smoke," she said, waving her hands in front of her. "You're blowing it in my face, you know?"

"I wasn't trying to. I was blowing it towards the door, but maybe a breeze caught it."

"Breeze, nothing. Stop smoking so early and get up. Enough's enough."

He watched her stack his coins into neat columns on the dresser, then pick up the newspapers off the floor and fold them.

"Your father wanted to know where the papers were this morning. He hadn't finished them. He paid for them, you know."

"You probably put them there yourself when I was asleep."

"There?" she said, pointing down. "On the floor like a slob?"

"Anyway, tell him there's nothing in them, so he didn't miss anything."

"That's for him to decide. For you, sure you say there's nothing, but there's plenty in them, plenty of good jobs."

She put the newspapers on a chair and began carpetsweeping the small round rug in the middle of the floor.

He felt hungry, but couldn't leave his bed while his mother was still in the room. She'd yell that if he could get up for his stomach then he could just as easily get up to make money for his food. He decided to light another cigarette. There was almost no pleasure in the world like smoking, he thought. It always took his mind off anything unpleasant. He might even be able to drive her out of the room if he blew more smoke in her direction. He reached over to the night table and fingered blindly through the cigarette pack. It was empty. He propped himself up and opened the night table drawers, but there were no cigarettes there, either.

"You take my butts, Ma?"

"Why, did you ever see me smoke?" she said, continuing to sweep the rug. "You do, like there's no tomorrow."

"But I'm sure I had them there; a couple of packs."

"News to me."

It was useless trying to talk to her. Always the same line; never a decent, understanding word. He got out of bed and rummaged through the top dresser drawer, but all he found there were three mangled packs, an empty carton, and some matchbooks. Next he searched all the kitchen shelves, where his mother usually hid the cigarettes she'd stolen from him when she thought he was smoking too much. She never dumped them, though, since she hated throwing out anything that at one time cost money and could still be used.

He sat down at the kitchen table with a coffee and prune Danish in front of him. He figured he'd looked at every possible hiding place, even picking through the garbage can under the sink on the theory that she'd really lost control of herself today and thrown away the cigarettes she'd taken from him. But wasn't he acting like a perfect idiot? Because how long had it been since his last smoke? Twenty minutes? So what the hell was he getting so worked up about? All he had to do was think the situation out, just as he had when something unusual came up at the store that Mr. Winston wasn't around to handle, and the crisis would be over.

He called Mr. Shalita at the candy store, two blocks away, asking him—practically commanding him in his new, deep authoritative voice—to send over a carton of Camels, a cold Pepsi, bag of pretzels and the latest racing car magazines. Mr. Shalita said he couldn't make deliveries till the boy got out of school—some three hours from now. Max said "That's sure a strange way of conducting a business," and politely canceled the order. He next called the one neighborhood supermarket, and when the person who answered said she couldn't take phone orders unless the customer had a charge account, he slammed down the receiver. His mother, he saw was now in the living room, grinning into the mirror she was wiping with some liquid from a spray bottle, though the mirror was as clean as anyone could get it.

"Hey, Ma," he said, "you know the name of that grocery on Tremont?"

"What do you need in a grocery we haven't got here?"

"Come on, you know the one. The store next to the Spotless Cleaners."

"Spotless, I know, but no other store next to it."

She knew all right. Maybe if he asked her nicely she'd order the carton from Mr. Shalita. That old guy would do anything for her, even lock the store and deliver the goods himself. But she'd only refuse and call him a nicotine addict and cigarette fiend. Forget the cigarettes and just read and sleep the next three hours, then phone Mr. Shalita and have him send the kid over with the order.

He went back to bed. That was the way to work things out: easily, decisively, using the brains God blessed you with. One day he'd look back at all this and have a fat laugh over it. He'd be sitting at some fancy poker table with a few business friends, and after winning a good-sized pot he'd tell them about this crazy smoking incident. It'd be a story to joke about with people who had the minds and experiences to understand. Didn't Einstein laugh with the world about the time he flunked an important math exam? And what about Bernard Baruch, who bundled an easy stock market deal just a short time before he made off with his first million-dollar killing. Both of them laughing up a storm about the worst failure to hit them before they decided to really become somebody. "And the same with me with my cigarette urge" he'd tell his cronies, as he picked up his second fantastic pot with four-of-a-kind—all kings.

He got out of bed a half-hour later and quickly showered, shaved, cleaned his teeth and brushed his hair. By the time he got back to his room the floor had been mopped, the bed stripped, his two pillows hung over the fire escape railing, and the place felt like an icebox from the airing his mother was giving it. All of it to create a symbol of sorts, he realized, but he could care less; he was only interested in dressing and collecting his wallet and change off the dresser and getting to the cigarette machine at the corner luncheonette. He stuck a tie and a waxpaper-wrapped schnecken and paper napkin into his overcoat pocket and, eyes down, walked past his mother as he left the apartment. He didn't want her pumping him for answers he was in no mood to give. When he reached the second-story landing, she yelled down the stairway from two flights above "Max? I'm having your father bring home a silver-tip roast for supper, so you'll try and be back by six?" He kept walking, when he got to the ground floor, she yelled "And don't bring home the *Post* tonight, even if you buy it. Your father always gets it, and you know how he hates seeing two of the same papers in the House. Max, you still there? If you are: best of luck."

UP
AND
DOWN
THE
DROSSELGASSE.

"Must we go now?"

The man nodded.

"Since I'd much rather stay here."

"So, stay."

"Now please be sweet to me, Hank."

"So, come. Because what do you want me to say? 'Of course, my dear, I want you to accompany me. What would a jaunt be without you?'"

"It's just I've always loved these small outdoorsy cafés—having nothing but strong black coffee, and maybe a dessert, and soaking up the afternoon sun. Oh, well." She stood up, brushing crumbs off her lap. "Look!" and she pointed to the cobblestone street when a motorbike drove past—a goggled priest arched over the handlebars like a racer, an attaché case strapped to the luggage rack.

But Hank was fingering through a palmful of several countries' coins.

"Wouldn't it be wonderful if we could transfer this exact setting to the heart of New York?"

"You'd still have lunch at the Brasserie three to four times a week."

"No, I wouldn't. We've nothing as quiet and quaint as this."

"Jes hold it there for a second, ladies and gents," and he put his hand over his eyes and waved the other in front of him: his tent-show swami routine. "I see a woman seated...at a restaurant table...why, it's Mrs. Patricia Lincoln Kahn. Dressed to her pretty eye teeth in authentic suede and fur and now blotting her lips on a cloth napkin after consuming a five-dollar omelet."

"I don't think they run them that high."

"Then a five-dollar cottage cheese salad topped with an enormous prune. Now there's a mouth-watering image if I ever created one. Enough. Bill's paid with all sorts of denominations. What the hell, it's one continent and they're among friends. Let's go."

"Which direction?"

"Let's see... Left, then another left to the river street and after a while through this cruddy old alley, which the guidebook refers to as ancient and historic. Till we get to the Drosselgasse—that main drag before, where we hit the third bierkellar up the street. I think it's called the *die* or *das* Rheinlander or something."

"Very original, since we're practically floating on that river."

"The Chinese have been known as ingenious though unfathomable people for ages."

"The Chinese?" Her eyes were drawn to a third-floor window across the street, where someone's bare arms reached through the curtains and drew in the shutters. She envied the woman, who she figured was about to settle down for a nap after a heavy German lunch. She turned to Hank to tell him she'd like to go back to the hotel and take a nap, and found him staring at her.

"Spying Nazi bastard," he said.

"Excuse me?" She pretended to look for someone behind her.

"That man you were looking at in the window there. You know what I mean," when she continued looking at him skeptically—"all of them, then. Spying's part of their precious Aryan blood."

"Nonsense. You're just going through some Jewish paranoia phase. Besides, that man up there was a woman."

"The women were just as bad. Because did I ever describe the Dutch museum photo of these German women laughing when a Kraut soldier pulled a rabbi's beard?"

"Only a few times. But why this sudden rage at the Germans? Before, you always thought they were industrious and intellectual. And then you never even had a third to tenth cousin in Europe during the war. Both sides of your family have been in the States so long they're almost considered Yankees. What nonsense."

"Anti-Semite."

"Oh, please—you're really speaking to the right person. Maybe my folks a little, and certainly my grandparents, but don't look at me."

"*Shiksa* anti-Semite. I still say it: you all are. But you can't change. It's in your precious Aryan blood also."

"Okay. Did you leave a good tip? The waiter gave us an extra free coffee, and they usually charge for that."

He snapped two more marks to the table. The waiter came up, took the check and the money off the table and said "*Danke schön*," bobbing his head and smiling a bit too generously as most German waiters tend to do, Hank thought. He really couldn't take their mannerisms or food or any of their customs and places of interest for that matter. After two months of touring Europe he didn't know why they had to end up here, their first German town after boarding the excursion boat in Holland for a trip along the Rhine. Though he'd sworn to his father, who still grumbled every time he saw a German car and who couldn't even stomach clicking the shutter of Hank's Zeiss-Ikon, that he'd never set foot in Germany. It was one of his father's stipulations for giving him the money to travel. The other was that on his return to New York he join his father's law practice.

"Actually, I like Germany," Pat was saying when they left the café and headed toward the river. "No matter what they did in the war or what your family thinks of them, this country's still pretty great."

"What stereotypical reasons do you have for this sudden national crush? Bach? Beethoven? The great Dürer? Or maybe even the songs of the Rhinemaidens."

"For one thing, they've been nicer to us here—just shopkeepers, waiters, our hotel clerk, even people with directions on the street—than in any country we've been to."

"If you mean they've been sycophantic and obsequious, which someone less clever than you might take for graciousness and help-fulness—then I say yes, I agree with you, you're right."

"Oh, stop the nonsense."

"And please stop misusing that inadequate word."

"But it is nonsense. I mean, try forming an opinion of your own once in a while, instead of sounding like Papa Kahn and your brother Niamey."

He looked away. Oh Jesus, she thought, he's going to start pouting again. "I'm sorry. Hank. Let's forget it."

"Excuse me?" he said as if he hadn't heard her. He'd stopped at a stone parapet that overlooked the river, and was watching a crowd of people walking and cycling off the excursion boat.

"Could you believe the tourists still flocking here like that?" she said, curling her arm around his. "Boy, are they ever in for a surprise."

"Maybe they all live here."

"Nobody lives in this dull town but waiters and bosomy barmaids."

"Then possibly because Rudesheim's a famous resort town. Say, now that can be the answer."

"Famous? Since when? I never knew it existed till that Thomas Cook man slipped it into our itinerary."

"And I promise never to reveal a word of that confession," and he fingered a cross over his chest. "Now what do you say?" and he pointed to the street that would lead them to the center of town.

"Let's go back to our room. We've had plenty to drink already, and I can see you're itching to get loaded again before dinner."

"Just one more sip with me and we'll go back to the hotel."

"I'll drink with you later—during dinner, and I'm serious now."

"Then maybe you better drink alone at dinner," and he took her arm out of his and walked away from her.

She caught up with him, and without saying a word they went through an alley till it opened up on the Drosselgasse, a narrow sloping street glutted with bierkellars and souvenir stands and coffee and pastry shops. She had a hard time keeping up with him, as he was anxious to get to the place he found last night in his solitary bar crawl through this section of town. Approaching the door of the Rheinlander, he stepped aside, extended his hand and bowed like one of the more fawning waiters they'd had, and let her pass him and descend the stairs. When she reached the bottom he galloped downstairs two steps at a time, tripping on the last step and falling.

"You hurt?" she said, helping him up.

"It's okay. I landed on my good shoulder for a change. It's these damn stone steps all the old bars seem to have."

"That's the third time you've fallen like that in a week, you know."

"I wish you'd stick to counting drinks like other wives."

"If you want," and she laughed, brushed some dirt off his sleeves and reached up on her toes to kiss his cheek. Then she took his hand and led him into the bar.

A large party of German men and women were drinking and toasting and singing what sounded like folk songs at a long oak table. Pat liked the looks of the place—it was low, snug and woody—and wanted to sit near the group and possibly strike up a conversation with then and be invited to sing along. She had a good soprano voice, perhaps too overtrained by a private voice teacher while she was in college, but she'd still managed to get into a folk-singing trio in one of the coffee houses off campus and make some money at it. But Hank tugged on her arm, just as she was about to suggest where they sit, and made his way to a two-seater at the other end of the room—a fairly dark spot tables away from any other customers. He studied the wine list. When the waiter came over and asked in German if they were ready, he ordered the most expensive bottle of the local wine. "*Und macht* sure it's *natur, jawohl?*"

"*Jawohl,*" the waiter said.

"*Und kanst du* try *und* keep doze people *über* der *von singen* like *katzen und hunds?*"

The waiter, folding up the wine list and standing it back up on the table, smiled and shrugged that he could only try and do his best.

"*Jawohl, mein kapitan*, you should've said," Hank said.

The waiter was still smiling at them as he left their table.

"You're always there with the quips," Pat said, "—the real *bon mots.*"

"Would you have preferred my jumping up and clicking my heels at him?"

"Now who's giving out with the stereotyped impressions? Officious and snotty as a lot of them are reputed to be, although I haven't seen it, they weren't all Nazis. Like the one who's waiting on us. I mean, what is he, nineteen, twenty?—so he was barely five when the war started. And this is his country we're in. So if you still insist on deriding him, let's go back to France or somewhere and knock the Germans from there."

"*Jawohl, meine* darlink," and he gave her the *seig-heil* salute.

"Cut that out, Hank. That's offensive to most people here. What makes it worse, it's not even funny."

"That's because you never understood my type of humor."

"Oh, I understand it all right. It's not like it's far out or subtle, you know."

"Just blow it out."

"No. I take it back. You just proved your humor is subtle."

He was going to answer her, when the waiter brought the wine, twisted the bottle around so Hank could see the label, wrapped a towel around it and drew the cork, and poured a little wine into his glass. Then he stepped back and stood at Hank's right, looking at him.

"I believe you're supposed to sniff and sip it and then tell him it's delicious."

"You know German better than me; you're the one with the Kraut background. Tell him to forget the stupid amenities and fill up my glass. I want to shoot the first one down, not pick at it like some fag."

"You're awful."

"Sure I'm awful. Because I'm in this awful country and it's making me feel awful that I'm here."

She smiled at the waiter and said "*Mein mann hier wisht das sie funen seine Glas voll, bitte.*"

"Ah-ha," the waiter said, smiling as he refilled Hank's glass and then Pat's. "*Das* is *viel besser*, is not?"

"*Mucho besser.*" Hank said. He slapped the table and said in a Texas drawl "Here's mud in your eye, slowpoke," and drank down the wine and held out his glass for the waiter to refill it.

"Oh, Jesus," Pat said, laughing to herself and looking away.

The waiter refilled Hank's glass. "Is good, *der Wein, nicht wahr?*"

"Hank gulped down this glass also, then loudly smacked his lips. "To tell you the dang-blasted God-awful truth, pardner, this here's just 'trocious wine—just disgusting stuff, but what could I do? I was thirsty."

The waiter beamed. "Thank you, sir, lady. *Vielen dank.*"

"Now tell him to beat it."

"You know he can understand some English, Hank."

"That was English? Come on, tell him to get lost. His breath's bad."

"*Mein mann sagt vielen dank auch,*" she said, trying to keep her weak smile from appearing apologetic. "*Sie sind sehr gut zu uns und wir...wir*...appreciate it. *Versteht* appreciate? *Von der herz,*" and she touched her blouse on the left side.

"Yes," the waiter said, looking perplexed but still smiling. "*Das herz.*" pointing to his chest. "I understand the heart very much. Thank you. Americans are very kind." He refilled Hank's glass and moved back till he stood by the bus table, holding the bottle and ready to pour the moment one of their glasses needed refilling.

"I thought I told you to tell him to beat it."

"He only means well. He's not busy, so I guess he thought he'd give us a little extra service."

"But he should know better than to hover around our table— making us feel uncomfortable with his lousy groveling act."

"I don't feel uncomfortable. And I see no reason for you getting upset."

"Are you going to tell him or do I have to in my own way?"

"Not another commotion—please. It's not as if he should vanish because we're acting like a couple of starry-eyed honeymooners."

He stood up, signaled for the waiter, and when the man eagerly strode over, grabbed him by his jacket's white lapels and said "So, you *versteht* English? Then beat it!" The waiter patted Hank's back as if telling him to forget whatever was bothering him, and pulling free of Hank's hold, leaned over to refill Pat's glass and pour a little wine into Hank's filled glass. When he stood erect again, Hank swung at his face but missed and fell across the table, his arm knocking both glasses to the floor when he rolled onto his chair and then toppled over with it. At the other end of the room the German party toasted to one another and began singing a new song—a loud cheerful one. Pat wanted to scream, to create total silence with her scream, but covered her shaking lips with her fist and bent down and pushed some broken glass away from Hank's hand as he struggled to get to his feet, the waiter holding him under an arm. When he made it to one knee and was resting in that position, Pat took the billfold from his inside jacket pocket, gave the waiter a ten-dollar bill and said to him "I am very sorry. *Sehr. Mein mann*...he meant no harm. Please understand. *Bitte versteht. Es tut mir leid*. Both of us. *Es tut mir leid*."

The waiter smiled at her and pocketed the money without looking at it. Then with the help of another waiter who'd just come running over, they lifted Hank into a sitting position and slid a chair under him. The singing had stopped, and when Pat looked over she saw most of the group looking at them.

"Sit up," she said.

"I'm sitting."

"You've really done it this time. My poor boy of a husband's really gone berserk and done it."

"Stop with the soap opera crap and help me get the hell out of here. I slugged down that rotten wine too fast and it went to my head."

"You'd never act like this in the States, You've acted like a boor often enough, but you'd never go this far because you know you'd never get away with it there."

"Well, I had good reason here. You saw what happened. Freaking creep wouldn't leave us alone. And you just wait till I get back to the States. Europe this time has given me renewed vigor, new balls."

"I wish we were going back tomorrow."

"What's the matter, Patty Pooh, aren't you having fun?" He rubbed her cheek affectionately and scanned the room, avoiding the embarrassed glances of their waiter and the glares of the older waiter, who'd raced back from the kitchen with a beer stein of coffee, which he handed to Hank.

"How much did it take to pacify the kid?" Hank said.

"Drink up the coffee. It'll do you good."

"I said, how much did you give him?"

"Ten," she whispered, "but only so he wouldn't call the police. He had a right to, you know."

He laughed. "Hell, for that amount of *gelt* it should've at least got a good crack at the Nazi punk."

"Will you stop being a moron?"

"Bottoms up, everybody." He raised the stein, sipped from it and put it on the table. "So"—grinning now as if that one sip had done the trick—"ready? I feel much better, and I know of a terrific *keller* across the street where this Yid can really get into a brawl. Get back at the butchering bastards the best way you know how, I always say."

"I asked you to stop it. And I think they're waiting for you to apologize, I hear it's the local custom after you've tried to kill someone."

"That tenner both apologized for me and paid for the wine."

"No, it didn't. And you really have to apologize to our waiter if you want me to leave here with you."

"Stop threatening me with the either-or shit. I want you with me—you're my darling schatzie and I've told you that—so let's get a move on."

"*Mein mann*," she said to the waiters, who'd been standing silently a few feet away, "*er kanst nicht gut Deutsch gesprechen*, am I being clear? I'm saying—*ich sage—konnen sie verstehen mir? Aber er sagt zu mir das er ist sehr traurig für alles diese—sehr.*"

"Please speak nothing of it," the older waiter said. "It happens. We are sorrowful too." The younger waiter nodded, smiled at her and gave her the check.

"*Danke schön*," She got the exact amount in marks out of her handbag and gave it to him.

"*Bitte schön*, madame," he said. The two waiters picked up the broken glass, cleaned the floor with a towel, cleared the table of everything but the wine list, and went back to the kitchen.

"Good God," Hank said, "did you catch those guys smiling so nicely at me? What in the world could you have told them?"

"That you were very sorry. And that you also wanted to say just how sorry you were in German but didn't know the language, so you asked me to say it for you."

He thought about it, then whistled. "There's one I never heard before. It's good; no, it's actually superb. You're a genius when it comes to making my apologies," and shaking his head in wonder how she could have come up with such a line, he started for the door. When he got there, he yelled back "So, der, *meine* sweetheart, *sie* comink?"

She was searching in her handbag for a tip, found five one-mark coins and put them on the table. Then seeing that not only wasn't Hank watching her but he was already past the door and hustling up the steps, she hurried after him.

"If you weren't always in such a damn rush," she said when she caught up with him on the street. "I can't run like you. I haven't got your long legs. And I've high heels on, Hank, high heels, so have a heart, will you?"

AN ACCURATE ACCOUNT.

I say "So I'll see you tomorrow."

She says "Not tomorrow. I need some time by myself."

"Then the next day."

"That day too."

"Hey, what's going on?" I say this jokingly but she doesn't take it as a joke. No smile; she looks serious. I say, not smiling this time, "What's up?" and she looks at me a little sadly. As if she's about to cry. Then a tear comes to one eye. I watch it well in the corner and go down her cheek. She's wiping the cheek when another tear wells in the same eye. I say "Why are you crying? What's wrong? You sick? About us, then? Something wrong with us? That has to be it. I recognize the signs. So, come on, speak."

"I think...this is what I think. I think..."

"Why are you crying, though?"

"Please let me finish. I'm crying because of what I'm thinking. I think you should get used to spending more time by yourself and with other people than me. I mean, every day with me."

"It's not just your work, then, that you want to be alone?"

"No. I think—"

"Uh-oh. I don't like the sound of it."

"It's been on my mind a long time."

"Not the sound or the sight of it, and it's sounding and looking even worse."

"I'm sorry, maybe it does sound bad. As for my face, that's how I feel. I've been meaning to tell you this for a while. We can't continue like this, indefinitely seeing each other day after day. It's reached its limit and doesn't seem to be going anyplace."

"What are you talking about? I want to marry you, live here and have a child by you."

"I'm sure you do. You've talked of it before. But I don't think that can work out. You just don't seem capable of it."

"I'm telling you, I am and it's what I want. That should be enough."

"You're devoted to your writing."

"I'm devoted to my writing for my work and other things, but to you for me emotional life and everything else. I'm devoted to you as much as I am to my writing, but in a different way. The two can go together."

"I don't think they can and I wouldn't want you to stop your writing."

"I don't have to."

"If you had a child you'd have to be making more money than you do from your writing."

"So I'll get a job. I've always made some kind of money, always been able to find a job."

"To make enough for you. True, I work, and make more than you. But if we had a child, I couldn't teach for a while, and there'd be so many other expenses after that, and you don't have enough "

"We'll save. What's the difference? We'll sacrifice. I'll sacrifice, though it wouldn't be a sacrifice. I love you. Do you love me?"

"Yes."

"You said, I don't know how many times—maybe just a few, but that you never loved anyone more than me. Has that changed?"

"No. It's been better with you than it has with anyone, but I can see it's not going to work out."

"How can you say that, after a happy morning, a happy evening, a great summer vacation—after we've been so close for almost a year? How can you so casually dump on it all?"

"In the end it seems we're just not suited for each other and it doesn't seem we'll ever be."

"That's ridiculous."

She's crying out of both eyes now. She says "Wait," and goes into the bathroom. For a tissue, I suppose. There's a stuffing up in my neck and I feel tears coming to my eyes too. I can't believe this is happening. I know that's trite to say, but the scene is suddenly very unreal. It's happened before, plenty of times. At least five, probably not too unusual for a guy who's 43 and never been married and been short of money for as many years as I. But I've never been happier with anyone more than I have with Lynn. I've been in love as much, but never happier. We've been so tight. She's perfect for me, or as perfect as a woman can be for me. I know I'm slightly neurotic and my compulsion to write can be a problem for the women I'm with, but so far she's put up with me and we get along very well. Again, this is trite, but it seems I'm in a dream. Or even that I've just awakened from a frightening one and am still a bit shaken from it. That's the image that comes to me while she's in the bathroom, maybe there for a tissue or to wash her face. Or to give herself more time to think what to do with me, or all three.

The toilet flushes. Maybe that's a ruse, maybe it isn't. She certainly didn't flush the tissue down it, as she always crumples them up and drops them in the wastebasket there. She comes out. She's wiping her eyes with a piece of toilet paper.

"No more tissues left?"

"Yes," she says. "The box was empty. You know everything, though, don't you? Or notice it. Listen, Michael—"

"I just can't understand any of it. I can't say I deserve it. I know I'm not easy being with sometimes, but I haven't been too bad. Everything so far between us has been good, I think, with not a single dispute between us."

"All true."

"Never a disagreement; not even a tiny one; none. So what you said before might make sense for you but it doesn't for me."

"We can continue to see each other but not as regularly."

"No. That's what the last one said. Diana."

"I don't care what Diana said."

"She said 'Let's see each other once a week,' after we'd been seeing each other seven days a week for three years."

"I told you, I'm not interested."

"I went along. It just dragged out. I don't want this to drag out. If you've made your decision, you've made it. It's not going to change. It's been my experience that once a woman makes a decision like that, at least when she makes it about me, it doesn't change. I'm going to look at it like this. I'm not talking about Diana anymore, so do you mind if I continue? It won't take long."

"Go ahead. I'm sorry for cutting in on what you were saying."

"This is the way I see it. The—our—relationship is the patient and we're the doctors. You want the patient to come in once a week or something. I think the patient should die."

"What?"

"That's not it," I say. "I was going to speak about it differently."

"Some metaphor!"

"I don't want the patient to die slowly, is more what I meant. The disease the patient has is inoperable, terminal, the rest. I don't want the patient to suffer. It's better the patient dies immediately. Ah, my imagery, metaphor, whatever it was, was bad. I can't think straight. I'm too sad, shaken up. I am. I probably look it and I am."

"I don't like this either. I hate that this has to happen."

"You look it too. The tears, your face and voice. Your key." I take my keyring off the piano. It's where I usually leave it and left it last night. Her apartment key's on it and I try getting it off.

"That's not necessary right now."

"It is." I can't get the key off. The ring won't open. "I'll get it when I get back to my place and mail it to you along with the money I owe you for the second month's cottage rent and utilities and some of your clothes. I can't believe all this," and I head for the door. "My things," I say, "I should probably take them," and I get a plastic shopping bag from the kitchen, go into the bedroom and bathroom and stick a few clothes and my shaving equipment and hairbrush in it and two books, and head for the door again. My duffel bag and typewriter and manuscript I was working on this summer and other books I already dropped off at my apartment when we drove in, just before we put her car in her garage.

She doesn't say anything when I think she might, and I unlock the door, don't say anything else or look at her, and leave.

Her building has an elevator but I like to walk the six flights downstairs. Now it's not a question of liking or not, I just do, as I don't want to wait for the elevator by her door and I just want to move. I think, when I'm rounding the stairs, didn't I see any signs where this was coming? I didn't. At least right now I don't see where there were any. Out of the blue, it came, out of the blue.

Round and round I go downstairs, and I open the door on the ground floor and I'm in the lobby. Frank, one of the doormen, is there, and he says "Hey, Michael, good to see you; when you get back?"

"Yesterday afternoon. Made it from Maine in one day."

"I was on duty yesterday. Probably on dinner break when you got in. Around six?"

"Around then."

"Get lots of work done?"

"Two months away; nothing much to do up there; it's the best time."

"But you're always working. Me too. This job and reading. Writing I leave to you guys so I can have something to do."

"What do you have there?" because I'd got him out of a lobby chair where he'd been reading a book.

"Socialism in South America. Maybe not for you, but I'm interested in economics, history, politics, those kinds of relations—international—and know nothing about it in South America, or not as much as I do in other places. How's Lynn?"

"Fine."

"I'll see her, but, tell her welcome back. Cool for this time of year, right?"

"I felt it upstairs. Had to shut some of the windows. I love it like this, breeze blowing directly into the apartment off the river and such."

"There'll be plenty more warm and even hot days left. It's only starting September. You get hot days in October."

"Not always, but we probably will. See you, Frank. You've been very nice."

"Hey, thank you; you too. I love talking to nice people who know books, and this building's loaded with them."

I wave, he does, and I leave.

When I'm walking to the subway and thinking about what happened upstairs, I start to smile. I don't know why. Then I think it could be because I'm not feeling hopeless, depressed or upset. Women breaking up with me has happened so many times the last twenty-plus years and every time it happened with someone I really liked I got tremendously depressed and upset, and this time I'm not. What does that mean? That I didn't love her as much as I thought I did or I feel some relief over the breakup and something inside is telling me that and therefore not to overdramatize the situation and get depressed and upset? No, I loved her a lot and wanted the relationship to go on but I guess I got upset one last time that last time with Diana and that was the last time I can get upset over something like that. Maybe. That after reacting the same way so many times it would just seem stupid to act that way again. Maybe. Probably this feeling won't last, though. We'll see, I hope it does.

I go into the subway station at a Hundred-sixteenth, buy a magazine from the newsstand on the platform, get on the downtown local and start reading an article on one of my favorite contemporary writers—one of the few I even like—an Austrian, who died of TB just last year. A few stations pass before I realize I haven't thought of Lynn since I started the article. That's a first. And it's not so much the article, which is stiffly written and full of literary jargon and has no new information about the writer or any original ideas. Before, after a breakup like this, the woman was on my mind all the time for at least a couple of days and of course I'd be constantly morose and also angry. But I don't have those feelings now. I feel pretty good, in fact. I go back to the article, which gets interesting at the end of it because of the writer's last tragic years.

I get off at Seventy-second and some guy standing at the station's entrance says "Got a quarter? I'm very hungry." He looks like he does need food and I give him some change and he says "Thanks," and I say "You're welcome, and take it easy," and he says "I'll try." Giving a panhandler change and a brief pep talk aren't things I would have done right after one of the previous breakups. Those times I would have felt more sorry for myself than I would for him and I'm sure I would have scooted right by. No, I don't feel too bad.

"Michael," someone says when I'm walking home, and I turn around and it's Annette. She used to go with my friend Ben. I say hello and we shake hands and I say "So how's it going? What've you been up to these days?" and she says "Nothing much, or same thing. My meditation and spiritual retreats and my work. Seen Ben?"

"Not for two months. Been away. But we wrote and phoned. He's doing fine. Likes his new job."

"Good for him. He was broke, last I heard. He's still not drinking too much, I hope."

"No, he cut out drinking and smoking, both cigarettes and dope."

"He must be seeing someone. It can't be just the job."

"He is."

"He's in love?"

"You really want to know?"

"What do I care? All right, I care a little, but that's been over a long time. Nah. Don't tell me about him. I don't care that much and it'll get back to him besides, not that I'd care if it did. He's totally out of my life, and good things have been happening to me too since I turned him loose. My play—the one I've been trying to sell for years? Not an easy one to peddle—a modern restoration comedy—but I found a backer. Good theater too, on West Fifteenth Street, we go into rehearsals next month."

"That's terrific."

"Better than terrific. It's Godsend-great. 'Eat your heart out, Benny boy, with your dismal satires,' I want to say, 'and while at it, kill your liver.' And they're interested in—it's a consortium of wealthy producers—the play I just finished. I'm on a roll that I hope never stops. How's Lynn?"

"She's fine. Filling in for someone at Princeton the next two years, so doing quite well. And publications in important journals in her field. She's on a roll too."

"Good for her. So, still together."

"To tell you the truth, I don't want to talk about it."

"Not going so well, then, huh? Too bad. You were crazy about her and it seemed the same for her to you. You don't seem too disturbed by it, so it's probably been awhile. Both Ben and I thought you two were the most perfect couple alive. We saw marriage, kids, side-by-side burial plots."

"We were, we are. Whatever the tense. She had doubts, though."

"Why, if she loves you? Money? Sex? Another guy?"

"Don't ask me. Anyway, you seem fine and you look good and I'm glad things are going so well for you. I gotta run, if you don't mind. Something at home."

"I'll send you an announcement of the play's opening. Lynn too. I'll get her address from the phone book. If it's a problem, you can come on different nights." She puts out her cheek, I kiss it, and she goes into the street to hail a cab and I go into a candy store to buy today's *Times*. I'll do the rest of my shopping later.

It wasn't that I didn't want to talk about Lynn, I think, heading up my block, but that I thought Annette was getting too nosy. Because who is she to me? When she was seeing Ben, I didn't even much like her. She always talked about herself and what she was doing and never asked what you were doing and she dumped on him all the time, paid some of his bills when he was short and then badmouthed him about it in front of people and also for dressing so sloppily and drinking too much and thinking he has talent as a playwright, and other things. "Why do you stay with her?" I asked him once, something I probably shouldn't have, and he said "The sex is good, and she's lively." God knows what she thought of me and my writing, and she no doubt thought I got the better of the deal when it came to Lynn. I feel, though, that if I bumped into someone now I actually liked and knew pretty well I'd even volunteer to speak about my breakup with Lynn today and say that for some odd reason it's not hurting one bit and also that I've no idea why she did it. It wasn't the sex, she didn't have another guy, and it can't be that she thinks I can only be devoted to my writing. So what was it? Maybe the money. That I didn't make enough, she didn't think I ever would, hard as I tried, and that frightened her when she thought of settling down with me, and did us in. It could be that. Or that and things I'm not seeing. That she's 32 and wants to have children and doesn't want to waste her time in a fruitless relationship. Anyway, can't be changed.

I get home and while I'm putting away my things, I think suppose she calls? It's possible; she did say she still loves me. So she could call to see how I'm taking it, worried that I'm not too despondent, that sort of thing. If she did, what would I say? I'd say, in the nicest way, that I'm okay, don't worry, but to keep it that way it's better for me That she doesn't call again. I wouldn't tell her I've barely thought of her since I left her apartment, or pined for her even once. I wouldn't want to hurt her feelings. I don't want to get even with her. That I'm taking it so well is enough for me. But she probably won't call. Almost definitely she won't. She'd know better. She'd think that calling me would be giving me some hope we could resume our relationship and maybe even eventually get married, and so on, and she wouldn't want me to think that. No, she's definitely not going to call.

I make coffee and get a stick of butter and sliced bagel out of the freezer, where I left them two months ago, and toast the bagel twice before it's completely unfrozen. I sit down with the coffee and buttered bagel and read the paper. I look up; after reading a few articles and reviews, and think I still don't feel bad at all. Either it hasn't hit me or it never will. I really can't say why. I've given myself a few reasons, but they don't seen enough. Have I become a cold fish? That's not it. And it isn't that I no longer love her. Hell, I love her as much as I've loved any woman, but what was different with her is I never wanted to marry and have a child with someone more. That so?

It's so. I also never had more laughs with any woman, enjoyed myself more with one, felt less tension than I did with any woman, and never respected and admired a woman more than I did her or thought I was luckier in being with anyone more, and lots of other things more. Never had an easier relationship, a more compatible and companionable and comfortable one. The three big C's. This one was as easy and smooth as can be till late this rooming when she dropped that news on me. If we had a disagreement, and we did have a few, rarely but a few, we worked it out almost immediately. There was never any anger or sulking or bitterness or continued bad feelings between us. I was confident that nothing would disturb our relationship, that it'd go on easily and smoothly and wonderfully and all the other things, seemingly forever. That we were as absolutely right for each other as two people could be. What Annette said, "Perfect together." Or was it "the most perfect couple alive"? We were close to being that, close, so how come I'm now not sad or even a little regretful? Really, I don't understand it. I'll miss her, won't I? Miss the sex, her body, presence, wit, intelligence, gentleness and goodness. Miss most everything about and around her, won't I? Her good friends, having dinner with her parents, the sane cottage she rents every summer, her two Siamese cats. Miss all that and more, won't I? I'll pass or go to places we've been together and think of her wistfully, won't I? See things, or think of them, I'll want to do with her and be sad I can't, won't I? All the things between two people who love each other and are so alike in many ways, right? So how come I'm not sad? I think I know why. I'm relieved, but relieved I'm not sad. But why aren't I sad? I don't know. I give up. But something unusual has happened to me. If I don't react the way I usually do, that's unusual. I think that's right. And maybe it is just because I couldn't allow myself to go through being sad over a breakup again. But could that be all? Ah, the hell with it. Maybe there's no sure explaining of it, at least for now.

Just then the phone rings. I think it's Ben. He knew I was getting back today and probably called Lynn's place and she told him I was here. I pick up the receiver. "Yes?"

"It's me," she says. "Before you say anything, I want to tell you I'm sorry about what happened."

"So am I. But what can we do? Nothing."

"Don't say that. I've thought it over."

"So have I."

"What did you think?"

"Things. But you called me. What is it?"

"You sound angry."

"I'm not. I'm feeling pretty damn good, in fact."

"You still sound angry. Not just your tone, but your choice of words. But I'm glad you're feeling good. I'm feeling very bad, though. I made a mistake, Michael. That's what I called to say. It could be I had to find out what my true feelings were about you and our future together by creating the worst scenario possible. Well, that I did, and I don't like it. When you left, I broke down. It's because I knew I'd made a grave mistake and that I do want to live with you and, if it continues to work out as well as it has before this morning, then for us to eventually get married and have a child."

"You thought all this in such a short time?"

"That's what you have to say?"

"I'm just asking," I say.

"Yes, it's what I thought after you left. It all came to me in a flash. My reaction, my thoughts. We'll work it out, sweetheart, we win. This is the bump we needed. If there isn't enough money, we'll deal with it. At first, we'll save on just having one apartment between us. You'll get a job and I'll do my best to keep working and I'm sure my folks will help us out. They want to be grandparents as much as you want to be a father. But we'll sacrifice, as you said. Both of us, not just you. But I first have to know how you feel about what I've said."

"I feel relief, but not about that. I wish you hadn't called, but you have. That you did call, I wish you hadn't said what you had, but you did. But I can't ever be with you again. Not see you, not be with you. The truth is, I can't ever be with anyone like that again. I never want to go through another relationship like ours. I only want to work as hard as I can at what I do for the years that I have on earth and then die. Okay, that's a lot of melodramatic bull. Simply put: staying involved with you or getting involved with someone else is obviously impossible for me. I see that now, this minute, because of this phone call, clearer than I ever have. Actually, I never saw it before; I'm only seeing it now. I'll miss you but love my unhappiness over missing you more than any future happiness I'd get from being with you. No, that's a bunch of bull too, and the quickest way to tell is that it's so aptly put. In fact, probably nothing much of what I said makes sense or isn't bull. I'm sure it's riddled with inconsistencies and contradictions and things like that. I don't even know why I'm saying any of it except for that; there is something there, in what I said, there's definitely something there, I just know it, and if the words and ideas are all mixed up and maybe incoherent, at least I know the feeling isn't. No, strike that last line out too. It was said for effect and makes no sense either."

She's crying.

"I'm going to hang up now, Lynn. If I don't I'll lose my resolve, if that's what it is, and say yes or maybe to something I feel deeply I don't want to. You just shouldn't have hit me with what you did and in the way and at the time you did it. Maybe that's all it comes down to. We were, I thought, so happy. The thoughts I had about, us after that never would have come to me, this phone call never would have come. Right now I'd be at my mother's apartment, which was where I was off to when you hit me with what you did. I'd be having a drink with her, maybe my second, and filling her in on what we did since she visited us this summer, and then gone to my apartment for the night or back to yours. No, mine. That's where my typewriter and manuscript and writing supplies are, and I wanted to write tomorrow morning after not having written for two days, one to pack and clean up the cottage, and the other to drive. That's what we planned, right?, when we dropped my things off at my apartment and then dropped the cats and your things off at yours and put the car in the garage and did some shopping. So I would have spent the night in my apartment, worked most of the day tomorrow and then gone to your place around late afternoon, most likely, since that's when I usually went and we usually saw each other every day. Too late for doing any of that now except for my going to see my mother. But I don't want to do that now either. I'm in no mood to, and she'd be glad to see me and have company and somebody to drink and talk with, and I wouldn't want to spoil it for her. I'll call her tomorrow and pretend we only just got back, or got back too late today to visit her, and see her then, tomorrow, when I hope I'll be in the mood more to visit her. If she's expecting me today and calls here tonight, I'll tell her I'm very tired after the long drive and I'll see her tomorrow. If she calls your place, tell her to call me."

"What is it with you?" She seems to have stopped crying. "You don't sound like yourself."

"Oh? I don't? Now there's a wise statement. Or bright, I mean bright."

"Even there. So cynical and a little mean. You never talked to me like that. Even when you were angry at me."

"I was once angry with you? I don't recall it."

"Several times. And I with you. But you're in a state I've never seen you in, and it doesn't become you."

"It doesn't? And I'm unbecoming? Well, you're wrong. But I am going to hang up. Please, I don't mean to hurt you, if that's what I'll be doing, but be prepared now for my hanging up."

I hang up. Tears come. First, a couple of drops, and I think it's over, and then I cry so hard my next-door neighbor, if she's home, must hear me. She probably is home; she usually gets back from work around six and then just stays there. I cry for a long time, five minutes, ten. Long for me. I'm usually a quick crier, and almost only at funerals and weddings and sad movies and when I think or talk about my dead brother and sister and father. I've never cried over a woman before. Is that right? Yes.

I wash my face in the bathroom, get a bottle of vodka out of the freezer, where I didn't mean to leave it when we went to Maine, and half-fill a juice glass with it. I drink it slowly. Now I'm just drinking to calm myself, but I think I'd like to drink enough where I eventually pass out. After a few sips, I put ice in the glass and open a small can of V-8 juice and pour some of it in because it's cheap vodka and it doesn't taste good straight. I make another drink and then a third and go to my work table with it. I take the typewriter out of its case, set it up with paper in it, and think I'll write a letter to her. I don't know what I'll say, but it'll have in it an apology for being cynical and a little mean and for acting so rude to her when she took the tine to call me. But I should call my mother, say we just got to the city and I'm very tired from the trip and I'll see her tomorrow around noon. "Maybe you'll let me take you out to lunch," I'll say. But I'll slur my speech and she'll know I'm getting drunk or already there and worry about it and ask a lot of questions, so I'll call her tomorrow and see her then. I start typing the letter.

"Dear Lynn: I don't know why I said what I did to you yesterday (it's now tonight. I know I'll never be able to completely explain it. I meant it or I didn't. Or meant some of it, though what part now I don't remember. (Yes, I've been drinking.) Drink or not, I know I love you but I also know that what you did to me today killed it for us forever. Oh, forever's too big a word. It's the wrong word. It's— Lynn.

I'm sorry and I know no apology will ever undo the harm I did. Again, slickly written in a momentary lucid moment, so don't believe a word I just said. I should give this up. I can't write. Can't write a letter now. I can barely find the right typewriter keys. I'm going to get up now and go to bed. It's early, it's still light out, so really not so long since I hung up on you, but I belong in bed. If I don't, I'll pass out at my work table. And I know I'm not going to mail this letter to you. How can I? I'll give it time, maybe things will get better. Though when I say 'it' and 'things,' what am I talking about? Us, us! Maybe we just shouldn't be together. That's what I think. I might send this letter after all, but tomorrow—I'm in no condition to go out now; even to finding a stamp and an envelope to stick this letter in—just so you'll get as accurate an account of what happened, or just my take on things, as you can. Then make your own decision. I'm sure what you decide, I'll want too, or at least I'll go along easily with it. I don't know if that's true. So, I'm sorry, believe me, very sorry, but that person who said all those things to you tonight was definitely me. Best ever, Michael, and of course, much love."

I think, after I fall on my bed and turn over on my back and feel myself drifting off, that I've ruined it with her for good.

YO-YO.

Hi.

Hi.

I'm sorry, did I startle you?

No, I think I startled myself.

I must have had something to do with it.

You just about had everything to do with it.

Isn't that close to what I just said?

I don't think so. My being startled came from my reaction at suddenly seeing you and being said hi to from you on your bike.

It still sounds close. But next time I won't rush up on you like that.

I don't think there can be a next time like that.

You mean next time you'll be ready for my racing down the street on my bike in the night and suddenly stopping and saying hi to you like that?

I mean next time I won't be surprised by my reaction at suddenly seeing you and your saying hi to me like that.

But if you're not startled or surprised by your reaction next time, then it'd mean you either saw or heard me or were told I'm racing down the street toward you on a bike.

What I think is that my surprise to my reaction at suddenly seeing and hearing you on your hike doesn't make sense.

I'd think that every reaction by someone rational to something real happening would have to make some sort of sense.

Well, they say it's not supposed to make total sense.

"They"? Who's "they"?

The people who talk about the things I'm now talking about,

such as my suddenly being surprised by my reaction at suddenly seeing you and hearing you say hi to me from your bike.

If you suddenly got surprised by my suddenly racing up to you on my bike on this empty street in the night and saying hi to you, then I think your surprised reaction to being surprised still makes sense.

Then the they who are they and not is they are wrong and you're right and I'm wrong. And though I still think I'm right by being wrong when I say they could be right when they say my reaction to my reaction doesn't make sense, it does make sense.

I think all this talk about what doesn't or does make sense is making less and less sense to me the more we talk. And if we're going to continue to talk we should both feel that what we're both saying makes sense.

All right, then—you biking back from work?

Yes, and you?

Walking back from the store.

Returning something? For I don't see any packages.

I didn't say what kind of store.

Was it a shoelace store where you bought just one pair of shoelaces?

A yo-yo store where I bought just one yo-yo.

Is it in your pocket?

No.

Up your sleeve? I can see it's not concealed in your hand.

It's in my mouth, its string end looped around a back bottom tooth. I bet you thought that lump in my cheek was my tongue.

Either your tongue or a large new sourball or even a larger sourball when new that had been slightly sucked.

I didn't say I went to a sourball store. And of course I couldn't have just come from a tongue store, as there are none.

I didn't say what kind of tongue I meant. For you could have gotten a tongue in a shoelace store. And if it were a sourball in your mouth, then had it left over from the last time you went to a sourball store.

I actually did have one left over. Till a minute before I first saw you, when I sucked down and swallowed the sour-ball in my right cheek to make room for the yo-yo I bought.

You could have put the yo-yo in your other cheek. Or if you like the right cheek for your yo-yos, then taken the sourball out and put the yo-yo in the right cheek and the sourball in the left.

I could have, but I only thought of putting the yo-yo in my mouth after I'd sucked down most of the sourball and bit into the little left and swallowed the pieces. Had I known I was going to bump in to you, I would have saved half the sourball I had left.

I don't eat sweets.

I could still give you half my yo-yo. It isn't a sweet or sour, comes apart easily and I'm sure in the short time it's been in my mouth, hasn't been changed in any physical or chemical way.

It would depend what flavor it is.

Wood.

I prefer plastic.

I think sucking a plastic yo-yo would make you sick.

But wood could give me splinters while plastic wouldn't.

If I can't give you a wooden yo-yo half, instead I can demonstrate my little yo-yo trick with the whole yo-yo in my mouth and its string end looped around my back tooth.

You only have one back tooth?

I've several. But the right lower's the one I choose for the loop to be around, as it's the biggest and I believe my strongest tooth. And because it's a bottom tooth, the string has less chance of slipping off than it would around an upper tooth which, if my lips or front teeth couldn't grab the departing string in tine or my tongue, couldn't pin it to my teeth or gums, the yo-yo would fall to the floor. And if the floor happened to be this sidewalk, the trick couldn't be tried again till the yo-yo was washed and the string, except for its loop end, had thoroughly dried.

I was only asking. Now I'm watching,

Well, as the yo-yo fully unwinds out of my mouth, I lean over a ways like this and do the walk-the-dog trick on the sidewalk and then jerk my head up so the yo-yo can rewind into my mouth. Then I close my mouth and stand straight and bring my feet and the inner condyles of my femora together again, or stand straight and bring the feet and condyles together and then close my mouth, and the trick's done.

That's quite a finish.

You're not in too much of a rush to watch it? If you are I could save the trick for another night when there might be a bigger moon and no clouds or perhaps during one of the hemisphere's rare auroras, or at least under or near a streetlamp.

I've time and there's plenty of light.

Or even on weekend or holiday afternoon when you're cycling down the street toward me and I happen to have a yo-yo in my mouth with its string end looped around that back tooth.

What I think is that you're dawdling on doing the trick because you don't have a yo-yo in your mouth.

Want me to open my mouth so you can see it?

Almost every time you opened your mouth to speak I saw you had no yo-yo inside. That is, once you said you had a yo-yo inside your mouth and I began making an effort to look for it.

Then I must have swallowed it.

Isn't that a risky thing to do with a yo-yo?

Why? My digestive track's like an alligator's.

Is an alligator's especially fit or equipped to digest yo-yos?

An alligator's or crocodile's or any of the large loricates who can digest an iron wrench without a problem.

That would be fine, if your yo-yo was made of iron and not wood.

The iron yo-yo I had was too prone to rust, didn't taste as good as the wood, and either chipped or dented a ceramic or linoleum floor tile if I landed it too hard, or my front teeth if I jerked, it back into my mouth too fast and without perfect control.

What about the string? Should I put my mind at ease because the string's also made of wood?

The string's made of string.

Then it must be a vegetable fiber, which shouldn't do your digestive system any harm if the wood doesn't.

I'm allergic to all fruits and vegetables, so I'm sure it wasn't either of those.

Maybe it was made of dried meat or fish.

Allergic to all animal flesh too—dried, fried or fresh. And anything grown in the ground except trees, shrub stems or the harder vines makes me unwell. But I think we better check whether the string's still in my mouth before we get upset. It could have come undone from the peg that joins the two yo-yo disks.

Doesn't seem to be inside.

Did you look way back to the right lower molars?

I envy you. From what I can make out, you haven't a filling in your mouth.

Forget about that. Is the string there or not?

Seriously, though, how can you have no fillings? You must be a few years older than I and so have had even more time to get cavities and impactions and lose a tooth or two. But you've all your teeth and apparently no cavity that large where the tooth had to be drilled and filled.

You didn't check the upper set.

I'd need a dentist's mouth mirror and penlight for that.

I could stand on my head on the sidewalk so you could see it.

I'd have to get on my knees to look, which would dirty my skirt.

What if I stood upside down on this car hood and opened my mouth extra wide?

You'd get dirty and probably slide off the hood and break some of your beautiful teeth.

Then I'll just have to take out the top set and show it to you in one piece.

You saying you've had less success with the upper set than your lower?

I'm saying I've two sets of uppers. One for taking out and showing people who are interested in upper sets or really any kind of sets, teeth, twins, etcetera. And a second set underneath the first for the prehension and chewing of food and as half of a defense and offense weapon and for clasping and carrying things.

You've got a pretty full mouth.

I'd even have more in it if I hadn't swallowed the yo-yo.

You forgot the string.

I didn't forget the string, just which side I put it in. For I occasionally loop its end around the lower left molar to give the right molar a rest if I'm doing the trick several times in a row. And the last time I looped the string around the tooth was a while ago.

Just waiting for someone to bike along to do the trick for?

All the hikers on the block but you have seen it, which was why it was in my mouth so long.

No new uni-, tri- or hydrocyclists move into the neighborhood in the last few days?

One, but he didn't stop pedaling long enough to be shown the trick to.

I'm sure there's a good reason why, but I better go.

You have to?

The babysitter leaves to babysit for her own child when my husband comes home at five. And after an hour of babysitting alone with his son, my husband can go wild.

Paints his face, dons a malamute's garb, does a snarling yipping dance—wild like that?

Just a few booming curses at my maiden and pet names. It isn't easy taking care of a sleepy-hungry two-year-old between five and six.

I bet it was even harder before he turned five.

You know, sometimes it can be difficult talking to you.

That's because I only have you for a few minutes. But at four I expect he got so out of hand now and then that you and your husband had to shout "four" and then duck, or just flee the house or crack.

No. We both had to shout "duck" and then fall on all fours in the house and quack.

You have more than one two-year-old who was four?

One's enough for the time being.

One might be enough, but there's nothing you can do about it once his second birthday comes.

It already has: three times. Which is the favor I want to ask of you, which I don't think I've alluded to yet. You see, tonight's Tim's second birthnight again and neither my husband nor I—

Bill.

Phil. And we don't want be around as we weren't for Tim's last three anniversaries, as we feel if we're not there when his birthnight comes, he'll always remain one.

One what? And how do you elude your son during the same day of his birthnight?

He was born at night, so we always assumed that's when his anniversary is. Though whenever we travel around the world and Tim's second anniversary comes, I always check my terrestrial calendar as to what hour and day it is where I am when it's nine at night in New York on November tenth.

But that's not tonight.

And I'm not at some other part of the world but New York.

And a good thing it is for me too. As I'm tired, grimy and thirsty and I'd hate right now to be talking to you so far away from my own kitchen, shower and bed.

Worse came to worse, you could always babysit for Tim while we're out trying to avoid him, and celebrate his second birthnight with him and later wash up and sleep on our couch.

If I spent the night with you all in another part of the world,

I might not have the time and means to get back to my job and room in New York.

You could make it your job to get back to your room by doing your yo-yo tricks in the streets.

But if I swallowed my yo-yo, the country I'd be stuck in with you might not carry them.

Then carry a few dozen lots in yourself and make your plane passage back by introducing the yo-yo craze to that country.

How does one go about introducing a yo-yo craze to a country? Does one say "Yo-yo craze, this is country. Country, I want you to meet yo-yo craze"?

I think it would be protocol in the host country to first introduce the country to the yo-yo craze and then the yo-yo craze to the country. After that, every five years you could reintroduce them the same way and become financially set for life.

But in those five years when I'd be away someone else might reintroduce the country to the yo-yo craze, and when I came back it would be old hat.

You're not missing my point? But say you were a couple of days late after the five years were up and someone got there before you with the reintroduction, start an old hat craze in that country.

You think I also have those in my mouth?

I didn't even see an old jacket, which is why I said I envy you so much. No matter how well I take care of my teeth, I get one to two cavities a year.

With me, no matter what I do, I can't get cavities.

I don't know why you'd do anything to get them. Though if you ever do get a cavity, I'll give you the name of a good dentist. If he's too busy to take on new patients, I'll try to give you my teeth with cavities in them in exchange for the equivalent of your perfect teeth. If by some luck I don't have cavities this year, I'll give you my old fillings, which you can then tell my dentist you want repaired or replaced for me.

I wouldn't have any place to put your fillings.

Since you swallowed your yo-yo, you could put the fillings in your cheek.

I would if I could loop a string end around one of them and this filling could spin out of my mouth and unwind and rewind like a yo-yo so I could do my walk-the-dog trick.

My dentist wanted to give me the unwinding-rewinding kind of fillings, but gold's the best I could afford.

Gold's rustproof, so it might taste a lot better than iron after a while and yet be just as digestible. But I think it would still break a front tooth or two if I lost control of it in the rewinding.

Now I see why you tried to get cavities. So you could always have fillings around in case you swallowed your yo-yo in a country which doesn't carry them and where you didn't have the foresight to carry any extras in.

You've got quite a memory.

Oh, I forget plenty of times. Like how Phil acts when it gets way past six and I'm not home when he's babysitting alone and he's past booming out curses to all my names.

I suppose the best thing then would be for you to get right home.

The very best thing would be for Phil not to get so upset after an hour of babysitting alone, so I wouldn't have to worry so much about rushing home.

Then I suppose the next best thing after that would be for you not to worry so much about how upset he gets after an hour of his babysitting alone when you're still not home.

No, I think the next best thing after Phil not getting so upset after an hour of his babysitting alone so I wouldn't have to worry so much about how upset he gets and have to rush right home, would be for me to simply go home.

Then the next to the next best thing, if the next best thing is your simply getting home, is for you not to worry so much about how upset he gets after an hour of his babysitting alone when you're still not home.

No, the next best thing after my simply getting home, is being home.

Then the next to the next to the next best thing, if the next to the next best thing is your being home, is your not worrying so much about rushing home.

No, I'd still have to worry about it.

But it would still be the next to the next best thing if you didn't.

It's so far from reality that there's almost no reason for me to even think about it or for you to catalogue it. And I really have to go.

That's the next to the very best thing on your list.

Is it? You mentioned my memory, but I don't know how you kept track. Anyway, right now it's the only thing.

If it is, then there isn't a list and thus no next to the best thing or next to the next or next to the next to the next best things.

You might be right. It's become too confusing to me with all these nexts and bests and not-nexts and thuses. And it's not that I don't want to talk about it. It's all been very stimulating. That must sound insensitive and forced. It's not easy talking the ordinary way with you. But I am married and have a child and responsibilities and a home and am loved by a man I'm in love with and who's the father of my child, so I'll have to do the only thing or the next to the very best thing or whatever thing or next you said it was on my list or list turned non-list and just go.

It's not that I don't want to have a child or responsibilities or a home, but I'm not married and right now have no prospects of such or am even seeing a woman, and I don't want to go.

So stay.

I think I will.

Then, nice talking.

Same here. But may I carry your bike up the stoop?

I don't see how you can if you stay.

I'll come back.

If you come back, you still haven't stayed.

Then I won't stay. I'll just carry your bike up the stoop to the building's vestibule or ground floor hallway and then come down again and go.

The bike's not that light. But carrying it up the stoop's good exercise for me after riding it back from work so lazily. I can do it myself.

I know, but I'd like carrying it up for you.

You're supposed to let women do what they can for themselves these days.

I know what I'm supposed to let women do these days, and what I want to do for this woman right now.

Look at you. You can suddenly get so serious.

Bike-carrying's serious business for me.

I'd think yo-yo carrying's the business you'd be more serious about. For no matter what the country you're in does or doesn't carry and no matter how many extra yo-yos you might carry in, it doesn't seem possible you could ever swallow a bike.

Should I leave it in the hall here or carry it to your apartment?

The landlord lets me keep it here. Was it heavier than you thought?

I never thought it would be heavy.

Did it turn out to be heavy?

It turned out to be light.

Not as light as your yo-yo, though.

Truth is, it's the yo-yo that's not turning out to be as light as I thought. Maybe it wasn't made of wood after all.

Laminated plastic perhaps?

One of your favorite flavors, if I remember, but I suddenly don't feel too good.

You're not serious again.

I am serious.

Probably you should take an antacid when you get home.

It's more than that.

A doctor?

A doctor wouldn't take me.

A city hospital?

I don't know if I could take a city hospital.

The emergency room of a private hospital would certainly take you, wouldn't they? But then you're not really ill.

This time, maybe it's you who's missing the point. My not wanting to swallow an entire city hospital is just a sensible precaution.

If the hospital's big enough, it might swallow you.

You're hardly comforting.

Because you can't be ill.

I can so be ill.

Then I don't know what to say.

If you can't think of anything, I can give you some things to say.

I think the best thing for me to say is goodbye.

And the next best thing?

There can't be a next best thing. I have to go. I've a home. A husband, a child, they're waiting for me. And if my son's napping, then just my husband. Thanks for carrying up the bike. Goodbye.

Then I don't know what's so good about it.

Then badbye or just bye.

Yes, that's probably just a goodbye.

Bye, then?

I wish we didn't have to say bye.

We didn't say bye. We said "badbye" and "just bye" and "then bye." And we didn't say these byes, only I did.

I mean I wish we didn't have to say goodbye.

But you still haven't said goodbye.

Then what I mean is I wish I didn't have to say goodbye.

What you really mean is you wish I hadn't and still didn't have to say goodbye.

No, that's not what I really mean.

Then what you really mean is you wish, after I said I hadn't and still didn't have to say goodbye, that I went upstairs and said my goodbyes.

Yes, that's what I mean.

That's what I said you meant.

And that's what I meant when I said "Yes, that's what I mean."

And that's what I meant when I said "That's what I said you meant." Anyway—bye.

But that's what I meant when I said "And that's what I meant when I said 'Yes, that's what I mean.'" Which is what I meant when I said "And that's what I meant when I said 'That's what I said you meant.' Anyway—bye." Anyway—bye.

And that's what I meant when I said "But that's what I said I meant when I said 'And that's what I meant when I said "Yes, that's what I mean."'"

But that's what I meant when I said "Which is what I meant when I said 'And that's what I meant when I said "That's what I said you meant."'" Anyway—bye.' Anyway—bye." Anyway—bye.

Bye.

NO

KNOCKS.

I go out into the street. Finally, it's a nice day. Rains came, went; sun now. I say hello to my landlord, Next-door neighbors. Wave to Mrs. Evans behind her window. Mr. Sisler sitting on his stoop across the street. Rob's boy walking their dog just before he goes to school. Mary Jane Koplowitz dumping her family's garbage on her way to work. Children, workers, cyclists, pedestrians, mailman. "Howdy-do. How are you? I feel great. Lovely day. What a relief after so much rain. Hiya. Morning. Hope the good weather holds. See ya. Take care. Hope you have a nice day." I walk down the block and say more of the same. "Hello. Morning. How's it going? So long. Have a great day." Friendly street. Living on it for years. People know who you are, what you do. What do I do? They know I do relatively nothing. Just about nothing. Nothing. They know. In other words, they also know what you don't do. I don't work. They know. No home projects or work for other people that keeps me home. They know that too. I walk, talk, read. I get up first. I have breakfast, wash, shave. Shower every day. No shower in the morning, then an evening shower. Then I go downstairs.

Not after my evening shower, though I might do that too, but after I do all those morning things. I never bother checking the mailbox anymore, on the way out or when I come back. There's never any mail. I'm waiting for the day the mailman says "Mr. Rusk, your mailbox is jammed full. I can't stuff any more mail inside. Please take the mail out so I can have room to put new mail in. At least take some of the mail out so I can have some room to put new mail in." That'll be the day. Day I might even look forward to. Do I? No, though once did. But it'll be a day, all right. What'll those letters be like? Say it happened.

And who'd write? Nobody. I know no one other than from the street and around the immediate neighborhood. No relatives, friends, old acquaintances. And I tell people who move off the block or out of the neighborhood "Just come back and visit if you want, but don't bother to write. I never bother opening my mailbox, so I'd never get your mail. Only day I'll open my mailbox is the day the mailman tells me it's too full to get another piece of mail in, but that'll be the day. But say that happened. I might only take out a few pieces of mail, or just one big one, to make room in the box, so I still might not get your mail." And I pay all my bills by cash and personally and on time. So no need for mail. I've none. No need for it and no mail. And the mailman's instructed not to put any junk mail in my mailbox. The instructions are on the building's vestibule letterbox for the mailman not to put any junk mail into my mailbox. Or they're on the vestibule mailbox for the mailman not to put any junk mail into my letterbox. One or the other. I'll go to the library one of these days to look up the difference in the dictionary between those two. If there isn't one, I'll find that out too. A difference. Mailbox and letterbox. Both I get my mail in, but which is which? And if the vestibule box that houses all the tenants' smaller boxes for mail is called a letterbox and those tenant boxes are called mailboxes, or vice versa, than what's the box on the street called that people put their mail in? Not only people. Yes, only people. I was going to say "Not only people but children too." But children are people too. Children are people, period. I don't know what could have been on my mind when I started to say "Not only people but children too." Caught myself this time. Other times also, but my mind's particularly sharp today. Not particularly. Not even sharp. Mind's just functioning a bit better than yesterday. Not even that. I can't really tell if it's functioning any better today than yesterday. Mind's functioning better now than when I woke up today. That's for sure, so that I can at least say. But now I'm at the corner. I look around. No one I know here. People, yes, but no one I know to talk to when I feel like talking to someone. I look all four ways. Up the block I just came down. Down the next block of this street that I don't think I'm going to continue on. Both ways along this avenue I'm now on.

Though who's to say where the avenue begins and sidestreet ends when one's standing on the corner where the avenue and sidestreet meet? I'm sure plenty of people can say. I can't. Not right now, at least.

But all four principal directions, in other words. East, west, etcetera. No one I know. No one who knows me. There's a difference there. Lots of people— Not lots. Several. A few, I'll say, claim to know me when I don't know them. Not claim. But they say they know me. They'll come over to me or just stop me and say "Hello" or "Good morning (etcetera), Mr. Rusk." In other words, that etcetera: all depending on the time of day in the time zone we're in. If, for example, they say "Good morning, Mr. Rusk," when it's obviously evening, then I figure they're poking or confused or even crazy or they made a simple word-reverse mistake, and I react according to how I feel at that moment about why they greeted me this way by my last name. If they use Mrs. or Miss before my last name, then no matter how accurate they are with the time of day, I ignore them or question them about the use of that conventional title of respect. But say they do say "Good morning, Mr. Rusk," when it's morning or close enough to it where I don't think the greeting is strange. If I look at them as if I don't know them—and usually when I look at them this way, I don't know them—they'll say "I know you but you don't know me." Sometimes they'll greet me and immediately say that about my not knowing them, even though I do know them and they know I do. And sometimes when I know them and they know I do, though they'll say I don't, I'll look at them as if I don't. Why will I give them that look when I do know them and why will they say I don't know them when they know I do? Couple of reasons, at least, that I can think of. But today none of that happens. So no one to talk to now unless I stop someone I don't know and who I know doesn't know me and start to talk to him, something I don't like to do.

If I walk uptown on this avenue, which is north, the chances of stopping someone I know in proportion to the number of people on the street will be much less than if I walk downtown, which seems to get more crowded the further south you walk, just as the streets seem to get less crowded the further north you walk. The chances of stopping someone I know in proportion to the number of people on the street would be greatest if I walked back to my block and kept walking up and down it and especially on my side of it, but I don't like going over the same route so soon after I came off it. I could cross the avenue and continue west along this same numbered street. But partly out of personal reasons, which I won't go into, and because the chances of stopping someone I know in proportion to the number of people on the street would be no better walking west than walking uptown, west seems the least likely direction to go except if I didn't want to stop or be stopped by someone. I could, of course, create many other routes other than just walking straight in one of the four principal directions. I could go north four blocks, then west till I hit the river, or south three blocks and east one and then south again till I get to the heart of the city; or south two blocks and east three and across the park and continue east till I hit the river that runs along the other side of the city, and so on. But I think the best chance, without going back to my side of my block and walking up and down it, of stopping someone I know or being stopped by someone I know or don't know but who says he knows me, is to walk downtown on the avenue I'm on.

So I walk south. I see no one I know on this avenue and am not stopped by anyone. I keep walking. Chances get less with each step that I'll meet someone I know or don't know but who says he knows me. I walk five blocks, six. Chances get even less, and after four more blocks, almost nonexistent. Then I'm so far away from my neighborhood—sixteen blocks—that I feel if I want to talk to someone now, and I think I do, the only way would be if I stopped someone I don't know, and chances are almost nonexistent here that he'd know me, and start up a conversation with him despite my dislike or reluctance or apprehension, or whatever it is, in doing so.

First person I see on the street, and I'm now twenty blocks from where I live, who I think I'd like to stop and talk to is a man. Not because he is a man. Though maybe because I'm a man I prefer to stop a man stranger to a woman, since I think a man would be less alarmed at being stopped by someone he doesn't know and feel more willing to talk to a stranger than a woman would, though I could be wrong. Are women less likely to be bothered or frightened by women strangers who stop to talk to them than by men? I'd think so. And what about men in regard to women strangers who stop them because they want to start up a conversation, or even for other reasons, like asking change for a dollar, let's say, or asking for a handout, or a donation of some kind? I'm not sure. But this man. I night now know why I prefer stopping a man I don't know, to a woman, but I'm less sure why I think I'd like to stop and talk to this man out of hundreds I've passed. It could be his clothes. One reason. He's dressed in a sports jacket and slacks, boots, big wide-brimmed western hat, and is carrying a closed umbrella and flat package, and has an overcoat over his arm. But closer I get to him from behind, more I think the flat package is a thin book and the jacket and pants are a suit made of a heavy fabric and the overcoat is a parker and the umbrella a black cane. When I get right up behind him and then am walking alongside him on his left, keeping in pace with him now, I see that the flat package *is* a book, on cytohistology, its cover says, another word, if I remember it and remember to look up, I should look up at the library one of these days. The other was what? I forget, though it came to me today and could come back. The cane's the closed umbrella I originally thought it was, but beige rather than black. Boots are western and well polished and recently heeled and have intricate stitching on them that looks like a lot of lassos. Parker is several djellabas that I supposed he's taking to a store to be cleaned, though that's a wild guess. His hat is still a Stetson-type, though leather instead of felt. Shirt's almost the same color as the suit and seems to be made of chamois cloth, while the suit's suede. Brown suede. Light brown. Darker brown leather buttons in a hatched pattern. Flap pockets. Same kind of buttons on the pockets. Or at least the left flap pocket has that button; the right one could be different or have come off, for all I know. A tie. Red. Stickpin. Gold. Cuff links. Just initials or one word: DAD. Or at least the left cuff link has those initials or that word; the right one could say MOM, for all I know, and also gold. "Hello," I say.

He stops. "Do I know you?"

"No. Do I know you?"

"Not as far as I know,"

"That's what I should have said. Not 'No.' But 'Not as far as I know.'"

"Then we definitely, or almost definitely, which could be undefinitely but not nondefinitely, don't know each other as far as we know, could that be right?"

"As far as I know it can't be 'We undefinitely don't know each other,' but on the other one you're right. Now as far as knowing each other, my memory does fail me sometimes. So we could still know each other. If we do, I've forgotten, and I'll have to leave it up to you to remember."

"My memory does fall short of me also," he says. "No, that's not the word. The words. My memory does fail me also, as far as I'm concerned. And that's not the expression. My memory occasionally fails me also, as it does everyone, but I'm almost sure I don't know you. Years ago I might have. But there comes a time when I have to say about someone I knew long ago but since then haven't spoken or written to or heard from in any way, or seen, and if I did see him, didn't recognize him, that I don't know him now."

"So we could have known each other once, you're saying?"

"Possibly," he says. "But our faces could have changed so much since then that we don't recognize each other now. And our eyesight, in addition to our faces or apart from them, and to a lesser degree as a recognizing factor, our voices, mannerisms, appearances and clothes. Anyway, to boil it down to the minimum: if I once knew you, I don't recognize you in any way now. How about you?"

"Same here all around. So how are you?"

"Do you mean, since I last saw you, if I ever did see you, or last to or heard from you, if I ever have?"

"Yes."

"I'm fine, since we last spoke, wrote or saw each other, if we ever did. And if we didn't, I can still say I don't think I've had a bad day that I can remember since I was born. That's not to say I haven't. My memory again. What it does say is that as far back and as much as I can remember, I haven't. Had a bad day, I'm saying."

"I can't say that."

"Well, it's over now, whatever it was, isn't that right?"

"I can't say that either."

"Broken love affair? Family tragedy? Professional or affinal crisis? Illness? Malaise? Something you read in the newspaper? Got in the mailbox? Witnessed, from your window? Saw in the street? Personal experience or experiences? Is one of those it, or are some to all of those them, and which can't be broached, right?"

"Personal experience, yes."

"A woman?"

"Can't be broached, yes."

"Yes, a woman?"

"Can't be broached."

"The woman? The subject?"

"Can't be broached, can't be broached."

"Too bad, then. That it happened. And that she or it can't be broached." Sticks out his hand. "Lionel Stelps."

"Victor Rusk."

Shaking of hands. Nicing of days. Changing of weathers. Preferences of sun to rain, city to suburbs, streets to parks, busier the better. What do you do's? Where you off to's? Going my ways? Okays. Walk. Talk. Seems he likes almost nothing better in life than to walk the streets too. To talk to people he knows or doesn't know but who know him, or to people he doesn't know and who don't know him but who like almost nothing better in life than to walk the streets and be stopped by people they know or don't know, and for many of the reasons that he and I do. Because we like people. Talking and listening to people. Because we like to be outdoors and preferably on the busy and hectic streets of the city with many kinds of people of both sexes and all sorts of age groups and occupations and pursuits. He's very much like me, in other words. Maybe that's why I wanted to stop him, when I ordinarily don't want to stop anyone I don't know and who shows no sign of knowing me. Not just his clothes. Not that I could have known much what he was like or what he almost liked doing best in life just by his clothes. Not that I really could see what his clothes were like, and especially the front part, from so far away in back when I first spotted him and thought I might want to stop him. Not that I even like to stop people who are like me in any way and who like almost nothing better in life than walking the streets to stop and talk to people or be stopped by people they know or don't know but who know them or show some sign they do. And as far as I know he isn't like me except for what he almost likes to do best in life and that he likes what helps contribute to it: mild weather, good health, sufficient sleep, crowded city streets, etcetera. His voice, face, hair, build, height, weight, age and just about everything else about him, and especially his clothes, aren't like me or mine at all. He's well-kempt, -shoed, -spoken, -bred, more mildly mannered than I, it seems, and he wears a hat. I don't own a single headpiece. Not even a winter cap, or hat with a brim of any kind to keep the sun off my face. Must be lots of people who do what we do, we say. Streets, walk, talk, people, stop, like to be stopped, and so on. Now the sun goes. I probably got a bit of a burn on my face today, which he didn't because of his hat. Continue to talk. He's lived a few more years in his apartment than I have in mine. Streets get less crowded, and not because we've passed through the heart of the city or it's that time of day. Bad sign, we say. Clouds come. We continue to walk. Three more blocks, four. Sky darkens. Talk about what we don't like to do most. Stay inside on nice days like this one was, for one thing. Not talking to anyone for hours, another thing. Day after day of unrelenting rain is probably the worst thing. Wind. Store awnings quaking. People hurrying. Signboards swinging. People running. They sense something. Finally, we do too. Or I just sense it, because it's possible he already did and wasn't saying. Maybe because he wanted to continue talking. "Pity," he says. Pats my shoulder.

"Pity is right," and I pat his shoulder.

"Though nice chat we had."

"Yes, while it lasted. No, that's not what I wanted to say or how I wanted to say it. One of those, not both. But I think you know what I mean without my going into it or repeating what I wanted to say the right way."

He doesn't say yes or no or nod or shake his head. He smiles, a weaker smile than the ones before, and sticks out his hand. I stick out mine and we shake. It starts to sprinkle.

"See you sometime," he says. "But I better run. Don't want to ruin my clothes."

"I guess I don't mind getting—" I begin to say, but he walks away. Put up his umbrella and is heading further downtown. That where he live? Maybe he was shopping in midtown. But he had no package. The djellabas. But they weren't bagged or wrapped. Maybe he came to midtown to get them from a friend, or even the umbrella or book or hat or he bought something that can't be seen in a pocket or around his neck or wrist. Or even his ankle. Men sometimes wear ankle bracelets, though that's the least likely prospect I mentioned. Or maybe he strolled all the way to around where I live and possibly beyond, and just to stroll—for exercise, let's say—and I caught him walking back to his home downtown. But that doesn't explain the djellabas. The book he could be carrying for any number of reasons. For instance, just to read in a stopping-off place like a café. What was the subject matter of the book again that I was going to look up? Forget. Such a long, complicated and unfamiliar word, I doubt I'll ever be able to remember it. Maybe he hurried off with that rain excuse because he knows something more about this area than I. I rarely get this far from my block. The last time was when? Can't remember. Well, lots of questions, and nothing like a little mystery in one's life. What's the mystery in mine? That personal experience I brought up and didn't explain? Bet he's wondering about it now. Woman, hmm, I can see him thinking. Actually, I can still see him walking downtown, the umbrella still protecting him. He's a block away but not many people between us. Then he disappears. Maybe he ducked in someplace to get out of the rain. Doesn't even want a few drops on his clothes, if that excuse was the truth. What I was going to tell him before he left was "I guess I don't mind getting caught in the rain as much as you." He would have asked why. I would have said "My clothes are quite old and used. First old, then used. I mean by that: made old by someone else, or who knows how many people, because who knows how many thrift shops they were in, then further used by me. In plainer language: I bought all the clothes I have on in a thrift shop. Several thrift shops, but they all came from one. Meaning: several different thrift shops, but they're all thrift-shop clothes. In even plainer language: they're worn, shabby, very cheap clothes that were the only ones I could afford in several very cheap thrift shops. What could be called work clothes if I worked. Worked at a laborer's job where one didn't need good clothes. In the plainest language possible: I don't mind ruining them; they're already ruined."

I look in all four directions, I seem to be one of the few pedestrians on the streets, and those that are on them are protected by rainwear or umbrellas or both. But why get wet? It's pouring now, so I mean why get wetter? I duck under a store awning. But why duck? Ducks take to rain, don't they? That might have elicited a laugh from that man. A good joke, I think, and I laugh out loud. Oops. Someone's under the awning with me. A woman, also with no umbrella or rainwear.

"Howdy-do," I say to her, "Nice day, eh?" She gives me the fisheye, looks away. One of those. Meaning: she is.

"Just a joke," I say. "Minor. Harmless. Didn't mean anything by it. Just the good mood I'm in. But some rain. Cats and dogs, yes? Bats and hogs, no." Fisheye, looks away. Still one of those. No letup. She nor the rain. Me too, I guess. Strangers. But maybe I'll get to her yet. In a good way, I'm saying. "Okay, I understand, madame. Takes all kinds, and I love that it does. But must say good-day. I must, not you. For ducks take to rain as they do to water, don't they? In fact, rain is water. Rainwater, of course." Fisheye, mutters, clutches her handbag closer to her, moves two steps away from me but still under the awning. I laugh to myself, but inside this time. Sort of to balance the last time I laughed out loud, which was to an inside remark.

I salute her goodbye and step into the rain. Really pouring now. Buckets. I start running north. Every so often I duck under a store awning or building overhang and try to make talk with someone there, and the awnings and overhangs I choose I choose because someone's there, but have no luck. Could be the clothes and that I'm so wet. And more I run, wetter I get. And there's nobody I know under these overhangs or who seems to know me. If they do, they're not saying, something I can also understand. A man so drenched and who keeps running in the rain without any protection can seem crazed. I run a few more blocks, keep ducking under overhangs, more because I'm tired than to talk to anyone, so some of the overhangs I duck under don't even have anyone there. Run a lot more blocks, but I'm really just jogging now, and walk fast and then at a normal pace the last five blocks till I reach my sidestreet. I run down the block—there's nobody out or at the window to wave to—and go two steps at a time up my building's stoop into the vestibule, where the landlady's mopping the floor under my mailbox or letterbox I don't open but do peek through and see nothing inside.

"Some day out," I say, but she's in no mood to talk. And when she's mopping while it rains she usually gets less in the mood with each succeeding dripping tenant. "Have a good day, though," I say, and run up the three flights of stairs to my apartment to do some undressing, showering, maybe soaking in a tub, drying, dressing, wet-clothes hanging, eating, resting and sleep. All that and more till later today or early tonight or tomorrow or tomorrow night or sometime this week, depending if the rain stops and if it's not too late in the day, I can go out again.

WALT.

"Don't worry; there'll be better days."

"No doubt."

"For both of us, I mean."

"I know, or at least I hope. But as you were going?"

She leaves. I putter around the house: sweep up, put away dishes, mop the kitchen and bathroom floors. She comes back.

"I got all the way to the bridge when I realize I forgot something."

"Forgot to stay away."

"Don't be nasty. I'll get it and then I'll go and I won't be back."

"Promise?"

But she's upstairs. Comes down with her hair dryer.

"Your hair dryer, no less. Oh, you really needed to come back for that."

"I thought why bother buying another one as long as I have one here. Because you weren't planning on using it, were you?"

"Oh sure, can't you see me under it with my five hairs on top and short side hair. But what you should've thought in your car was why have a dryer at all?"

"You can't let up?"

"You can't dry your hair with a towel?"

"With a trowel, that's how I'd like to dry your hair. Anyway, my dryer makes drying quick and easy. Saves me time for more important things."

"Like prolonging affairs?"

"One affair. The others weren't even minor romances. Not even mini-minor ones. Just tosses in the hay if there was hay."

"A turn or toss in the sack, then."

"If the sack's supposed to be the mattress on the bed, then for most of them, that's correct."

"The sack is the bed. Old word for it, and the tossing or turning business, old expression. I think it comes from the navy—if not the expression, then the word, or maybe both."

"You were in the navy?"

"You saying you didn't know?"

"I thought it was the marines."

"Navy. Private first class."

"I know they don't have privates."

"Sailors don't have privates? Oh, new joke if it isn't an old one. They've privates, privies and privileges as in liberties, or they did when I was junior grade."

"You were an ensign, now I remember. Well, I salute you, Ensign Wilkerson, and say ahoy there or whatever the nautical term is for goodbye."

"Shove off."

"Shove off. Okey-doke and adieu, my dope, as the French navy might say," and she leaves.

"Screw you too, once my hope, now my rope. Good riddance, my former deliverance, and…and…nothing. Just nothing." I throw a coffee mug, only dish I didn't wash and put away, through one of the front windows. She comes back.

"You know, I was opening my car door when I heard the crash. At first I thought let him get his anger out. It's good for him. Then he'll be calm, like seas are calm after a storm, which all JGs are familiar with, right? Then I thought hell, I still own half this house, so my warning to you. Ensign Wilkerson, first class jerk, is don't go busting up any more of it or I'll get my rear admiral on your ass, or whatever the legal officer is in navy talk, for more than just a divorce. In other words—"

"In other words, go hang myself or slit my own throat, you were going to say?"

"No."

"Ah, you were always so considerate and sweet: property, more important than people, in your book. To that I say, screw property, yours and mine, jointly or singly held," and I throw a lamp through another front window. She runs to the phone, looks in the directory, and dials.

"Police? I'm in your precinct. Thirty thirty-five Waverly, and my husband is tearing up our house and I want him arrested... Yes, it's a domestic dispute. It always is if it's between husband and wife, but that shouldn't stop you from coming here. It's half my house, and after he gets done destroying it, I fear he's going to start on me... Good. Edith Wilkerson, his is Walt. Please hurry." She hangs up.

"So you're going to stay after all."

"Till the police arrive and then just long enough to have you put away in jail or a mental institution. In fact, the hell with my beating it out of here. You're the one who'll have to go and be barred from this house for life, even if I'm the one who carried on and am ending this marriage." She picks up the receiver and dials. "Mrs. Silbert, please." That's her lawyer. "Miriam? It's Edith. Walt's destroying our house. Literally, I mean. I was in the process of leaving...No, I don't think his breaking up the place is natural." I pick up the extension. "He's on the extension so watch what you say. He's already broken two front windows that are full pane, not little French ones, and I've called the police and would like you to be over here soon as you can,"

"I can't come now, Edith. I'm tied up all day."

"Then get a writ out against him, or something, but quickly, because I don't want him staying here. He's going to wreck the whole house, I know it."

"Did he threaten that?"

"Ask him. I told you he's on the extension."

"You also told me to watch what I say. Okay. Walt, this is Miriam Silbert, Edith's lawyer who's handling her divorce. You've received several letters from me and notices from the court with my name on them, so you know who I am. My question is, are you planning on doing further harm to the house?"

"And her lawyer. And the police who come here. Everything. The front and back yards and basement and Edith too. I am going to murder her."

"Walt, just what you're saying now could land you in jail for a while and provide even additional grounds for a divorce, so try to be reasonable and answer me."

"All right. I'll only murder her lawyer."

"I'm serious, Walt. What my advice is—"

"Lawyers always have advice. Don't you people have marital and social and psychological problems of your own?"

"Of course. I was born poor to insane parents and had a miserable childhood and adolescence and got divorced twice. That's neither here nor there except for the experience and know-how and insights into human nature it gave me. Now I'm happy."

"You know this creep Edith is supposedly in love with?"

"I am in love with him, no supposedly," Edith says.

"Edith, let me talk to Walt. You're in business, Walt. You know that a lawyer, even in court under oath, can't divulge what a client's told her. Especially not to the client's contestant."

"Her client, his contestant, party of the first tart, the second fart. Bull. Divulge. Bulge. Bilge. Reveal. God, you people are creeps. You ought to be her lover, not lawyer."

"And what's that supposed to mean? Little more of it and you'll be hauled into court by me."

"It was nothing. Silliness. Senselessness. Man in distress. You were about to suggest? Perhaps that I leave this house for a hotel, agree to the divorce proceedings and give in to everything and make your work easier than pie-eating, yes? Okay, I will. I did I do and now I will. But no big settlement in her favor, you hear? I'll pay half the divorce costs and that's it. Two kids in college and I'll do my best to keep them there, but to only pay half. My share of the house and all its belongings I'll give free and clear to the three of them, but let the kids work for the rest of their college costs if Edith can't come up with it. It'll do them good. You worked. I worked. Edith didn't ranch but she'll have to now."

"Times have changed, Walt," Miriam says.

"Why? Because schools are much more expensive now? So pay is a lot more also than in your day or mine."

"There aren't that many available jobs for college students. That's why they do unpaid internships."

"Manure. Kids can always find work. Picking dead tree leaves out of pachysandra bushes or whatever pachysandra is. A ground covering. An herb. A friend of mine has a son who did that last month for four bucks an hour, imagine that?"

"Walt, I'm very busy. Appointments and meetings. We'll talk about leaves and manure another time."

"But I'm divulging the dog-eared ruth, Miriam, the ragtagged forsooth."

"You are what?"

"Nothing. I'm crazy. Rather, feeling rather crazy today. Where's the nearest lamp? There's still one front window to blow out."

"Walt?"

"He's left the phone, Miriam. I think he went looking for a lamp. Here he is, unplugging one now. No, ripping it out of the wall. Hold it. I've got to stop him."

She tries to stop me. I shove her to the floor. She jumps up and grabs the lamp by the cord while I hold it by the top. Tug, pull. "Walt, Edith." I hear Miriam on the phone. Edith now has the lamp by the base. I drag the lamp to the phone with Edith pulling back at her end and say into the receiver "You don't think I should do it, Miriam?"

"If you mean throw the lamp through the window, of course not."

"Strangle Edith with the lamp cord, I mean."

"Miriam, will you get someone here to restrain him?" Edith yells a few feet from the phone.

"Walt, I'm hanging up now and calling the police to get over there right away. Maybe Edith didn't tell them how serious it is."

"Too late. They're here." I hang up. The doorbell rings. "Go answer it, please. I'm bushed, and you invited them."

"Only when you put the lamp down and promise to back off."

"I promise." I put it down. She goes to the door. I throw the lamp through the one front window left. Two cops come in with drawn guns. "Welcome, strangers."

"He's tearing up the house," Edith says.

"We can see," one of them says. "You want to relax a second, Mr. Wilkerson?"

"And your names, my friendly police?"

"I said to relax; now cool it."

"I think I'm allowed to have your names. You're in fact both supposed to be wearing name tags above your badges."

"That's in the city, not here in the country." They've put away their guns.

"You want me to relax and cool it, I want your names."

"As you say. Allen and John."

"You were born and went through life without cognomens?"

"Those are our last. I'm Jim and he's Russell."

"Howdy, fellas. I'm Walt Wilkerson. I live here. I broke those three windows, as you must've heard. You at least heard the third being broke. Or created those three holes. No, the panes will have to be replaced, so they've more than holes; they're broken for life. This is my wife, Edith. Show them the sunny side of your teeth, Edie. We were married twenty-one years ago, or are about a week shy of that anniversary date. Or maybe just I'm shy, but she's not, for lately she's had many dates and this month she's taken up seriously with another man. Before then, just dates with others. Maybe six altogether. I can't say she's had those six altogether, though I'm sure in pairs and maybe even one as a trio they've been in the altogether. As you can see I've become quite torn up about it, which I've begun demonstrating by tearing up this house. But they were nothing-much affairs, the previous six. A night. Maybe two. A morning or three. A couple of summer weeks when she met them on the beach and. I could only come out weekends because I worked. We have two children who used to vacation with us when they were younger, Sue and Chuck. You can chuck Chuck and though I don't think Suzie's thinking of suing me, I'm sure her mother and brother are. Insufferable kid, Chuck, but Sue's okay. Both are away in college and spending plenty of money and getting so-so grades. Neither thinks much of me and my work or have much to speak about with me, and though the feeling wasn't mutual, it's become so the last year. I'm naturally mad at what's happened to me, or if you listen to my wife, just mad naturally. Mostly because she told me last night about the quick six and this recent heartthrob and that he's the main reason she instituted the divorce. Now she's going to try to institutionalize me. Hot flash: fat chance. Edith, dear, could you get these men coffee and cake while we talk?"

"I wish they'd just take you away."

"I think I've a better solution," Jim says. "How about if we try to settle the dispute without your having to press charges or our booking him at the station house and both of you going through the whole court scene?"

"I'm sorry, fellas. If pressing charges is the single best way of getting him out of here, that's what I want to do."

"I won't go without a row," I say.

"Don't tempt us," Russell says. "So far we've let you run off at the mouth and scare the daylights out of us with your third broken window there, and now we're having a nice discussion. But don't speak about making tough."

"I know judo and other martial arts."

"No, he doesn't," she says, "or never showed it. It's true he was in the navy during some Asian war, although I thought it was the marines. An ensign."

"Long time ago. Garbage barge. Skippered it around the bigger ships and smaller destroyers. But I was a lousy sailor. Bad sea legs. I also can't stand to fight. The judo and stuff was just for mental discipline and body tone, I'm really a peaceful man experiencing a painful crisis. But if your wife suddenly told you she's slept with six other men in the last year and in the last few months with one in particular and that she hates your guts and sight and said all this in the dark of your bedroom moments after you told her how much you still adore her and long to make love with her, I doubt either of you would have taken it any better than I."

"I never married," Russell says.

"Then you, Jim."

"I was. To be honest, splitting up was the next best thing that ever happened to my wife and me, the first being our brood."

"You see, Walt?" she says. "If the marriage isn't working out, why postpone the divorce?"

"That's how we felt, Mrs. Wilkerson."

"Oh, do call her Edith," I say. "Anything more than that, she'll begin to mind."

"We had three kids. Bing, bang and boom, that's how quickly they seemed to come. But we'd gotten hitched too young. So, very amicably, no dillydallying with legal advice or anything, we decided, after we'd seriously talked it over, and have continued to honor our original arrangement once we knew the marriage was through—"

"Yes, yes," I say, "that was you two, but with me it's different. I still love my wife and think a reconciliation can be made."

"That's absurd and a lie, Walt," she says.

"Will you just get these men some coffee?"

"No, thanks," Jim says. "We just had breakfast."

"I wouldn't mind a cup," Russell says.

"Heat up the Danish also. Please, they work hard and are probably hungry." She goes into the kitchen. "Can I speak plainly with you guys, man to men?"

"Of course," Jim says. "That's what we're also here for."

"It's not only my tender feelings for her or that I can't see myself suddenly living alone after so many years of marriage, kids, barracks, barges, college dorms and with my siblings and folks. Or even those six brief liaisons and now the one long one. But then when a woman tells you she's never loved you and in fact could never stand you and you're that and this when you always thought you were this and that, well—"

"You got agitated," Jim says.

"The windows. The everything. I even threatened to kill her and her lawyer both."

"Shouldn't do that."

"Don't I know. It's all wrong. But man—a person, is only human. If we didn't get excited sometimes, we'd explode. Or we'd be automatons, if that word's still used."

"Even so—three windows. It's going to cost a lot. This house jointly owned?"

"She can have everything—that's not my point. But only after I bust a little more of it up first."

"No can do," Russell says. "The house has to be totally yours to destroy. Even if it is, if your destroying it is disturbing the peace of your neighbors, you'd be breaking another law and so can't destroy your own house. It sounds unfair. You should be able to do with your own property what you want, right? But if you live around people, you have to show respect for them if that's the norm of the land and the law."

"Wait till your divorce settlement comes through," Jim says. "Then, if you get the house and still feel the same way, do it with as little noise as possible and staying within the building safety code. Bust up the whole inside if you want—we won't stop you. The outside might be a different story. For instance, something like a very neglected lawn or façade that's beginning to depreciate the property value of the rest of the neighborhood, I think they can get you for that too."

"Then I ought to swing along with the divorce, say all my threats were said in a fit of anger and I didn't mean them, and try to get this house. If I do, I can do what

I like inside it providing I don't cause too much of a ruckus or make the place structurally unsound and its exterior isn't visually offensive to my neighbors. I got it. Thanks a lot, guys. I think that should be all."

"We have to speak to Mrs. Wilkerson first before we leave," Russell says. He goes into the kitchen.

"You like your job?" I ask Jim.

"Very much, and it pays okay."

"Ever remarry?"

"Me, I freelance now and have plenty of fun."

"You meet them at bars?"

"Bars, parties, friends' homes, workplace and on vacations. No shortage of great ladies out there, I found."

"Still see the kids?"

"On my days off. I take them or just visit. My ex-wife has a much better disposition to me when I get there, now that I'm gone."

"You still don't desire her when you see her?"

"Why should I? I have my own women now, she her men, so between us it's all business and concerns and tales of the kids. When you first divorce you can't believe you'll think this way, but soon it becomes second nature with you no matter how hard you fight it."

"Can I get that down in writing?"

"As long as you don't ask me to do it in blood. Look, to me with your sense of humor and clear moments coming up more now than then, your problem is just emotional and temporary. Off the record, you're still pretty young; not old, at least. So you have kids college age. So will I in twelve years, and you still got your energy and if you lose twenty pounds and keep cogging around a bit and let the hair on one side grow out and comb it over your head in a concealing way, you'll have a good face and figure too. And living in this house and neighborhood must mean your standard of living's way up there also, so you'll survive. Better than that, you'll thrive. Women go for guys with money to burn. Maybe we weren't made for living with just one person all our life, something only this generation's finding out."

"Oh, they knew it in early Greece and ancient Rome."

"There you are; you've brains too. Think of your splitup as almost a renewed lease and blessing. But now let me ask you a few questions. You going to pack your bags now, go to the city and take a room there and let Mrs. Wilkerson live peacefully in the house for the time being? Because if you insist on staying and she presses charges to force you to leave, the judge, as they usually are with the wives, will be more sympathetic to her than to you."

"Yes, I'm going to do exactly as you say." I head for the door.

"Wait till Russell comes back. And don't you think you should put on your socks and shoes?"

I get my keys off the wall hook and open the door.

"Now I said to hold it, Walt. That means stop right there."

Their car's blocking mine. Edith left the keys in hers and I get in it. Jim and Russell rush up to the car as I back out of the driveway to the street. "I said to halt," Jim says. He unsnaps his holster.

"Don't be a fool," Russell says. "We'll get him later." I drive off, waving to them as I go. Edith is at the door. I drive down the street. There's the tricycling McQuire kid and Gretchen raking her lawn. And the Beinstock triplets in their stroller, three of them in a row. Cute. Abe Eaton. Myra Skintell. Mrs. Nichols. "Hiya, Mrs. Nichols," I yell out the window.

"Morning, Walt," she says. Nice lady. Always there when we needed her or one of her children to babysit. All seemingly happily married couples and contented boys and girls. So Edith and I and our kids didn't make it. Or at least I didn't with them. So, that's what happens sometimes.

I drive to town, park and go into the smoke shop where I know there's a phone. Two men at the magazine stand look at me and then at themselves as if they think I'm a bit off. Sure, the bare feet and the only shirt I have on is an undershirt and it's late fall. Well, so I'm doing seething out of the norm, but not against the law, I don't think. I say to them "You'd be in bare feet too and only this skimpy shirt if you went through what I did today. First my wife tells me about her six and one lovers. Next I knock out three front windows of my house and threaten not only her life but her lawyer's. The cops are after me for fleeing what might be considered the scene of a crime, which is knowing out my windows and threatening my wife's life or just escaping in her car, which might not be a crime if it's considered jointly owned, but anyway, before they said I could go."

"Shouldn't you be going back to square things with them?" the younger man says.

"Mind your biswax, Pete," the other man says.

"He told us, so I'm just suggesting to him."

"Do what I say; don't get involved."

"Ah, the attitude of the day," I say. "Stay cool, your nose clean, hands off, once removed—no, I don't know what I'm saying. But that's what I hear a lot from the guests and call-in folks on the radio talk shows, going into the city and on my way back. You know, to and from work? But I don't believe it, do you? We're all still earth dwellers and not very far from our origins and so pretty much the same, isn't that so?"

"What?" Pete said.

"Now I told you, Pete," the other man says.

"My dad says to keep my trap shut, so I will, but I can't make out half what you're saying."

"Your father? How nice. Hello, sir. Walt Wilkerson here. May I ask your name?"

"Hyram Falk. This is Pete."

"Glad to meet you both." I shake their hands. "What are you reading?"

"Just magazines," Pete says.

"Good for you. Excuse me; I got to make an important phone call." I dial Information, get Miriam's work number and call her, "Miriam, I'm about to make your job much easier and also make it possible for Edith to pay your exorbitant fees. I'm going to burn down my house now so she can collect all the insurance money from it and, though I'll contest it to make it look authentic, a quick divorce because of the mental cruelty inflicted on her by my burning the house down with all her things in it."

"Don't, Walt," she says. "The authorities will say you did it only to get the insurance money for Edith, and then she'll get nothing. Besides, she called before and said your house is being watched and that the police of your town and the surrounding ones are out looking for you. She suggests, and I go along with it, that you plead temporary insanity and that I represent you in criminal court. Believe me, it all looks bad now, but everything will work out."

I do. It doesn't. Six months in the clink for resisting arrest and attempting to run over an officer. Lies, but what can I do? After that, too much to drink and everything goes down the tubes. Wife and kids are already gone, but now business, savings, friends. Ten, twenty years pass. Cheap rooms, rotten food, crummy jobs, too many times fired or laid off, for entertainment: watching lousy television on thirdhand TVs. I don't want to go into it that deeply anymore. I get sick, liver and kidneys fail, I get worse—throw in the heart and lungs—but I don't do anything to control or prevent it. With each succeeding operation I tell the surgeons not to worry if it looks bad for me on the table: just put me away for good, something I'd do myself but can't. They say Hmm, interesting entreaty, they'll think seriously about my suggestion but I should know that in the last years of some of their 90-year-old patients there was nothing they liked more in life than sitting out on a porch or sidewalk under a warm sun. Finally, the one who's to operate on me today says he'll take away my life support system under anaesthesia as he's a great believer in mercy killing too. So that's where I am now. Men's ward of the city hospital and soon on my way to the operating room. Since there's no one to say this for me, I'll say it myself: "May he rest in peace forever; I mean me."

I wake up in the recovery room. "Sonofabitch lying doctor," I try to say. One of these days I'm going to be gutsy enough to do myself in. But by then I probably won't have the strength.

IN
MEMORIAM

.

He phoned the newspaper and said to the woman who answered "I'd like to place a notice in your In Memoriam space." She said "The In Memoriam notices are handled by the Obituary section of the Announcements department. Hold on and I'll connect you."

"Obituaries, Ray Kelvin speaking."

"I'd like to place an In Memoriam notice, Mr. Kelvin. You have a pen handy, because I've the notice all set?"

"Just a second, sir. What's the name and address of the person we're to bill this to?"

"That would be me. Stanley Berwald. B-e-r-w-a-l-d. Three-seventy-six President Street. Brooklyn."

"Is there a middle initial?"

"It's 'O,' but it'll get to me without it."

"And repeat the address, Mr. Berwald?"

He repeated it.

"Zip code?"

He gave the zip code.

"Finally, your phone number."

Phone number.

"What date do you want the notice to appear?"

"February 10th."

"Now, if you'll write down the cancelation number in case you later want to change or cancel the notice, we'll go ahead with the wording."

"I'm not going to want to cancel or change it. I'm going to give you this notice and when you send me the bill, I'll pay right away and that'll be the end of it."

"You probably won't cancel or change as you say," Kelvin said. "In Memoriams, in fact, have the lowest cancelation and change rate of any of our announcements, obituaries being the next. But there have been placers like yourself in both categories who also had no intention of changing or canceling their notice, but who later, after the paper's closing time for canceling or changing one for the next day's edition, called and wanted to do just that. Even that we change the name and address of the person we're to bill the notice to when the bill's already been sent out—we get some of those also."

"You won't have that problem with me. I've lived in the same apartment the last thirty-eight years and don't plan to move, and nobody but me knows the notice's being placed. And I've worked most of the night composing it, so it's the one I've decided on without question."

"The paper, no matter what the circumstances, still requires me to give a cancelation number for each notice, both for our protection and yours. The number I give will be the only way the paper and you can identify and locate your notice once I've put it through. We're also required to give cancelation numbers to all death, birth, marriage, engagements, memorial services and thank-you-for-your-condolences announcements. Also for help and situations wanted, personal and commercial notices, real estate, auction sales, merchandise offerings, business opportunities, automobile and pet exchange and. anything else in the line of classified ads. We use this system because we haven't the filing space or staff to keep any records of announcements and classified ads other than the cancelation numbers, which are automatically processed into our computers and then removed once the announcement and ad charges are paid."

"It seems you've made your system a lot more complicated than it need be, and probably at the expense of the customer."

"The system actually simplified the placing and taking of announcements and ads. And the fees for them are much less than they'd be without the system, if you've any idea what filing and office space rent for in this part of the city and what kind of payroll it'd take to keep a staff of bookkeepers and filing clerks for this department, not that it's so easy to hire them. But what do you say we finish up with your notice, Mr. Berwald? There could be another caller with a notice or announcement he or she wants to get in before closing time."

"After all you've said, I'm not so sure my notice will get in on the day I want it to or won't get mixed up in the real estate or help wanted sections or canceled soon after I get off the phone."

"Not anything to worry about. Because of the early closing time for In Memoriams, as compared to obituaries, let's say, typographical errors or misplacing an announcement almost never happens. The most likely error, though chances of it are extremely rare, is that your notice will get lost between the time I type it up and dispatch the original copy to the printers and the carbon to the accounting department, both by pneumatic tube, which is usually done within twenty minutes after our call's completed, depending on the length of the notice to type and how busy the tube is. This also further illustrates how important the cancelation number is. Call us before I've dispatched your notice, and without cancelation number or anything else, I or one of the other announcements reporters will be able to locate your In Memoriam at one of the three places it could be: still in my typewriter, typed up and on my desk waiting to be inserted into the pneumatic tube cylinders, or in the cylinders and waiting to be placed in the tube to the printers and Accounting. But call without cancelation number after the cylinders have been sent and you could end up with two published In Memoriam notices and bills, if you're calling to change the wording of the notice, or one bill and published notice if you wanted the original notice and bill canceled."

He gave the number.

"Keep it in a safe place till you get your bill, which takes about a month," Kelvin said.

"That's a long time. Suppose I lose it before then?"

"If you lose it but don't cancel or change before your notice's in the paper, then nothing will go wrong and the notice will appear as you requested it."

"Suppose it doesn't appear as I requested it? I don't want, for instance, to be paying for something that puts someone else's In Memoriam above my name."

"That won't happen. But in the rare chance it did, you'd call this department and give your cancelation number to whoever answers the phone and say your notice appeared incorrectly and you don't want to be billed for it or that you already sent a check for it and want to be reimbursed. We've a policy here where if the announcement isn't printed as directed, the customer doesn't pay a cent. What happens then is that the person you speak to sends down your cancelation number to Accounting, which keeps copies of the announcements for sixty days and then stores them on microfilm for ten years. If they find your notice didn't appear as it should have, which means the way I wrote it up, then you're reimbursed. If it appeared the way you gave it to me, which is why I'm being so meticulous about it, then of course you're expected to pay in full."

"Suppose it doesn't appear on the day I specifically wanted it to, what do I do then?"

"Again, you call this department, give your cancelation number to the person who answers and tell him what the problem is. He'll find the copy of your notice in Accounting through your cancelation number check it with the In Memoriams that ran the day you requested yours to and, if the newspaper was in error—and even if your In Memoriam ran the day before or after you wanted yours to—you'll be reimbursed in full. So, if everything's clear to you now, Mr. Berwald. I'll write up your In Memoriam. What' s the name of the person the notice is about, last name first?"

"My wife. Same as mine. Berwald. Sarah with an a-h."

"Do you want to add her middle name or initial or her maiden name in parenthesis or without?"

"Good idea. It's Wiener," and he spelled it. "And no parenthesis. Just Sarah Wiener Berwald. That's how she went."

"Would you read the notice to me? Slowly, as I'm not a fast typist."

"'Sarah, darling. Today is a year, a year of pain, sorrow and loneliness. Only God knows how much I miss you. What can I say? I am so lost without you. My dearest Sarah, no one will ever take your place in my heart. I love you so. Forty-seven years of beautiful memories. I speak to you with tears every night. I will mourn you until I join you. Love, Stan.'"

"Let me read back the notice, Mr. Berwald, and then quote you the charges. 'Berwald, comma, Sarah' with an a-h. 'Wiener' with an i-e. 'Sarah, comma, darling. Today is a year, comma, a year of pain, comma, sorrow and loneliness. Only God knows how much I miss you. What can I say, question mark. I am so lost without you. My dearest Sarah, comma, no one will ever take your place in my heart. I love you so. Forty-seven years of beautiful memories. I speak to you with tears every night. I will mourn you until I join you. Love, comma, Stan.'"

"That's right. And all the commas seem fine."

"The notice will be printed in both editions of the newspaper on February 10th, will take eighteen lines in the In Memoriam column, and the charges, to be billed to you at Three-seventy-six President

Street, Brooklyn, New York, 11231, will be sixty-eight dollars and fifty-three cents."

"That's okay."

"Thank you, Mr. Berwald."

"You're welcome."

The following stories in this collection appeared in different form in the following periodicals, to which the author and the publisher extend their thanks: *Ambit* ("Getting Lost"), *Asylum* ("Nothing New," "Ass"), *Atlantic Monthly* ("The Neighbors"), *Bennington Review* ("The Bussed"), *Big Moon* ("Shoelaces," "End of a Friend"), Black Ice ("One Thing"), *Boulevard* ("An Accurate Account," "Who He?"), *Box 749* ("The Killer"), *Brooklyn Sun* ("Night"), *Cake* ("The Former World's Greatest Raw Green Pea Eater"), *Caution Horse* ("No Knocks"), Center ("The Talk Show"), *Chouteau Review* ("Sex"), *Confrontation* ("Dream"), *Continental Drift* ("Knock Knock"), *Croton Review* ("Burglars"), *DeKalb Literary Review* ("Mr. Greene" in earlier version: "Mourning Crane"), *Departures* ("Next to Nothing"), *Failbetter* ("No Knocks"), *Fantasy & Science Fiction* ("A Home Away from Home"), *Fiction Network* ("The Wild Bird Reserve"), *Flyway* ("End of a Friend"), *Genesis* ("An Outing"), *Glimmer Train* ("Contac"), *Idaho Review* ("Wait"), *Iowa Review* ("The Leader," "The Cleanup Man," "Question"), *The Hopkins Review*—preview issue ("In Memoriam"), *Kansas Quarterly* ("Getting Lost," "Long Made Short"), *Little Magazine* ("The Argument"), *Memphis Review* ("Biff"), *Montana Review* ("For a Quiet English Sunday"), Mundus Artium ("Evening"), *New England Review* ("Can't Win"), *Nitty Gritty* ("An Outing"), *North American Review* ("Overtime"), *Ohio Journal* ("Stories," "She," "The Baby"), *Other Voices* ("Starting Again"), *Pale Fire Review* ("Yo-Yo"), *Periodical Lunch* ("Jackie"), *Per Se* ("Pale Cheeks of a Butcher's Boy"), *Playboy* ("Produce" in earlier version: "Berry-Smashing Day at the C &L," "The Young Man who Read Brilliant Books," "What is All This?"), *Quarry West* ("Getting Lost"), *South Carolina Review* ("The Phone," "Piers" in earlier version: "Paul"), Southwest Review ("China"), *Stanford Magazine* ("The Good Fellow"), Sun & Moon ("Meet the Natives," "The Chocolate Sampler"), *Sycamore Review* ("Long Made Short"), *The Fault* ("Leaves"), *Urbanite* ("Mr. Greene"), *Washington Review* ("Reinsertion," "Storm") and *Westbere Review* ("Dawn"). "No Knocks" also appeared in Best of the Web 2009, and "The Young Man who Read Brilliant Books" appeared in the *Playboy* anthology *Just My Luck*.

5.

he wants: where she suddenly appears, they quickly get the
miraculousness of her being there out of the way: "I don't
know how it happened either," she says. [...] not knocking
it, though since it gives me the chance to see you and you
the chance to do something for me I very much want done."
He asks what; she says "It's not up to me today." He says
"Come on, Mom, don't [...] and on ceremony [...] liked to say.
You [...] to to [...] and [...] know how much
time [...] together, [...] so [...] and she says
"Maybe if [...] ed [...] ess, [...] still don't think it
proper for me [...] right out [...] with it. He says "'Proper'?
What kind of word is that for [...] that we're [...] king about? I'll
do whatever you want me [...] back [...] I know [...] ing you'd
want would be within reason, but you got to let me know what
it is," and she says "Please, dear, let's not argue over semantics
now." He says [...] did [...]? Oh, the 'proper.' Okay, here's
a good guess. You want to see your granddaughters, and she
says "That'd be very nice, I can't tell you how much that would
mean to me, but it'd be too frightening for them, and it wasn't
what I had in mind." "Then I give up. I was always bad at
guessing games unless I got help," and she says "Do you know
today is?" "The date? November 14th. Is that the old Armistice
Day? No, that used to be the Eleventh. It's your birthday;
I knew that." "You're flipping me again. You don't want to

Self portrait of the author, 10.27.05